A MAN

OF

PARTS

ALSO BY DAVID LODGE

FICTION

The Picturegoers
Nice Work
Ginger, You're Barmy
Paradise News
The British Museum is Falling Down
Therapy
Out of the Shelter
Home Truths
Changing Places
Thinks . . .
How Far Can You Go?
Author, Author
Small World
Deaf Sentence

CRITICISM

Language of Fiction
The Novelist at the Crossroads
The Modes of Modern Writing
Working with Structuralism
After Bakhtin

ESSAYS

Write On
The Art of Fiction
The Practice of Writing
Consciousness and the Novel
The Year of Henry James

DRAMA

The Writing Game
Home Truths

A MAN OF PARTS

a novel

DAVID LODGE

VIKING

VIKING
Published by the Penguin Group
Penguin Group (USA) Inc., 375 Hudson Street, New York, New York 10014, U.S.A.
Penguin Group (Canada), 90 Eglinton Avenue East, Suite 700, Toronto, Ontario, Canada M4P 2Y3
(a division of Pearson Penguin Canada Inc.)
Penguin Books Ltd, 80 Strand, London WC2R 0RL, England
Penguin Ireland, 25 St. Stephen's Green, Dublin 2, Ireland (a division of Penguin Books Ltd)
Penguin Books Australia Ltd, 250 Camberwell Road, Camberwell, Victoria 3124, Australia
(a division of Pearson Australia Group Pty Ltd)
Penguin Books India Pvt Ltd, 11 Community Centre, Panchsheel Park, New Delhi – 110 017, India
Penguin Group (NZ), 67 Apollo Drive, Rosedale, Auckland 0632, New Zealand
(a division of Pearson New Zealand Ltd)
Penguin Books (South Africa) (Pty) Ltd, 24 Sturdee Avenue, Rosebank, Johannesburg 2196,
South Africa

Penguin Books Ltd, Registered Offices: 80 Strand, London WC2R 0RL, England

First American edition
Published in 2011 by Viking Penguin, a member of Penguin Group (USA) Inc.

10 9 8 7 6 5 4 3 2 1

Copyright © David Lodge, 2011
All rights reserved

Publisher's Note
This is a work of fiction based on real events.

LIBRARY OF CONGRESS CATALOGING IN PUBLICATION DATA
Lodge, David.
  A man of parts : a novel / by David Lodge.
    p. cm.
  ISBN 978-0-670-02298-4 (hbk.) — ISBN 978-1-84655-497-1 (trade pbk.)
  1. Wells, H. G. (Herbert George), 1866–1946—Fiction. 2. Wells, H. G. (Herbert George), 1866–
1946—Relations with women—Fiction. 3. Novelists, English—19th century—Fiction. 4. Novelists,
English—20th century—Fiction. I. Title.
  PR6062.O36M36 2011
  823'.914—dc22   2011013902

Printed in the United States of America

To Jim Crace

who guessed the subject of this book
before I had written a word of it.

Parts PLURAL NOUN *1. Personal abilities or talents:* a man of many parts. *2. short for* **private parts**.

Collins English Dictionary

He could imagine as existing, as waiting for him, he knew not where, a completeness of understanding, a perfection of response, that would reach all the gamut of his feelings and sensations from the most poetical to the most entirely physical, a beauty of relationship so transfiguring that not only would she—it went without saying that this completion was a woman—be perfectly beautiful in its light but, what was manifestly more incredible, that he too would be perfectly beautiful and quite at his ease . . . In her presence there could be no self-reproaches, no lapses, no limitations, nothing but happiness and the happiest activities . . . To such a persuasion half the imaginative people in the world succumb as readily as ducklings take to water. They do not doubt its truth any more than a thirsty camel doubts that presently it will come to a spring.

This persuasion is as foolish as though a camel hoped that some day it would drink from such a spring that it would never thirst again.

H.G. Wells, *Mr Britling Sees It Through*

A young mind is like a green field and full of possibilities, but an old mind becomes more and more like a cemetery crowded up with memories.

H.G. Wells, Looseleaf Diary, April 28, 1942

Nearly everything that happens in this narrative is based on factual sources—'based on' in the elastic sense that includes 'inferable from' and 'consistent with'. All the characters are portrayals of real people, and the relationships between them were as described in these pages. Quotations from their books and other publications, speeches, and (with very few exceptions) letters, are their own words. But I have used a novelist's licence in representing what they thought, felt and said to each other, and I have imagined many circumstantial details which history omitted to record.

D.L.

PART ONE

I

In the spring of 1944 Hanover Terrace, a handsome row of Nash town houses on the western perimeter of Regent's Park, is looking distinctly war-worn. Its cream stucco façade, untended since 1939, is soiled, cracked and peeling; many windows, shattered by bomb blast or shock waves from the anti-aircraft guns on Primrose Hill, are boarded up; a house towards the end of the terrace, hit by an incendiary bomb, is a gutted shell, stained with smoke. The elegant arcade running the length of the building, which serves as a communal porch for the front doors of the houses, is chipped and flaking, as are the massive Doric columns supporting the building's central feature—a pediment framing statuary of classical figures engaged in various useful and artistic pursuits, two of whom have lost their heads and one an arm. The goddess who formerly stood on the apex of the pediment, clasping an orb, has been removed as a potential danger to people below if she should be suddenly toppled by an explosion; and the cast-iron railings that, smartly painted in black and gold, used to divide the service road and its shrubbery from the park's Outer Circle, were long ago cut down and taken away to make munitions.

Only one house, number 13, has been permanently occupied throughout the war by its owner, Mr H.G. Wells. During the London Blitz of 1940–41 he was frequently teased with the suggestion that this might prove an unlucky number, to which he responded, consistent with a lifetime's contempt for superstition, by having a bigger '13' painted on the wall beside his front door. He stubbornly refused to move to the country, saying 'Hitler (or in male company, "that shit Hitler") is not going to get *me* on the run', and stayed put in Hanover Terrace as, one by one, his neighbours slunk off to safe rural havens and their houses were occupied by sub-tenants or left empty.

As long as he was physically able to do so H.G. put on a tin hat and took his turn at fire-watching from the roof of Hanover Terrace, partly from a sense of patriotic duty and partly from a personal solicitude for the Aubusson carpet in his drawing room. It also gave him a gloomy satisfaction to observe from, as it were, a grandstand seat, the fulfilment of his prophecy as far back as 1908, in his novel *The War in the Air,* that future wars would be dominated by air power and involve the destruction of cities and civilian populations by indiscriminate bombing. Admittedly he had been mistaken in assuming that this strategy would be carried out mainly by enormous airships, big as ocean liners, rather than aeroplanes, but given the state of aeronautical engineering in 1908 that was not such a wild guess, and certainly didn't seem so a few years later when German Zeppelins appeared in the night sky over England. Penguin Books considered *The War in the Air* still sufficiently relevant to the current war to reissue it in 1941, with a brief new Preface by himself that concluded with an epitaph he wished to have inscribed on his tombstone: 'I told you so. You *damned* fools.'

Fire-watching is beyond him now, but there is little need for it. In the spring of 1944, the sirens seldom sound. The unexpected resumption of German night raids at the beginning of the year turned out to be just a token retaliation for the carpet-bombing of German cities by the British and American air forces and soon petered out. Now there is only the occasional hit-and-run daylight raid by some fast low-flying fighter-bomber that slips under the radar shield, and these rarely get as far as central London. Nazi Germany has more important things on its military mind: grimly resisting the advance of the Russian armies in the east, and preparing to repulse the invasion of occupied France which everybody knows is imminent. London is safe again, and one by one the leaseholders of Hanover Terrace are creeping back to reclaim their property, viewed with some contempt by H.G. who has been here for the duration, keeping to his routine, writing his books, answering letters, going for a daily constitutional—across the road and into the park, to the Zoo or the Rose Garden, or down Baker Street to the Savile Club in Brook Street, pausing for a browse in Smith's bookshop on the way.

Lately he has had to give up these excursions—even the Rose Garden is too far. He is not well. He has no strength. He has no appetite. He rises late and sits in an armchair in the small sitting room, or in the sun lounge, a glassed-in balcony at the back of the house, with a rug over his knees, reading and dozing intermittently, woken with a start by the sound of his book sliding to the floor, or by his daughter-in-law Marjorie, who has acted as his secretary ever since his wife died, coming in with some letters that need answering or just to check that he is comfortable. In the evenings he is visited by his elder son Gip, Marjorie's husband, or by Anthony, his natural son by Rebecca West, born on the first day of the First World War. He is conscious of these three people going in and out, scrutinising him with worried frowns. For some time he has had a nurse in the house at nights; now his physician Lord Horder has recommended that they employ a day nurse as well. He wonders if he is dying.

One evening in April, Anthony West rings up his mother. She receives the call at her home, Ibstone House, the surviving wing of a Regency period mansion, with its own farm attached, in the country near High Wycombe, where she lives with her husband Henry Andrews, a banker and economist now working at the Ministry of Economic Warfare.

'I'm afraid I've got some bad news,' Anthony says. 'Horder says H.G. has cancer of the liver.'

'Oh God!' says Rebecca. 'How awful. Does he know?'

'Not yet.'

'You're not going to tell him, I hope?'

'Well, I've been talking it over with Gip. We think we should.'

'But why?'

'H.G. has always believed in facing facts. He's not afraid of death. He's said so on many occasions.'

'It's one thing to say it . . .'

'I don't think we should discuss this over the phone, Rac,' Anthony says, using the nickname she acquired when she married Henry and they began calling themselves Ric and Rac after two French cartoon dogs. 'I wish I could have come over and told you in person.'

'Because you're feeling dreadful?'

'Because I thought *you* would feel dreadful.'

'Well, of course I do,' says Rebecca, bridling slightly. Their conversations tend to be barbed with little implied or inferred accusations and rebuttals, which often turn into bigger ones.

'I can't get over to Ibstone at the moment,' Anthony says. 'We're short-staffed in Far East and I'm very busy.' He is currently working as a sub-editor in the Far Eastern Department of the BBC's Overseas Service.

Anthony summarises Horder's prognosis: H.G. might experience some remission, but he probably has only a year to live, at the most. They argue again about whether he should be told, until Rebecca irritably terminates the call. She goes to her study and records it in her diary, concluding: *'My chief anxiety is that Anthony should not be hit too hard by this news. I have made my peace with H.G. I have not forgotten the cruel things he did to me, but our affection is real and living.'* Her diary is written with one eye on her future biographers, who will quote from it.

Anthony rings up Jean, a pretty young brunette with superb breasts who works as a secretary at Bush House, with whom he is having a passionate affair, and tells her the news about his father. She is sympathetic, but unable to enter fully into his emotions because she has never met H.G., and she cannot be introduced to him or to the rest of the family because Anthony is married to Kitty, who is running their farm and looking after their two children while he works at the BBC, and Kitty is at present unaware of Jean's existence. Meanwhile Anthony when he is working in London lives in the mews flat at the end of the rear garden of number 13 Hanover Terrace, known in the family as 'Mr Mumford's' after some former tenant long gone and probably dead.

'Have you told your wife about us yet?' Jean asks Anthony, lowering her voice so her flatmate Phyllis won't hear. Their affair is consummated mainly in this flat, situated conveniently near Bush House, in daytime hours snatched when they are free and Phyllis is at work.

'Not yet.'

'When will you?'

'I have to wait for the right moment.'

'There'll never be a right moment. You just have to do it.'

'I can't while we're all absorbing this news about H.G.'

'Well . . .'

'I love you, Jean.'

'Love you too. But I hate this hole and corner thing.'

'I know, but be patient, darling,' he says.

Some days later Rebecca receives a phone call from Marjorie, asking her to come and see H.G. 'Would he welcome that?' Rebecca asks. The wounds of their parting in 1923 or '24 (it was never clear to either of them exactly when it became final) after a stormy and passionate relationship that had stretched over a decade, have healed, and they have been on friendly terms in recent years, but knowing that he has a life-threatening illness makes a visit potentially stressful. 'He said he would like to see you,' says Marjorie. 'Then I'll come,' says Rebecca. 'Does he know about his . . . ?' 'Yes,' says Marjorie.

Rebecca takes with her a basket containing eggs and butter and cheese from the Ibstone House farm, precious largesse which the housekeeper receives gratefully. 'Mr Wells can't stomach the dried eggs any more whatever I do with them,' she says. 'A nice fresh egg soft-boiled might tempt him.' H.G. has had a bad night and is not quite ready to see Rebecca when she arrives, so she is shown into the long drawing room on the first floor to wait. She has never liked the house: it is grand but cold and rather gloomy, with dark polished parquet floors and beige walls, furnished with impersonal good taste, like an expensive hotel. There is an Aubusson carpet in the drawing room and a Tang terracotta horse on the mantelpiece but they express the owner's wealth, not his personality. H.G. never did have much visual taste, she reflects. He was obsessed with functionality in domestic architecture, but indifferent to décor, a fanatic for plumbing, but a poor judge of pictures. The house lacks a woman's touch—Moura Budberg, his mistress when he bought the lease in 1935, wisely refused either to marry or to cohabit with him, and she has had no successor. Even his study, which Rebecca peeps into on her way to visit the lavatory, with its mahogany desk bearing a green-shaded reading lamp on a heavy ziggurat base, a matching inkstand and a leather-bound blotting pad, might be the office of the chairman of a bank—except that on the polished surface of the desk there are two foolscap manila folders, creased and dog-eared from use, one to each side of the blotter, which look as if they contain manuscripts rather than accounts.

In the ground floor cloakroom she examines her fifty-year-old face in the mirror for new wrinkles, and combs her greying hair. She refreshes her lipstick, powders her nose, and shapes her eyebrows with a licked finger, feeling a little foolish at this display of vanity—but one wants to look one's best when meeting an old lover, even if he is sick and dying. She is amused to observe a notebook and pencil lying on top of a cabinet next to the W.C.—it was always H.G.'s habit to have notebooks scattered around whatever house he was occupying, in case some thought occurred to him which he could scribble down before he forgot it. She peeps inside the notebook, but the pages are blank.

The small sitting room to which she is summoned when H.G. is ready is cosier than the drawing room, but she finds him in low spirits, worried and depressed. He is slouched in an armchair beside a fire of smouldering slack, his neatly slippered, size five feet peeping from under the rug covering his legs. Anthony and Gip have told him that he has cancer, but not the prognosis. 'I want to know how long I have left,' he says plaintively, 'but they won't tell me. Even Horder won't tell me.'

'That's because they don't know. You could live for years, Jaguar.' Long ago, when they were lovers, they called each other 'Panther' and 'Jaguar' in bed and correspondence, and she thinks the name will please him, but to her dismay it upsets him even more. A tear trickles from one eye down his cheek and loses itself in the roots of the moustache, now grey and rather straggling, with which in his prime he would tickle intimate parts of her anatomy.

'I don't want to die, Panther,' he says.

'Nobody wants to.'

'I know—but we must. Of course one must. I'm ashamed of myself.' He sits up in his chair, smiles, reaches over and squeezes her hand. 'Thank you for coming to see me.'

'I brought you some eggs from the farm.'

'That was kind,' he says. 'And how are you? Are you writing?'

'Only journalism. I can't concentrate on anything more substantial with the war going on and on . . .'

'You managed to finish *Black Lamb and Grey Falcon* in spite of the Blitz.'

'I had to. But it totally exhausted me. And what about you, Jaguar?'

'Oh, I shuffle pages about. I have a couple of things on the go, but I'm not sure I shall finish either of them. Nobody's interested in me now, anyway.'

'Nonsense,' says Rebecca, dutifully.

H.G. asks after Henry. 'He's working very hard at the Ministry on plans for post-war reconstruction,' says Rebecca. 'I must say it's very reassuring to see him with his gaze fixed so confidently on the future, while the rest of us are biting our nails about the present. And how is Moura?'

'She's in the country, staying with Tania.'

'Has she been to see you, since . . . ?'

'Since Horder pronounced the death sentence?'

'Don't, Jaguar!'

'I told Gip Moura wasn't to be put in the picture yet. She's not been feeling too well herself lately, and went down to Tania's to rest and recuperate. I don't want to upset her unnecessarily.'

'I see.' Rebecca ponders this information, uncertain whether to feel flattered or used that she has been summoned to comfort the stricken H.G. in preference to his mistress—if that is what Moura still is. The exact nature of their relationship has always been an enigma—to H.G. as much as anyone, he claims.

'To be honest,' he says, 'I was afraid that if she was told I'm dying she'd come over all Russian on me, like some Gorky character, get maudlin drunk on brandy, and make me even more depressed than I am already.'

'I know what you mean,' Rebecca says with a smile. Moura, Baroness Budberg, does seem like a character who has stepped from the pages of a Russian novel, trailing melodramatic, barely credible stories of love and adventure: that she walked across the ice between Russia and Estonia at the time of the Revolution to get to her first husband and their children; that he was murdered on his estate and she later married the Baron to obtain an Estonian passport, paying his gambling debts in return and divorcing him shortly afterwards; that she was the lover of the British secret agent Robert Bruce Lockhart, and was suspected with him of involvement in the 1918 plot to assassinate Lenin, but found protection as secretarial assistant to Maxim Gorky. Rebecca knows this last detail is true because H.G. stayed with Gorky on a visit to Russia in 1920, and his confession to her on his return that he had slept with Moura, who lived in the Petrograd apartment, provoked one of their most divisive rows. Years after their relationship had come to an end, and his wife Jane was dead, H.G. met Moura again, decided she was the love of his life, helped her to settle in England, and tried in vain to persuade her to marry him. Anthony, who likes Moura and approves of her relationship with H.G., nevertheless believes she is a Soviet spy, as do several other people. Rebecca is uncertain whether to believe this or not: although Moura might have been a Mata Hari once, it is difficult to see the matronly, slightly dowdy fifty-year-old woman of today in that role. But being herself an outspoken critic of Soviet Russia, she keeps a wary distance from Moura.

These thoughts and memories slide across Rebecca's mind as she chats to H.G. on light, neutral topics, until she notices his eyes are almost closed. 'I don't want to tire you,' she says. 'I'll be on my way.' She stands, stoops and kisses his cheek. It is no longer as smooth and plump as it once was, but his skin still smells faintly and pleasantly of walnuts, as it did when they first became lovers. Somerset Maugham asked her once, with a smile that was half a sneer, what had been the secret of H.G.'s sexual attraction, a man twice her age, not especially good-looking, only five foot five in height, and tending to corpulence, and she answered: *He smelled of walnuts, and he frisked like a nice animal.*

As she is leaving the house, smiling at the recollection of this remark, she meets Gip in the front hall, coming in from outside, and her smile fades. She berates him and Anthony for upsetting their father by telling him he is dying.

'He kept asking questions,' says Gip. 'I don't like lying to H.G. He brought us up, Frank and me, to tell the truth. It's the basis of good science.' Gip is Reader in Marine Biology at University College London.

They glare at each other with mutual dislike. It makes Rebecca feel almost physically sick to look at him, he so resembles his mother, the petite, dainty, self-effacing Jane, who clung on to her husband in spite of his many infidelities, and inspired in him an unshakeable loyalty. Hard as she tried, she could never persuade H.G. to divorce Jane. Of course it suited him very well to have a wife who looked after his every comfort and entertained his friends and typed his manuscripts and kept his accounts in order while he went off whenever he felt the urge and bedded whoever took his fancy, but no self-respecting woman would have tolerated the situation. Rebecca never doubted that if Jane had told H.G. he must choose between the two of them, he would have divorced Jane and married herself. She would have been a fit consort for him, his intellectual equal, and a great deal of emotional misery would have been avoided, not least for Anthony.

'Anthony agreed that we should tell H.G.,' says Gip.

'I know,' says Rebecca. 'But I think he regrets doing so. He sounds overwrought when I speak to him on the phone.'

'Well of course he's upset,' says Gip. 'Anthony is very devoted to H.G.'

'Anthony has a reverse Oedipus complex,' Rebecca bursts out. 'He has wanted to kill his mother and marry his father ever since he found out who his father *was*. Because I had to bring him up, I was the one he blamed for being sent to boarding school, and being bullied and teased and miserable, while H.G. was always the godlike Uncle-figure who descended from time to time in his motor car distributing presents and whisking him off to theatres and restaurants.'

'Yes, well . . .' Gip says. 'It must have been difficult for Anthony.'
'It was difficult for *me*!' Rebecca almost shouts.

Left alone in the small sitting room, H.G. stares into the fire, wondering what the world will say about him when he dies. The obituaries, of course, have already been written. Given his age and distinction, they will have been on file in the newspaper offices for years, revised and brought up to date periodically, ready for publication when the time comes. The time has come rather sooner than he expected when he wrote a humorous 'auto-obituary' for a BBC radio series in 1935. It was published in the *Listener* and reprinted in newspapers around the world. *'The name of H.G. Wells, who died yesterday afternoon of heart failure in the Paddington Infirmary, at the age of 97, will have few associations for the younger generation,'* it began. *'But those whose adult memories stretch back to the opening decades of the present century and who shared the miscellaneous reading of the period may recall a number of titles of the books he wrote and may even find in some odd attic an actual volume or so of his works. He was indeed one of the most prolific of the "literary hacks" of that time . . .'* He pictured himself in the early 1960s as a *'bent, shabby, slovenly and latterly somewhat obese figure'* hobbling round the gardens of Regent's Park with the aid of a stick, talking to himself. *'"Some day," he would be heard to say, "I shall write a book, a real book."'* This piece was intended, and generally received, as a *jeu d'esprit,* a disarming exercise in self-mockery, but it doesn't seem so absurdly wide of the mark now.

Of course the real obituaries, when they appear in due course, will be long, and respectful, paying tribute to his many achievements, his hundred-odd books, his thousands of articles, the originality of his early scientific romances like *The Time Machine* and *The War of the Worlds*, the controversial impact of his treatment of sexual relations in novels like *Ann Veronica* (the irregularity of his own sexual life would be discreetly veiled), the warm Dickensian humour of novels like *Kipps* and *The History of Mr Polly,* the remarkable accuracy of many of his predictions (the inaccuracy of many others would be tactfully passed over), the global success of the *Outline of History,* his morale-boosting journalism in two world wars, his hobnobbing with leading statesmen, his presidency of the international PEN association, his tireless campaigning for science, for education, for the abolition of poverty, for peace, for human rights, for world government . . . Yes, there is plenty for them to write about. But there will be an inevitable dying fall to the tributes, a sense of anticlimax, a perceptibly bored perfunctoriness in the record of the last twenty-five years, and an implication that he published too many books in that period, of diminishing quality. All the emphasis will be on the first half of his life—up to, say, 1920. That was the terminal date of his influence according to George Orwell, in his *Horizon* article a few years ago: '*Thinking people who were born about the beginning of this century are in some sense Wells's own creation . . . I doubt whether anyone who was writing books between 1900 and 1920, at any rate in the English language, influenced the young so much.*' He recalls the words without difficulty, having returned so often to the article, 'Wells, Hitler and the World State', fingering it like an old wound that still aches.

—**But that's a pretty impressive achievement, isn't it? To have created a whole generation of thinking people . . . ?**

He has heard this voice frequently of late, but when he looks round there is nobody else in the room, so it must be in his head. Sometimes the voice is friendly, sometimes challenging, sometimes neutrally enquiring. It articulates things he had forgotten or suppressed, things he is glad to remember and things he would rather not be reminded of, things he knows others say about him behind his back, and things people will probably say about him in the future after he is dead, in biographies and memoirs and perhaps even novels.

—**Something to be proud of surely?**
—Not the way Orwell served it up. He said that what made me seem like an inspired prophet in the Edwardian age, makes me a shallow, inadequate thinker now. He said that since 1920 I have squandered my talents slaying paper dragons.
—**He did add, if I remember rightly, '*But how much it is, after all, to have talents to squander.*'**
—That was just a sop, to try and draw the sting at the end. He probably added it in proof, because he'd just remembered that Eileen had invited Inez and me to dinner.

He had first met Orwell through the novelist Inez Holden, who was renting Mr Mumford's at the time, 1941, and a few days before the dinner party she had given him the latest issue of *Horizon* with the essay about himself in it, saying, 'I think you'd better read this before next Saturday, H.G., because George will assume you've seen it. Don't take it too hard—he does admire you really.' The article had upset him. It started by attacking his early journalism about the war, and admittedly he had been rash in affirming that the German army was a spent force just before it began to rampage through Russia, but what really stung was the assertion that '*much of what Wells has imagined and worked for is physically there in Nazi Germany. The order, the planning, the State encouragement of science, the steel, the concrete, the aeroplanes are all there.*'

—Well, they are, aren't they?

—Yes, but with an entirely different intention behind them. It's a travesty of what I have advocated and worked to bring about—as I told him at that dinner party.

He had taken *Horizon* with him to dispute the article, and saw immediately that Orwell had his own copy to hand, evidently prepared for a duel. They sat face to face at the table and he took Orwell through the text paragraph by paragraph, while Inez and Eileen listened nervously and the remaining guest, William Empson, got increasingly drunk. Honours were about equal by the end of the evening, but shortly afterwards Orwell gave a radio talk in which he said that H.G. Wells supposed that science would save the world, when it was far more likely to destroy it. Enraged by this second assault he fired off a note to Orwell care of the BBC: '*I don't say that at all, you shit. Read my early work.*'

—Such as?

—Such as *The Island of Dr Moreau*. Such as *The Sleeper Awakes*. Such as *The War of the Worlds*. It's not science that saves Earth from the Martians. It's the accident that they lack immunity to earthly bacterial infection.

—But in other books you claim that the application of science can save the world.

—The *application*, yes. Progress all depends on a benign application of science. But our literary intellectuals have never had any faith in that possibility. Eliot, for instance, who's at the opposite pole to Orwell in every other way, agrees with him about that.

—T.S. Eliot said some complimentary things about you in that article in the *New English Review*.

—But the tone of the whole piece was patronising, and at the end he said, '*Mr Wells, putting all his money on the near future, is walking very near the edge of despair.*' Christians like Eliot have never expected anything better from humanity than blitzkriegs and concentration camps, because they believe in original sin. So they can calmly contemplate the end of civilisation, put their feet up, and wait for the Second Coming.

—**Why do these fellows bother you so much?**

He stares into the heart of the fire, glowing dully under a coat of grey-white ash.

—Because I'm afraid they may be right. I *am* very near despair.

'The old man is muttering to himself again,' the day nurse says to the night nurse, as they change over that evening.

'What about?'

'Don't ask me,' says the day nurse. 'I can only make out the odd word. "Obituary" is a favourite.'

—**Still brooding about your obituaries?**

—I think atheists suffering from a terminal disease should be allowed to read their obituaries. In confidence, of course, and with no right of reply—except perhaps to correct matters of fact.

—**Why only atheists?**

—Well, if you believe in an afterlife, one of the things to look forward to must be finding out what your contemporaries really thought of you, eavesdropping on conversations as a ghost, reading the obituaries over people's shoulders . . . Unless they get all the newspapers delivered daily in heaven. Or the other place. Whereas we shall never find out. It's frustrating.

—**What d'you want to find out? Whether you are considered a great writer?**

—Lord no, I gave up that ambition long ago—left it to Henry James and his ilk. I demolished the whole idea of literary greatness in *Boon*, remember? '*Decline in the output of Greatness, due to the excessive number of new writers and the enlargement of the reading public, to be arrested by establishing a peerage of hereditary Novelists, Poets and Philosophers . . . The Nobel Prize to be awarded to them in order of seniority . . .*'

—**So . . . what then? A great thinker? A great visionary? A great man?**

—Not a great anything. The whole idea of greatness is a nineteenth-century romantic deathtrap. It leads to the rise of tyrants like Hitler. We have to value the collective over the individual, serve the Mind of the Human Race, not try to impose our personal will on it. I've been saying that for the last thirty years, but no one has paid any serious attention. If they had, we wouldn't be in the mess we're in now, with Europe being rapidly reduced to rubble.

—**Something good may come out of the war. This idea of setting up a United Nations organisation, for instance—the obituaries should give you some credit for your contribution to that.**

—It would be nice to think so. But it's a long way from World Government. Without a change in the collective mind-set it will be as useless as the League of Nations was.

Shortly after her visit to H.G., Rebecca invites Anthony to meet her for tea at her London club, the Lansdowne. They have not met for some time and she is struck unfavourably by his appearance. At thirty he is still handsome in a bulky, fleshy sort of way, but today his cheeks seem unnaturally fat, almost swollen, and his hair needs washing and cutting, falling lankly forward over his forehead. His clothes look crumpled and grubby, no doubt because he is living away from home and Kitty's housewifely care so much of the time. When they get on to the subject of H.G., and whether it was right to tell him he has an incurable cancer, his speech seems to her theatrical, inauthentic. He makes offensive remarks in a manner designed to make them seem compassionate, taking her hand and saying, 'I don't want to hurt you, Rac, I would rather do anything than that, but you shouldn't involve yourself in H.G.'s welfare. The truth is, it's a long time since you were the centre of his life.' 'I know that perfectly well,' she says indignantly. 'I took steps to remove myself from the centre of his life twenty-one years ago. Why are you putting on this show?' 'I just mean that H.G. is much closer to Gip and Marjorie than to you,' he says. 'They must make the necessary decisions.' 'I don't have to pretend to agree with them,' she says. When she asks after Kitty and the children Anthony looks slightly shifty as if he is concealing something. She will soon discover what it is.

.   .   .

In the middle of May, Rebecca receives a brief note from Kitty saying that Anthony has asked her for a divorce. '*It was quite out of the blue. He said after supper last Sunday, when the children were asleep, that he had met someone at the BBC and wanted to marry her. I said, "That's a pity my love, as you are married to me." I thought he was joking. But he's not.*'

Rebecca is outraged and dismayed. She likes and admires Kitty, a gifted painter and a beautiful woman, whom Anthony wooed and won in the most romantic fashion in 1936, proposing on the second occasion they met, and persisting on subsequent occasions until she capitulated. It seemed to Rebecca at the time a typically impulsive, quixotic move on Anthony's part, but for once it turned out well. Kitty, older and considerably more mature than Anthony, convinced him to give up his ambitions to be a painter because he would never be really good at it, and to become a writer instead, like his parents, and although he has yet to produce anything of consequence he has shown some flair in reviewing novels for the *New Statesman*. They have seemed happy together, especially after Anthony resolved his feelings about the war, which were divided between his pacifist principles and a reluctance to seem to shirk patriotic duty, by becoming a dairy farmer, a reserved occupation. He has taken to farming surprisingly well, as has Kitty, but about a year ago he accepted the offer of a part-time job with the BBC which seemed to him a more dignified contribution to the war effort, and now it has led to this silly infatuation. 'Who is she?' Rebecca demands of Anthony on the telephone, but he refuses to tell her. 'I want to meet her,' says Rebecca. 'Well, you can't,' he says. 'This is nothing to do with you, Rac. It's between Kitty and me.' 'How can you think of deserting those two adorable children?' Rebecca says, referring to Caroline aged two and a half and Edmund aged one, on whom she dotes. 'Well, you wanted H.G. to desert *his* children,' Anthony replies. Rebecca slams down the phone in a fury, and then regrets doing so, as she has more questions she wanted to ask. For instance, does H.G. know about this latest folly of his natural son?

H.G. does indeed know, because Anthony tells him, and receives a tongue-lashing on the evils of divorce that takes him by surprise. 'But you divorced your first wife,' he points out, 'and were very happy with your second, I believe.' 'That has nothing to do with it,' says his father, his voice rising to a high-pitched squeak, as it always does when he is agitated. 'Isabel and I had no children.' 'Kitty and I will share time with the children,' says Anthony. 'Kitty is not vindictive. She's really been very reasonable about this.' 'It's more than you deserve,' says H.G. 'You're a fool. I don't understand you. I never have.' 'I'm in love,' Anthony says. H.G. gives a snort of derision. 'I should have thought you of all men would have understood that,' Anthony says.

H.G. is silent, and glancing at him Anthony sees that his eyes are closed. Whether he is asleep or feigning sleep there is no way of knowing, but he does not stir when Anthony adjusts the rug over his feet and miserably leaves the room. He finds the night nurse in the kitchen, chatting to the housekeeper, and tells her that he is going back to Mr Mumford's.

—I suppose he has a point.
—What?
—You've had more than your fair share of love affairs in your lifetime.
—I had a lot of affairs. Love didn't come into most of them. As far as I was concerned—and for most of the women too—it was just a mutual giving and receiving of pleasure. The idea that you have to pretend to be in love with a woman in order to have sex with her—which we owe to Christianity and romantic fiction—is absurd. It has caused nothing but physical frustration and emotional misery. The desire for sex is constant in a healthy man or woman and needs to be constantly satisfied. Love, real love, is rare. As I said in *Experiment in Autobiography*, I've only loved three women in my life: Isabel, Jane and Moura.
—Didn't you love Rebecca?
—I was *in* love with her. And before her with Amber. But that's a different matter. The most dangerous of all.
—Why dangerous?
—You *think* you've found the perfect partner at last—soulmate and bedmate . . .
—What you call the 'Lover-Shadow' in that secret Postscript you've written to your autobiography.
—Exactly.
—You'd been reading Jung.
—Yes, but it's not quite the same as his Shadow. It's a person, someone who embodies everything lacking in your persona, with whom you could

achieve the perfect fulfilment which you have always dreamed of. But when you think you've found her, common sense goes out of the window. It's as if you've taken a potion, or are under a spell—like the lovers in *A Midsummer Night's Dream*. It's a kind of madness. If that's what's happened to Anthony there'll be a smash.

Anthony lets himself out of the back door of the blacked-out house and makes his way down the path with the aid of his shaded torch, inhaling the scents of hyacinth and lily of the valley invisibly in blossom, until he reaches the wall at the end of the garden. In defiance of blackout regulations he elevates the beam of his torch and plays it over the frieze drawn on the wall in lines of black paint by H.G. in his cartoon-like 'picshua' style, depicting the rise and fall of the Lords of Creation, a line of figures in profile beginning with prehistoric monsters and ending with men in top hats. Underneath is written *'Time to go.'*

There is a door in the wall which reminds Anthony of one of H.G.'s short stories, about a man who in childhood came upon a door in the wall of an anonymous London street opening on to a paradisal garden, full of sunshine and flowers and pleasant companions, which he longed fruitlessly to revisit for the rest of his days. There is no paradise behind this door— only Mr Mumford's, a rather poky flat, in need of redecoration, furnished with odds and ends that Anthony remembers from Easton Glebe, H.G.'s country house in Essex, which he used to visit in the 1920s in his school holidays: a faded sofa with a tear in the upholstery, a gate-leg table, a revolving bookcase, and—whimsically mounted on the wall, like a trophy—a battered hockey stick, memento of many riotous games organised by H.G. in his prime for his weekend house-party guests. Banal, shabby objects, but the visits to Easton Glebe which they evoke *had* seemed like glimpses of paradise to the unhappy schoolboy.

He rings Jean, but the number is engaged, probably by Jean's flatmate Phyllis who has interminable conversations with her mother most evenings. He sits down on the faded sofa and, to pass the time, takes from the revolving bookcase a thick omnibus edition of H.G.'s short stories, and turns to 'The Door in the Wall'.

It begins: *'One confidential evening not three months ago, Lionel Wallace told me this story.'* Lionel Wallace was a successful forty-year-old politician who at the age of five or six escaped from his home and got lost in the streets of West Kensington. He came across a green door in a high white wall covered with Virginia creeper, a door that, once opened, led him into an enchanted garden. *'There was something in the very air of it that exhilarated, that gave one a sense of lightness and good happening and well-being; there was something in the sight of it that made all its colour clean and perfect and subtly luminous. In the instant of coming into it one was exquisitely glad . . . everything was beautiful there . . .'* Two friendly panthers approach the little boy and one rubs its ear against his hand, purring like a cat. A tall fair girl picks him up and kisses him, and leads him down a shady avenue to a palace with fountains and all kinds of beautiful things and playmates with whom he plays delightful games, though he can never remember later what they were. Of course his story is not believed and he is punished for lying and running off from home on his own. For the rest of his life he yearns to return to the garden, but when he searches for the door in the wall he cannot find it, and when, on several occasions, he passes it by chance he does not stop to go through it because he is bound on some urgent worldly business—a scholarship exam at Oxford, an assignation with a woman that involves his honour, a crucial division in Parliament. These opportunities have become more frequent of late. *'Three times in one year the door has been offered me—the door that goes into peace, into delight, into a beauty beyond dreaming, a kindness no man on earth can know. And I have rejected it.'*

As Anthony reaches this point in his reading, the telephone rings. It is Jean. He is annoyed to be interrupted just a page or two short of the story's ending, which he has forgotten, and fails to put the usual note of tenderness into his voice in their exchange of greetings.

'Is something the matter, darling?' Jean asks.

'No. I was just deep in one of H.G.'s stories.'

'Well, I'm sorry to intrude,' she says ironically. 'Shall I ring back later?'

'No, no, of course not,' he says. 'I'm a bit upset, to tell you the truth. I've just had a rather painful telling-off from the old man.' He gives her a brief précis of his conversation with H.G.

'He's got a bit of a nerve, hasn't he?' says Jean. 'He wasn't exactly a model of matrimonial fidelity himself, from what you've told me.'

Anthony gives a dry chuckle. 'No indeed. But he didn't like it when I sort of reminded him of that.'

'Perhaps I should meet him,' Jean says. 'If he's so susceptible, perhaps I could win him over.'

'Not now, darling,' Anthony says hastily. 'Not yet.'

When the telephone call is over, he returns immediately to the story to find out what happens to Wallace. Oh yes, it comes back to him. He is found at the bottom of a deep shaft under construction for an extension to the London Underground, having gone through a door, carelessly left unlocked, in the temporary hoarding enclosing the building site, and fallen to his death—either accidentally or, more probably, deliberately. *'We see our world fair and common, the hoarding and the pit. By our daylight standard he walked out of security, into darkness, danger, death. But did he see like that?'*

Meanwhile, in the small sitting room of the main house, the interlocutor has turned interrogator.

—You only loved three women in your life: Isabel, Jane and Moura?
—Yes.
—Two wives and one mistress.
—I wanted to marry Moura after Jane died.
—But she refused.
—Yes.
—Perhaps she was afraid you wouldn't want to have sex with her any more if you were married.
—What do you mean by that?
—Well, both your marriages were sexual failures, weren't they?
—I would say disappointments rather than failures.
—Isabel disappointed you in bed?
—I was starving for sex when we married, but she couldn't respond. I was an inexperienced lover, and she was a deeply conventional young woman.
—So fairly soon you sought more exciting sex with other women? Like that little assistant of hers?
—I didn't seek out Ethel Kingsmill, she took the initiative. But yes, she showed me that there were women in the world who had the same appetites as I had.
—And a year or so later you left Isabel for your student, Amy Catherine Robbins—'Jane' as you curiously renamed her.
—I didn't like the name Catherine, which she used because she didn't like 'Amy', so I chose a new name for her.

—Not a very romantic one though, was it? No erotic associations. 'Plain Jane' . . . Jane Austen . . .

—What about Jane Eyre? She was passionate enough.

—Do you like that novel?

—No, since you ask. But—

—You left Isabel for Jane, and eventually married her, but as you say in your *Autobiography* she turned out to be just as disappointing in bed as Isabel. Isn't it rather puzzling that you exchanged one sexually inhibited spouse for another? As Oscar might have said, 'once is unfortunate, twice looks like carelessness'.

—What are you getting at?

—Perhaps secretly, subconsciously, you never really wanted a fully sexual woman as a wife. Perhaps you only really enjoy sex when it is wild, unlicensed, transgressive. Perhaps Moura suspected that.

—Nonsense!

—Is it?

'He's talking to himself again,' Marjorie says to Gip when he calls at Hanover Terrace one afternoon, as he often does on his way home from University College. Quietly she leads him to the door of the small sitting room, which is ajar, and he stands in the passage for some minutes, listening. He cannot catch more than a few words and phrases, but the dialogic rhythm of the old man's voice reminds him of something his brother Frank used to do in early childhood.

'He had an imaginary friend he used to talk to,' Gip says to Marjorie when they are back in the room that serves as her office. 'I used to eavesdrop on him, because if he thought he was observed he would immediately clam up. If there was anything on his mind—if he'd done something naughty, for instance, and was wondering whether he would be found out or whether he should own up—he would discuss it with this other boy, putting the arguments on both sides of the question. I was fascinated. It was like listening to a radio play—though of course there was no radio in those days. Maybe H.G. is doing something similar, but in second childhood.'

'Well it's an interesting theory,' says Marjorie. 'We must ask Frank what he thinks next time he comes.' Gip's younger brother, a documentary film maker currently employed as a civil servant, allocating accommodation to bombed-out families, spends much of his time commuting in and out of London from his home in the country, and is able to visit Hanover Terrace only occasionally. The main responsibility of looking after H.G.'s welfare has fallen on Gip and Marjorie, but they do not complain. They are both devoted to him.

A few days later Rebecca comes to see H.G. again, deploring Anthony's irresponsible behaviour. H.G. tells her he has done his best to dissuade their son from breaking up his family, but without success.

'Why for heaven's sake can't he be content with an affair, like anybody else?' Rebecca complains. 'Kitty wouldn't have minded if he'd been discreet—she more or less told me as much on the phone.'

'I couldn't agree more,' H.G. says. 'But Anthony is silly, theatrical and childish. Whether that's some innate weakness of character, or the fault of his upbringing, it's hard to say.'

'I hope you aren't blaming me,' says Rebecca.

'I blame myself for his existence.'

They are both silent for a moment, remembering the circumstances of Anthony's conception: a passionate embrace in the drawing room of his flat at St James Court, his hands under her clothes, her eager response . . . but there had been a servant in the apartment whose presence inhibited him from leading her to his bedroom where he kept contraceptive sheaths, so he pressed on, intending to rely on withdrawal, but lost control at the crucial moment. The same thought is in both their minds. What misery, what years of anger and frustration and recrimination had flowed from that brief spasm of pleasure! And still persist . . .

'If Anthony insists on going through with this stupid divorce,' Rebecca says, 'I think you should emend your will and leave some money to Kitty.'

'I've been thinking along the same lines,' says H.G. 'Enough to provide comfortably for the children.'

'It won't, of course, provide them with a father,' says Rebecca.

H.G. shrugs. 'It's all I can do.'

Travelling home from Marylebone to High Wycombe in a stuffy first-class railway compartment, in the company of three elderly businessmen with bowler hats, peeping at her from time to time over their evening newspapers, Rebecca is overwhelmed by dread, the sense of a curse working itself out in delinquent fathers over several generations. Her father deserted his family when she was eight, going off to South Africa on some vague business venture and disappearing without trace, leaving his wife to bring up Rebecca and her two sisters on barely adequate means. Then she herself had to bring up Anthony on her own—admittedly with more generous financial support from his father, but H.G. kept his distance and his freedom—and now Anthony is planning to leave Kitty to bring up *his* children on her own. And what was the reward for the mothers whose lives were pinched and frustrated by the responsibility thrust upon them? They became the object of their children's displaced resentment, *that* was their reward. She never gave up hope that her beloved Daddy would somehow return to the family with an honourable explanation for his absence, like the father in *The Railway Children* (how she had wept over the ending of that book!), until she was thirteen, when they heard that he had died. Later she learned from her mother that he had been an incorrigible philanderer, seducing their own housemaids and resorting to prostitutes. She recognises in retrospect that she was a difficult, disruptive child and adolescent, always quarrelling with her sisters and criticising her mother; Anthony was the same when he was growing up—hero-worshipping his absent father and blaming her for all the miserable experiences of his schooldays. She can so easily imagine little Caroline and Edmund in years to come repeating the same mistake, adoring Anthony and inflicting the same undeserved punishment on Kitty, as she struggles to bring them up, run the farm and, if she is lucky, find a little time for her art. The feminism Rebecca campaigned for all her adult life has liberated women sexually— the bolder spirits among them, anyway—but it has not redressed this fundamental imbalance in the relations of men and women: the female instinct to nurture their offspring and the male instinct to spend their seed promiscuously. H.G. is simply a more intelligent and more successful version of her father. Even Henry has disappointed her in this respect. Unfailingly kind and protective, admiring and supportive of her work (gamely escorting her round the wilds of Yugoslavia in dirty trains and flea-infested hotels when she was researching *Black Lamb and Grey Falcon*), possessing impeccable manners, and enough money to allow her to live in some style, he is in every respect the perfect spouse, except that he is prone to infatuations with pretty young women, and he hasn't made love to her since 1937. Lying beside him in bed one night she cried out in the dark: 'Why don't you make love to me any more?' But he was asleep, or pretended to be, and said nothing. She has had other lovers herself, of course, since then, though none at present. She reflects despondently that her sexual life may have come to an end.

In June the war takes a dramatic turn, on the home front as well as abroad. On June 6th the long-awaited Allied invasion of France takes place—not, as was expected, at Pas-de-Calais but on the beaches of Normandy. The nation is gripped by excitement and suspense, eagerly consuming every morsel of strictly controlled news about the event. After a few days it seems that the operation has been successful, the Allied forces have obtained a secure foothold, and reinforcements and supplies are pouring in via the ingenious prefabricated Mulberry harbour. This surely is the beginning of the end of the war, long though the wait has been since Churchill famously described the battle of El Alamein as the end of the beginning. But then, just as people are starting to relax and celebrate, the bogeyman Hitler, like some demon king in a pantomime, produces a new weapon from his arsenal to show he is not done for yet: the V1, so-called by Goebbels, the first of two *Vergeltungswaffen*, 'retaliation weapons' designed to exact retribution for the Allied bombing of German cities. (No one knows yet what the V2 will turn out to be.) The V1s are small pilotless aircraft, painted an ominous black, with a bomb-shaped fuselage carrying a ton of high explosive and short stubby wings. They are propelled by a jet engine, mounted above the fuselage like the handle on a flatiron, which makes a distinctive droning sound, causing them to be nicknamed 'buzz-bombs' or 'doodlebugs' by the British public. At a pre-set moment the engine cuts out, and the weapon falls to the ground. The heart-stopping seconds of silent suspense between the cutting out of the engine and the noise of an explosion as the missile hits its random target is a new source of stress for long-suffering Londoners.

This is a development in aerial warfare that H.G. has not foreseen. The V1s fly fast and low at all hours of the day and night, when they reveal their presence by a tongue of fire spurting from the jet engine. Anti-aircraft guns are of little use against them, and only the latest Spitfires and Typhoons can match their speed and shoot them down or tip their wings to send them spinning into the sea or open country (a difficult manoeuvre, but to shoot is to risk being blown up oneself). The V1 offensive began on the 13th of June, and by the end of the month two and a half thousand have been launched, of which about a third came down or were brought down in the

24

Channel, a third in south-east England, and a third reached London. The numbers increase in July. It seems as if a new Blitz is beginning. Plans are made to evacuate women and children from the capital. The leaseholders of Hanover Terrace slope off back to their rural bolt-holes. Various friends and acquaintances urge H.G. to move to a safer location, but he dismisses these suggestions with scorn. The V1 offensive seems to have a tonic effect on his health. His appetite improves. He becomes more mobile, walking around the house and even, in fine weather, having short outings in the Park.

Moura visits him one day without notice, letting herself into the house with her latchkey, so it is a surprise, and a pleasant one, though she herself looks flustered. She travelled up to London that morning from her daughter's home near Oxford to find her own flat with its windows blown out by blast from a V1. It was a shock, she says, and she asks for a brandy to calm herself. 'Leave the bottle,' she instructs the housekeeper when the drink is brought, and winks at H.G. Her capacity for brandy is legendary. When she pronounces 'Hanover Terrace' in her unique Anglo-Russian accent it sounds like 'Hangover Terrace', but he has never known her to be hung over—only the men who tried to keep up with her drinking the night before. 'Why don't you move in here till your flat is made habitable?' he suggests, but she shakes her head, and pours herself another brandy. 'No, I will go back to Tania's.' He does not suspect her of running away from the V1s. If only half of the lethal dangers she claims to have encountered and survived in her lifetime are to be believed—well, on reflection, probably half is about the right proportion, so say a quarter—if only a *quarter* of the perils she claims to have lived through are to be believed, there could be no question of her courage and nerve. 'You could have the guest bedroom as long as you like,' he says. She wags her finger at him. 'Aigee! You are trying to break our agreement.'

Normally he was the one who dictated the terms of 'treaties', as he called them, with his women, but not with Moura. This one went back to the mid-1930s. She was willing to be his mistress, and to appear at his side in society, but she would not marry him and she would not live with him. When, after one of their many arguments, he said sulkily that in that case he wanted his latchkey back, she handed it to him on the spot. Subsequently she borrowed it for some particular reason and he did not ask her to return it, so she retained her freedom to come and go as she pleased. If they made love in Hanover Terrace after spending the evening together, she would leave him afterwards and go home by taxi. How often he had watched her from the bed as he telephoned for one and she put on her clothes by the dim light of a shaded table lamp—all except her stays, which she rolled up and put into a paper bag before leaving, because she couldn't be bothered to struggle into them for the taxi ride.

'Did you ever leave your stays in the taxi?' he asks her on a sudden impulse.

'What are you talking about?' she says.

'When you went home after we made love here, you didn't put your stays on, you used to put them in a paper bag. I wondered whether you ever left them on the back seat of the taxi, and what the driver would have made of them if he found them.' He smiles, but Moura doesn't seem to be amused. Perhaps she doesn't care to be reminded of her need for corsetry. She was a slim, lissome young woman when he first met her, but has an ample, slackly curved body in middle age.

'What nonsense you talk, Aigee!' she says. 'Be serious. How are you—really?'

'I'm feeling much better,' he replies, 'and all the better for seeing you.' He does not see the need to tell her of Horder's diagnosis, which he is beginning to distrust.

'And the flying bombs? They don't frighten you?'

'Not a bit.'

'But you must have your windows covered. Promise me.' He agrees, reluctantly because it will make the house so dark, but there is always the glazed sun lounge, which cannot practicably be protected from blast.

All through July he writes regularly to Moura to assure her that he is surviving the V1 bombardment in good heart: '*Sweet little Moura, everything you told me to do I am doing. Everything you told me not to do I do not do. And so I am still alive although there was one doodlebug this afternoon which fell apparently on the edge of the world because I heard no more of it . . . All my heart & love, Aigee . . . Dear little Moura, we had a near one last night but all your injunctions are scrupulously obeyed & we are now living in a boarded up and windowless home. Physically I get stronger and stronger every hour. All of my warmest love to you, your devoted Aigee . . . Sweet my Moura, the robot bombs come in increased quantities but thanks to my punctilious observance of your instructions no harm has come to me (or to anyone else in the house) . . . I go on working & I grow more & more self reliant every day . . . I love you my dear & am as ever your Aigee.'* The repeated references to Moura's instructions about boarding up the windows are designed to bestow on her a kind of wifely status in his domestic arrangements. He has always been haunted by the fear of loneliness, of being without a woman companion devoted to his welfare, and he hasn't entirely abandoned hope of persuading Moura one day to move into Hanover Terrace.

Sometimes he sits at the desk in his study, opens one of the two manila folders placed on its surface, and turns a few pages of the typescript it contains, making an occasional note or emendation with a fountain pen. These two works in progress, which he has been composing in tandem for some months, reflect his fluctuating moods as he turns from one to the other. One is a short text entitled *The Happy Turning.* It begins *'I am dreaming far more than I did before this chaotic war invaded my waking hours',* and goes on to describe a recurring dream based on the daily constitutional he used to take in the Park when he was well.

> *I dream I am at my front door starting out for the accustomed round. I go out and suddenly realise there is a possible turning I have overlooked. Odd I have never taken it, but there it is! And in a trice I am walking more briskly than I ever walked before, up hill and down dale, in scenes of happiness such as I never hoped to see again.*

It is a slight, sunny prose fantasia, a carnivalesque reworking of his story 'The Door in the Wall'. It owes something to the idea of 'dreaming true' in George du Maurier's *Peter Ibbetson,* and even more to Henry James's tale 'The Great Good Place'. They are all secular myths of transcendence, of paradise regained. *'Nobody is dead in this world of release, and I hate nobody.'* He meets and chats companionably with Jesus, whose *'scorn and contempt for Christianity go beyond my extremest vocabulary',* and who asserts that his greatest mistake was having disciples. *' "I picked my dozen almost haphazard. What a crew they were! I am told that even those Gospels you talk about, are unflattering in their account of them." '* Sometimes he dreams of *'a purely*

27

architectural world. I apprehend gigantic facades, vast stretches of magnificently schemed landscape, moving roads that will take you wherever you want to go instead of your taking them . . .' But unlike the futuristic cityscapes of his utopian fictions, which people seemed to find so cold and inhuman, especially as visualised in Korda's film *Things to Come,* in his dream *'endless lovely new things are achieved, but nothing a human heart has loved will be lost'.* He ends up in the Elysian Fields, discussing *'the Beautiful, the Good, and the True'* with a group of poets, painters and artists, but this episode, probably to be the conclusion of the book, is still incomplete.

The tone of the other text is very different. It is entitled *Mind at the End of its Tether.*

> *The writer finds very considerable reason for believing that his world is at the end of its tether . . . The end of everything we call life is close at hand and cannot be evaded. He is telling you the conclusions to which reality has driven his own mind, and he thinks you may be interested enough to consider them . . . Foremost in this scrutiny is the abrupt revelation of a hitherto unsuspected upward limit to quantitative material adjustability . . . The writer is convinced that there is no way out or round or through that impasse. It is the End . . . The limit to the orderly secular development of life had seemed to be a definitely fixed one, so that it was possible to sketch out the pattern of things to come. But that limit was reached and passed into an incredible chaos . . . Events now follow one another in an entirely untrustworthy sequence. No one knows what tomorrow will bring forth, but no one but a modern scientific philosopher can accept this untrustworthiness fully. Even in his case it plays no part in his everyday behaviour. There he is at one with the normal multitude. The only difference is that he carries about with him this harsh conviction of the near conclusive end of all life . . . It does not prevent his having his everyday affections and interests, indignations and so forth . . . Mind may be near the end of its tether, and yet that everyday drama will go on because it is the normal make-up of life and there is nothing else to replace it.*

Nothing could illustrate this paradox more vividly than Anthony's marital crisis and its repercussions. While the fate of Europe hangs in the balance in Normandy, where the Allied forces are bogged down and unable to advance, hampered by bad weather, which has broken up the Mulberry harbour, grounded air support for the invasion force, and turned the deep lanes of the Normandy *bocage* into mud, while V1s dart noisily across the skies of south-east England in ever-increasing numbers, to expire lethally like heavy birds stricken with heart attacks above the roofs of London—while these events, which are signs and portents to the scientific philosopher, are in progress—what most exercises the minds of Anthony and Rebecca and Kitty and their close relations, and what they talk and telephone and write letters about obsessively, is this drama in their personal lives. Whose fault is it? Anthony's or Kitty's? Or the Other Woman's? What is to be done? How will it all end?

Rebecca arranges a meeting between Anthony and Henry, hopeful that her husband's calm counsel will be more effective than her own in bringing Anthony to see sense. Anthony agrees but then cancels the appointment. Rebecca criticises this evasive behaviour and points out that there are financial aspects to Anthony's proposed divorce on which Henry's advice would be useful. 'Then let Henry speak to Kitty,' Anthony says, and arranges for them to meet for lunch one day early in July at the Carlton Grill. Although she has not been invited, Rebecca insists on accompanying Henry, and he is too apprehensive of her temper, when crossed, to resist. Kitty, already tired of the stream of letters Rebecca has been sending her, comprehensively condemning Anthony and promoting herself as Kitty's chief ally and protector, resents her unexpected appearance in the Carlton Grill bar and retaliates by taking Anthony's side in the discussion that follows. Four years older than Anthony, but secure in her blonde good looks, Kitty refuses to play the role of the injured spouse, and adopts a philosophical view of the situation, saying 'such things do happen—men fall in love'. 'But Anthony is not acting normally,' Rebecca retorts. 'I can tell when I speak to him on the phone that he is not in his right mind.' 'That's funny, that's exactly what Anthony says about you,' says Kitty tartly. 'And I wish you wouldn't get at Anthony about Caroline and Edmund,' she adds. 'Surely,' Rebecca asks, 'I have a right to tell him I think he will regret leaving his children?' 'No,' says Kitty. 'That's a matter between Anthony and me.' 'Mayn't I even offer an opinion?' says Rebecca. 'No,' says Kitty, 'that's my business, not yours. You shouldn't interfere.'

Henry coughs and says he will see if their table is ready. But there is no table to be had—it seems there was some misunderstanding between Henry and Anthony about reserving it—so they get a taxi to the Ritz. On the way

Kitty goads Rebecca further, remarking that Anthony shows signs of maturing at last, and she is hopeful that he will grow out of his current infatuation. Rebecca says she is a fool—Anthony is utterly irresponsible and mentally unstable. Over lunch, of which not much is eaten, the more Kitty defends Anthony the more hysterical Rebecca grows in her denunciation of her son. He is evil and vile and brings nothing but suffering on everyone he is involved with. There is something fundamentally base about him. She wishes she had never brought him into the world. She wishes he were dead. Gradually the diners at the tables around them fall silent, awed and fascinated by this torrent of eloquent vituperation. Eventually Henry beckons to the head waiter and together they escort Rebecca from the dining room and put her into a taxi to Marylebone station, Henry returning to apologise to Kitty and finish his lunch. 'I'm afraid Rebecca is under considerable strain,' he says.

When Kitty describes this episode to Anthony by telephone that evening he rocks himself in his chair, groaning and laughing with his eyes squeezed shut, visualising the scene, half appalled and half elated at having his prejudices against his mother so thoroughly vindicated. Relaying the story immediately to Jean he embroiders it, as a novelist might, to heighten the effect, so that in his version Rebecca is lifted from her chair by Henry and the head waiter and carried bodily from the dining room with her legs kicking in the air, still shrieking anathemas against Anthony, until the swing doors close on her, a detail he likes so much that he believes it actually happened. Jean however seems to find the story more alarming than amusing. 'I don't think I could ever face meeting your mother,' she says down the line. 'It would be like going into a house where you know there's an unexploded bomb, waiting to go off.' 'Don't worry, darling,' Anthony says. 'She'll calm down eventually.' And indeed by the time Henry gets back to Ibstone that evening he finds Rebecca in a comparatively submissive mood. He reproaches her for her behaviour in the Ritz dining room and accuses her of making an unprovoked attack on Kitty. 'I'm sorry I lost my temper,' Rebecca says, 'but in fact she provoked me a great deal. I don't think you can have heard everything she said—you know you're getting deaf, Ric.' This she has found is a sovereign way to silence Henry since he cannot deny that his hearing is deteriorating and therefore cannot be sure that he hasn't missed some vital bit of information.

. . .

At the end of July there is good news at last from the Second Front. American armoured forces break out of the Cherbourg Peninsula, rout the German defences around St Lô, spread out through Brittany and race towards Paris, which is liberated on August 25th without German resistance. British and Canadian troops take Caen and push swiftly into north-eastern France. H.G. arranges to publish part of *The Happy Turning* in a magazine, the *Leader,* in October. But hopes of a swift end to the war are dashed in September by the costly failure of the airborne attempt to secure three bridgeheads over the Rhine at Arnhem. In the same month the second of Hitler's *Vergeltungswaffen,* the V2, is launched against London. There is absolutely no defence against these huge rockets with a 2,000-pound high explosive warhead, and hardly any warning of their approach, since they travel at five times the speed of sound. If you should happen to look up at the right moment you might see a small red glow in the sky seconds before there is a devastating impact on some unfortunate street or office block or store, but that is all. In a way the V2s are less frightening than the V1s because there is no pause for fearful suspense and no possibility at all of taking shelter. Either your number is on the warhead or it isn't, and if it is you will never know. This breeds a kind of fatalism in the population, a tendency to ignore the crump of an incoming rocket unless it is very near, or to register the sound of its detonation with a mere shrug or grimace. H.G. did foresee the development of rocket weapons in his early books, but not quite on this scale. He closes the *Happy Turning* folder and opens the one containing *Mind at the End of Its Tether.*

> *Hitherto, recurrence has seemed a primary law of life. Night has followed day and day night. But in this strange new phase of existence into which our universe is passing, it becomes evident that events no longer recur. They go on and on to an impenetrable mystery, into a voiceless limitless darkness, against which the obstinate urgency of our dissatisfied minds may struggle, but will struggle only until it is altogether overcome.*
>
> *There is no way out or round or through.*

Meanwhile Anthony's marital crisis remains unresolved. Kitty calmly declines to co-operate in obtaining a divorce, and Anthony finds he has no will to force the issue. One evening, as he sits in silence with H.G., lost in troubled thoughts about Jean, and Kitty and the children, trying to do moral and emotional equations in his head which never come out, Anthony glances at his father, who has been dozing in his armchair, and is startled to see that the bright blue-grey eyes are open and glaring at himself.

'Hallo, H.G.!' he says. 'Woken up?'

'You look worried,' says his father.

'Well, naturally . . . I don't want to hurt Kitty, or the children. I want to do what's best for everybody.'

'It's not those Nazis in the BBC then?'

'What Nazis?'

'The ones who are blackmailing you.'

After a few more questions Anthony ascertains that H.G. believes he is being manipulated by Nazi agents who have infiltrated the BBC.

'That's complete nonsense, H.G.,' Anthony protests.

'Is it?' says his father sceptically, and closes his eyes again.

It doesn't take Anthony long to trace this bizarre fantasy to Rebecca. The publication in 1941 of *Black Lamb and Grey Falcon*, half a million words on the history, topography, ethnography and culture of Yugoslavia, established her as an authority on that country as long as Britain supported its royalist government in exile and the Serbian General Mihailović's resistance campaign against the German occupation, her sympathies being emphatically pro-Serb. But now that Churchill has switched Allied support to the Croat Tito's communist partisans she feels isolated and vulnerable to attacks by left-wing commentators and politicians. She has mentioned this concern to Anthony, and hinted that the pro-Tito faction in the Foreign Office might get at her by throwing suspicion on his role in the BBC. He had paid little attention to this typically paranoid suggestion at the time, but now he sees a connection with H.G.'s crazy delusions which makes him reach immediately for the telephone.

'Rac—have you been talking to H.G. about my being blackmailed by Nazi infiltrators at the BBC?'

'Of course not. Whatever gave you that idea?'

'You've had no conversation at all with H.G. about my position in the BBC?'

There is a pause before Rebecca resumes in a more defensive tone. 'Well, as you know, I'm concerned that my enemies might exploit your past record to discredit you and compromise me . . .'

'What do you mean—my record?'

'They know that you were a pacifist for a time, and they've probably found out that you were under police surveillance as a suspected spy at the beginning of the war.'

'That was a total farce, as you know, Rac!'

He and Kitty had come under suspicion when they were entertaining some Belgian friends at their Wiltshire farm. Overheard Flemish was mistaken for German, flapping curtains were interpreted as semaphored signals, and the farmhouse was searched for incriminating evidence by frowning rustic constables who solemnly impounded Anthony's foreign books, maps, guides, and a collection of toy soldiers given to him in childhood by H.G.

'It may have seemed farcical to you, but they only suspended the investigation because I had friends in high places, like Harold Nicolson and Harold Laski,' says Rebecca.

'But have you been talking about this to H.G. lately?'

'I may have mentioned it,' she admits.

'Well, he's converted it into a crazy conspiracy theory of his own about Nazi infiltrators at the BBC blackmailing me. I'd be much obliged if you would disabuse him.'

'Well, I'll try . . . But it sounds like the onset of senility, I'm afraid.'

'Just do it,' says Anthony and slams down the phone.

Whether she did or not he is unable to ascertain. He swears to his father that there is no conspiracy of any kind against him, and enlists Gip and Marjorie in support, but H.G. continues to goad him with allusions to 'your Nazi friends at the BBC' from time to time. Whether these barbs are prompted by dementia or conscious malice, Anthony is unable to decide, but this additional source of friction between them causes him pain and does nothing to improve relations between himself and his mother.

Then suddenly, in October, the crisis in Anthony's marriage is over. After sex one afternoon in Jean's flat, lying in the bed amid the tangled sheets, smoking a cigarette, and watching Jean put on her stockings, examining each one carefully for ladders, Anthony mentions that H.G. is altering his will to leave some money to Kitty and the children in the event of a divorce. Jean is disconcerted by this information. 'Will it be taken from what you were to get?' she asks. Anthony says it will, as seems only fair. Jean disagrees. She doesn't see why the money should have to be deducted from Anthony's inheritance, since his father must be jolly rich. 'Not all that rich,' he says. 'H.G. doesn't earn a huge amount from his books these days, and when he did he spent it freely and gave a lot away.' 'All the more reason to make sure you get your fair share of what's left,' Jean says. Anthony accuses her of being mercenary. Jean takes offence. They have a blazing row, and she asks him to leave. He says he won't come back. She says that's fine by her. Who knows if H.G.'s will was the real *casus belli*, or whether both of them were tired of the affair and looking for a pretext to end it?

Anthony continues to live at Mr Mumford's because Kitty, understandably, is unwilling to have him back in the matrimonial home at once, and requests an interval for reflection. Anthony tells Rebecca, when she visits him one day, that he is hopeful they will get together again in due course. Rebecca is relieved, and makes a kind of peace with Anthony. H.G. is pleased not to have to concern himself with the matter any longer. He wants to think about his life, free from distraction.

As the year wanes, as the air becomes colder and the blackout plunges London into pre-industrial gloom at an earlier and earlier hour, the revived energy he felt in the summer begins to fade. He becomes more withdrawn, living inside his own head. The other people in the house, the nurses, the cook-housekeeper, the woman who comes in daily to clean, and his small family entourage of Marjorie, Gip and Anthony, observe him slumped in his armchair in the small sitting room, staring into space, muttering to himself, or sitting at his desk in the study, turning over papers, getting up occasionally to take down a book from the shelves, or rummaging for letters and photographs in drawers and filing cabinets. They do not know what is going on in his head. The mind is a time machine that travels backwards in memory and forwards in prophecy, but he has done with prophecy now. His mind is at the end of its tether, he cannot bear to look forward into the chaos ahead. He looks back, at his life: has it, taken all in all, been a story of success or failure? In trying to answer this question it is useful to have a second voice. He can, for instance, interview himself about his past, lobbing easy questions and answering them expansively, as he used to do in the days when journalists were still interested.

2

—So when and where were you born?

—On the 21st of September, 1866, at Atlas House, in Bromley High Street—an undistinguished place, Bromley, halfway between a town and village, about ten miles south of London and soon to be swallowed up by it. 'Atlas House' was the ridiculously pretentious name of a china shop, a chronically unprofitable business which my parents were conned into taking over from a relative. Neither of them had any aptitude for commerce. My mother had been a lady's maid in a great house before she married, and my father an under-gardener on the same estate. He was also a very good cricketer—turned professional and played for Kent after they married. That brought in some additional income, and he sold cricket gear from the shop, but not very profitably. Who would think of going to a china shop to buy a cricket bat?

—What's your earliest memory?

—Looking up through the barred window of our kitchen at the feet of people going past on the pavement. We lived above and behind the shop and the house was built on a slope, so our kitchen and scullery were below ground level. The whole house was dark, cramped and insanitary. There was a dangerously steep staircase that led from the back parlour down to the kitchen and the scullery, which had a single pump-driven cold tap. There was an open gutter in the yard where the domestic waste water soaked away into a cesspit under the outdoor jakes, just a few yards from the well that provided fresh water for the pump.

—But by the age of thirty-four you had done well enough to build your own spacious house overlooking the sea at Sandgate, near Folkestone, designed by a distinguished architect—

—And by me as well. It was the first private house in the country in which every bedroom had its own lavatory attached. That was my idea, and I had to fight Voysey every inch of the way to get it. But without the experience of growing up in that jerry-built horror on Bromley High Street, I probably wouldn't have had the vision to build Spade House. It gave me a lifelong obsession with domestic architecture, and a hatred of the badly designed houses which spread all over suburban England in the late nineteenth century like some kind of brick-and-mortar leprosy. My poor mother wore herself out trying to keep Atlas House clean and decent, but she hadn't a chance. There were vermin behind the wallpaper and in the furniture—you could squash them if you saw them, but you could never get rid of them.

—So, growing up in poverty—

—It wasn't real poverty. We never starved, but we had a poor diet, which stunted my growth, and made me susceptible to illness. We never went barefoot—but we wore ill-fitting boots and shoes. It was a kind of genteel poverty. I was never allowed to bring my friends home to play because they would see that we couldn't afford a servant, not even the humblest skivvy, and the word would get round the neighbourhood. My parents scrimped and saved so they could send me to the cheapest kind of private school, and avoid the shame of a board school, where I might have had better-trained teachers.

—Were you aware that you had talents which were being stifled by this environment?

—Dimly. I discovered from books that there was a more exciting, fulfilling world elsewhere, but I despaired of ever getting access to it.

—What would you say was the lowest point in your life at that time?

—Well, there are a lot to choose from . . . But I think it was my first day at the Southsea Drapery Emporium, the day I arrived to begin my second apprenticeship. I was fifteen. I'd left school at fourteen, because my parents couldn't afford to go on paying the fees even though Bromley Academy's were as low as they came. When I was about eleven my father had an accident and broke his leg, which put a full stop to his cricketing career, so money was very short after that. My mother was set on making me into a draper, like my two older brothers, but I behaved so badly in my first apprenticeship, at Windsor, that I was fired after a few months. By this time my mother had returned to Up Park, the big country house near Midhurst in West Sussex where she'd been a maidservant before she was married. She was offered the job of housekeeper, which was an unexpected stroke of luck for her, and she was able to accommodate me there for a while. I had a trial as apprentice to a chemist in the town of Midhurst, which I found more congenial than drapery, but my mother couldn't afford the higher premium, so it didn't last long. Long enough, though, for me to be sent to Midhurst Grammar School for a few private lessons in Latin from the headmaster—just so I could read prescriptions and the labels on the bottles—and when the family at Up Park got restive about my continuing presence my mother boarded me at the school as a pupil for some weeks while she looked for another draper's apprenticeship for me. She had a faith in that branch of retail trade that was almost religious. But I'd had a taste of something resembling real education at Midhurst Grammar, and I'd discovered the library at Up Park, a wonderful place, with cliffs of books so high you had to scale them with a moveable ladder, books like *Gulliver's Travels* and Plato's *Republic*. In the attic next to my bedroom I found the components of an old reflecting telescope which I managed to put together, and mounted at my bedroom window to look at the craters of the moon—perhaps *The First Men in the Moon* had its genesis there. The family that owned Up Park made little use of their library and none at all of the telescope, but the glimpses I had of their civilised, leisured existence excited my adolescent mind and opened up all kinds of horizons previously hidden from me. I didn't know what I wanted from life exactly, or what I could achieve, but I knew it had to be something more fulfilling than working in a shop . . . Where was I?

—Your second draper's apprenticeship.

—Yes. That's why my first day was so depressing—because it *was* the second one. I remember taking my valise up to the dreary dormitory where the apprentices and junior assistants slept, its eight iron beds and four washhand stands with chipped enamel basins lined up on the bare floorboards, waiting for someone to come and show me over the premises and knowing in advance what they would be like—the windowless basement dining room illuminated by naked gas jets, its walls damp with condensation and the smell of the previous night's cabbage still lingering in the air, where I would have a bread-and-butter breakfast at half-past eight in the morning after working for an hour getting the shop ready for opening time, and where I would return for my dinner after a long day of humping bales of cloth and kowtowing to toffee-nosed customers and being ordered about by the senior shopwalkers. '*Forward, Wells!*' That's what they used to bark when they wanted you for something . . . The dormitory windows overlooked a narrow featureless cul-de-sac that resembled a prison yard, and peering down at it I felt like an old lag returning to serve a second sentence—a four-year sentence, because my mother had paid nearly the whole premium in advance. That was my lowest moment.

—And what would you say was the most important turning point in your life?

—Getting out of there. The place was exactly as I had feared. If you've read my novel *Kipps* you'll know what it was like. Wage-slavery, made all the worse somehow—worse than a factory or a mine, where the manners would be as rough as the work—by the fact that the nature of the trade required us to mimic the gentility of our customers. I was suffocating in an atmosphere of false gentility and petty cash—what a redolent phrase that is, *petty cash*! Everything was petty in that world—the ideas, the conversations, the flirtations, the ambitions. It was as if the eternal verities were measured out and cut up in yards and inches, and their price calculated down to the last three-farthings. Anything but the most proper behaviour, not only in working hours, but in our meagre spare time, could cause instant dismissal. The fear of losing your 'crib' as it was called, and falling into the abyss of poverty, hung over the shop assistants as well as the apprentices—over everybody except the Boss, and very few had any hope of becoming a boss themselves. There's a gloomy character in the novel called Minton, a senior apprentice, who says to Kipps, *'I tell you we're in a blessed drainpipe, and we've got to crawl along it till we die.'* That was taken from life, only the chap who said it to me called it a 'bloody drainpipe'. I stuck it for two years, but by then I'd had enough . . . I knew the only way out of the drainpipe was through education. I was clever, but I wasn't educated. I thought wistfully of my brief time at Midhurst Grammar and I knew there were persons called ushers, who acted as teachers to younger pupils while receiving some tuition themselves. So I wrote to the headmaster, a man called Byatt, and asked if he would take me on in that capacity. Now Byatt knew I was clever because he had coached me in Latin and I'd astonished him by learning more Latin in five weeks than most of his beginners managed in a year. He thought I could be useful to him, so he offered to take me on as a student-teacher, without pay, but with board and lodging provided. One Sunday, my day off work, I walked the seventeen miles to Up Park, and told my mother what I wanted to do. Of course she resisted the idea. She wept and argued and pleaded with me to give the drapery apprenticeship 'one more try'. I don't think it was the thought of losing the premium that worried her most—it was the uncertainty of an unqualified teacher's future, and above all my apostasy from the retail trade in drapery.

—What about your father? What did he say?

—He was furious at the prospect of my forfeiting the premium, but his opinion didn't really matter. He lived alone in Atlas House after my mother went back to Up Park, making a pretence of running the shop until it was finally declared insolvent. He was a broken man really, after the accident—cricket was all he lived for, and he'd been good at it. He's the only player who ever clean-bowled four batsmen with successive balls in first-class cricket. You'll find it in Wisden. But my mother was always the dominant partner in the marriage, and she made all the decisions. Legally I was still a child, and Byatt couldn't take me on without her agreement. I had to return to Southsea that Sunday evening, but I told her that if she wouldn't let me go to Midhurst I would kill myself.

—Did you mean it?

—I believe I did. I'd thought a lot about suicide in Southsea, and what would be the best method: drowning, I decided. It was the only other way out of the drainpipe, as far as I could see. My mother could tell I was serious, and it shook her. As a pious Low Church Anglican she regarded suicide as the unforgivable sin, whereas I had no such scruples—I'd never had much faith in the Christian God, even as a child, and I lost it completely when I was about fifteen.

—For any particular reason?

—I used to go to different churches in Portsmouth on a Sunday, to sample the various services, and one day I went into the Catholic cathedral and heard a sermon on Hell given by some Monsignor in a long skirt which disgusted me—it was just sadistic, designed to fill people with terror—you know the sermon in Joyce's *A Portrait of the Artist as a Young Man*? It was like that. I gave Joyce's book a good review many years later—it brought back that Sunday morning in Portsmouth cathedral so vividly. That was when I shed what little religious faith I still had. I used to scare the other apprentices by making atheistical remarks in the dormitory and challenging the Deity to strike me dead with a thunderbolt if He existed.

—Did you tell your mother that you were no longer a believer?

—No, though she probably guessed from the suicide threat. Fortunately Byatt improved his offer and proposed to pay me twenty pounds a year, rising to forty in the second year if I gave satisfaction. My mother conceded defeat. I left the Southsea Drapery Emporium and went to Midhurst Grammar School. Ironically I had to agree to be confirmed shortly after I got there, because all teachers at the school were required to be members of the Church of England. I hated submitting to the mumbo-jumbo, acting out a lie, but there was no alternative. There were other turning points in my career, but that was the crucial one. Everything else followed from that act of faith in my own potential, that insistence on getting myself educated.

—You gave satisfaction at Midhurst Grammar, then?

—I certainly did . . . Byatt was a good man, and I owe him a lot, but he exploited me to some extent. He got grant money from the government, you see, for every exam one of his pupils passed in a science programme which was being promoted by the Education Department at the time— four pounds for a first-class mark, two pounds for a second and so on. Byatt put me in for everything he could think of, and I had to mug up an incredible range of subjects—physiology, botany, geology, mathematics, chemistry, physics . . . I acquired a grounding in pretty well the whole range of modern science—it was elementary, but it served me well later. I crammed myself out of textbooks, just to pass the exams. But I did more than pass—I got a First in nearly every subject I went in for. I was pleased of course, and Byatt was delighted, but I didn't realise what a remarkable achievement it was until I was invited to apply for a scholarship to study for a degree at the Normal School of Science in South Kensington, and got it—one of only five for the whole country. Poor old Byatt was furious because I applied without telling him, and accused me of breaking my contract, but the chance of studying under the great Thomas Huxley was too good to miss. That was when I first realised that my brain had more than ordinary powers of assimilation.

—But the subtitle of your autobiography is 'Discoveries and Conclusions of a Very *Ordinary* Brain'.

—Yes, well, a little modesty always goes down well with the British public . . .

—And when did you think that you might make your mark on the wider world as a writer?

—Oh, when *The Time Machine* came out, definitely. Up to that point I was just a journalist—turning out articles and sketches and stories tailored to the market. I'd given up teaching as a career. It was a boom time for newspapers and magazines, the 1890s, and if you had a fund of fresh ideas and a certain facility with the pen, you could make a decent living as a freelance. But, as it happened, in 1894 a number of my regular sources of income—the magazines and editors who liked my work—suddenly dried up, and I was strapped for cash. It was a difficult time. Jane and I were waiting for my divorce from Isabel, and we'd moved out of London for her health, which was delicate, as indeed was mine, and we took digs in Sevenoaks under the suspicious nose of a landlady who before long found out we were living in sin but couldn't actually accuse us without admitting she'd been reading my correspondence, so she just tried to make life uncomfortable for us . . . Anyway, that was the situation when I dug out a story I'd once drafted called 'The Chronic Argonauts'—not exactly a catchy title, eh?—and completely rewrote it as *The Time Machine.* Luckily William Henley, who'd been a patron of mine in the past, but had been out of a job for a while, was appointed editor of a new magazine called the *New Review,* and he took *The Time Machine* as a serial. He offered me a hundred pounds for it. A hundred pounds! That was a fortune to us. And when it was published as a book it was a tremendous hit. I remember one of the magazines, the *Review of Reviews* I think it was, said, 'Mr H.G. Wells is a genius'. You couldn't ask for more than that for a first book. It's never been out of print since.

He opens one of the glass-fronted bookcases in his study where he keeps first editions of his novels and takes out *The Time Machine,* a slim crown octavo volume published by Heinemann, in a pale grey cloth binding, with the title and a line drawing of a sphinx imprinted on the front cover in purple. It is a habit he has acquired lately, going to the bookshelves, taking down one of his books from the past and opening it at random to see how it reads, like putting a sample in a test tube and holding it up to the light. But this test isn't truly random, for the book falls open where it has been opened many times before, at one of his favourite passages, where the Time Traveller drives his machine, now positioned on a beach, nearer and nearer to the death of the sun and the end of life on earth.

> So I travelled, stopping ever and again, in great strides of a thousand years or more, drawn on by the mystery of the earth's fate, watching with a strange fascination the sun grow larger and duller in the westward sky, and the life of the old earth ebb away. The darkness grew apace. From the edge of the sea came a ripple and

whisper. Beyond these lifeless sounds the world was silent. Silent? It would be hard to convey the stillness of it. All the sounds of man, the bleating of sheep, the cries of birds, the hum of insects, the stir that makes the background of our lives—all that was over . . . The sky was absolutely black. A horror of this great darkness came on me . . . Then like a red-hot bow in the sky appeared the edge of the sun. I got off the machine to recover myself. I felt giddy and incapable of facing the return journey. As I stood sick and confused I saw again the moving thing upon the shoal—there was no mistake now that it was a moving thing—against the red water of the sea. It was a round thing, the size of a football perhaps, or, it may be, bigger, and tentacles trailed down from it; it seemed black against the weltering blood-red water, and it was hopping fitfully about. Then I felt I was fainting. But a terrible dread of lying helpless in that remote and awful twilight sustained me while I clambered upon the saddle.

—The saddle . . .

—Yes, amusing isn't it, that I modelled my time machine on a bicycle? I suppose today I would make it more like a car—or an aeroplane. But it was the age of the bicycle when I wrote the tale—motor cars were still prototypes, and aeroplanes non-existent. The bike was the acme of mechanised transport for most people, certainly one everybody could relate to. And there's something poetic about the bicycle, something slightly magical. I once saw a picture of a man pedalling with his bike mounted on a set of rollers, for exercise, and that gave me the idea: time was passing, and he had the illusion of movement as the wheels went round, though he stayed in the same place. But supposing he were actually moving *through* time, and the appearance of the place changed accordingly . . .

—How do you find it reads now?

—Pretty well, I must say. It's very much of its period of course, the 1890s, *fin de siècle,* the so-called Decadence. Pessimism was fashionable among the literati, and I wanted to be taken seriously as a literary writer in those days. Remember that languid exchange of dialogue in Wilde's *Dorian Gray*: ' "*Fin de siècle*" . . . "*Fin du globe*" . . .' *The Time Machine* caught that mood. But it still makes the hairs on the back of my neck prickle, that black thing with tentacles hopping fitfully about in the blood-red shallows, the last vestige of animal life on the planet, evolution having gone into reverse.

—It's a very bleak image.

—Entropy *is* bleak. Sooner or later our solar system will run out of energy and life on earth will end. But actually it will be later rather than sooner, so much later that it's hardly worth worrying about, because long before that point in time human beings will either have wiped themselves out by some other means, or they will have moved off this planet and colonised some other bit of the universe.

—**Which do you think is more likely?**

—At this moment, the former, definitely. And when I wrote *The Time Machine* I would have said the same thing. But for many years in between I was more hopeful about the future of mankind, and our ability to survive even the death of the planet.

—**As you said in your lecture at the Royal Institution, in 1902, '*A day will come when beings, who are now latent in our thoughts and hidden in our loins, will stand upon this earth as one stands upon a footstool, and shall laugh, and reach out their hands amidst the stars.*'**

—Yes. It caused quite a stir, that lecture.

—**Was that what got the Fabian Society interested in recruiting you?**

—It certainly helped, but they were already interested. They'd been reading *Anticipations,* which was published the year before.

He goes across to the bookcase of first editions, takes down the plump octavo volume in its dark red binding and opens it at the title page.

—*Anticipations of the Reaction of Mechanical and Scientific Progress upon Human Life and Thought,* to give its full title.

—**You were generally optimistic in that book about the improvements in human life that scientific progress would bring about.**

—Yes.

—**But in *The Time Machine,* in the main story, which is set in the distant future—**

—802,000 AD.

—**You imagine that humanity has by then split into two races—**

—On reflection, much too distant. I very much doubt whether human civilisation will survive that long.

—**Two races: the Eloi, an effete, pastoral people who live an apparently idyllic life of graceful indolence on the surface of the earth, and the cannibalistic Morlocks, workers who labour in underground factories by** day and emerge only at night to cull the Eloi, whom they rear as cattle, for meat . . . It's a kind of dark satire on the socialist dream of overthrowing industrial capitalism: the proletariat have become the dominant class but exploit the upper class in a peculiarly horrible way. What happened to make you turn, in the space of five years or so, from that nightmarish vision, to the confident prediction in *Anticipations* of a benign social system, attainable within a century, when everybody would be middle class and inhabit a suburban paradise of motor cars and labour-saving domestic appliances?

—The short answer is that I started to make some money—thanks to *The Time Machine.* That book was written out of thirty years of poverty, poor diet and bad health, and if it projected a bleak view of the long-term future that was because my own short-term future seemed bleak to me. I had a defective lung with suspected TB and a damaged kidney. Jane wasn't in much better shape. Neither of us expected to live more than ten years. When *The Time Machine* was a success I exploited it for all it was worth, turning out novels and short stories like a man possessed, to make the most of the time I thought I had left. In that same year, 1895, I published another novel, *The Wonderful Visit,* and a book of short stories. Two more novels the following year, *The Island of Dr Moreau* and *The Wheels of Chance. The Invisible Man* and another collection of short stories in '97 and *The War of the Worlds* in '98. Not to mention countless journalistic articles and reviews. Some of the fiction was as dark and frightening as *The Time Machine*—I still enjoyed putting the wind up my readers, disturbing their complacent trust in things-as-they-are, showing how thin and fragile the veneer of civilisation would prove if some completely unforeseen catastrophe happened, like an invasion of aliens from Mars, or a huge comet which enters our solar system and threatens to collide with the earth, as in my story, 'The Star'. But I always reprieved the world—the comet just misses the earth, the Martians are killed off by bacteria—and there's a suggestion at the end of these tales that a new human solidarity comes out of the horror and suffering.

Meanwhile our lives—Jane's and mine—were improving rapidly. My divorce came through in the same year that *The Time Machine* was published, so we were able to marry and quickly raised our standard of living, moving from house to house and place to place until we ended up in Sandgate. In a few years I had made enough money to build a house there on a prime site, but I still didn't expect to enjoy a long life. I had it designed with some of the bedrooms on the same floor as the living rooms because I was sure that fairly soon I would have to lead an invalid existence in a wheel-chair and be unable to manage stairs. It's true! But by the time the house was built Jane and I were feeling the benefit of a few years of good food, sea air, exercise and domestic comfort. We walked and cycled long distances. We learned to swim and play badminton and tennis. We grew strong and healthy. Gradually it dawned on us that our lives were stretching out ahead of us much further than we had ever envisaged, full of pleasing possibilities. I thought to myself—not in so many words, but it was the underlying drift of my thinking: if I can transform my life in this way by having a bit of luck as a writer, why shouldn't the majority of men—and women—have their lives transformed by a more rational arrangement of society? It's poverty, bad diet, bad health, that keeps them crawling along the drainpipe till they die, and makes them die sooner than those in more privileged circum-stances. My escape from the drainpipe radicalised me, it made me want to take our arteriosclerotic social system by the scruff of the neck and give it a good shake—make it see that things didn't *have* to be ordered in such a way that most men and women led cramped lives of soulless drudgery. It didn't need a violent revolution to change that—just a revolution in think-ing. By the application of scientific intelligence and common sense to the mechanisms of industrial society we could peacefully accomplish a more equitable distribution of its benefits. It was an argument that appealed strongly to the Fabians, who called themselves socialists but rejected the Marxist model of achieving socialism through class warfare, so they invited me to join them, and from my point of view they offered the most conve-nient channel to get my ideas across to the people that mattered. We were natural allies. Or so it seemed in 1903 when I joined the Fabian.

    —**But the alliance didn't last.**

    —No.

    —**Why was that?**

    —Several reasons, which seem obvious in retrospect, but weren't at the time. We agreed that the poverty or near poverty in which most people lived was intolerable, and that wealth needed to be redistributed by the state taking over many of the functions and resources of capitalism and private land ownership. We both believed this could be accomplished by legislation rather than revolution. But the Fabians put their faith in something they called 'permeation'—that is, they would put forward these ideas in print and public debate which would gradually permeate the thinking of politi-cians and the main political parties. 'Gradually' was the operative word.

—Hence the name of the Society.

—Yes, named after the Roman general, Fabius Cunctator, 'Fabius the Delayer'. That choice of name tells you a lot about the Society. I think at heart they never really wanted a socialist state, especially the more prosperous members. They liked to think that they were helping to bring it about in the distant future, but the idea of actually living in it, without servants for instance, without private property, secretly frightened them. I was more impatient. I wanted to get something *done.*

—**You were willing to give up Spade House, and your servants?**

—I wouldn't have had to give up the house, under the sort of system I envisaged. I would have simply paid rent to the state, instead of owning it. And as for servants, I explained in *Anticipations* how rational house design and labour-saving devices—central heating, electric sweeping machines, automatic dishwashers, and so on—would make them unnecessary.

—**But you still have servants yourself.**

—Well, we haven't got a socialist state, or anything like the technologically advanced society I envisaged. You can't catch me out like that! I was often criticised by people on the Left, especially in the Labour Party and the Trade Union movement, for enjoying a high standard of living while calling myself a socialist, and I always gave the same answer: I'm ready to surrender my privileges at the same time as everybody else, and in the meantime I don't see what use it would be to deprive myself of them voluntarily. My greatest extravagance was working countless unpaid hours for the socialist cause.

—**You say you were impatient to get things done. What did you think the Fabian Society should do?**

—Well initially I thought they should work more actively with the Labour movement, put up candidates for Parliament, but I changed my mind about that later. I judged that the Labour Party as long as it was controlled by the trade unions would always be a fundamentally conservative force, obsessed with improving wages and conditions in the workplace, never fundamentally questioning the nature and organisation of the work itself. More and more I came to the conclusion that progressive change would only come about by empowering a new political elite, a body of dedicated managers with a scientific education who would run the state.

—**Those you called 'Samurai' in *A Modern Utopia*? The guardians of the World State.**

—Yes, but the idea was already adumbrated in *Anticipations* as the 'New

Republic'. Later I called it 'The Open Conspiracy'. It was always the same idea, the vision of a just and rationally governed global society from which war, poverty, disease and all the other ills of human civilisation would be eliminated.

—**But not for everybody. Not for the chronically poor, unemployed, sick, retarded, criminals, addicts of drink and gambling—what you called 'the People of the Abyss'.**

Suddenly the interviewer sounds more like an interrogator.

—No, not for them. People physically or mentally incapable of taking advantage of the new opportunities for a happy, useful life, would have to be . . .

—**Eliminated?**

—Well, they couldn't be allowed to be parasites on the rest of the community, obviously. They would have to be discouraged or prevented from breeding.

—**As you wrote in** *Anticipations*: **'To give them equality is to sink to their level, to protect and cherish them is to be swamped by their fecundity.'**

—Exactly.

—**And you also wrote: 'the nation that most resolutely picks over, educates, sterilizes, exports, or poisons its People of the Abyss . . . will certainly be the most powerful or dominant nation before the year 2000.' Isn't 'poisons' a rather shocking suggestion?**

—You've taken that out of context. Listen to the whole passage: *'The nation that most resolutely picks over, educates, sterilizes, exports, or poisons its People of the Abyss; the nation that succeeds most subtly in checking gambling and the moral decay of women and homes that gambling inevitably entails; the nation that by wise interventions, death duties and the like, contrives to expropriate and extinguish incompetent rich families while leaving individual ambitions free; the nation, in a word, that turns the greatest proportion of its irresponsible adiposity into social muscle, will certainly be the most powerful or dominant nation before the year 2000.'*

—**Which one will that be, do you think?**

—I've no idea. Not Britain, by the look of it. Maybe China, if they can cure their passion for gambling.

—**But 'poisons' . . . Aren't you advocating murder there?**

—I was thinking of something like euthanasia, painless voluntary termination. Such people, for whom there is no hope of a happy fulfilled life, would be persuaded that death was a preferable alternative. 'Poisons' was an unfortunate choice of word, one I've often regretted. It's been thrown in my face many times, especially recently, with these reports that the Nazis have been gassing gypsies and mental defectives.

—And Jews. Mostly Jews, in fact.

—I've never regarded the Jews as collectively undesirable. I state that quite categorically in *Anticipations*. Here, on page 316: *'I really do not understand the exceptional attitude people take up against the Jews.'* And I go on to list all the things that people object to about Jews and argue that you can find them equally in other races. I'm anti-Zionist, but not anti-Semitic.

—What about on the next page: *'As for the rest, those swarms of black and brown, and dirty-white and yellow people, who do not come into the new needs of efficiency? As I see it . . . they have to go.'* Go where? Did you mean die, or be killed?

—Die, or die out. It's obvious that the earth cannot support a desirable quality of life for all its inhabitants if the global population goes on expanding as it is at the moment, especially in parts of Africa and the East. There will have to be a world authority capable of controlling population growth by one means or another: contraception, sterilisation, euthanasia. If that doesn't work, famine, or war provoked by shortages of food and water, will bring about the same result more brutally.

—Did the Fabians object to these parts of *Anticipations*?

—Not that I recall. In those days eugenics was rather fashionable on the political Left.

—So that wasn't why you fell out with them?

—No. It was more a matter of policy and personalities. And sex. Basically they couldn't take my views on sex, or not so much the views themselves as the fact that I acted on them.

—How was that?

—It's a long story.

PART TWO

t is a very long story, one that began years before he ever heard the word 'Fabian', and it is another voice that tells it in his head, not an interlocutor or an interrogator or an interviewer, but a novelist, a novelist both like and unlike himself in earlier years when he wrote quasi-autobiographical novels, novel after novel, about men who were seeking some kind of explanation of what was wrong with the human world and what might be done to redeem it and how they might take a leading part in that redemptive process—religious language which superficially might seem to contradict his lifelong hostility to institutional religion, the repressive, fearful Low Church Protestantism of his mother, for instance, or the reactionary dogmatism of the Roman Catholic Church, but he has always regarded his sense of mission as essentially religious, often puzzling or scandalising his secular friends and acquaintances when he so described it. Any devotion to an idea that subordinates the individual's aspirations to the collective good, the idea of socialism for instance, or the idea of a World State, is in his opinion essentially religious. It does not entail allegiance to a Church, or even a God, though there was a period in his life, embarrassing to recall, when he attempted to co-opt God into his programme for saving the world from self-destruction, in books like *God the Invisible King,* published in 1917, one he has never taken down from his bookcase to sample, well aware that he would not be pleasantly surprised.

The best of his novels about men seeking to understand what was wrong with contemporary society, and to find some useful role for themselves in it, was *Tono-Bungay,* published in 1909; in fact he regards it as his best novel of any kind, judged by normal literary criteria. The novels that followed were more polemical and discursive, and, with the exception of *Ann Veronica,* which was centred on its heroine, their heroes were so humourlessly high-minded that he privately referred to these books as his 'prig' novels. *The New Machiavelli, Marriage, The Passionate Friends, The Research Magnificent* were some of their titles, all about men progressing from youth to maturity who were to some extent idealised versions of himself: taller, more handsome, from a higher social class, and considerably more punctilious in their relations with the opposite sex. These men invariably experienced a conflict between their personal sense of mission, whether intellectual or political, and their desire for union with a particular woman. Usually the woman proved to be an obstacle to the fulfilment of the mission, which could only be overcome by her being converted to it or by dying or by some act of renunciation by the hero.

Women, and his relationships with them, had been at the heart of his difficulties with the Fabians. There were differences of opinion about political ends and means between himself and the leading lights of the Society which were always likely to be causes of conflict, but it was his sexual conduct that provoked the final breach and continued afterwards to dog his lone efforts to make the world see sense. The women, and the relationships, were recognisably reflected in the novels—recognisably, but not truthfully. The element of lust, so important in his own sexual life, was almost entirely missing from these books, only occasionally discreetly hinted at and mostly veiled by high-romantic love talk in which the phrase *'Oh, my dear . . .'* figured largely, the ellipsis gesturing towards intensities of emotion which the reader was obliged to imagine unassisted. The satisfaction of lust could not, of course, be truthfully described in fiction without inviting prosecution as a pornographer, and he was not one of those modern novelists, like James Joyce and D.H. Lawrence, who had striven to extend the boundaries of the permissibly explicit. Although *Ann Veronica* had been denounced in the press and from pulpits as a depraved and depraving book when it was published in 1909, that was because the virginal young heroine frankly declared she wanted sexual union with the married hero, not because of any description of their eventual enjoyment of it. In that respect the novel was as pure as the Lambs' *Tales from Shakespeare*. In fact he had never felt any urge to describe the sexual act and its variations in his fiction—it was the sort of discourse he preferred to keep private, confined to love letters and pillow talk. Even the secret Postscript he had written to his autobiography, a memoir of his sexual life to be published after his death by his executors when all the women mentioned were also deceased, was not revealing about what he did with them in bed. That was partly because the manuscript was typed up by Marjorie, and there were limits to how much information of that kind even an honest man, unashamed of his sexuality, wished to share with his daughter-in-law. The novelist in his head has no such inhibitions, but what interests him is not the mechanics of copulation but the operation of sexual desire in a man's life, his life, how it could sometimes be a mere blunt brutal impersonal need for a woman, almost any tolerably attractive woman, assuaged in minutes, and at other times focused obsessively on a particular woman with tormenting pangs of longing and jealousy that lasted for months and years, disturbing and disrupting the serious business of improving collective life.

He must have had well over a hundred women in his lifetime, some on only one occasion, and he has forgotten the names of the majority of them. He was never able to decide whether he had a more powerful sex drive than other men, or was just more successful than most in satisfying it. Perhaps both hypotheses were true. So where did it come from, this sexual appetite? There was no obvious genetic or environmental source. Reading his mother's diary after her death he found no hint of erotic awakening in the account of her early married life, only pleasure in young motherhood, heavily overlaid with pious Christian sentiment. His father was a virile-looking man, and more pleasure-seeking than his wife, but his passion was sport, especially cricket, and for social recreation Joe Wells sought the male companionship of the public house. When he was old enough to observe and reflect on such things, in adolescence, his parents' marriage seemed to him completely sexless; they slept in separate bedrooms, and if this was, as he later suspected, a method of birth control, his father seemed to acquiesce in it. His brothers had been, as far as he knew, sexually unadventurous. Sexual matters were never discussed in the home, which was a matriarchal society in microcosm, four men ruled over by a determined little woman who imposed a rigid code of puritanical decorum in word and deed. The smutty jokes and anecdotes that circulated at school had disgusted rather than excited him. So what could explain his inveterate and inexhaustible desire for women, which began before he even knew the facts of life, and persisted into old age?

The first to affect him in this way were virtual, ideal and classical. These were allegorical figures representing the nations of the world in Tenniel's political cartoons in the bound volumes of *Punch* which his father borrowed for him, along with many other books, from the library of the Bromley Literary Institute, when he was laid up for weeks in the front parlour of Atlas House at the age of seven or eight, recovering from a broken leg. A friendly young man, showing off his strength at the local cricket ground, had tossed little Bertie in the air for fun, but failed to catch him, and he fell on to a tent peg which broke his tibia. It was a curious coincidence that both father and son suffered a broken leg within a few years of each other, and with momentous consequences—catastrophic for the former, liberating for the latter. For that licensed orgy of promiscuous reading, in a home where this activity was normally regarded as a form of idleness—devouring works of history, natural history, popular science, adventure fiction, and bound volumes of *Punch,* as fast as his father could feed them to him—had laid the foundations of his future career as a writer. From the cartoons of *Punch* he acquired a precocious interest in domestic and international politics, but the personification of the nations—Britannia, Erin, Columbia, La France—as beautiful half-naked Grecian deities, with exposed breasts and thighs, also stirred feelings in him that he could not put a name to. All the women he knew were impenetrably covered in fabric from their chins to their feet. It was Tenniel's drawings that first gave him an inkling of what might be found under those layers of cloth, and he furthered his knowledge in early adolescence by inspection of the plaster reproductions of classical statuary in the Crystal Palace at Sydenham, goddesses even more scantily covered than Tenniel's figures, with folds of drapery carved in the act of sliding from their magnificent hips, and all the more affecting for being three-dimensional. He took these images of women home with him stored in his memory and comforted himself in bed at night by conjuring them up in the form of flesh, willing the drapery to fall from their hips, a scenario which, if he turned on to his stomach and pressed his penis against the mattress, would provoke a delicious gush of spunk (as the rougher boys at school called it) without his incurring the guilt attached to actual masturbation. Not that he knew then the words 'penis' or 'masturbation', but when his mother, stripping his bed on washday, asked him sternly if he had been 'touching himself', he could honestly answer in the negative.

These encounters with virtual women implanted in him a devotion to the idealised female form and a longing to embrace the naked body of a beautiful woman, naked himself. The longing was intensified when he came across an old leather-bound edition of Milton's *Paradise Lost* in the library at Up Park illustrated with engravings, one of which showed Adam and Eve in Paradise before the Fall, with Eve's long tresses only half concealing her breasts, and a flower dangling from her hand barely covering her private parts, while Adam's crotch was screened by the bough of a judiciously planted sapling. His arm was extended to lead Eve to their 'Nuptial Bowre' and although Milton was exasperatingly unspecific about what happened there and wrapped it up in stately poetic diction, it sounded thrilling:

> . . . *transported I behold,*
> *Transported touch; here passion first I felt,*
> *Commotion strange, in all enjoyments else*
> *Superior and unmov'd, here only weake*
> *Against the charm of Beauties powerful glance.*

But it was many years before he was able to fulfil his dream of the naked embrace, years during which his sexual experience advanced very slowly and in a furtively titillating, frustratingly unconsummated fashion, always conducted through or under layers of clothing. There was for instance Edith, the youngest daughter of Alfred Williams, a distantly related 'uncle' who ran a school in Wookey, Somerset, with whom he stayed for a while at the age of fourteen in the period between his two apprenticeships, helping out as an unpaid classroom assistant. Several years older than himself and obsessively interested in sex, of which she had no practical experience but about which she possessed a good deal of information, Edith took it on herself to quiz him on his knowledge of the facts of life, and to correct his misapprehensions with a degree of detail that seemed to excite her as much as it embarrassed him. One hot day when they were sitting on a riverbank in the shade of a willow tree, she lay back on the grass, closed her eyes, and gave him permission to feel between her legs under her skirt to learn how women were made, and that was when he first discovered that they had pubic hair. The sensation was something of a shock and caused him to withdraw his hand with an abruptness he later regretted, but when he attempted to repeat the experiment at the next opportunity she slapped his face.

He had similar confusing experiences at the lodging house in Westbourne Park where he lived in his first year as a student at the Normal School of

Science, sent there, ironically, by his mother because the landlady was known to her as the daughter of a piously Evangelical friend in Midhurst. This woman had in fact lapsed from the high moral standards of her parents and presided over a louche household in which the Sabbath was dedicated to the rites of Hymen rather than Jesus Christ. After Sunday lunch, a roast joint accompanied by beer and stout ale, the children were packed off to Sunday School with the servant girl, and the landlady and her husband and a married couple who were lodgers would retire to their bedrooms for a 'lie-down', though not before exchanging a good deal of badinage and innuendo about what this phrase denoted, leaving him in the company of a young woman called Aggie who was related in some way to the landlady. 'Be good!' the married couples would cry to the two young people as they departed, with leering smiles which were clearly an incitement to be the reverse. Even Aggie seemed to expect this, though she imposed strict limits on his exploration of her person when he fondled her on the sofa and attempted to undo various buttons and hooks on her apparel. 'Oi! Stoppit! Not that! Not there!' she would say, slapping and tugging at his hands. 'What sorter gal jer fink I am?' But she never showed any real indignation, or made any attempt to leave the room; she seemed content to spend the afternoon fending off his advances as if it were a recognised parlour sport, a kind of sedentary wrestling. Why he persevered he didn't know, for she was not pretty and hadn't an idea in her head, but there was nothing else to do and nowhere else to go on a Sunday afternoon in winter if you were as penniless as he was.

The landlady herself seemed disposed to be more accommodating. One day she came into his bedroom to change a pillowcase and was surprised, or pretended to be surprised, to find him there. She was wearing a loose house-dress unbuttoned at the neck which gave him a view of her uncorseted breasts swinging freely as she stooped over the bed, and when she saw him staring she held the pillow coquettishly up to her chest. Some badinage followed and a playful struggle for the pillow in the course of which he managed to get his hand inside the dress. She reproached him for his impudence but did not immediately remove the hand. 'Anyone would think you was a grown man, the way you carry on,' she said. 'I *am* a grown man,' he said boldly. He did not add, 'and in need of a woman', but he had some hopes that she might supply that need in due course. Luckily for him, before that could happen, and possibly embroil him in a very ugly situation, he was whisked away from the house by a niece of his father who worked at a department store in Kensington and had been asked to check up on his welfare. She quickly gauged the moral tone of the establishment, and arranged for him to move to his Aunt Mary's lodging house in the Euston Road. And there he met his cousin Isabel, on whom all his romantic and erotic longings would be focused over the next six or seven years.

He was having tea with his Aunt Mary and her sister Aunt Bella in the parlour of the lodging house on the Euston Road, a visit preparatory to moving there, when the door opened and a young woman of his own age came quietly in and stopped, hesitating, as she noticed him.

'This is your cousin Bertie, Isabel,' his Aunt Mary said to her.

He stood up and shook her hand, which felt cool and soft in his, and she smiled timidly and murmured a greeting. She seemed to him extraordinarily beautiful and wonderfully clean and fresh in appearance in spite of having been at work all day in Regent Street where she had a job retouching photographs. She had delicately modelled features and deep-set brown eyes surmounted by a head of densely curled dark brown hair. She wore a simple Pre-Raphaelite-style dress of dark blue wool which showed she had a slim waist and hinted at a shapely bosom. The thought that he was going to live in the same house as this vision filled him with joy.

The house itself offered only one small improvement on the one in Westbourne Park: it had a bathroom of sorts, with a temperamental gas-fired geyser that spat and dribbled hot water into a tub, which lodgers could use once a week at a fixed hour. But both houses were of the same type, replicated thousands of times all over the inner suburbs of London: meanly proportioned imitations of the upper-class town house, originally built for middle-class families with servants and ill adapted to multiple occupancy. His attic bedroom at Aunt Mary's house had no fireplace and no other means of heating. Freezing draughts blew under the ill-fitting door and across the bare boards of the floor in winter, so that he sometimes studied with his stockinged feet resting in the open bottom drawer of the chest of drawers, wrapped in his underwear. But for the time being Isabel's presence in the house made all its imperfections and privations bearable.

That they were cousins made it natural for them to be frequently in each other's company without for some time arousing the suspicions of their elders that this was more than ordinary friendliness. They left the house in the morning together and he accompanied Isabel as far as the photographer's premises in Regent Street before proceeding to South Kensington. On Sundays Isabel would put on her best outdoor clothes while he donned the top hat and tail coat he had acquired at a discount from the Southsea Drapery Emporium, and they would walk in Regent's Park, or visit an art gallery or a church. Yes, a church! Isabel was not devoutly religious but she regarded occasional churchgoing as an index of conventional respectability, and he loved her enough to sit through the doleful hymns and boring sermons, preferably in a crowded pew so that he could squeeze up close and feel her thigh against his.

Isabel was impressed by his talk, different from anything she had heard before in her life, full of wild radical ideas imbibed from attending William Morris's socialist soirées in Hammersmith, and astonishing scientific facts acquired from his courses at college: the evils of industrial capitalism, the vastness of the universe, the fossil evidence for evolution . . . She could not contribute more to these outpourings than an occasional expression of wonder and timid doubt (she refused to believe, for instance, that some of the stars she saw in the sky no longer existed, and that it was only the light they had emitted before their extinction, travelling across millions of miles of space towards the earth, that she observed) but she accepted his learned disquisitions as a kind of tribute to herself and a token of his devotion. For his part it was enough that she was his sweetheart, on whom all his vague dreams and ambitions for the future could be projected. He was well aware of being no great catch as a swain. He was pitifully thin from a poor and insufficient diet—there was a photograph of himself standing next to the skeleton of a great ape in Professor Huxley's laboratory in which it was hard to tell whether he had any more flesh on his bones under his shabby clothes than the grotesque relic beside him. Acutely conscious of his physical shortcomings, he was grateful that he could walk out with such a beautiful girl on his scrawny arm. They kissed and cuddled when the opportunity arose, but if he became a little too ardent for her comfort she found ways, infinitely more delicate and tactful than Aggie's, to disengage herself from his embraces. He was resigned to a long, chaste courtship: given Isabel's character and their family relationship no alternative was imaginable.

He had passed his first-year examinations with distinction, but the amount of time he spent with Isabel during his second year at college caused him to neglect his studies, which had become inherently less interesting as he passed from Professor Huxley's scintillating classes to those of a dull and dry professor of physics. In the evenings he skimped studying in his cold bedroom so he could hasten down to the back parlour where Isabel would be sitting by the fire, ready to chat, and when the weather turned warmer they would go out for evening walks in the Park. The consequence was that he failed one of his second-year exams, and did poorly in others. He was in some fear of losing his grant and his place on the course, but was allowed to continue into the third year. In spite of this warning he did not apply himself diligently to preparing for his final examinations. He was more interested in reading books about socialism, making provocative speeches to the College Debating Society, starting up a student magazine, writing stories, essays and poems, and other extracurricular activities, including his courtship of Isabel.

He shouldn't have been surprised when he failed two papers that summer and therefore left the College without a degree, but he was—surprised and shocked. It was a humiliating, morale-shattering setback, which indefinitely postponed the possibility of marrying Isabel, and he directed some of his chagrin at her when he broke the news. They were in Regent's Park, sitting on a bench in the dusk of a summer evening. He slumped with both hands in his trouser pockets, not holding one of hers as usual, gazing glumly across the lake.

'What will you do now, Bertie?' she asked anxiously.

'I'll have to get a teaching post in a private school somewhere,' he said.

'In London?'

'Anywhere that's not fussy about qualifications. In fact it might be better if it was a long way away,' he said.

'Why?' She looked at him anxiously.

'Since there's no realistic prospect of our getting married, I'd rather not be tormented by the daily sight of you,' he said, not seriously expecting that she would throw herself into his arms and offer to assuage his frustration, but out of a cruel wish to make her share something of his own bitterness. In this he was successful. She wept quietly, but said nothing. The park keeper's doleful bell, signalling that the gates to the Inner Circle would soon be locked, tolled the end of their idyll.

After he had made numerous applications to pedagogic agencies one of them found him a post as usher at an establishment called Holt Academy, near Wrexham in Wales. Its brochure was promising, but the reality was deeply depressing: the classrooms were shabby, the food disgusting, the accommodation dirty, the headmaster incompetent, and the pupils mainly local farmers' sons with no interest in learning anything. A miasma of deep provincial dullness hung over the village and the featureless surrounding countryside. A few days after his arrival he wrote to a college friend, Arthur Simmons, thinly disguising his dismay under facetious misspelling: '*I am hier in this gloomy neighbourhood & I wish I was dead. The boys are phoolish & undisciplined to an astonishing degree and the chemistry cupboard is not worthy of the name.*' A month later he escaped from the place, but only through a mishap which threatened to fulfil his rhetorical death wish. A lout of a pupil maliciously fouled him when he joined in a football game, inflicting an injury which caused him to pass blood later. After a few days' recuperation he returned to the classroom but soon collapsed, coughing up more blood. The injury appeared to be a crushed kidney, but the local doctor suspected he might also be consumptive. His mother arranged for him to convalesce at Up Park, where he had another haemorrhage almost as soon as he arrived, seeming to confirm the diagnosis.

His convalescence was not entirely idle. He took the opportunity once more to stock his mind from Up Park's extensive library, and when he moved on from there and took refuge with another friend from college days who lived in the Staffordshire Potteries, an area improbably reputed to be healthy for consumptives, he made some tentative efforts at literary composition, including the first draft of a tale about travelling in time. But he was steeped in self-pity at the prospect of dying with all his aspirations unfulfilled, and without ever having had carnal knowledge of a woman. He discovered later that because consumption is an almost painless illness it encourages a dangerous passivity in its victims, and realised that he had been half in love with easeful death when in fact he was beginning to recover his physical strength.

The turning point occurred one brilliantly sunny day in the late spring of 1888, when he went for a walk in a small wood on the outskirts of Stoke where the fuming chimneys of the potbanks were invisible and wild hyacinths were blooming in profusion. He passed a pretty girl on the footpath, and raised his hat, meeting her eyes with frank admiration. She smiled shyly and walked on, while he stopped and looked back at her, appreciating the swing of her hips under her skirt. He lay down on a grassy bank among the hyacinths and inhaled their heady perfume. He imagined himself making love to the pretty girl, naked under the trees, like Adam and Eve in their nuptial bower, and then he substituted Isabel for her in his mind's eye. He said to himself: 'I have been dying for nearly two-thirds of a year, and I have died enough.' He returned immediately to London and began to look for a job.

Suddenly he was filled with renewed energy, ambition and confidence. Over the next couple of years he obtained a teaching post at a private school in Kilburn, and then a much better paid position as tutor with a correspondence college that served external students of the University of London, where he made himself invaluable as a designer of teaching materials and editor of the house journal, and taught a course in biology for London-based students. Before long he was earning £300 per year. He became an external student himself, and obtained his B.Sc., taking first-class honours in Zoology, thus wiping out the humiliation of his expulsion from the Normal School of Science. He began to project for himself a career in education, but he had not given up his literary ambitions, and succeeded in placing an essay of scientific speculation called 'The Rediscovery of the Unique', developed from a paper he had given to the College Debating Society, with the prestigious and progressive *Fortnightly Review*. He sent the letter of acceptance to Simmons with a jubilant note scribbled on the back: *'Is this the dove with a sprig of bay? Is it poor Pilgrim's first glimpse of the white and shining city? Or a mirage?'* It was not a mirage, but all this effort took its toll on his health and he had two more serious episodes of illness, one with another haemorrhage. On each occasion he went back to work, after short periods of convalescence, with undiminished zeal, driven by the need to save enough money to marry Isabel and at last consummate his love for her.

In spite of that unhappy conversation on the bench in Regent's Park they had not formally parted when he left London, because they had never been formally betrothed. He wrote to her occasionally during his time at Holt and Stoke, in the tone of a friend not a lover, letters to which Isabel responded in the same style, but when he returned to London he picked up the threads of their old relationship as if nothing had interrupted it. Isabel, for her part, had acquired no other beau in the meantime. Before long he was lodging with his Aunt Mary once more. As he prospered the family accepted that it was only a matter of time before he and Isabel married, and living in close proximity to her he became more and more impatient for this conclusion.

He imagined their wedding night with excited longing, but also some anxiety about his own inexperience. One evening, after working late at the College, instead of going home as usual, he acted on an impulse to walk down to the West End and find a prostitute. The woman he selected proved to be not as young and comely as she had seemed when she accosted him coaxingly in a shadowy street behind the Haymarket. She led him up a dirty staircase of creaking bare boards to a narrow, sparsely furnished room, and lit the gas jet. He saw that she was a mature woman with a tired, heavily painted face and when she flashed him a professional smile she revealed a disconcerting gap in her front teeth. She stripped off her clothes without coquetry and squatted over a basin of water to wash herself with a rag cloth as if her private parts were no more interesting or sensitive than a soiled plate. Nevertheless the brazenness of the action excited him, and he stared, hypnotised, at what he had only known by touch under Edith's skirt. 'Ain'tcher goin' to take yer togs off, then?' she said. And, as he hesitated, added knowingly: 'This yer first time, is it ducky?'

'Yes,' he murmured, and turned his back to remove his jacket, shoes, trousers and drawers. He kept his shirt on: this was not to be the ideal, idyllic naked embrace he had dreamed of for so long, but merely a mechanical practice for that event. His erect penis stood out rudely between the tails of his shirt in spite of his efforts to conceal it. 'My, you've got a big one for a little chap,' the woman said, as she lay back on the bed and spread her knees. It was the first intimation he had that he was unusually well endowed in this respect, for he had had no opportunities to compare himself with other males since boyhood. Encouraged by the remark, he lay on top of the woman and began to butt at her crotch with his rigid member, but with little effect until she took it in her practised hand and guided him in. The act ended instantly, with an unstoppable, intensely pleasurable ejaculation, but it was accomplished. He was a man. Isabel seemed to sense it when he next looked at her. She flushed and lowered her eyes, as if she had perceived in his the gleam of a new knowingness in his desire for her, and shrank timorously from it.

He resorted to prostitutes again on a few occasions, simply for physical relief, using the rubber contraceptive sheaths which were readily available from seedy barber's shops, backstreet pharmacists and purveyors of dubious reading matter—partly as a precaution against infection, and partly to get

62

used to handling them, for he had no intention of starting a family as soon as he married. 'Suppose we have children, Bertie?' Isabel said once, trying to persuade him to wait longer, and save more money. 'We won't,' he said. 'But how can you be sure?' 'There are things one can use,' he said. 'Things?' she echoed fearfully, as if she imagined that hard pointed instruments were somehow involved. 'Rubber sheaths,' he said, 'which the man puts on.' 'Oh, Bertie,' she whispered, blushing and covering her face with her hands. 'Don't.' What did she mean by that monosyllable: *Don't use them* or *Don't embarrass me by mentioning them*? It did not occur to him until much later that she probably meant: *Don't imagine I'm looking forward to this sex business as eagerly as you are.*

They were married on the last day of October 1893, in church. To salve his secular conscience he made a token effort to persuade Isabel to have a civil wedding in a register office, knowing full well that she and her mother would never agree. Isabel had made her conditions for marriage clear— enough money in the bank to afford a decent home of their own, and a 'proper' wedding. He had fulfilled the first one, taking a lease on an eight-roomed house in Wandsworth, an undistinguished but respectable suburb in south-west London, and he was not going to postpone their union any longer by making an issue of the second. There was a wedding breakfast— actually more of a meat tea—for family and friends in a restaurant round the corner from the church, but no honeymoon. The wedding night was spent in their new home.

It wasn't the rapturous naked embrace he had dreamed of for so long. Isabel was shy of exposing herself to his hungry gaze. She used the bathroom first—their house boasted a proper bathroom with an efficient hot water system—and while he took his turn she disrobed and got into the double bed, pulling the covers up to her chin. When he prepared to get into bed beside her she asked him to turn out the light first, and when he stripped off his nightshirt and took her in his arms he found her swathed in a lawn cotton nightdress which she refused to take off. 'I don't want to, Bertie. Don't make me,' she begged. He was obliged to push the folds of linen up round her hips in order to enter her at last, and she gave a gasp of pain as he thrust through the hymen and spent, almost as quickly as with his first prostitute. Early the next morning, with a faint light coming through the curtains, he threw the covers off the bed, drew the nightdress up and over her weakly protesting head, and took her again with passionate urgency, trying in vain to arouse in her some reciprocating response. She winced and whimpered faintly under him as he plunged in and out, but that was all she did, and when he collapsed and rolled off her she pulled the sheet up to cover herself and turned away, weeping. 'I'm sorry, dearest,' he said, appalled, and putting his arm round to comfort her. 'I didn't mean to hurt you.' 'I know, dear,' she murmured, wiping her eyes on a corner of the sheet. 'I know you have to do it.' After a few minutes she sat up on the edge of the bed with her back to him and put her nightdress on again.

And that, sadly, set the pattern of their intimate life. He made allowances for her innocence and inexperience, trusting that in time she would begin to get some pleasure from intercourse and return his caresses, but she remained a passive partner in the act of love, regarding it as a kind of licensed assault inscrutably ordained by the Creator for the propagation of the human race, which women must therefore endure. He wondered gloomily if all women who were not prostitutes took the same view, but this hypothesis was pleasantly disproved one afternoon by Miss Ethel Kingsmill, a young woman who was an assistant and pupil of Isabel's in the art of photographic retouching. Since her marriage, Isabel had worked at home for her old employer in Regent Street, collecting and delivering work once or twice a week, and her mother, Aunt Mary, had moved in with them to help with the housekeeping. As he himself often worked at home, all eight rooms were needed. Ethel was frequently in and out of the house, and always gave him a nice smile and a warm greeting when he encountered her in the hallway or on the stairs. She was quite attractive in a vivacious, wide-mouthed way, with a neat figure which she dressed in a showier style than Isabel: striped blouses with puffed sleeves and skirts that fitted closely over the hips. When she brushed past him on the staircase on her way to the photography workroom on the top floor there was a hint of coquetry in her movements and a saucy gleam in her eye. The conviction grew in him that little Ethel Kingsmill was no innocent virgin, and that she was interested in himself.

One afternoon he was marking biology exercises in his study when there was a knock on the door and on his invitation to 'Come in!' Ethel Kingsmill opened it and took a step into the room. 'I'm going to make myself a cup of tea, Mr Wells,' she said. 'Would you like one?'

'That's very kind of you,' he said. 'Aunt Mary usually brings me one about this time.'

'She's gone shopping,' said Ethel. 'Up the West End.'

'Has she?'

'And Mrs Wells is at the shop in Regent Street.'

'Yes, I know. It's her day for that.'

They looked at each other with the consciousness that they were alone in the house together.

'So what are you doing with yourself?' he asked.

'Mrs Wells left me some work, but I've finished it,' she said, and added cheekily: 'What are *you* doing?'

'Marking students' essays,' he said.

'Can I see?' Without waiting for permission she came across to the desk where he was sitting and looked over his shoulder at the essay he was correcting in red ink. She read the title aloud, '*The Fertilization of Flowering Plants*,' and giggled. 'All about the birds and the bees, is it?'

'Something like that,' he said, looking up at her from his chair with a smile.

'I think human beings have more fun,' she said.

'How do you know?'

'You'd be surprised.'

There was a long pause while they looked into each other's eyes, trying to read each other's thoughts and intentions. 'You know, I don't think I would be surprised,' he said. Suddenly he took her hand, pulled her down on his knee and kissed her on the lips. She responded warmly.

'I think that's what you came in here for,' he said. 'Am I right?'

'I've always fancied you,' she said, 'ever since the first day I came here. Couldn't you tell?'

'I have noticed, lately,' he said. 'And I must say I fancy *you*, Ethel. What shall we do about it?'

She put her mouth to his ear and whispered, 'Whatever you like.'

He took out his pocket watch and looked calculatingly at it. 'It's a quarter-past three,' he said. 'When did Aunt Mary go out?'

'Two o'clock. She won't get back till four, earliest, because she likes to have tea out. And Mrs Wells is never back before half-past four.'

'You seem to have it all worked out,' he said, smiling. 'Shall we move over to the couch?' His heart was beating fast with excitement.

'You will be careful, won't you?' she said, as he led her over to the ottoman couch where he would occasionally read or rest. 'I don't want to get into trouble.'

'Don't worry,' he said. 'I'll use something.'

'Oh, good,' she said.

He went to the locked drawer in his desk where he kept a supply of French letters, and when he turned round she had taken off her skirt, petticoat and stays, and was draping them carefully over a chair. The sight of her standing there, demurely bloused from the waist up, wantonly déshabillé below, inflamed him further and he knelt to pull down her drawers and bury his face in her belly. She laughed as he did so—laughed! Isabel never laughed when he made love to her; nor, for that matter, did she speak or move. This girl raised her hips to meet his thrusts and cried aloud, 'Oh! Lovely lovely lovely!' as she reached the climax of her pleasure, doubling his own.

They did not undress completely, in case Isabel or her mother should return earlier than expected and they had hastily to dress again. But otherwise it was a kind of sex he had always dreamed of without knowing whether it existed: not the solemn rapture of the nuptial bower—that was a different dream—but sex as release and recreation, with an eager partner, without shame, without guilt, and without any commitment. No vows, promises, formulaic declarations of love, to justify the act, because it needed no such validation. They had just finished putting their clothes back on when they heard the front door of the house slam shut behind Aunt Mary. He raised his finger to his lips and Ethel slipped out of the room, pausing only to blow him a kiss at the door. He heard her going downstairs, greeting Aunt Mary and saying she was just about to put the kettle on for a cup of tea. What a cool little minx!

When he retired to bed that night, lying beside the sleeping Isabel before falling asleep himself, he wondered drowsily if there had been some veiled, allusive talk about sex and marriage between the two women—if, say, Isabel had referred obliquely to his being *very demanding that way*, from which Ethel had inferred that he might welcome a more enthusiastic partner and thus been emboldened to enter his study that afternoon. Whatever the explanation, he gave thanks to Venus Urania for the visitation, and slept well that night.

He had hopes of renewing the experience, but—whether by chance or because of some suspicion of Isabel's or Aunt Mary's—Ethel and he were never left alone in the house again before her apprenticeship was concluded a month or so later. It remained a bright episode in his memory, and an incentive to look for other opportunities of the same kind. There would be many in due course, but for the time being he was weighed down with family worries and responsibilities. His mother, who had become seriously deaf and increasingly incompetent as housekeeper at Up Park, was dismissed from her position with a sum of £100 by way of compensation, and reluctantly joined her husband in the cottage he had rented for his father near Up Park when the Atlas House shop went bankrupt. His two brothers had also run into difficulties in their careers and required his assistance. He was soon spending a third of his income on his family.

More and more he felt oppressed by the role that circumstances and the expectations of his relatives were imposing on him: the role of the breadwinner, the hard-working husband, the dutiful son and brother, working every hour God gave him, travelling up and down the District Line between Wandsworth and Charing Cross in carriages packed with similarly harried and oppressed married men, hurrying along the crowded pavements of the Strand and Kingsway to the headquarters of the University Correspondence College in Red Lion Square, writing letters, marking exercises, teaching classes in biology, and then back again on the train in the evening, still working with papers balanced on his knees if he was lucky enough to get a seat, and retiring after dinner to his study to work on a biology textbook from which he had hopes of earning enough to relieve the anxiety of meeting all his financial obligations. When he went to bed at last, tired but tense, needing the release of sex to relax his body and clear his mind, Isabel was usually asleep; and if she was not, or he woke her up with an importunate embrace, she did no more than passively submit, cautioning him not to make a noise in case her mother in her bedroom on the other side of the landing should hear, because she was a light sleeper.

The erotic disappointment of his marriage was all the more bitter because, gripped by his pent desire for Isabel during their long courtship, he had omitted to notice that she was uninterested in or positively hostile to the ideas that absorbed him, like scientific education, or social and economic reform, and the various schools of socialist thought dedicated to this aim. She was incorrigibly conventional in her values and ambitions. She wanted only a modestly comfortable, impeccably respectable style of life, with a nice house, nice furniture and nice clothes. 'Nice' was her favourite adjective of approbation. And she was nice herself as everybody agreed, including himself. She was gentle, kind, loyal, unselfish. But he realised with dread that they were totally incompatible in body and soul. What on earth had possessed them to marry? It was all the fault of the social system, which put its oppressive weight behind an outmoded morality based on archaic religious dogma, preventing young people from exploring their sexuality freely with each other before they made any permanent commitment.

In this mood he was susceptible to the admiration of his female students at the College in Red Lion Square, and of one in particular who joined his practical biology class in the autumn term of 1892. Her name on the register was Amy Catherine Robbins, but she called herself 'Catherine' to her friends, and to him of course she was 'Miss Robbins'. She was extremely pretty, not unlike Isabel in looks, but with lighter coloured hair, and more delicate and fragile in build. Her family background was several notches up the social scale from himself and Isabel—middle-middle rather than lower-middle class—and she had had better schooling. When she joined his course she was wearing black in mourning for the recent death of her father, who had evidently left his wife and daughter in straitened circumstances, and it was her intention to support herself and her mother by qualifying as a teacher, which invested her with a certain pathos and heroism in his eyes. He was also taken with her looks, which the black clothes rather enhanced than otherwise, and impressed by her sharp mind and fluent speech.

Miss Robbins lived with her mother in Putney, not far from Wandsworth, so she often walked down to Charing Cross station with him after his class to catch a District Line train. One day he suggested they might pause for a cup of tea at the Aerated Bread Company's teashop in the Strand, and without a second's hesitation she agreed. These teashops were a relatively new and very welcome amenity: clean, decorous establishments where a man might chat to an unchaperoned young woman without any embarrassment to either party. He learned on this occasion that her father had been killed in an accident on the railway line near Putney.

'It's not clear what happened—he was found beside the line, apparently hit by a train,' Catherine said. 'He may have been trying to cross it, because he often walked in the woods nearby. The coroner's verdict was accidental death, but of course one can't help wondering if it wasn't an accident, especially as his business affairs were in such a bad state. But I don't breathe a word of that kind to Mother—or to anyone else.'

Except her tutor, it seemed. He felt moved to share a similar confidence. 'I sometimes wonder if my father didn't try to take his own life,' he said, and described the rather improbable accident which had caused Joseph Wells to break his leg, falling off a ladder resting precariously on a bench in the yard of Atlas House, allegedly in an effort to trim a vine on the back wall of the building—an uncharacteristically foolish thing for him to attempt. 'If he didn't actually intend to take his life, I think he was wilfully careless—didn't care whether he lived or died. He was not a success as a shopkeeper, and he was past his prime as a cricketer.' It struck him that he had never confided this thought to anyone before. There was something in this young woman's attentive, clear-eyed gaze that inspired trust and drew confidences.

A pause for refreshment and conversation with Miss Robbins at the ABC teashop on the way home became a regular occurrence, and he soon discovered that she was interested not only in science but also, like himself, in modern literature and radical ideas. She had read the plays of Ibsen and 'The Soul of Man under Socialism' by Oscar Wilde. She aspired to be a New Woman, in the currently fashionable phrase, and believed passionately in the rights of women to higher education, to the vote, and to ride bicycles in bloomers. When he advocated a state endowment for motherhood which would make wives financially independent of their husbands, subtly implying that it was an original idea of his own rather than Tom Paine's, she almost swooned in admiration. She professed to be a free-thinker as regards religion, and approved Free Love in principle—the principle that the union of a man and a woman who sincerely loved each other should not be obstructed or regulated by the state or a church. He was conscious that he was something of a 'crush' for her, and that there was an element of risk in the closeness of their association but, dissatisfied as he was with his domestic life, he thought he was entitled to enjoy the harmless adoration of a pretty and intelligent pupil, and he regarded their tête-à-têtes in the ABC teashop as little oases of civilised leisure in a desert of dutiful toil.

The toil, however, took its usual toll. In the middle of May, hurrying home—alone on this occasion—to Charing Cross, he started a cough that ended with his bringing up blood in the gentlemen's lavatory beneath the concourse of the mainline station. He managed to get home, but collapsed and took to his bed. The doctor was called and prescribed opium pills and ice-bags on the chest. Isabel conveyed a message to the College that he would have to cancel his classes for the remainder of the academic year; privately he knew he would have to give up teaching for good, and try to earn his living as a writer in future. Miss Robbins called at the house a few days later to enquire anxiously about his health. Isabel was out and Aunt Mary conveyed the student's good wishes to the invalid in his bedroom. 'The young lady seemed very concerned,' she remarked. 'Yes, well, it's fellow feeling,' he said. 'She is thought to be consumptive herself.' 'Is she, poor thing, what a shame,' Aunt Mary sighed. 'Such a pretty girl.' He thanked Miss Robbins by letter, illustrated with a comic drawing of himself sitting up in bed in his nightshirt, looking miserable and dishevelled, and invited her to call again in a week's time, when his wife would be at home and he might be able to venture downstairs and talk to a visitor. Occasional visits and correspondence continued throughout his convalescence and afterwards.

Isabel could see that the girl worshipped him, but she did not seem to feel threatened, and indeed made something of a joke of it. He thought he understood the reasons for her composure. Miss Robbins was very young for one thing, and delicate in health for another. There was not a hint of coquetry in her manner when she was with him and she was always very respectful to Isabel and her mother. He knew he was not the easiest person to look after when he was ill, so a regular visitor who could distract him with college gossip and intellectual conversation was very welcome to his womenfolk. He was advised, however, to move further out of London for the sake of his health, and in August he leased a mock-Tudor house in Sutton, where one could breathe air that blew unpolluted off the North Downs. This new location was some distance from Putney, and Catherine's visits became less frequent, especially after the new academic year began. Isabel remarked on this one day with a certain complacency, adding, 'I expect she's found herself a nice young man.' 'Oh, I don't think so,' he replied—then added quickly: 'Well, you may be right. But she's a very serious student—her mind is focused on getting her degree.' In fact, he was quite certain that Catherine had not found herself a young man because, unknown to Isabel, he was still seeing a good deal of her himself, in London.

He was now busily engaged in writing short stories and humorous articles for newspapers and magazines. He didn't have much luck with the stories, and the articles were his main source of income. Reading a novel by J.M. Barrie called *When a Man's Single* while he was convalescing at Eastbourne in June had given him the impetus: there was a character in it who explained that the surest way to get published as a freelance journalist was to write amusing short essays on commonplace topics like pipes, umbrellas and flowerpots. He immediately dashed off a piece entitled 'On the Art of Staying at the Seaside', and sent it to his cousin Bertha Williams, Edith's older sister, who worked as a secretary, to type it up for him. He submitted it to the *Pall Mall Gazette*, whose editor promptly printed it and asked for more of the same kind. In the months that followed he produced some thirty articles on subjects like 'The Coal Scuttle', 'Noises of Animals' and 'The Art of being Photographed'. It wasn't the most elevated form of literary composition, but it was a start—and the articles paid quite well in proportion to the time they took to write. He published them in a number of different journals, and it was necessary for him to travel up to London quite often—the house was conveniently near Sutton station—to cultivate his contacts with editors, deliver manuscripts and obtain new commissions; and although he had resigned from his position at the Correspondence College he was still associated with that institution and had occasional business with his former employer. These trips afforded numerous opportunities to meet Catherine, and to treat her to lunch at a restaurant or tea at the ABC teashop. In fine weather they would stroll in the Embankment Gardens beside Charing Cross station.

One unusually warm afternoon in November of that year, 1893, they were sitting side by side on a bench overlooking the Thames, which was at the turn of full tide, bearing its customary freight of barges, ferries, pleasure boats and rubbish down towards the sea. 'It's like a frontier, the river,' he remarked. 'See what a difference there is between the buildings on this side, and those over there.' He pointed to the low, irregular outline of wharfs, cranes, warehouses and factories with their smoking chimneys on the south bank. 'We have the Houses of Parliament to our right and Somerset House to our left—noble, dignified, expensive architecture, which says, "*This is London, this is history, this is where power is.*" Across the river it's like an industrial slum—buildings thrown up and thrown together higgledy-piggledy to serve the needs of commerce without any planning, any concern for their appearance or the convenience of the people who labour in them. And beyond those buildings are real slums, tenements where people live in disgusting squalor, and beyond them again streets and streets of cramped terraced houses, or town houses divided up into apartments they were never designed for, that are not much better. Vast tracts of London are the same—the East End, for instance—but only here do the two worlds confront each other so starkly. This great ugly bridge'—he gestured at the rusty hulk of the Charing Cross railway bridge—'is like an iron arm, the arm of the underprivileged masses thrusting its fist across the water into the face of the English ruling class—but it can't quite reach—or the blow gets softened, absorbed, it becomes just a conduit for the wage slaves who flow in and out of the City every day . . . I'm afraid I'm losing control of my metaphor!' He laughed and turned to look at Catherine, who was gazing at him in adoration.

'No, it's wonderful!' she said. 'It's wonderful to listen to you talk. Mrs Wells is so lucky!'

'Mrs Wells isn't interested in my ideas, I'm afraid,' he said wryly.

There followed a silence in which they both pondered the implications of this remark. He took out his pocket watch and examined it. 'I'd better catch my train home,' he said.

'Give Mrs Wells my regards,' Catherine said.

'Catherine . . .' He used her first name now when they were alone together, though he had not invited her to call him 'Herbert' or 'Bertie'. He had never much liked the former name, and the latter would have sounded just a little too familiar. She had solved this delicate problem by not addressing him by any name.

'Yes?' she prompted.

'Mrs Wells doesn't know that I meet you when I come to London.' He saw a gleam of excitement light up her eyes. 'I think it's best if she doesn't. She might misinterpret the nature of our friendship.'

'Of course,' said Catherine, dropping her eyes. 'I understand.'

'Good.' He stood and offered his hand to help her up, but she remained seated.

'But it's more than friendship to me,' she said, without looking up at him. 'I love you.'

He sat down again, sighed, and took her hand between his two. 'Catherine . . . I'm a married man.'

'I know,' she said, looking straight ahead as if delivering a memorised speech. 'I don't expect anything from you. I don't expect you to leave your wife and run away with me. I know it's hopeless. But I just want you to know. And now you can catch your train home.' She burst into tears.

Then of course he had to comfort her, hold her hand again, and in the gentlest possible way tell her that although he valued her regard, and was moved by it, there was nothing to be done about it, unless they were to stop seeing each other, which he would regret.

'Oh no, not that! It would kill me,' she said. 'I'm sorry I spoke. It was stupid of me.'

'No, it was very sweet of you. But we must draw a line under it.' She nodded agreement. 'And now I really *must* catch my train,' he said, 'and you too.'

In the days and weeks that followed, his thoughts often reverted to this conversation, and it was a shared, unvoiced descant to their talk on subsequent occasions. He was fairly confident that if he tried to seduce Catherine he would succeed, because she simply wouldn't have the will to resist, but the consequences would be grave. She wasn't an Ethel Kingsmill, experienced and fancy-free, with whom one could have an enjoyable tumble with no commitment. She was a virgin—he had never met a girl who was at once so intensely virginal in manner and appearance, and so uninhibited in discussing matters like Free Love and birth control—and she would not surrender her virginity except for unconditional love. Nor could he imagine her being content to be a covert mistress, sharing her lover with a wife. No, if he were to begin an affair with her it would soon come out, and there would be a smash. So he must restrain himself, though it was difficult to resist the temptation to take the ardent young girl in his arms and kiss her when they were alone together under the trees in a park, or in some alley after dark with deep shadows between the gaslights. He gave himself credit for his restraint, being aware of how much less scrupulous other men were, especially in the literary and bohemian circles on whose edges he now moved. And sometimes, when his sense of being trapped in a marriage that would never be fulfilling grew almost unbearable, he allowed himself to speculate whether a smash wouldn't be the best solution for all concerned. *'I don't expect you to leave your wife and run away with me,'* she had said, but the negative statement had left the trace of a positive lingering in his consciousness. Suppose he did just run away with her? Could the consequences be worse than the dreary future, foreshortened by poor health, which extended before him now, like a narrow, high-walled cul-de-sac?

At this juncture Catherine herself took the initiative: she invited Isabel and him to spend a long weekend with her mother and herself at their home in Putney, in mid-December. The invitation was sent, very correctly, to Isabel, who was nevertheless puzzled by it. 'Why has she invited us?' she said, passing the letter to him over the breakfast table. 'Just to be friendly,' he said, quickly scanning the letter, which was as much of a surprise to him as to Isabel. 'As she says here, she hasn't seen much of us since we moved to Sutton. And her mother would like to meet us.' 'What will we do there, for a whole weekend?' Isabel asked. 'I don't know,' he said. 'Chat, eat, go for walks, play cards—what people usually do on such visits.' 'We never have people to stay, except for family,' said Isabel, which was true. 'Well, perhaps we should,' he said. 'Perhaps we should entertain more. We're getting into a rut.' He presumed that Catherine had not consulted him about this invitation so that he couldn't discourage it—but what was the motive behind it?

It became apparent in the course of that weekend that, consciously or unconsciously (he inclined to the former hypothesis), she was nudging their relationship into the open and forcing matters to a crisis and some kind of resolution. She was dressed in her most charming and elegant attire, and was the most gracious of hostesses, her mother being content to take a back seat in this respect. 'Amy has done it all,' Mrs Robbins would say with a self-deprecating gesture, when any compliment was offered on the food provided, or on the arrangements for the guests' comfort. 'It is all Amy's doing—such a resourceful girl—I don't know what I would do without her,' for all the world as if she were showing off a marriageable daughter to a suitor. Then without doing or saying anything which was flagrantly re-vealing, Catherine conveyed by countless nuances of speech and behaviour that she was on terms of considerable intimacy with him. She revealed that she knew exactly what his tastes in food were—what kind of jam he fa-voured on muffins, for how many minutes he liked his eggs to be boiled, and whether he preferred white or dark meat from a roast capon. She ap-pealed to him to confirm her remarks on various features and amenities of London, including the ABC teashop in the Strand, as if alluding to shared experience. She referred to books he had lent to her, and arguments they had had about them. Mrs Robbins did not seem to find this degree of fa-miliarity surprising, assuming (he supposed) that she had acquired it chez Wells, but he could see that Isabel was startled and disturbed by it. He felt both alarmed and excited by the little drama that was being played out in full view of the oblivious widow. How far would Catherine dare to go, and how would Isabel react to the provocation?

When they retired to the guest bedroom that night she immediately challenged him. 'You and that girl seem to see a good deal of each other in London.'

'Catherine? I see her from time to time, when I have occasion to go into the College.'

'And into the ABC teashop in the Strand?'

'It's near Charing Cross—we walked to the station at the same time once or twice and stopped for a cup of tea.'

'And how long have you been calling her "Catherine"?'

'Oh, I don't know, I can't remember,' he said lightly. 'Since I'm no longer her teacher, "Miss Robbins" seemed excessively formal. Why do you ask?'

'If you can't see you must be blind,' Isabel said. 'That girl is setting her cap for you.'

He forced a laugh. 'Don't be silly, dear, she's just being nice.' It was not with any ironic intent that he invoked her own favourite adjective, but it provoked her into making some very uncomplimentary remarks about Catherine in a voice which he had to beg her to moderate in case they were overheard. She went to bed in sulky silence, and turned her back on him without saying goodnight.

The next day did nothing to improve the atmosphere. Isabel was barely polite to Catherine at breakfast and even the imperceptive Mrs Robbins seemed vaguely to sense that something was not quite right. For his part he felt obliged to disguise his wife's ill humour by an extra effort to be amusing and sociable, but as he could only achieve this by interaction with Catherine, responding to her cues, and engaging her in badinage, the effect was to deepen Isabel's suspicions even further. It had been agreed in advance that they would make an excursion to Kew Gardens, Catherine pointing out that the glasshouses and hothouses provided a weatherproof diversion in mid-winter, but these structures, crowded with exotic trees, vines, shrubs, flowering plants and cacti, also offered an excellent opportunity for her to display her botanical knowledge in conversation with him about the peculiarities of the various species. Poor Isabel was excluded from these discussions by her ignorance of the terminology, and obliged to trail behind the two scientists in vacuous conversation with Mrs Robbins. He was conscious of Isabel's smouldering resentment, but somehow felt helpless to do anything about it—or perhaps simply disinclined to do so. The truth was, he was enjoying himself going round the glasshouses with a pretty girl who knew what she was looking at and could talk about it, and he didn't see why he should forgo the pleasure. It gave him a vivid sense of what it would be like to have such a woman as a mate—someone who would share your interests and concerns, help you with your work, and identify with your ambitions.

Isabel was ominously silent on their journey back to Sutton, giving monosyllabic responses, if any at all, to his remarks. But when they got home she gave vent to her feelings, declaring that she was hurt and humiliated by the way he had carried on with Catherine. He defended himself, saying she was making an unreasonable fuss.

'Unreasonable?' Isabel echoed. 'Anyone can see that the girl is in love with you. The question is—are you in love with her?'

The directness of the question took him by surprise. 'I don't know, I haven't allowed myself to think that thought,' he said, but even as he spoke he realised he was not telling the truth. Catherine was the one bright spot in his grey life, his meetings with her the only thing he really looked forward to, she was the one person who never bored or irritated him. 'I think perhaps I am,' he said.

'Well then,' Isabel said. 'You must choose between us.'

She issued the ultimatum calmly, clearly, resolutely. If he wanted to stay married to her, he must promise to cut Catherine out of his life and never see her again. Suddenly his fate, his future, which had seemed so dully predictable, was open to thrilling, dangerous new possibilities. He turned and paced the floor of the drawing room to conceal what might look like an expression of elation on his face.

'This is very sudden, Isabel,' he said. 'I will have to think about it.'

She rose from her chair. 'Don't keep me waiting too long,' she said. 'Meanwhile I'll sleep in the spare bedroom.'

The next day he went up to a foggy London early in the morning and hung around the College until Catherine appeared. She was surprised to see him. 'We must talk,' he said. 'I've got a lab class now,' she said. 'All right, I'll wait,' he said. 'No, I'll come,' she said, sensing the urgency of his mission. 'I'll cut the lab.'

They walked into Lincoln's Inn Fields, and perambulated the gravel paths, as the benches were too wet to sit on. It was a grey, damp day, and moisture dripped from the leafless boughs of the trees. Barristers in black gowns and clerks carrying stacks of legal papers loomed out of the mist, stared at them as if sensing their drama, and retreated into it again. He told her of Isabel's ultimatum.

'So what will you do?' she said in a scarcely audible whisper.

'I can't give you up,' he said.

'Oh!' she murmured. She staggered and seemed about to faint.

He took her in his arms and kissed her. 'I love you, Catherine,' he said.

'You know *I* love you,' she said, leaning against him. 'I'm so happy.'

'But listen to me, my darling. It won't be easy. It will be very hard. We'll be living together "in sin" as they say.'

'I don't care. It will be a marriage of true minds.'

'You're so sweet,' he said, and kissed her again. 'But there will be a scandal. Your mother will be distraught.'

'Oh, poor Mother!' Catherine exclaimed, but it was with a kind of laugh. 'Yes, she will be upset, but I can manage her.'

'Your whole family will be outraged. I shall be cast as the black-hearted seducer.'

'They can't stop me. I'm twenty-one.'

'You're a wonder,' he said, and kissed her once more.

'Tell me what I must do,' she said.

'Nothing, for the moment. First I must speak to Isabel. Then I will look for rooms for us somewhere. Then—the sooner the better—you must join me. It will be best if you do it without telling your mother—slip out of the house and leave her a letter. Otherwise she will try to stop you somehow, even though you *are* twenty-one.'

'You mean—elope?' Her eyes shone with the romantic thrill of the word.

'Exactly.'

'But not till after Christmas,' she said. 'I couldn't bear to leave Mother all alone at Christmas.'

He agreed readily, since Christmas was little more than a week away. He escorted her back to the College and then, with just a squeeze of her hand, since it would be reckless to embrace in the environs of the place, took his leave, and made his way back to Charing Cross and the train to Sutton.

Isabel accepted his decision with sad resignation. 'I knew which of us you would choose,' she said. 'I was never clever enough for you, Bertie, and I never could be.'

'It's not that, Isabel,' he said, when he should more truthfully have said: *It's not only that.* 'It's that we are not suited to each other as lovers—you know what I'm talking about. Maybe it's because we are cousins. I love you, I think you are a wonderful and beautiful woman, but it is more like a brother-and-sister love than married love.'

'And you think she will satisfy you that way?'

'I believe so, yes,' he said.

'Have you slept with her?'

'Of course not!' he said. 'She's not that kind of girl, anyway.'

'Well, I hope you'll be happy, Bertie,' she said.

In a curious way he never admired Isabel more than in the week their marriage collapsed, and it would have been easier to part from her if she had acted the role of the wronged wife, screamed abuse at him, thrown things, hit him, and given way to hysterics. Her calm dignity in the crisis made him feel guilty at deserting her, and he was aware, from a conversation in raised voices he overheard, that Aunt Mary, so far from supporting her daughter, thought she was being a fool—'driving him away', as she put it, 'just on account of a flirtation with a silly young girl'. There were moments when his own resolution faltered, and if Isabel had responded to his speech about brother-and-sister love by stripping naked in front of him in their bedroom that night and inviting him to take her as roughly and passionately as he liked, who knew what might have happened? But it was not in her nature to do any such thing. So he went on preparing for his departure.

He came to an agreement with Isabel to remit a regular amount of money to her on a monthly basis. 'That will do until we get a divorce,' she said. The word 'divorce' had a slightly chilling effect on his spirits. 'Must we divorce?' he said. 'Must we bring the law and lawyers into what is essentially a private matter of emotional cross purposes?' 'Don't you want to marry the girl, then?' she said, surprised. 'We don't believe in marriage as an institution,' he said. 'Well, I do,' Isabel said. He registered the implication that she herself might want to re-marry one day, and found the idea so disturbing that he hastily banished it from his mind.

He went back to London to look for accommodation for himself and Catherine, and found a pair of rooms in Mornington Place, Camden Town, on the ground floor of a terrace house. It was slightly depressing to feel himself slipping back into the lodging-house era of his life, but there was no hope of renting anything better, since he would have to support Isabel as well as Catherine for the foreseeable future. In a nearby cafe he wrote a letter to Catherine giving her the address of the lodgings, and instructed her to meet him there on Boxing Day. 'Don't give the address to your mother, of course—tell her she can write to you at Camden Town general post office. Wear a plain ring on your ring finger and remember you are "Mrs Wells" to our landlady,' he wrote. Even apostles of Free Love must needs be discreet. He walked back to Charing Cross past shop windows in the Strand festooned with gaudy Christmas decorations and stacked with

Christmas gifts. The sound of carol singers announcing tidings of comfort and joy in Trafalgar Square carried faintly to his ears.

He could have wished the crisis in his marriage had occurred at a different season, for the approach of Christmas and its associated rituals and festivities seemed like a mocking, ironic commentary on their domestic misery. 'Do we have to have a Christmas dinner?' he said, appalled to see a turkey being prepared in the kitchen on Christmas Eve. 'We've got to have something,' Isabel said with a shrug, 'so it might as well be a turkey. Mother is very fond of a turkey, she looks forward to it every year.' 'As long as we're not going to pull crackers and wear paper hats,' he said, and immediately regretted his sarcasm as Isabel flashed him a look which said very clearly, *And whose fault is it that we're having a horrible Christmas?* The three of them, Isabel, Aunt Mary and himself, ate the roast fowl and its usual accompaniments almost in silence, with his trunk packed and waiting in the hall for his departure next day. He was very nearly sick after the meal.

He crept out of the house early in the morning while Isabel was still asleep—or if not asleep, in bed. He couldn't face saying goodbye to her in person, and instead left her a note, as tender as he could make it without seeming hypocritical. He pushed his trunk to the station in a wheelbarrow, and gave a porter a shilling to return it to the house. At the ticket office he asked out of habit for a 'return to Charing Cross' and quickly amended the request to a single fare. Once he was seated in the train, and it began to move, his spirits lifted. A new life lay ahead, full of risk, uncertainty—but also freedom! And a new female body, slim, pliant, nubile, to hold in his arms and introduce to the pleasures of physical love.

Catherine arrived in the early afternoon in a hansom cab with two valises. She looked pale and anxious, threw herself into his arms as soon as they were alone together, and clung to him as if to a mast in a storm at sea. Minutes passed before she spoke.

'I had to tell Mother,' she said at last. 'I couldn't just leave her a letter. It seemed cowardly.'

'How did she take it?' he asked.

'How do you think? She sobbed and she wept and she went down on her knees and begged me not to go to you. It was terrible.'

'My poor darling,' he said. 'But you came. My brave girl!'

'She only stopped the hysterics when my cab arrived and I said I would go and get the lady next door to look after her—then she suddenly pulled herself together. It was the thought of having to explain everything to a neighbour . . .'

'Better than smelling salts,' he said with a smile, and then corrected his expression in case it seemed too flippant a remark.

'I left her prostrate on the sofa, with a handkerchief soaked in eau de cologne pressed to her forehead. Fortunately cousin Jemima and her husband are visiting for tea today, so she will have some support.'

'Tea!' he said. 'What a good idea. I will ask our landlady to make us some. Tea and muffins.'

The landlady, who was German, seemed to have guessed that he and Catherine were very recently married, if married at all, and it probably took no great discernment on her part to draw this inference from their self-conscious behaviour. She was however well disposed towards them—almost too well, in fact, serving the tea and muffins, and later their supper, with many significant smirks and nods and gestures. She had a way of looking gloatingly at them and rubbing her hands together that was almost indecent, and he could see Catherine shrinking uneasily from her attention. He had a sense that if Mrs Scholtze could have infiltrated their bedroom unobserved she would have sprinkled rose petals on their mattress.

He had in fact already decided that he would not attempt to consummate their union that first night. Catherine had suffered enough stress that day, and he wanted to avoid a repetition of the debacle of his wedding night with Isabel. Besides, his need was not so urgent as it had been on that occasion when he released the pent-up desire of years. After Mrs Scholtze had carried away the supper trays, bidding them an almost visibly salivating goodnight, he turned the key in the door, and Catherine, hearing the click of the lock, looked at him with a kind of tense solemnity, as if steeling herself for an ordeal. He embraced her and said, 'I think, dearest girl, we should not become lovers in the fullest sense tonight. Let us wait until you are more rested and relaxed. Tonight, let us just sleep in each other's arms. Would you like that?'

'Oh yes!' she said instantly, relief flooding her face.

Their accommodation was the original dining room of the house, divided by folding doors left permanently closed to create a living room in the front half and a bedroom in the back. He allowed her to undress and get into bed before he joined her. A single candle on the chest of drawers dimly lit the room. Catherine, her hair down and spread out over the pillow, wearing a nightdress buttoned up to the neck, smiled timidly at him, and then turned her head to stare modestly at the wall when he began to undress. He pulled on his nightshirt before he removed his trousers and drawers, blew out the candle and got into bed beside her. When he drew her into his arms she snuggled up to him with a contented sigh and if she felt his erection through their nightwear she did not shrink away from it. Perhaps she didn't know what it was. Only when he began to stroke her back through the thin fabric of her nightdress, and allowed his hand to slide down and cup her buttock did she stiffen as if startled. But nobody, he reflected, had touched her there since she was a baby. He removed his hand and placed it in a more decorous position and, obviously exhausted by the emotions and exertions of the day, she soon fell asleep, leaving him to plot the manner in which he would, in due course, possess her. A pleasure postponed was a pleasure enhanced.

In the event it was postponed longer than he anticipated. The next day Catherine could not resist going to the Camden Town post office to see if her mother had already sent a message to her there. Indeed she had, but as Catherine turned away from the counter with the envelope in her hand she saw cousin Jemima's husband, Reginald, watching her with a triumphant expression. She had been ambushed. She hurried from the post office, but he caught up with her outside and demanded to be taken to their lodgings to confront 'the bounder who has seduced you'. 'He didn't seduce me. I went to him of my own free will,' she said. 'If there was any seducing it was mine,' she added boldly. 'You should be ashamed of yourself,' Reginald said. 'Your mother is beside herself, she can't stop weeping. We are seriously concerned for her sanity—read for yourself.' He pointed to the letter in her hand. 'I will read it in my own good time,' she said. 'Now kindly leave me alone, or I will call a constable.' She turned her back on him and walked swiftly away, and he did not attempt to detain her. All this she told her 'seducer' on her return to the house in Mornington Place, laughing and crying as she did so.

He praised her courage and called her his 'heroine'. He proposed they should go to bed immediately and make love. But she said she was too upset by the incident, and her perturbation was increased by reading the tear-stained letter from her mother.

'She says she will kill herself.'

'Nonsense. Just emotional blackmail,' he said.

'I know, but I must see for myself,' she said.

Catherine went immediately to Putney, and sent a telegram later that day: 'MOTHER POORLY STOP AM STAYING WITH HER FOR ONE OR TWO DAYS STOP TRUST ME STOP ALL LOVE CATHERINE.'

In spite of the concluding words of the message he was apprehensive that once she was back in the family home pressure would be put on her to stay there and give him up, especially if her relatives discovered she was still *virgo intacta*. He began to regret that he had been so chivalrously considerate of her maiden sensibility, for he would look, and certainly feel, very silly indeed if he found himself all alone in a shabby London lodging house, having deserted his wife without securing his mistress. These misgivings turned to alarm the next day when Reginald and his brother Sidney called on him, having somehow obtained the Mornington Place address. They were rather large and intimidating men, dressed like undertakers in top hats and black overcoats with black kid gloves, and they issued vague threats of legal action against him for abduction or enticement if he did not sign a document promising not to contact Catherine again. He laughed in their faces and told them, with more confidence than he felt, that nothing could keep himself and Catherine apart. It was a relief when she returned next day and learned with indignation of her relatives' intervention, of which she knew nothing. 'It's outrageous,' she said. 'They had no right to interfere.' 'They didn't get this address from you then?' he asked. 'Of course not,' she said. 'Uncle Reginald must have followed me here from the Camden Town post office that day. Did you think I would tell them?' 'No, no,' he said, 'not willingly, but I thought they might have bullied you.' 'I wouldn't have told them if they had used thumbscrews,' she said, and she looked at that moment like some virgin martyr in an old painting calmly defying her tormentors. He was suddenly overwhelmed with gratitude for her steadfastness and with relief that she had returned to him and he folded her in his arms. 'Tonight we will be lovers,' he whispered, and she murmured her assent.

2

—But it wasn't the rapturous shared experience you had hoped for, was it?

—I didn't really expect it would be. I said to her 'The first time it may hurt, but after that you will feel pleasure. More and more pleasure as time goes on.'

—But she didn't.

—No. She tried, for my sake—that night and the nights that followed. She tried harder than Isabel. She took off her nightdress to please me. She let me have a lit candle on the chest of drawers when we made love. But it was like teaching someone to swim when they're terrified of the water—she lay beneath me with every muscle in her body tensed, her arms round my neck, holding on for dear life, like someone afraid of drowning. As time went on she became a little more pliant, a little more responsive, but not much. When we went abroad for the first time, in '98, to Italy, I picked up a copy of Aretino's *Postures* in a bookshop in Florence, but she wouldn't look at them, let alone try them.

—Did she ever have orgasms?

—I don't think so, no. Sometimes, later on in our marriage, after we made love she claimed she had enjoyed it, but I was never convinced. Basically, she lacked lust. Whereas for me sex is the joyful relief of lust. It's an animal thing. I like to be like an animal in bed with a woman, to bite and lick and wrestle before I take her. Jane hated that, she couldn't join in the animal game. She was too fragile, too delicate, too fastidious.

—But you knew what kind of a girl she was before you eloped with her. 'Catherine' wasn't the sensual type.

—I suppose I thought I would awaken her sexually. And when I failed at first, I presumed it was just the effect of her upbringing, which was repressed, prudish, fanatically 'respectable', in an English middle-class Low Church suburban way. She'd rebelled against that intellectually with all her New Woman stuff, but not with her body. And then it wasn't the most auspicious setting for a sexual initiation, that pair of rooms in Mornington Place, with no bathroom in the house, and a landlady who acted like a procuress . . . We got out of there pretty smartly. Jane found us lodgings in Mornington Street, just round the corner, with a nicer landlady, but the rooms were almost identical and there was still no bathroom. We had a tin tub just big enough to stand up in. I used to tease Jane by peeping at her though a crack in the folding doors while she was having a strip-wash, and offering to come in and scrub her back. We were like a couple of kids, really, playing at 'mothers and fathers'. We were full of our own audacity in defying the world. Living together without being married made even the most decorous lovemaking seem daring. We were acting out a sort of Shelleyan rebellion against a hypocritical, repressive social order—we gloried in our freedom from property, duties, responsibilities. Not that we were idle, far from it. Our landlady provided us with our meals on a tray, so we were free to read and write all day if we wanted to. Jane helped me research my journalistic articles, wrote them out in a fair hand, and posted them to my cousin to be typed.

    —She didn't go on with her studies. She didn't get her degree.

    —She couldn't. It would have caused a scandal at the College. She took typing lessons instead, so she could type up my manuscripts and save us money. And she wrote a few little things herself which got published after I polished them a bit. We were a team. We got a thrill out of waiting for the post, wondering whether there would be an acceptance in one of the envelopes—or a cheque! We desperately needed money, and journalism seemed the best way to make it, until *The Time Machine* was published and my boom began. We moved out of lodgings to our first proper home, in Woking, and then to Worcester Park—quite a substantial house that was, with a name, 'Heatherlea', not just a number, and a half-acre of 'grounds' rather than a garden. We sniffed victory then—I mean victory over the people who had disapproved of our elopement and tried to keep us apart. Jane's mother, who had sold her own house, helped with the expenses and moved with us into Worcester Park for a time. She was finally reconciled to our union when Isabel and I got divorced and I married Jane as soon as the decree came through. We both agreed there was no point in continuing to live in sin for the sake of a principle—

fighting prejudice on that particular issue just consumed too much time and energy.

—It didn't worry you that for the second time you were getting married to a woman who couldn't satisfy you sexually?

—I think I hadn't yet come to that conclusion about Jane. Or perhaps I didn't want to admit it to myself. Everything else in our partnership was going so swimmingly, I didn't want to bring that problem into the open, and neither did Jane. We conspired together to ignore it for some years. We developed a childish private language, and a sort of mythology, to avoid confronting the true nature of our marital relations. It involved pet names and amusing burlesques on our domestic life, in doggerel verse or in my little comic 'pichuas'. She was 'Bits' or 'Miss Bits', an imperious and practical-minded female, and I was 'Bins' or 'Mr Bins', a weaker character who was usually in the wrong and rather afraid of her. It started when we were living together and continued into our marriage. I still remember some of the 'pomes':

> *Our God is an Amoosing God. It is His Mercy that*
> *This Bins who formerly was Ill is now quite well and Fat*
> *And isn't going bald no more nor toofaking and such*
> *For all of which this Bins who writes congratulates him much.*

That one ended:

> *I sits and sings to Lordy God with all my little wits.*
> *(But all the same I don't love 'Im not near what I love Bits.)*

We had a lot of fun with this kind of thing. We were substituting fun for the lust that was missing from our marriage.

—So you looked for lust elsewhere. When did that start?

—I think it was when we were living at Woking, through my old friend from Bromley days, Sidney Bowkett. I hadn't been in touch with him since we left school, but one day I read a report in the newspaper about a playwright of that name who was the defendant in a case of plagiarism. I knew it must be him because it's an unusual name and as a boy he was always dreaming of going on the stage. He'd been touring a play in the provinces allegedly based on George du Maurier's *Trilby*, which of course was already a tremendous hit as a play in London, with Beerbohm Tree. I can't remember what happened in the case—I think he lost—but I wrote to him and he turned up one day at our house in Woking, surprised to find that his old school chum was the rising young novelist H.G. Wells. He had married a very attractive blue-eyed Jewess, an actress called Nell de Boer, and they were living in a cottage at Thames Ditton, not far from us, so I began to see quite a lot of him. We went for cycle rides through the Surrey lanes, talking about life and art and women, especially women. Bowkett was a great one for the ladies, or so he would have me believe, and regaled me with very vivid accounts of his conquests. Frank Harris was another acquaintance in those days who liked to boast in the same way. It was very coarse talk, but inflaming. I began to hanker after something a bit gamier in that line than I was getting at home, and before long I obtained it—with Nell Bowkett, in fact, when I called at their cottage one day and found Sidney was in Town on theatrical business. Or maybe it wasn't business—Nell had no illusions about his faithfulness and was disposed to get her own back, and I was very ready to oblige, on more than one occasion. I put the two of them into *Kipps,* years later, as the Chitterlows, suitably cleaned up to make a couple of Dickensian comic characters, though by that time they were separated. Nell Bowkett was the first of my adventures in adultery—I mean as regards Jane. I hadn't been faithful to Isabel either, of course. There was Ethel Kingsmill, and some other casual encounters after her. I was faithful to Jane until Bowkett turned up in Woking and started putting ideas into my head.

—But that wasn't for very long, was it? Less than two years after you eloped with her?

—True. But it wasn't until some time later that I took every opportunity to 'get' women.

It was some time before he overcame the diffidence ingrained in him by his humble background, his small stature, his chronic ailments, and the squeaky voice from which he could never entirely eradicate a trace of the 'common', and realised that his increasing success and fame as a writer made him attractive to women. It was not until he and Jane had settled in Sandgate, and started to build Spade House, that he began to appreciate this fact, and by that time his increasing prosperity had made good his physical deficiencies to a considerable extent. He would never be tall or handsome, but there was now a spring in the step of his small, well-shod feet, there was a smooth sheen to his skin, and strong muscle beneath it, firmed by regular exercise. Even his moustache had grown less straggling, more glossy and dense. He was told by several women that the gaze of his slightly hooded blue-grey eyes was peculiarly penetrating and had an almost hypnotic power over the subject on which it was turned. And it gave him confidence in the game of seduction that when their clothes were off he could rely on his *membrum virile* ('the Honourable Member for Sandgate' as he sometimes personified it in amorous badinage) to rise impressively to the occasion. But it was the glamour of his literary reputation above all, and the possibility of intimate access to the man behind the books, that attracted susceptible women to him like the action of a magnet on iron filings. In most cases he found he only had to ask in order to receive, and sometimes they asked first. For example, that Australian woman—he couldn't remember her name, only her golden curls, above and below, and the way her body was marked out like a map in sharply defined areas of pale and suntanned skin—who was visiting London and wrote to him care of his publishers to say how much she had enjoyed reading *Kipps*. She also invited him to call at her lodgings and spend some hours with her which she hoped would be mutually enjoyable—after reading *Kipps* of all novels, with one of the most sexually innocent heroes in contemporary fiction! And it *was* a very enjoyable afternoon.

Once they were settled in Sandgate he often spent two or three days midweek in London, staying overnight in a small flat he leased in Clement's Inn, meeting publishers and editors, lunching or dining with friends, going to literary parties. In this way he encountered ladies who were very willing to have sex with him, and as long as they were mature and experienced, with the same frankly hedonistic attitude to the activity as himself, there were no unpleasant repercussions. Women like Ella D'Arcy, for instance, the green-eyed, red-haired author of wryly elegant short stories frequently published in *The Yellow Book*, or the novelist Violet Hunt, not quite as beautiful as she had been when Ellen Terry reportedly described her as 'out of Botticelli by Burne-Jones' but still alluring, whom he consoled after the unhappy end of a long-term love affair. Such discreet, sophisticated ladies caused him no embarrassment or notoriety. It was the young ones, the young virgins who wanted to be initiated into the mystery of sex by the celebrated writer and radical thinker, it was they who got him into hot water and blew his public career off course: Rosamund, Amber, Rebecca . . . And there was Dorothy, too, Dorothy Richardson, though she hesitated longer than the others before asking him to relieve her of her virginity, and was more discreet about the consequences.

—We will come to the young virgins in due course. There are still some questions to answer about the wives. You say in your autobiography that Isabel thought *'lovemaking was nothing more than an outrage inflicted upon reluctant womankind'*, but in another place in that book, discussing Jane's inability to respond to your sexual needs, you say, *'there arose no such sexual fixation between us, as still lingered in my mind toward my cousin'*. Isn't there some contradiction there?

—Not really. I was frustrated by Isabel's frigidity, I resented it, and I took my revenge in trivial infidelities, but it didn't make her innately less desirable to me. I admitted in the autobiography that even while I was arranging to elope with Catherine I might very well have changed my mind if Isabel had made an effort to bind me to her.

How strong the tie still was he didn't really discover until three years later. He and Isabel corresponded from time to time about practical matters concerning their divorce, but did not meet until 1898. Early in that year she wrote to tell him she had bought a small poultry farm in the country near Virginia Water, and was planning to run it with the help of her Aunt Bella. She had been reading *The War of the Worlds* with amazement: *'Where in the world of all that's wonderful do you get your ideas from? And you make them so realistic too. It's marvellous.'* Some months later she wrote again to say that she was in a little difficulty over meeting some bills and asked for his help. The sum involved was not very large, and he could easily have just sent her a cheque, but he felt an irresistible curiosity to see her again, so one fine day in June he put his chequebook in his pocket and cycled over from Worcester Park to the farm. He was now a keen cyclist and thought nothing of a ride of some two hours' duration.

He was completely unprepared for the emotional effect of the meeting. It was partly the setting—she seemed so at ease in the country, caring for her chickens, taking her favourites in her arms and stroking their feathers, calling them by their names, and then leading him round the garden, pointing out the vegetables and flowers she had planted, stooping to pull up a weed or stretching to deadhead a rose bush. She seemed more beautiful and blooming than ever, and he realised that this pastoral world was where she really belonged, not in the dingy, soiled streets of London where he had courted her. She bore him no resentment for deserting her nor jealousy towards Jane, and it struck him that very few women in her situation would have been so magnanimous. They spent a wonderful day together, in relaxed and friendly conversation. She had read most of his books and stories published over the past few years and was full of simple, unfeigned admiration for them. He could hardly believe it, but he felt himself falling in love with her all over again, and possessed with the mad idea of reclaiming her, reversing everything that had happened. He deliberately left it too late to cycle home before sunset so that she had to invite him to stay the night, and after Aunt Bella had retired to bed he tried to persuade her to make love. She stared at him with wide-eyed astonishment.

'What *do* you mean, Bertie? Have you forgotten that I never pleased you in that way?'

'It was all my fault. I was a clumsy, impatient lover then. It would be different now. I could make up to you for those unhappy nights. Let me, please.'

'But how can we?' she said simply.

He could hear Aunt Bella moving about in her bedroom upstairs, and thought that was perhaps the reason for her hesitation. 'We can go out into your barn,' he said. 'I saw a heap of straw there to lie on. Or out into the fields for that matter—it's a dry night.'

'I think you've lost your senses, Bertie,' she said firmly, like a mother speaking to a wilful child. 'We're divorced, and you've married again, and that's an end of it.'

She made up a bed for him in a spare room, where he slept restlessly and woke early. He tried to creep out without disturbing her, just as he had left the house in Sutton that miserable Boxing Day morning, but she heard him and came downstairs to the kitchen and insisted on making him a breakfast. 'You can't cycle all that way on an empty stomach,' she said sensibly. He gave her the cheque he had intended to leave on the table, for an amount which she said was too much, but he persuaded her to accept it. They embraced and he wept in her arms. She stood at the door of the farmhouse and waved to him as he rode away, indifferent to the beauty of the dawn sky and the milky mist rising from the fields, feeling drained and empty, convinced that he had lost all chance of lasting happiness in his life and that it was all his own fault.

In time he appreciated how sane and sensible Isabel had been, and what a moral and emotional mess they would have found themselves in if she had yielded to his pleas. But five or six years later he heard that she had married again; had been married in fact for a year. He presumed she had kept the information from him out of an empathetic sense that it would upset him, which it certainly did. For several days he was gripped by a frenzy of jealousy. The idea of another man possessing that body, and perhaps summoning the joyful response that he had failed to awaken, was intolerable. He destroyed every trace of Isabel that he possessed, every letter, every photograph, every memento of any kind, made a holocaust of them in the garden of Spade House, watched by his puzzled two-year-old son, and from a window by Jane, who knew very well what he was doing and why, but had the sense to say nothing.

Another few years later, when he was deeply involved with Amber Reeves, he met Isabel again and found that the 'sexual fixation' had vanished, this time for good. From then onwards he was able to relate to Isabel on easy, friendly terms in which there was not a scintilla of jealousy or desire. She and Jane got on well together, and Isabel stayed with them from time to time at Spade House and later at Easton Glebe. She used to help Jane on these occasions with typing his manuscripts and filing his papers. It pleased him to see their heads bent together over these tasks. It seemed a tribute to their maturity and civilised good sense that the three of them could calmly enjoy each other's company after all the emotional storms of the past.

—It's interesting that you employed several of your women as secretaries or amanuenses after you no longer had sexual relations with them. As well as Isabel, and Jane of course, there was Amber who contributed to the *Outline of History* in the twenties and to *The Work, Wealth and Happiness of Mankind* in the thirties, and you paid Dorothy Richardson to proofread your books for many years . . .

—In most cases it was an act of friendship, to help them out financially.

—But it also allowed you to feel that in a way you still owned them, they were your pensioners, like elder concubines in the harem.

—That's a ridiculous suggestion! Jane acted as my secretary from the very beginning. She made it her occupation, and she got satisfaction from it. Dorothy really needed the money in the thirties, when her sales as a novelist were declining. I paid her fifty pounds to go over the manuscript of *Experiment in Autobiography* like an editor, and she was jolly glad of it.

Amber was delighted to be published in those books. As to Isabel, I helped her financially all her life, one way or another, although when she remarried I wasn't legally obliged to give her a penny. She helped Jane when she was staying with us as a way of expressing her gratitude.

—Still, one can't help seeing a kind of pattern in your life. Once you have possessed a woman, married her, or made her your mistress, you tire of her more or less quickly; her very availability makes her less satisfying sexually, so you seek out another, or several others, for excitement, passion, release. Isabel became desirable again when she was no longer married to you.

—I'll be the first to admit that I need novelty and variety in my sexual life. In all aspects of life, actually. There's something innately restless about my temperament. I called it the 'fugitive impulse' in the autobiography: as soon as I feel settled in a place or a relationship, I begin to feel bound and constrained, and have an urge to escape. *That* rather than sexual frustration was basically why I left Isabel and ran off with Jane, and when I saw Isabel again years later, beautiful and blooming, it struck me like a thunderbolt that our unsatisfactory sex life had been all *my* fault, because I was such an inexperienced and insensitive lover at the time, and I felt an overwhelming desire to make amends, to reverse the past. An absurd idea, but not basically a selfish one. And I didn't tire of Jane as a lover because we got married. We were sexually incompatible from the beginning, and eventually we had to face the fact. We could have separated and divorced, but in every other way we were perfectly suited to each other and very happy in each other's company. So we came to an understanding. We would remain married, Jane would remain my beloved wife, the caring mother of my children, efficient mistress of my household, gracious hostess to my friends, the indispensable manager of my business affairs, and I would have occasional discreet affairs with other women, *passades* as the French call them— passing fancies. It was a very civilised solution.

—Yes, so you say in the autobiography. But it wasn't quite as cut and dried as that, was it? There was the letter she wrote to you after the birth of Gip, for instance. A love letter.

—I don't remember it.

—Yes you do. The one she signed 'Your shameless wife in love.' You kept it. You know where it is.

He goes, rather reluctantly, to a filing cabinet where correspondence and other documents relating to Jane are stored in chronological order, and finds the letter without difficulty. It is undated, but headed 'Spade House'. He reads it.

—*'Dearest, dearest, dearest, dearest—do not forget me—do not fail me. My dear love do not doubt. Do believe in me a little—till I make you quite believe—till I can show you. Oh, but I love you and I am just longing for the time to come. My very dear. Your (shameless) wife in love.'*

—**That doesn't sound like a woman who has come to an 'understanding' with her promiscuous husband.**

—No, we hadn't got to that stage yet.

—**And it doesn't sound like a woman who was frigid. What do you think she meant by 'shameless'?**

—I don't know. I wondered at the time.

He received the letter at the post office in Ramsgate about three weeks after Gip's birth. Jane's labour had been long and painful, the birth difficult, and he had found the experience profoundly upsetting. This, then, was how the act of love, one of the most exquisite sensations in life, fulfilled Nature's blind purpose: in blood and sweat and cries of pain. He was not present at the birth of course, but he heard Jane's cries from his study, and he saw the evidence of her ordeal as soon as he was admitted to the bedroom: the bloodstained sheets in the laundry basket, and Jane's pale, exhausted face against the pillow, her hair lank and dark with perspiration. The doctor congratulated him and the nurse beamed as she cradled the newborn infant under his nose. He felt a thrill of wonder at the sight of his son, and a wave of tenderness for the wife who had borne him, and he kissed her reverently on the forehead. But almost at once a different reaction set in. Everything in the household revolved around the new inhabitant. His feeding, his excretions, his sleeping, his crying, were subjects of inexhaustible interest and concern, from the discussion of which he himself was largely excluded. The infant's daily bath was a ritual of almost religious ecstasy for the group of ministering women, which soon included his mother-in-law. The home he had designed as a haven for productive work and civilised leisure was suddenly transformed into something between a crèche and a hospital. The 'fugitive impulse' cut in. He felt an irresistible urge to escape the suffocating atmosphere of child-centred domesticity—to jump on his bike and pedal away as far and as fast as he could manage.

Jane was not well pleased when he told her he was going off on a cycling trip just a few days after she had given birth. Where? When? For how long? she asked. He said he would visit his parents to tell them they were grandparents, and after that he didn't know quite where he would go or when he would return. He just knew he had to get away, probably for two or three weeks. Jane sulked. She said she didn't understand how he could leave her without reason at such a time, nor would her mother, nor would the servants. It would be very embarrassing and humiliating for her. He said he was sorry, but he had to get away, and he did, the very next morning. When he came to her room where she was resting in bed, to say goodbye, she did not speak, and when he tried to kiss her she turned her face away and the kiss landed on her ear. He put a couple of books and a minimum of clothing and toilet utensils into the pannier bags of his bicycle and set off on the open road with a feeling of enormous relief. After visiting his parents at Liss in Hampshire, where they now lived in a cottage superior to the one near Up Park, he explored Sussex and Kent, avoiding main roads, favouring quiet lanes through pleasant countryside, staying at rural inns or seaside guesthouses. He wrote postcards home at frequent intervals, giving Jane the name of his next port of call, and at these stopping-places he collected a series of letters from her, the tone of which quickly changed from cool to warm. It was clear that she was in a growing panic, fearing that the ill feeling provoked by his sudden departure might harden into a permanent estrangement.

Sexual relations between them had been suspended for some time because of Jane's pregnancy, an abstinence made easier because he normally slept in the dressing room that adjoined their bedroom in Spade House. He often woke early with new ideas for some work in progress spinning in his head, and he could turn on the light, put on a dressing gown, and write at his desk without disturbing Jane, sometimes working through till breakfast time. When he felt in the mood for intercourse, which might be provoked by something he had read, or written himself, during the day, or by an encounter with some desirable but unattainable female, or if he were made aware by a glance or remark by Jane that a considerable time had passed since he had last demonstrated his love in this fashion, he would say when she prepared to go to bed, 'Shall I come to your room tonight?' and she always responded with a demure smile and a nod, unless it was the wrong time of the month. He decided that the upper-class custom of spouses having separate bedrooms had much to recommend it, not only for the freedom it gave him to work in the small hours, but because it retained a certain aura of romance for the sexual act which the habitual proximity of the marital bed tended to dissipate. The exercise of conjugal rights became a kind of assignation. It gave him a frisson of excitement, and guaranteed an erection, as he undressed in his bedroom, to think of Jane lying under the sheets in the room next door, freshly bathed and perfumed, waiting for him. He sensed that she also found the arrangement congenial, and that now she feared he might never come through the door that separated their rooms again. *Oh, but I love you and I am just longing for the time to come . . . Your (shameless) wife in love.* Sitting on the bed in his Ramsgate lodging house, he was both aroused and puzzled by this letter. She had never spoken to him in such language face to face. Obviously she wanted to say that she was looking forward to resuming sexual relations. But what did she mean by 'shameless'? That she would eagerly co-operate in all the variations he had vainly urged her to try in the past?

When he returned home there was an emotional reconciliation, but it was some time before Jane intimated that she had fully recovered from the physical effects of the difficult birth and was ready to receive him in her bed once again. He for his part was solicitously tender and gentle in his love-making at first, and all was well, but when he became more adventurous she was as unhappy as always. Either the 'shameless' letter, and all it promised, had been written under the pressure of emotion which evaporated as soon as he returned home, or she had simply meant by the epithet that she was not ashamed to grovel before him to retain his love. So they resumed tepid conventional intercourse, and it was not long before she conceived again, both of them having agreed that little George Philip, now known familiarly as 'Gip', ought to have a brother or sister. It was a brother, as it turned out, and in due course the boys proved excellent playmates.

—And you made another little dash for freedom about that time, didn't you? You went off on a walking tour in the Swiss Alps with Graham Wallas for a month, just before Frank was born.

—Well, as Jane's time approached we both became more tense and anxious, remembering what a hard time she had had with Gip. I thought it would be better if I cleared off—relieved my 'fugitive impulse' in advance as it were—and came back in time for the birth. It worked out very well. I had a great holiday and returned home fit and happy, ready to face all the domestic upheaval of a new infant.

—Having dallied with one or two compliant chambermaids en route.

—Yes. Wallas was very shocked. He reproached me for my loose behaviour. Like many of the older Fabians he was liberal in principle but essentially puritanical at heart.

—**Did you tell Jane about the chambermaids?**

—I don't think so, no.

—**So when did you and she arrive at your 'very civilised solution'?**

—It's hard to say. Although I sometimes referred to it as a 'treaty', we didn't sit down at a table one day and hammer out an agreement. It wasn't like that. Probably I said something after we'd had a tiff, or more likely I wrote her a letter, when I was away from home—we often communicated more frankly in letters than in conversation—about how much I loved and depended on her but that I needed other women from time to time, for purely physical relief, and I didn't want to deceive her about it, but I didn't want to rub her nose in it either, so couldn't we just accept that, and enjoy the other wonderful things in our marriage? She didn't agree immediately, but she didn't reject the idea either, and we came back to the topic from time to time. One evening—a summer evening, it was still light, I remember, with a sunset glow on the garden—we were sitting quietly in the drawing room at Spade House, I was reading and she was doing some sewing, and she suddenly said, as if we had just been discussing the matter, though in fact it hadn't been mentioned between us for some time, 'I wouldn't mind as long I know what you're doing, who the women are that you're going with. But you have to be completely honest with me. I hate the idea of being deceived. I hate the idea of other people knowing and pitying me or laughing at me behind my back.' Of course I was very glad to agree. It was a great relief to both of us—I'd only concealed my *passades* out of a misguided wish to spare her feelings. I think that was the turning point. After that relations were much easier between us.

—**Who was the first woman you told Jane about?**

—I think it must have been Dorothy. But that was a special case—because she was Jane's friend.

Dorothy Richardson had been a close friend of Jane's at school—Southborough House in Putney, an excellent institution, to judge from these two alumnae, with an unusually liberal curriculum. They had lost touch with each other since leaving it, but once Jane was comfortably settled in Heatherlea she felt an impulse to resume contact and wrote to Dorothy suggesting they meet in a teashop in London (the same ABC in fact where his relationship with Jane had effectively begun). From this meeting she returned home full of excitement at the reunion, and of the story Dorothy had to tell, which Jane related to him that evening as soon as she had taken off her hat and coat. 'Poor Dorothy! Her father was suddenly ruined a few years ago, had to declare bankruptcy—just like Daddy, only instead of her father it was her mother who fell into a frightful depression—and cut her throat with a bread knife while Dorothy, who was looking after her, was out for a few minutes. Can you imagine anything more horrific? But she seems to have got over it. Anyway, I've invited her to lunch next Sunday. You'll enjoy meeting her. She's quite clever, I think. Reads a lot.'

'My books?' he asked.

'I don't think so, but she's heard of you of course. She was quite impressed that I'm married to you.'

Dorothy duly appeared the following Sunday and revealed herself to be not only quite clever, but also pretty in a rather stiff, doll-like way, with a solemn countenance that would occasionally light up with a delightful dimpled smile. She called Jane 'Amy' which was how she had been known at school, though her nickname there was apparently 'Perky'. He chortled at this revelation, and Jane chided Dorothy for letting it out—'Now he'll tease me to death,' she said. 'No I won't, Perky,' he said, eliciting a dimpled smile from Dorothy. He was amused to observe how Jane enjoyed showing off her new house and her new husband to her old school chum, and that Dorothy was clearly much more interested in the husband than in the house. She had evidently looked into his work since the meeting with Jane, and made some intelligent references to it without fawning. She confessed an ambition to 'write' herself one day, but earned her living as receptionist to a dental practice in Harley Street.

The visit was a success, enjoyed by all three of them for different reasons, and Dorothy never declined an invitation to repeat it. After they moved to Sandgate she was often a weekend guest at Spade House, sometimes alone and sometimes as one of a large party, listening to the literary and political chatter of the other visitors with a faintly sceptical air and occasionally making a deflating contribution of her own. He was impressed by her refusal to be awed in the presence of loquacious luminaries like Bernard Shaw, Arnold Bennett, Frank Harris and Fordie Hueffer, and he only gradually came to realise that this self-confidence was based on an impregnable egotism. She was insatiably interested in herself, in her own consciousness and her own identity, and relegated the rest of the universe in importance beneath that supreme subject.

She was clearly fascinated by him, but it was a fascination in which there appeared to be as much antagonism as attraction. She argued with him constantly, attacking his faith in science and progress, which she regarded as lacking a personal and spiritual dimension. She herself had no consistent ideological allegiance—she attended Fabian meetings occasionally, had an anarchist male friend, an exiled Russian Jew called Benjamin Grad, whose pronouncements she sometimes quoted, and for a time invoked against himself the arguments of an idealist Cambridge metaphysician called McTaggart. She wrote him long letters candidly exploring her thoughts and her reading, to which he replied briefly but promptly, encouraging her to develop her ideas into essays or stories. Underneath these intellectual exchanges there was a sexual cat-and-mouse game in progress of which both were aware, though she seemed unwilling to admit it. Whenever he took advantage of their being alone together to lay a hand on hers or put an arm around her waist she always calmly detached herself and continued their conversation without interrupting its flow. He was not used to meeting this kind of resistance from women who were obviously attracted to him, and it spurred him to greater efforts at seduction.

He thought a propitious moment had come early in 1905 when they were walking on the Folkestone Leas one afternoon, having left Jane at home looking after Gip, who had a temperature. They were caught by a sudden rainstorm funnelling up the Channel from the west, and took refuge in a shelter looking out over the sea. It was not the season for visitors and they were all alone. He turned the conversation to the subject of sexual relations, or as the pundits of press and pulpit often referred to it, the Sex Question. She, typically, turned it to her own sex question.

'I'm a virgin, you see,' she said with startling candour.

'Really, Dorothy? You surprise me,' he said, though in fact she didn't. 'That young man, Benjamin, you go about with—I thought perhaps you were lovers.'

'No, Benjamin won't sleep with me unless I marry him, and I don't want to be married.'

'You offered to sleep with him without being married, and he refused?' She nodded. 'Benjamin seems to be a very unusual kind of anarchist,' he said. 'A very unusual young man of any persuasion, come to that, to turn down a girl like you.'

'Yes, he is,' she said. 'He spent a year in a mental asylum once.'

'Ah,' he said. 'Then you are quite right not to marry him.' He put his arm round her shoulder and was encouraged when she did not shrug it off.

'It's not that I desperately want to have sex with him, quite the contrary. We get along very well without it. But I sometimes wonder if I ought to have the experience if I'm going to be a writer.' She turned her head and looked at him solemnly. 'What do you think?'

'I think you should,' he said.

He leaned forward and kissed her on the lips. She did not resist or try to turn her face away but she did not respond either. She accepted the kiss thoughtfully, like someone being offered a new kind of food, letting the taste linger on her palate while she decided if she really liked it.

'No,' she said. 'I couldn't—not with you. Jane is my friend.'

'Jane won't mind. We believe in Free Love,' he said.

Dorothy thought for a moment, and then stood up. 'No, it wouldn't feel right. It's stopped raining—shall we go back?'

But some weeks later he received a letter from her addressed to him at the Reform, saying that she had just come back from a wonderful holiday in Switzerland and it would be nice to meet some time soon in London. There could be only one reason for her to write to him at his club—to prevent Jane from seeing her telltale handwriting on the envelope. Dorothy had evidently changed her mind.

He took her to dinner at a restaurant in Soho which Frank Harris had recommended, with private rooms that could be accessed without going through the main dining room. You rang a bell beside a plain door in a side street, and a waiter led you up a flight of stairs into a room with a small round table laid for two, a decanter and glasses glinting under a chandelier, red velvet curtains drawn over the windows, and a divan in the shadow beyond the circle of light for post-prandial relaxation . . .

—Dorothy described that room in her novel, *Dawn's Left Hand*.

—And very accurately, considering it was written twenty-five years later. She must have made notes as soon as she got home that night.

—She described you both undressing after dinner, you humming tunelessly to yourself as you folded your clothes, and her finding she didn't like your body when she saw you naked. '*His body was not beautiful. She could find nothing to adore . . . with the familiar clothes, something of his essential self seemed to have departed . . .*'

—Yes, I could see that in her face. It put me off my stroke, I have to say. I mean, I never flattered myself I looked like Michelangelo's David in the nude, but at least I was better endowed. It really put me off the way she stared at me. She seemed extraordinarily self-possessed for a woman who was about to lose her virginity. Standing there, stark naked, with her hands at her side, showing no embarrassment, no shyness, no desire. It was like a cold douche, just when you don't need one. For the first time in such a situation I feared I would be impotent. And she seemed to sense this, because she softened and came over and put her arms round me, and then she said a very strange thing.

—*'My little babe just born.'* **It's in the novel. What did she mean by it?**

—I've no idea. It's clear from the book that she didn't know either. I simply repeated it to her, and then I said, 'Let's just lie down in each other's arms,' and that's what we did. We pulled a rug over ourselves and slept for a couple of hours, and then we dressed and went out to an Italian café she knew and had coffee.

Later, as he put her into a cab, and pressed a sovereign into her hand for the fare, he said, 'Come to Sandgate next weekend.' She said, 'I can't, I'm going to my sister's,' so he said, 'Then come the weekend after,' and she agreed. He knew he had to act as soon as possible to make up for the evening's debacle, and he was mindful of the conversation he had recently had with Jane, when she said he must be open with her about the women he went with. He hadn't put it to the test yet, but it had occurred to him while he was drinking coffee with Dorothy, scarcely attending to her chatter with the *padrone*, that this might be an opportunity to do so.

At home the next day, as they were sitting in the drawing room after dinner, he with his newspaper, Jane with her sewing, he said: 'I saw Dorothy in town yesterday. I treated her to a meal.'

'Did you? How is she?'

'Very well. She had a wonderful holiday recently, in the Bernese Oberland.'

'Oh, good. She needed one, I think. She was looking jaded last time she was here. She'll soon look like a real old maid.'

'Well, that's the thing. She's tired of being a virgin.'

Jane raised her head from the sock she was darning and stared at him. 'She told you that?'

'Her Russian boy-friend seems a spineless fellow, he won't oblige. She wants me to make love to her.'

'And do you want to?'

'Yes,' he said, simply. 'You must know there's always been a kind of sexual attraction between us . . .'

'Of course. She's obsessed with you.'

'But she would never admit it. It's always been a barrier between us, an irritant, a source of frustration—it's why we're continually arguing, the argument is sublimated sex. It's why there's always a sort of tension in the air when she's here. I'd like to get rid of it.'

'Then you'd better,' Jane said, and bowed her head over the sock.

After a pause, he said: 'I invited her down for the weekend after next.'

'That's all right,' Jane said calmly. 'We've nothing arranged for that weekend.'

'Good,' he said, and turned the page of his newspaper.

Nothing more was said between them on the subject, nor did he say anything explicit to Dorothy when she arrived on the appointed Saturday. But the three of them were all aware of what was going to happen. They went through their usual routine of a walk after lunch and book chat over tea, but it seemed to him that they moved as if in a trance and spoke by rote. After dinner the two women played piano duets for him, as they often did, and he lounged in his armchair musing on their curious relationship. They enjoyed scoring points off each other, and making sharp little jokes at each other's expense. Dorothy teased Jane for being too much the fussy housewife, forever plumping cushions and straightening curtains and re-arranging flowers in vases, while Jane criticised Dorothy for her dreami-ness, her impracticality, her passive acceptance of a dead-end job. He always felt they did not really like each other, probably never had even as school-girls, yet there was a symbiosis between them which was stronger than liking, and it was epitomised by the spectacle of them playing the piano together, concentrating, co-operating, for his pleasure. He felt like a pasha in his seraglio, who had summoned his two favourite wives to entertain him, and for a while he indulged in a fantasy of enjoying both of them si-multaneously that night, though it would be hard to imagine two less likely participants in an orgy.

What followed was done quietly and discreetly. He bade Jane goodnight in her room, kissed her gravely, and retired to his own bedroom where he read for an hour. Then, wearing only a bathrobe, he went softly along the corridor to the other end of the house where the guest bedroom was situated. The door was unlocked, as he expected. He entered quietly and shut it behind him. 'It's cold in here,' he said. 'You must have a window wide open.' She said nothing, but showed she was awake by making a slight noise as she moved in the bed. It was almost pitch dark in the room but he did not attempt to turn on a light or pull back the curtains—he had no intention of letting her see him naked this time. He felt his way towards the bed, and dropped his robe to the floor. As his eyes accommodated to the darkness he saw her lift the bedclothes, and he got in beside her. She was naked too, and lying on a towel—a thoughtful touch, if a shade clinical, like a patient laid out on an operating table. He did what he had come to do, and it was soon accomplished. It was not ecstatic, and he had not expected it to be. He got out of bed and put on his robe. 'Goodnight, my dear,' he said, and stooped to kiss her. 'I'm not here,' she said, speaking for the first time. 'You'll come back,' he said, 'and it will be better. Don't attach any importance to these preliminaries.'

In fact they never slept together in Spade House again. They met a couple of times in London in a seedy hotel near Paddington station, but Dorothy always seemed uncertain whether she really wanted an affair with him. Then she moved from her lodgings to share a one-bedroom flat with a member of a women's club she had joined, a formidable forty-year-old spinster called Miss Moffat, as if to ensure that she couldn't receive him in her own bed, and he began to lose patience with her. The only positive thing that had come out of the episode was that his understanding with Jane now seemed to be on a firmer footing.

—But you didn't tell her about *every* woman after that . . .

—Well, no, I didn't. But if it was anyone she knew, or might meet, or might hear about, I told her. It made a great difference. I think she felt empowered by knowing, in a curious way. In due course she accepted my having long-term mistresses as well as *passades*, in fact even gave me advice about them, and wrote friendly letters to them, and sent them presents. Some people found that quite extraordinary, extraordinarily tolerant or extraordinarily depraved, but it was consistent with the Free Love principle on which we eloped together.

—So it was a kind of open marriage, but open only on your side.

—Jane didn't want to have lovers.

—Are you sure? She wrote some short stories about women trapped in unsatisfying marriages, longing for romantic adventure. You collected them in *The Book of Catherine Wells*. Could we have a look at that?

He goes to the bookcase and takes down *The Book of Catherine Wells. With an introduction by her husband, H.G. Wells,* published in 1928 a year after her death from cancer. Chatto & Windus made a nice job of it. The three photographic portraits of Catherine at different stages of her life are not printed on the page, but mounted like photos in a private album. How beautiful she was!

—But how sad she always looked in photographs, even snapshots. Do you have a single one of her smiling?
—I don't know.
—You would if you had one.
—I remember her smiling and laughing in life. That's enough for me.
—This late story of hers called 'In a Walled Garden'—an interesting echo there of your own story, 'The Door in the Wall', only in her case the garden is a prison, not a paradise. The heroine is married to a dull, egotistical poet and man of letters called Bray, who changes her first name to suit his taste, just as you changed Catherine to Jane, and who doesn't satisfy her sexually—
—But that's because he made love to her 'delicately and reverently'— hardly my style.
—Well, isn't that typical of the way writers conceal their autobiographical sources? Simply reverse the facts: instead of a too rough lover, a too timid one. Jane learned that trick from you. And anyway it doesn't affect the fundamental *donnée* of the story, that the heroine is sexually unfulfilled, so that when a handsome young photographer comes to take a portrait of her husband, who is absent, she falls instantly in love with him. *'Mate of mine! Found! Found!'* she thinks. She resolves to take the initiative next time he calls, but he doesn't return, and she never sees him again. So she decides to seek fulfilment in motherhood instead. The last line is: *'But it was not Bray's child she desired.'*
—Yes, well, I admit when I read that story I felt a twinge of discomfort. It was published in a magazine with a very small circulation, but I could imagine it being passed around among my friends—and enemies—and being chuckled over. *'Jane getting her own back, I see!'* 'H.G. getting a taste of his own medicine.' That sort of thing. Of course I didn't say anything to Jane about that aspect of the story. She showed the first draft to me in

manuscript, as she always did, and I confined myself to purely literary comments. I remember questioning '*Mate of mine! Found! Found!*' A bit out of character, I felt, a bit too D.H. Lawrence, but she stuck to it.

—**You could hardly have complained about the content, considering how often you portrayed unsatisfactory marriages in your novels, some of the wives bearing a resemblance to Jane in various ways.**

—Absolutely. She never complained to me about that either. It was part of our understanding that I was free to make use of our lives in fiction. If you're writing about contemporary life there's really no alternative but to draw on your own. But that story, and a few of the others, did make me think, rather sadly, especially after her death, that there was an unfulfilled hankering for romance in Jane—or rather Catherine. That was why I called the book, *The Book of Catherine Wells*.

—**Catherine was the woman with unfulfilled romantic longings. The part of herself she suppressed when she accepted your renaming of her as 'Jane'.**

—That's a somewhat prejudicial way of putting it. I don't think she had a libido to suppress. As I say here, in my introduction to the stories: '*Desire is there, but it is not active aggressive desire. It is a desire for beauty and sweet companionship. There is a lover, never seen, never verified, elusively at the heart of this desire. Frustration haunts this desire.*'

—**But suppose it had been more active and aggressive. Suppose it hadn't been frustrated indefinitely. Suppose she *had* taken a lover?**

—Then I would have gone mad with jealousy.

—**You admit it.**

—Othello would have paled in comparison.

—**In spite of your belief in Free Love.**

—I believe in it as an ideal to aspire to. Unfortunately it's always liable to be undone by jealousy. I preached against jealousy in many of my books, but I could never entirely free myself from it. On occasion it has totally possessed me—when Isabel remarried, for instance, and when Moura went back to see Gorky in Russia in '34 and lied to me about it—but Jane never gave me any provocation of that kind.

—**Very fortunate for you.**

—It was.

Strangely, the only moment when he feared to discover some infidelity on Jane's part occurred a few weeks after she died, in October 1927, and after her final illness had brought them together more closely than for many years. He was in the south of France, where he spent a good part of the year in those days, when he received a telegram from Frank telling him that Jane had been diagnosed with incurable cancer. She had been unwell for some time, but made light of it and, typically, had booked herself in for an exploratory operation without telling him, so as not to be a bother. He came home to Easton Glebe immediately, and spent the next five months with her as she slowly declined, admiring her fortitude, her patience, her lack of self-pity, and doing his best to care for her. She wished only to survive to see Frank married, but sadly she died on the day before the one appointed for the wedding, to be held at Easton as the bride was a local girl. The couple were married privately, the wedding celebration was cancelled, and there was a funeral a week later to which he invited a large number of friends, and at which he made an exhibition of himself, blubbing noisily as a friend, the classical scholar T.E. Page, read a eulogy which he had composed but did not trust himself to deliver. *'We have come together in this chapel today,'* it began, *'to greet for the last time our very dear friend, Catherine Wells. We meet in great sadness, for her death came in the middle season of her life when we could all have hoped for many more years of her brave and sweet presence among us. She died a victim of cancer, that still unconquered enemy of human happiness. For months her strength faded, but not her courage nor her kindness. To the end she faced her destiny with serenity and with a gentle unfailing smile for those who ministered to her.'*

For several years past she had rented a small flat in Bloomsbury, not far from the British Museum, as a kind of haven, a place that was only for her. Neither he nor any other member of the family had ever been inside it. She did not make use of it very often and seldom spent more than a few hours there at a time. She used it for writing—it was difficult for her, she said, to write her own things when she was at home at Easton or in their London flat, surrounded by the evidence of his own prolific literary career, and engaged in helping him manage it. He understood that, and encouraged her to take the flat, 'A Room of One's Own' as Virginia Woolf would call it a few years later, in the title of a book he liked better than most by the same hand. He had made a little joke to Jane when he paid for the lease about trusting her not to use it as a love nest, provoking a faint smile and a shake of the head in response. He had never entertained the slightest suspicion of her doing any such thing—until the day, not long after her funeral, when, as part of the melancholy business of sorting out her affairs and disposing of her effects, he took the keys from her bureau drawer neatly labelled with the address in Bedford Place and went there to clear the flat of her belongings.

On his journey he was suddenly afflicted with a dread of discovering in the flat some evidence of a secret romantic life, of a lover whom she had met there unknown to him. He told himself the idea was ridiculous, but he could not shake it off. Perhaps it was his own fictional imagination that fuelled the suspicion—it would be just the kind of reversal that a novelist would think up, the serial adulterer confronted with the evidence that he had been cuckolded by his submissive little wife when he could no longer accuse her . . . or perhaps it was the operation of his own bad conscience, punishing him with these disturbing thoughts for not loving Jane enough while she was alive. Whatever the reason, he was almost trembling with apprehension when he arrived at the house, and had some difficulty fitting the keys into the locks on the front door and the door to Jane's flat.

As soon as he stepped inside, however, his fears evaporated. It was a small sparsely furnished studio apartment, with a narrow divan bed, a bureau desk and chair at the window, an easy chair, a bookcase, and a chest of drawers. There were a few prints on the walls, still lifes and seascapes, and a vase of dried flowers on the hearth next to the gas fire. Everything was neatly in place—the bed concealed under a tightly fitting coverlet, the cushions on top symmetrically distributed, the implements of writing tidily arranged on the surface of the desk. It was a room as eloquent of chastity as a nun's cell. In the drawers of the desk he found the manuscripts of her stories and poems, most of which she had shown him, and the ones that he had not seen before contained no hints of unsuspected amours. But collectively they did suggest a wistful regret that there was an area of life, the area of passion, from which she knew she had been excluded. It was an intimation that rose from the handwritten pages, as delicate and intangible as the faint trace of her favourite perfume in the trapped air of the room. Sitting there at her desk, he resolved to collect the best of these writings into a book that would be a memorial to her.

—So when did sexual relations between you and Jane cease?

—I don't know. I can't remember. It wasn't something we agreed explicitly. The intervals between intercourse got longer and longer, and eventually it just stopped.

—But you must have some idea of when that was.

—It was probably about 1907, 1908. Maybe 1909.

—The time of your affairs with Rosamund Bland and Amber Reeves.

—But it wasn't as if Jane was jealous or angry with me over those girls, and said 'Never come to my room again.' In fact she was an absolute brick. I couldn't have survived that time without her support, during the Amber affair especially. That nearly broke me, you know. I was mad with anxiety—everything I'd worked for over the past decade seemed to be spinning out of control: my literary career, my political mission, my private life, all at the same time.

—Well, you brought it on yourself.

—Yes, I brought it on myself.

PART THREE

By 1902 he had achieved a position in the world that he would not have dreamed possible ten or even five years earlier. He owned a fine house, architect-designed to his own specifications, and although the building of it had been attended with many petty frustrations and delays, this trade having seemingly made few improvements in its methods and working practices since the construction of the Pyramids, the final result had been worth waiting for. It was a house designed for comfortable and convenient living, rather than boasting of the owner's social status. The front elevation was simple, the porch and front door modest in their proportions. The principal object of interest to be seen from the windows on that side was the Sandgate Lift, a funicular system ingeniously worked by hydraulic power which conveyed passengers up to and down from the heights of the Folkestone Leas—fascinating to those of a technical cast of mind, but of no picturesque value. The glory of the house was its rear aspect, which faced south, its white-painted rough-cast surfaces reflecting the light and absorbing the warmth of the sun. There was an inviting terrace and two lawns, one big enough for badminton. Beyond the rim of the garden the land fell away steeply to give a view between trees of the English Channel, and on the western edge of the property there was a small brick building with its back turned to the house and a decoratively tiled roof, intended by Voysey to serve as a gardener's shed, which he himself had quickly commandeered and converted into a satellite study. In the summer months when the weather was fine he would rise at dawn and go out there to write for some hours before breakfast, glancing up from his foolscap pad from time to time to enjoy the view of Sandgate High Street stirring into life far below, the wooded hill that rose up behind the village taking the light of the rising sun, and the waves breaking soundlessly on the shingle beach that stretched westwards along St Mary's Bay to Dymchurch. Inhaling the fresh sweet sea air that came through the open door he would sometimes recall the bedroom in Mornington Street where he had a small writing table squeezed in between the bed and a chest of drawers, overlooking a squalid yard hemmed in by the sooty backs of other identical houses, and reflect with satisfaction on how far he and Jane had travelled since then.

In literal terms London was only seventy miles distant, and though the South Eastern Railway Company contrived to stretch that out to a two hour and fifteen minute journey, it was not tedious enough to deter week-end guests, of whom there were many. Gissing came, Bennett came, and as the Fabians began to woo him, Beatrice and Sidney Webb came, and the Shaws, and other luminaries of the Society. He enjoyed entertaining his friends and acquaintances from the metropolis, mixing badminton with book talk and charades, and Jane was an efficient if slightly over-anxious hostess. Not that the locality lacked its own literary celebrities. Henry James was not far away in Rye, and they had been on friendly terms ever since he and Jane first came to the area in '98, when he was laid up in New Romney with the last spasm of his kidney ailment. The damaged kidney finally dematerialised there, leaving him with one healthy organ which had served its purpose adequately ever since. James and his guest Edmund Gosse cycled over from Lamb House to visit him and kindly enquire whether he was in need of financial assistance from the Royal Literary Fund. They were pleased, and visibly impressed, when he told them he was not, and already planning to settle in the area and build himself a house with the royalties from his novels.

It was fortunate that at the outset of his brief career as drama critic for the *Pall Mall Gazette* a few years earlier he had reviewed James's disastrous play *Guy Domville* kindly, since this allowed a friendship to develop between them based on mutual admiration and—since their work was so different in character, and their ages so widely separated—a blessed absence of rivalry. It was conducted chiefly through correspondence, since James always found some excuse to decline invitations to Spade House, perhaps fearing that he would not be able to praise it convincingly (the information that every bedroom had its own lavatory seemed to disturb him) but the baroque extravagance of his epistolary style was a compensation. '*You, with a magnanimity already so marked as to be dazzling, sent me last summer a beautiful and discouraging volume which I never mustered the right combination of minutes and terms to thank you for as it deserved—and then perfectly aware that this shameful consciousness had practically converted me to a quivering pulp, you let fly the shaft that has finished me in the fashion to which I now so distressfully testify'*—thus did James magnificently apologise for not having acknowledged receipt of *When the Sleeper Wakes* before receiving *Tales of Space and Time.* They had got into the habit of exchanging copies of their new books and compliments about them. The older writer's fulsome praise was invariably qualified by some hinted reservation, itself disguised as a compliment. *'I re-write you, much, as I read—which is the highest tribute my damned impertinence can pay an author,'* James wrote after reading, rather late in the day, *The Time Machine.* But it pleased him to have this intimate connection with the most distinguished, if not the most popular, exponent of the novel as a form of art in the English language.

There were two other literary novelists of growing reputation living in the same corner of England, where East Sussex met West Kent, whom he had soon got to know and like: Ford Madox Hueffer and Joseph Conrad, who were themselves friends and on occasion collaborators. Collaboration seemed unlikely when you saw them together—Hueffer tall, blond, moustached, with extrovert bohemian manners, and Conrad short, dark, bearded and prickly. He privately nicknamed them the Walrus and the Carpenter, on account of Hueffer's prominent front teeth. 'Fordie', as he was familiarly known, was always seeking to co-opt other writers in his mission to modernise contemporary English writing, and the Polish Conrad, a retired sea-captain, brought a Continental European seriousness and a treasure chest of adventurous experiences to this project, though the nuances of English comedy of manners eluded him. 'My dear Wells, what is all this about Jane Austen?' he would ask, frowning and gesticulating. 'What is there *in* her? What is it all *about*?'

With James, Hueffer, Conrad and himself all living in the same area there seemed to be the makings of a new literary coterie, and for a brief time it was augmented by Stephen Crane, the brilliant young American author of *The Red Badge of Courage,* and the beautiful Cora who passed as his wife but was in fact married to another man, and rumoured to have run a brothel in the Wild West of America. The Cranes came to England in 1897 and rented a huge ramshackle mansion at Brede, near Rye, where they threw a memorable New Year's party in 1899/1900 which spread over three days of feasting, wassailing, games and theatricals. Henry James was invited but prudently declined. There were so many guests that the men and women had to sleep in segregated dormitories, and, in stark contrast to

Spade House, Brede Place had only one WC, which was reserved for the ladies, so in the early morning gentlemen were to be seen making their way to the nearby woods with a thoughtfully abstracted air, pretending not to notice each other. In spite of these inconveniences most of the guests enjoyed themselves, though poor Crane himself was obviously very ill with the tuberculosis which caused his death six months later in a Swiss sanatorium. He missed Crane sorely, a brave, delightful man, whose tragically premature death, which might so easily have been his own, made him feel all the more blessed by good fortune.

So there he was in 1902, the proud owner of Spade House, a paterfamilias with a healthy son, respected in the local community (he had been approached about becoming a Borough magistrate), enjoying a crowded and various social life, on friendly terms with a widening circle of important writers and thinkers, and increasingly celebrated as a writer and thinker himself. *Anticipations* was selling as fast as a novel, and his lecture at the Royal Institution in January, 'The Discovery of the Future', was rushed into print for the benefit of the hordes who had been unable to get tickets for the event. But in the same year he wrote another book of a very different kind, which puzzled many of his new admirers when it was published, a short novel entitled *The Sea Lady*. It was a variation on the Undine myth that playfully mixed incompatible elements of fantasy and realism, but had a serious theme. A middle-class family called the Buntings who occupied a house on the beach at Sandgate saw one day a beautiful young woman swimming in the sea, apparently in difficulties. She was rescued and brought ashore wrapped in a blanket, the blanket concealing a tail. She charmed everyone, especially a young man called Charteris destined for a successful career in Parliament on the Liberal benches. He fell in love with the mermaid, to the dismay of his fiancée, Adeline, who was devoted to the novels of Mrs Humphry Ward and committed to improving the Condition of the Poor, an ambition mocked by the Sea Lady: *'What is the Condition of the Poor? A dreary tossing on the bed of existence, a perpetual fear of consequences that perpetually distress them, because they do not know what a dream the whole thing is . . . .And what does she care for the Condition of the Poor after all! Her dream is that she be prominently Doing Good, asserting herself, controlling their affairs amidst thanks and praise and blessings.'* The Sea Lady's enigmatic motto was, *'There are better dreams.'* Charteris vacillated between the claims of Desire and Duty, and finally succumbed to the former, sinking beneath the waves in the arms of the Sea Lady.

The idea for this book sprang from an experience on the beach at Sandgate in the summer of 1900. While Spade House was being built, they were renting a villa called Arnold House, one of a row whose back gardens extended down to the shore, very convenient for mixed bathing, an activity still regarded as somewhat daring by conservative Sandgate. One fine morning he went for a stroll along the beach at low tide and was making his way back to his garden gate when he heard a call of 'Uncle Bertie!' from the direction of the sea. He turned and saw, wading through the shallow breakers towards him, a vision of transcendent beauty, Botticelli's *Birth of Venus* come to life.

She was May Nisbet, the daughter of E.F. Nisbet, who had been drama critic of the *Times* when he himself was reviewing plays for the *Pall Mall Gazette*. Nisbet had in fact written a devastating review of *Guy Domville* which Henry James still recalled with pain, but he never confessed to James that he knew the reviewer personally. They met frequently at first nights, and the experienced journalist had taken a liking to him and given him a few tips of the trade. In due course they became sufficiently friendly for Nisbet to confide that he had an illegitimate daughter at school in Goudhurst in Kent, and when he fell suddenly ill he sent a message begging 'My Dear Wells' to look after this girl after his death, news of which had swiftly followed. He had accordingly continued to pay the school's fees, invited the girl to Sandgate for occasional holidays, and bade her call him 'Uncle Bertie'. She had been a gawky, pimply adolescent when she first became his ward, but this summer, aged seventeen, she had blossomed into a striking beauty. Now, striding towards him in a wet bathing costume and lit by the morning sun, she seemed like a young goddess. Her costume was a simple schoolgirl's garment, without the frills and furbelows of high fashion, rather too small for her, and all the more revealing for that. It covered her from neck to mid-calf, but clung like a second skin to every contour of her perfect young body—even, he noticed as she came smiling up to him, the nipples of her swelling breasts. She seemed the epitome of clean, healthy, sun-kissed young womanhood, and he was swamped by a wave of impossible desire for her.

'Good morning, Uncle Bertie,' she said, tugging off her bathing cap and allowing her long fair hair to tumble about her shoulders. 'Aren't you going to bathe?'

'*No, I want to peel that costume from your limbs and lick the salt water from every inch of your delicious body and then make urgent ecstatic love with you here on the sand like a satyr with a nymph on some Aegean island,*' he wanted to say, but in fact he said, 'Maybe later. I prefer to go in when the tide is up.'

Perhaps she became conscious that he was staring at her rather fixedly as he spoke, for she blushed and looked round for the towel and bathing robe which she had left higher up the beach. 'I'd better go in and change,' she said.

'Yes, don't get chilled,' he said. He could not resist adding, 'You've become a beautiful young woman, May.'

She blushed again and smiled shyly, and mumbled something that sounded like 'Thank you.' He watched her, appreciating the alternate rise and fall of each buttock under the clinging short skirt as she moved up the beach, until she found her towel and robe on the dry shingle and covered herself. Only then did she look back at him and wave, and he waved back.

May had a certain musical ability, and had gratefully accepted his suggestion that she should train to be a school teacher of music at his expense, but she was a rather dim and unimaginative girl, whose only attraction was her physical beauty. If he had applied himself to seducing her he would probably have succeeded, but of course the idea was utterly out of the question for reasons of honour and common sense. During the rest of that holiday he confined himself to flirting with her in a sentimental avuncular way, amusing himself by seeing into what bashful pleased confusion even the mildest compliment would throw her. But the image of her rising from the sea like Aphrodite stayed with him, and out of the longing it had triggered in him that morning, he developed the story of the Sea Lady and her fatal allure.

The meaning of the story was ambiguous, and he himself was not quite sure what it was. The Sea Lady was immortal, but her immortality was a burden to her. She envied human beings '*because you look towards an end*', but criticised them because '*the little time you have you use so poorly*'. Her siren attraction proved fatal to the hero, but she was given all the best lines in the book. Was it a fable illustrating the destructive effect of sexual love, or celebrating its transcendent power? He didn't really know. It was as if, hesitating on the threshold of a new phase in his life, he was suddenly afflicted by doubts which he tried to work through and throw off in this fantasy. The exercise was effective inasmuch as by the end of that year he had decided to join the Fabian Society and thus committed himself to the cause of radical politics. He could, he was well aware, have settled down at Spade House to build himself a comfortable career as an Edwardian man of letters. A future of quiet, satisfying work, varied by entertaining gossip and mutual admiration at literary societies and dinners, awaited him if he followed that route, leading eventually to a knighthood and a clutch of honorary degrees—but he knew it would not satisfy him. He would continue to write, yes, but he had already experienced the thrill of success in that line, and the prospect of spending the rest of his life merely striving to maintain his place in the literary pecking order with book after book did not appeal. He wanted to achieve something more, something that would touch the lives of people who did not read literary novels, and that meant engaging in political life. He wanted to leave the world in a better state than the one he had been born into. Later he would see the Sea Lady, and the transfigured May Nisbet who inspired her, as forerunners of other young women in his life who upset that mission.

Their next-door neighbours at this time were an amiable family called Popham, with whom he had taken some liberties in portraying the Bunting Family in *The Sea Lady*. Mrs Popham's brother and occasional guest was Graham Wallas, a lecturer at the recently established London School of Economics, and it was through meeting this man that he first got drawn into the Fabian orbit. They took an immediate liking to each other, having many ideas and aspirations in common, though temperamentally they were chalk and cheese. He shared Wallas's aim of creating a 'Great Society' through education, while Wallas for his part was excited by the radical vision of a New Republic in *Anticipations*. Wallas, who was older than himself, had joined the Fabian Society a couple of years after its foundation in 1884, and been a member of its Executive ever since, though of late, he confided, his influence had waned as the Webbs and Bernard Shaw became dominant. 'I feel the Fabian has lost its way,' he said, in the course of a stroll along the Sandgate beach. 'We can't seem to make up our minds about any serious issue. We were split over the Boer War. We're split over tariff reform. We're split over female suffrage. We debate endlessly and never settle anything. Membership has fallen well below seven hundred, which is our limit, and they're mostly middle aged or elderly. We need some new ideas, Wells, and I'm not the only one on the Executive who thinks you may be the man to give them to us. I can tell you that Shaw and the Webbs are reading *Anticipations* with keen interest. I'd like to introduce you to them.'

'I've met Shaw,' he said, 'though I doubt whether he will remember. I walked home with him after the first night of Henry James's *Guy Domville*. We were both drama critics at the time.'

'All the better,' said Wallas. 'And I'll wager he will remember you.' He added conscientiously, 'Or I would if I were a betting man.' He had lost his Christian faith as an undergraduate at Oxford, but his evangelical upbringing had left its mark.

Another overture came in a letter from Edward Pease, the Secretary of the Fabian Society, enquiring if he had met the Webbs: '*they are the pioneers of your New Republic. We have lived for years on Webb's idea of politics. We want someone else who can also think ahead, and that is why I welcome "Anticipations".*' The Webbs were invited to Spade House for the weekend and a polite mutual appraisal ensued which seemed to satisfy both parties. The Wellses were invited to dine at the Webbs' London home, an invitation repeated on several occasions, though usually he went alone. He knew he could never love the Webbs, and wondered a little if anybody loved them, or whether they loved anybody, except each other in a tepid sort of way. Wallas told him they had spent their honeymoon in Dublin studying the history of the Irish Trade Union movement, and he was not surprised. They seemed an ill-matched couple on first acquaintance, she tall and willowy and upper middle class, he short, squat and lower middle class, but they were a formidable team. Sidney had a civil servant's mind: a tireless capacity for painstaking work, and the ability to absorb and correlate facts and statistics. Beatrice was more intelligent and intuitive. But they spoke, or rather wrote, with one voice (their accents revealed their very different social origins), and they never seemed to publish anything that didn't have both their names over it. They also had access to a remarkable pool of influential people, whom they brought together under the auspices of a dining club called the Co-efficients, which he joined at their invitation. At one of their own dinners he sat down with Herbert Asquith, a leading light of the Liberal Party, John Burns the trade union leader, the Shaws, and Lady Elcho, one of the 'Souls', a circle of intellectually enlightened aristocrats who revolved around the Conservative Prime Minister Balfour, and this contact led to an invitation to a weekend house party at Stanway, the Elchos' charming seventeenth-century house in the Cotswolds.

Jane accompanied him and, somewhat overawed herself, was impressed by his confident handling of the social challenges of the occasion. He knew not to be surprised when the servants unpacked your bags on arrival and how much to tip them when you left on Monday morning. He knew when you should go to your room to dress for dinner and exactly how long before it was served you should go down to the drawing room. 'I know how to do it because I used to observe it all from the servants' point of view when I was a boy,' he explained to her. It was one of many reasons why he looked back in gratitude for the times he had spent at Up Park, as a delinquent apprentice and convalescent schoolteacher, while his mother was house-keeper there. Chance had given him an insight into the history and structure of English society which normally would never have been vouchsafed to a youth of his class. The country house, with its army of servants, its deferential tenants and villagers, and its extensive acres of land, stolen, requisitioned or enclosed in the distant past, inherited by a privileged few and owned as if by divine right, was the clue to England. It embodied a civilised but rigidly stratified social system that had hardly changed in the last two hundred years, and assumed it would go on for ever, unconscious that its foundations were being sapped by social and economic change. He had begun to brood on the idea of a novel which would examine the desta-bilising impact of the new industrial and commercial oligarchy on the tra-ditional land-based aristocracy and gentry, but it would be some time before he managed to write it. For the time being he was more exercised by the urgent political need to distribute the use of land and the benefits of the industrial revolution more equitably, and the Fabian Society seemed the best instrument available to further that project.

He joined it in February 1903, sponsored by Graham Wallas and Ber-nard Shaw. Shaw remembered very well their walk together through the West End to Camden Town after the notorious first night of *Guy Domville*, when the unfortunate author, taking his bow after the final curtain, was booed by the gallery. 'You told me that you had just sold a story called *The Time Machine* for a hundred pounds,' Shaw said when Wallas re-introduced them to each other in the dingy cellar offices of the Fabian in Clement's Inn, off Fleet Street. 'The title left an impression on my mind—so did the size of the fee, which was more than *I* had ever earned for a single piece of writing—and I've followed your subsequent career with interest. You've done very well, I must say.' 'And you too,' he replied. When they first met, Shaw had been struggling to get his plays performed, but in recent years he had achieved recognition as the most interesting contemporary British playwright, and also a very entertaining one, whose plays filled theatres. 'We've both done well,' said Shaw, 'but it's taken me longer.' There was a ten-year age gap between them, and Shaw seemed bent on adopting a kind of fatherly stance towards the new recruit to the Society, which was made easier by the circumstance that he was nearly a foot taller. 'It's good to have you on board, Wells,' he said, looking benignly down his gingery beard. 'We need shaking up. We need new blood in the membership. You're the man to attract young people.' This was all very flattering, but he sensed that Shaw would use him to make reforms in the Society which he thought were necessary but which he could not initiate himself without alienating his old friends on the Executive, and would put the brakes on any proposals that he considered too radical.

He had no intention of being Shaw's puppet, but he gave none of the Fabian Old Guard, or 'Old Gang', as the veterans of the Executive were familiarly called, any cause for alarm with the first paper he delivered to the Society. 'The Question of Scientific Administrative Areas in Relation to Municipal Undertakings' was more interesting than its title (which might have been composed by Sidney Webb or intended as a parody of his style) suggested, a development of his argument in *Anticipations* that the increasing speed of communications in the modern world was making the received notions of regional and national boundaries obsolete, leading inevitably in due course to the establishment of a World Government. But it was uncontroversial, the idea of world government being too remote a possibility to disturb the Fabians. Among the new friends who congratulated him afterwards on his 'maiden speech' were two long-serving stalwarts of the Society, Hubert and Edith Bland.

He and Jane had been introduced to the Blands by Graham Wallas some months previously, at Dymchurch, a few miles along the coast from Sandgate, where they had a holiday home. 'You must meet the Blands,' Wallas had said early in their acquaintance, evidently considering this would be an enticement to joining the Fabian. And indeed it was: seldom had he and Jane taken to new friends so quickly and enthusiastically.

He was eager to meet them from the moment Wallas mentioned that Edith was the children's writer 'E. Nesbit', author of *The Treasure Seekers*. He had been aware for more than a decade of the existence of an E. Nesbit who wrote poetry and short stories, often for children, without taking much interest in any of this work. He didn't read contemporary poetry, had as yet no children to entertain, and the adult fiction by E. Nesbit which he sampled seemed second-rate. But in 1898 or '99 he happened to pick up and leaf through a copy of the *Pall Mall Magazine* which contained the first episode of *The Treasure Seekers,* and his attention was caught by its opening:

> *There are some things I must tell before I begin to tell about the treasure-seeking, because I have read books myself, and I know how beastly it is when a story begins, '"Alas!" said Hildegarde with a deep sigh, "we must look our last on this ancestral home"'—and then some one else says something—and you don't know for pages and pages where the home is, or who Hildegarde is, or anything about it. Our ancestral home is in the Lewisham Road.*

When he read this he chuckled appreciatively, and not because he was writing a novel called *Love and Mr Lewisham* at the time. Lewisham was a name he had borrowed for purely alliterative reasons from a railway station on the line between Bromley and Charing Cross. He read on:

> *It is semi-detached and has a garden, not a large one. We are the Bastables. There are six of us besides Father. Our Mother is dead, and if you think we don't care because I don't tell you much about her you only show that you do not understand people at all. Dora is the eldest. Then Oswald—and then Dicky. Oswald won the Latin prize at his preparatory school—and Dicky is good at sums. Alice and Noël are twins: they are ten, and Horace Octavius is my youngest brother. It is one of us that tells this story—but I shall not tell you which: only at the very end perhaps I will. While the story is going on you may be trying to guess, only I bet you don't.*

This struck him as extraordinarily fresh and original writing for children, which could be enjoyed just as much by the parents who would read it to them. Children would respond to the colloquial, truth-telling style of the young narrator, adults (and perhaps older and more sophisticated children) would respond to the literary parody, and the witty bathos of 'our ancestral home is in the Lewisham Road'. This double-effect was sustained throughout the serial, which he followed intermittently in the *Pall Mall*

Magazine. The basic situation was that the Father's business was in trouble and money short, so the children thought up ways to restore the family fortune which were derived from storybooks, and therefore hopelessly unrealistic, thus often getting themselves into trouble, but occasionally being unexpectedly rewarded by kind and knowing adults. It was not entirely clear—the novel equivocated cleverly on this point—whether the children really believed their schemes might work or were engaged in a form of play, compensating for, and made possible by, the loss of their mother. The pleasures of fiction were held within a frame of reality until the very end, when a happy ending was contrived by a blatantly improbable and sentimental twist in the plot, of which the narrator (who turned out to be Oswald) said disarmingly, 'I can't help it if it is like Dickens, because it happened this way. Real life is often something like books.'

He was not surprised that the story was a huge popular hit. It was in fact E. Nesbit's breakthrough book, and she quickly consolidated its success with a sequel, *The Wouldbegoods,* and another story, *Five Children and It,* which had a different cast of characters. What did surprise him was to discover that the author was a woman. 'I always thought "E. Nesbit" was a man,' he confessed when they first met. 'Writers who use initials instead of first names usually are. Like me, for instance.' 'I'm not the first woman writer to use that device to get attention when submitting work to publishers, Mr Wells,' she replied, 'and I won't be the last. What did you think the "E" stood for?' 'Ernest,' he said off the top of his head. 'I hope I don't seem an earnest sort of writer,' she said. 'No, no, quite the contrary,' he said hastily. 'It was your subtle humour that first appealed to me.' Nevertheless he sometimes addressed her as 'Ernest' as their friendship developed. She was a woman who attracted affectionately mocking nicknames—'Madam', 'Duchess' and 'Aunt' were some of them, inspired by a tendency to bossiness in her manner.

If he had invented the Blands as characters in a novel, he certainly wouldn't have given them that surname. Edith was tall, statuesque and handsome, with a head of luxuriant brown hair, softly braided and gathered symmetrically at each side of her head. In youth she must have been a real beauty of the Pre-Raphaelite type, and although motherhood had given her a matronly figure in her mid-forties she could still in repose remind you of Rossetti's languorously pensive maidens. She favoured long, flowing dresses in bright colours and wore a large number of silver bangles on her arms, each one given to her by Bland to mark the publication of a new book. She smoked incessantly, rolling her own cigarettes, with materials that she carried around in a cardboard box on which the name of a well known corset-maker could be discerned, and inserting them into a long cigarette holder which gave an extra theatrical flourish to her gestures. On occasion she would smoke a cigar. But she was also energetic and athletic, enjoying badminton, swimming, horse-riding, and pedalling a tricycle. He felt that in many ways they were kindred spirits. Edith was as prolific and work-driven as himself, and she too liked to write her quota of words in the early part of the day in intense solitary concentration, and then be free to exercise and amuse herself for the rest of it in company, the more the merrier. Like him she was impulsive, restless, easily bored, and subject to sudden changes of mood.

Hubert Bland was an equally idiosyncratic and larger-than-life figure, but it was more difficult to fit the various parts of him together to form a consistent, interpretable character. He had been one of the small group who broke away from an idealistic utopian society called 'The New Life' to found the Fabian Society in 1884, and had been its honorary treasurer ever since, but he was not a typical member. His views were a strange mixture of the progressive and the reactionary: he believed the Fabians should work towards the formation of an independent socialist party, and had helped Annie Besant organise the famous Bryant & May match girls' strike, but he was a fervent Imperialist and opposed to women's suffrage on the grounds that once capitalism was abolished they would not need the vote. He claimed to be a Roman Catholic and scrupulously abstained from meat on Fridays, but was never observed to go to church on Sundays. His appearance was striking, but verging on the exaggeration of caricature: the caricature of a choleric retired colonel, say, or a Tory financier. He was a big, burly man, with silver hair and eyebrows, but a dark, possibly dyed moustache above a rather grim, down-turned mouth. He wore a monocle screwed into one eye through which he would glare intimidatingly at anyone who opposed him in argument. He was not a man you would want to pick a fight with, for he was a proficient boxer and, according to Wallas, kept a rifle in his London home, with which he would sometimes demonstrate his strength by lifting it down from its rack using just one hand to grasp it like a revolver. He habitually wore a black frock coat and a top hat, and presented himself as a man of business, though on enquiry this seemed to amount to little more than his having once worked in a bank. In fact he was a journalist and essayist, and a good one, with a fluent affable style and a wide range of reference, and for many years he had written a regular column in the Manchester *Sunday Chronicle* which had a large loyal following in the north of England. He had collaborated with his wife in a variety of literary and journalistic enterprises ever since they married, but lately Edith had become the chief earner of the household in her own right, a change of status that Hubert perhaps did not relish, and countered with his blustering and domineering manner.

He did not really take to Hubert, but tolerated his foibles for the sake of friendship with Edith. The Blands were both about ten years older than him and had started their family earlier in life. They had four children: Paul and Iris, who were twenty-two and twenty-one respectively when the two families first met, Rosamund who was sixteen, and John who was three. There had been another boy, called Fabian, who would have been seventeen, but he had tragically died two years earlier after an operation to remove his adenoids. The two grown-up children were rather withdrawn, Paul in a diffident and Iris in a sullen way, but Rosamund was an attractive and outgoing girl, with a well-developed figure for her age. John was too young to show much character but was a promising playmate for Gip. He was looked after by a nanny-cum-housekeeper called Alice Hoatson, often addressed familiarly as 'Mouse', who was also a companion and assistant to Edith, and treated as a member of the family rather than a servant, going everywhere with them. In spite of age differences, the Wellses and the Blands had much in common. Both couples had achieved prosperity through the profession of writing, without the security of a private income or the benefit of a conventional upper-class education (neither of the Blands had been to any kind of university); both were sociable and gregarious, and both, in spite of differences on particular issues, shared the same broadly progressive agenda. But the Blands performed their lives with a flamboyant *élan,* and a bohemian disregard for convention, which made him feel that he and Jane were a little suburban and bourgeois in comparison. He didn't go so far as to envy the Blands their style of life—it was too reckless and rackety for his taste—but occasional immersion in it added a welcome colour and variety to his and Jane's existence.

Dymchurch, where the two families first met and mingled, was a pleasant, sleepy little village, sheltered from sea breezes by its low-lying situation and blessed with a superb sandy beach. The Blands had been coming there every summer for years, at first staying in lodgings, and then acquiring a cottage of their own. But to appreciate the full, complex texture of the

Blands' existence you had to know them in the setting of their London home. Not that it was properly speaking in London—it was in Eltham, Kent, and surrounded by fields—but London was creeping inexorably nearer, and it was connected to the metropolis by trains which stopped at a station that was conveniently close to the house and indeed named after it: Well Hall.

Edith, who had raised her family in a series of terraced and semi-detached houses like the Bastables' home on the Lewisham Road, gradually increasing in size and amenities but always irredeemably banal, had found in Well Hall the house of her dreams, a dwelling fit for a writer, especially a writer of books for children. It was built in the eighteenth century of red brick, and now thickly covered with ivy—perhaps to advantage, because it was not a particularly beautiful house, but it was unique and built on a site of historical interest. 'The original Tudor house belonged to the Roper family,' Edith told him, when showing him round the property for the first time. 'Thomas More's favourite daughter, Margaret, married William Roper, and she is said to have brought her father's head back here after he was executed, and buried it in the garden.'

'Really? Where?' he asked eagerly.

'Oh, nobody knows,' Edith said. 'Why are you so interested?'

'I've been reading More's *Utopia*,' he said. 'I'm planning to write a modern Utopia, and I've been looking at the classic examples. More's is easily the best.'

'And we have a ghost,' said Edith.

'Of course!' he said. 'What would a place like this be without a ghost? Like a modern house without plumbing.'

'Actually I wouldn't mind having some modern plumbing installed in Well Hall,' she said. 'But we've already spent a fortune making the place habitable. It was terribly dilapidated when we bought it.'

'And the ghost? Is it Thomas More looking for his head?'

'No. It may be Margaret. She—I'm sure it's a she—plays the spinet very quietly in the next room—it's always the *next* room, no matter which room you are in yourself. But she's not at all frightening. Sometimes when I'm working very intensely I hear a faint sigh, and I have a sense she's looking over my shoulder at what I'm writing, but when I look round there's nobody there.'

'And is it a sigh of satisfaction or a sigh of disappointment?'

'Sometimes one and sometimes the other.'

'It's probably a projection of your own feelings about your work at the time.'

'Yes, I thought you would say that. You don't believe in ghosts, do you?'

'No, but I recognise their usefulness to writers of fiction,' he said.

Well Hall was three storeys high, and had a rickety balcony at the back overlooking a garden large enough to accommodate tennis and badminton, and surrounded on three sides by a moat, which afforded swimming and punting in summer and skating on frosty days in winter. There were shrubberies beyond the moat, two huge cedars where owls perched and hooted, an overgrown orchard, and outhouses which were used to accommodate guests when the bedrooms in the house were full up, for the Blands entertained on a large scale. Those invited to dinner came down by railway from Cannon Street, changing at Blackheath, and often missed the last train back, either because the meal started late or because they were enjoying the subsequent entertainments—dancing, charades, dumb crambo, devil-in-the-dark—too much to tear themselves away. If you were invited for the weekend it was advisable to catch an early train down and bag a bedroom before the main party arrived. Dinner was served on a long table in the great hall behind the front door, so this was kept locked and visitors were greeted with a notice saying 'The Front Door is at the Back.' On Sunday evenings there were regular political symposia at which speakers like the Chesterton brothers and Hilaire Belloc would debate with Shaw and Bland and younger Fabians before an audience of up to forty people.

Sometimes he observed signs of concern on Bland's part at the cost of all this hospitality, but since it was Edith's boom that was funding it, there was no way he could object. She loved playing the generous hostess, and was always attended by one or more adoring young men. How platonic these relationships were was a matter for speculation and gossip. She was rumoured to have had a passionate affair years ago with the poet Richard Le Gallienne, threatening to run away with him after a row with Bland, and according to Wallas she was before that in love for a time with Bernard Shaw. 'I think he reciprocated up to a point,' said Wallas, 'because he was aware that Bland was not the most faithful of husbands, but he didn't want to get deeply involved. She pursued him though. She used to waylay him at the British Museum, and he managed to keep her out of his lodgings only by leading her on exhausting walks around London.' Bland was still a far from faithful husband to judge by the Fabian gossip about him, though how he reconciled this behaviour with his public pronouncements on sexual morals was one of the many enigmas of the man's character. One way and another it was a highly unconventional household, and he often wondered with amusement what the eager purchasers of E. Nesbit's tales about the children of respectable middle-class mummies and daddies would think if they wandered into Well Hall and observed the authoress presiding over one of her parties.

In 1904 Edith had another great hit with *The Phoenix and the Carpet,* brought out as usual just in time for the Christmas trade. It added a new dimension to her work in seamlessly combining the fantastic with the recognisably real—more deftly, he had to admit, than *The Sea Lady.* He wrote a letter, jocularly addressed to '*Steamed Madam,*' of sincere congratulation: '*Go on every Xmas never missing a Xmas, with a book like this, and you will become a British Institution in six years from now. Nothing can stop it. Every self-respecting family will buy you automatically and you will be rich beyond the dreams of avarice, and I knock my forehead on the ground in the vigour of my admiration at your easy artistry.*'

He himself had just completed, with some difficulty, a novel in the Dickensian mode of comic realism entitled *Kipps,* with which he had been struggling on and off for several years. It was really the story of his own life as it might have been if he had lacked talent, intelligence and willpower. Arthur Kipps, like Bertie Wells, was a miserably unhappy apprentice in a seaside draper's shop with no hope of escaping from a life of penurious drudgery by his own efforts. An unexpected legacy enabled him to assume the life of a gentleman, but without the benefit of a proper education or any innate gifts he proved quite incapable of playing the part, and was exploited and humiliated by the genteel people with whom he now mixed. At one point in the composition of this novel he had intended Kipps to be converted to socialism and find redemption in that, but as he became increasingly involved in the political debates of the Fabian it became more and more difficult to fuse that kind of discourse with the genially comic authorial voice of the book he was writing. Over the same period he was working on *A Modern Utopia,* a much more appropriate vehicle for his own political thinking, so he decided that Arthur Kipps should find happiness in the end by marrying a servant girl and settling down to run a small bookshop. When he sent off the manuscript to his agent Pinker he admitted that the last section of the novel was '*scamped . . . a thing of shreds and patches, but it is quite handsomely brought off*'. He was confident that the first two-thirds were better than anything else he had written in that mode, and certainly funnier; and he believed that once you had your readers well and truly hooked, they would forgive many faults. Pinker's reaction confirmed this, and the book was promptly accepted by Macmillan for publication in the autumn of 1905.

A Modern Utopia was published before it, in the spring of the same year, and caused a considerable stir, especially among the Fabians. It was continuous with *Anticipations* in asserting that mankind had the means at hand to banish poverty and disease if it only had the will and wit to do so—'*Science stands, a too competent servant, behind her wrangling underbred masters, holding out resources, devices, and remedies they are too stupid to use*'—but it was much bolder in speculating on the kind of society that might evolve if this were combined with a radical change in the system of human governance. His basic narrative device was an application of the theory he had heard aired by speculative physicists, that there might be other universes in existence, parallel to the one we know. Suppose it were possible to pass from one to another, where you might find your familiar world changed for the better, and meet your own double, similarly transformed. This is what happened to the narrator of *A Modern Utopia* and his rather stupid companion, a botanist. While walking in the Swiss Alps they looked down a precipice towards Italy and '*behold! In the twinkling of an eye we are in that other world*'. It is a world of order and rationality, beauty and convenience, peace and health of mind and body, and of course it has a world government—not democratically elected but formed from a 'voluntary nobility' modelled on the Guardians of Plato's republic. He called them Samurai, a caste of austere, dedicated and gifted men and women who administered human affairs for the common good. Below the Samurai there were four classes, characterised by their nature: the Poetic, who were creative, the Kinetic, who had practical intelligence, the Dull, who had no special gifts, and the Base, who lacked moral sense. The first three were directed by the Samurai to contribute appropriately to the commonweal, while the Base, being inclined to crime, were obliged to live on remote, secure islands, inflicting their baseness on each other. There would be no prisons in Utopia because '*no men are quite wise enough, good enough and cheap enough to staff jails as a jail ought to be staffed*'.

He enjoyed describing his ideal society in detail, especially its rules concerning sex and marriage, in which some of his current negotiations with

Jane about their relationship were reflected. In his Utopia marriage was reserved for those who wished to have children, and sexual intercourse was otherwise not a matter with which the state was concerned, effective contraception being freely available. Married women were paid by the state for motherhood, and thus independent, but since it was necessary to know the parentage of children, they were required to be faithful to their husbands on pain of divorce. Married men however were free to have sex with other women provided their wives did not object. The chief source of ordinary novelistic interest in the book was the character of the botanist, a miserable fellow tormented by sexual frustration in the real world because he was too hamstrung by conventional morality and manners to take the woman he loved, and who loved him, away from the man she had mistakenly married. This made the botanist unresponsive to the appeal of Utopia, and his refusal to meet his own utopian double triggered the abrupt return of both him and the narrator to a dirty and depressing London where newspaper placards proclaim the latest crises and atrocities, and '*a ragged and filthy nursing mother, with her last addition to our Imperial People on her arm, comes out of a drinkshop, and stands a little unsteadily, and wipes mouth and nose comprehensively with the back of a red chapped hand . . .*'

The book was widely reviewed and discussed, and it strengthened his position in the Fabian, especially among younger members who responded enthusiastically to the boldness of its vision. He expected more criticism from the Old Gang, since he was well aware that his elitist Utopia bore little resemblance to orthodox models of socialism, but their reaction was on the whole surprisingly favourable. In fact neither the Webbs nor the Blands were enthusiastic supporters of the democratic system as it currently existed, nor did they have much faith in extending more power to the uneducated masses. They saw themselves in an ideal world—the Webbs in particular saw themselves—very much as his Samurai, selflessly administering sweetness and light to the community by the practical application of their superior intelligence, without having to answer to anybody else. Only the sexual mores of his Utopia caused a slight raising of eyebrows and pursing of lips, an intimation of trouble to come.

In June of that year his mother died, after a fall on the stairs in her cottage. For some years she had been sinking into senility, and unable fully to comprehend the scale of her son's rise in the world. There was a photograph

taken by Jane of the two of them sitting together on the sunny terrace of
Spade House just a year before she died which eloquently expressed their
relationship and her state of mind. He was relaxed, dressed in a soft Jaeger
woollen suit, with his legs crossed and a hand on one knee, but leaning
sideways and forward in an effort to get her attention, while she, dressed in
a full-skirted, all-enveloping black dress and cap, the image of the recently
deceased Queen Victoria in her widowhood, was looking away from him
with an expression of bewilderment and fear on her white, round face. She
obviously could not believe that this splendid and luxurious new house
could belong to her Bertie, or that he had come to possess it by honest
means. Her own father had deceived her mother and her siblings about his
financial status and died bequeathing them nothing but a mortgage and
numerous other debts. She clearly expected the bailiffs to turn up at any
moment and begin moving the furniture out of Spade House, and nothing
he told her about the income he was earning from his books, or the exalted
company he kept, would dispel her anxiety. His stories of meeting lords and
ladies and cabinet ministers on equal terms were as fantastic and incomprehensible to her as his scientific romances had been when she was still able
to read them. 'Fancy,' she would murmur incredulously at anything and
everything he told her. 'Fancy that.'

It grieved him when she died that she had never understood or really
appreciated his success. It had been achieved by dint of a struggle of wills
between them in which he had been victorious, and he would have been
pleased if she had been able to acknowledge that he had been right, and
herself wrong, and to take pleasure in the admission. Then they would have
been finally reconciled. But it was not to be. When she was laid out for
burial, swathed in a white lace shawl, he kissed her forehead, cold and hard
as marble, and took several photographs of her before the lid was screwed
down on the coffin. But these were not consoling mementoes: her lips were
tightly set in what could only be described as an expression of comprehensive disappointment with what life had given her. Among her effects he
found a diary going back to her youth which was a long litany of com-
plaints, especially against her father, whose fecklessness had compelled her
to go into service, and her husband, who had taken her away from the
comfortable position she had attained in that occupation and condemned
her to years of unpaid servitude as a housewife in a home only one notch
better than a slum. The single joy in her life had been her daughter Frances,
'Possy', who died of appendicitis at the age of nine, and she decided that

her third and last son had been sent to her to replace this saintly child, an expectation that he had signally failed to fulfil. As he read he was divided between pity for his mother's unhappy life and dismay at what an ungenerous, self-centred, unctuously pious person it had made her.

He was upset by his mother's death, but unwilling to share these thoughts with Jane, or anyone else. He was irritable and restless in the weeks that followed the funeral, unable to get on with a new book he had started called *In the Days of the Comet*. He bickered with Jane about household matters, and shouted angrily at his boys when they made too much noise in the garden outside his study window, making little Frank cry. 'What's the matter with you?' Jane asked. 'I need to get away,' he said. 'Where will you go?' 'I don't know,' he said. 'Maybe to the Reform. I could work in the library there.' He had been elected to this famous club, another feather in his cap, in March. He packed a few clothes and the manuscript of *In the Days of the Comet* in a valise and set off for London, but on the journey the idea of staying at the Reform in the middle of July, when everybody he knew among the members, like Arnold Bennett and Henry James, would be in the country or abroad, did not appeal. He needed company, sympathetic company. He thought of Edith Bland.

He didn't wire in advance, but arrived uninvited and unannounced at Well Hall, carrying his valise, and said to Edith, when she came downstairs to see who had called, 'Hallo, Ernest, I've come to stay for a few days.' Her face lit up with a smile of pleasure. 'What a lovely surprise!' She took his hand and kissed him on the cheek. 'You may be wondering why—' he began, but she waved away his explanations. 'We're always delighted to see you, H.G. Stay as long as you like.'

That evening the family put on charades based on the titles of his books to amuse him and make him feel at home. Paul sat at a table reading textbooks and taking notes while young John, dressed as Cupid, mimed taking shots at him with a bow and arrow. He guessed 'Love and Mr Lewisham' immediately but pretended to be puzzled for a while to let the actors have their fun. An item performed by Edith and the housekeeper-nanny Alice Hoatson kept him guessing longer, till he exclaimed 'Anticipations!' Rosamund, now eighteen and a striking young woman, with a pretty face and a buxom figure, did 'The Sea Lady', miming the breaststroke while pursued around the room by Hubert Bland wielding a shrimping net. He couldn't resist contributing to the entertainment with a couple of improvisations on Nesbit titles, which were warmly applauded. He hadn't enjoyed anything so much for weeks, and retired to bed in good spirits. 'You won't mind if I'm not in evidence tomorrow until the afternoon,' Edith said as she wished him a good night. 'I work in the mornings.' 'So do I,' he said. 'That's perfect then,' she said.

He had been given two bedrooms: one on the first floor in which to sleep, and another on the second floor in which to write, with a desk at the window which looked towards the front gates and a cottage dignified with the name of 'The Lodge'. But the weather was fine that week, and both he and Edith worked most days in shady nooks of the garden, well separated so as not to distract each other. If he took a stroll to stretch his legs and meditate the next sequence in his novel he would sometimes catch sight of her sitting in an arbour, her head bowed over a foolscap pad, driving her pen rapidly over the pages, stopping, crossing out, looking up into the sky for inspiration, and then writing again. Sometimes she would work on into the middle of the afternoon, before breaking off for tea and a game of badminton or a punt on the moat. She was under considerable pressure, writing two serials simultaneously and struggling to keep an episode or two ahead of her deadlines. *The Railway Children* had been running in the *London Magazine* every month since January and the book was due to be published in time for Christmas; *The Amulet* had been appearing in the *Strand* since May and would finish in the same month next year. It used the same kind of magical device as previous tales to transport its English children from modern London to distant times and places where they had perilous adventures.

'The amulet is in fact your time machine,' he observed slyly one afternoon when they were chatting about their work.

'I admit the debt, H.G.,' she said, 'and I shall soon be incurring another. I've been re-reading *A Modern Utopia,* and like it much better than I did the first time. I'm planning a chapter in which my characters travel into the future, where children cry if they can't go to school because it's so nice.'

'I look forward to that,' he said, laughing.

They were sitting in the garden after tea in the shade of a chestnut's thick foliage, eagerly listened to by Rosamund, who had ambitions to follow in her mother's footsteps and was clearly enthralled by this dialogue between the two writers. The others who had taken tea had gone back into the house, leaving only the three of them at the wooden table, apart from the wasps that were feasting on the jam-smeared plates. Edith sucked on her cigarette holder and blew smoke at them.

'I'm enjoying *The Amulet* enormously,' he said, 'especially when you bring the historical characters back into modern London. The Queen of Babylon trying to recover her jewels from a case in the British Museum . . . great fun! But you know, Ernest, I think *The Railway Children* is going to be your masterpiece.'

'Oh, I agree!' said Rosamund. 'It's so moving as well as funny. I'm always dying to read the next episode.'

'That's because it's got a strong plot that runs through the whole story, Rosamund,' he said. 'What has happened to the Father? What has he done? Will he return to his family? We want to know.' He glanced at Edith.

'Well, don't expect me to tell you,' she said, smiling. 'What about you, H.G.? What's *your* new novel about?'

'It's set in the future and it's called *In the Days of the Comet*. Did you know that Encke's Comet is due to make a reappearance next year?'

'Never heard of it, I'm afraid,' said Edith, and Rosamund also shook her head.

'But you've heard of Halley's Comet—that's due again in 1910. It was thinking about these comets that gave me the idea for this novel. Their shining tails contain a great deal of gas, and it's been discovered lately that this gas may be stripped from the tail if the comet passes into the gravitational field of another astral body, like the earth. I imagine a huge comet that is getting closer and closer to the earth, and causing a great deal of alarm and panic—because if it collided with the earth the effect would be devastating, perhaps the end of the world—and it's happening just as war has broken out between England and Germany. There's also a love-story plot that's driven by jealousy. What happens is that the comet doesn't collide with the earth, it just brushes past it, enveloping the world in its gas, which has a strangely beneficial effect: it puts humanity into a deep sleep from which they awake born again, realising what fools they've been, and that there is no need for war and jealousy, and begin to rebuild the world accordingly.'

'Another Utopia, then,' Edith said.

'Yes, but with a more exciting story than the last one.'

'It sounds wonderful!' Rosamund said, gazing at him wide-eyed.

Later that day, before dinner, he went for a stroll with Edith. They passed beyond the confines of the moat and wandered through the overgrown and largely untended grounds until they came to an old summerhouse, and sat down on an ancient wicker sofa, where a most interesting conversation took place.

'Why didn't you like *A Modern Utopia* the first time you read it?' he asked her.

'I didn't like the idea that married men could have affairs but their wives couldn't.'

'You think married women should be able to have affairs too?'

'No. I don't think either of them should,' she said. He was surprised by this answer, which did not accord with what he knew about the history of her marriage, but he could hardly say so. Noting his silence, she said: 'I mean I know they do, the flesh is weak, the heart is susceptible . . . I won't claim that Hubert and I have been entirely . . . But I don't think it should be publicly approved, taken for granted, as it is in your Utopia. I think we must uphold the traditional principle that sexual intercourse should be restricted to married couples.'

'Even though we know it isn't?'

'Yes. If you had daughters like Rosamund you would agree with me. Young girls like her know everything and fear nothing. They don't believe in religion, they read any books they like, Darwin, Marx, French novels, Havelock Ellis I wouldn't be surprised, because we've brought them up—I mean liberal progressive people like us have brought our children up—in complete intellectual freedom. It makes them terribly vulnerable. I don't worry about Iris, even though she is at the Slade, where all kinds of things go on. She's a level-headed girl, and she's being courted by a very nice man in the civil service . . . But Rosamund . . .'

'But you and Hubert are Roman Catholics, aren't you? Hasn't that . . . ?'

He left the question unfinished, but she inferred it without difficulty: 'We were received fairly recently. Hubert in 1900 and I two years later. It was much too late to affect Rosamund's upbringing. She's a terrible little pagan, I'm afraid.'

He was surprised by this reply, because Bland had given him the impression that he belonged to an old Catholic family in the north of England who had been deprived of their wealth and property by the Reformation. He did not probe into this discrepancy however, but risked a direct question on a matter which puzzled him more: 'I don't wish to be rude, Ernest, but why did you both join an institution that is adamantly opposed to almost every principle the Fabian stands for?'

Edith looked a little embarrassed. 'Yes, our friends who knew were surprised, some disapproving. Hubert had always been attracted to the Roman Church in a rather romantic, literary way, but he didn't do anything about it until Fabian died. You know about that?'

'Yes, I was very sorry to hear about it.'

'I had a baby born dead once—that was bad enough. And one is always terrified of illnesses in infancy. But to lose a son at the age of fifteen, with his whole life before him . . . and he was such a lovely boy, my darling, my favourite . . .' To his dismay, she began to weep.

'Ernest—Edith—I'm sorry. Forget my impertinent question,' he said. 'Let's talk of something else.'

'No, no, it's good to talk about these things occasionally,' she said, taking a hanky from her sleeve and wiping her tears away. 'You see it was such a stupid, unnecessary death, that was what made it so unbearable. It was just a minor operation, carried out at home, so minor that we had forgotten all about the appointment and Fabian was digging in the garden when the surgeon and the anaesthetist arrived, and I had to send him to have a bath and get into pyjamas so the operation could take place. The doctors left him sleeping off the chloroform. There was a muddle. I thought Hubert was with him, he thought I was with him. When Hubert went into the bedroom poor Fabian was dead—he had choked and suffocated while still under the anaesthetic. The poor child died alone. You can imagine how Hubert and I felt. We were devastated to lose our darling boy, and it was all our own fault.' She wept again.

'You mustn't think that, Edith,' he said, and put his arm round her shoulders to comfort her. 'It was just damned bad luck.'

'I know,' she said, sniffing and blowing her nose. 'And it's kind of you to say so. But that's how we felt. Hubert took it very hard. I think he decided to become a Catholic because he wanted absolution—they have confession you know, the real thing, not like the pale imitation you get in the C of E. When you're received you have to confess the sins of your entire life, and they are forgiven. It seemed to work. He was able to forgive himself. He recovered his old energy and spirit. So I decided to follow him into the Church.'

'And did it work for you too?' he said.

'Up to a point,' she said. 'But not as well as it did for Hubert. To speak the truth, we're not really very good Catholics, either of us. We don't go to mass very often—hardly at all in fact. But it's a comfort to belong. It's nice to know the Church is there if you ever need it, in the great crises of life and death, when the Fabian, frankly, isn't much help.' She smiled sadly at him. 'Dear H.G., how kind you are to listen patiently to all this. And what extraordinary eyes you have.'

They both became conscious at the same time that his arm was still round her shoulder and their faces very close together. It seemed natural to seal the conversation with a kiss, and it was far from being a chastely decorous one. It was full on the lips and lasted some time, during which he put his other arm round her waist. When it ended Edith leaned her head on his shoulder and they were silent for some moments as he wondered, and presumed she was wondering, what to do next. Then Edith sighed, sat up, and separated herself from his supporting arm. 'Perhaps we should go back to the house,' she said.

He was fairly sure that if he had acted first he could have enjoyed more kisses, and who knew what might have followed? '*The flesh is weak, the heart is susceptible . . .*' Edith was a passionate woman, and Bland was conveniently absent on business in the north of England connected with his journalism. But on reflection he was relieved that he had not taken the opportunity to initiate a *passade* with her. His reasons were ungallant. She was taller than him by several inches and when he clasped her briefly in his arms he had taken the measure of her body's considerable bulk under her flowing robe. When he imagined making love to her naked on a bed the picture he summoned up was faintly ludicrous. So it was as well that nothing irrevocable had been said or done between them in the summerhouse, and he could maintain an innocently friendly relationship with her, rendered more intimate by their conversation, but with no emotional complications. When Bland came back from his trip to the north he was able to look his host in the eye without a qualm.

Bland was in excellent spirits, for reasons that became evident when they went, at his suggestion, for a 'breather' after a late dinner delayed for his return. It was dark, but a full moon allowed them to follow the footpaths without the aid of a lamp. The moon cast sharp shadows of trees on the lawns, and prompted the thought that if a comet were as bright in the night sky every object would have two shadows, angled in different directions: he made a mental note to work that into his novel. Bland led him to a corner of the moat-enclosed garden that was screened from the house by trees and bushes, stopped beside a heap of compost and unbuttoned his fly. 'I always like to piss in the open air, when I have the opportunity, don't you?' Bland said.

'Well, there are some things I enjoy doing more in the open air,' he said, as he followed suit. It was not his natural style of humour, but whenever he was with men like Bland—Frank Harris or Sidney Bowkett, for instance—he found himself drawn into it, while rather despising himself for competing on this low level.

Bland gave a knowing laugh. 'And you don't mean badminton!' He spread his legs, leaned back slightly, and released an arc of urine which glittered in the moonlight and fell with a soft hiss on the compacted mound of leaves and grass cuttings. 'Personally I prefer a nice big bed, with firm springs,' he said. 'Speaking of which . . . I made good use of such a bed last night, belonging to a young lady of my acquaintance in Manchester. I took her to heaven three times in as many hours.' He finished his lengthy micturition with a grunt of relief, shook his penis, stowed it away in his trousers, and began to button himself up. 'Not bad for a man of my age, eh, Wells?'

'Not bad at all, Bland,' he said, having already finished and adjusted his dress.

'What's the most times you've done it in one night?' Bland asked, as they walked on.

'I don't know,' he said. 'I lose count after it gets into double figures.'

Bland roared with laughter and clapped him on the back. 'You rogue! But if you prefer it al fresco you should try Blackheath one warm night, near the gates to Greenwich Park. All kinds of interesting ladies are to be met there.'

He couldn't resist asking Bland how he reconciled these adventures with the teaching of his adopted religion. 'Isn't it a sin according to your faith, Bland?'

'Of course it is. It's very wicked,' he said. 'But it's knowing that it's a sin that makes it meaningful. For you fellows who don't believe, it's no more significant than a sneeze. For us it means risking our immortal souls. Fortunately there's always confession.'

He wondered if Bland were joking, but it appeared that he was entirely serious. He couldn't help reflecting that if Bland was saving up his sins for a deathbed confession, it would take a perilously long time to get through all of them, but managed to keep the thought to himself.

He stayed at Well Hall for a week, and made excellent progress with *In the Days of the Comet*. In the late twentieth century the elderly narrator, Willie Leadford, was recalling his life before the great Change which was brought about by the comet. Willie was a character much like himself when he was a young man, intelligent but hampered in his ambitions by the disadvantages of his humble background, and sexually frustrated. He set these early chapters in the Potteries, risking an accusation of poaching on Arnold Bennett's territory, because he associated that place with one of the lowest points in his own life. But Willie's home was closely based on Atlas House in Bromley:

> *A scullery in the old world was, in the case of such houses as ours, a damp, unsavoury, mainly subterranean region behind the dark living-room kitchen, that was rendered more than typically dirty in our case by the fact that into it the coal-cellar, a yawning pit of black uncleanness, opened and diffused small, crunchable particles about the uneven brick floor. It was the region of 'washing-up', that greasy damp function that followed every meal; its atmosphere had ever a cooling steaminess and the memory of boiled cabbage, and the sooty black stains where saucepan or kettle had been put down for a minute, scraps of potato-peel caught by the strainer of the escape pipe, and rags of a quite indescribable horribleness of acquisition, called 'dish-clouts,' rise in my memory at the name.*

Recalling his mother's life of drudgery and self-denial in this squalid environment, he worked through the complex emotions stirred up by her death and resolved them into a poignant portrait of a woman who was a victim of her society. '*She had been cowed into submission, as so many women of that time had been, by the sheer brutality of the accepted thing. The existing order dominated her into a worship of abject observances. It had bent her, aged her, robbed her of eyesight so that at fifty-five she peered through cheap spectacles at my face and saw it only dimly, and filled her with anxiety . . .*' In Willie's furiously jealous pursuit of his former sweetheart Nettie, and her new love, the upper-class Verrall, he explored his feelings for Isabel after their divorce and at the time of her remarriage. As always, writing these things as fiction, with the freedom to change, enhance, and with hindsight interpret one's own experience, was cathartic.

As he was strolling in the garden before lunch on his last day he met Rosamund, and had a strong feeling it was not by accident. He was walking under the shade of a pergola when she appeared at the other end and came smiling up to him, like a pretty wench who had stepped out of some pastoral idyll, her bare feet shod in sandals, wearing a straw hat and a loose blue muslin dress with a neckline that showed her remarkable bosom to advantage.

'Finished work for the day, Mr Wells?' she said.

'Yes, I've come to the end of a chapter, and I'm not ready to start the next one. I'll leave it till I get home tomorrow.'

'I just heard you were leaving us. What a shame, it's been lovely having you here. You've become one of the family.'

'It's been lovely for *me*,' he said. 'But I have a family of my own—I really must get back to them. Shall we . . . ?' He gestured to a bench seat, and they sat down. 'Well Hall is a perfect haven for a writer,' he said.

'Well, it may be for you . . .' she said, with a faintly sulky set of her lips and jaw. Like her mother she had a sensuously fleshy chin reminiscent of Rossetti's beauties, though not their hairstyle: hers was short and fair and gently waved.

'I believe you have literary aspirations yourself, Rosamund.'

'Yes. Well, actually I have published a couple of little children's books.'

'Really? I didn't know. Congratulations.'

'Oh, they're nothing—I don't boast about them. Little books for little children. One is called *Cat Tales* and one is called *Moo-Cow Tales*. Just hackwork, really—Edith got me the commissions. It was useful pocket money, but that's all. I want to write something more grown-up, more original, but it's hard when you've got two famous and successful writers like Edith and Hubert for parents, looking over your shoulder. And then they fuss so if I want to go out on my own anywhere. How am I ever going to be a writer if I don't get some experience?'

'It will come. You have your whole life before you,' he said benignly. 'Meanwhile your home should give you plenty of ideas.'

'What do you mean?' For a moment he saw a look of surprise, almost alarm, in her brown eyes.

'It's such a romantic place. Steeped in history. Thomas More's head buried somewhere in the grounds, for instance, nobody knows where. That should be good for a story. I'm surprised Edith hasn't written it.'

'Oh *that* . . .'

'Why don't you have a try yourself?'

She looked at him with a cheeky smile. 'If I did, would you read it and give me an opinion?'

'Certainly.'

'Then I will!' she said, clapping her hands. 'Thank you. I'll have to read up about Thomas More.'

'Be sure to read his *Utopia*,' he said.

'Isn't it rather boring?'

'Not at all. The chapter on marriage is particularly interesting.'

'Why?'

'Read it and you'll find out.'

'I will,' she said.

A voice, probably Alice's, calling 'Ros-a-mund' was heard, coming from the direction of the house.

'Bother,' said Rosamund, 'I expect she wants help with lunch. Excuse me.'

'Of course,' he said, and watched her walk down the tunnel-like pergola. At the end she stopped, turned and waved, reminding him of something, or somebody.

He returned to Spade House in excellent spirits and immediately wrote Edith a 'roofer' as, for reasons obscure, a letter of thanks was called in the Bland family's argot. It began: '*Dear Lady, A roofer! The thing cannot be written! Jane I think must take on the task of describing the departure of a yellow, embittered and thoroughly damned man on one Thursday and his return on the next, pink—partly his own, and partly reflected*', and it ended: '*Fine impalpable threads of agreeable association trail from Lodge to stairway, hold me to your upstairs and downstairs bedrooms, take me under the trees of your lawn, and to your garden paths . . . It was a bright dear time. Yours ever, H.G. Wells*'

That visit marked a new phase of intimacy in the relations between the Wellses and the Blands, who, flush with Edith's royalties, had acquired a bigger summer home in Dymchurch: a red-brick Georgian house with

Dutch gables called Sycamore House, though with characteristic insouciance the Bland family always referred to it as 'the Other House' to distinguish it from the cottage it replaced. They were frequently in residence there in August and September, and numerous visits were made and returned between the two families. There was badminton at Spade House, and French cricket on the flat hard sand of the Dymchurch beach when the tide was out; there were cycle rides through the lanes of the Romney Marshes and pot luck meals and hilarious charades. He dispensed literary advice to Rosamund in confidential chats, enjoying her lavish praise of his own work. She never managed to get the story about Thomas More's head into a shape she was willing to show him, but she did read the chapter on marriage in *Utopia*. 'And what did you think of couples who are contemplating marriage being allowed to see each other naked before they commit themselves?' he asked her. 'I thought it was a jolly good idea,' she said. 'I wouldn't mind at all, if it were done decently, as in the book, with chaperones. What do you think, Mr Wells?' 'I think there would be many fewer unhappy marriages if it was a custom in our society,' he said, 'but the English are so prudish about nakedness.' 'Yes, I asked Iris if she wouldn't like to see her Austin naked before she got engaged to him and she told me not to be disgusting. And she's drawing naked models all the time at the Slade! Well, not quite naked.' She giggled. 'Apparently the men wear little pouches.' 'And what about the rest of More's *Utopia*?' he asked. 'I didn't find it very interesting, I'm afraid,' she said. 'I much prefer yours. The ending, when they come back to sordid London is so wonderful.'

'I hope you will be sensible with that young girl,' Jane said, as they were coming home from the Other House that day, having observed him and Rosamund deep in conversation in the garden. 'Don't worry, my dear,' he said. 'She's a nice girl, but I'm not in love with her.' 'It's *her* falling in love with *you* I'm worried about,' Jane said. 'It would be a shame if anything upset the nice relationship we have with the Blands.' 'Have no fear, I agree entirely,' he said. And he did agree. There seemed to be a symbiosis between the two families that was helpful to the writers at the heart of each. In October Jane accompanied him to Well Hall for the first time, and they stayed for a weekend which went very well, Edith writing afterwards: '*Oh my dears—oh my dearie dears! Virtue must have gone out of you both during this good weekend, for quite unexpectedly, and with a most thrilling suddenness I find that I have finished* The Railway Children *which have sat on my bent and aged shoulders for nearly a year!!!!!! Thank you so much. This, as you per-ceive, is a* roofer!'

In December Edith sent him an advance copy of *The Railway Children* and he sat down in his study and read it in a single sitting, quickly at first, reminding himself of the early chapters he had already read in serial form, then more slowly and appreciatively. His provisional judgment had been correct: it *was* Edith's masterpiece, with a depth and a unity that none of her previous books, for all their merits, possessed, and in his opinion was destined to become a classic.

Three children were abruptly uprooted from their comfortable London home because of the unexplained disappearance of their father, and obliged to live in near-poverty with their mother in a country cottage. The nearby railway line was their main source of amusement—waving to the passing trains, and making friends with the staff of the local station. Three-quarters of the way through the story the eldest, Bobbie, discovered from an old newspaper that her father was in prison; wrongfully, her mother assured her, but she had to conceal this knowledge from her siblings. As so often in the author's work, a good deed by the children brought into the story a benevolent old gentleman who steered it towards a happy ending by orga-nising an appeal against the father's conviction, but never before had Edith played so skilfully with the reader's desires, expectations and emotions at the climax.

There comes a day when the three children go down the fields to wave at the 9.15 train as usual and are astonished when all the passengers smile and wave back at them with their newspapers. Unable to concentrate on her mother's lessons later that morning, Bobbie goes down to the station to ask after the signalman's sick little boy. On the way everyone she meets smiles knowingly at her but says nothing, conspiring with the author to keep Bob-bie unaware of what is about to happen. Daringly, the author addresses the reader: *'Of course you know already exactly what was going to happen. Bobbie was not so clever. She had the vague, confused, expectant feeling that comes to one's heart in dreams. What her heart expected I can't tell—perhaps the very thing you and I know was going to happen—but her mind expected nothing.'* Thus did the writer simultaneously admit the convention-bound nature of fiction and at the same time claim a superior truthfulness for her own story, thus did she exquisitely delay the climactic discharge of emotion when Bob-bie, sitting on the station platform, idly watching the passengers alight from the 11.54 suddenly sees –

'Oh! my Daddy, my Daddy!'

That scream went like a knife into the heart of everyone in the train, and people put their heads out of the windows to see a tall pale man with lips set in a thin close line, and a little girl clinging to him with arms and legs, while his arms went tightly round her.

The story ended on the next page, for Edith did not make the mistake of trying to describe the heroine's relief and happiness or how it was shared with the rest of the family.

Bobbie goes into the house, trying to keep her eyes from speaking before her lips have found the right words to 'tell Mother quite quietly' that the sorrow and the struggle and the parting are over and done, and that Father has come home.

There were a few more lines, but he read them with difficulty, tears streaming down his face.

Jane came into his study at that moment and looked at him in astonishment. 'Good heavens, H.G., whatever is the matter?' she cried.

'Nothing,' he said, wiping his eyes and cheeks with a handkerchief. 'I feel such an ass, blubbing over a children's book. But I couldn't stop myself.' He held up the copy of *The Railway Children*. 'That woman plucks at your heartstrings like a harpist.'

Jane laughed. 'Well, it's certainly an achievement to make *you* cry over a book for children.'

'Wait till you read the last chapter—I bet you'll do the same,' he said. He brooded for a moment over the way the trick was done. That switch of perspective from Bobbie to the passengers on the train, for instance, when she screams and embraces her father with her legs as well as her arms and you are reminded that she is, for all her emotional maturity, a child— brilliant! But it wasn't simply a matter of technique. 'Tell me,' he said, 'did anything I've written ever make you cry?'

Jane thought for some moments, her eyes unfocused as she cast her mind back over the years and the titles of his novels and stories. 'No, I don't think so,' she said at last, and seeing that he looked glum, added comfortingly. 'It's not your forte, H.G.'

2

The personal and social entailments of belonging to the Fabian were much more interesting and rewarding than its official activities, which consisted mainly of rather boring meetings at which senior members gave papers and aired views which were already well known to the audience, who debated them along predictable lines. There seemed to be little will to rethink the function and strategy of the Society radically, and he began to wonder if he had made a mistake in joining it. A familiar fugitive impulse gripped him, and in the spring of 1904 he thought he saw in the current controversy over tariff reform an opportunity to escape with honour. The charismatic Conservative politician Joseph Chamberlain was campaigning effectively for a protectionist British Empire, an idea which the Fabian Executive pragmatically decided not to condemn, but which his friend Graham Wallas, as a faithful Liberal, opposed on principle. When Wallas resigned from the Society over this issue, he seized the opportunity to tender his own resignation on the same grounds. Shaw, however, persuaded him to withdraw it in a letter which artfully combined sarcasm with flattery, declining to believe that he cared a fig about tariff reform, but urging him to persevere with the Society because they needed him. He accordingly wrote to the Secretary Pease withdrawing his resignation while making it clear that he disapproved of the Society in its present form and was staying on only in order to turn it upside down.

Throughout 1904, and much of 1905, he concentrated his efforts on trying to persuade the Fabians to re-examine and revise their precious 'Basis', the manifesto drawn up by Wallas, Shaw, Bland and other founding fathers of the Society, which had acquired for the Old Gang the same status as the Ten Commandments had for the Israelites. The main virtue of this document was its brevity, for it could be printed on a single sheet of paper, in spite of saying the same things several times in different ways. *'The Fabian Society consists of Socialists,'* it began. *'It therefore aims at the reorganization of society by the emancipating of Land and Industrial Capital from individual or class ownership, and the vesting of them in the community for general benefit.'* The next two paragraphs repeated the same objectives with very little additional detail, and confidently predicted that *'the idle class now living on the labour of others will necessarily disappear, and practical equality of opportunity will be maintained by the spontaneous action of economic forces . . .'* It concluded: *'It seeks to achieve these ends by the general dissemination of knowledge as to the relation between the individual and society in its economic, ethical and political aspects.'*

The main feature of this document was its vagueness as to the means by which its aspirations were actually to be carried out, which was an advantage inasmuch as it encouraged many middle-class intellectuals who thought of themselves as progressive to put their names to it without any real fear of having to surrender their private property to the state, but a disadvantage in that it postponed indefinitely any action other than giving lectures and publishing pamphlets. And the definition of socialism in narrowly economic terms excluded mention of urgently needed social and cultural reforms—for example, ending the subjection of women. His radical views on this issue earned him the friendship and support of one of the leading female members of the Fabian, Maud Reeves, the wife of William Pember Reeves, the Agent General for New Zealand. They had come to England in the late nineties with good progressive credentials—he as a former minister in the New Zealand Liberal Government and author of a scholarly book on *State Experiments in Australia and New Zealand,* she for her participation in a successful campaign for female suffrage in her native country, the first in the world to give women this right. They were quickly welcomed in Fabian circles, where they already had several contacts, and although Reeves could not take an active role in the Society's affairs because of his diplomatic status, Maud was not thus inhibited.

She was a vivacious, elegant, intelligent lady and he developed a friendship with her in which there was not an iota of the mutual sexual attraction that was always latent in his relationship with Edith Nesbit. Perhaps for this reason she was remarkably unguarded in discussing with him general issues to do with sex and marriage, once casually mentioning apropos of male conservatism in these matters that, 'Will would never consider contraception and refuses even to discuss it.' His inference from this and other remarks was that their sexual life had ended with the birth of their third child, a son, just before they came to England, and that this was not a source of grief to her. Certainly Pember Reeves did not seem like a man to set a woman's pulse racing with desire: he had a long, lugubrious countenance like a bloodhound, looked older than his age, was morose in temperament, stiffly correct in manners, and very conscious of his status, all the more so when his title was elevated to High Commissioner. He had fallen out with his political colleagues in New Zealand and been removed from office, with the sop of a diplomatic post in Britain which he tried to make appear more important than it was. Notwithstanding his support for the cause of female suffrage, Reeves ruled his family as a patriarchal autocracy—or imagined he did. In fact Maud and her two teenage daughters managed to live fairly unrestricted lives by simply not asking his permission for doing as they liked—the young girls, for instance, going about London without chaperones—relying successfully on his imperceptiveness and official preoccupations to escape detection.

In spite of Reeves's lack of personal charm the two families got on very well together, and Maud was particularly keen to develop her friendship with Jane, who had joined the Fabian as soon as Frank was weaned. Visits were exchanged, and the Reeves family spent a whole week in Sandgate in the summer of 1904, taking a house in the village to be near the Wellses. He enjoyed talking to their two girls, especially the older of the two, Amber, who was just seventeen and not only very pretty but also very intelligent. It was typical of her father's essentially conservative temperament that he tried to discourage her from going to Cambridge when she left school as she wished, offering her instead the enticement of a presentation at Court and a 'coming out' in London. 'As if I would want to be a debutante!' Amber said scornfully as he walked along the shore with her and her sister Beryl one day. 'Curtseying to Royalty in a white dress, and dancing with boring young men at balls night after night.' 'So you'll go to Cambridge?' he said. 'Of course!' 'Good for you, Amber. What will you study?' 'I haven't decided yet,' she said. 'What do you think I should study?'

There was nothing he liked more than holding forth about education to a captive audience such as Amber and her sister provided, and he delivered an extempore lecture on the contrasting merits and limitations of the sciences and the humanities. 'Ideally,' he concluded, 'you should be able to study both at university. But such is the prejudice of this benighted country that you have to choose between them, so I suppose it's a matter of intuition—what sort of knowledge you desire most.' *'Tell Mr Wells that he ought to have been a finishing governess,'* Maud wrote in her thank-you letter to Jane afterwards, *'How those girls revelled in him and how excellent was his influence!'*

A year later, when they met at the Reeveses' big house in Kensington, Amber told him she was going up to Newnham College in the autumn to read Moral Sciences. 'What are they?' he asked her. 'Science isn't moral or immoral—only the uses that are made of it.' 'Oh, it's nothing to do with natural science, it's the Cambridge name for philosophy,' she said airily. 'Philosophy, ancient and modern, with a bit of psychology thrown in. Plato and Aristotle, Bentham and Mill, Kant and Hegel. That sort of thing. I'm looking forward to it.' 'What made you choose that?' he asked. 'I was browsing in a bookshop in Charing Cross Road, and I happened to open a book by Kant where he demonstrated how to demolish the claims of the Roman Catholic Church by reason. I decided philosophy was the subject for me.' 'What's the name of the book?' he said, 'I'd like to read that demolition myself.' She blushed. 'I'm afraid I don't remember,' she said. 'I didn't buy the book—I couldn't afford it.' 'Well, you must look up the reference in the Public Library and send it to Mr Wells,' said Maud, overhearing this conversation, 'or he will think you're just making it up to impress him.' 'Don't be so mean, Mother! I'm *not* making it up!' said Amber, and flounced out of the room. Maud raised her eyebrows and sighed. 'Young girls! They're so sensitive.'

For Maud the excitements of Fabian politics filled the place that love affairs occupied in the lives of other women with unrewarding husbands, and she enthusiastically supported him in his mission to reform the Society. 'I'm not making much progress,' he complained to her one evening in the autumn of 1905, as they were chatting after a rather boring paper by Sidney Webb on statistical analysis of the birth and death rates in the borough of Lambeth. 'The Old Gang are blocking my attempts to have the Basis debated at a Special General Meeting. I sent a motion to the Executive, but it bounced back.'

'That's not the way to proceed,' she said. 'You should give a paper to the Society which is a kind of manifesto for change. Call it . . .'

'The Faults of the Fabians,' he suggested, as she hesitated.

'Perfect. That would establish you as a leader of the movement for reform in the eyes of the membership. The Executive would have to respond.'

'The trouble is,' he said, 'I'm not a good public speaker. No, I'm not,' he insisted as she began to demur. 'I've no illusions on that score. I haven't got the right voice for the job—it goes high-pitched and squeaky under pressure. And I can't speak from notes or extempore like Shaw, in perfectly formed sentences—I have to write a speech in advance and read it out, which isn't half so effective.'

'If *you* write it, H.G., with passion and conviction, it *will* be effective,' she said. 'As long as you don't gabble and swallow your words, which I admit you are prone to do when you are nervous. As long as you can be heard, you will be listened to.'

In the end he succumbed to her flattery and her enthusiasm, and agreed to give a paper on 'The Faults of the Fabians' in the New Year, on the 12th of January. But not long afterwards Balfour called a general election for the same month and the Executive decided that a talk on a subject of such controversial importance to the Society should be postponed to February when it would not be overshadowed by national politics. 'In the meantime, if you have something less portentous to hand, Wells, to give us on January 12th, that would of course be very welcome, since the hall has been booked,' Pease said. He did not fail to notice the slightly sarcastic choice of epithet, 'portentous'. Although Pease had been among the first to invite him to join the Fabian there had always been an element of condescension in his manner, and of late, since his own intention to turn the Society upside down had become overt, the manner had become distinctly cool. But, as it happened, he did have something to hand, a magazine article he had just drafted entitled 'This Misery of Boots', which could be easily adapted for the purpose, and he accordingly offered it to Pease, who accepted the suggestion with a prim smile as he wrote down the title.

As he foresaw, it worked very much to his advantage that he delivered 'This Misery of Boots' before his more challenging critique of the Fabian. It was a light-hearted piece with a good deal of humour in it, but it also expounded the fundamental principles of socialism in a very accessible way, and it went down a treat with his audience. He began with a little vignette of his underprivileged upbringing, how his first infant apprehension of the wider world was the sight of people's variously shod feet moving past on the pavement outside Atlas House, glimpsed through the high barred window of its underground kitchen, which perhaps explained his later preoccupation with boots as an index of quality of life. He then proceeded, in a kind of pastiche of Sidney Webb's analytical method, to suggest that one in five of the population of these islands were suffering on account of their boots, and then discriminated between the various kinds of discomfort caused by new boots, badly fitting boots, boots made from unseasoned leather, the various species of chafe they produced, the different pains and injuries occasioned by uneven heels and worn soles, by splits and leaks and holes . . . The audience was laughing merrily until he reminded them that 'these miseries of boots are no more than a sample. The clothes people wear are no better than their boots; and the houses they live in are far worse. And think of the shoddy garments of ideas and misconceptions and partial statements into which their poor minds have been jammed by way of education! Think of the way *that* pinches and chafes them!' The audience applauded.

He continued with his parable. He knew a man (it was himself) who by good fortune had raised himself from the class who buy their boots and clothes out of what is left from a pound a week after food and accommodation have been paid for, into the class that can spend seventy or eighty pounds a year on them, so his feet are perfectly comfortable. But the thought of the multitudes so much worse off than himself in this matter of footwear gave him no sort of satisfaction. *Their* boots pinched him vicariously, because this misery of boots was not an unavoidable curse on mankind. "There is enough good leather in the world to make good sightly boots and shoes for all who need them, enough men at leisure and enough power and machinery to do all the work required, enough unemployed intelligence to organize the shoe making and shoe distribution for everybody. What stands in the way?' What stood in the way was private property and private capital, which controlled the whole process from the acquisition of raw leather to the sale of the finished product in order to extract profit at every stage. Only Socialists had the remedy. 'The whole system has to be changed, if we are to get rid of the masses of dull poverty that render our present state detestable to any sensitive man or woman. That and no less is the aim of all sincere Socialists: the establishment of a new and better order of society by the abolition of private property in land, in natural productions and in their exploitation . . . if you funk that, then you must make up your mind to square your life with a sort of personal and private happiness with things as they are, and decide that "it doesn't do to think about boots."'

The hall erupted in prolonged applause when he finished, and he saw Maud beaming approval at him from the front row as she joined in, with

Jane beside her clapping for all she was worth, her eyes shining with pride. He took some questions, which he dealt with adequately, if not as adroitly as he would have wished, and then the meeting dispersed. 'That was wonderful, darling,' Jane said as he joined her, and Maud concurred: 'Yes. Well done, H.G. It was the perfect curtain-raiser for "The Faults of the Fabians".'

'That may not go down so well,' he said, warding off hubris.

But it did.

The general election resulted in a landslide victory for the Liberal Party, who won 400 seats to the Conservatives' 129 and, taking into account alliances with other groups, had a working majority of 358. Most significant of all, from the Fabian point of view, was the election of 29 Labour MPs. For the first time socialism had a substantial representation in Parliament. This was a cause of some embarrassment to the Old Gang, because ten years earlier they had rebuffed an approach by Ramsay MacDonald when he asked the Executive to help finance the launch of a Parliamentary Labour Party, on the grounds that, given the dominance of the two major parties, this would be a waste of time and money, and they had used a large bequest in their possession at the time to found the London School of Economics instead. He felt the tide of events was now running with him. The huge Liberal victory indicated that the nation was disillusioned with the old order and eager for change, and the Fabian was in danger of being left behind by the wave of popular sentiment if it did not urgently remodel itself, and seize the historic opportunity. There could not have been a more favourable moment for him to deliver his talk on 'The Faults of the Fabians'. Not surprisingly, the hall in Clifford's Inn was packed on the appointed evening, the 9th of February.

From the outset of his talk he attacked the Society's insularity and complacency. 'I see our Society, with its seven hundred odd members, apparently under the impression that these seven hundred odd are the only thoughtful and authoritative socialists in existence in England,' he said. 'I want myself tonight to correct this extraordinary mistake some of us make.' While the tone of 'This Misery of Boots' had been genially humorous, this second talk was written in a satirical mode. The Society, he said, 'strikes an impartial observer as being still half a drawing-room society, which by a wild, valiant effort took a central office in a cellar in Clement's Inn, and exhausted its courage in that enterprise'. (Laughter) He mocked the rambling, inconsequential information distributed to members, and deplored the failure to actively recruit new ones. 'We don't advertise, thank you: it's not our style. We cry socialism as the reduced gentlewoman cried "oranges": "I do hope nobody hears me." '(More laughter) All the faults of the Fabians could be traced back to its origins. 'It met socially—to this day it meets socially. It has never yet gone out to attack the unknown public in a systematic and assimilatory way. At a certain stage in its development it seemed to cease. It ceased to grow, ceased to dream, ceased to believe in any possible sort of triumph for socialism as socialism. It experienced just that arrest of growth one sees in a pot-bound plant.'

Then he attacked one of the tablets of the law, the famous quotation attached to the Basis, about the Roman General, Fabius Cunctator, from whom the Society derived its name: *'For the right moment you must wait, as Fabius did most patiently when warring against Hannibal, though many censured his delays; but when the time comes you must strike hard, as Fabius did, or your waiting will be in vain, and fruitless.'* Though it was got up to look like a translation from some Roman historian, nobody had ever managed to find the source of this passage and it was generally admitted to be a fabrication. No one seemed to have noticed that it was also untrue. A little research in Plutarch revealed that Fabius never *did* strike—it was left to Scipio to carry the war against Hannibal victoriously to Africa, in spite of everything Fabius did to obstruct him. 'You see how dangerous and paralysing the Fabian tradition can become. I don't suggest for a moment it has become so, to any extent, in this society'—the disclaimer of course deceived nobody—'I offer this merely as a warning.' To have their precious piece of Fabian scripture turned against them in this way was a body-blow to the Old Gang—he glimpsed Pease looking stony-faced and Bland glowering at him through his monocle—but his erudite dispatch of its credentials amused and impressed the younger members. He concluded with a number of specific proposals: to publish a set of tracts to attract new members, to aim at a membership of 10,000 instead of 700, to increase revenue on the same scale, to give young members a more active role in the Society's affairs, and to establish local branches throughout the country. He sat down to enthusiastic applause. After some discussion it was agreed that a Committee of Enquiry should be set up under his chairmanship to draft proposals for the reorganisation of the Society and revision of the Basis which would be put to a General Meeting.

Four members of the Executive more or less sympathetic to him person-ally were appointed to the committee, including Sydney Olivier and Shaw's wife Charlotte. Charlotte would of course report back to her husband and do whatever he told her to do, but Olivier was a man of independent judg-ment, and now that Wallas had resigned over the tariff reform issue, the Executive member with whom he felt most at ease. A high-ranking civil servant in the Colonial Office, the urbane and distinguished-looking Ol-ivier combined administrative expertise with an interest in literature, and wrote accomplished light verse himself. The others on the committee were known supporters of reform, including Maud Reeves. Olivier was ap-pointed chairman and Jane secretary. The setting up of this promising com-mittee seemed like a victory at the time, but in due course it was used as another instrument of delay by those on the Executive who felt threatened by his criticisms.

Committee work was never to his taste, and was an inefficient use of his time, but he buckled down to it and after several meetings he drafted a document which won the approval of his colleagues. The new Basis would commit the Society to three main objectives: transfer of land and capital to the state, equal citizenship of men and women, and 'the substi-tution of public for private authority in the education and support of the young'. Essentially this last meant endowment of motherhood by the state, thus freeing women from the tyranny of the patriarchal private family, but the committee under Sydney Olivier's guidance thought it prudent to adopt a more abstract formulation. 'The members might ac-cept maternity allowances for married women,' Olivier said at their last meeting, 'but if you mean unmarried mothers would be eligible too, Wells—' 'I do,' he answered promptly. 'Then I fear many of them would regard it as an encouragement to immorality,' said Olivier. 'Best leave it vague.'

In forwarding the draft to Pease early in March he requested that it should be put to a General Meeting before the 27th of the month when he had to leave for an extensive tour in the United States. Pease wrote back to say that this was impossibly short notice to set up such a meeting and it would have to wait until he returned, and in the meantime the proposals would be circulated to the membership. But when he got back from Amer-ica at the end of May he was told by Pease that there had been so many queries from members about the revised Basis, especially concerning the third proposed objective, that it was desirable he should himself explain and elucidate the document to members before it was put before a General Meeting; and since people would soon be dispersing to their various summer retreats this exercise would have to be postponed until the autumn. There was a speaking date available in mid-October in the Society's programme—would he be willing?

The spirit of Fabius Cunctator lived on.

The procedural reeling and writhing of the Executive was all the more exasperating because he had had a highly successful visit to America and came home full of energy and confidence. He had gone out there to give lectures and to write a series of articles on his travels for the London *Tribune,* which he planned to turn quickly into a book called *The Future in America*. He was lionised everywhere he went—New York, Boston, Chicago, Washington—and even had a private meeting with the President, Theodore Roosevelt, in the White House. He liked America, and responded positively to its brash, bustling, egalitarian, can-do ethos, which the President, referred to universally and affectionately as 'Teddy', personified. It was a young Empire in the making, but its very rawness made one wonder if it held any promise of permanence and fulfilment. Was burgeoning America a giant childhood or a giant futility, merely the latest in the long succession of political experiments that had risen and fallen over the ages? When he was bold enough to touch this note in conversation with Roosevelt, as they strolled after lunch through the White House garden, its trees and shrubs heavy with blossom, he was intrigued—and flattered—to discover that the President, for all his publicly expressed confidence in the American future, was not free from moments of pessimism and was familiar with *The Time Machine*. 'I know that this country, which is now on an upward ascent of prosperity and power, will one day be in decline,' Roosevelt said, leaning on a garden chair, with one knee on its seat, and addressing him over its back as if from a public platform, 'but I choose to live as if that is not so. Suppose your tale of the future is right, and it all ends in your butterflies'—he meant the Eloi—'and Morlocks. That doesn't matter now. The effort's real. It's worth going on with. It's worth it.'

He was impressed by this declaration, and encouraged by it; it was, after all, the principle on which he had turned his back on the career of a dilettante man of letters and joined the Fabians. But a fat lot of thanks he had received from their senior officers. Didn't a man who was famous enough to have such a conversation with one of the most powerful statesmen on the planet deserve a little more respect? Thus he grumbled to himself as he wrote a curt letter to Pease accepting the invitation to address a meeting in October.

He had another reason to remember the day when he met Teddy Roosevelt. After he left the White House, that warm spring afternoon, a familiar sensation overtook him, a languorous longing for fleshly contact and physical relief, rewarding himself for an assignment successfully accomplished and obtaining a temporary release from the burden of thought. He hailed a cab and asked to be taken to a gay house. 'White or coon?' said the driver. 'Coon,' he said, after a moment's hesitation. It was the first time this invidious word had passed his lips, though he had heard it frequently in the last few weeks, casually applied to coloured people by the white population. It sounded strange to his own ears in his high-pitched English voice, as though he were ordering a regional dish in some foreign country, which in a way he was: he had never had intercourse with a coloured woman before. 'The best place of its kind there is,' he added as he got into the car. 'Sure thing. I know one with real class,' said the driver.

Before long he found himself in a lavishly furnished drawing room, with blinds adjusted to admit light but frustrate observation and a ceiling fan silently revolving above his head, buying drinks for a bevy of attractive ladies in various states of undress, and with complexions in various shades of black and brown, as he discussed with them the beauty of the spring weather and the progress of the Washington monument currently under construction. A slim dark-eyed young woman sitting apart in a satin shift, whose light brown skin was as flawless as sand left by the withdrawing tide, attracted his attention and he sat down beside her. Conversation flowed easily between them and soon he followed her to her room. Her name—her professional name, anyway—was Martha. She told him she was of mixed blood, white, native Indian and Negro, and she had been trying to learn Italian from a book which she showed him. She was saving up to go to Italy where she planned to live for a while and then return to America and pass as Italian. Given her features and light colour, this was not an implausible project, though it was a shame that she felt driven to it. He had been shocked by the antipathy of many white Americans he met on his travels, especially those from the southern states, towards their coloured fellow citizens (whom he personally found very friendly and likeable, whether they were hotel porters or intellectuals), but his attempts to shake their prejudice by pointing out that genetically these descendants of slaves and slave-owners must have much more in common with themselves than the hordes of white immigrants streaming into the country from Europe were not well received.

He found himself getting more and more intrigued by Martha and her story, which might have been made up by a novelist, and she was obliged to remind him gently of his reason for being with her. Her style of lovemaking was not the exotic experience he had anticipated in the cab, but it was graceful and accomplished. If her sighs and moans of pleasure were acted, they were very convincing, and spurred him to a very satisfying climax. 'I like you,' she said afterwards. 'Will you come back here?' 'I will try,' he said, and the words would have been sincere if he hadn't known he was departing from Washington the next day. When he laid a large denomination dollar bill on the bedside table she asked him if he meant to leave so much, and when he confirmed it she said sadly, 'Ah, then I know I will never see you again.' He couldn't stop thinking about her for the rest of the day, and even entertained a mad plan of arranging to meet her in Italy until common sense suppressed it. Common sense, and a letter from Jane which he received the next morning:

> *I feel tonight so tired of playing wiv making the home comfy &*
> *as if there was only one dear rest place in the world, & that were in*
> *the arms and heart of you. There is the only place I shall ever find*
> *in the world where one has sometimes peace from the silly and*
> *wasteful muddle of one's life—think: I am thinking continually of*
> *the disappointing mess of it, the high bright ambitions one begins*
> *with, the dismal concessions—the growth, like a clogging hard*
> *crust over one of home & furniture & a lot of clothes & books &*
> *gardens & a load dragging me down. If I set out to make a comfort-*
> *able home for you to live & do work in, I merely succeed in contriv-*
> *ing a place where you are bored to death. I make love to you and*
> *have you for my friend to the exclusion of plenty of people who*
> *would be infinitely more satisfying to you. Well dear, I don't think*
> *I ought to send you such a lekker, it's only a mood you know but*
> *there's no time to write another and I have been letting myself go*
> *in a foolish fashion. It's all right you know really only you see I've*

had so much of my own society now & I am naturally getting sick of such a person as I am. How you can ever stand it! Well!

Your very loving Bits

This letter disturbed him, moved him, and puzzled him, in almost equal proportions. It seemed to be several letters that had got intertwined: one of tender yearning from a lonely wife; one expressing deep dissatisfaction with a life dominated by petty domestic concerns and material possessions; another complaining that she could never succeed in satisfying his needs however hard she tried; and yet another blaming herself for inflicting these negative thoughts on him. The apology at the end did not cancel out the implied accusations of the preceding lines, and the assurance that *'it's all right you know really,'* did not allay his concern that she could admit such a degree of unhappiness, even transitorily. It troubled him that he, the champion of women's rights in public debate, should provoke such an outburst from his own wife. It seemed that she was not really reconciled to the understanding they had reached, or he thought they had reached, about his freedom to rove where other women were concerned, and he resolved to be especially kind and loving to her when he returned home.

And so he was, for a time, sharing her bed every night, not necessarily to make love, but holding her in his arms as they dropped off to sleep. Soon, however, accustomed habits reasserted themselves. He was busy with his book on America and the proofs of *In the Days of the Comet,* and would wake in the small hours with his brain racing, and get up and go into his dressing room to write, so that after a while it became sensible to sleep there. And although he did not immediately begin to seek out other women, it was not long before new opportunities, temptations and obligations arose.

The Blands were at Dymchurch for much of the summer and he and Jane saw them from time to time, but not as frequently as before. Relations had cooled perceptibly since he gave his talk on the 'Faults of the Fabians'. It had evidently taken Hubert Bland some while to realise that he was entirely serious in announcing his intention to shake up the Fabian, an ambition that inevitably implied a condemnation of those who had guided it till now, but his talk, and its enthusiastic reception, had finally opened Bland's eyes. The

Webbs, he thought, had not yet made up their minds about him—they were clearly piqued by his presumption, as a comparative newcomer, in making such scathing criticisms of the Society and such sweeping proposals for change, but they probably doubted that he had the will or the leadership to sustain the attack; while Shaw continued to play the game of puppet-master, trying to keep the peace by pulling strings from above, without so far intervening directly. With Pease, Bland was now his chief opponent on the Executive Committee, and when they met socially there was little warmth in Hubert's handshake or behind the glint of his monocle. Fabian politics were however in recess for the summer, and it was possible to avoid contentious matters when the two families met. Edith, he noticed, looked uncomfortable when the conversation veered in that direction and was quick to change the subject. In spite of her husband's manifest flaws of character she seemed to be genuinely impressed by his intellect, and always deferred to him on ideological issues—opposing votes for women, for instance—and he could very easily imagine what Hubert would have been saying privately to Edith about the recommendations of the 'Wells Committee' (as the Enquiry Committee was invidiously referred to by Pease) for the revision of the Basis. Although when they met she still gave him a friendly greeting, and smiled when he kissed her hand with ostentatious gallantry or addressed her as 'Ernest', there was not the same intimacy between them as there had been previously, a change which he regretted.

His relations with Rosamund, however, developed in the opposite direction. While he had been in America the Fabian Executive had set up a sub-group for young members to discuss and debate matters of special interest to them, called, with characteristically twee humour, the Fabian Nursery (one could easily imagine the self-approving giggles with which this name had been mooted and approved), and Rosamund was Secretary of the committee for this new body. Ostensibly a positive response to one of his own proposals at the conclusion of 'The Faults of the Fabians', it was actually an attempt by the Executive to claim the credit for the initiative and to keep its activities under their own wing. But in this hope they were to be disappointed, if his first conversation with Rosamund after he got back from America was any indication.

They met at the Other House one weekend when the Blands were entertaining a number of visitors from London, and he and Jane were invited over to join them for an informal tea party. Rosamund was in good spirits, excited by her new office, and very confident now of her attractiveness to men. He observed her flirting with Cecil Chesterton, G.K.'s less famous and less amiable brother, and attracting disapproving glances from Clifford Sharp, a young journalist who was the chairman of the Nursery Committee, before she noticed his arrival and came bouncing and smiling across the room to greet him. 'I want to ask you a favour,' she said. 'Will you give a talk to the Nursery in the autumn on Sex and Marriage? The committee was unanimous that I should ask you.' He told her that he had agreed to address a plenary session of the Society on this topic in October and had to save his powder for that, but would be glad to talk to the Nursery on some other subject. 'Socialism and the Arts, perhaps?' She looked a little cast down. 'All my friends will be disappointed. We so admire what you are saying about the oppression of women and relations between the sexes.' 'Well, I daresay I could work something in about that,' he said with a grin. 'Oh, good,' she said. 'I'll let you have some possible dates. And how are you getting on with your novel about the comet?'

'It's virtually finished,' he said. 'It comes out in September. I'm correcting the proofs, but I want to add an epilogue.'

'You said at Well Hall last year that there was a love story in it. What kind of love story?'

He hesitated, but his head was full of the book and the temptation to talk about it to a comely young admirer was impossible to resist. 'If I tell you, will you keep it to yourself?'

'Of course!' She flushed with pleasure at the idea of being entrusted with this secret.

He looked round the crowded drawing room. 'I can't tell you here—too noisy. And too nosey! Let's go into the garden.' They passed through the open French windows into the overgrown garden and sat down on a bench screened from the house by giant hollyhocks.

'Well, the hero, Willie,' he began, 'is a young man from an impoverished background, rather like mine in fact, and is in love with a beautiful girl called Nettie, but she falls in love with a handsome young chap called Verrall. Willie is furiously jealous, and as Verrall is well-off there's class hatred as well as sexual jealousy in his bitterness. He pursues the young lovers to the seaside—'

'Are they lovers, then? Not married?' Rosamund interjected.

'Yes, lovers. They have gone to live in an isolated community by the sea where such unions are not disapproved of. Willie tracks them down. He has a gun, and intends to murder them.'

'Oh!' Rosamund clasped her hands together, and pressed them against her bosom.

'And the climax of his quest coincides with the outbreak of war between England and Germany. There is a night scene. A huge naval battle is going on out at sea—guns booming and flashing on the horizon. The comet is shining down, bigger than ever, huge, flooding the beach in an eerie light. Willie sees the two lovers taking a midnight swim in the sea, coming out of the surf in their tight bathing costumes, all the beauty of their young bodies revealed.' He paused, struck by a thought. The description of the bathers derived from his memory of May Nisbet emerging from the sea at Sandgate, and he realised now whom Rosamund had reminded him of, that day when she turned and raised her hand at the end of the pergola at Well Hall.

'Wonderful,' Rosamund breathed. 'I see it vividly.'

He went on with his summary. 'In a paroxysm of insane jealousy, Willie follows them to their cottage with the gun in his hand. And then, on the way, he is suddenly overcome by a kind of cloud of green vapour and falls to the ground unconscious. That's the end of Part One. Part Two begins with him coming round out of what feels like a refreshing sleep. In fact he has been unconscious for days. He is a changed man. His heart is full of peace. The simplest thing—a wild flower, a stalk of ripe barley—fills him with joy. As he explores the world he finds that everyone has changed in the same way, under the influence of the green gas left by the comet as it narrowly missed the earth. He discovers the Prime Minister in a ditch—a bit of a stretch for the long arm of coincidence, but in this kind of novel you can get away with it—who now sees the folly of war and vows to put an end to it. He arranges a truce with Germany. He convenes a conference to draw up a constitution for a World State—'

'But what about Willie and the lovers?' Rosamund asked.

'He meets them of course, and all his jealousy has vanished. They immediately become firm friends, all three. But there is a snag: Willie and Verrall like each other—but they *love* Nettie. They have a man to man talk, and they agree that one of them must give up his claim to her, and obviously Willie's is the weaker. But then Nettie says, "Why must it be one or the other? I love you both, for different reasons. Why does love have to be so exclusive, one woman owned by one man. Why can't we be a unit of three equals"—or words to that effect.'

Rosamund was clearly excited by this turn in the story. 'You mean, she offers to belong to them both—in every way?' she said, wide-eyed.

'Yes—she hints as much. But the men can't contemplate the possibility. The old male possessiveness is too deeply ingrained in them. So Willie sadly goes on his way, and dedicates himself to assisting with the great task of remaking human civilisation, razing the filthy old cities and building light, clean new ones.'

'Oh,' said Rosamund. 'What a shame. Poor Willie.' She unclasped her hands and let them fall to her lap.

'But he meets a nice woman called Annie, and marries her and has children by her, and they join Nettie and Verrall and live happily ever after as a kind of extended family.'

'Oh, well, that's not so bad then,' Rosamund said, smiling.

He did not tell her, since he had not yet decided how to write it, that in the epilogue he was going to make it clear that Willie and Nettie finally became lovers, but not exclusively so, the two couples amicably cohabiting in a world that had come to accept Free Love as the norm.

'Perhaps we should rejoin the party,' he said. 'People will be wondering what we are up to.'

'I don't know what you mean, Mr Wells,' she said flirtatiously.

'I think it's high time you stopped calling me Mr Wells, Rosamund,' he said. 'My friends call me H.G.'

Another blush of pleasure flooded her cheeks. 'Thank you, H.G.!'

It crossed his mind that seducing Rosamund would be as easy as plucking a ripe peach from the tree.

But he did not act on this intuition immediately; never, in fact, for you could hardly call what happened a seduction, unless he himself was the object of it. Rosamund sent clear signals in further encounters between them that she was eager to know sexual love, and would like nothing more than to be initiated by a mature, experienced lover whose discretion could be relied upon and whose intellect she revered. He hesitated to respond, conscious of the dangers inherent in his relationship with the Blands. She was a good-looking young woman in a plump, wholesome, nubile way, but he did not feel an irresistible desire for her, and as if perceiving this she set about making herself interesting to him by some astonishing revelations about her parentage.

These were triggered by a casual remark he made about her eyes one evening at Spade House. She had brought young John Bland from

Dymchurch to play with Gip and Frank, and they were staying overnight. While the boys were put to bed and dinner was prepared under Jane's supervision, he poured himself and Rosamund schooners of Madeira and suggested that they take their drinks out on to the terrace. But there was a chilly east wind blowing, so they moved to the garden shelter (as he now called his shed-cum-study) and sat looking out through the open door as the sun declined towards the sea in the west. She raised her glass to the light and commented on the beautiful colour of the wine: 'It's the colour of your eyes, Rosamund,' he said. 'And your mother's.'

'You mean Edith?' she said. 'Edith is not my mother.'

He gaped at her. 'Edith is not your mother?' he repeated. 'Then who is?'

She looked at him over her glass, as if both pleased and scared by the effect of her words. 'If I tell you, you must keep it as a secretest secret.'

'All right.'

'Alice,' she said.

'*Miss Hoatson?*' He was astounded. But . . . you don't look like her. You look much more like Edith.'

'I know,' said Rosamund. 'It was very convenient when I was adopted—the same colour eyes and everything.'

'And who is your father?' he asked.

'Daddy, of course,' she said.

'Hubert! Good Lord . . . How long have you known?'

'He told me when I was eighteen. And afterwards Alice filled in a lot of the details.'

Then, having sworn him again to secrecy, she unfolded a story so extraordinary that for a while he wondered if she was making it up, but he was soon convinced of its truth.

'Alice was a friend of Edith's in the early eighties,' Rosamund began. 'She worked for a pittance on a women's magazine Edith used to write for. Edith became pregnant soon after Fabian was born—too soon—and Alice moved in with her and Daddy to take some of the domestic strain off Edith as her time approached. Sadly the baby was born dead. Edith was terribly upset—Alice told me Daddy had to practically tear the poor little corpse from her arms to see to the burial—and Alice stayed on in the house, not Well Hall of course, a much smaller one in Lewisham, or perhaps it was Lee, they were always moving house in those days . . . anyway Alice was a huge support to Edith in this crisis. But she soon had a crisis of her own to cope with: she was with child herself—me. She didn't tell Edith who the father was—just that it was someone she couldn't possibly marry—so Edith suggested she should move in with them permanently as a kind of housekeeper, have the baby under their roof, and she and Hubert would adopt it and bring it up as their own child. So that's what they did. It seemed like the perfect solution. Daddy was very glad to go along with it.'

'As well he might be,' he could not resist interpolating, as Rosamund took a sip of her Madeira. 'It got him out of a very sticky situation, I'd say. When did Edith discover the truth?'

'I think when I was about six months. Apparently there was a terrible row, but she had become too attached to little me by then to reject me—at least that's her story. Daddy told me she threatened to have me adopted by somebody else, and he said that if I went he would go too. But Alice thinks Edith suspected all along he was the father. She knew Daddy's naughty ways with women and she made no attempt to discourage his attentions to Alice—rather the contrary, because Alice had an admirer whom Edith didn't like, so she encouraged Daddy to see him off. She's not very consistent, you know, Edith.'

'Neither is your father, Rosamund, I'm bound to say,' he remarked. 'I've heard him singing the praises of monogamy more than once.'

'No, you're right . . .' she said. 'They're both full of contradictions. I suppose that's why they still love each other, in spite of everything. Because they do, you know, in their odd way. But whenever there was tension between them, I think the fact that I was Alice's daughter, not Edith's, would open up like an old wound, and add to the bitterness. My childhood memories are full of rows between them, with Edith suddenly bursting into tears, usually at the dinner table, and flouncing out of the room and going to her bedroom, and Daddy groaning, 'Oh *God*!' and going upstairs to pacify her.'

'But you never guessed the truth when you were a child?'

'No. Not even when Fabian died—I was thirteen—and I overheard Edith having hysterics and screaming, "Why did it have to be Fabian? Why couldn't it have been Rosamund?"'

'She said that? How terrible for you,' he said, genuinely shocked.

'It *was* terrible. But I never suspected the reason until Daddy told me.'

'And then?'

'Then, in a way, it was a relief to understand what I had always felt intuitively, that I was Daddy's favourite child, but Edith's least favourite. It was inevitable—how could she feel for me as she felt for her own children? If I outshone Paul and Iris in any way, she would naturally resent it. Oddly enough she was never the same about John, I suppose because he came so long after.'

'John?' he said, bewildered.

'Yes, John is Alice's child too,' Rosamund said calmly.

'By Hubert?' Rosamund nodded. 'Good God,' he murmured.

'We're quite an unusual family, you see,' Rosamund said.

A phrase he had heard frequently on his travels in America, '*You can say that again*', came to mind, but he did not utter it. Instead he put his free hand on hers and squeezed it. 'You poor girl,' he murmured.

They sat in silence for a while, looking out at a spectacular scene: dark purplish clouds edged with gold barred the setting sun, whose broken rays were reflected in the foam-flecked sea. Then the sound of a dinner gong which someone, probably Jane, was holding at an open window, carried to their ears on the east wind.

'We'd better go in,' he said.

As they stood up he saw that her eyes were wet. 'My poor girl,' he said again, and opened his arms to give her a comforting hug. She fell into them instantly, and he felt the soft, warm pressure of her breasts through his thin summer jacket as she clung to him. The only way he could think of to bring the embrace to a conclusion was to kiss her on the cheek, but she turned her head and pressed her lips warmly to his.

'Dear H.G.,' she said. 'It's such a relief to talk about these things to someone you can trust.'

He didn't consider that his vow of secrecy applied to Jane, and as soon as Rosamund had returned to Dymchurch he told her everything that he had learned from his conversation in the garden shelter, omitting only the embrace which concluded it. Slightly to his surprise, Jane was disposed to be sympathetic to Edith's part in the saga. 'After all,' she said, 'it was generous of her to agree to bring up Alice's child as her own . . . and the second one too. You could see that ménage as being based on a kind of Free Love—like your characters at the end of *In the Days of the Comet*.' She had just read the epilogue he had written to this novel.

'But that presupposes a completely transformed society,' he said, 'when Free Love is universally accepted, and everything between men and women is open and above board. The Bland household is the reverse of that. Well Hall turns out to be a house of lies—of concealment and hypocrisy.'

He felt that very strongly when he next returned there, not long afterwards. The Blands were hosting a big summer party to celebrate the engagement of their daughter Iris to her civil servant. The Wellses had been invited to stay for the weekend and had accepted, both parties tacitly agreeing to conceal the tensions that now existed between them. On the surface it was a gay occasion. The sun shone down on the ivy-covered walls of the old house and its gardens in the late afternoon, and as dusk fell light poured from the open windows and Chinese lanterns hanging from the trees were reflected in the moat. There was a splendid cold buffet laid out between silver candlesticks in the big hall, prepared by two Swiss male cooks whom the Blands now rather grandly employed, and the drawing room was cleared for dancing to piano and violin. 'Isn't it wonderful!' Maud Reeves cried enthusiastically as she greeted him, throwing out her arm to embrace the whole occasion, and of course he agreed. But in truth Well Hall no longer seemed the idyllic demi-paradise it had been for him a year before. Rosamund's revelations had cast a retrospective shadow over his previous perceptions of the place and its inhabitants, making the latter seem no longer charmingly eccentric, but devious and dangerously irresponsible. The death of the adolescent Fabian, for instance, when you thought about it, was not a tragic accident, but the consequence of culpable carelessness. Imagine forgetting that your son was booked to have a surgical operation, however minor! Fabian would have eaten breakfast that day—why would he not?—contrary to standard procedure before an operation. He probably choked on his own vomit while coming round from the chloroform, alone and unattended, while Edith was no doubt scribbling away in her room, lost in the dreamworld of one of her stories, and Hubert was, what, probably rogering Alice Hoatson . . .

At this point in his thoughts Alice herself came up to him, where he stood alone on the terrace overlooking the moat, and asked him if he didn't want to go into the house and partake of the buffet. He said he would when the crowd around the table had diminished. She seemed disposed to linger and talk—rather to his surprise, for in all the time he had known the Blands he had seldom exchanged more than a few words with her. She was appropriately nicknamed 'Mouse', for she was small in stature (and seemed especially so when standing beside the Blands) and quiet and self-effacing in manner. He had never known anyone who made so faint an

162

impression on one's senses, like a figure slightly out of focus at the edge of a family snapshot. Now that he knew something of her personal history she had become an object of great interest to him, but it was difficult to connect the melodramatic story Rosamund had related with this diminutive, grey-haired, softly spoken woman of utterly unremarkable looks.

They chatted for a while on trivial topics, and then she startled him by saying: 'I've been pleased to see that Rosamund and you are becoming great friends.'

'Well, I er, I do my best to help her with her writing, you know,' he stammered, though in truth she had still not shown him any work in progress, and he had been too busy with his own to urge her to do so.

'Yes, that's very kind of you. I'm not sure she has real talent in that direction, but we shall see. Apart from that, it's good for her to have a mature man like you to confide in.'

'Is it?' he responded lamely, quite confounded by the tone and drift of her conversation.

'Yes. She's a very pretty and popular girl, and the young men flock round her, but she's not ready to commit herself, quite rightly. I'm afraid that Edith and Hubert will try to marry her off as soon as they can, to make her safe, like Iris.'

'Safe?'

'You know what I mean: respectable. In spite of their own free and easy ways, they like to keep up appearances. They will encourage some young man to court her. Clifford Sharp, for instance—he's keen on her.'

'Is he?' He felt a little stab of jealousy at this information. He had had a few conversations with Sharp and found him a dour character, ambitious to make his mark on the Fabian, but lacking originality and charm.

'She needs time to discover herself, to become a woman without becoming the property of some man.'

'I couldn't agree more,' he said, sincerely.

'So that's why it's good that she has a friend like you to counsel her, tell her about life. The only mature man she is close to is Hubert. And Hubert . . .' She sighed. 'Well, Hubert is Hubert.'

There was a wealth of implication in this cryptic utterance, but he didn't have the nerve to try and draw it out. The tenor of her remarks about Rosamund betrayed at every point a mother's concern in a way he had never detected in her speech previously. It seemed certain that Rosamund had told her that she had revealed their secret relationship to him, but he dared not ask in case he was wrong.

'Yes, Hubert is Hubert,' he said with an air of profound and sympathetic understanding.

They heard the sound of Edith's voice through an open window calling inside the house: 'Mouse! Mouse! Has anyone seen Alice?'

'I must go, Mr Wells,' she said, and flitted away in the dusk like a shadow.

Later that evening he danced with Rosamund—having first, for form's sake, waltzed with Jane and Edith. To Rosamund as they parted he murmured, 'I'm going to take a breather on that seat in the pergola,' where ten minutes later she joined him, approaching hesitantly until he called her name. There was barely enough light to see by from the hazy half-moon, filtered through the bramble roses that covered the pergola.

'Golly, it's dark under here, H.G.,' she said, sitting down beside him.

'Your eyes will accommodate soon,' he said. 'I wanted some privacy.'

'Is that so you can kiss me again?' she said archly.

'No,' he said, 'so we won't be overheard. I had a rather extraordinary conversation with Alice, earlier this evening. Or rather, she had it with me. She seemed to assume that I know—know she's your real mother.'

'Yes, I told her I had spoken to you, in confidence of course,' Rosamund said.

'Ah, I thought so . . . She seemed to approve.'

'Yes, she does,' Rosamund said. 'She thinks you're a counterbalance to Daddy.'

'A counterbalance?' For the second time that evening he felt the conversational ground shifting under his feet. As she didn't answer, he said: 'She did say something cryptic about your father.'

'What's "cryptic" mean?'

'Difficult to interpret. She said, "Hubert is Hubert."'

'Yes, Hubert is Hubert,' Rosamund said, nodding. She kicked off her shoes and wriggled her feet. 'Gosh my feet hurt. New shoes.'

'Rosamund,' he said gently, 'I must know what you are talking about.'

After a long pause she said: 'It's just that lately he's been very affectionate towards me in a way that I feel is . . . more than fatherly. I don't mean that he's done anything rude, but . . . it's just, when he kisses me, or gives me a hug, which he's always done a lot, ever since I was a little girl, well he squeezes just a little too hard, or he goes on just a little too long, especially if we're on our own. It makes me feel uncomfortable, but I don't know how to stop it. I know that if I said the slightest thing about it to Daddy he would get into the most frightful paddy and accuse me of having a depraved imagination . . . And maybe it *is* my imagination . . .'

'Have you spoken to Alice about this?' he asked.

'Not explicitly, but she knows, I can tell . . . she doesn't miss anything.'

'Then it isn't just in your imagination,' he said.

'No, I suppose you're right,' she said. 'But it's so difficult to know what to do when you're a girl who is . . . who hasn't . . . who isn't experienced . . . you understand?'

'Yes,' he said. 'I understand.'

'You hear so much talk about sex, and read about it in books, and you don't know what or who to believe, and anyway, words can never tell you what it's actually *like*. Is it wonderful, or just ordinary?'

'It's both wonderful and ordinary,' he said.

They then had a long conversation about sexual love, in which she asked most of the questions and he gave most of the answers, until he put a question himself: 'Do you mean you would like me to make love to you, Rosamund?'

'Yes, H.G. I want you to.'

'Even though I'm not in love with you? I like you, but I'm not in love with you.'

'I don't care. *I'm* in love with *you*. I have enough love for both of us.'

She threw herself into his arms at that, and seemed to assume that he would complete her sexual education on the spot, or in some unoccupied outbuilding on the estate, but he calmed her down and counselled caution. As the Blands were soon returning to Dymchurch he said he would think of somewhere near there where they could safely meet, and let her know. 'But if you should change your mind in the meantime, just—'

'I won't,' she said, and silenced him with a kiss.

3

In the first summer of the new century, when Spade House was being built, he had rented a cottage in the flat fields below the village of Lympne on the northern edge of the Romney Marshes, as a place to which he could retreat, to think and to write, when Arnold House and its environs became too noisy and busy. It was the most basic kind of accommodation for the poorest kind of agricultural worker, just two bare rooms, with an outside earth privy and a well for water, but it served its purpose and cost him only a few shillings a week. He had furnished it with a table and chair, a couch and a few other bits and pieces, bought second-hand so cheaply that he left them there when he gave up the lease. He began *The First Men in the Moon* in that cottage, and had his narrator Bedford, sole survivor of the lunar expedition, splash down in the sea near Lympne when he returned to earth in his anti-gravity sphere, and recover in the hotel there. Back home in Spade House, following his conversation with Rosamund in the scented darkness of the pergola at Well Hall, he cycled out one day to inspect the cottage and found it unoccupied, with his furniture undisturbed. The farmer who owned the building was willing to let him rent it again on the same reasonable terms.

It was an ideal place for discreet assignations with Rosamund while the Bland family was in residence at the Other House, in an isolated situation at the end of a rutted cart track, equidistant from Sandgate and Dymchurch. Jane was not surprised when he took the cottage again as a writing retreat—she was used to his sudden flights from domesticity—but when he mentioned casually one day that Rosamund had called on him there she grasped the implication immediately. 'I hope you know what you're doing,' she said. 'Perfectly,' he said. He thought of it as completing a young girl's education at her request. The Blands did not apparently see anything suspicious in

Rosamund's new enthusiasm for taking solo cycle rides in the country—which is to say that Edith didn't, because Hubert was fortunately detained in London a good deal of the time, and if Alice Hoatson guessed what was going on she kept it to herself. The cottage was not the most comfortable of love nests, but its rustic simplicity conferred a kind of pastoral innocence on their trysts. The couch was somewhat damp, but he dragged it out into the sun and it soon dried. The roof leaked in one place, so he put a bucket under it when it rained, and they washed themselves in the water, which was softer and warmer than from the well.

The lovemaking was sometimes a little too like a tutorial for it to be fully transporting for him—Rosamund being prone to ask if she was 'doing it right' at inappropriate moments—but naked she was a sight to arouse any red-blooded man. Her beauty was already at its full-bloomed, voluptuous perfection, and he felt privileged to enjoy it before it was overblown. She would arrive usually a little while after him, flushed and breathless from the cycle ride, or more likely with excitement and exaltation at the consciousness of being a grown-up woman at last, secretly meeting her lover. He was surprised and amused by how rapidly she progressed from bashful maiden modesty to bold confidence in the ritual of disrobing, soon being quicker than himself to strip off her clothes. Reclining on his couch, its dowdy upholstery covered with an old Liberty throw brought from Spade House, she would turn her dark brown eyes up at him with a coquettish smile that hesitated between that of a licentious mistress and a naughty schoolgirl, her full, widely separated breasts standing out proudly from her torso, reminding him of a copy of Goya's 'Naked Maja' he had seen on the wall of a brothel once. They met perhaps half a dozen times in the cottage that summer, and on the last occasion she forgot to worry about whether she was doing it right and came to a genuine, uncontrollable climax, crying out in surprise and joy. 'You said it was both ordinary and wonderful,' she said afterwards, 'but that was extraordinary and wonderful.' He felt something like a teacher's complacency at the end of a successful lesson.

There was barely room enough on the couch for them to lie together after sex, and certainly not to sleep, so they remained clasped together while Rosamund uttered in a rambling monologue whatever thoughts were passing through her mind. Sometimes these involved further startling confidential revelations about her family, about Hubert in particular. It appeared that he had seduced one of her school friends when the girl was staying with them at Well Hall. 'How old was she?' he asked. 'Oh, seventeen, I think . . . It wasn't entirely Daddy's fault, Georgina rather threw herself at him, but then the silly girl started boasting about it at school and it got back to her parents, who were furious of course, but they decided it was better to hush it up rather than make a public fuss.' He was astonished by this further evidence of Hubert's lechery and his uncanny ability to avoid exposure and disgrace. But he was restrained in his comments because Rosamund was unwilling to criticise her father and appeared to regard his philandering as the consequence of a magnetism he was unable to control. 'You can have no idea, unless you're a woman yourself. He makes you feel that you are the only person in the world who matters to him. Alice told me she always found him completely irresistible, and Mother did too, I'm sure. She was pregnant with Paul when they married. Alice told me.' He was uneasily aware that Hubert's womanising had certain parallels to his own, but the great difference between them was that he did not pretend to believe in marital fidelity, he did not pretend he was in love with all the women he slept with, and he was often the pursued rather than the pursuer, as in the case of Rosamund. And Dorothy Richardson.

In August Dorothy unexpectedly initiated a renewal of their dormant affair. She invited herself to Sandgate and took the first opportunity to inform him of the latest crisis in her personal psychodrama. She was no longer sharing a flat with the formidable and unsympathetic Miss Moffat and had made a new friend, a young woman called Veronica Leslie-Jones, with whom she felt an immediate and reciprocated affinity, and who had recently moved in to live with her. Although Veronica had a male lover she made it obvious that she was also physically attracted to Dorothy, and Dorothy was disconcerted to find that she herself felt, for the first time in her life, feelings of genuine sexual desire—for Veronica.

'You mean, you never felt genuine sexual desire for me?' he said.

'Well, yes, up to a point,' she said reflectively. 'But it was nothing like this. With you I was always self-conscious, my mind detached from my body, observing its reactions.'

'Yes, I noticed.'

'But with Veronica . . . the mind–body thing dissolves. It's an intense feeling of wanting to merge one's identity with the Other, as if we were twins or something in another incarnation—not that I believe in reincarnation.'

'I should think not,' he said.

'I feel very confused,' she said. 'Does this mean that I'm a lesbian?'

'It could mean you are bi-sexual,' he said.

'I don't want to be bi-sexual,' she said vehemently, 'I don't want to be a freak. I don't want to be a lesbian either, for that matter.'

'What do you actually do with Veronica?' he said.

'We embrace,' she said. 'And talk. That's all—so far.'

This conversation took place in his garden-shed-study, which seemed to lend itself to acts of secular confession. 'What do you want me to do about it?' he said.

She pulled a face. 'You're so cold. You don't love me, do you?'

'I never said I did, Dorothy,' he said. 'I like you. I find you attractive. I have tried to make you happy. But you're a difficult subject.'

'Is that why you lost interest in me?'

'I rather thought you'd lost interest in me,' he said.

'No, I didn't,' she said. 'There's a way in which ever since I've known you, you obliterate other men. You still do.'

'So . . . what?'

'Make love to me again.'

It seemed that she wished him to rescue her from lesbianism, and honour required that he should at least try—in any case he had pleasant memories of her compact body, dusted with fine golden hairs, and welcomed the opportunity to reacquaint himself with it. So he fitted her in between assignations with Rosamund, sometimes in the cottage, sometimes at venues in London. Once they walked for a day in the country near Tunbridge Wells, and at his suggestion made love in the bracken somewhere between Eridge and Frant. He always derived a special thrill from making love in the open air—it went back, perhaps, to his adolescent fantasies of Adam and Eve's nuptial bower—and one of the first indications of his and Jane's sexual incompatibility had been her flat refusal to indulge him in this respect, not even in a secluded part of their garden at Worcester Park. Dorothy however agreed nonchalantly, stepped out of her drawers, lay down on the coat he spread on the springy bracken, and opened her knees to him, talking all the time about a Russian novel she had been reading. Nothing much changed in this new phase of their relationship apart from the settings of their encounters. Dorothy made more of an effort at physical abandonment in the act of love than in the past, but as soon as it was over she resumed her tireless introspection or lectured him, criticising his materialistic philosophy, correcting the cockney vowels in his speech, and even criticising his prose style.

'Listen to this,' she said one afternoon when for once they were in her flat, and in her bed, Veronica being away for a few days. She reached across him to the bedside table for an advance copy of *In the Days of the Comet*, which he had sent her a few days earlier, and sitting up, naked but for her rimless pince-nez spectacles, began to read out a marked passage, one that had given him particular pleasure to write, describing the scullery in Atlas House. '*It was the region of "washing-up", that greasy, damp function that followed every meal; its atmosphere had ever a cooling steaminess and the memory of boiled cabbage, and the sooty black stains where saucepan or kettle had been put down for a minute, scraps of potato-peel caught by the strainer of the escape pipe, and rags of a quite indescribable horribleness of acquisition, called "dish-clouts," rise in my memory at the name.* That's a terrible sentence.'

'What's wrong with it?'

'It's far too long and congested, for one thing—you should have started a new sentence after "*meal*", instead of putting a semicolon there. And there's intrusive assonance—"*indescribable horribleness*", for instance. But the real problem is the repetition of "*memory*". When it first occurs we presume that it's the subject of the long complex main clause that follows, but when we eventually come to the predicate it's "*rise in my memory*" and we are confused. How can a memory rise in a memory? So we go back to the first "*memory*" and discover that it isn't a subject after all, but an object, the metaphorical object of "*had*": "*its atmosphere had ever . . . the memory of boiled cabbage*".'

'"*The memory of boiled cabbage*" is a good phrase,' he protested.

'It's good in itself,' she said, addressing him over her pince-nez like a severe schoolmistress. 'But because it's separated from the verb by another, non-metaphorical object, "*a cooling steaminess*", we don't connect it back to "*had*" on first reading, but presume it is the subject of a new clause. The grammatical ambiguity spoils the effect.'

He took the book from her hands and read the passage for himself. He had to concede that she was right, and thought to himself that he might in future ask her to read his galley proofs and suggest emendations. Jane, who was also a better grammarian than himself, was too deferential to make many editorial suggestions when she typed his work. He composed rapidly, the words flying off the end of his pen, and lacked the necessary patience to tune and polish his style like, say, Henry James—though for different reasons you had often to read *his* labyrinthine sentences more than once to make sense of them.

James had visited Spade House at last, staying for a weekend in August. *'Delightful to me is the sense of the end of my grotesque Years of Delay to tread your charming halls,'* he wrote, when confirming the time of his arrival. He had sent a previous request to inform *'Mrs Wells, with my best remembrance, that my dietary is the easiest mere tissue of feeble negatives. I eat but little here below, but I eat that little long.'* This was a reference to his 'Fletcherising'— the practice of chewing solid food at inordinate length before swallowing it, recommended by an American quack called Fletcher. Gip and Frank, when they had the opportunity, watched this performance with fascination. Gip called James 'the Egg Man' because he had three coddled eggs for breakfast, and perhaps because he looked somewhat egg-shaped these days, with his symmetrically curved paunch, clean-shaven oval face, and big balding brow. He was however an amiable and gracious guest, praising the appointments of the house with a gallant effort at sincerity. 'My dear fellow, you have borrowed—or anticipated—the best features of my native country's domestic interior design, while avoiding its vulgarity,' he pronounced after a tour of the property. Even the lavatories attached to every bedroom attracted a commendation that was only slightly tongue-in-cheek—'a veritable sanitary utopia!'

Each of them had recently undertaken a tour of the United States, and both were shortly to publish books based on these experiences. 'Yours will of course sell much better than mine,' James said with a sigh, and he could not plausibly contest this prediction. The disappointing sales of James's books, especially the three major novels he had published in recent years— *The Wings of the Dove, The Ambassadors* and *The Golden Bowl*—were a constant cause of complaint in correspondence, and also of a certain embarrassment in their relationship. Writing to praise *The Ambassadors,* he had tactlessly mentioned the sales of a book of his own short stories, and James had responded dolefully, almost accusingly, *'My book has been out upwards of a month and, not emulating your 4,000, has sold, I believe, to the extent of 4 copies.'* He sympathised and did his bit to promote the appreciation of James's work—warmly recommending *The Wings of the Dove* to Arnold Bennett, for instance, and choosing *The Golden Bowl* as one of his Books of the Year for the *Bookman*—but there was never any hope that James would be a popular writer.

James had written in generous and gratifying praise of *Kipps* a year ago, comparing him favourably with Dickens, Thackeray and George Eliot, though as usual there was a hint of reservation beneath the extravagant encomiums. '*What am I to say about Kipps but that I am ready, that I am compelled, utterly to <u>drivel</u> about him? He is not so much a masterpiece as a mere born gem—you having, I know not how, taken a header straight down into mysterious depths of observation & knowledge, I know not which & where, & come up again with this rounded pearl of the diver.*' The more one thought about this metaphor, the less credit it gave the novelist for artistry, and the more it seemed to attribute his achievement to luck. He was grateful, nevertheless, for the words of praise, and a little surprised that James did not take him to task for the scamped concluding chapters. When he mentioned this in conversation his guest looked a little shifty, and he suspected that James had not in fact read to the end of the novel. Never mind—he himself had never finished *The Golden Bowl*. They were both prolific writers and obviously hadn't enough time to read every word the other had written.

James indeed was concerned that his friend was squandering too much of his time on politics. His detailed account of his struggles with the Fabian Old Gang was heard with polite interest at first, soon shading into boredom and disapproval. 'These committees and cabals, these motions and amendments, these debates and dryasdust reports, they are death to the creative impulse, my dear Wells,' James declared. 'The job of the artist is to enlighten and enrich the collective consciousness by the exercise of his imagination in his chosen medium. *That* is his proper contribution to politics.'

'Art for art's sake?' he questioned.

'Art for Life's sake!' James said, with the air of a man laying down a trump card.

'I want to change the world,' he said, 'not just describe it. One has to start somewhere, and I decided to begin by changing the Fabian.'

The first indication he had of the struggles ahead was a flurry of correspondence from members of the Executive in September. Charlotte Shaw wrote to say she had decided that she could not after all sign the Enquiry Committee's report, obviously bowing to pressure from her husband. He replied curtly that she had betrayed him. Pease wrote to say he could not approve the publication of 'This Misery of Boots' as a Fabian tract unless offensive personal remarks about Shaw and the Webbs were deleted. He declined to censor his own text. Sidney Webb wrote to say that although the committee's report contained '*much that is interesting and well put*', he did not believe the Society would accept its proposals, because they would be too expensive to implement and no members of the Executive would be willing to serve on the three 'triumvirates' which the Report suggested should manage different aspects of the Society's affairs in its place. He replied that they would see. Then Shaw wrote two letters in quick succession, neither of which made any mention of Charlotte's defection.

The first took Pease's side in the dispute over 'This Misery of Boots', and reminded him that he had declared to Shaw himself his intention of deleting the personal jibes for publication. He decided to capitulate, though not with the grovelling urgency recommended by Shaw: '*Write to Pease by return of post—wire—take a motor car and tell him in person, with ashes on your hat.*' The second was written a few days later, during which time Shaw had evidently read *In the Days of the Comet*. It was an extravagantly long letter, scintillating with characteristic wit, and he could not restrain his admiration for Shaw's eloquence even as he winced under his irony. It began with a playful pretence that the addressee's recent churlish behaviour was motivated by jealousy: '*May I without indelicacy ask whether Jane has been unusually trying of late? Can it be that during your absence in America that Roman matron has formed an attachment for some man of genius nearer home—I will name no names, but, say, one whose more mature judgment, more majestic stature, more amiable disposition, and more obvious devotion to her person, has placed you at a disadvantage in her eyes?*' Shaw then suggested how the problem might be resolved by acting out the solution hinted at in the conclusion of the new novel. '*What is all this in the <u>Comet</u> about a <u>ménage à quatre</u>? What does it mean? Why does the book break off so abruptly? Why not take some green gas and be frank? I have never concealed my affection for Jane. If the moroseness and discontent which have marked your conduct of late are the symptoms of a hidden passion for Charlotte, say so like a man. She takes a great interest in you—one which might easily ripen into a deeper feeling if ardently cultivated.*' Shaw developed his conceit at considerable length, concluding: '*Do not let a mere legal technicality stand between us. If you would like to make it a group marriage, and can get round Charlotte, and Jane doesn't mind (if she does, I can at least be a father to her), you need apprehend no superstitious difficulties on my part.*' This facetious scenario was all the more absurd because it was widely rumoured in Fabian circles that the Shaws' union was a *mariage blanc,* but he recognised that Shaw was alerting him to the possible scandal that his novel might cause, and felt a qualm of premonitory uneasiness even as he smiled at these lines.

The letter then went on to discuss his campaign for wholesale reform of the Fabian, and cunningly pointed out the possible drawbacks of victory. He didn't believe for a moment Shaw's claim that all the Old Gang except Pease were longing for an excuse to resign from office and be free of the work it entailed—most of them had far too much ego invested in their status—but it was true that if they resigned en bloc out of animosity to himself he might be left with a crippling executive responsibility. Having frightened him with this vision, Shaw exhorted him to learn the arts of political persuasion. *'You must get the committee habit . . . if you are ever to be anything more than a novelist bombinating in vacuo except for a touch of reality gained in your early life. We have all been through the Dickens blacking factory; and we are all socialists by reaction against that; but the world wants from men of genius what they have divined as well as what they have gone through.* He agreed heartily with that, but could never be a dedicated com-mittee man, and had no faith in the committee as an instrument of radical change. That was why he had proposed the Society should be run by elected triumvirates who would exercise the kind of privileged power enjoyed by the Samurai of *A Modern Utopia.* But if he did not accept all Shaw's argu-ments, he was impressed and moved by the time and effort expended on them, and wrote back: *'You write the most gorgeous letters. I bow down. You are wonderful. The amazing thing is that just at one point the wonderfulness stops short. Why <u>don't</u> you see how entirely I am expressing you in all these things? Fall in with my triumvirates. (They'll never elect me).'* This last was a hope, as well as a prediction: he saw his function as providing a blueprint for change and did not want the responsibility of office, though if elected to one of the triumvirates he would of course have to shoulder the burden for a year or two.

It was not long before the scandalous potential of *In the Days of the Comet* teased out by Shaw was realised. The anonymous reviewer of the novel in the *Times Literary Supplement,* summarising the conclusion of the story, observed with sly malice, *'Socialistic men's wives, we gather, are to be held in common, no less than their goods.'* This was quickly followed by a report in the virulently right-wing *Daily Express* which quoted the *TLS* review as evidence that the ultimate goal of socialism was Free Love, and incited a couple of clergymen to condemn him for promoting it. It was unwelcome publicity, coming at a most inopportune time, just as he was girding himself to lead the Fabian into a new era—he was due to give the lecture solicited by Pease, which he had decided to call 'Socialism and the Middle Classes', in October, and to move the adoption of his committee's report at a General Meeting in December. The Fabians individually held different views on sexual morality, and many of them, like the Blands, led unconventional lives in this respect, but collectively they believed in keeping up the appearance of respectability, some on principle, and all because they feared that the Society's political mission could be jeopardised if it were associated with sexual promiscuity and the undermining of traditional marriage. He had to admit that this fear was not unfounded. 'Free' and 'love', two of the noblest and loveliest words in the English language, when joined together possessed an extraordinary power to shock and outrage not only conservative journals and newspapers, but the British public in general, including large sections of the working and lower middle classes whose economic plight the Fabian was dedicated to alleviating. Something in him rebelled against hypocritically supporting the sexual status quo while waging war on all other aspects of a repressive social system, but he had taken to heart Shaw's homily on political pragmatism. What could be done? He had another look at the passage in the novel's Epilogue which had caused all the trouble, where the narrator of the dream-like frame story, a representative of unenlightened early-twentieth-century man, questioned the aged Willie about his eventual reunion with Nettie:

> *I felt a subtle embarrassment in putting the question that perplexed me . . . 'And did you—?' I asked 'Were you—lovers?'*
> *His eyebrows rose. 'Of course.'*
> *'But your wife—?'*
> *It was manifest he did not understand me.*
> *I hesitated still more. I was perplexed by a conviction of baseness. 'But –' I began. 'You remained lovers?'*
> *'Yes.' I had grave doubts if I understood him. Or he me.*
> *'And had Nettie no other lovers?'*
> *'A beautiful woman like that! I know not how many loved beauty in her, nor what she found in others. But we four from that*

time were very close, you understand, we were friends, helpers, personal lovers in a world of lovers.'

'Four?'

'There was Verrall.'

Then suddenly it came to me that the thoughts that stirred in my mind were sinister and base, that the queer suspicions, the coarseness and jealousies of my old world were over and done for these more finely living souls. 'You made,' I said, trying to be liberal-minded, 'a home together.'

'A home!' He looked at me . . . 'I forgot,' he said. 'You are pretending the old world is still going on. A home!'

And Willie threw open a great window to reveal the transformed world of the future in which the stifling individual home was as obsolete as the stifling traditional family.

This was undoubtedly pretty radical stuff. There was no point in denying that it celebrated group marriage against a general background of tolerated promiscuity. The best he could do was to define the Epilogue as not the depiction of a practically achievable society such as socialists were aiming to build, but as a prophetic vision of a totally transformed human nature. Accordingly he wrote a letter for publication in the *TLS* in which he said, '*The intention of my book is to achieve an effect of contrast, to tell in dark and despairing tones, with an intensifying note of urgency, of the life of the present, and then to get an immense sense of release, of light coming, of dawn, freshness freedom and purity . . . the end is not Socialism at all, but a dream of human beings mentally and morally exalted. Given a change in human beings, and it is not my base imagination only, but an authority your reviewer would probably respect that assures the world there would be "no marrying nor giving in marriage".'* He was particularly pleased with this invocation of the New Testament, and used it again in writing a more robust letter of complaint to the *Express.* Dorothy wrote to say that the sentence in the *TLS* letter was ungrammatical, and that she planned to review *In the Days of the Comet* for a little anarchist magazine called *Crank,* edited by a friend of hers.

He picked up several indications from correspondence and casual conversation that his opponents in the Fabian were rubbing their hands with glee at the controversy stirred up by the new novel. *'That will teach the little upstart not to be so cocky,'* they were saying to themselves, and to each other. *'The membership will think twice before letting a Free Lover take over the Society.'* But if they thought he would respond by retracting his views on sex and marriage in his October lecture, they were mistaken. Instead he described the current confusion in society about these matters as an opportunity to forge a new sexual ethic based on socialist values and aspirations, such as the abolition of private property and equal citizenship for women. The basic unit of society was the Family, but the family was currently represented in the state only by its male head, whose relationship to its other members was one of ownership. 'Every intelligent woman understands that, as a matter of hard fact, beneath all the civilities of today, she is actual or potential property, and has to treat herself and keep herself as that . . . Socialism involves the responsible citizenship of women, their economic independence of men, and all the personal freedom that follows . . .' The phrase 'personal freedom' was as near as he came to endorsing Free Love, and the only occasion on which he used that bogey term was to airily dissociate himself from it. 'Socialists would have forwarded their case better if they had been more outspoken. It has led to preposterous misunderstandings; and among others to the charge that Socialism implied Free Love. I believe that a modest but complete statement of the Socialist criticism of the family and the proposed Socialist substitute for the conventional relationships might awaken extraordinary responses at the present time.'

Rosamund and her friends in the Fabian Nursery had publicised the meeting energetically, so it was well attended by a mainly young or youngish audience, at least half of them women, who responded enthusiastically to the vision he held forth, and their smiling eager faces looking up and nodding agreement as he spoke inspired him to a more than usually effective delivery. He concluded: 'To begin to speak plainly among the silences and suppressions, the "find out for yourself" of the current time, would be, I think, to grip the middle-class woman and the middle-class youth of both sexes with an extraordinary new interest, to irradiate the dissensions of every bored couple and every squabbling family with broad conceptions, and enormously to enlarge and stimulate the Socialist movement.'

The applause at the end was long and loud, though Pease, Bland and other older members sat on their hands and looked sour. The Webbs clapped politely—they could hardly do otherwise, since he had accepted their invitation to stay with them overnight, as he sometimes did when

Fabian business took him to London. When he stepped down from the platform he was mobbed by an excited crowd of admirers, Maud Reeves and her daughter Amber being among the first to shake his hand. 'Wonderful, H.G.!' Maud smiled. 'Yes, wonderful, Mr Wells,' Amber echoed. 'It was really inspiring.' 'Shouldn't you be in Cambridge, Amber?' he said. She was now in her second year and had matured strikingly in looks and manner. 'I got permission from College to come down for this,' she said. 'I wouldn't have missed it for worlds.' 'Amber is starting up a University branch of the Fabian,' Maud said. 'Yes, will you come and speak to us next term, Mr Wells?' Amber said eagerly. 'It would be a tremendous boost for the Society.' 'Amber! Don't pester Mr Wells with that now,' Maud reproached her. 'Well, if I'm free, I'd be glad to,' he said to Amber. 'Write to me about it.' The young girl beamed triumphantly. 'Thank you!' From the back of the crowd Sidney Webb attracted his attention. 'I'll get a cab, Wells,' he called out. 'Don't be too long—supper is waiting for us.'

When he extricated himself from the throng he went to fetch his hat and coat and overnight bag from the gentlemen's cloakroom and on his way back through the labyrinthine corridors of Clifford's Inn he was waylaid by Rosamund, who drew him into an empty unlit office and ardently embraced him. 'That was absolutely brilliant, H.G.!' she said when they came up for air. 'Thank you, my dear,' he said, clasping her plump warm body tight against him. It was some time since they had made love. The cottage near Lympne had become too cold and uncomfortable for assignations as the season changed—he was afraid to light a fire in case the smoke attracted inquisitive visitors—and he told her it would be too risky to meet privately in London in case they were observed. In truth he had rather hoped that the affair would quietly lapse because he was growing bored with her puppyish devotion, but at that moment, euphoric with the success of his speech, adrenaline still coursing through his veins, nothing would have pleased him more than to discharge his excitement in a bout of passionate copulation with Rosamund. If he hadn't been conscious of the Webbs waiting for him outside, he might have taken her then and there, up against the door or sprawled over the desk. 'When will we make love again?' Rosamund sighed, as if reading his thoughts. 'I don't know, my dear. I'll think about it.' 'I don't mind that the cottage is cold and damp,' she said. 'Well, I do,' he said with a smile. 'One day I'll take you to a really swish hotel. We'll have a huge four-poster with Egyptian cotton sheets and a marble bathroom and piped heating.' 'Oh, lovely,' she cried. 'Where?' 'Anywhere you like,' he said recklessly. 'Paris?' 'All right, Paris,' he said. 'But at this moment the Webbs are waiting for me in the Strand with a cab, and they will be getting very impatient. You'd better linger here for a few minutes. Goodnight my dear Rosamund.' He kissed her again and left her sadly alone in the darkened room.

The Webbs' home in Grosvenor Street was a substantial but charmless town house furnished and decorated with dark durable paper on the walls and hemp matting instead of carpet on the floors. Beatrice congratulated him on a very well received lecture, but she could not restrain herself from taking issue with it over supper, a plain, nourishing repast served by their tall, largely silent Scottish housekeeper. To do her justice, Beatrice tried to be fair to his views, but a deep-seated puritanism, or perhaps it should be called idealism, made her recoil from them. Though like most intelligent people of her generation she had shed her Christian faith early in adult life, she retained its dualistic opposition of flesh and spirit, its fear of the former and privileging of the latter. She still believed in prayer—to whom, or what, was not clear. When he challenged her once on this point she answered him with Matthew Arnold's formula, *the Eternal not ourselves that makes for righteousness*, and in this respect her prayers had been efficacious. He had never known a woman whose motivation for her every action, down to carpeting her floors with matting, was so consciously righteous. She was however extremely intelligent, and pounced on the rhetorical sleight of hand by which he had dismissed the Free Love issue.

'I don't really see that there would be any difference in actual behaviour between your "proposed Socialist substitute for the conventional relationships" and what is called Free Love,' she said over dessert.

'In a narrow behavioural sense, no there wouldn't be,' he admitted. 'But the experience would be qualitatively different in a socialist state.'

'I wonder,' she sighed sceptically. 'Don't imagine that I fail to see the attraction of Free Love. I know I could love other men besides Sidney –' she glanced smilingly towards her husband to indicate this was a mere hypothesis, but he had his head down over his helping of treacle pudding—'and perhaps it might be intellectually stimulating to have an intimate relationship with another man who has the same aspirations as oneself. Perhaps it would extend one's understanding of human nature –'

'It would, Beatrice, I assure you,' he said cheekily.

'But for every illicit union in which there is an educative and life-enhancing effect on the couple concerned,' she said earnestly, 'there are a hundred—a thousand—in which the only motive is the gratification of lust. Human beings are so volatile and irrational where sexual desire is concerned, that I fear the consequences of removing the traditional constraints on it. I believe men and women will only evolve upwards by subordinating their physical desires and appetites to the spiritual and intellectual side of human nature. That is the faith that sustains me.'

He was tempted to speak up for lust, but thought better of it. 'Have you read my new novel?' he asked.

'No,' she replied, 'not yet. I've read *about* it of course.'

'Ah well, you have obtained a very distorted view of it. The point of the ending of that novel is that the characters who are enjoying what we call Free Love have already evolved in exactly the way you hope humanity will develop. They are like gods. Sex for them is no longer a dirty furtive business carried out in secret and surrounded with shame. It is blessed. It is a gift you give freely to those you love, and receive in return. It has a valued place in people's lives, but it doesn't dominate them and torture them and obsess them. It leaves them free to get on with the business of perfecting collective life.'

'Well, I must read it,' said Beatrice, visibly impressed.

Not so Sidney. 'Some more treacle pudding, Wells?' he asked. He was always bored by what he called airy-fairy discussions of this nature.

Beatrice was true to her word: at the end of the month she wrote him a brief note to say she had read *In the Days of the Comet*. It had not changed her mind about Free Love, but it had finally convinced her that women should be enfranchised, and she had written to Dame Millicent Fawcett, leader of the moderate, non-violent suffragettes, to pledge her support. A letter from Dame Millicent in the *Times* a few days later made this information public. He was surprised and delighted: surprised because there was not much about the suffrage issue in his novel, and delighted because it was a significant blow to the patriarchal caucus in the Fabian. Maud Reeves was overjoyed. The tide seemed to be moving in his favour again, and he felt in good heart for the General Meeting which had been arranged for the 7th of December. He decided to take a break from Fabian politics, and to go to Venice, unaccompanied, to start a new novel, an ambitious and partly autobiographical condition-of-England novel provisionally called *Waste*. He chose Venice because he didn't know anybody there and it would be empty of visitors in November, and told Jane he didn't want to be disturbed with any letters or telegrams except in the direst emergency. He took a room on the top floor of the Grand Hotel with views of San Giorgio and the Salute across the misty lagoon, and wrote without interruption for three weeks.

There was a formidable heap of mail waiting for him on his desk when he returned home, and a parcel with his complimentary copies of *The Future in America*, published in his absence. He had dedicated it to Dorothy Richardson under her initials, 'D.M.R.', hoping this would make up for his rather neglecting her of late. Jane was surprised to see the dedication, which he had inserted in the proofs. 'Why?' she asked. 'Dorothy knows nothing about America, and she's not interested in it.' 'Just for friendship's sake,' he said. 'Won't people think that your friendship must be rather a close one?' Jane said. 'Nobody will recognise her behind the initials,' he said. 'Very few people know her middle name is Miller.' Spotting an envelope with Dorothy's handwriting on it he plucked it from the pile. It contained not, as he anticipated, a letter thanking him for the dedication, but a cutting of her unsigned review of *In the Days of the Comet* severed from the pages of *Crank*. Yet that was in its way a kind of letter, since a strain of personal grievance against himself for not taking her seriously enough ran through it. Dorothy expressed a hope that one day he would write the great novel of which he was capable, but this one was not it, and in order to succeed he would have to overcome the limitations of all his work in the depiction of women. They were almost without exception, *'one specimen carried away from some biological museum of his student days, dressed up in various trappings, with different shades of hair and proportions of freckles, with neatly tabulated instincts and one vague smile between them all'*. It was, he thought, possibly the first time in literary history that a book had been unfavourably reviewed by the dedicatee of another book by the same author. He sensed more trouble ahead from difficult Dorothy.

There was a more welcome letter from Henry James congratulating him on *The Future in America*—'*I have done nothing today but thrill and squirm with it and vibrate to it almost feverishly and weep over it almost profusely (this last, I mean, for intensity of mere emotion and interest)*'—though as usual a backwash of reservation followed the foaming wave of compliment: '*what primarily flies in my face is you and your so amazingly active and agile intellectual personality—I may even say your sublime and heroic cheek—which I can't sufficiently resist to feel (as much as I want to), that you tend always to simplify too much . . .*' And as usual there was a wistful reflection on James's failure to make an equivalent mark with his own latest publication, *The American Scene,* which poignantly happened to be on the same subject. '*I think you, frankly,—or think the whole thing—too <u>loud,</u> as if the country shouted at you, hurrying past, every hint it had to give and you yelled back your comment on it; but also, frankly, I think the right and only way to utter many of the things you are delivered of <u>is</u> to yell them—it's a yelling country, and <u>my</u> semitones, in your splendid clashing of the cymbals (and <u>theirs</u>), will never be heard.'* James! There was nobody like him.

The good humour this letter put him into was abruptly shattered by one from Rosamund. She wrote in her round, schoolgirlish hand to say that Edith had found a compromising letter from himself making an arrangement to meet at the cottage back in August.

> *She must have gone through my bureau drawers—she's totally unscrupulous about invading people's privacy—and came across that old letter. I know you told me to destroy all your letters, and usually I do, but I wanted to keep one from you as a kind of proof of our love, proof that I was not dreaming the whole thing . . . I used to take it out and look at it and kiss it sometimes. Fortunately there was nothing very explicit in it, but it did say you had enjoyed our last time in the cottage together and that you would be there again 'next Wednesday' and it was signed 'With love, H.G.' Of course there was the most awful row, Daddy was absolutely furious, and they cross-questioned me and made me cry, but I think you would have been proud of me because I didn't admit that we were lovers. I said we had a very intimate friendship and that you used the cottage to write but it was a convenient place to meet and talk occasionally and that Alice had told you she approved of our friendship. I'm not sure that they believed me but they decided not to force the issue any further, but I'm under a cloud here, and they watch me like hawks, so be warned. All my love, Rosamund.*

He swore softly, screwed up the letter and tossed it into the wastepaper basket. On second thoughts he retrieved it, smoothed it out and showed it to Jane. 'I was afraid something like this would happen,' she said. 'You can't say I didn't warn you.' 'No, I can't and I won't,' he said. 'But what shall I do about it?' 'Nothing,' Jane said. 'Except stop seeing the girl, of course.' 'Oh well, that's no great sacrifice,' he said. 'And hope she does nothing foolish,' Jane added. 'So far she seems to have behaved very well in the circumstances.' 'I think she may even be enjoying it, in a curious kind of way,' he speculated hopefully. 'She obviously sees herself as the heroine of a novel.' He was thinking to himself that perhaps for Rosamund this was the best way their affair could end, with a dramatic climax of love thwarted by tyrannical parents rather than a slow cooling of interest on his part.

But another letter in the pile, from Sydney Olivier, gave further cause for anxiety—and anger. Olivier wrote to warn him that Pease and Bland, alarmed by the success of his lecture on 'Socialism and the Middle Classes' were lobbying energetically against him in the run-up to the General Meeting, and that Hubert Bland was spreading scandalous stories about him among senior members of the Fabian, namely, that he had betrayed his oldest friend, a certain Sidney Bowkett, by having an adulterous affair with his wife, and that Bland had recently discovered Wells had designs on his daughter Rosamund and had only just succeeded in foiling his dastardly plans. *'I know it's pretty rich for Bland of all people to accuse you of libertinism,'* Olivier wrote, *'and of course I've no idea whether his allegations have any basis. But I thought I should warn you of what he is up to. Everyone knows Bland is a womaniser, I mean everyone in the Fabian who matters. It's been going on for so long that it's taken for granted among us, as a rather pitiful character trait, like a weakness for drink. But we all know Bland is never going to have control of the Fabian's policy and future development. He's regarded as harmless, therefore. You are not. You matter. Take care.'*

This letter provoked another, louder oath. Sidney Bowkett! How in God's name had Bland got to know Bowkett, and dragged out of him that ancient grudge on account of Nell? Probably a chance meeting in the saloon bar of some Manchester hotel; he vaguely remembered hearing many years ago that Bowkett had moved to the north. As for Rosamund, he now realised why Bland had not wrung from her a confession that they were actually lovers—it allowed him to accuse Wells of plotting seduction without compromising his daughter's honour. It was a damned awkward situation. He could not deny Bland's accusation about Bowkett because it was true, and he could not deny that he had tried to seduce Rosamund without unchivalrously revealing that she had taken the initiative in their affair. He could not defend his conduct by pointing out that both women were adults who slept with him of their own free will without reviving the Free Love controversy.

The very next day he went up to London and confronted Pease in his clammy underground office in Clement's Inn. 'I understand Bland has been spreading stories about me,' he said. 'Really? What kind of stories?' Pease said suavely from behind his desk. 'Don't pretend you haven't heard them,' he said. 'I really can't answer your question unless you tell me what you are referring to,' said Pease. 'Then perhaps I could clear up any misunderstanding.' 'I believe you know very well what I'm talking about,' he said. 'I just want to say that if you and your friends on the Executive want a dirty fight, you can have one. I know a thing or two about Bland's private life which I shall have no hesitation in broadcasting to the world if he doesn't stop slandering me.'

'Bland of course is a Roman Catholic,' said Pease. 'I understand that the Romans make a distinction between slander, which is false, and detraction, which is true. He told me once that detraction is considered the greater sin, because it cannot honestly be withdrawn.' He smiled. 'An interesting paradox, don't you think?'

They duelled like this for a few more minutes, Pease parrying his bluster by pretending not to know what he was talking about while obliquely indicating that he knew very well, until he burst out, 'Damn you, Pease, and damn your friends. I know you look down on me because my parents were in service and I didn't go to public school and Oxbridge and I still have some cockney vowels when I speak, I know you call me a "common little cad" behind my back—'

'I assure you I have never said anything of the kind,' Pease said haughtily.

'Well, if you don't say it, you think it,' he said. 'Common I may be, but I'm not a cad. If you want a prize cad, you need look no further than Bland.' And with that he walked out, not feeling very pleased with himself. He had relieved his feelings, but at the cost of exposing his own weakness and insecurity. It had been a mistake to come.

On his way out he passed through the General Office and observed Rosamund in conference with young Clifford Sharp beside the Fabian Nursery noticeboard. She saw him and turned pale. Sharp shot him a hostile glance. The patter of a typewriter faltered and stopped as its operator observed the encounter with barely disguised interest, an indication of how far down the Fabian hierarchy gossip had carried. He greeted them formally—'Good morning Miss Bland, good morning Sharp'—and did not linger, pretending he was late for another appointment. It was raining outside and he had forgotten to bring an umbrella. As he hesitated under the arched entrance of the Inn, peering at the leaden sky, Rosamund rustled up behind him. 'Oh, H.G.,' she said, laying a hand on his arm. 'Did you get my letter?' 'Yesterday,' he said. 'I only got back from Venice yesterday.' 'I didn't know you were away,' she said. 'I've been so worried. I thought you were angry with me.' 'I'm not angry with you, Rosamund,' he said. 'I'm angry with Edith for reading a private letter not addressed to her, and with your father for spreading malicious gossip about me. This is the last thing I need before the General Meeting next week.' 'I know, it's awful,' she said. 'What shall we do?' 'Well, you could begin by not running after me in public places,' he said unkindly. 'It only encourages the gossip.' 'I'm sorry,' she said, and looked as if she was about to cry. He glanced around to check that they were unobserved, and took her hand. 'Be strong, my dear. Be dignified. We have done nothing to be ashamed of.' 'No,' she said, nodding eager agreement. 'Ignore the gossip, don't answer intrusive questions.' 'Right,' she said. 'But will we be able to see each other again—alone, I mean?' 'I fear not,' he said. 'Not for a long time. Not until this has all blown over.' 'And then will you take me to Paris?' 'Maybe,' he said, smiling, and thinking to himself that he was as likely to take her to the moon. 'But you promised,' she said. 'Did I? Then of course I will, one day,' he said, squeezing her hand, and giving her a quick peck on the cheek. It seemed the only way to escape before they were observed engaged in a suspicious tête-à-tête.

The hall in Clifford's Inn was far too small for the General Meeting, so Essex Hall was hired, and several hundred members—more than a third of the total membership, which had increased significantly since he began to take a leading role in its affairs—crowded in on both levels. An excited buzz of chatter filled the air until the chairman, one Mr H. Bond Holding, banged his gavel and opened the meeting. Two substantial documents had been circulated to everyone present: the Report of the Committee of Enquiry (as the 'Wells Committee' was officially known) and the Executive's reply to it. The Report proposed a new Basis and a more efficient executive structure, attacked the policy of 'permeation', and urged that the Society should greatly expand its membership, rename itself the British Socialist Society and join similar bodies in putting up candidates for Parliament. The Executive's response, in which the hand of Shaw could be detected, welcomed constructive criticism, but wondered how the more ambitious proposals were to be funded. They were unimpressed by the revised draft of the Basis, defended the doctrine of permeation, and thought that a direct intervention in Parliamentary elections would be premature. Shaw proposed a long and complex motion which approved a cautious move forward in the direction indicated by the Enquiry Committee while positively committing itself to very little.

His own speech was in the form of an amendment, endorsing the 'spirit and purport' of the Report and calling for the election of a new Executive to implement it. Strictly speaking Sydney Olivier, as chairman of the Enquiry Committee, should have spoken to the Report, but in the euphoric aftermath of his October lecture on 'Socialism and the Middle Classes' he had insisted on performing this function himself. His confidence had taken several knocks since then, and he felt nervous, sitting on the platform listening to Shaw's smoothly turned sentences uttered in a mellifluous Irish accent, as his own time to speak approached. Then all his old faults as a public orator returned in their worst form. Avoiding eye contact with his listeners, he mumbled into his moustache or piped into the rafters; he stumbled over his notes, and fumbled his jokes. He felt himself steadily losing the audience's goodwill and went on for over an hour, far too long, in a hopeless effort to recover it. When he had finished there was no time for a proper debate. Webb made a short speech saying that it seemed members had to choose between an Executive that had enjoyed their confidence for many years and an untried and inexperienced new leadership. Sydney Olivier said the Society was in danger of becoming a 'small, hidebound, learned body' if it did not reform its constitution. The chairman declared it was now too late in the evening to bring the debate to a conclusion, and adjourned it for a week.

He was cast down by his own performance and apologised afterwards to Olivier and other colleagues on the committee. 'Don't despair,' Olivier said. 'It was not your finest speech, Wells, but all is not lost. There are a lot of young people in the Society now who are hungry for change.' Shaw evidently thought so, because in the following week he circulated a message to all members of the Society making it clear that if the Executive were defeated by Wells's amendment they would all resign, *with the most serious consequences to the Society*. Olivier shook his head over this missive. 'Shaw is very cunning. He's making your amendment into a vote of no confidence in the Executive. The members will never vote to chuck them all out in one go. It would be like multiple parricide.'

On the eve of the second meeting he had a conversation with Maud Reeves which tended to confirm Olivier's misgivings. She was due to speak first in the resumed debate, and warned him, with obvious embarrassment, that she would not be pressing for the adoption of his amendment, but advocating a compromise between the two contending parties. 'I'm very sorry, H.G.,' she said, 'but I just can't support what has now become such a divisive amendment that it could lead to the collapse of the Society.' 'I understand, Maud, don't feel bad about it,' he said. 'Oh, but I do,' she said. 'You've been such a stalwart supporter of the women's cause that I hate to let you down now. But Shaw says that with Beatrice's recent change of heart it's very likely that equal citizenship will soon be incorporated in the Basis, without any need to tear the Fabian apart.' So Shaw had been getting at Maud privately. And he had a shrewd idea that she was also under personal pressure from her husband not to support a takeover of the Society by someone whom Reeves would regard as a dangerous proponent and, in the light of recent gossip, exponent of Free Love. But he sympathised with the difficulty of her position, and told her not to worry. 'I think there's enough momentum for change for us to carry the day,' he said. 'And I believe Shaw is bluffing when he threatens that the Executive will resign en bloc if they're defeated.'

There was an even bigger audience, and even more excitement in the air of Essex Hall, when the second session of the General Meeting commenced on the 14th of December. After Maud had made her diplomatic, conciliatory statement, a number of people spoke from the floor against the amendment and in support of the Executive, among them Clifford Sharp, who had formerly supported the movement for reform, and Hubert Bland, who made some sarcastic remarks about middle-aged men pretending to speak for the interests of youth when in fact promoting their own. But there were also speeches praising the Report, and the atmosphere in the hall was tense as the clock ticked on towards the critical vote.

It was nine when Shaw rose to speak, and as Olivier had predicted, he immediately made the issue one of confidence. 'If Mr Wells will withdraw his amendment, the Executive would be happy to debate the Report's substantive proposals one by one,' he said. 'But the amendment ties the acceptance of the Report to the dissolution of the present Executive—in other words, dismissal with dishonour—which would necessarily lead to our resignation, while the Committee of Enquiry has made it equally clear that, if defeated, they would abandon their effort to regenerate the Society.'

There was uproar in the hall as several voices disputed this interpretation of the amendment, and he himself sprang to his feet to say that he had no intention of resigning, whatever happened. 'I am very glad to hear it,' said Shaw, with the triumphant air of a man watching the jaws of his trap close on a victim, 'because it means that I can pitch into Mr Wells without fear of the consequences. But this meeting still has to choose between the annihilation of the Executive and the unconditional surrender of Mr Wells.' And he proceeded to review the whole history of the dispute in a flagrantly ad hominem fashion, attacking 'Mr Wells' for using misrepresentation, invention and personal insult to advance his cause, but all delivered with a genial smile and the apparently effortless wit of which Shaw was a master. The audience had acquired a reassuring sense that there were after all to be no resignations and no irreversible damage to the Society that evening, and settled back to enjoy the entertainment. At one point, speaking of the constraints under which both parties had worked, Shaw remarked, 'During his Committee's deliberations Mr Wells produced a book on America. And a very good book too. But whilst I was drafting our reply I produced a play.' He stopped speaking and looked abstractedly up at the high ceiling, long enough for the audience to think that he had lost his thread, then said: 'Ladies and gentlemen, I paused there to enable Mr Wells to say "And a very good play too."' There was a great burst of laughter from the house, which he himself had to suffer with a forced grin to avoid seeming a bad sport, and at that moment the occasion passed irretrievably from a serious debate to something more like music hall.

When Shaw sat down to huge applause, the chairman turned to him and said, 'Mr Wells, I wonder whether in the circumstances, you would like me to proceed to take a vote, or . . .'

He glanced at Sydney Olivier, who shook his head. 'No,' he said, 'I withdraw the amendment.' At which there was another long round of applause, and the meeting came to an end.

4

The result of the meeting of 14th December was, of course, a humiliating defeat for him personally, even though no vote was taken. If he hadn't been lured into declaring on the platform that he had no intention of resigning he might well have done so, in disgust at having been beaten by purely rhetorical means, not on the issues. No substantive discussion of his committee's proposals had taken place. But that was in a way a reason to persevere, as several of his allies in the Society urged, and even Shaw, his adversary in the debate and chiefly responsible for trivialising it, took this line. A few days after the meeting Shaw wrote, making no apologies for his own part in it, but assuring him that *'you can easily retrieve the situation if you will study your game carefully, or else do exactly what I tell you'*. He pointed out that there were more meetings scheduled to discuss the Executive's views on the future of the Society, at which members of the Wells committee might well succeed in getting their ideas adopted in a modified form, and recommended that he should stand for the Executive at the annual elections in March. He didn't know whether to resent or admire the cool cheek of a man who presumed to offer constructive advice to the still smarting victim of his devious tactics in debate.

For the time being he turned his back on the Fabian and threw himself into writing. He resumed work on *Waste,* now entitled *Tono-Bungay,* the name of a patent tonic medicine on which the narrator's uncle built an ephemeral fortune. This character, Edward Ponderevo, was based on his own Uncle Williams, the Wookey schoolmaster and father of Edith and Bertha, a kind-hearted, genial man with a moral blind spot, who had hurriedly to close his school to avoid prosecution for fraudulent misrepresentation of his qualifications. The stupendous success of Ponderevo's worthless tonic was based entirely on mendacious advertising and aggressive marketing, but instilled in him delusions of grandeur which he would act out in the acquisition and construction of more and more extravagant houses for himself and his wife, until his financial bubble collapsed and he fell into bankruptcy, taking with him the thousands of small investors who had trusted him. He personified a new kind of irresponsible capitalism that was becoming a feature of the Edwardian Age, creating what his nephew George, the narrator of the novel, called *'the most unpremeditated, subtle, successful, and aimless plutocracy that had ever encumbered the destiny of mankind'.*

He put a good deal of his own experience into the character of George—an upbringing as the child of a servant in a great country house, the struggle to get free of this humble background through a scientific education, problems with sex and marriage in a repressive and hypocritical society—and gave himself room to analyse and generalise about the condition of England by making George present himself from the outset as an amateur novelist: *'I warn you this book is going to be something of an agglomeration. I want to trace my social trajectory (and my uncle's) as the main line of my story, but as this is my first novel and almost certainly my last, I want to get in, too, all sorts of things that struck me, things that amused me and impressions I got—even although they don't minister directly to my narrative at all . . . I must sprawl and flounder, comment and theorise, if I am to get the thing out I have in mind.'* Whether this excuse would satisfy Henry James was doubtful, but he believed the tone and texture of the narrative voice, the insistent imagery of disease, degeneration and decay in the social fabric, would give the book unity.

Early in the New Year, however, he was seized with another idea. He had got to know a young man of unusual experience and talents called John William Dunne. The son of a British General, he had been brought up in South Africa, where he was apprenticed to a farmer, and served in the Imperial Yeomanry in the Boer War, after which he came to England and trained as an aeronautical engineer. He designed a revolutionary kind of monoplane with swept-back wings, based on his observation of seabirds, which impressed the War Office sufficiently for them to employ him at their research unit in Aldershot, though they did not authorise production of a prototype and eventually the idea was shelved. From Dunne he gleaned much interesting information about new developments in aeronautics and their potential applications in warfare—notably the progress of Count Ferdinand von Zeppelin's dirigible rigid airship in Germany. After a number of failures and crashes, the prototype had recently succeeded in staying airborne for eight hours. 'These airships would make a perfect platform for weapons, and could be built to enormous size, giving them almost limitless range,' Dunne told him. 'You mean, the Germans could bomb London from them?' he asked. 'They could bomb New York eventually,' Dunne assured him.

He could not get this vision out of his head: the proud skyscrapers of New York crumbling and collapsing under a ruthless bombardment from the air, whole blocks on fire, panic in the streets . . . Soon his imagination had conceived the outline of a novel in the same genre as *The War of the Worlds,* which would tap into current British anxieties about German imperialism and the accelerating arms race between the two nations. Typically, both nations were preparing to fight the next war with the weapons of yesterday, not tomorrow, building more and more, bigger and bigger battleships. It was obvious if you talked to men like Dunne that air power was destined to supersede naval power, and that the speed, range and mobility of the former would result in the rapid globalisation of warfare. He sketched a narrative in which a conflict between Britain and Germany rapidly drew in America, Japan and other countries, and consisted mainly of the wholesale destruction of large cities by aerial bombing, leading to the total collapse of civilisation. Narrative continuity was to be provided by the character of a cockney cycle-repairer who stowed away in an airship and found himself the involuntary witness of a German surprise raid on New York and the mayhem that followed. The moral, as always, would be that only a world government could ensure the benevolent, not destructive, application of new advances in science and technology. But what excited him was the prospect of once again summoning up an apocalyptic vision of the complacent, familiar present-day world disintegrating under the devastating impact of unprecedented force. It would be a harmless but satisfying discharge of the violence he would like to do to the Old Gang and their followers.

There was also a mundane reason to pursue this new project promptly: namely, his bank balance was dangerously low. He and Jane liked to entertain in style. They had a houseful of guests nearly every weekend, and the cost of food and drink and hot water *ad libitum* piped to every bedroom mounted up. He was in the process of adding a tennis court to the amenities of Spade House, which entailed extending and levelling his property, at considerable expense. His involvement in Fabian affairs over the past year had absorbed a great deal of time that would otherwise have been devoted to profitable authorship. *Tono-Bungay* was not a book he could toss off quickly. It was his most ambitious attempt to write a literary novel that would become a classic, but for that very reason it progressed relatively slowly by his own standards and was unlikely to be a best-seller when it was published. Putting all these considerations together there was a strong case for turning out *The War in the Air* quickly, while the idea was still bubbling in his head. Accordingly he sent an outline to his agent Pinker and said he could write it in a few months if somebody would give him an advance of £1,200, and knowing that his usual publisher Macmillan wouldn't put up that kind of money, he wrote to him personally, describing the projected novel as a 'pot-boiler' which he proposed to publish with a less distinguished house. Macmillan raised no objection, George Bell & Sons came up with the ready, and he contracted to deliver the book by September.

As his anger and frustration at the outcome of the December meetings subsided, he resumed a cautious involvement in Fabian affairs. He agreed to be nominated as a candidate for the forthcoming Executive elections, and Maud Reeves persuaded Jane to stand as well, and also to join a women's group she was forming within the Fabian. In February Maud succeeded in getting the Executive to approve in principle the incorporation of equality of citizenship for women into the Basis, to be ratified at a general meeting in six months' time, and she saw Jane as a useful ally in ensuring that this victory was followed through.

In the same month he fulfilled his promise to address the Cambridge University Fabian Society which Amber Reeves had started in collaboration with a young man at Trinity called Ben Keeling who was already a member of the rather sleepy 'town' branch of the Society. More than ever he was struck by what an impressive young woman she had grown into— clever, articulate and beautiful, with brown eyes, a straight Grecian nose set in a heart-shaped face and a mass of dense crinkly black hair, which had earned her the family nickname of Dusa, short for Medusa. She was working hard, she told him, as she walked him round the grounds of Newnham before his lecture, and desperately keen to get a First in Part One of the Moral Sciences Tripos in the summer. She would sit Part Two a year later. 'Women are not allowed to take their degrees, of course,' she said, 'but we take the same exams as the men and our results are published with theirs.

It's always such a thrill when a woman does well, it makes the men so sick.' 'How ridiculous that you can't take your degree!' he expostulated. 'You should have gone to London University.' 'Well, it wouldn't be quite as nice, would it?' she said, with a gesture that took in the quietly elegant halls, built in Queen Anne style of red brick with white sash windows and gables, spaciously set out among lawns and shrubberies, and he had to admit she was right. 'Anyway,' she added, 'I wanted to get away from home.' 'What about your Part Three?' he asked. 'There is no part Three. Part Two is Finals.' 'So why is it called Tripos?' 'I believe it was in three parts once,' she said. 'They say it goes back to medieval times, when students were given a three-legged stool when they graduated, one leg for each year.'

It seemed to him typical of Cambridge University that it wrapped up a degree course in philosophy in this mystifying fossilised language. The whole place—he stayed overnight and explored a little—aroused in him powerful contradictory feelings of attraction and repulsion, envy and derision. It was visually ravishing, even in winter; the fine architecture of the colleges, their quiet courts and time-worn cloisters, the green, groomed Backs, the willow-hemmed river, all blended together with a grace and beauty that had taken centuries to mature. And it was exhilarating to walk the cobbled streets of a town so clearly dedicated to the life of the mind, lavishly provided with booksellers, thronged by young people in gowns hurrying to lectures, or chattering and arguing with each other in teashops. He felt pangs of resentment and regret as he compared the ambience of the place with his own student days, the long daily trek through filthy noisy indifferent London to the bleakly utilitarian classrooms and laboratories of the South Kensington Normal College. How he would have loved to study here! But it was of course an environment steeped in privilege, and its retention of archaic and obsolete terminology, of peculiar customs and shibboleths, were methods of exclusion and defences against change. If I had the power, he thought, after a morning spent asking his way from strangers in the street, I would pass laws forcing the colleges to display their names on their frontages, and forbidding the pronunciation of 'Caius' as 'Keys'.

But when he gave his talk—a bolder and more explicit version of his lecture on 'Socialism and the Middle Classes'—in a room packed with young people, mostly undergraduates, many of them literally sitting at his feet, he was disarmed by their admiration and enthusiasm. There was no need for him to feel inferior or excluded because he had not enjoyed their privileged education and his voice retained a trace of cockney vowels and glottal stops. To them he was a genius, a prophet, with a much broader vision than their tutors and professors, and a better grasp of the real world they were preparing to enter and hoped to improve. They lapped up his arguments for political, economic and sexual reform through the application of reason and scientific expertise. They were not of course representative of the student body as a whole. He was aware that not all undergraduates were as earnest and thoughtful as these—there were plenty of arrogant-looking young men in Cambridge whose overheard conversation, conducted in braying public school accents, indicated that they were more interested in rowing and hunting than ideas. Ben Keeling had more than once been threatened with a ragging by undergrads of that type. But these eager young Fabians were the hope of the future—especially the young women. They were the brightest and the best of their gender and generation, and conscious of carrying the standard for women's rights, taking it from the hands of earlier generations who had struggled valiantly in the teeth of prejudice to obtain higher education for women. The CFS was in fact, Amber told him, the first Cambridge society to admit women as equal members from its foundation. After the meeting the committee bore him off to a convivial supper in Keeling's rooms in Trinity where he fielded their questions and entertained them with anecdotes and was, he felt, particularly brilliant. Amber, radiant with the success of the evening, and the kudos she had acquired in the eyes of her friends by enticing this lion up from London, thanked him effusively afterwards. 'You were absolutely wonderful, Mr Wells,' she said, shaking his hand. 'I do hope you'll come to Cambridge again, if we have the cheek to invite you.' 'I think I would,' he said, smiling. 'I find it has many attractions.' Of which Amber herself was certainly one. But having just extricated himself from an embarrassing entanglement with one young female admirer, he was not minded to get involved with another, even though she was more beautiful and much more intelligent.

He had in fact already begun a new relationship with a woman who was four years older than himself, the novelist Violet Hunt. They had known each other socially for some time because they had many literary friends in common, and contributed to the same magazines, so were often invited to the same parties. In late 1906 these encounters became more frequent and more flirtatious. Both of them were recovering from setbacks in their lives—he from the Fabian defeat and the associated Rosamund imbroglio, she from the recent death of her first lover, and the aftermath of being jilted by her second—and both were seeking consolation in a new amorous affair without entailments. Early in the New Year he wrote to invite her to lunch at Torino's in Soho, which had private rooms upstairs: *'Be nice to a very melancholy man on Tuesday please. Come and Torino at one. I'm rather down, cross, feeble . . . No afternoon appointments.'* She took the hint in her acceptance, mentioning that she would also be free in the afternoon. Thus began an affair which brought much uncomplicated pleasure to both parties.

Violet was the daughter of Alfred William Hunt, a watercolourist associated with the Pre-Raphaelites and often confused with the painter Holman Hunt on that account. Violet, whose own looks, with her long chin and mass of hair, were somewhat Pre-Raphaelite, grew up knowing this circle of artists and their mentor Ruskin. She told him that when she was thirteen, on hearing that the great love of Ruskin's later life, Rose La Touche, had tragically died, she volunteered to marry him in Rose's place. 'Mama wrote to Ruskin, whom we knew quite well, to tell him of this offer, thinking he would be amused. He received it gratefully and with complete seriousness—said he would think about it and let us know. He had a penchant for very young girls, of course, and waited for years for Rose to grow up, but he decided not to wait for me.' This was typical of the many anecdotes with which she entertained him when they lay together resting languorously after sexual intercourse in some room in London hired for the purpose. Long practised in amorous adventure, Violet greatly extended his knowledge of restaurants with *cabinets particuliers*, and hotels and lodging houses willing to rent out rooms by the hour, a secret metropolitan network of accommodation for illicit sex. *'Do you know of any convenient place for sin in Kensington?'* he wrote to her once when he was arranging an appointment at the Natural History Museum. *'If so, write here and tell me and I'll wire you if I can get away.'* He received the address of a private hotel near the South Kensington Underground station by return of post.

They both believed in Free Love, but Violet's experience had begun earlier and she had been tutored by one lover in particular, a man called Crawfurd, one-time diplomat and minor man of letters, who was a dedicated libertine. He was also, by her account, an unmitigated cad, who used her as his mistress for many years because he was married, and when his wife died promptly married another woman with money instead of Violet. Some years had passed since this happened, but the pain of rejection and betrayal obviously still hurt. At the time they lunched together at Torino's she was grieving for her first lover, the painter George Henry Boughton, another married man with whom she had fallen desperately in love at the age of seventeen and pursued until he yielded to her importunate devotion. He eventually ended the affair in order to save his marriage, leaving her heartbroken, but his recent death had revived all her old tender feelings for him, and made her yearn for the comfort of someone else's arms.

Violet had been a New Woman before the phrase was ever coined, fearlessly seeking her own erotic fulfilment from an early age, and prepared to pay the price that a hypocritical society exacted. Her novels dealt with the experience of similar young women, similarly placed, but the code of sexual reticence she was obliged to follow drew much of the potential sting from those he had sampled, sentimental stories of amorous intrigue redeemed by a cynical epigrammatic wit reminiscent of the plays of Oscar Wilde. She claimed Wilde had been an admirer in her youth and was once on the brink of proposing to her. Henry James, rather surprisingly, was a friend of her maturity, and entertained her occasionally at Lamb House. 'I stimulate his imagination,' she explained. 'He knows what a depraved life I lead and milks me for lubricious stories of London Society, which he is too frightened to investigate for himself.' She quoted a characteristic letter from the Master declining an invitation to visit her in London: '*You are Society, and I am more and more contemplative detachment—hanging on to the world after the fashion of a very obese spider by a thin thread of my own independent weaving.*' They laughed together over this wonderfully vivid simile. 'It deserves to be illustrated by Max Beerbohm, don't you think?' said Violet. 'H.J. calls me the Great Devourer because of my appetite for social life, and the Purple Patch because of a purple overcoat I wore once, but also as a sly hit at my prose, I don't doubt.' It was true that Violet sometimes let her verbal facility run away with her in her novels, and that nearly all of them were a little too long for what she had to say, but there was no doubt about her fertility of invention within a fairly narrow compass.

At forty-five she had already lost the beauty for which she had been admired in her younger years, and painted heavily to disguise a poor complexion, but her body was still slim and limber, able to adopt any attitude in bed he suggested, and to demonstrate a few that were new to him. Her years with Crawfurd had made her shamelessly versatile in the art of love, and she did not hesitate to use her mouth and tongue to arouse him for an encore when they had time to indulge in one. 'Now I know the real reason why Henry James calls you the Great Devourer,' he said, watching her complacently as she performed this service, and causing her to choke with laughter. He liked a woman who laughed in bed. Violet was the ideal partner for a *passade*. Unlike Dorothy Richardson.

He continued to see Dorothy at infrequent intervals for rather perfunctory sex followed by long discussions of her emotional, psychological and philosophical problems. She was still locked in the curious triangular relationship with her celibate lover Grad and her ardent bi-sexual flatmate Veronica, and no nearer to resolving the question of her own sexuality. He wished he had never got involved with Dorothy, and blamed himself for doing so. He had undertaken a kind of therapeutic responsibility for her without having the necessary time and patience to exercise it, distracted as he was by his clandestine affair with Rosamund and his disputes with the Fabian Old Gang, not to mention the books he was trying to write at the same time. Sex for him was ideally a form of recreation, like tennis or badminton, something you did when you had completed a satisfactory bit of work, to let off steam and exercise the body instead of the mind for a while, but that was not what Dorothy needed, or at least wanted, from their assignations. He decided to put this to her one afternoon when they met at the hotel near South Kensington Underground station usefully recommended by Violet Hunt. When booking the room he had ordered a bottle of hock to be placed there in an ice bucket. Instead of getting into shirtsleeves and taking off his bow tie as soon as they were in the room, as he usually did, he remained fully dressed, gestured her to sit down in one of the two armchairs, and uncorked the bottle of wine. She looked at him with a wry, knowing, humourless smile.

'I know what you're going to say,' she said.

'What is that?' he replied, filling the two glasses and giving her one.

'You're going to say we should put a stop to this.'

'Well, it's not making you happy, Dorothy, so it doesn't make me happy either,' he said, sitting down in the other chair facing her. 'Of course we can go on being friends—you and I and Jane. But let's face the facts. Sex between us has been a failure. I don't know whether it's my fault, or . . .'

'Whether I'm a lesbian?'

'I don't know. Sometimes I think you are not really interested in sex at all, per se.'

'Sometimes I think that myself,' she said.

'There you are, then. Wouldn't it be best to stop seeing each other—like this, I mean? Go back to our old open friendly relationship. Forget we ever tried to be lovers.'

'That may be difficult,' she said. 'You see, I think I'm pregnant.'

'*What?*' He sat up abruptly, spilling wine on his trouser leg. 'Are you sure?'

'Well, I haven't been to a doctor yet. But it's two months now since my last . . . you know. I'm fairly sure.'

His brain whirred, considering the implications and options at lightning speed. Was it his child? Almost certainly, and he couldn't risk mortally offending her by asking. When had it happened—and how? He didn't recall any mishap with a split French letter or a mismanaged withdrawal. Of course no method was one hundred per cent reliable . . . But suppose it was a hysterical pregnancy, that she was imagining the whole thing? He went across to her, perched on the arm of her chair, put his arm round her shoulder and kissed her forehead. 'My dear Dorothy,' he said. 'How wonderful.'

'Wonderful?' She sounded surprised.

'Wonderful that you and I should bring a new life into the world. He will be very clever.'

'He?'

'Or she. Of course, I will give you all the support you need.'

'You will endow my motherhood?' she asked ironically.

'Exactly. I can't make an honest woman of you, in that revolting phrase . . . but I will give you everything you need to bring up the child.'

She blinked at him as if she was about to cry. 'I didn't think you would be so nice about it,' she said. 'Thank you, but I will manage on my own.'

'Why should you? You're not well off, and I am.'

'I prefer to be independent,' she said.

'Well, we won't argue about it now. Have another glass of hock.' He refilled her glass. 'Here's to the new life.'

'You are an extraordinary man,' she said.

'And you are an extraordinary woman, my dear,' he said. 'How are your friends? Mr Grad and Veronica—do they know?'

'No, of course not, nobody knows, except you—now. Benjamin will be shocked—he probably won't speak to me again. Veronica will probably be delighted and want to adopt the child when she and Philip marry.'

'And would you wish that?'

'No. I would like to have a child of my own.'

'Splendid!' he said.

'It's not at all splendid,' she said. 'It's a mess. What will Jane say?'

'Jane will take it in her stride,' he said. 'Nothing to do with me surprises her any more.'

Nevertheless he did not put this presumption immediately to the test by speaking to Jane—wisely, as it turned out. Some time later he received a brief note from Dorothy to say that she had had a miscarriage. *'Perhaps it's just as well,'* she wrote. *'But I have been very ill, and feel wretched. I have been off work for weeks and would like to give up Harley Street completely. I would like to live in the country and write.'* He sent her a sympathetic letter and a cheque, and offered to give her proofreading work which she could do at home. He said that he hoped they would continue to be friends and that she would always be a welcome guest at Spade House. Whether she had really had a miscarriage, or in fact had not been pregnant, he would never know, but he was simply relieved that their unsatisfactory affair had finally come to an end by mutual consent, and that scandal had been avoided. As far as he was aware, nobody except Jane had known it was going on. The relief he felt at this turn of events was, however, soon overtaken by a new cause of scandal—or rather, the revival of an old one—which upset his tentative rapprochement with the Fabian.

He and Jane were both elected to the Executive at the end of March. He came fourth in the ballot, rather to his surprise, close behind Sidney Webb, Pease and Shaw, which showed that he still had considerable support among the membership in spite of his defeat at the December meetings. The new Executive agreed to set up a small subcommittee consisting of himself, Shaw and Webb to tackle once again the task of revising the Basis. He dashed off a draft and sent it to his two colleagues, but predictably they quibbled with him and between themselves about his formulations and he resigned himself to a long and probably inconclusive process. He converted his draft into a proposed Fabian Manifesto and circulated it to seventy-two senior members, but only twenty-six of them responded positively. His strongest supporters in the Society were the young. Amber Reeves, down from Cambridge for the Easter vacation, was telling everyone about how brilliant his talk of February had been, and asked him if he would give some public lectures under the auspices of the CFS in the autumn. Her opportunity to make this request, to which he agreed, was a meeting of the Fabian Arts Society at which Rosamund was also present, and in retrospect he wondered whether she had observed how very much at ease Amber was in his company and felt a pang of jealousy. The young women were equal in their admiration for his ideas, but Amber was able to discuss them more articulately, with a confident range of intellectual reference, and Rosamund, who had never been encouraged to think of going to a university, must have enviously registered this difference.

Up till then, Rosamund had been very sensible about keeping her distance from him to allow the gossip about them to subside, contenting herself with the occasional knowing smile when their eyes met across a crowded room, or a covert squeeze of his hand when she had occasion to shake it. She seemed to accept that their relationship was indefinitely suspended, if not, as he rather hoped, concluded. Occasionally the memory of their last private conversation, in the archway to Clement's Inn, returned to worry him with the thought that his final words on that occasion had been imprudent, but it was not until after the meeting of the Fabian Arts Society and Amber's return to Cambridge that he received a letter from Rosamund reminding him of his 'promise' to take her to Paris, and asking when the trip was to take place. He arranged to meet her in the Constable room of the National Gallery, where they could pretend if necessary that they had bumped into each other by chance. He could see that she enjoyed the little charade this plan entailed, their greeting each other with pleased surprise and sitting down on a bench under the bored supervision of a uniformed member of the gallery staff. But when he told her that he hadn't realised she had taken the Paris idea so seriously she looked stricken. 'You didn't mean it, then?' she said.

'Well, I meant it at the time. But it was more of a wish than a promise. Something that would be fun, but . . . I mean, can you really see us doing it?'

'Yes, I can,' she said. 'I think of it constantly.' She spoke emphatically, and the attendant showed signs of interest in their conversation. He raised his finger to his lips and she continued in a lower tone. 'It's the last thing I think of before I fall asleep and the first thing when I wake up. I remember exactly what you said we would have—a hotel room in Paris with a huge four-poster bed with Egyptian cotton sheets, and a marble bathroom, and piped heating.'

'Did I say that?'

'Yes.'

There was a long pause while she looked at him yearningly. 'Then we'd better do it,' he said, and the way her face lit up was, for a moment, sufficient reward for his reckless commitment.

Why on earth, he wondered later, had he made it? Gallantry? Honour? Pity? Probably vanity, when you came down to it. He knew Rosamund would despise him for the rest of her life if he backed out of his pledge, and though he had no desire to continue their romance, he did not relish living with that knowledge. The whole justification for their affair in his own conscience was that he, the older, experienced man, would initiate her into the ways of love, and then gracefully retire at the appropriate moment, to allow her to explore relationships with people of her own age. There would be sadness at parting, but no bitterness and resentment. The only way he could think of achieving such a conclusion now was to make the Paris excursion the occasion of it. He would say to her something like: '*We will have one weekend of ecstatic love, in exotic, luxurious surroundings, and then, for both our sakes, part for ever as lovers, contenting ourselves with the memory of that last, perfect time together.*' It sounded terribly like a line of dialogue from one of Violet's novels, but it would almost certainly work.

Accordingly he started to make plans, and after a while he began genuinely to look forward to the adventure and to derive some satisfaction from his own finesse in planning it. He decided they would travel to Paris not by the usual route from Charing Cross or Victoria, crossing the Channel via Dover or Folkestone to Calais, but from Plymouth, where the transatlantic liners stopped to disembark passengers before proceeding to Cherbourg. They would be far less likely to run into anyone they knew, and although the journey would be longer, it would be more comfortable and give Rosamund the extra treat of a few hours in the first-class dining room and saloon of a Cunarder. He booked a passage for two on the *Luciana* under the names of Mr & Mrs Herbert, and tickets for the boat train from Paddington. As an extra precaution he counselled Rosamund to disguise her appearance by wearing a hat with a veil, while he himself planned to wear a scarf which he could wrap around his lower face if necessary. Having decided to spare no expense to make the trip a memorable one, he booked a suite at the Ritz in Paris. He corresponded with Rosamund via the Fabian Nursery office in Clement's Inn, and she sent her replies to his club. They agreed on a weekend and constructed their alibis. Rosamund arranged a fictitious visit to a sympathetic ex-school friend; he told Jane that he was popping over to Paris to do some research for *The War in the Air*, which wasn't entirely untrue—he was thinking of destroying the centre of Paris by aerial bombing at some point in the story and it would be easier to imagine on the spot how the Eiffel Tower might most spectacularly topple to the ground when its massive feet were blasted away.

To avoid meeting Rosamund publicly on the station's concourse, he directed that they should rendezvous on the train, sending her a first-class ticket and seat reservation, and money for a cab. He arrived at Paddington early, feeling tense, wondering whether she would turn up or lose courage at the last moment, and slipped into the buffet to down a calming brandy at the bar. As soon as the Plymouth train drew in he took his seat, getting up from time to time to put his head out of the window and look down the platform towards the ticket barrier. There were not many people coming through, and he was hopeful that they would have the compartment, a smart new one with opulently stuffed and buttoned leather seating, to themselves. At last he saw Rosamund approaching in the distance, in a wide-brimmed hat with veil and a light-coloured travelling costume, preceded by a porter carrying her valise, and he ducked back into the compartment, sat down and pretended to be deeply engaged in reading the *Times*. A few moments later he heard the porter say, "Ere we are, Miss. Sure you wouldn't prefer a Ladies Only compartment? I can find you a seat in one of them, easy.' 'No thank you, this will do perfectly well,' Rosamund said, sounding remarkably assured. The porter opened the door, entered the compartment with a ''Scuse me, sir,' and lifted Rosamund's valise on to the luggage rack. He heard the man thank her as she tipped him on the platform, and lowered his newspaper. Only then did he see her, framed in the open door. She laughed as he grasped her hand and helped her up the step into the compartment. 'Why are you wearing that thick muffler on such a lovely day?' she said. 'It was supposed to be a disguise,' he said, pulling it off. 'But you look wonderful, my dear.' And she did, radiant and rosy-cheeked as she threw up her veil. He was no longer acting a part—he felt a surge of desire for her, and a triumphant pride in having organised this amorous escapade so successfully. He closed the door, hoisted up the window, and pulled down all the blinds on the platform side. Then he took her in his arms and kissed her warmly, and she responded with equal ardour. They sank down on to the leather upholstery with their arms round each other. 'I was beginning to fear that you had changed your mind,' he said. 'Never!' she said. 'I've been dreaming of this for months, and now it's actually happening, I can hardly believe it. Just think, tonight I will be in Paris with you.' 'In a four-poster bed,' he said, and kissed her again as she blushed delightfully. He had a vivid mental image of them romping together amid the goosedown pillows, like lovers in the antique erotic prints you could buy on the Left Bank. What naughty fun they would have!

'Did you get away from Well Hall without any problems?' he asked.

'Absolutely . . . nobody suspected anything. And your instructions were so good! I had a little trouble getting a cab at Cannon Street . . .' She was in the middle of telling him the details of her journey when the door of the compartment was suddenly opened from outside and Clifford Sharp appeared, looking up at them from the platform. They sprang apart and jumped to their feet. Rosamund spoke first: '*Clifford!* What on earth . . . ?' Sharp regarded them for a moment with a smirk of satisfaction, then turning his head called out, 'Here they are!'

What followed resembled not a scene from one of Violet Hunt's novels, but the melodramatic climax of some shilling shocker from the railway bookstall: villain foiled in the nick of time by outraged father and chivalrous admirer in dastardly attempt to abduct innocent maiden. All it lacked was a horsewhip in Hubert Bland's hand when he appeared at the open door, glaring through his monocle like Polyphemus, his black moustache bristling, his face puce with anger under the thatch of white hair. 'Out you get, young lady!' he snapped.

Rosamund shrank back into the corner seat furthest from the door, and shook her head. 'No, I won't,' she said tremulously.

Bland clambered into the compartment as if intending to drag her bodily from the train, and he placed himself protectively in front of her. 'Get out of my way, Wells,' Bland said menacingly, 'I'll deal with you later.'

'Rosamund is an adult,' he said, 'capable of making her own decisions about where she travels and with whom. You have no right to treat her as if she is your chattel.'

'And you have no right to seduce an innocent young girl—a married man old enough to be her father,' Bland retorted. 'Thank God I was able to prevent you—for the second time! Get out of my way.'

'Rosamund and I became lovers last summer,' he said, 'by her own wish and consent—ask her.'

Bland was momentarily silenced, glowering, breathing heavily, his bulky shoulders heaving under his tight frock coat, like a bull preparing to charge. Clifford Sharp remained standing guard at the open carriage door, through which late-arriving passengers, sensing that some drama was in progress, shot curious glances as they passed.

'It's true, Father,' Rosamund said from behind his back.

'Then you should be ashamed of yourself,' Bland snapped. 'I never thought a daughter of mine would surrender her honour to a cad like this . . . cad.' His journalistic gift for elegant variation had temporarily deserted him.

'Of course you've always set her a shining example of chaste behaviour yourself, haven't you, Bland?' he said—rashly, because the man responded by grasping the lapels of his jacket and throwing him on to the seat, pushing past to seize Rosamund by the hand.

'Don't, Father! You're hurting me!' she exclaimed as she was pulled to the door. When he tried to impede them Bland punched him in the chest making him stagger and sprawl back on the seat. 'Oh, don't hit him!' Rosamund wailed as she was dragged off the train, and she burst into tears.

'Get her valise,' Bland ordered Sharp, who obeyed smartly. 'You'll hear more of this, Wells,' he snarled, before whisking the weeping Rosamund out of his sight.

Winded, he got slowly to his feet. Whistles blew and he heard the sound of carriage doors slamming shut. He managed to lift his own valise off the rack and alight from the train moments before it pulled out of the station, sending gouts of smoke and steam into the curved vault. Further down the platform Rosamund was being escorted—almost frogmarched—towards the exit by the two men. She turned her head and threw a helpless pitiful glance over her shoulder before she was jerked forward into a throng of people and disappeared from his view. Poor Rosamund. What a cruel awakening from her dream. He sat down on a bench to recover his composure and to consider how he was going to make a clean breast of this absurd and humiliating episode to Jane.

Jane was as quietly critical and stoically forgiving as she usually was when he made a fool of himself, though she had an additional provocation to feel resentful when Edith Bland, no doubt egged on by Hubert, wrote a very offensive letter holding her responsible for his debauching of their daughter. '*Whether you knew of it or not, (and I find it difficult to believe you had no suspicions) you must be aware of his habitual philandering, and your toleration amounts to encouragement,*' she wrote. He wanted Jane to fire back a reply citing examples of Hubert's habitual philandering, some of which were certainly known to and tolerated by Edith, but Jane maintained, rightly as it turned out, that a dignified silence was the best response. In spite of Hubert's parting threat on the Paddington platform, it seemed that the Blands had decided not to make a public fuss about the episode, no doubt because they wanted to protect Rosamund's reputation and because Hubert was conscious of his vulnerability to counter-attack. He and Jane braced themselves for a storm of public scandal which did not materialise.

The humiliation of the incident continued to rankle, however, and he couldn't help wondering how their plan had been discovered. He had his suspicions, which he was unable to discuss with Rosamund because all social contact between the two families was at an end, and even at Fabian gatherings she was always watchfully guarded by Sharp or her parents. The Blands however still spent a good deal of time at the Other House that summer, and he received a letter from Rosamund asking him to meet her in Dymchurch on a day when she knew Edith, Hubert and Alice would be out on an excursion to Hastings. He cycled over and they met by arrangement beside an abandoned fisherman's hut known to them both, at the back of the beach some distance out of the village. Rosamund looked a little thinner than usual, but still healthy and rosy-cheeked. They embraced tenderly, but not passionately, and he sensed with some relief that she accepted that their affair was over.

It was a dull overcast afternoon, and chilly for the time of year, so there were few holidaymakers about. He leaned his bike against the wooden wall of the hut and they walked westward together along the beach on the hard sand left by the low tide and talked. Rosamund said that life had been pretty hellish at Well Hall immediately after Bland had marched her back there to be arraigned by himself and Edith, but that gradually things had quietened down. 'Daddy still hates *you*, I'm afraid, more than ever,' she said. 'When he was criticising my morals I said it was the pot calling the kettle black, and he's convinced you've been feeding me with slander against him.'

'Slander is lies,' he said, recalling his conversation with Pease. 'I've told you only the truth, and only half of what I know.'

'And most of that I knew already,' Rosamund said, with a wry smile. It puzzled him that she didn't seem to bear any deep grudge against her father either for his hypocrisy or for the violent way he had treated her—or for that matter for the assault on himself. 'I do hope Daddy didn't hurt you,' she said, adding as if to excuse him, 'I'm afraid he doesn't know his own strength.'

'I had a bit of bruise for a while,' he said.

'Oh dear. I thought you were awfully brave, to stand up to him,' she said, and he felt better.

'How did he find out about our excursion to Paris?' he asked.

'I don't know. He wouldn't say.'

'I suspect Sharp,' he said. 'Why else was he with Hubert that day?'

'Daddy says he asked Clifford to go with him, to make sure he didn't do something he might regret.'

'Like pushing me under a train?'

Rosamund laughed. 'Something like that.'

'I think Sharp must have steamed open my last letter to you when it was delivered at the Fabian offices, and found out the details of our arrangement, and told your father.'

'You could be right,' Rosamund said. She looked slightly embarrassed. 'Clifford of course has always been very keen on me, and very protective. He never approved of our friendship.'

'No, I was aware of that.'

'I expect I'll end up marrying him,' she said.

'Really? Why?' He was shocked, for he had never liked Sharp. There was something too calculating about the way he had set about making a career for himself in the Fabian, taking charge of the Nursery and appearing to support change while retaining the trust and respect of the Old Guard. He did not seem to be a happy person or capable of making a woman happy.

'Well he's clever, and we share the same ideas, and he loves me—or he says he does,' Rosamund said. 'Daddy and Edith think I should marry him. So does Alice.'

'You surprise me. She told me once she thought you shouldn't be rushed into marriage. I agreed with her.'

'Yes, well, Daddy was terribly cross with her for encouraging me to be friends with you, and blames her for what happened between us, so Alice is in disgrace and has to go along with what they say. They think Clifford is being rather fine in still being willing to have me, in spite of knowing we were lovers, and that I ought to be grateful and marry him.'

'That's old-fashioned nonsense!' he said. 'Don't do it.'

206

'Well, I shan't be in a hurry to, anyway.'

'Make sure you see each other naked first,' he said.

Rosamund laughed. 'Clifford would have kittens at the very idea!'

'Then he will be no good to you,' he said.

At that moment the clouds parted briefly and a bright sunbeam streamed down through the gap like a searchlight and cast its reflection on the calm sea. They stopped and admired the effect. 'I think I'd better get back before they return from Hastings,' Rosamund said.

They walked back to the fisherman's hut mainly in silence, each lost in their own thoughts of what they had shared together. They embraced again on parting, and she wept a little. 'Thank you, for everything,' she said. 'I'm sorry I got you into trouble.'

'Others would say I got *you* into trouble,' he said.

'I know. It's not fair. I hope you don't blame me too much.'

'I don't blame you at all. Rosamund—promise me something.'

'What?'

'That, if you're ever stranded, if you're ever in need—you'll tell me.'

'All right, H.G., I promise.' She hugged him once more, turned on her heel and trudged away through the soft dry sand at the top of the beach. Cycling back to Sandgate along the coastal road, into the darkling east, he wondered why Rosamund, with all her radical views, her belief in Free Love and women's rights, didn't just walk out of her oppressive home. Perhaps she would when she was twenty-one, but somehow he doubted it. She just wasn't brave enough, or clever enough, to break free from the strange sinister spell the Blands had cast over Well Hall, where nothing was as it seemed and distinctions between fact and fiction, truth and lies, were blurred and confused. She was still locked into a childish relationship to Hubert and Edith, idolising him and feeling rejected by her. As he pedalled, musing on Rosamund's plight he thought it might be interesting to write a novel one day about a young woman who *did* act out her radical principles and assert her independence in defiance of parental authority and social disapproval, especially in the matter of choosing a mate for herself, and when he got home he made a few notes.

Charlotte Shaw wrote to invite them to share a house in Llanbedr in Snowdonia where the Fabian Nursery were holding a Summer School—their latest experimental initiative. He declined, since Rosamund and Sharp were likely to be there, but he was glad to receive the invitation, whose genial tone implied that no rumour of the Paddington melodrama had reached the Shaws' ears. This impression was confirmed when Shaw wrote him an immensely long letter a few weeks later wholly devoted to the story of how, bathing with his friend Robert Loraine off a Welsh beach, they had been buffeted by strong waves and swept out to sea, unable to swim back to shore, and the thoughts that went through his head when he believed he would drown. It was like a good short story—vivid, gripping, and highly amusing. He wrote back: *'Wasted chances! You shouldn't have come out. There you were—lacking nothing but a little decent resolution to make a distinguished end. You should have swum to Loraine, embraced him & gone to the bottom—a noble life wasted in an insane attempt to rescue an actor-manager. I could have sailed in with one or two first class obituary articles and put you right with America and Germany . . .'*

The summer passed at Sandgate in the way he liked, working hard on weekdays, and entertaining a jolly group of guests most weekends, with tennis now available as an additional diversion to badminton and bathing, and charades and improvised theatricals indoors when the weather was inclement. If it was a large party, guests were found lodgings in the village. An up-and-coming Liberal politician called Charles Masterman and his charming wife Lucy were accommodated in this way. Masterman had published a rather good study of urban poverty called *The Abyss*, based on the experience of actually living in a slum tenement for a period, was an admirer of his work, and had written an enthusiastic review of *Kipps* in the *Daily News*, 'in spite of having my name taken in vain in that novel' as he remarked, referring to a rather unsavoury character called Masterman. 'Yes, I apologise for that,' he said. 'Actually he was a much nicer character in the original plan of the book—he was to convert Kipps to socialism. But my idea of the ending changed.' 'I really don't mind,' Masterman said tolerantly. 'What are you writing at the moment?' When he described *Tono-Bungay* Masterman showed keen interest and he promised to give him a copy as soon as it was available.

The Reeveses came down to Sandgate with the delightful Amber and her younger sister and brother, and also stayed in the village. Their presence was another reassuring sign that they had no knowledge of the Paddington episode, as was their agreement that Amber could stay on at Spade House on her own for several days, at the special request of Gip and Frank, who were enchanted by her. She spent hours with them playing the floor games with bricks and soldiers he had invented, as totally committed to this activity as when arguing points in philosophy with himself. Amber was in the best of spirits, having obtained the desired First in Part One of her Tripos. Her father now preened himself on her academic achievements, and carried about in his notecase a letter from the great Gilbert Murray, who had read a paper on Ideals which Amber delivered to the Newnham Society, sent to him by her classics tutor, Jane Harrison. 'Listen to what Murray said,' Reeves bade him, unfolding the letter with a flourish.

' "*It seems to me quite the best college paper on the subject I have ever read—I mean as treated by a young person and from a non-metaphysical point of view. She seems to start where our generation left off—just the thing that new generations ought to do and mostly don't. I have no doubt that you are proud of her.*" And we are!' Reeves added, as he stowed the letter away. He seemed to have conveniently forgotten his former reluctance to send Amber to Cambridge.

Violet Hunt was an occasional visitor that summer, and they carried on risky games of hastily snatched kisses and intimate touching, concealed from other guests by the shrubbery or in his garden shelter. Dorothy, rather to his surprise, invited herself one weekend in August when Violet happened to be there, and Violet complained that she was in constant terror of seeing her sharp little eyes peering at them through the leaves of a laurel bush or the skylight of the shelter. 'You don't know what a jealous woman is capable of,' she said, when he laughed at her. 'Dorothy may disapprove of you, Violet, but she has no reason to be jealous,' he said. 'It is all over between us in that line. We are just friends now.'

Dorothy in fact had finally resolved the problem of her sexual identity and stressful relationships with Veronica and Benjamin Grad in the most Dorothy-like way, as she told him when he was able to give her a private audience in the garden shelter. It appeared that very recently Veronica's fiancé, Philip, a man considerably older than herself, had died suddenly of a heart attack. Dorothy, herself barely recovered from her miscarriage, had nursed the grief-stricken Veronica through this tragedy, and in the process she had a sudden, almost miraculous inspiration. 'I knew that both Veronica and Benjamin wanted to possess me completely, but Veronica had also wanted a male lover in Philip, and Benjamin wanted to possess me only if we were married, while I didn't want to be married or possessed by anybody. That was why we were locked in this exhausting three-cornered struggle for fulfilment. But now that Philip was dead I suddenly saw the solution: Veronica must marry Benjamin!' She beamed at him triumphantly as she said this. 'Really?' he said, suppressing a temptation to smile. 'Yes! That way Veronica and Benjamin can possess me spiritually in possessing each other physically—it will be a mystical marriage of three.' 'Like the Trinity?' he risked saying. But she saw nothing amusing in the analogy. 'Exactly.' 'And what do they both think of this idea?' he asked. 'They think it's wonderful,' she said. 'In fact they are already engaged.' 'And will you live with them in a platonic *ménage à trois*?' She shook her head. 'No. I've found a place to live cheaply in Sussex, with some awfully nice people who look after me tenderly. I'm going to live there very frugally and quietly and write.' She told him she was going to write a novel which would be a faithful record of the consciousness of a young woman like herself. 'The psychological novel has been dominated by male authors,' she declared. 'Even the best of them, James, Conrad—none of them really gets us, women I mean. There is always the male idea of order imposed on the stream of thought, the final clinching main clause, the stamp of the full stop at the end of the periodic sentence. I want to do something much more flowing and organic, the way a woman thinks and feels.' 'Well, I wish you luck, Dorothy,' he said sincerely. It didn't sound very promising.

His own work went well, and he finished *The War in the Air* on schedule at the beginning of September. Before taking up *Tono-Bungay* again, he and Jane had a well-earned holiday in Switzerland, walking in the Alps. In spite of her slight frame Jane was an agile and enthusiastic walker, with stamina that more than matched his own. They both loved the mountains, the crystal clear air, the sublime views of snow-capped peaks receding into infinity, the peaceful silence broken only by the distant sound of cow bells and church bells rising from the valleys below, the feeling of health and well-being these things instilled. In the course of this happy, companionable interlude, tired but euphoric at the end of the day, they came together as man and wife as they hadn't done for some time at home.

But from this healing and restorative break he returned to an unwelcome revival of the controversy over *In the Days of the Comet*. William Joynson Hicks, the Conservative candidate in a forthcoming by-election in October for a Lancashire seat, standing against a Liberal of declared socialist sympathies, had circulated a scurrilous pamphlet warning the electorate that voting for a socialist was the beginning of a slippery slope that ended in sexual promiscuity—citing as evidence that old canard in the *TLS* review of *Comet,* about wives being held in common in the socialist Utopia. This smear was picked up and given much wider circulation by an article in the *Spectator,* 'Socialism and Sex Relations', by the editor, St Loe Strachey, a high-minded Tory moralist and leading light of the National Social Purity Campaign, who wrote, *'we find Mr Wells, in his novel, making free love the dominant principle for the regulation of sexual ties in his regenerated State. The romantic difficulty as to which of the two lovers of the heroine is to be the happy man is solved by their both being accepted. Polyandry is "the way out" in this case, as polygamy might be in another.'* He was drawn into another tedious round of correspondence in the *Spectator* and various newspapers that repeated the story with variations, and was obliged to trot out once again the defence of his novel that he had employed a year before, which in the repetition seemed somewhat strained even to himself. At one point in the brouhaha, which lasted for several weeks, he resorted to threatening a libel suit against Joynson-Hicks, who then admitted that the defamatory pamphlet had been prepared by his agent, a certain well-named Bottomley, and that he himself had not actually read *In the Days of the Comet* at the time, but relied on the *TLS*'s description of it.

In the end he received enough half-apologies from his accusers, and enough support from sympathisers, to feel he had survived this new attack on his reputation, but it rattled him. He became aware that rumours of the Paddington fiasco were circulating after all in Fabian and literary circles, with fantastical distortions and elaborations—that he had been eloping with Rosamund to live with her in France, that she had disguised herself for the occasion as a boy (as if that voluptuous bust could ever be plausibly concealed under male clothing) and that Hubert had given him a public thrashing on the platform at Paddington station. A coolness in the manner of his old friend Graham Wallas when they met, and a look of distaste on Sidney Webb's face when they passed and saluted each other on opposite sides of the Strand one day, suggested that both had heard some of this gossip. Shaw had evidently received a less highly coloured but prejudicial account of his affair with Rosamund—he suspected Edith was the source— and wrote to reproach him for sullying the public image of the Fabian and jeopardising its mission by his irresponsible philandering. He wrote back: *'I think you do me an injustice—I don't mean in your general estimate of my character—but in the Bland business. However you take your line. It's possible you don't know the whole situation. But damn the Blands! All through it's been that infernal household of lies that has tainted the affair and put me off my game. You don't for a moment begin to understand, you've judged me by that matter and there you are!'*

When Shaw responded by trying to make a case for Hubert Bland's integrity and chivalrously protective attitude towards the 'innocent little person' of Rosamund, he lost his temper and fired back a furious riposte:

> *The more I think you over the more it comes over me what an unmitigated middle Victorian ass you are. You play about with ideas like a daring garrulous maiden aunt, but when it comes to an affair like the Bland affair you show the instincts of conscious gentility and the judgment of a hen. You write of Bland in a strain of sentimental exaltation, you explain his beautiful romantic character to me—as though I don't know the man to his bones. You might be dear Mrs Bland herself in a paroxysm of romantic invention. And all this twaddle about 'the innocent little person'. If she is innocent it isn't her parents' fault anyhow.*
>
> *The fact is you're a flimsy intellectual, acquisitive of mind, adrift and chattering brightly in a world you don't understand. You don't know, as I do, in blood and substance, lust, failure, shame, hate, love and creative passion. You don't understand and you can't understand the rights or wrongs of the case into which you stick your maiden judgment—any more than you can understand the aims in the Fabian Society that your vanity has wrecked.*
>
> *Now go on being amusing.*

As soon as he had posted the letter he regretted its intemperate tone. He had said things which would not be easy to forgive or withdraw, and it would be a long time before he could hope to be back on easy terms with Shaw. He was sorry for this, but he had been oppressed by a sense that enemies were circling in the darkness beyond his tent, plotting, gossiping, rumour-mongering against him, and Shaw's second letter had goaded him beyond endurance. Only when he was among the young Fabians in Cambridge did he feel free from this poisonous atmosphere. If they knew anything about his affair with Rosamund, they didn't show it, and didn't regard it as their business. They knew about the campaign against him in the press of course, but they regarded him as a hero, a martyr for daring to question the old sexual ethics based on repression, ignorance and the double standard. The three lectures he gave there in October, a kind of personal credo summarising his interpretation of socialism, were well attended and warmly received. 'Are you going to publish them, Mr Wells?' Amber Reeves asked him after he had delivered the last one. 'There was so much to take in—I would love to be able to read them.' 'Well I have thought I might work them into a short book, when I can find the time,' he said. 'Wonderful!' she said. 'What will you call it?' 'I was thinking perhaps, *First and Last Things*. What do you think?' 'Perfect!' she said. 'I can't wait to see it.'

Before they parted, she asked him to give her regards to Jane, and recalled how much she had enjoyed her visit to Spade House in the summer, especially playing floor games with the boys. 'I've invented some new ones since then,' he said. 'Wasn't there talk of your coming to visit us again, on your own?' 'Yes, there was,' she said, and the way her eyes brightened told him that she had intended to jog his memory. 'I could come in the Christmas vac, any time except Christmas itself,' she said. 'Right ho,' he said, smiling at her eagerness. 'I'll remind Jane and she'll write to you.' 'Thank you!' she said, ecstatically. She really was a very charming girl, completely unaffected in spite of her beauty and her brains, and it was impossible not to take pleasure in her frank admiration. He looked forward to entertaining her *en famille* at Spade House and demonstrating his new games, but he must of course be careful how he managed their relationship. Very careful.

5

Dear Mr H.G.,

Thank you very much for your letters and Mrs Wells for her love. Getting letters from you is a tremendous joy and makes me work hard for days. I am working quite hard at Moral Science and very hard at Fabians. We have affiliated at length to both the Fabians and the S.L.P. but the whole University rang with the struggle. The men are frightfully pleased with themselves because they brought in a Socialist motion at the Union and were only defeated by 100–70. I am in evil odour with the authorities for the moment because I said revolutionary things at a public meeting—the one you were to have spoken at. I was too frightened to know what I did say, with two chaperones glaring at me, but the men are delighted. By the way Mr Keeling says if you don't come next term you will be a skunk. If you don't come I shall be so unhappy that I shall fail in my tripos. If you could see how I love getting letters from you, you would write again some day.

Yours ever,
Amber Reeves

'Amber thanks you for sending her your love,' he said, as he finished reading this letter.

'I thought I recognised the handwriting on the envelope,' Jane said. 'May I read it?'

'Of course.' He passed the letter to her across the breakfast table, and spread butter and marmalade on a second slice of toast as she read it. Outside it was a grey February morning, with a blustery wind that dashed raindrops against the windowpanes at intervals with a sound like handfuls of gravel, but the dining room was warm and cosy.

Jane chuckled at something in the letter. 'I'd love to know what it was she said that shocked the chaperones.'

He had the same wish, but instead of saying so he grumbled: 'It's absurd that women undergraduates can't go anywhere in Cambridge without chaperones, even to lectures.'

Jane finished reading the letter and passed it back to him. 'The girl is in love with you, of course,' she said. 'I hope you realise that.'

He munched his toast meditatively before he replied. 'Do you think so?'

'It's obvious from the last few lines. In fact it was obvious to me when she was here after Christmas.'

He glanced at the end of the letter again. 'I didn't make love to her, though.'

'You told her to call you "H.G.",' Jane said. 'That was as good as a kiss to her.'

He smiled. 'She starts her letter "Dear Mr H.G.", which sounds rather funny. She obviously thought it would be too cheeky to say "Dear H.G."'

'But she didn't want to go back to the formality of "Mr Wells",' Jane observed. 'You must remember, dear, that I can read the minds of your young women admirers like a book. I've been there myself.'

'I haven't encouraged her. I've actually *dis*couraged her, by pulling out of that meeting.'

'Only because you wanted to go to Arnold's play.'

'Well, Arnold is an old friend,' he said.

'You don't have to explain to *me*, dear,' Jane said.

Arnold Bennett's play *Cupid and Common Sense*, a dramatisation of his novel *Anna of the Five Towns*, had been given two performances by the Stage Society in London at the end of January and the only one they could attend clashed with the public meeting of the Cambridge Fabian Society he had half promised to participate in. He had a professional as well as a personal reason for wanting to see the play, because he and Arnold had a long-standing but as yet unfulfilled plan to collaborate on an original dramatic work, but he had felt a little guilty—no, not exactly guilty, but regretful about pulling out of the Cambridge engagement, because he didn't like to think of Amber being disappointed in him. So he had sent her two letters in quick succession to make up for it, and had now received this wistful appeal for more, with its tantalising hint of what he had missed by his absence. Bennett's play had been enjoyable, but nothing comparable to hearing Amber make a revolutionary speech.

The receipt of her letter disturbed his thoughts for the rest of the morning, but the second post brought another one from Cambridge which calmed him. 'That's a coincidence,' he said to Jane, as he quickly scanned it. 'A young man I met in Cambridge, Rupert Brooke, one of Amber's Fabian friends, is inviting me to talk to a group in his rooms at King's. He's said to be a very promising poet, and certainly looks the part. I think I might go.'

'Can you spare the time?' Jane asked.

'These young people are worth it. They're the hope of the future. And I learn something myself from talking to them.' So he said yes to Rupert Brooke, taking the earliest of the dates that were offered him, and a few days afterwards had a similar invitation from a Mr Geoffrey Keynes of Pembroke College, which could be conveniently combined with the other engagement, making a stay of a few days.

He was in a restless, febrile state of mind such as usually followed the completion of a book, and looking for distractions like these. He had at long last finished *Tono-Bungay*, or at least got to the end of it and written the concluding words: *'I have come to see myself from the outside, my country from the outside—without illusions. We make and pass. We are all things that make and pass.'* Jane was engaged in typing up the final chapter. After he had read it through there would be some rewriting to be done, and more retyping, but essentially the thing was finished. It was to be serialised in a new literary magazine provisionally called the *English Review*, which he had been planning with Hueffer and Conrad, and in which he was going to invest some money in return for a share of the profits. The idea was to provide a platform for new writing that was truly 'modern', and Fordie had the taste and the contacts to make a success of it. All agreed that the first instalment of *Tono-Bungay* would be an ideal lead item for the inaugural issue, being an ambitious and experimental work by an established author with a large following. He was thinking that his next novel might be on the theme he had vaguely entertained a year ago, of a young woman who dared to assert her independence in defiance of parental and social disapproval. He had it in mind to draw in the topical issue of the suffragette movement, which had lately taken a more militant turn, but the project was still at the tentative, note-making stage. In the meantime he occupied himself with expanding his Cambridge lectures of the previous autumn into *First and Last Things*.

He saw Amber several times when he went to Cambridge and found her more captivating than ever. She was clever and articulate and beautiful, but what he most admired was her fearlessness—exactly the character trait he had in mind for the heroine of his next novel. She questioned everything and took nothing for granted, which naturally alarmed those who were *in loco parentis* to her. On his last afternoon he visited her at Newnham and was introduced to Miss Jane Harrison, the tutor who had passed her paper to Gilbert Murray. 'We think very highly of Amber,' she said confidentially to him when the girl was out of earshot for a few minutes. 'But we wish she were not quite so headstrong. She does tend to rush in where angels fear to tread.' 'But she's no fool,' he ventured to say. 'No indeed, I used the proverbial phrase loosely,' she said blushing slightly. 'We all hope she will get the Double First she deserves.'

Amber herself did not use the bright student's customary spell for warding off hubris, deprecating one's prospects of success. On the contrary she said she would drown herself in the Cam if she didn't get a First in her Part Two. Having introduced him at Newnham as an old friend of her family she was allowed to give him tea in her rooms in Clough Hall, which were smaller than Ben Keeling's, but bright and comfortable, with chintz curtains and floral wallpaper. There were piles of books and magazines on every surface and socialist posters on the walls. She sat him down in the one upholstered armchair and squatted on a leather pouffe beside the fire to toast muffins on the end of a fork.

'Why does getting a First matter so much to you?' he asked her.

'Partly vanity, and partly to annoy the men,' she said. 'But also because I want to do postgraduate research at the London School of Economics.' She had an interesting thesis topic in mind, the question of Motivation in social service: what motivated those who chose to work in this area of local and national government, poor relief, community health, and suchlike? Was it idealism or professionalism? Were they driven by a vision of what an ideal society should be, or by a practical concern to improve the conditions of life for the masses? It was a subject very close to the bone of the Fabian, full of fascinating possibilities, moral and psychological as well as philosophical.

'Have you read William James's latest book, *Pragmatism*?' he asked.

'No, but I really want to,' she said eagerly. 'I love Schiller's *Studies in Humanism*, and he's a great admirer of James.'

He was acquainted with the work of the Oxford don F.C.S. Schiller, and had met the man himself when he gave a paper to the Oxford Philosophical Society in 1903, so was able to take this reference in his stride. 'Yes, they have a lot in common. But "humanism" is such an over-used and abused word that I don't think it serves Schiller well. James's "pragmatism" is more precise.'

'Tell me about it,' she said, laying the toasting fork aside, and giving him her full attention.

'Well, he makes an interesting distinction in the first chapter which might be a useful tool for analysing Motive, a distinction between the tough-minded and the tender-minded.'

Amber smiled. 'That doesn't sound like philosophical language!'

'But it's what I like about William James—he uses ordinary language to make difficult concepts intelligible.'

'Not like his brother, who uses difficult language to make ordinary concepts unintelligible,' Amber said.

He laughed. 'Very good! Arnold Bennett would agree with you. Have you read a lot of James—Henry, I mean?'

'Not much, I have to admit,' she said. 'I loved "Daisy Miller" when I was a girl, and some of his other stories, but I tried *The Wings of the Dove* and gave up halfway.'

'A pity—the last section is the best. The book has its longueurs, admittedly.'

'It seemed like one long longueur to me,' she said. 'I much prefer *your* novels. Once you start reading them, you don't want to stop.'

'Well thank you, Amber,' he said. 'But as I said to Arnold, there are things in *The Wings of the Dove* that I couldn't do, and *he* couldn't do.'

'The question is, are they worth doing?'

'Well, of course, that's always the question. Which only posterity can definitively answer. But about *Pragmatism* . . .'

She listened attentively as he outlined James's distinction between two basic types of mental make-up. The Tender-minded was rationalistic, idealistic, optimistic, religious, monistic, dogmatic. The Tough-minded was empiricist, materialistic, pessimistic, irreligious, pluralistic, sceptical. Idealist philosophers and Christian apologists were typically tender-minded. Scientists and engineers were tough-minded. 'You might find you can classify people in the social services that way,' he concluded.

'Yes, I can see that might work,' she said, thoughtfully. 'Thank you. But which type are you?'

'Well, basically tough-minded. Most people who've had a scientific education are. But the point is that both are unsatisfactory on their own. As James says, quite rightly, the tender-minded are on the back foot these days, mainly because of Darwinism and advances in the physical sciences. But tough-mindedness alone leads eventually to pure materialism, which doesn't satisfy the human spirit, because it leads only to death—death of the individual and in the long run the death of the planet. So no hope. The tender-minded offer transcendence in one form or another—God, the Absolute Mind, personal immortality . . .'

'But those ideas have no logical foundations,' Amber objected.

'Exactly. But we can't just dismiss them. There must be some non-materialistic principle to make life meaningful, purposeful, hopeful. Pragmatism, James says, values an idea not in the abstract but for what its practical consequences are. For instance, does it or does it not contribute to the betterment of human life? Socialism triumphantly passes the pragmatic test.'

'It's both tough-minded and tender-minded?'

'Exactly.'

'That's all extremely interesting. I must obviously read *Pragmatism* as soon as possible,' said Amber.

'I expect Wallas would look after you at the L.S.E,' he said.

'I did speak to him about my thesis idea—at a party at Christmas—but he thought it was a rather ambitious project for a young girl like me. I need to get a First to really impress him.'

'Well, I'll tell him how impressed *I* am, already,' he said.

She blushed, and dropped her eyes, and there was silence between them, suddenly charged with sexual feeling. He broke it by saying that he knew an officer of health called McCleary who would be a good source of information and that he could put her in touch with him when the time came. 'Thank you, H.G.!' she said, raising her big dark eyes to him again, and smiling, her composure regained. 'You're so kind.'

He mused on that moment of charged silence as he travelled back to London in the evening, staring through the blurred reflection of his face in the train window at the dimly visible flat fields of Cambridgeshire. There was no doubt that the girl was in love with him; the question was whether he was falling in love with her. His sexual life was dormant at present— surprisingly so, because when he finished a big project like *Tono-Bungay* he normally let off steam in that fashion. But his affair with Violet Hunt was over. She had begun one with Hueffer, a really serious relationship by all accounts, and ironically enough he had been responsible in a way. She had shown him some short stories which he thought were rather good, more honest and less prolix than her novels, and he had suggested that she offer them to Hueffer, for the *English Review*. Hueffer liked the stories, they met, and now they were apparently besotted with each other and wanted to marry. It was a pity that Fordie already had a wife from whom he was estranged, but no doubt they would work something out in due course. He wished them well, and had no jealousy or regrets in relation to Violet, for their affair had run its natural course. So he was at a loose end as regards female company. He encountered opportunities for new *passades*, but somehow he didn't have the urge to follow them up. Whenever his thoughts wandered in that direction, the image of Amber would pop into his head, laughing, arguing, and gesticulating with her friends, kneeling on the floor of the playroom in Spade House, building a fort for toy soldiers with the boys, or silently absorbed in a book, unaware she was observed. And now there would be another image: Amber squatting by the fire with a toasting fork in her hand, talking philosophy. If he wasn't already in love with Amber Reeves, he was certainly dangerously near the brink.

She wrote very shortly after his return home to say how much she had enjoyed their talk in her rooms, and how greatly she appreciated his support and encouragement. He was virtuously restrained in his reply and subsequent correspondence, keeping to a tone of avuncular-tutorial concern for her welfare, and he resisted the temptation to find new reasons to go to Cambridge. Instead he threw himself back briefly into Fabian politics. He and Jane were both re-elected to the Executive in March, rather to his surprise, because he had attended hardly any meetings in the past year. But the ordinary members didn't know that, and a significant number obviously still regarded him as their spokesman. He felt an obligation to their loyalty, and picked up once again the much-chewed but currently dry bone of the Basis. Apart from the addition of the clause about equal citizenship for women which had been approved last September, thanks mainly to Maud Reeves's efforts, the Basis remained unchanged from its original form, and the small committee of himself, Shaw and Webb, charged a year ago with the task of revising it, had achieved nothing. Accordingly he got out the papers and wrote yet another draft, with which he was rather pleased, and sent it off to his two colleagues, only to get dismissive replies from both to say that they saw much in the document with which they disagreed but were too busy with other matters—Poor Law reform in Webb's case—to respond fully. He fired off a furious missive to Webb saying *'You two men are the most intolerable egotists, narrow, suspicious, obstructive, I've ever met'*, which Webb evidently passed to Shaw who favoured him with one of his patronising, sarcastic homilies: *'There is an art of public life which you have not mastered, expert as you are in the art of private life.'* The effect of this correspondence was to make him wish he had never allowed his name to go forward for re-election on to the Executive. He had really had enough, more than enough, of being treated by the Old Gang like some promising but disruptive young pupil at the back of the class. He made up his mind to resign from the Fabian, but he would choose his own moment, one that would not make him look as if he were merely sulking.

Early in April Jane received a letter from Maud Reeves to say that she was worried about Amber, who was at home for the Easter vacation and showing signs of nervous tension about her forthcoming exams, not eating or sleeping well. *'I feel I should be looking after her more, but the trouble is I have so many speaking engagements for the suffrage movement that I'm rushing up and down the country and often away for days at a time, and Will of course is always busy with his work. I know she loves staying with you and H.G.—she was in raptures about her visit after Christmas—and I wonder if you could bear to have her again for a few days. The sea air and your company I'm sure would do her the world of good.'*

'What shall I say?' Jane asked him when she had shown him this letter.

'Invite her, of course,' he said. 'Let her stay as long as she likes. The boys will be delighted.'

'And you, H.G.?'

'Well of course, I'm always pleased to see Amber. You too, I think?'

'Oh yes. I'm very fond of Amber. If I had a daughter I would wish her to be like Amber.'

'Well then! Let her come—and everybody will be happy.'

When Amber arrived she showed no signs of the nervous prostration her mother had indicated. She ate with appetite, slept soundly, and seemed to have her usual energy. She 'revised' in the mornings while he was working, and in the afternoons went for walks with him which she told Jane were as good as revision, if not better, because they talked about books and ideas. In fact their conversation became increasingly personal and intimate as the days passed. She told him about her childhood, how she had hated London after the open air life of New Zealand—'no freedom, no seashore, just streets and streets of sooty brick houses'—and described a home life surprisingly lacking in warmth, both physically and emotionally. Physically because both Maud and Pember had been Christian Scientists in youth and had never quite renounced faith in the power of mind over matter, so they kept the windows in the house open all through the winter, even if members of the family had colds, and when the girls reached the menarche they were given no special concessions or cosseting when they had their periods but on the contrary were made to take especially long bracing walks, in all weathers. Amber mentioned this without embarrassment, glancing at him to see if he was shocked—which he was not, of course; but he was impressed by her candour and the trust in himself it implied.

They were walking along the seashore, crunching the shingle under their feet, as Amber reminisced in this vein. Maud's commitment to the cause of women's rights had not apparently made her a compassionate mother. 'Once when I complained that she didn't really love me, she boxed my ears and said she had more important things to do than fuss over ungrateful children. And in spite of all her progressive ideas about women's rights, she never helped me or Beryl much with the problems of growing up. She was too embarrassed to talk about sex to either of us—she thought it was enough that we had the run of Father's library and could look up anything we wanted to know.'

'And did you?'

'Oh yes, of course. But encyclopaedias and medical textbooks can only tell you so much.'

She stopped and turned to look at a commotion of gulls soaring and swooping above something, a shoal of fish probably, in the sea.

'They don't tell you about love,' she said. 'They don't tell you about desire.'

'No, you have to go to novels for that,' he said.

'But novelists don't tell you what you really want to know—they're not allowed to.'

'True,' he said. 'In the end you must find out for yourself.'

'I want to,' she said. 'But it's difficult.'

Neither of them dared to look each other in the face as they spoke. Their

222

relationship was like a bowl that had been slowly filling with unacknowledged feelings until now it was brim full—the surface tension was actually convex, and it only needed one more drop to set the whole thing overflowing unstoppably.

The moment came two days later, when they were effectively alone together in Spade House. Mrs Robbins was unwell, and Jane had gone up to Putney to visit her, staying overnight and leaving the two boys in the charge of himself and Amber and the servants. Amber threw herself into the role of surrogate mother with enthusiasm and to the boys' great delight. But when they had been played with, fed, bathed and put to bed, and she had read them a story and kissed them goodnight, and returned to the drawing room, she became more subdued and pensive. It was a mild spring evening and he suggested they go out into the garden before they had their own supper. They strolled up and down the lawn, and then sat down on the garden bench outside his shelter, looking out over a sea wrinkled by dwarf waves and stained by the orange glow of the declining sun. He made conversation on the topic of the Altrincham by-election, which he had been thinking about that morning. Winston Churchill, required by parliamentary rules to stand for re-election because of his recent appointment as Liberal President of the Board of Trade, was opposed by his own adversary of the previous year, the Conservative Joynson-Hicks, and by a socialist candidate called Irving sponsored by the Social Democratic Party, an extremist faction in the Labour movement. Irving had no hope of being elected, but would split the progressive vote. He was minded to write an open letter to the electorate of Altrincham urging socialists to vote for Churchill as the best way of furthering the cause of socialism in the long run, and he wanted Amber's opinion on this project, which was likely to arouse controversy among the Fabians, because it was the Society's official policy to support all socialist candidates in parliamentary elections. It was the kind of issue which would normally engage her eager interest, but her responses to his exposition were listless, abstracted, almost bored. 'What's the matter, Amber?' he said. 'You don't seem yourself this evening.'

'Don't I?' she said.

'No. Is it because you've got to go home soon?'

'No, not exactly,' she said.

'Is it because you're worried about those exams? You really don't need to be.'

'No,' she said. 'I couldn't care less about the beastly exams!'

He knew intuitively where the conversation was leading, but forced an uncomprehending laugh. 'Well, this is a change! What is it then?'

After a long pause, she said, in a small voice, without looking at him: 'I'm in love, if you really want to know.'

'I see.' After an even longer pause, he said: 'And who are you in love with?'

'*You* of course! You!' She turned and threw her arms round his neck, and sank sobbing on to his breast.

He cradled her in his arms, pressing her body against his for the first time, feeling its heat under her thin dress. 'Why are you crying, Amber?'

'Because I love you, and you don't love me.' She spoke indistinctly, her face still buried in his shirt-front.

'But I do love you, Amber,' he said.

'You mean, like a father . . .' she mumbled.

'No, like a lover.'

She sat up and stared at him. 'Do you really?'

For answer he kissed her.

'Am I dreaming?' she said when she opened her eyes.

'No,' he said, and kissed her again.

'But what about Jane?' she said. 'You love Jane.'

'Yes I love Jane, and Jane loves me, but there are many kinds of love, Amber. You've read *A Modern Utopia*, you've read *In the Days of the Comet*, you know my views on free, healthy, life-enhancing sexual relationships. Jane shares them.'

'You mean . . . she wouldn't mind?'

'She won't mind,' he said.

Nevertheless he had a scruple about consummating their new relationship in Jane's absence and without her knowledge, in her own home. Instead he proposed to Amber that they lay naked in bed together that night, without making love, as a kind of rite of betrothal. 'And if you decide afterwards that you don't after all want to go any further, then you must say so, and I will understand,' he said. 'Oh, I won't,' she said. 'But I think it's a wonderful idea. It's so . . . so . . . fine!'

He came to her room when the one housemaid who lived in had gone to bed and was sure to be soundly asleep. Amber was waiting in the pitch dark, wide awake and naked under the sheets. They embraced and lay in each other's arms, exploring and gently stroking each other's bodies like blind people. It was an intensely erotic experience. 'Is that your . . . ?' Amber whispered. 'That is my erect penis,' he said, 'a column of blood, one of the marvels of nature, a miracle of hydraulic engineering.' 'It's enormous,' she said. 'Will it hurt me when you . . . ?' 'It may hurt a little the first time,' he said. 'I don't mind anyway,' she said. 'I want it inside me. I want you inside me.' In his younger days he would have found it difficult to restrain himself from satisfying her wish instantly, if only to avoid an embarrassing ejaculation, but at the age of forty-one he had attained a measure of control over his sexual reflexes. 'And I want that too, my darling,' he said, 'but if we wait, it will be all the sweeter when it happens.'

It happened one afternoon some days later in a rented room in Soho, on a bed that creaked and twanged under their every movement, but the seedy setting didn't matter. Amber was wonderful. In the daylight that filtered through the thin curtains her body was as delectable as it had promised to be under his blind touch in Spade House, shapely but lithe, with a delta of dense black pubic hair that set off her milk-white skin. She gave a cry that mingled pain and pleasure as he penetrated her, and when he had spent she wanted immediately to do it again. He smiled at her ignorance of male physiology. 'I'm afraid at my age—at any age, actually—an interval is required,' he said. 'Let us sleep now.' When they woke they made love in a more leisurely way, and she had a rapturous orgasm. 'You have a natural aptitude for love, Amber,' he told her, without flattery, as they lay side by side, sated and happy.

'Call me Dusa,' she said. 'My intimate friends call me Dusa.'

'All right—Dusa. I love your Medusa hair—in both places.' He stroked her pubes and she giggled. 'But what will you call me? "H.G." sounds a bit formal in bed.'

'I'll call you "Master",' she said. 'Like the young Samurai to their teacher. Would you like that, Master?'

For an answer he turned and kissed her. Would he like it! The word on her lips was enough to stir his limp penis into life again.

In the remainder of her Easter vacation they snatched every opportunity to meet in the Soho lodging house for joyous copulation, and when she returned to Cambridge for the summer term good fortune provided a perfect excuse for meeting her there. Ben Keeling was giving an informal dinner party in honour of Sir Sydney Olivier (as he now was, following his appointment as Governor of Jamaica) accompanied by his wife and his two elder daughters, one of whom, Marjery, was at Newnham and a friend of Amber's. He and Amber were both invited to this event and he arranged to escort her to it. He arrived at Newnham in time for tea and took advantage of his trusted status at the College to possess his young mistress in her bedroom in Clough Hall, covering her mouth with his hand to stifle the sounds of her ecstasy lest they reach the ears of the virgins and spinsters passing on the staircase or in the gardens below the open window. 'Bite on my hand, bite me,' he hissed, and she did; the indentations were still discernible on the cushion of his thumb hours later, if anybody at the party for the Oliviers had looked closely. They arrived late, with the meal already in progress, and were greeted with a cheer, but he was ragged a little for his open letter to the Altrincham voters, recently published, and had to defend himself, sitting beside Amber on a window ledge with their plates on their knees because all the seats at the table were taken. This company was used to his presence in Cambridge by now and their arrival together raised no eyebrows. Only Olivier met his glance with a quizzical and faintly admonitory regard.

The next day he went to hear Amber give a paper to the Moral Science Society in which she developed an argument of her favourite philosopher, Schiller, challenging the presumption in logic that A is either B or it is not B, whereas in reality nothing is permanent and fixed. A is always becoming more or less B, and vice versa. It is only the human mind that has to hold a thing still for a moment before it can think it. He listened rapt with admiration and pride in his possession of this peerless creature, who could so effortlessly move from sensual abandonment to the lucid analysis of problems in epistemology. After the meeting she accompanied him to the station to catch his train, and waiting for it to arrive they paced the platform which pointed like a long finger towards London, resisting with difficulty the temptation to link arms or hold hands in case they were observed.

'When will we meet again, Master?' she said.

The name was like balm to his soul whenever she uttered it, but the question she asked had been bothering him. 'I don't know, Dusa,' he said. 'I can't keep popping up to Cambridge without arousing suspicion. And anyway, you've got to revise for your Part Two.'

'I'd much rather revise with you than here,' she said. She was thought-fully silent for a few minutes, and then came up with a plan. There were no more lectures and tutorials for students taking examinations, who were left free to prepare on their own. 'The consequence is that Newnham is like a mental sanatorium at this time of the year, girls going mad with anxiety or overwork and having nervous breakdowns all over the place . . . It's infec-tious. I could easily persuade Mother and Father that I would be far better off revising on my own, in a cottage in the country somewhere. You could meet me there.'

'Well, it's worth a try,' he said.

It seemed to him unlikely that the Reeveses would agree, but when he got home to find a letter from Macmillan accepting *Tono-Bungay* for the ad-vance he had demanded, he felt that Fortune was favouring him, and that the ruse would succeed. He told Jane that he was thinking of getting away for a week soon, to work on a new novel.

'And will Amber be joining you?' she said.

This was the first open acknowledgement by either of them that he was having an affair with Amber, though Jane had clearly sensed that a new relationship had been formed between them as soon as she returned home from visiting her mother in April. 'I hope so,' he said.

'Shouldn't she be preparing for her examinations?'

'Well, that's exactly the point.' He repeated the arguments that Amber was going to put to her parents. 'I'll work on my novel, and she will do her revision.' As she looked sceptical, he added: 'She'll be able to concentrate much better that way, Jane. She's head over heels in love with me. And I with her, to be honest.'

'I know,' Jane said with a sigh. 'I could see it coming. I knew there was nothing I could do to stop it.'

'Why should you want to stop it? She's a lovely girl. You like her. She worships you. She wouldn't do anything to hurt you. She understands com-pletely that this doesn't affect our marriage.'

'Maud's letter makes me feel we have betrayed their trust.'

'Nonsense! You mean the good fairy letter?' Maud had sent a gushing letter of thanks after Amber returned home from Sandgate: '*Thank you so much for your goodness to Amber. I think she is much better. She adores you both and talked of nothing else when she came back. She has gone to Cambridge full of spirits and confidence. I hope she will realise all her desires, dear soul. You are good fairies to all those young people.'*

'Yes, that letter.'

'We didn't invite Amber down here so that I could seduce her. Maud asked if she could come—no doubt prompted by Amber. Amber has behaved exactly as you did in '93, my dear, when you invited Isabel and me to Putney for the weekend. She fell in love and went after the man in question.'

'Not exactly,' said Jane. 'Isabel wasn't prepared to share you with me. Nor was I, for that matter.'

'And that was why there was so much pain,' he said. 'We've matured since then. We've conquered jealousy.'

Jane thought for a moment, and then gave a shrug of acquiescence. 'Well . . . Just be careful, H.G. Promise me you'll be very, very careful.'

'I promise,' he said, and gave her a hug and a kiss. 'You and I and Amber are exceptional people. We can make this work.'

He woke early the next morning and went out in the summer dawn to his garden shelter to write. He was finishing off *First and Last Things* with a chapter on sex and marriage. He wrote:

> *The ordinary civilised woman and the ordinary civilised man are alike obsessed with the idea of meeting and possessing one peculiar intimate person, one special exclusive lover who is their very own, and a third person of either sex cannot be associated with that couple without an intolerable sense of privacy and confidence and possession destroyed. But that does not abolish the possibility that there are exceptional people somewhere capable of, to coin a phrase, triangular mutuality, and I do not see why we should either forbid or treat with bitterness or hostility a grouping we may consider so inadvisable or so unworkable as never to be adopted, if three people of their own free will desire it.*

Amber's ruse worked, as she said, 'like a dream'. A fictitious cottage in Epping Forest was fictitiously rented for a week, shared with a fictitious fellow student, while they occupied rooms he found in Southend-on-Sea, a cheerful cockney resort on the Thames estuary where the landladies were broad-minded. They both worked in the mornings, sworn to silence. In the afternoons if the weather was fine they took books down to the beach and bathed and talked about the ground-breaking thesis she was going to write at the L.S.E. In the early evening they worked again for a few hours until it was time to sup in a nearby cafe or restaurant, and so to bed. They made love every night of their stay, and on the last morning, when it was time to leave, and their luggage had been taken down to the cab which had arrived earlier than appointed, they hesitated on the landing, looked at each other with the gleam of the same lascivious thought in their eyes, and went back into the room for a last quick coupling.

There was a chaste interval while Amber went back to Cambridge to sit her examinations, and then she was free to return to London occasionally while she waited for her results. He rented a bed-sitting room in Eccleston Square, Pimlico, a more salubrious venue than Soho, and they met there every week or so for a day of sensual indulgence, and sometimes a night too if she could contrive an alibi for her parents. She was a partner after his own heart, who frankly enjoyed the physical release of sex, liked to give vocal expression to her pleasure, and brought a surprising degree of athleticism to her embraces, which she attributed to the classes in jiu-jutsu that she had enrolled in, along with other emancipated young Cambridge women, under a Japanese instructor. She could effortlessly cross her ankles behind his neck when lying underneath him, and with her feet planted on a firm mattress arch her back like a drawn bow, strongly enough to lift his weight. When they went for walks in the country, he discovered with delight that she shared his penchant for spontaneous copulation in the open air, in copses, under haystacks, in churchyards—once even in the bell tower of a church itself—the risk of discovery giving an extra spice to what he referred to familiarly as their 'sinning'.

If it was a sin it seemed immune from divine punishment, for Amber was awarded a Double First in July, and showered with congratulations from the great and the good of Cambridge and further afield. Towards the end of that month she came to stay at Spade House, a time chosen to coincide with the fruition of a long-mooted plan to entertain William James, who was visiting his brother in Rye with his daughter Peggy. Henry was always rather possessive of his relatives when he had them to stay, perhaps disliking to mix them up promiscuously with his literary friends for fear they would transmit family secrets, but he had agreed to release his brother and niece for a couple of days. '*There is staying with us a Miss Reeves who is just your daughter's age,*' he wrote in a letter to William James confirming the arrangements. '*She has recently achieved a transient notoriety by getting a First in Part II of the Moral*

Sciences Tripos at Cambridge, and is so accomplished she can speak Hegelian.' On the appointed day he took Amber with him in a hired car to pick up William and his daughter. When they arrived at Lamb House, they found themselves in the middle of a farcical altercation between the two brothers, Henry red with indignation and William defensive but unrepentant. William had discovered that G.K. Chesterton, whose writings he admired, was staying in the house next door, and unable to restrain his curiosity had put a ladder against the wall, and peeped over into the neighbour's garden in the hope of seeing the author of *The Napoleon of Notting Hill* and *The Man Who Was Thursday* taking the air. Henry had just caught him red-handed in this shocking breach of etiquette, and ordered the gardener to take down the ladder at once. 'It is not done—tell him, please, Wells, that it is simply not done in England to spy on one's neighbours.'

'I was not obviously spying, Henry,' William said mildly. 'I was pretending to be trimming the vine which grows along the wall—I had provided myself with a pair of secateurs for that purpose.'

'But you are not a gardener, William. You are my brother and my guest, and it is not appropriate—I would go so far as to say it is absolutely unacceptable—at least in this country—for a gentleman to ah, ah—impersonate a gardener in order to—to—to . . .' (Henry James groped for *le mot juste*) 'to *violate* the privacy of his neighbours. Is that not so, Wells?'

'Some people might think it was a little eccentric, but perhaps not Chesterton, who has a few eccentricities himself,' he said diplomatically. 'Why don't you just invite G.K. to call?'

'Because I don't know him!' was the answer. 'We haven't been introduced.'

There was no more meticulous guardian of traditional English manners than this American expatriate. But after further huffing and puffing, Henry James calmed down sufficiently to release William and Peggy into his care, and they set off in the hired car, only to see approaching them on the coastal road outside Rye the unmistakeable figure of Gilbert Chesterton, tall, corpulent and untidily dressed, with coat flapping open and greasy curls protruding from under a panama hat, out for a walk with his wife. He stopped the car, made introductions, and a convivial conversation took place at the end of which Chesterton invited William to call on him one evening—'and do bring your brother'. They resumed their journey with William delighted to have made his acquaintance in a way to which Henry could take no exception.

Amber maintained an admirable poise in the midst of all these excitements but she was thrilled to have met so many distinguished authors all in one day. William was kind to her, congratulating her on her Double First, questioning her about her postgraduate research topic, and drawing her out on the merits and limitations of F.C.S. Schiller. Poor Peggy James was somewhat eclipsed by Amber's brilliance, and the two young women managed only a polite pretence of friendship during the visit. Peggy was quite personable in a shrinking sort of way, and intelligent enough, but diffident and reserved. He gathered from William that she had recently had some kind of nervous illness, taking after her Aunt Alice, the James brothers' neurasthenic sister who had died some fifteen years ago, and although she was now recovered she lacked vitality. She didn't swim or play tennis and her attempt at badminton was embarrassing. She watched Amber and the boys playing floor games with interest, but did not take part. She was really a bundle of negatives, poor girl, with the words 'old maid' written all over her in prediction of her future fate, and it seemed almost cruel to put her in proximity to Amber, bursting with health and confidence and appetite for life.

Amber seemed to him a golden girl that summer and autumn, an almost mythical creature, such as the gods of classical Greece coveted and descended from the heights of Olympus to ravish in human disguise or in the form of some animal or bird. Every week or so she gave herself willingly to be ravished, in the Eccleston Square love nest or wherever else opportunity afforded, and he worked all the better in the intervals with the memory or anticipation of these passionate assignations at the back of his mind. It was not just his lust that she excited, but also his creative and intellectual ambition. She called him 'Master', but he looked forward to the day when she would be not just his pupil but his collaborator. She would give his nonfictional work the philosophical rigour it often wanted, and do the kind of sociological research for which he lacked time and patience. And she wrote a short story that summer, about a young wife dismayed to discover how much independence she had forfeited by getting married, which showed distinct promise in that kind of writing, even though his efforts to get it published failed. They were to do great things together. It seemed to him that he had finally achieved a kind of equilibrium in his life: work, love and domesticity balanced in perfect harmony between himself, Amber and

Jane. The key of course was the absence of jealousy between the two women, who got on wonderfully well together. There was a tacit understanding that he did not make love to Amber at Spade House when Jane was there, while Amber for her part never challenged Jane's sovereignty over the household, but made herself useful in unobtrusive ways.

Once when he and Amber were lying together in bed at Eccleston Square after a very satisfactory ravishment, and congratulating themselves on their happiness, he asked what had brought her to the point of confessing that she was in love with him, and her answer was interesting. 'It was because Jane was away, and we had to look after Gip and Frank. I found myself in Jane's place for a day, keeping you company, telling the servants what to do, putting the boys to bed, and so on . . . I suddenly felt on my pulses what it would be like to be married to you, to belong to you, to be part of your everyday life . . . And I knew that the next day Jane was coming back, and the day after that I had to go home and give up all hope of ever having you. Because it never occurred to me that both of us could have you in different ways. So I fell into a terrible despair, and when you started on about Winston Churchill in the garden I just couldn't bear it and blurted out that I was in love with you. Which I thought would be the end.' 'Instead of which it was only the beginning,' he said, and kissed her.

He put quite a lot of Amber into the heroine of his new novel. The young Catherine Robbins was also a source, and there was a little of Rosamund in the portrait, but Amber was present to his imagination as he wrote, like an artist's model.

> *Ann Veronica Stanley was twenty-one and a half years old. She had black hair, fine eyebrows, and a clear complexion; and the forces that had modelled her features had loved and lingered at their work and made them subtle and fine. She was slender, and sometimes she seemed tall, and walked and carried herself lightly and joyfully as one who commonly and habitually feels well, and sometimes she stooped a little and was preoccupied. Her lips came together with an expression between contentment and the faintest shadow of a smile, her manner was one of quiet reserve, and behind this mask she was wildly discontented and eager for freedom and life.*

He made Ann Veronica's struggle for personal liberation more difficult than it had been for Amber Reeves. Amber had taken advantage of her father's absorption in his official duties and her mother's enlightened feminist principles to obtain a considerable degree of independence for herself even before she went up to Newnham, and once there she made the most of her distance from home to increase it. Veronica was less fortunate. She was a dependant of a deeply conventional widower father, and lived at home under the watchful eye of his spinster sister, both of whom obstructed her attempts to explore the world and relationships with the opposite sex. Only rebellion could release her from a life of stifling conformity to their bourgeois prejudices and prudery. Early in the story Ann Veronica, denied permission to attend a fancy dress ball of which her father disapproved on moral grounds, ran away from her suburban home, took a room in central London, and enrolled to study biology at the Imperial College of Science in South Kensington. There she met and fell in love with her biology lecturer, a man called Capes, who reciprocated her feelings, but hesitated to respond because he was estranged from a wife who would not divorce him, even though he had been unfaithful to her. Meanwhile she was courted by and rejected an effete poetaster called Mr Manning whom her father favoured, and resisted seduction by a plausible libertine called Mr Rammage, who artfully compromised her by lending her money to subsidise her studies.

He enjoyed creating the character of Rammage, who was in many ways a prejudicial self-portrait. This middle-aged man had had many '*feminine experiences, disturbing, absorbing, interesting, memorable affairs. Each one had been different from the others, each had had a quality all its own, a distinctive freshness, a distinctive beauty. He could not understand how men could live ignoring this one predominant interest, this wonderful research into personality and the possibilities of pleasing, these complex, fascinating expeditions that began in earnest and mounted to the supremest, most passionate intimacy.*' This was very much the style in which he would justify, if challenged, his own womanising; but by depicting Rammage as the villain of the story, preying on the innocent Ann Veronica, he aimed to puzzle those who would try to read the novel as a *roman-à-clef,* and make the character of Capes, his real surrogate in the story, appear by contrast more conventionally honourable and acceptable as a hero. To further confuse such readers he threw in a minor character, the well-known author and Fabian polemicist 'Wilkins', who was obviously identifiable as H.G. Wells.

Alone in London, Ann Veronica was taken up by a fervent suffragette and promiscuous dabbler in 'advanced' thought called Miss Miniver, who introduced her to a number of different groups—Fabians, Tolstoyans, proponents of Dress Reform and Food Reform, as well as the suffragettes themselves—but when Miss Miniver asserted that advanced people tended to 'generalise' love, Ann Veronica shocked her by asking if she didn't want the love of a man.

> Miss Miniver looked over her glasses at her friend almost balefully. 'No!' she said at last, with something in her voice that reminded Ann Veronica of a sprung tennis racket. 'I have never yet met a man whose intellect I could respect.'
>
> 'But if you had?'
>
> 'I can't imagine it,' said Miss Miniver. 'And think, think'—her voice sank—'of the horrible coarseness!'
>
> 'What coarseness?' said Ann Veronica.
>
> 'My dear Vee!' Her voice became very low. 'Don't you know?'
>
> 'Oh! I know. But don't we all rather humbug about the coarseness? All we women, I mean. We pretend bodies are ugly. Really they are the most beautiful things in the world.'
>
> 'No,' cried Miss Miniver almost vehemently. 'You are wrong! I did not think you thought such things. Bodies, bodies! Horrible things! We are souls. Love lives on a higher plane.'

This conversation marked the end of Miss Miniver's influence over Ann Veronica. She found that falling in love with Capes consisted in part of a powerful physical attraction to him. As he sat at the microscope, 'she became aware of the modelling of his ear, of the muscles of his neck and the textures of the hair that came off his brow, the soft minute curve of the eyelid that she could see just beyond his brow', and this in turn made her aware of her own beauty and desirability when she undressed and looked at herself in the mirror.

That was about as far as he had got with the story by the end of August, but he had the rest of it well mapped out: Ann Veronica was to throw herself into the militant suffragette movement, get herself arrested and imprisoned, and come to the conclusion that she did not really belong among the martyred women because they hated men and she didn't. She would be obliged to humble herself to her father in order to escape the toils of Rammage, but in the end triumphantly assert her independence by overcoming the scruples of Capes and running away with him. He had very clearly in his mind a scene in which he would say bluntly, *'What is it you want?'* and she would answer *'You!'* And then they would travel to the Swiss mountains, his favourite location for the evocation of happiness, and enjoy an idyllic, unlicensed honeymoon. On the 15th of September he whetted Macmillan's appetite to see the novel by writing to him that it was *'the best love story I have ever done'*.

The next day he finally resigned from the Fabian. Describing it through the eyes of Ann Veronica (attending a big meeting of the Society at Essex Hall, she *'was struck by the oddest mixture of things which were personal and petty with an idealist devotion that was fine beyond dispute'*) had confirmed his belief that he would never be able to work within it without frustration and friction. At the back of his mind too was a sense that his relationship with Amber would be more easily and comfortably concealed if he were no longer attending Fabian meetings and mixing in Fabian circles. He wrote to Pease to say that he was resigning from the Executive and the Society and would continue only as a subscriber, receiving information about events and publications. He gave as his principal reason the Society's refusal to incorporate endowment of motherhood into the Basis, but also deplored its repudiation of the principle of compensation for owners of private property and capital, which he believed was essential for the orderly advance of socialism in Britain. The opportunity to convert the British middle classes to socialism, he wrote, *'found us divided in theory and undecided in action, and it is to other media and other methods that we must now look for the spread and elaboration of those collectivist ideas which all of us have at heart'*. His resignation was accepted with alacrity and a sigh of relief emanating from Clement's Inn that was almost audible in Sandgate. It might have been received with less joy if the Old Gang had known that he was already sketching out the plan of another new novel, about a man who became disillusioned with Fabianism and sought to transform society by forming an elite of powerful but dedicated leaders like the Samurai of *A Modern Utopia*. By the end of the month he had finished *Ann Veronica* in a furious burst of creative energy and sent it off to Macmillan.

In mid-October Macmillan wrote: *'I am sorry to say that after very careful consideration, we do not see our way to undertake the publication of* Ann Veronica. *I could give you the reasons, but as I know you resent literary criticism from a publisher—I refrain from doing so.'* He was sure that the reasons were *not* literary-critical, and to elicit them replied meekly that he would be really glad to have Macmillan's criticisms and was sure they would be illuminating. Macmillan admitted a few days later that *'it seems to me a very well written book and there is a great deal in it that is attractive, but the plot develops on lines that would be exceedingly distasteful to the public which buys books published by this firm'*. This reaction was not wholly unexpected—the novel was bound to be controversial, and Macmillan was a cautious and conservative man by temperament—but he had hoped that the spirited sincerity of the heroine and the absence of inflammatory descriptions of physical passion would have overcome the publisher's doubts.

The rejection was disappointing, but it did not shake his faith in the book, and the disappointment did not last for long. On the very same day he received a letter from Stanley Unwin, who had just joined the firm of his uncle J. Fisher Unwin, and was, as he said, *'disposed to speculate in futures'*. Did Mr Wells have any plans for a new book not yet under contract to a publisher? Mr Wells did, and wrote back by return: *'Very well, what will you give for <u>all rights</u> (serial and book) American, British & colonial of the version in English of a novel by me which I have in hand, more or less at the present time. It is to be called <u>Ann Veronica</u>. It is to be the love story of an energetic modern girl who goes suffragetting & quarrels with her parents. It can be delivered in a state fit for negotiation before the end of this year . . .'* He went on to boast of the excellent sales of his other recent publications, the splash he expected the forthcoming *The War in the Air* to make, and concluded: *'Put up a firm offer of £1500 payable Oct. 1st 1909 & <u>Ann Veronica</u> is yours. We will eliminate the agent.'* He always enjoyed getting involved in the financial bargaining aspect of authorship (it was perhaps the only trace of the successful life in trade that his mother had hoped for him), and he took satisfaction in the subtle manipulation of verbal tense by means of which he concealed from Unwin the fact that the novel was in fact finished and had already been rejected by another publisher. He did not feel guilty of serious deception; after all, it could do with some more work. His self-advocacy was swiftly rewarded with a contract that satisfied all his stipulations.

That fortuitous approach from Fisher Unwin and its sequel was the last piece of unalloyed good luck that he enjoyed for some considerable time, both professionally and privately—not counting the acquisition shortly afterwards of a treasure of a governess for the boys, which was not entirely

236

due to luck anyway, but also to Jane's judgment when she interviewed Miss Mathilde Meyer in London among several other candidates. Now aged seven and five respectively, Gip and Frank were too old to be left in the charge of the nursemaid Jessie, and needed a more regular educational regime than he and Jane could provide in the intervals of their busy lives, but neither of them was in a hurry to expose their sons to the vagaries of English private schooling. They also shared a common belief that the boys should be encouraged to learn foreign languages from an early age, when the ability to do so was at its optimum. Miss Meyer, who was Swiss, and spoke French and German fluently as well as English, was ideally qualified for this task. She had had no idea that the Mrs Wells who had offered her the position was the wife of the famous author until she presented herself at Spade House and was shown into a room lined with his books and framed photographs of himself, while the maid went to fetch Jane from the garden. Miss Meyer had been teaching at a dull school for girls in Bognor up till then and never entirely lost an air of wonder at her good fortune in joining their household. This made for easy relations between employer and employee, as did the fact that the governess, though unexceptionable in appearance, was entirely lacking in sex appeal as far as he himself was concerned. Under the stimulus of her instruction the boys made such rapid progress in the two new languages that to her great concern they began to combine them into a macaronic dialect of their own, but when he suggested that she spoke to them exclusively in French or German in alternate weeks the problem disappeared.

Meanwhile the *English Review* project began to unravel as Hueffer revealed himself to be a hopeless businessman, who did not keep proper accounts, did not answer letters promptly, lost manuscripts, and reneged on promises. Fortunately he perceived the extent of this incompetence in time to pull out of co-editing and investing in the venture, but he had contracted to give Hueffer the serial rights in *Tono-Bungay* for a consideration of twenty per cent of the magazine's profits in the relevant period. It became evident that it was unlikely to make any profit whatsoever under Hueffer's editorship, and could only be published at all with the help of loans from his rich friends. Delays to the launch of the *English Review* meant delaying publication of *Tono-Bungay* to ensure that at least the first instalment of the serial would precede the book, and eventually the publication of the latter had to be postponed till the New Year. These frustrations hung like an inauspicious cloud over the prospects of a novel on which he had staked his claim to be taken seriously as a literary novelist of the first rank, and they were all the more acute because Arnold Bennett at last produced a real masterpiece that autumn, *The Old Wives' Tale.*

There had always been an element of competition in their friendship—both being immensely popular writers of fairly humble social origins, they were continually bracketed together and compared by critics—a rivalry which they managed to keep amicable by cheerful criticism of each other's work tempered with praise that was not always sincere. But in this case he had no criticism to make, and his praise was genuine. '*It is the best book I have seen this year—and there have been one or two very good books,*' he wrote to Bennett, '*and I am certain that it will secure you the respect of all the distinguished critics who are now consuming gripewater and suchlike, if you never write another line. It is all at such a high level that one does not know where to begin commending . . . But the knowledge, the detail, the spirit! From first to last it never fails.*' Bennett replied in his more economical and somewhat opaque epistolary style: '*What am I to say in reply to your remarks? Considerable emotion caused in this breast thereby! Also no doubt a certain emotion in yours, as you cannot write such letters often!*' Which was true, and it had cost him some effort in the suppression of envy to do so. He did not regard *The War in the Air,* which came out in the same month, as one of the very good books published that year, or expect Bennett to identify it as such. The novel did what he had hoped and expected of it: it sold well, was favourably reviewed in the popular papers and somewhat patronisingly by the quality press. *Tono-Bungay* was the book he would put in the scales against *The Old Wives' Tale,* and he deeply regretted ever letting the bumbling Hueffer anywhere near it.

In his discontent he turned to the two women in his life for different kinds of solace: with Jane he could complain about Hueffer's delinquencies confident that she understood all the factors involved—finance, publicity, sales, critical reception—and identified sympathetically with his anxieties, while with Amber, who had little experience of or interest in the processes of publishing, he could find relief and release in occasional bouts of passionate lovemaking. That continued to be wonderful, but the post-coital peace it brought was transient, and could not disguise the evidence of Amber's casual conversation that she was not making much progress with her research. She was registered at the L.S.E as a postgraduate student, but this was a solitary existence very different from the one she had enjoyed at Cambridge, with its full programme of lectures and tutorials, its abundance of extracurricular activities, the watchful pastoral care of the Newnham academic staff, and the constant stimulus and support of her peers. She lived at home and worked either there, alone in the big chilly Kensington house, while her parents and siblings were out pursuing their various vocations, or in the Round Reading Room of the British Museum, intimidated rather than inspired by the book-lined walls and galleries supporting the great dome, by the huge leather-bound volumes of the Catalogue, heavy as paving stones, ranged in concentric circles at the hub of the floor, and by the industry of the scholars who occupied the desks around her, reading intently and taking notes busily as if they knew what they were doing. She had been allocated a supervisor—not Wallas, but Professor L.T. Hobhouse, a distinguished man recently elected to the first chair of sociology at the L.S.E., but he did not really take to her project, and gave her little help in carrying it out. He told her to produce a draft outline and specimen chapter for him to comment on, but she seemed unable to buckle down to this assignment and get it done.

Instead the main focus of interest in her life was their affair, and she couldn't keep the secret to herself. He understood her desire to confide in her mother and agreed that she should do so, trusting that Maud's theoretical belief in female autonomy would extend to her own daughter, who was now twenty-one and legally as well as morally a free agent. According to Amber, Maud was shaken by the revelation, and fearful of the possible consequences, but reluctantly accepted their relationship as a *fait accompli* and helped to conceal it from Pember Reeves, hoping no doubt that it would eventually end without his ever knowing anything about it. In truth, it would have been difficult to avoid arousing Reeves's suspicions without Maud's co-operation in covering Amber's tracks, though she was unwilling to admit that she knew anything about the matter. On the rare occasions when they were in the same company Maud was politely friendly to him but carefully avoided any opportunity for private confidences, and Jane had the same experience. 'Not that I was seeking a tête-à-tête,' Jane said to him as they came away from such a party. 'In fact I was rather afraid that she would cut me—as most mothers would in the circumstances. But she just smiled vaguely and chattered aimlessly until someone else came up.' He had a theory that Maud was treating her daughter's affair and its ramifications rather as Christian Scientists treated illness and its symptoms, as unreal illusions which would go away if you ignored them.

His first intimation that Amber had taken others into her confidence came from Sydney Olivier, who was home from Jamaica on leave in December. They met for lunch at the Reform, and Sydney startled him by asking him quite early in their conversation, in a casual familiar tone, 'And how is Amber?'

'Amber Reeves? She's well, I believe,' he faltered. 'Why do you ask?'

Olivier smiled sardonically above his bowl of oxtail soup. 'I understand you are very close to her at present.'

'Who told you that?' he said, busying himself with his potted shrimps.

'My daughter Marjery, who was told by Amber herself.'

'Ah,' he said, concealing his dismay as best he could. 'That was very indiscreet of Amber. I trust Marjery has respected her confidence.'

'It's a bit late for that, I'm afraid, Wells,' Olivier said. 'Marjery is not the only one Amber has confided in. Even the dons know. The whole college is agog with speculation about your affair.'

'Damn!' he said quietly, and glanced at the neighbouring tables to see if anyone had overheard Sydney's remarks. He had been aware that Amber was making trips to see her old friends at Cambridge from time to time between their trysts in Eccleston Square, and evidently she had been unable to resist boasting to them about her thrilling affair.

Olivier finished his soup and wiped his neatly trimmed beard and moustache with a napkin. 'I thought something might be up when I saw you walk into Ben Keeling's rooms with Amber last May, looking like the cat that has eaten the cream,' he said. 'As the father of four daughters I should deeply disapprove—and I do! But my baser self feels a certain admiration for your success with beautiful and gifted young women half your age. How do you do it?'

'I'd like you to know, Olivier,' he said earnestly, 'that this is no casual seduction. We are deeply in love. Jane knows all about it—'

Olivier's eyebrows lifted. 'Jane knows? And she doesn't mind?'

'She and Amber get on famously together. We are acting out in personal relations what other so-called "advanced" people profess to believe in but are too timid to practise.'

Olivier shook his head. 'Well I wish you luck, Wells. But I don't think you can start a sexual revolution single-handed.' He paused before adding drily, 'If "hand" is the applicable word in this context.'

This news spoiled a lunch he had been looking forward to, and he was unable to appreciate—indeed he scarcely attended to—Olivier's exposition of the social, political and economic problems of Jamaica. As soon as he

240

could politely do so, he parted from him and hastened to the British Museum hoping to find Amber there. He had to renew his reader's ticket, which had expired, before he could enter the Reading Room and look for her. The light was fading outside the high windows. It was a foggy day and some of the fog had seeped into the great domed space, increasing the gloom, so that the desk lamps seemed like so many street lamps in a miniature city of crescents and circuses as he prowled in search of Amber. He found her at last, staring vacantly into space, chewing on a pencil, with a thick volume open before her. She started when he touched her shoulder, and her face lit up when she recognised him, then paled as she registered his frown. 'What is it?' she said. 'We must talk,' he whispered, conscious of disapproving looks from the neighbouring readers, and waited as she gathered her books together and took them to the desk where they would be reserved for her for the next day.

To obtain some privacy he led her out of the building to one end of the great pillared portico, deserted on this damp, dispiriting afternoon apart from a few sooty-winged pigeons strutting about, sat her down on a bench, and reproached her for her indiscretion.

'I only told a few of my closest friends . . . and a couple of the dons,' she protested, 'and I swore them all to secrecy.'

'Oh yes, and of course *they* swore *their* friends to secrecy when they told them, and so on,' he said. 'You must know by now that gossip spreads like wildfire in Cambridge. I don't know why you still spend so much time there.'

'Because I'm lonely in London,' she said. 'I know we can only meet occasionally, and I put up with that, but I must talk to *somebody* the rest of the time and most of my friends are in Cambridge.'

He was conscious that they seemed to be drifting towards their first lovers' tiff, but he couldn't stop himself from pressing on: 'All right. But why talk to them about *us*?'

'Because it's the thing in my life I care most about,' she said frankly, with her big dark eyes fixed on his; and immediately his heart melted and he took her in his arms and kissed her.

After a little love talk, and another kiss, he said, 'I'm sorry that you feel lonely at times, Dusa. Don't you have any friends in London?'

'Only Rivers,' she said. 'If you mean a friend I can really talk to.'

'Rivers?'

'Rivers Blanco White.'

'Oh, him!' He knew this young Fabian, a nice enough fellow who had been at Cambridge and was currently at one of the Inns of Court, eating his dinners and preparing to be a barrister, but in putting his question he had been thinking of female friends. 'You know him well?'

'Very well,' Amber said. 'He wanted to marry me when I was in my second year at Cambridge.'

'*What*? You never mentioned that before.'

Amber shrugged. 'I didn't see any reason to. It seems a long time ago—I was a different person then.'

'But you turned him down?'

'Not exactly. We talked it over, and decided it was not a good idea—which it wasn't. We were both far too young and immature—I certainly was. Rivers is a few years older than me. He'd already graduated, and was studying law before going to Lincoln's Inn. But he was in love with me and afraid that he would lose me if we didn't get engaged before he went down.'

'Were you in love with him?'

'Well, I thought I was, but really I think I just wanted to sleep with him. Which would of course have been the sensible thing for us to do,' she said, smiling reminiscently at some memory, 'but I knew he would be shocked if I suggested it and Rivers was far too conventional and chivalrous to suggest it himself. He even felt guilty about kissing me when we weren't engaged.'

What kind of kisses? he wanted to ask—passionate kisses, open mouth kisses, tongues squirming, bodies pressed together, limbs intertwined . . . ? He was suddenly swamped by a wave of jealousy which he was ashamed to reveal, and asked a trivial question instead. 'Where did he get that ridiculously tautologous name, as a matter of interest?'

'There was an ancestor, an Irishman called White, who emigrated to Spain in the eighteenth century and changed his name to Blanco, but Rivers's great-grandfather, Joseph Blanco, left Spain around 1810 to settle in England and called himself Blanco White.'

'It sounds like a schoolboy's nickname,' he sneered. '"Rivers" is pretty odd too, for that matter.'

'It's an old family name, his second given name. He was actually christened "George".'

'Do you still see him?'

'Oh yes, quite often. We take the Tube sometimes to the end of the line and go for walks in the country.'

He stared. 'Why did you never mention this to me before?'

Dusa gave him a sly, feline glance from under her long lashes. 'I thought you might be jealous,' she said.

'Hmmph!' He looked away, across the courtyard now lit by gaslamps, each with a halo of irradiated fog. Visitors and scholars leaving the Museum as closing time approached were descending the broad steps and making their way towards the Great Russell Street gate, the scholars distinguishable by their briefcases. 'Should I be?' he asked.

'Of course not! I'm in love with *you*. Rivers knows that.'

'You told him?' He swivelled round to face her accusingly. 'You told him about us too?'

Amber looked defensive again. 'I had to,' she said.

'Why?'

'To stop him from trying to make love to me again.'

'So he is still in love with you, then?'

'Well, he thinks he is. But our friendship is purely platonic.'

'As far as you're concerned, perhaps. But what about him? What does he think of your relationship with me?'

'He disapproves of course, but—'

'Disapproves! I wager he does! In his position I'd like to kill me!'

Amber laughed. 'You needn't be afraid of that! He's a lawyer.'

'It's not funny, Dusa,' he said, severely. 'He may not literally try to murder me, but he could do a lot of damage. Suppose he tells your father?'

'He won't. I swore him to secrecy before I told him—and unlike my Cambridge friends he takes an oath seriously.'

'Hmmph!' he grunted again.

'Are you cross with me, Master?' she said in a small voice.

'Well, yes, I am,' he said. 'With all these people knowing about us . . . sooner or later there's going to be trouble.'

'I'm sorry, Master. But I love you—that's all that matters, isn't it?'

After which there was nothing to do but take Dusa to Eccleston Square in a brougham and quell his jealousy and his doubts by possessing her with as much violent passion as she could bear. In the cab he whispered into her ear exactly what he intended to do, and felt her trembling with a mixture of excitement and fear. She fought him with spirit, and afterwards they kissed each other's scratches and bite marks tenderly, and cuddled like babes. She was a girl in a thousand.

·   ·   ·

He had little doubt that the rumour-mills of London were now busy linking his name with Amber's, but no gossip came directly to his ears, partly because he kept clear of the metropolis over Christmas and into the New Year. The holiday was enlivened by a new kind of war game he had invented for toy soldiers, of which the boys now had a fine collection—whole uniformed armies, or at least battalions, of cavalry and infantry. The recent invention of a breech-loading toy cannon, obtainable from Hamley's, which when carefully aimed could actually knock down several soldiers at a time with a small projectile at a range of up to twelve feet, had enormously expanded the possibilities of this kind of play. He had devised a game, based on timed turn-taking for manoeuvring and firing, which could take several hours to complete, and absorbed adults as thoroughly as it did Gip and Frank—in fact rather more so, as Jane was wont to observe when she went looking for her husband and his male guests and found them lying on the floor of the attic playroom, pushing toy soldiers around a miniature landscape constructed of wooden bricks, cardboard, and evergreen twigs, with a river marked on the lino in blue chalk, arguing vociferously about the rules, with Gip and Frank reduced to mere spectators.

Masterman, who came down with Lucy to stay in the village in January, was thoroughly taken with the game, and contributed a few refinements to the rules. He had come to Sandgate to start a new book called *The Condition of England*, and had been reading the serialisation of *Tono-Bungay* in the *English Review* with great excitement. 'It's exactly a fictional equivalent of the book I want to write,' he said. 'I intend to quote copiously from it if I may.' He gave Masterman an advance copy on his departure and soon received a gratifying response, '*I read it on the train back to London, and I could scarcely refrain from shouting out and brandishing it in the faces of the bewildered passengers, as I realised I had got hold of a masterpiece.*' Beatrice Webb was less enthusiastic in acknowledging her copy, and said she had preferred *The War in the Air*, a perverse judgment which provoked him into a dismissive response to the reciprocal gift of the first volume of the *Minority Report of the Poor Law Commission* on which she and Sidney had been labouring for several years. '*You don't by any means make the quality of your differences from the Majority Report plain, and your case in the slightest degree convincing. Perhaps I have been led to expect too much, but at any rate, I am left wondering what it is you think you are up to,*' he wrote, to which she responded ironically: '*What an interesting letter—I enshrine it with due honour in my diary.*' Somewhat chastened he replied, '*Perhaps my letter was a little ungenerous but the provocation to hurt your good piece of work as you treated mine and to be just wilfully unsympathetic was too great,'* and was relieved when she wrote back apologising for her remarks about *Tono-Bungay* and even inviting a renewal of contact between them. He had no intention of getting involved with the Webbs again, but the rapprochement was welcome inasmuch as it implied that if they had heard about his relationship with Amber they were not going to make a fuss about it.

The early reviews of *Tono-Bungay* when it was finally published in February were mixed. The one that gave him most pleasure was surprisingly in the *Daily Telegraph*: *'Unless we are greatly mistaken,'* the anonymous reviewer wrote, *'Tono-Bungay is one of the most significant novels of modern times, one of the sincerest and most unflinching analyses of the dangers and perils of our own contemporary life that any writer has had the courage to submit to his own generation.'* Bennett was similarly laudatory in *New Age,* but then he would be. The *Spectator,* given its record of hostility to himself and his work, was better than he had anticipated: while deploring his *'dreary or lurid harping on the sex problem'*, it praised *'the passages in which Mr Wells is stirred to eloquence by the contemplation of the grandeur or the squalor of London, and by the magic of its ancient river. The romantic side of the mad game of modern commercial and journalistic adventure; the dodges of forcing worthless wares on a gullible public and getting rich quick,—all this is described with the utmost verve.'* When he saw the name of Hubert Bland over the review in the *Daily Chronicle,* he braced himself for a verbal thrashing, but Bland was too experienced a journalist to betray any personal animus, and was aware that a tone of bored disappointment by a former admirer would be more wounding. Bland found the novel *'rather incoherent, not to say rather chaotic . . . Mr Wells's habit of letting his pen wander at large is growing upon him. Presently the artist who gave us* Love and Mr Lewisham *will be no more. We shall have only a greatly inferior Sterne.'*

After all the effort, hope and anxiety expended on and generated by this novel, its publication was anticlimactic. It was not unanimously acclaimed as a masterpiece, but not universally damned either. His faith in the novel was unshaken by the criticisms, but it would have to make its mark gradually, over time. Meanwhile he got on with the revision of *Ann Veronica.* Among other things he added an epilogue in which Ann Veronica and Capes were shown four years after their elopement, back in London, married (Capes's wife having agreed to a divorce) and affluent (he has had a success as a playwright), giving dinner to Mr Stanley and his sister, recon-

245

ciled at last with Ann Veronica—who is expecting a baby. It was a fairly contrived happy ending, designed to appease any apprehensions Fisher Unwin might have about the reception of the book by the circulating libraries, and he was not particularly proud of it, but he salved his conscience by giving Ann Veronica a long speech on the last page in which she felt a kind of dread of the life she saw before her of respectability and riches, and appealed to her husband: *'Even when we are old, when we are rich as we may be, we won't forget the time when we cared for nothing, for anything but the joy of one another, when we risked everything for one another, when all the wrappings and coverings seemed to have fallen from life and left it light and fire. Stark and stark! Do you remember it all? . . . Say you will never forget!'*

During these early weeks of the New Year he continued to see Amber in London, and as an occasional guest at Spade House, without any ripples of comment or condemnation reaching him. He began to feel that he had overreacted to the discovery of her indiscretions in December, until, at the end of February, there was a sudden alarming development. He got a wire one evening sent from a post office in Kensington saying 'FATHER KNOWS. I MUST SEE YOU. DUSA.' He wired back 'ECCLESTON SQUARE TOMORROW ELEVEN AM', and slept badly that night.

Amber had a latchkey to the flat and was waiting for him when he arrived, huddled by the gas fire. It was a cold, overcast day outside the grimy windows, and the familiar room looked shabby and cheerless without the promise of sexual release which usually brought him there. They embraced, and she clung to him as if reluctant to let go, but eventually they sat down and she told him what had happened.

'Rivers went to Father and told him we were lovers.'

'*What?* But you swore him to secrecy!'

'I know.'

'The little shit!' The expletive burst out before he could suppress it. 'Excuse my language, Dusa, but really that was very dishonourable. He swore an oath.'

'Well, it wasn't exactly an oath,' she said sheepishly. 'More like a promise, and he warned me yesterday he was going to break it. Of course I begged him not to, but he said he couldn't stand by and see me "ruined" and do nothing to stop it. He said he was going to tell Father that he was still in love with me and wanted to marry me if I would give you up. He seemed to think that made it all right to break his word. I said I wouldn't dream of marrying him under any circumstances, but it made no difference. He went straight round to Father's office and told him. And then of course there was a terrible scene at home. He ordered Beryl and Fabian to go to their rooms, got Mother and me into his study, locked the door and raged at both of us for an hour. Poor Mother was in tears. He said I had disgraced the family, that Mother had connived at my dishonour and deceived him, and we had both dragged the reputation of New Zealand womanhood through the mud. I won't tell you what he said about you . . .'

'I can imagine,' he said grimly. 'What did *you* say?'

'Well, of course, I defended you. I said I loved you, and it was mutual. That Jane knows and is happy about it. That we have a very special relationship between the three of us which we believed could be a model for future generations. And that I was twenty-one and free to make my own decisions about how I lived.'

'And what did he say to that?'

'He threatened to turn me out of the house, and cut me out of his will, like a character in a Victorian melodrama, and Mother said if he wanted to create a scandal that was the best thing he could possibly do, and he backed down a bit, and blamed her for encouraging me to go to Cambridge, which he said was the start of my moral decline. Then he began to sing the praises of Rivers, and said he was a very fine young man, and that I was very fortunate that he was still willing to marry me in spite of my being "damaged goods" as he charmingly put it, and that if I had the slightest remnant of a conscience, and the smallest consideration for myself and the family, I would accept Rivers's proposal immediately, in which case a scandal might be averted, and he would be prepared to forgive me.'

'And what did you say to that?'

'I said I wouldn't marry Rivers if he was the last man on earth. Which isn't true actually, because I'm fond of him and I know he is doing what he thinks is right, according to his lights, but I wanted to make it clear that nothing could come between you and me.'

'And it won't, Dusa,' he said, stretching out and covering her hand with his. 'I won't let it.'

They made love that morning after all, not with their usual joyous abandon, but simply, almost sadly, as a pledge of their determination not to be parted. In the ensuing days and weeks, however, he began to feel less confident of the outcome. Pember Reeves was no more capable of keeping his outrage to himself than Amber had been capable of keeping her love story to herself. He heard from several sources that Reeves was telling his friends that 'the blackguard Wells' had seduced his daughter, and vowing revenge. The High Commissioner was said to have obtained a gun with the intention of shooting him, and according to one lurid version of the tale sat every lunch hour in the bow window at the front of the Savile Club, to which they both belonged (Pember Reeves had in fact proposed him there), waiting with a loaded revolver for the blackguard to turn up, and so alarming the members that they begged him to resign. This was all palpable nonsense, since he himself had prudently resigned from the Savile the previous summer. But there was certainly some substance to the rumours, and for Amber the situation was deeply stressful. The poor girl was under intense pressure from her father either to marry Blanco White or to insist that he must marry her himself after divorcing Jane. 'Otherwise,' he thundered at her, 'there will be no place for you in decent society.' Maud, who had been shaken by the public exposure of the affair, and had a guilty conscience about her own part in it, suspended her feminist principles and sided with her husband, urging the merits of Blanco White, though she conceded that Amber might yet save herself from social disgrace if she only cut off all relations with himself immediately. 'But I can't give you up, and I don't want you to divorce Jane—I couldn't contemplate that for a moment,' Amber wailed in one of their many conversations on the subject. 'So what can I do?' He suggested she should leave home and live independently in a flat which he would pay for, but the persona this proposal summoned up was obviously too close to the stereotype of the kept mistress for her to be comfortable with it.

One day late in March Amber contacted him at the Reform by telephone and asked him to come immediately to the room at Eccleston Square. She sounded in an emotional state. 'I've come to a decision, Master,' she said.

'What decision, Dusa?'

'Come,' she said, and the line went dead.

He took a cab to Pimlico, filled with dread that she was going to say they must part. The idea of losing Dusa, of losing that loving, desirable, intelligent creature, of never holding her naked in his arms again, and still more the thought of her naked in Blanco White's, with her ankles locked behind his neck, was simply unbearable. But when he let himself into the room and she smiled at him and held out her hands to him he knew that the decision she had come to was not what he had feared. It was however a shock.

'Give me a child!' she said.

'A child? Why?' he said.

'If I'm pregnant they can't make me marry Rivers, because he wouldn't have me. And if I bear your child I will always have something of you, whatever happens.'

'Dusa, you're wonderful!' he said embracing her, euphoric with relief, and carried away by the reckless romanticism of the idea. His mind was already busy with plans to adopt the child, perhaps even pretend that it was Jane's, while Amber lived with them as companion, secretary, collaborator . . . if the Blands could get away with it, why not themselves?

So they set about the business there and then, all the more joyfully for not having to take any contraceptive precautions. They were truly two in one flesh at last, with no membrane of rubber between them. Amber gave a great shout when she climaxed, and afterwards, as she was lying limply in his arms, she said: 'I'm sure I've conceived.' He laughed. 'Only the Virgin Mary knew as soon as that,' he said. 'You may mock,' she said calmly, 'but I felt it happen deep inside me.' 'Well, to make sure, we should repeat the procedure as often as possible,' he said, and arranged to meet her in the flat the next day.

The following afternoon he was the first to arrive, and watched from the window as she came round the corner of the square and approached the house. She was hurrying, but her movements and expression seemed anxious rather than eager, and when she entered the room he could tell immediately that she had unwelcome news.

'Promise you won't be angry with me,' she said.

'What have you done now, Amber?' he said.

'Dusa.'

'What have you done, Dusa?'

'I saw Rivers this morning,' she said. 'I told him I was carrying your child.'

'For God's sake, Dusa!' he exclaimed. 'You can't possibly know that— you won't know for a month or more. Why on earth did you say it?'

'I told you yesterday I was sure, but even if I'm wrong, sooner or later it will be true. I didn't want to have to wait for weeks to tell him. I wanted to get it over with—I mean his ridiculous chivalrous plan to save me from your clutches by marrying me. I was sure he would recoil from me with disgust if I told him I was pregnant by you.' She paused significantly in her narration.

'You mean, he didn't recoil?' he said.

'He looked horrified, and he said some things about you I won't repeat, and he paced up and down for a bit without speaking, but eventually he said it didn't make any difference. He still loves me and wants to marry me.'

'Does he?' he said grimly. He was beginning to feel rather intimidated by this young man's dogged persistence.

'And he said he would tell Father accordingly.'

'Oh God!' he groaned.

'What I'm afraid of is that Father will try to force me to marry Rivers to save the family's name. Not that he can, of course . . . But the scenes will be horrible. Mother will support him, I know she will. What shall we do?'

He thought for a few moments. 'We'll have to hide somewhere,' he said at length. 'Run away to some place where we can't be got at, where we can be calm and think things out. We'll go to France for a while.'

Amber's face brightened, and she clapped her hands. 'France! What a lovely idea.'

Jane as usual was a brick, albeit a puzzled and somewhat sceptical one. 'You're going to elope with Amber to France and have a baby with her?' she said when he announced their plans. 'Is that a good idea, H.G.? Is that going to help the situation?'

'We're not "eloping", Jane, in the normal sense of the word,' he said. 'We just want to be alone and left in peace for a while to think things through. Amber doesn't want me to leave you—she's always made that absolutely clear.'

'Yes, I know. I trust Amber, and I like her. But will a baby solve anything? Or will it just be another problem?'

When he had finished expounding the arguments for Amber's great 'decision', which sounded weaker to his own ears the more he elaborated them, she shook her head and said, 'Well, I think you're both mad, but I see you've made your minds up. What do you want me to do?'

'Just hold the fort. Tell people I've gone away to do some writing. Don't tell them where.'

'Where *are* you going?'

'I thought Le Touquet,' he said. 'That way I can pop back from Boulogne any time it's necessary.'

6

Blanco white could not immediately carry out his intention of telling Pember Reeves that his daughter was pregnant because the High Commissioner was out of London on official business, so the lovers had a couple of days in which to plan their departure to France. Amber packed a pair of valises and left the Kensington house unobserved to meet him at Victoria station. There she posted a brief letter to her parents saying that she was 'going abroad' for a time with her lover, that they need not worry about her and should not try to trace her. Then they took the boat train for the Folkestone–Boulogne crossing, and some hours later arrived at the holiday villa on the outskirts of Le Touquet which he had rented from an agency in London for two months. It looked like a doll's house that had been blown up to life size, built of white clapboard with red shutters, and had a little veranda sheltered from sea breezes by the grass-covered sand dunes which ran along this part of the Pas de Calais coastline. At low tide the sea was almost out of sight, leaving a vast plain of hard packed sand on which children flew kites and young men sailed sand yachts with nonchalant skill. They went for long walks on the beach, and when the tide was up braved the chilly sea to swim, towelling each other dry before an open fire in the villa, and making love on the hearthrug afterwards. In the evening they strolled into the town to dine in a bistro and sometimes, if the night air was mild, sat on the dunes with his arm round her waist and her head on his shoulder, watching the beams of two lighthouses sweeping across the water and highlighting the crests of the waves.

It was a kind of honeymoon, but like all honeymoons it had to come to an end, and in fact the air of idyllic enchantment they seemed to breathe at first lasted barely a week. They had, after all, come here primarily to make some serious decisions about their future, but the more they talked the less likely it seemed that they could agree on a plan. His idea of a discreet *ménage à trois* on the Bland model was on reflection impracticable—their affair was already too public for that to succeed. He was all for setting up a separate home for her and their child in London, and bravely defying any public disapproval, but Amber said it would not be fair on the child. On the other hand she couldn't contemplate living alone in France with their infant, visited at intervals by himself, nor would he wish to subject her to such a lonely and restricted life. He was grateful that Amber consistently maintained that she didn't want him to divorce Jane, because it was a solution he recoiled from, but it would be surprising if the thought did not sometimes occur to her that circumstances might force it upon them. It became more and more obvious to him that the child was the factor which caused all projected plans to fail. Of course there was no certainty that Amber was pregnant, though she continued to be confident that she was, and he had to assume that she would eventually conceive unless he reverted to using sheaths, which would be in effect a hurtful rejection of her grand romantic gesture as well as very likely a futile exercise.

The deadlock in their discussion of this issue exacerbated the minor tensions and irritations which increasingly arose in their day-to-day life together. He was used to having his creature comforts quietly and efficiently managed by Jane. In Spade House meals were always served on time and were always palatable and sustaining; there was an unfailing supply of freshly laundered shirts and underlinen in his chest of drawers; fires were laid and beds were made, shoes were polished and clothes were pressed, by a small team of servants. He was prepared to undertake some of these tasks in the circumstances, but not all of them. Amber however was completely lacking in domestic skills. Maud, she told him, had never cooked a meal in her life, considering that she had more important things to do, and therefore had not instructed her daughters in this skill. Amber couldn't even boil an egg that wasn't too hard or too soft for his taste, and although she washed her own linen and underwear she bluntly refused to wash his. She was a stranger to the art of ironing. Her French was excellent for the purpose of food shopping, but she had no idea what to do with the produce once they got it home. Things improved somewhat when they located a laundry in the town that would collect and deliver, and hired a woman who came in daily to clean the house and prepare their midday meal, and there were plenty of decent restaurants in the town for supper, but breakfasts of coffee and rolls without fried eggs and bacon made a cheerless start to the day. So much time was consumed in performing unaccustomed tasks, or making up for the lack of amenities in their domicile, that he was able to do very little serious work, and this made him nervous and irritable.

Jane forwarded mail to him every day, with its reminders of the complex social and professional life he had abandoned, and seductive invitations he was forced reluctantly to decline. One engagement made before they fled to Le Touquet was a lunch in London in mid-April in honour of Anatole France organised by a group of his English admirers to celebrate his sixty-fifth birthday, and he insisted on attending it. His plan was to cross the Channel to Folkestone the previous afternoon and stay the night at Spade House, in order to dress and groom himself appropriately next morning for the lunch, and to return directly to Le Touquet from London. Going home was a queer experience—intensely enjoyable in some ways, disturbing in others. It was very pleasant to enjoy home comforts again, including a full English breakfast before he set off for London, but his sons' joy at his return and their disappointment when they learned of the brevity of his stay made him feel guilty. It was his custom when bidding them goodnight, perched on the edge of their beds, to sketch little humorous 'picshuas' with his fountain pen, which referred to incidents in the course of the day, or were variations on a repertoire of favourite themes, like 'How to Avoid Being Eaten by a Crocodile' or 'The Good Dadda and the Bad Dadda', the one which Gip requested for that evening. He had brought each of them a toy sand yacht from Le Touquet, and depicted the Good Dadda as a man weighed down like Santa Claus with presents for his children, while the Bad Dadda turned his back on his two sons and wouldn't let them play with their own toy soldiers. They put on a show of being amused, but he could tell they both thought a Good Dadda was one who stayed at home and a Bad Dadda was one who was always going away.

The lunch for Anatole France, held in a private room at the Savoy overlooking the Thames, went off well. He deliberately arrived a little late, just before they sat down, to avoid any inquisitive personal questions from guests who might have picked up rumours of an elopement. But no one looked surprised to see him, so he assumed that he was not, for the time being, the object of gossip. Arnold Bennett was there, and he managed, in the gentlemen's cloakroom, to have a confidential word with him about Amber. 'You do believe in living dangerously, don't you, H.G.?' Arnold said in a tone which implied, *Rather you than me.'* 'I believe in living,' he said, rather more jauntily than he felt.

Afterwards he decided to return to Sandgate to change from his best suit, which would be no use to him in Le Touquet, into more casual clothes, and to stay another night. He wired Amber to say he would be returning the next morning, but after breakfast (eggs, bacon, kidney, tomato, mushrooms . . .) the boys clamoured for a holiday from lessons and a war game on the schoolroom floor, and he indulged them. The game, which lasted into the afternoon, was a way of extending his enjoyment of the comforts of home while avoiding too much private talk with Jane. She was naturally curious about how things were going in France, but had the tact not to press him. He told her something in vague general terms, making light of the problems and inconveniences of his domestic life with Amber, and concealing their failure so far to arrive at any satisfactory plan for the future. He suspected however that she was not deceived on either count.

He got back to Le Touquet in the evening to find Amber in a sulky and resentful mood at being deserted for much longer than she had expected, and when, a few days later, he hankered after accepting an invitation to one of Lady Desborough's weekend house parties she turned on him.

'You prefer Lady Desborough's company to mine, then?' she said.

'Not at all, Dusa,' he said. 'I want to go because she hinted that both Asquith and Balfour are going to be there—the Prime Minister and the ex-Prime Minister. It will be a fascinating conjunction, especially with Lloyd George's budget plans in the air. It's an opportunity to eavesdrop on history. I wish I could take you with me.'

'Why can't you?'

'You know very well why, Dusa. Don't be silly. The invitation is to me and Jane. If I turned up with you on my arm it would cause huge scandal, and embarrass Lady Desborough.'

'Are you proposing to take Jane, then?'

'She wouldn't want to go,' he said, though in fact his mind had been playing with just that possibility. 'She finds these grand country house parties rather intimidating.'

'And what am I supposed to do with myself while you're enjoying yourself among the aristocracy?'

'Well, you could do some work on your thesis,' he said—unwisely, for it inflamed Amber's temper all the more to be reminded of her lack of progress on that project.

'My thesis? My *thesis*?' she almost screamed. 'How am I to work on my thesis in a French seaside resort, without books or a decent library?'

'Well, you should have brought some books with you,' he said. And the row degenerated into a petty argument about what it was or was not feasible to pack into two valises at short notice for an excursion abroad of indeterminate duration, ending with Amber in tears and himself apologising for being a beast and promising to decline the invitation. They sealed their reconciliation by going to bed early to make love.

The next day, when he was reading on the veranda, she came out and told him that her monthly period was a week overdue and she was sure she was pregnant. 'Can you be certain so soon?' he said, looking up from his book. 'I'm usually as regular as clockwork,' she said. 'Aren't you pleased?' 'Of course I'm pleased, Dusa,' he said. 'Well you don't look very pleased,' she said sulkily, all the tenderness of the night before apparently forgotten. 'I'm delighted if it's true,' he said. 'It's just that Jane never said anything to me until she was at a rather more advanced stage.' 'Oh that's just like Jane,' Amber said. 'Always so considerate. She probably didn't want to disturb you. I'm sorry I interrupted your reading for such a trivial reason.' And she flounced back into the house. He was filled with misgivings about the future: they had only been living together for three weeks and already they were squabbling serially. And for the first time Amber had shown a little spasm of jealousy towards Jane—that was a very worrying sign. But how could he extricate himself from this relationship with honour and with no injury to Amber? He went for a long solitary walk on the beach to consider the question. There was only one possible solution as far as he could see.

At the beginning of May he announced that he had to go back to England again to attend to urgent business matters with Jane and to reassure the boys. Amber agreed reluctantly and accompanied him on the electric tram that connected Le Touquet to Boulogne harbour to see him off, waving forlornly from the quay as the packet boat drew away. He didn't go immediately to Sandgate, but to London, and took a cab from Victoria station to Lincoln's Inn, where Blanco White's chambers were situated. He was told Mr Blanco White was in court, but should be back in an hour or so. He said he would wait, and did so for an hour and a half, the object of occasional curious glances from the clerks, who evidently recognised his name and perhaps knew something of the scandal associated with it. Blanco White gave a start when he came into the outer office, with a bulging briefcase in one hand and more papers under his arm, and saw him rise to his feet. 'May I see you for a few minutes—privately?' he said. Blanco White nodded. 'Please follow me,' he said curtly, and led him up a narrow staircase of worn bare boards to a tiny office where there was scarcely room for the desk and two chairs that faced each other across it. Blanco White removed a pile of briefs from one of the chairs and bade him sit down, then seated himself on the other side of the desk. He was a pale-faced young man of unexceptional looks, neither handsome nor ugly, with dark hair symmetrically centre-parted and flattened down with Macassar oil, and a longish chin that gave his countenance a look of determination. 'What can I do for you, Mr Wells?' he said.

'I suppose you hate me,' he began. 'I wouldn't blame you—in your position I'd feel the same.'

'I don't hate you,' Blanco White replied evenly. 'I disapprove of you. I think your conduct towards Amber has been disgraceful. But I don't hate you. Lawyers shouldn't hate—it warps one's judgment.'

'Well, I will try to emulate your dispassion,' he said. 'I don't mind admitting that I have harboured some uncharitable feelings towards you in recent months. If you hadn't gone to Mr Reeves and told him all about me and Amber, contrary to your promise to respect her confidence—'

'I did what I considered to be my duty,' Blanco White said.

'Quite so. Anyway, I didn't come here to reproach you. What's done is done, and what matters is the future.'

He had had plenty of time to prepare his speech. Hard as Blanco White might find it to believe, he hadn't seduced Amber in the usual melodramatic sense of the word, an older man exploiting a young girl's innocence. He had fallen genuinely in love with her and she with him. His wife knew about the relationship and all three of them were true friends. It had been Amber's idea—a bad idea, he realised too late—to seal their attachment, when it seemed under threat, by conceiving a child. It was not absolutely certain that she was pregnant but it seemed very probable. They had gone away to France to think over the situation in peace and quiet, and to formulate a plan for the future. He had to admit that they had failed. He had come to the conclusion that English society was simply not ready to tolerate an experiment in human relations such as they—himself, Jane and Amber—had attempted. The only secure future for Amber and her child was marriage, and he couldn't marry her because he was already married with a wife and children he couldn't bear to be separated from.

'Shouldn't you have thought of that earlier?' Blanco White interjected.

'Perhaps,' he said, suppressing the impulse to defend himself. 'The point is this. I still love Amber, but it seems to me that the best way I can express that love is to let her go—into the care of a man who will cherish and protect her.'

'You mean myself?'

'Exactly.'

Blanco White was silent for a moment before he said: 'I love Amber. I have always loved her since we first met. I have several times offered to marry her in spite of her deplorable relationship with you. She has consistently refused me.'

'I think I could persuade her that it is the best thing to do,' he said. 'If you are still willing.'

'I am willing—and if there is a child, I would adopt it as my own.'

'That's very handsome of you.'

'Provided of course that she terminates her relationship with you.'

'Of course,' he said.

They didn't actually shake hands on it, but that was the understanding between them when he left.

He spent the night at Spade House and explained to Jane that the experiment of living with Amber on the Continent for a few weeks had been a total failure and that he thought she should marry Blanco White. 'I see,' she said calmly. 'You don't seem surprised,' he said. 'Nothing you do could surprise me any more, H.G.,' she said. 'But will Blanco White marry her?' 'Yes, I saw him this afternoon,' he said. 'The problem will be persuading Amber.'

He took a boat from Folkestone to Boulogne the next morning, and arrived at the villa in Le Touquet to find Amber reclining on a chaise longue in the front parlour, covered with a blanket and wearing a martyred expression. It appeared that she had fallen down the stairs in the middle of the night, as she groped her way to the lavatory in the dark, hurting herself in the process. Fearing that she might have endangered her baby she had remained lying against the bottom steps until Marie, the woman who cleaned and cooked for them, arrived in the morning. Seriously worried by this account, he immediately summoned a doctor, who examined Amber carefully and declared that she had sustained no serious injury and that it was very unlikely that the foetus, if there was one, would have been affected. When the man had gone he asked Amber why she hadn't got Marie to fetch a doctor as soon as she arrived, and the answer, that she didn't trust

Marie to get a good one, was unconvincing, especially as the doctor he summoned himself was recommended and fetched by Marie. When he pointed this out she accused him of harrying her with pointless questions instead of sympathising with her plight. He couldn't suppress the suspicion that the accident on the stairs had in fact been a minor one, which Amber had wanted to present in the most dramatic way possible, to make him feel that it was somehow his fault for being absent. 'You don't really care about me,' she complained. 'You go off back to England whenever you feel like it, leaving me here all on my own at night. It's not fair. It's certainly not kind.'

'Well, I'm sorry, Dusa, but I can't live here like an exile,' he said. 'I have a family and a career to look after in England—I have to go back from time to time.'

'Well then I don't see the point of us being here.'

The unsayable had been said—fortunately by Amber. They contemplated it in silence for a moment, until he said: 'It's not really working, is it?'

Amber slowly shook her head.

'Then we'd better go back,' he said.

'But to what?' she exclaimed. 'To where? It's easy for you to say, "go back", but I can't live with you and Jane, not permanently, and I can't go home—I can never go home now. I don't want to live alone in some poky London flat waiting for you to call on me when you can spare the time from "your family and your career",' she went on, sarcastically echoing his own words, 'afraid to go out and meet people in case they cut me or, even worse, pity me, as it becomes obvious that I'm pregnant. What do you suggest I do?'

'You could marry Blanco White,' he said.

She stared. 'You're not serious?'

'Quite serious. I saw him yesterday in London. He's a very decent young man, and he's still keen to marry you.'

Amber threw back her head and gave a slightly hysterical laugh. 'Oh is he really? So you went to see him and offered to give me back to him, did you? Without consulting *me*. The great champion of women's rights, the fearless critic of the patriarchal family, is prepared to get rid of his trouble-some mistress by palming her off on some chivalrous lawyer she doesn't love. Did you offer to give me a dowry as an incentive? Or has money already changed hands?'

He had expected a tirade like this, and patiently absorbed her anger and her insults, waiting for her to run out of steam. The energetic way she strode up and down and gesticulated while she raged at least reassured him that she had sustained no serious injury. Then slowly he began to chip away at her resistance to the idea of Blanco White as a spouse. All right, she didn't love him, not in the way they loved each other, but there were many happy marriages founded on affection rather than passion, his own being an example, and she had admitted more than once that she liked Rivers, and valued his affection and loyalty to her. He was a fine young man, serious and responsible, and had every prospect of a successful legal career. And he was ready to provide for the child, to adopt it as his own—that was the crucial thing. There wasn't another man in England who would do the same. He went on and on in this vein for two hours or more, countering every objection Amber could raise, demonstrating that no other solution was possible, until she said wearily at last, collapsing on to the chaise longue and closing her eyes, 'All right, I give in. It's obvious that you want me off your hands.'

'That's not true, Dusa,' he said.

'Yes, it is. Tell Rivers I'll marry him.'

This was the hardest moment for him in the epic argument. He longed to take her in his arms and tell her that he still loved her and that giving her up was the hardest decision he had ever had to make in his life, but he was afraid that if he did so there would be another reconciliation, another passionate consummation, and they would be back where they started. So he hardened his heart, and said, 'When will you meet him?'

'The sooner the better,' she said, her eyes still closed as if to block out visions of the future.

He went into the town and sent a telegram to Blanco White to say that Amber had agreed to marry him and asking if he could meet her at Folkestone next day off the packet that departed from Boulogne at twelve noon. He received a reply the same evening, '*WILL MEET AMBER AT CUSTOMS STOP AM APPLYING FOR SPECIAL LICENCE.*'

He escorted Amber to Boulogne in the morning and saw her aboard the boat. It was an overcast day, chilly for May, and the sea beyond the harbour had a sullen grey aspect, flecked with whitecaps. Amber was pale-faced, having brought up her breakfast earlier from either anxiety or morning sickness, and expressed the hope that she wouldn't be punished for her sins by seasickness as well. She had evidently decided to conceal whatever emotion she was feeling behind a brittle ironic wit, and he had a feeling that he was more likely to break down at their parting than she was. He placed her in a corner of the first-class lounge and made her comfortable with a rug obtained from a steward. The ship's hooter sounded a warning blast. 'You'd better get off the boat,' she said. 'It would be too silly if you had to hand me over to Rivers in the Folkestone customs shed like a bartered bride.' When he leaned forward to kiss her goodbye, she presented her cheek, not her lips. 'Goodbye, Dusa,' he said. 'Safe journey.' 'Goodbye, Master,' she said, and at last there was a note of tenderness in that name. He hurried away before he made a fool of himself by bursting into tears.

In a shop near the harbour he bought a bottle of cognac, and that evening drank himself into unconsciousness, something he did very rarely. He was woken the next morning by Marie's entrance into the parlour where he had fallen asleep fully dressed on the chaise longue. He spent a miserable day suffering from combined headache and heartache until he went for an icy swim in the late afternoon, after which he felt better, and slept reasonably well that night without the assistance of alcohol. But it was not until the following day, after receiving an economical telegram from Blanco White, '*MARRIED YESTERDAY AT KENSINGTON REGISTER OFFICE*', that he began to plan a life without Amber.

First he summoned Jane and the boys to join him immediately, to make use of the rented villa. Gip and Frank were delighted to have this unexpected seaside holiday, and he enjoyed taking them for walks along the beach, shrimping in the pools left by the outgoing tide, and getting them to practise their French in shops and *glaciers.* Marie was somewhat shocked to discover that there was another, genuine Madame Wells, but adapted to the change of regime quickly, recognising in Jane someone who knew very well how to run a house. Blessedly relieved of all domestic concerns, he made a start on a new novel. It was to be a funny novel, somewhat in the style of *Kipps,* with no politics or sex problems or big ideas, about a hen-pecked, indifferently educated, unsuccessful, small-town shopkeeper who would eventually and almost accidentally rebel against his fate. It began:

> '*Hole!*' *said Mr Polly, and then for a change, and with greatly increased emphasis:* "*Ole!*" *He paused, and then broke out with one of his private and peculiar idioms.* '*Oh! Beastly Silly Wheeze of a hole!*'
>
> *He was sitting on a stile between two threadbare-looking fields, and suffering acutely from indigestion.*

The book was a kind of escape from all the preoccupations of his private and public life in recent years, converting the experience of frustration and disappointment they had caused him into liberating, life-enhancing comedy. He chuckled a good deal to himself as he wrote; but there were also times when he would be suddenly reminded of Amber, overwhelmed by the sense of what he had lost, and he would carry on writing some farcical scene with tears wetting his cheeks.

As the days passed he became more and more certain that he did not want to go back to Spade House and pick up the threads of his accustomed life there. The place had been spoiled for him for ever by the failure of the great experiment in 'triangular mutuality' between himself, Amber and Jane. Giving up Amber had been necessary, but it had been a negative achievement, a kind of defeat. He had to start a new life in a new place. He outlined his plan one evening to Jane: they would move to London. It was the obvious place for both of them to be. He was sick of the hours wasted travelling up and down on the wretched South Eastern Railway. He would be at the centre of literary life, and she would have easy access to the concerts and art exhibitions that she liked to attend. 'But the boys will miss the sea and the countryside,' she objected. 'They've been so happy and healthy there.' 'We'll get a house in Hampstead,' he said. 'Near the Heath—plenty of fresh air and walking there—and near the new Tube station—the West End only twenty minutes away. Perfect!' He did not mention—though it was a consideration he privately added to the balance in favour of the move—that now his great love affair was over he would more easily find consolation in the opportunities for *passades* that the capital afforded.

Jane put aside her doubts, as she usually did when he had made up his mind to do something, and played her part in persuading the boys of the superior attractions of London over Sandgate. He couldn't wait to get on with the business, and took them all back to Spade House a week before the villa's lease expired. He knew that Henry Arthur Jones was a frequent resident at the Folkestone Hotel, which he evidently found a congenial location in which to write his very lucrative plays, so might be tempted by the idea of a place of his own on the same part of the south coast. He accordingly wrote to him: '*It just occurred to me that you might like to think of buying my house. Don't be alarmed! But I want very much to leave this place and live in London soon by reason of a web of almost impalpable reasons that affect people of our temperament, and the house is therefore in danger of going very cheap.'* Henry Arthur Jones took the bait, and negotiations for the sale proceeded with unexpected smoothness.

He and Jane went to look at houses for sale in Hampstead, and his choice fell on one in Church Row, a street of elegant Georgian town houses which led from the main thoroughfare of the village to the parish church of St John, and was conveniently near the Underground station. Its architectural design—basement kitchen, a pair of rooms divided by folding doors on the ground floor, another pair on the first floor, and two floors of bedrooms above—was one that he had often criticised in the past, and he was conscious of a certain inconsistency in choosing it, but it was part of his wish to open a wholly new chapter in his life. He had created a model modern house at Sandgate, and had enjoyed his years in it, but now he fancied something different, something old, dignified, and steeped in history. Church Row, which had seen so many famous residents in its time, and the church itself, with its memorial to John Keats and the graves of John Constable and George du Maurier among others in its churchyard, had the kind of ambience he desired. He felt a twinge of conscience at condemning his servants to labour in a basement kitchen, and climb so many flights of stairs, but he had plans to modernise it and make it as easy to run as such a home could be, and although it had fewer bedrooms than Spade House, they would have fewer guests to accommodate than in the past, since most of their visitors at Sandgate came from London. Thus and thus did he quell any doubts he entertained or Jane voiced. He made an offer which was accepted, but he bought the house in Jane's name, renouncing the usual privileging of a husband over his wife in the matter of property. At least, that was how he presented it to Jane; but it also made him feel freer in spirit knowing that, if the 'fugitive impulse' should ever possess him again, her home would be secure. They would not get vacant possession till August, and it was still only June, but he tempered his impatience for the move by reflecting that they would enjoy one last summer beside the sea, and got on with *Mr Polly*.

Then there was a surprising development, heralded by a letter in his post one morning with Amber's familiar handwriting on the envelope. He had banished all thought of Amber since she left: if ever his mind veered in that direction, triggered by some memory or chance association, he wrenched it back to focus on another topic. In particular he savagely stifled any private speculation about what she and Blanco White might be doing, or where they might be living, and no information on this matter had reached him from outside sources. Jane quickly learned not to say idly, 'I wonder how Amber is getting on?' He thought he had managed to draw a line under their affair, but the mere sight of her handwriting was enough to make his heart beat faster. He tore open the envelope and read the brief note inside. It said that she was married to, but not living with Rivers, for reasons too complicated to explain in a letter. She was staying temporarily with friends in Hertfordshire, and he could visit her there if he cared to hear the full story. She was definitely pregnant, and suffering from morning sickness, but otherwise well and hoped that he and Jane were too. The letter was addressed to 'Dear Master' and signed 'Dusa'.

The news that Amber was not living with Blanco White jolted him with a powerful charge of irrational satisfaction. But why wasn't she? He showed the letter to Jane. 'Oh dear, they must have broken up already,' she sighed. 'Amber seems to live from one crisis to another.' 'I must go and see her,' he said. 'Is that wise?' Jane said, giving the letter back to him. 'I don't care whether it's wise or not, I must know what's happened,' he said, and wired Amber to say he was coming to see her the next day.

She was staying in a village near Hitchin with the family of an old school friend whose parents (the friend herself was absent) received him with wary and somewhat disapproving looks and ushered him into the drawing room where Amber was waiting. She looked surprisingly well, and as beautiful as ever, and he knew at once that he had not expelled her from his system—she was in him like a virus, in his body, blood and brains. Only the presence of her hosts checked his impulse to embrace her. It was a fine day, and they went out through the French windows into a land-scaped garden and found a bench at the bottom in the shade of an oak tree, where she told him her story.

It was full of drama, and emotional twists and turns that would have strained the credence of a novel reader. The self-possessed manner with which she parted from him at Boulogne had been, as he suspected, a pre-tence. Inwardly she had been depressed and despondent, a mood that deep-ened into despair as the packet churned its way towards England. What was she doing, going to marry a man she didn't love, with another man's child in her womb? Was it fair to Rivers, never mind herself? She felt she had messed up her life irretrievably, and a lot of other people's lives as well. She was seriously tempted to throw herself into the sea and end it all. 'I actually tried to climb the ship's rail to see if I could bring myself to do it, but my skirt was too tight. I was saved from suicide by my vanity,' she said with a wry smile. A steward spotted her struggling with her skirt with one foot on the lower rail, and escorted her away from danger. He locked her in a cabin, came back shortly with a cup of tea, and chatted to her until the boat docked. 'I would like to thank that man,' he said. 'I would like to give him a reward. What was his name?' 'I've no idea,' she said. 'But he was very nice. He didn't tell me off. He just said, "Nothing's really as bad as it seems when you're down, Miss," and then chatted about his family.'

As she lined up on the deck to disembark she wondered if perhaps Blanco White had had second thoughts too, and would not be waiting to meet her—but he was there, reliable as always, at the end of the customs shed, in a dark suit and a bowler hat, with a furled umbrella in his hand, as if he had just stepped out from Lincoln's Inn. He greeted her shyly, kissed her on the cheek, and asked how the crossing had been. She didn't tell him that she had nearly thrown herself into the sea halfway through the voyage. As they walked to the boat train preceded by her porter he told her that he had made an appointment for them to be married in the Kensington register office at eleven o'clock the next morning, and had booked her into a nearby hotel for the night. She was taken aback by the short notice and asked if it had to be so soon. 'There's no point in delaying,' he said. 'I know your parents will be delighted when we tell them we are married, but if we tell them in advance they'll want to be involved, and they would expect you to live with them in the meantime. Do you want that?' 'No,' she said, emphatically. 'Let it be tomorrow, then.' 'We will have to postpone a proper honeymoon, I'm afraid,' he said with a nervous smile. 'But I've got tomorrow—Friday—off, so we'll have a long weekend at least. I've booked us into a hotel on the Thames, near Henley. Then one of the KCs in my chambers has very generously offered us the use of his pied-à-terre in Bloomsbury until we've found somewhere ourselves.'

There were other passengers in their compartment whose presence inhibited further conversation on any but the most banal subject, and in fact they passed the journey mostly in silence. Rivers was plainly pleased with himself for the efficiency of his arrangements, but Amber was appalled as the full consequences of her decision became real to her for the first time. The word 'honeymoon' had sent a shaft of apprehension through her. It wasn't that she found the idea of sex with Rivers repulsive, but it was bound to be extremely embarrassing, both of them being conscious that she had been until yesterday another man's mistress, and was probably pregnant by him. She had a shrewd suspicion that Rivers was not sexually experienced, and might very well be a virgin—so how would they manage the wedding night? Should she help him and risk shocking him by her immodesty, or leave him to humiliate himself by his own clumsy efforts? It didn't bear thinking about, but she could think of little else until they got to the hotel in Kensington, by which point she had made up her mind what to do.

He had booked for her a small suite with a separate sitting room, so she ordered tea to be served there, and told him to stay while she changed from her travelling costume. Then over tea and scones she made a frank declaration: she would marry him next day, but on one condition, that until her child was born it would be—she was about to say '*un mariage blanc*', but just stopped herself from making the dreadful pun—an unconsummated marriage. Anything else, she said, would be indelicate, indecent, it would make her feel like a harlot being passed from one man to another. But after nine months or so of chaste companionship, after her child was born, and adopted by him as he had generously offered, she thought they could begin to have a real marriage. She fully expected him to reject this condition, and half hoped that he would, but to her surprise he welcomed it with visible relief. It seemed that similar thoughts had been exercising him, and he agreed with everything she had said. He cancelled the honeymoon weekend and they moved directly into the borrowed flat. 'But the chaste companionship didn't really work,' she said. 'It didn't last two weeks.'

Amber was happy with the arrangement, but Rivers increasingly was not, for reasons he could empathise with. To live in close proximity to that delightful creature, to share a small flat with her, to glimpse her dressing and undressing, however discreet she tried to be, and not to be able to make love to her, must have been an intolerable strain. At first Rivers negotiated permission for certain modest embraces and caresses, but when he showed signs of wanting to go further she resisted and accused him of breaking their contract. Rivers said he found the situation intolerable, and she said in that case they should live apart until the baby was born. He was reluctant to accept this solution, but while he was brooding on it she wrote to her friend in Hertfordshire and secured an invitation to stay with her. The loan of the flat was due to terminate soon and fortunately they had not yet committed themselves to other accommodation, so she packed her valises and told Rivers she was leaving. And that was her story to date.

'Where is Rivers?' he asked.

'He's gone back to his bachelor rooms at the Inns of Court,' she said. 'He visited me here last week. He's been to see Father and Mother, and told them that we are married but living apart by mutual agreement until the baby is born.' She stroked her stomach, not yet visibly altered, in a tender, automatic gesture as she pronounced this last phrase. 'They were pleased he's made an honest woman of me of course, but a bit concerned about how I'm going to manage on my own while we are separated.'

'And how *are* you going to manage, Dusa?' he said.

It soon became clear that she had invited him to Hertfordshire to get his advice and assistance on this point. She could not stay with her friend's family much longer without imposing on them. She had very little money, not enough to find decent accommodation for herself in which to prepare for the birth of their child, and she couldn't ask her father to increase the modest allowance he made her without putting herself back under his authority—or risking his cutting it off altogether. Rivers had offered to find her rooms in London somewhere, but she feared that this might prove the thin edge of a wedge of renewed intimacy and corresponding tension.

'You can stay with us as long as you like,' he said.

'Thank you, but that wouldn't be a good idea,' she said, shaking her head. 'If it got back to Rivers, and my parents—and it would be bound to—there would be terrible ructions. Rivers would say you'd gone back on your word, and with reason. What I'd really like is a place of my own in the country—somewhere like this village, I love it here. Somewhere Rivers could visit me, but not too often.'

'Leave it to me,' he said.

There were times in the next few weeks when he felt more like an estate agent than a writer. He was selling his own house, and arranging to buy another in Hampstead, as well as looking for a country cottage for Amber, all at the same time. *It eats up time and brains,* he wrote to a new friend, Elizabeth Robins, asking for her help in the third of these tasks. She was a distinguished actress, and a friend of Henry James, in whose first play she had starred, but she was better known these days as a feminist novelist and playwright. He had met her recently at a dinner party and on discovering that she had some property in the country near London he sought her help in finding a suitable cottage for Amber. When in the course of their correspondence Miss Robins learned the facts of his relationship to the young woman on whose behalf he was acting, she delivered some sharply disapproving remarks about Free Love and recommended him to be quit of the entanglement. He replied angrily: *'Have you ever in your life known what it was to have a community of flesh & blood & pain & understanding with another human being? You can't get quit.'* In spite, or possibly because, of this outburst, Elizabeth Robins shortly afterwards offered for rental a cottage belonging to herself at Blythe, a hamlet outside the village of Woldingham, in a lush bit of Surrey near Caterham. He went to see it, and it was perfect—a thatched cottage with leaded casement windows and a walled garden with fruit trees. He wrote to Elizabeth Robins: *'I wrote you a cross rude letter & I bow beneath your feet. (But you were wrong about me.) I'm putting Amber into Blythe.'* By early July Amber was installed there. He paid for a six-month lease, renewable—the baby was due early in the New Year—and undertook if necessary to subsidise Pember Reeves's allowance to cover her living expenses.

'What exactly are you trying to achieve?' Jane asked him one day, watching him frowning over the lease. 'To help the young couple, of course,' he said. 'To bring some stability into a very volatile situation.' Which was true up to a point, but it was also true that by taking the initiative in the matter of the cottage he had found a loophole in the terms of his surrender of Amber to Blanco White, who was resentful of his intervention, but lacked the means to offer Amber an acceptable alternative. The marriage had not been consummated, and Amber was living apart from her husband to bring *his* child into the world. This surely gave him a moral right to continue to see her. And who could say what might happen in the future? Divorce would be easy if Dusa and Blanco White both desired it. And if she liked the country life as much as she claimed, perhaps the idea of being his mistress, with a home of her own, might not seem so alien to her as before. He wrote jauntily to Arnold Bennett at the end of July, congratulating him on a new play which had just opened in London, *'and bye the bye, it may interest you to know that that affair of philoprogenitive passion isn't over. The two principals appear to have underestimated the web of affections and memories that held them together. The husband, a perfectly admirable man, being married attempted to play a husband's part. Violent emotional storms ensued and I think it will be necessary out of common fairness to give him grounds and have a divorce—and run a country cottage in the sight of all mankind. I tell you these things to strain your continence, knowing you will tell no one.'* But in August he wrote to reassure Miss Robins that *'There will not be a divorce—a quite satisfactory treaty has been made about that. I shall be about at Blythe a good deal and Blanco White will come down for weekends. Everybody is going to be ostentatiously friendly with everybody & honi-soit-qui-mal-y-pense. Amber seems likely to be very happy in Blythe.'* He took care to add: *'At present she has two puppies & my two little boys to satisfy her abounding maternity—while we move to Hampstead.'*

To send Gip and Frank, accompanied by Miss Meyer, to stay with Amber for two weeks while he and Jane attended to the move from Sandgate was not only very convenient—it was the best possible advertisement for their enlightened attitude to sexual relations. If people who regarded such arrangements as depraved could read Amber's letter to Jane as the boys' visit approached its end, and note the complete absence from its language of any hint of tension, animosity or jealousy—on the contrary the sustained tone of relaxed affection between the two women—they might be forced to revise their opinions. Jane had passed it to him at breakfast. *'Dearest Jane, Many thanks for your sons. They have been perfectly delightful and I'm awfully sorry they are going . . . I tried to wring from the boys some admission that perhaps they would like to come again . . . You'll come yourself as soon as you really get over the house, won't you? . . . Did you know that one rub of Wood Milne shoeshine keeps boots bright for days? I see from a bill head on my desk that it does. Thought you might find the hint useful . . . Dear Jane what ought one per week prepare ahead for four people? Rivers and H.G. and visitors.'* He sometimes thought that if he could publish the complete correspondence of Amber and Jane in the *Times* the controversy about Free Love and their own practice of it would subside like a punctured balloon, but since that was impossible he did his best by soliciting the support of respected and influential people such as Elizabeth Robins. There was no way to stop the circulation of rumours and reports of his elopement to France with Amber, her pregnancy, the hasty marriage to Blanco White, and its sequel, especially in Fabian circles, so he wrote to as many potential sympathisers as he could think of, putting his side of the story in a favourable light.

The Reeveses' relief at the marriage of their daughter quickly evaporated when they learned that her seducer was still seeing her and paying the rent for her cottage, and there was a good deal of sympathy for them among the Fabians. The Old Gang obviously regretted that they couldn't expel him from the Society because he was no longer a member, but Pease wrote frostily to Jane requesting that she resign her position on the Executive in view of circumstances well known to her, which threatened to bring the Society into disrepute. The Webbs were particularly appalled by these circumstances and began to interfere. Sidney, using Shaw as an intermediary because he was too angry to write himself, deplored his inflammatory self-justifying letters, and declared that the honourable thing for him to do would be to find an excuse to go abroad for a year. But Shaw passed on the message in a tone of urbane detachment that would have displeased its originator. *'Webb is pretty savage with you for writing to keep up the agitation. He wants you to go away to the East for a year, and write a book about oriental marriage customs, to keep you from making mischief with occidental ones,'* he wrote, and took a surprisingly sympathetic line about his continuing involvement with Amber and Blanco White: *'It is entirely proper that the young couple should have the friendship of such a distinguished man if they are lucky enough to get it. And A. is such an ungovernable young devil that nothing short of a liberal allowance of interesting society will ever keep her from the wildest adventures. So if you will follow the negative part of Webb's program (no more letters) and omit the Asiatic part, matters will proceed very properly, gossip or no gossip.'* He was delighted to receive this letter, so different in tone from the lecture Shaw had given him about the Rosamund affair, and replied at once: *'My Dear Shaw, occasionally you don't simply rise to a difficult occasion, but soar above it & I withdraw anything you would like withdrawn from our correspondence of the last two years or so . . . Matters are very much as you surmise. Amber has got a little cottage in Blythe, Woldingham. B.W. works in London, & goes down in his leisure time. I like him and am unblushingly fond of her & go down there quite often. The Reeves don't know how often & the heavens will fall if Reeves finds out.'* Pember Reeves was more incensed than ever with 'the blackguard Wells and his paramour', as he apparently referred to them in conversation with his friends, and it was in fact hard not to feel some compassion for him. Disappointed in his hopes of returning to political life in New Zealand, he had resigned as High Commissioner earlier that year to accept an appointment as Director of the London School of Economics, only to find at the outset of his first academic year in post that the whole institution was buzzing with the scandal surrounding its most celebrated postgraduate student, his daughter.

It was reassuring to have Shaw on his side at this time, especially when Beatrice Webb began to get involved, writing peremptorily to Amber early in September, *'You will have to choose—and that shortly—between a happy marriage and continuing your friendship with H.G. Wells.'* Astonishingly, she seemed to have only recently heard of the whole history of their affair—Sidney must have shielded her from the gossip as long as he could. She declared that the Webbs' friendship with himself was at an end, and commenced a vicious defamatory campaign against him, as he discovered one day when he was staying with Sydney Olivier, home on leave from Jamaica. Olivier, opening his mail at breakfast, gave a chuckle as he was perusing a letter, and passed it to him: 'Here's something that will make you laugh, Wells.' It did not. It was a circular letter signed by both the Webbs but obviously written by Beatrice, to *'all our friends who have daughters between the ages of fifteen and twenty'*, warning them of the predatory sexual habits of H.G. Wells where innocent young girls were concerned. He immediately fired off a brace of furious letters to Sidney, threatening a libel action, which according to Shaw frightened him into making Beatrice desist from her poisonous letters—but not from involvement in the affair.

When he arrived at the Blythe cottage one day towards the end of September Amber greeted him with the announcement, 'Beatrice Webb was here yesterday.'

'Really? What did she say?'

'She said I should break off all relations with you and live either with Rivers as his wife, or if I don't want to do that, live with my family, and that if I go on seeing you in this irregular way I will eventually be cast out of decent society, and probably end up as fallen women usually end up in novels. Well, she didn't say that in so many words, but that was the gist of it.'

'Beatrice Webb is an interfering bitch with the soul of an old maid, married to another old maid,' he said angrily. 'She looks at you, radiant with the expectation of motherhood, and feels only envy and spite. What business has she coming down here?'

'Well, I asked her to, actually,' Amber said.

He stared. 'Why on earth did you do that?'

'I used to like the Webbs. They were important influences on me when I was a young girl, and I admired Beatrice particularly. I was rather touched when she wrote to me the other day, giving me her advice. I wanted to try and explain how we saw things. It wasn't any use, though.'

'Of course it wasn't.'

'But she sincerely wanted to help. When I said there was no possibility of my going back to live with my family she offered to try and arrange a reconciliation, and she really meant it.'

'Beatrice can't help us—she's stuck in a rigid moral framework built on foundations in which she herself doesn't really believe.'

'She kept saying—"But you have to choose, my dear girl—between Blanco White and Wells—you can't have them both, society won't let you. If you want your husband, you must go back and live with him. If you want Wells—though I can't imagine why you should—you'll have to divorce your husband, and Wells his wife," and I said, "Well, I've got them both at present, Rivers and H.G., and we get along very nicely together." And she said, "You don't mean to say that your husband will tolerate that state of affairs indefinitely?" And I said, "Well, we have hopes of him," and she threw up her hands in dismay—or surrender.'

He laughed. 'Good for you, Dusa!'

In fact Blanco White's view of the situation was obscure. It was understood between them that his own relationship with Amber was now chaste, and this was also the basis of his self-justifying missives to friends and enemies. He and Amber had not cheated on this contract, in spite of some temptation early in her residence at the cottage, and as her belly swelled it ceased to be an issue. Pregnancy in a curious way gave her back a kind of virginity, or at least chastity. She presided over the cottage like a Virgin Queen, with himself and Blanco White as courtiers dancing attendance on her, and she obviously rather enjoyed the role. She beguiled the time when she was alone by writing a novel, and even began to learn a few housewifely skills from Esther, the very competent cook and 'general help' they had hired locally. Blanco White was polite and friendly to him in a reserved sort of way on the rare occasions when their visits to the cottage coincided, but they avoided discussion of personal matters, talking instead about politics, mainly the long-running struggle between the government and the Lords over Lloyd George's 'People's Budget', which threatened a constitutional crisis and had the whole country enthralled. Considering the amount of gossip and attention the young man must be attracting as he went about his professional work, he was conducting himself with admirable dignity and restraint—but what would he want after the baby was born? It was hard to imagine him approving an arrangement he and Amber speculatively discussed, of her continuing to live at Blythe as Mrs Blanco White, perhaps with a female companion for respectability's sake, visited discreetly by himself and her husband at different times. He thought that Blanco

271

White must have in mind a future less like the conclusion of *In the Days of the Comet,* but was not inclined to press him on the matter and risk disturbing the delicate balance they had achieved at Blythe.

He had brought with him to the cottage an advance copy of *Ann Veronica: A Modern Love Story*, which Fisher Unwin were about to publish as their leading title of the season, and he presented it to Amber with a twinge of misgiving. He had not shown it to her before in any form, feeling that it was Jane's prerogative to read his work first, and Jane when she read the proofs had said, 'You know this will be taken as the story of you and Amber, don't you?' He had rejected the prediction, pointing out all the differences between the fiction and reality which he had taken care to establish. 'Ann Veronica comes from a much more suburban background than Amber, and is much more naïve. She goes to London University not Cambridge, and studies biology not philosophy—' 'Mere details,' Jane said, 'that anyone can see through.' 'And there are two characters much more like me, or people's notion of me, than Capes is,' he continued, 'and Capes is divorced by his wife in the end but we're not going to get divorced—ever.' And he gave her a kiss to underline the point, which pleased her. Still the conversation unsettled him, and he knew in his heart that he had kept the novel from Amber's eyes out of a fear that if she saw it she would demand changes and deletions that he could not bear to make. Lately she had been expressing curiosity about the book, and he could postpone showing it to her no longer. She took the volume, elegantly bound in reddish brown cloth with gilt lettering and decoration, exclaiming 'At last!', and opened it by chance at the dedication page. '*"To A.J."* Who is that?' 'A composite of Amber and Jane, of course,' he said. She smiled, and said she would take it up to bed and begin it before she went to sleep.

The next morning she came down late to breakfast looking pale and haggard, with the book in her hand, having sat up all night reading it. 'Ann Veronica is me,' she said accusingly. 'This is our story.' 'No, it's not, Amber,' he said testily, and went through the same arguments he had used on Jane, with the same lack of success. It always annoyed him that people didn't understand that fiction could only be made out of life, and there wasn't a decent novel written by anybody which didn't have a good deal of the writer's experience in it, but that didn't license them to treat the whole thing as biography. 'They will, though, given half a chance, and you've given them much more,' Amber said. 'Even the name "Ann Veronica" sounds like an anagram of mine.' 'But it isn't,' he pointed out pedantically.

'It's near enough,' Amber retorted. 'And she takes a course in jiu-jutsu! All my Cambridge friends will recognise that. Why did you put it in?' 'I don't know,' he said feebly. 'And this is the worst possible time to publish it!' she said. 'It's bound to draw attention to our relationship.' She was of course absolutely right, but until now he had managed to exclude from his consciousness this obvious truth. 'Can't you stop it?' she asked. 'I'm afraid not, Dusa,' he said. 'It's too late. The books are already in the booksellers' stockrooms, the review copies have already been sent out. We must just batten down the hatches and sit out the storm.'

And a storm there was, though it built up slowly. The early reviews of *Ann Veronica* in the *TLS* and the *Athenaeum* were favourable, but there was a warning of what was to come in the *Daily News,* from R.A. Scott-James. *'As a novel it is a brilliant and interesting one,'* he wrote. *'But as everyone knows, Mr Wells uses the novel as a medium for expressing his views. I maintain that Mr Wells's psychology is wrong in its foundation. He is right in his protest against the modern world, against its lack of opportunities for development, but it is not frustrated sex impulses which are responsible for the evil; they are merely a symptom; you will not put things right by promoting some mighty sex-passions.'* This was a fair point, responsibly argued. But a review by the pseudonymous 'John O'London' in *T.P.'s Weekly* took a more populist and polemical line. *'Decidedly, then,* Ann Veronica *will be read and talked about this winter by the British daughter. All I can say is that I hope the British daughter will keep her head. That Mr Wells's story may do considerable mischief is too clear.'* John O'London feared that the British daughter, faced with temptation, might quote and act on Ann Veronica's words to her married lover: *'To have you is all-important, nothing else weighs against it. Morals only begin when that is settled. I don't care a rap if one can never marry, I'm not a bit afraid of anything—scandal, difficulty and struggle . . . I rather want them. I do want them.'*

In retrospect this speech seemed something of a hostage to fortune. He and Amber now had plenty of scandal, difficulty and struggle to bear, and neither of them found it pleasant. The novel was banned by the circulating libraries, denounced by the National Social Purity Crusade, the Young Women's Christian Association, the Mothers' Union, and the Girls' Friendly Society. It was anathematised from the pulpit, one canon declaring that *'I would as soon send a daughter of mine to a house infected with* diphtheria or typhoid fever as put that book into her hands.' The same kind of public condemnation that had been visited on *In the Days of the Comet* now descended on *Ann Veronica*, but with increased intensity, fuelled by gossip that the central love affair in the story corresponded closely to one in which the author was currently involved. The revised ending he had added to the novel in which Ann Veronica was legally married to a divorced Capes and reconciled with her father and aunt made no difference to the outrage of the moralists, and was frequently picked on by literary critics as contrived, so that he regretted now that he hadn't been more honest and left his principals living in sin.

All this controversy was of course good for sales, and Fisher Unwin were rubbing their collective hands as the orders poured in, more than compensating for the circulating library ban. But the sales figures did not compensate for his own discomfort. He was conscious that he had become an object of pity and a cause of embarrassment to some of his friends, and that they were avoiding him. He received fewer invitations to social events, and when he put in an appearance at his clubs, members he recognised at a distance seemed mysteriously to disappear from sight if he took his eyes off them. If he was not mistaken, Henry James performed this vanishing trick at the Reform one day, and sent a letter subsequently, acknowledging the gift of *Ann Veronica,* in which his attempt to praise and damn the novel in the same long exhalation of breath was more than usually strained: '*The quantity of things <u>done,</u> in your whole picture, excites my liveliest admiration—so much so that I was able to let myself go, responsively and assentingly, under the strength of the feeling communicated, and the impetus accepted, almost as much as if your "method" and fifty other things—by which I mean sharp questions coming up—left me <u>only</u> passive and convinced, unchallenging and unenquiring (which they <u>don't</u>—no they don't!)*'

His old adversary John St Loe Strachey, editor of the *Spectator,* had a much more decided opinion of *Ann Veronica*, though he waited till late November to deliver it. The piece was unsigned, but his style of magisterial condemnation was unmistakeable from its title, 'A Poisonous Book', onwards.

> *The loathing and indignation which the book inspires in us is due to the effect it is likely to have in undermining that sense of continence in the individual which is essential to a sound and healthy State. It teaches in effect that there is no such thing as a*

woman's honour, or if there is, it is only to be a bulwark against a weak temptation . . . If an animal yearning or lust is only sufficiently absorbing, it is to be obeyed. Self-sacrifice is a dream and self-restraint a delusion. Such things have no place in the muddy world of Mr Wells' imaginings. His is a community of scuffling stoats and ferrets, unenlightened by a ray of duty or abnegation.

Strachey concluded by brushing aside possible defences of Ann Veronica's conduct by quoting Samuel Johnson. '*Boswell tells us of a conversation in which he defended with sophistical excuses a woman who had betrayed her husband. Dr Johnson cut him short with his immortal—"My dear Sir, never accustom your mind to mingle virtue and vice. The woman's a* ———, *and there's an end on't."*'

He had hopes of keeping this review from Amber's eyes, but he discovered when he next visited her that some anonymous person had sent it to 'The Occupier' of the cottage in Blythe, and she had it ready to show him. 'I've seen it already,' he said. 'It's vile.' 'What word is represented by the dash at the end, I wonder?' she remarked, affecting a detached curiosity. 'I believe it's "*whore*",' he said. 'But Strachey is too mealy-mouthed to print it.' 'I see,' she said, and flushed perceptibly. A few minutes later she said she was feeling tired, and went to her room, obviously upset. He cursed the malicious person who had sent the review. At first he suspected Beatrice Webb, but on closer examination the hand on the envelope looked more like that of Hubert Bland, who could have got the address from Beatrice, and would certainly be gloating over the hostile reception the novel was getting, and want to make sure Amber saw this particularly wounding specimen. By a strange coincidence Rosamund Bland had at last got married that month to Clifford Sharp, just as the publication of *Ann Veronica* brought the scandal of his affair with Amber to the boil—or perhaps it wasn't coincidence, perhaps the spectacle of them heading for a public smash had frightened Rosamund into matrimony with the man her parents favoured. But it was a queer repetition: his two young mistresses married off to faithful younger swains in the same year.

He received a letter from Violet Paget, a friend to him and his work for many years, who wrote under the name of 'Vernon Lee'. Rumours of the scandal in which he was enmeshed had reached her ears, and she wrote expressing concern. He replied summarising the situation candidly, and concluded: *'There you are! You won't for a moment tolerate it I know—nobody seems going to tolerate it—I won't leave my wife whose life is built up on mine or my sons who have a need of me. I won't give up my thinking and my meeting with my lover. I mean somehow to see my friend & my child & I mean to protect her to the best of my power from the urgent people who want to force her to make her marriage a "real one".'*

It was a relief to write this letter, but he was well aware as he read it through how illogical and impracticable his defiant stance would seem to the recipient. He sent the letter anyway, but he was beginning to weary of the struggle, feeling like a stag at bay, bleeding and exhausted, surrounded by yapping hounds. He suspected that Amber and Jane were beginning to weary too, though neither of them admitted it. Jane did not visit Amber at Blythe, but corresponded with her and bought baby's clothes which he took down there. It was fortunate that they had just moved to London, for in Sandgate Jane would have been the object of local gossip; their Hampstead neighbours were less inquisitive, or concealed their curiosity behind more urbane manners. But he was guiltily aware that some of Jane's London friends and acquaintances had 'dropped' her, or found excuses not to accept her invitations.

As to Amber, she became more and more passive and contemplative as her pregnancy advanced, moving slowly about the cottage as if drugged, her thoughts focused on the coming child. Sometimes she would take his hand and place it on her belly to feel the baby kick, and then he would gently stroke the convexity through her smock, round and round in circles with the tips of his fingers—it was the closest they came to making love these days. 'Do you want a boy or a girl?' he asked her as he was doing this, sitting beside her on a sofa facing the fire, one dark afternoon early in December.

'I don't mind,' she said.

'I hope it's a girl,' he said. 'I'd like to have a daughter, as brave and beautiful as you.'

She smiled. 'And what would you call her?'

He thought for a moment. 'Anna Jane,' he said eventually. ' "Anna" because it's about as close as you can get to Amber without causing confusion—'

'And because of Ann Veronica?' she interjected.

'Perhaps . . . And "Jane" because she's been such a brick in all this.'

'Very well, if it's a girl "Anna Jane" shall be her name,' said Amber. 'Providing Rivers agrees of course.'

'Of course,' he said. But the reminder of Blanco White's prerogative depressed him somewhat, and he continued stroking her belly in silence.

'He was here yesterday,' she said after an interval.

'Was he? He doesn't usually come in midweek.'

'He wants me to go back to him,' she said.

'Does he?' he said, trying not to show how much this statement disturbed him. 'And do you want to?' He stopped the massage.

'I don't know,' she said. 'Sometimes I think, for the baby's sake, I should. I'm very isolated here, when neither you nor Rivers is down.'

'I'll arrange for you to have a proper nursemaid when you bring the baby here,' he said—it had already been agreed that she should go into a nursing home at his expense to have the baby.

'Thank you, H.G., but . . . it's not just the baby,' she said. 'Rivers is not prepared to go on like this. He said to me yesterday, "This nonsense has got to stop before you have the child." '

'Did he? He's got on a very high horse suddenly. What did you say to that?'

'I said he'd have to talk to you.'

'Rivers can talk to me until he's blue in the face,' he said, 'but he won't make me give you up.'

'He seems to think he can.'

'How?'

'I don't know,' she said.

When he got back to Hampstead the following day there was a letter from Blanco White, requesting a meeting at his chambers; not so much a request, in fact, as an order, giving him a number of possible times in the coming days. He chose the earliest and made his way by Tube to Lincoln's Inn the next morning with a sense of foreboding. This confidently assertive Blanco White, described by Amber and expressed in his letter, was a quite new persona, and there must be some reason for it.

When he presented himself at the chambers he was not directed to the crowded little office at the top of the stairs where they had had their previous conference—how long ago it seemed!—but ushered into a kind of boardroom with a big rectangular table of dark polished wood and upright chairs, and left there for some minutes to twiddle his thumbs and stare at the glass-fronted cabinets full of legal books, before Blanco White appeared with several manila folders in his hands. 'Good morning,' he said stiffly, and sat down on the opposite side of the table. He placed the folders on the polished surface and squared them up with his hands. 'Thank you for coming,' he said, without a trace of warmth in his voice. 'I don't think I will detain you for long. I am speaking, you understand, as a lawyer representing myself as Amber's husband. The charade at Blythe has gone on long enough. Amber must return to me as my wife, and you must sign an undertaking not to see her or communicate with her for a minimum of three years. I have it here.' He slid one of the folders across the table.

'Amber must decide for herself,' he said without touching the folder. 'But I'm damned if I'll sign any such undertaking.'

'Then I will sue you for libel,' Blanco White said calmly. 'I have here'—he patted the remaining folders—'a number of sworn affidavits from highly respected persons stating that they recognised the character of Ann Veronica in your novel as a portrait of Amber, and it is a plainly defamatory portrait. You have no doubt read the article in the *Spectator*— "the woman's a whore, and there's an end on't," and similar comments in other journals.' The lawyer's countenance was impassive, but there was a gleam of triumph in the eyes.

He attempted a derisive laugh, he blustered and jeered, he said he would see Blanco White in court, and he walked out of the room leaving the folder with the undertaking unopened on the table. But he knew in his heart he had lost. There was no way he could defend a libel suit without Amber being required to appear in court as a witness, and he couldn't possibly put her through such an ordeal even if she were willing. He went directly from Lincoln's Inn to Blythe and told Amber of Blanco White's ultimatum.

'Did you know he was going to do this?' he asked her.

'Not exactly, but I knew he was going to bring matters to a crisis of some kind,' she said.

'And do you want to go back to him and give me up?'

'I don't want to give you up, Master,' she said. 'But I think perhaps we have no choice. We've come to the end of the road. It's been a great adventure, and I shall miss you terribly, but for the sake of our child—and for Jane's sake, because it isn't fair to expose her to the horrible gossip and slander any longer—I think it will be best.'

She began to weep, and he put his arms round her and wept too.

He delayed the process, he quibbled over the terms of the undertaking, reducing the term of three years to two, he withdrew his offer to pay for the nursing home (Pember Reeves would have to pick up the bill), but he signed the undertaking in mid-December, by which time Amber had left the cottage and been admitted to the nursing home in London to await the birth of her child. Since the legal agreement did not take effect till the beginning of the New Year he visited her there and accompanied her on walks in nearby Hyde Park, but this was his last gesture of defiance. He sought distraction from the inevitability of their parting in the preparations for the family's first Christmas in the new house, and Jane arranged a pre-Christmas lunch party on the 22nd of December for Arnold Bennett, Robert Ross, Constance Garnett, the Sidney Lows, William Archer—and May Nisbet, whom they still entertained at holiday times by long tradition. Henry James was invited, but sent an unconvincing apology, no doubt disturbed by the spreading ripples of scandal. He asked Arnold to arrive early and took him into his study to tell him the whole story of the last nine months. 'I don't know how you could stand the strain of it, old man,' Arnold observed finally. 'Neither do I,' he said candidly. 'There were times when I nearly cracked up, I can tell you.' 'But now it's all over, you must feel some relief.' 'I feel numb,' he said. But he managed to simulate enough cheerfulness at the lunch to make it go off pretty well.

The next day he received a letter from Violet Paget, responding to his defiant one. As always, what this lady had to say was thoughtful and thought-provoking. Although she had found his story *'easy to understand, easy to sympathise with, even easy to excuse, it jars with some of the notions deepest engrained in me. My experience as a woman and as a friend of women persuades me that a girl, however much she may have read and thought and talked, however willing she may think herself to assume certain responsibilities, cannot know what she is about as a married or older woman would, and that the unwritten code is right when it considers that an experienced man owes her protection from himself—from herself.'* Violet was no prude or puritan, but a lesbian who did not conceal the fact from her friends. If *she* thought this way, there had really never been any chance that he and Amber could have carried off their daring experiment in human relations. Violet added that *'In all this story the really interesting person seems to me to be your wife, and it is her future, her happiness for which I am concerned,'* a sentiment for which he blessed her. The only good he could see in the end of the affair was that Jane was quietly and untriumphantly relieved that the long struggle was over.

On New Year's Eve he received a message that Amber had given birth safely to a baby girl, and he wrote to Violet with the news:

> Dear Friend,
>
> I have a little daughter born this morning. You wrote me the kindest letter & I clutch very eagerly at the friendship that you say is still mine. I don't think there is any faultless apology for Amber & me. We've been merry & passionate—there's no excuse except that we loved very greatly and were both inordinately greedy of life. Anyhow now we've got to stand a great deal—of which the worst is separation—& we're doing it chiefly for love of my wife & my boys.
>
> Best wishes for the New Year
> H.G. Wells

PART FOUR

PART FOUR

I

—It was strangely appropriate that Amber gave birth on the day you finally had to give her up, the last day of the year—the last day of the *decade* indeed—marking the end of a chapter in your life.

—And it also marked the end of my association with the Fabian.

—Though you'd already resigned, in 1908.

—I resigned over policy issues. But what you might call sexual politics continued to be a cause of contention between me and the Old Gang, apart from Shaw. My affair with Amber, following on from the one with Rosamund, brought their disapproval to the boil. When it became public they turned their backs on me completely. There was no further possibility of my collaborating with them to convert Britain to socialism.

—Was it ever likely in the long run?

—Probably not, in hindsight. But we might have come to that conclusion in an amicable, reasonable manner, and without wasting so much time and energy on futile intriguing and backbiting.

—In *Experiment in Autobiography* you take some of the blame for that. '*No part of my career rankles quite so acutely in my memory with the conviction of bad judgment, gusty impulse and real inexcusable vanity, as that storm in the Fabian teacup.*'

—It *was* partly my fault. But it was because I believed in the sexual liberation of women, and acted on that belief, that we fell out. I didn't seek scandal, I didn't boast about my relationships with women to whom I wasn't married, but if these affairs became public knowledge through no fault of mine, I refused to deny or apologise for them. It was my openness, or brazenness as they saw it, and the fact that Jane supported me, that shocked and frightened people like Pease and the Blands and the Webbs. But of course I couldn't write openly about that in the *Autobiography*.

—Granted that you were trying honestly to live out your belief in Free Love, wasn't it rather tactless to do so with the virgin daughters of prominent Fabians?

—I didn't pursue them: they went after me. And I could never refuse an overture from a woman—it just isn't in my nature.

—You weren't getting your own back on your opponents in the Fabian by deflowering their daughters?

—There might have been a bit of that in the affair with Rosamund, I suppose. It started just after Pease and Bland and Sidney Webb began to block my attempts to reform the Society. I can't say I was irresistibly attracted to her, and there was a kind of satisfaction in undertaking the sexual education of this girl under her hypocrite father's nose. But Amber was a genuine love affair. I missed her horribly after we had to part.

—These were both very young women, half your age. Looking at the matter from the point of view of those who disapproved, your affairs put them under tremendous emotional pressure, alienated them from their parents for long periods, thrust them into the complexities of adult relationships before they were fully mature, and made them objects of wounding gossip and scandal. Was this fair on them?

—Well, all I can say is that neither of them bore me any resentment. I had a letter from Amber to that effect just before the war which pleased me greatly.

He looks in a filing cabinet where he keeps especially valued private correspondence and soon finds the letter, filed under 'Blanco White, Amber' and dated August 25th 1939. She had written to thank him for a copy of *The Fate of Homo Sapiens*, just published.

> *Dearest HG, We got back last night from Wales to find your book—it will be something to occupy our thoughts, a god-send. At a time like this, when life as we know it seems to be ending for all of us, one's thoughts go back, and even if there were not the book to thank you for I think I should have written to thank you—What you gave me all those years ago—a hope that seemed perfect to me, the influence of your mind, and Anna Jane—have stood by me ever since. I have never for a moment felt that they were not worth the price.*

—Generous words.

—Amber is a very generous person.

—**You don't think she might have had a more distinguished career if she hadn't been led or pushed by you into adultery, motherhood, and marriage before she was twenty-four?**

—She's had a fulfilling life since then.

—**But she was one of the brightest students of her generation. She might have had a brilliant academic career without the distractions of her involvement with you.**

—I know that's what they said at Cambridge, and probably still say, but Cambridge always thinks it is the hub of the intellectual world. It isn't. Amber has had a very creditable career. She found her métier as a lecturer in philosophy and psychology at Morley College, teaching adults, ordinary men and women—especially women—who were excluded from conventional university courses but hungry for knowledge.

—**A worthy achievement, but not really a fulfilment of her promise.**

—I don't think Amber was ever going to develop into a really original philosopher or sociologist—she's one of those people who reach their peak as students, who are quick to take hints and tips from others and synthesise them into something that looks bright and new, but she lacked the persistence and self-belief necessary to produce the real thing. She did good work for me in her contributions to *Work, Wealth and Happiness,* but it was essentially a deft digest of secondary sources.

—**What about her novels? She published several after you split up.**

—They were perfectly competent, and one of them, *A Lady and Her Husband,* which came out in 1914, was really good—about the cosseted middle-aged wife of a successful businessman who suddenly wakes up to the wage-slavery on which her quality of life is based. But the others were rather formulaic. In the end she lacked the courage to confront and explore her own personal experience in fiction.

—**Perhaps she didn't want to embarrass Blanco White.**

—Perhaps. But if you want to be a true novelist you can't afford scruples of that kind. I've embarrassed a few people in my time.

—**Indeed. Including Amber.**

—She forgave me for Ann Veronica. But I don't suppose Blanco White would have forgiven her for portraying him in a novel. In the end a woman writer has to choose between putting her marriage or her vocation first, especially if there are children—and Amber chose her marriage.

—Considering its inauspicious beginnings, it has lasted remarkably well.

—It certainly has. Ironic that Blanco White was made a Divorce Commissioner when the Divorce Law was liberalised. He's Recorder of Croydon now, I believe. Not a glorious legal career, but a solid one. He's an honest fellow.

—Did *he* forgive you?

—I don't think so, not really, but he finally agreed to shake hands and put his feet under my table at a rather sticky lunch party at Easton Glebe in the twenties, and after Jane died it became easier to meet him and Amber socially.

—You didn't meet Rosamund socially.

—No.

—She had a rather unhappy life after her affair with you.

—Don't blame me—blame her parents for pushing her into marriage with Clifford Sharp. He became an alcoholic—lost his job as editor of the *New Statesman*, and was never able to hold down another one. Rosamund remembered that I had warned her against marrying him.

The few letters he possesses from Rosamund are filed under 'Bland', conveniently next to 'Blanco White'. He takes out one dated 29th January. There is no year on it, but it must have been about 1929. She was writing to ask permission to use his portrait on a cigarette card. Sharp was in New York, looking for a job, and she was at home, desperately hard up and staving off creditors, working part-time in an advertising agency. '*Strangely enough I remember I gave you a promise on the seashore at Dymchurch twenty-two years ago that I would tell you if ever I was stranded. You told me then that Clifford would be no good to me. How horribly terribly right you were! Of course a promise like that doesn't mean anything on either side, except that I remembered it & you probably didn't.*'

—I did, of course.

—You gave her the permission?

—And a cheque, though she hadn't asked for any money. Neither did Amber, after we parted, not for Anna Jane nor herself—though I wish she had, because I discovered later that she'd been terribly poor early in the first war. They were both very straight, honourable young women, who truly loved me and didn't want to sully their affection with any mercenary obligation.

There is another letter from Rosamund in the file, sent years earlier, prompted by seeing a portrait drawing of him by William Orpen. *'Clifford came home the other night & thrust a page of "The Tatler" under my nose, saying, "There's H.G. for you". And it really was. Orpen is awfully clever. He had put down all that is essentially you & nobody did that before. This is the real H.G. who writes unforgettable and darling things, the H.G. one loves & always loved and couldn't misunderstand. This was once my H.G. & I think in one deep place in me is still my H.G. Now that I have put that it seems rather cheek because it is really the other way round. Last winter I made a discovery. I was ill in bed for five months, fairly sure I wasn't going to recover and during the better times I re-read your earlier books—all that I read at nineteen or twenty. I found that what I thought of as "Rosamund" was simply something made up of H.G. Wells. It was a shock to find that there was no "I" at all, that thoughts and feelings I had supposed my own were all to be found in you.'*

—It was sweet of her to say so, but I was sorry she had such a weak sense of her own identity. She became a disciple of that charlatan Ouspensky at some point.

—**Didn't she write a novel too?**

—Yes. A very strange one. *The Man in the Stone House.* The heroine is a twelve-year-old girl who falls innocently in love with a writer of detective stories. He hates women because one betrayed him in the past, but finds himself reciprocating the girl's love. In the denouement another little girl is murdered by a child molester, and the writer murders *him* and goes off round the world planning to return when the heroine will have grown up. It begins like one of Edith's stories for children and then turns into something adult and dark. Rosamund actually called herself "Rosamund E. Nesbit Bland" on the title page.

—**Hoping her mother's name would help sales no doubt.**

—Well it didn't, I'm afraid.

—**And she didn't write any more novels?**

—No. A pity, because *The Man in the Stone House* is well written in parts.

—**It's a rather sad story, her life.**

—The whole family's history was sad, after Edith's boom came to an end. They'd squandered all the money on lavish entertaining, so when her sales declined they became hard up and had to sell the Other House. Edith became obsessed with the theory that Shakespeare was really Francis Bacon and frittered away a lot of time on that, and Bland was going blind, so his earnings fell off too. He was totally blind when he died in 1914.

—D'you think it was syphilis?

—It crossed my mind, given the kind of life he led.

—**The existence of syphilis is perhaps the most cogent argument against Free Love.**

—It needn't be if precautions are taken. I always used sheaths when prudence dictated it. But Bland probably didn't because it was against his absurd religion.

—**Did you see Edith after he died?**

—She wrote out of the blue a year later, in the middle of the war, and told me that she was selling vegetables at the gates of Well Hall to make ends meet. It was the first contact I'd had with her since my affair with Rosamund. I've lost the letter, but I remember she said, *'Don't you think there ought to be a time limit for quarrels?'* I think she was hoping I would visit her.

—**And did you?**

—No. I couldn't forget or forgive her vicious letters to Jane after the Paddington station episode. I replied politely, with belated condolences for Hubert's death, but didn't propose a meeting. I heard she married again a few years later.

—**A sailor, wasn't he?**

—A sort of sailor. Tommy Tucker. He was a marine engineer in charge of the Woolwich Ferry and known as 'Skipper'. The children thought he was a bit déclassé, I believe, but he looked after her till she died in 1924. They had to sell Well Hall after the war and lived in a couple of converted air force huts on the Romney Marshes near Dymchurch, which they called the 'Long Boat' and the 'Jolly Boat'.

Berta Ruck told him the story after Edith died—Berta who had been a frequent guest at Well Hall in the glory days, and whom Edith had helped with her early attempts at writing romantic fiction. They quarrelled about something, as one did with Edith, and had no communication for fifteen years, until one day Berta got a letter from Iris Bland to say Edith was seriously ill, and went down to visit her. Skipper said 'Welcome aboard!' when he opened the door of the Long Boat, or perhaps it was the Jolly Boat. Berta said it was as if Edith had passed into one of her own stories, living in picturesque genteel poverty, but there was no happy ending up the author's sleeve. She was dying of lung cancer. She was very pleased to see Berta, and be friends again, and Berta visited her several times before she died, and read to her. The first time, Berta said, it was from *Jane Eyre,* and the second time Edith asked for a chapter from *Kipps.* He was touched by that, and regretted that he hadn't taken the opportunity to be reconciled with her when she wrote to him about having a time limit for quarrels.

—Many people thought you changed after 1910—that you became rather hard. Outwardly cheerful, sociable, but more selfish, more calculating, less forgiving.

—I had to become hard. I'd been under extreme stress for the past year over the Amber affair, I'd been vilified and slandered publicly and privately, and I'd lost her in the end. I'd uprooted my family and settled in London to begin a new life. I'd given up the hope of using the Fabian as a way of getting my ideas into the public domain. From now on my books would be the only vehicle. I was on my own. I had to be hard.

The first book he published in the new decade, in the spring of 1910, was *The History of Mr Polly,* a novel that bore no obvious trace of the sexual scandals and ideological controversies in which he had been involved over the past few years. Mr Polly and the other principal characters were all lower middle class, poorly educated, and sexually innocent or unadventurous. Perhaps for that reason the novel received a rather muted reception, as if the reviewers were puzzled or disappointed by the absence of controversial content, and only gradually did it prove to be one of his most popular novels. It was seen by the critics as a throwback to earlier work like *Kipps*—which to some extent it was. But this comic idyll conveyed a quite subversive message to those who knew how to read it: that a man could break all the rules of law and society and still live happily ever after. Mr Polly intended to escape from a barren marriage and an unrewarding occupation by committing suicide, setting fire to his shop in the process so that his widow would get the insurance money, but he bungled the operation, failed to kill himself, set fire to several other shops as unsuccessful as his own, whose proprietors gratefully received the insurance, and made himself into a hero by rescuing an old lady from one of the burning buildings. He pocketed most of his own insurance money and deserted his wife to live like a tramp, settling down eventually as the odd-job man and chaste companion of the motherly landlady of a riverside inn, and successfully fought off a violent rival claimant by a mixture of luck and cunning. In the denouement the rival stole Mr Polly's clothes but was accidentally drowned, and his corpse identified as that of Mr Polly, who was thus enabled to live at the inn under a new name for the rest of his happy life, while his wife benefited from yet another insurance policy. It was the most immoral story he had ever written, but the British public received it without a murmur of disapprobation because there wasn't a word in it about sex.

The next novel, however, *The New Machiavelli*, which he had been working on in tandem with *Mr Polly*, was a very different and much more provocative book. It was written in the loquacious, discursive, first-person style of *Tono-Bungay*, combining the narrator's personal history with a broad-ranging survey of the condition of England, but with a much more political slant. The novel in fact drew closely on his own disillusioning involvement in politics over the past decade. The hero, Richard Remington, studied Political Science at Cambridge and became a radical journalist in London, where he met and married Margaret, a woman with ambitions to be the wife of a leading politician, and stood successfully for Parliament as a Liberal. Disillusioned before long with both the Liberal and Labour parties, Remington decided that his ideal state—'*England as our country might be, with no wretched poor, no wretched rich, a nation armed and ordered, trained and purposeful amidst its vales and rivers*'—could only be achieved by recruiting the powerful men of business who actually made the wheels of modern society turn, the more idealistic of whom might be persuaded to form a Samurai-like elite of dedicated leaders. To this end he crossed the House to join the Conservative Party, and started up a progressive Tory faction, with its own publication, the *Blue Weekly*, assisted in this enterprise by an attractive and unconventional young woman called Isabel Rivers. By this time he was estranged from his wife, who never satisfied him sexually or shared his political vision, and soon he was in love with Isabel and she with him. When their affair became the subject of scandal his career was jeopardised, and to save his reputation Isabel prepared to marry a man she respected but did not love. In the end they could not bear to part, left London, '*the slovenly mother of my mind and all my ambitions*', and went to live on the Ligurian coast where, comparing himself to Machiavelli in exile, Remington wrote the story of his life.

In the latter part of the narrative he relived the drama of his relationship with Amber, but rewrote its actual, anticlimactic conclusion to make his fictional self appear more of a tragic hero, in the tradition of 'all for love, or the world well lost'. In the earlier part he settled some scores with the Fabians, especially in the characterisation of Altiora and Oscar Bailey, a couple who ran a political salon from a house very like the Webbs' home in Grosvenor Street.

> *She was a tall and commanding figure, splendid but a little untidy in black silk and red beads, with dark eyes that had no depths, with a clear hard voice that had an almost visible prominence, aquiline features and straight black hair that was apt to go astray like the head feathers of an eagle in a gale . . . Oscar had none of the fine appearance of his wife but he had a quite astounding memory for facts and a mastery of detailed analysis. He soon achieved the limited distinction that is awarded such capacity, and at that I think he would have remained for the rest of his life if he had not encountered Altiora . . .*

He was in no doubt that these characters would be identified as portraits of Beatrice and Sidney Webb, but was confident that he had said enough flattering things about them, especially about Beatrice, to take the edge off the sarcasm and ensure that they would not sue him for libel. And although he could not deny that the concluding sequence of the novel closely paralleled the climax of his affair with Amber, what he wrote about Isabel in the book was a kind of love letter to Amber which she would treasure rather than resent, with intimate details drawn from their life together (such as Isabel's habit of calling Remington 'Master') that only she would recognise; and he did not think Blanco White, having won one crucial contest with him by threatening a libel suit, would risk all the unpleasant publicity of another for little gain.

Publishers however were extraordinarily pusillanimous about the book. Macmillan had contracted to publish it on the basis of the author's description and did not find time to read it until the proofs came in, when he was horrified by the narrator's candour about his sexual life, and found 'twice as much reason' for rejecting the novel as in the case of *Ann Veronica*. The publisher tried to persuade first Heinemann and then Chapman and Hall to take the book off his hands, but both declined for fear of libel suits, even after he sent Amber a copy of the novel and she wrote him a helpful and friendly letter saying she and Blanco White saw no grounds for legal action in it. Eventually John Lane, who was something of a specialist in publishing risky books of literary merit, took the novel, and brought it out in January 1911. They were both thoroughly vindicated: there were no libel suits, and he even heard indirectly that Beatrice Webb had been impressed by the book and declared the caricatures of herself and Sidney to be 'really very clever in a malicious way'.

The novel attracted considerable attention when it was serialised in the *English Review* in the latter part of 1910, and was widely reviewed when it was published in January 1911. It was generally received as an impressive but flawed novel, though the flaws were differently identified by different critics: it was the looseness of the narrative structure, or the tedium of the hero's long digressions on political and social issues, or the malicious portraits of real personages, or the excessive attention to the hero's sexual problems, or something else. Henry James sent from America, where he had accompanied his brother William in his final illness, one of his characteristic homilies disguised as panegyrics: '*Your big feeling for life, your capacity for chewing up the thickness of the world in such enormous mouthfuls, while you fairly slobber, so to speak, with the multitudinous taste—this constitutes for me a rare and wonderful and admirable exhibition, on your part, in itself, so that one should doubtless frankly ask oneself what the devil, in the way of effect and evocation and general demonic activity, one wants more.*' But of course, James did want more—or rather less, less matter, more perfectly formed. '*I make my remonstrance—for I do remonstrate—bear upon the bad service you have done your cause by riding so hard again that accurst autobiographic form which puts a premium on the loose, the improvised, the cheap and the easy.*' He did not want to argue, let alone quarrel, with Henry James, because of the respect he felt for the older writer, and because he empathised with him at this time of grief for the recent death of William, so he responded graciously to his criticisms, trying to perform the same trick as H.J. by receiving them as tributes: '*So far as it is loving chastisement I think I wholly agree and kiss the rod. You put your sense of the turbid confusion, the strain and violence of my book so beautifully that almost they seem merits.*'

Nevertheless, he was conscious that the novels he intended to write in the future would be of roughly the same kind as *The New Machiavelli*, and would never satisfy the accepted criteria for literary fiction. He felt it expedient therefore to issue a manifesto for a different kind of fiction, using as his platform a public lecture to the Times Book Club on 'The Scope of the Novel', presenting himself as the member of a new movement whose work was going to supersede the novel of character and personal relations. *'We are going to deal with political questions and religious questions and social questions. We cannot present people unless we have this free hand, this unrestricted field . . . We are going to write about business and finance and politics and precedence and pretentiousness and decorum and indecorum, until a thousand pretences and ten thousand impostures shrivel in the cold, clear, draught of our elucidations . . . Before we have done, we will have all life within the scope of the novel.'* The event was reported in the *New Age* by Arnold Bennett, the only other potential member of this new movement he could have named if challenged, who described the audience somewhat flippantly as *'the "library" public in the mass . . . a thousand women and Mr Bernard Shaw',* but approved his argument and gave it valuable publicity by his article.

The New Machiavelli was also the occasion, or pretext, for the entry of another significant woman into his life: the Countess Elizabeth von Arnim. He had been slightly acquainted with her since 1907, when Constance Smedley, feminist author and founder of the very successful Lyceum Club in London for Women Artists and Writers, introduced her to him, and he had long been well aware of her reputation as a writer—how could one not be? *Elizabeth and her German Garden* had been the literary sensation of 1898. A short, stylish narrative that was published as a novel but read as if it were autobiography, rendered all the more teasingly enigmatic by the fact that no name other than the one in the title appeared on the title page, it told the story of an English, or at least English-speaking, woman married, not altogether happily, to an impoverished Prussian Junker referred to throughout as *'the Man of Wrath',* who had made her the mother of three little girls with scarcely more than a year between them, referred to as *'the April baby, the May baby and the June baby'.* To escape the tedium of life in a city apartment Elizabeth took to spending much time in her husband's neglected and unproductive country estate in Pomerania, where she created in the teeth of many obstacles and discouragements a beautiful English garden as a refuge and a joy for herself, and where she entertained various guests whose egotism and insensitivity were observed with subtle Jane-Austenish irony. The book proved irresistibly readable, especially to women, who relished the narrator's spirited resistance to her husband's patriarchal prejudices, but English male readers also appreciated its mischievous satire

293

on German manners, and both sexes enjoyed Elizabeth's descriptions, lyrical and comic, of her horticultural enterprise. The mystery of the work's authorship added to its appeal. It quickly became the best-selling book of the season, went through eleven reprints in its first year, ten more in the second, and (he learned on good authority) in due course earned the writer £10,000 in royalties. Jane was enchanted with the book and made him read it, which he did in one sitting and pronounced it clever but slight, a verdict in which there was an element of professional jealousy since its sales made those of *The War of the Worlds*, published in the same year, look comparatively modest.

By the time he met the author her identity was widely known. She had published several more books, not so successful as her first but not negligible, and borne two more children to the Count. At that first meeting, however, he gathered that the Man of Wrath was languishing under the oppression of illness and financial troubles, and Elizabeth was in command of the family and the main source of its income. She was petite, with a neat figure that curved in and out at the right places in spite of all her childbearing, and features that were pleasant to look at without being beautiful or even conventionally pretty. As he had expected, she was amusing company, but there were glimpses of real intelligence and unexpected talents—as a musician, for instance—beneath the small talk. He liked the little Countess, but when she invited him to lunch with her at the Lyceum Club, where she was staying, he declined politely, having too many other pressing claims on his time and attention, mostly connected with the Fabian, to cultivate this new acquaintance. Later Constance Smedley, evidently prompted by Elizabeth, wrote to say that the latter had been hurt by the refusal and was still very eager to meet him again, even if it meant travelling to England especially for the purpose, and he sent her a bland message apologising for any unintended discourtesy and issuing an open invitation to visit him in Sandgate at any convenient opportunity.

Elizabeth found one quite soon. That summer she brought her children to England for an original kind of touring holiday through the southeastern counties in hired horse-drawn gypsy caravans, with the intention of making a book out of it. The holiday was cursed by the wettest summer in living memory, and while the party was taking shelter from the bad weather at Leeds Castle they motored over to Spade House for lunch, after which the von Arnim children played floor games with Gip and Frank while the adults chatted, Jane and Elizabeth getting on very well together.

The weather which had inconvenienced the von Arnims became a source of incidental comedy in the novel based on the holiday, called *The Caravaners*, which was received with acclaim when it was published a year or so later and created an imitative cult of such holidays among literary folk.

He heard no more from or about the little Countess until 1910, when he learned indirectly that her husband had died, and that she had moved to England with her children to pursue her literary career. She demonstrated her versatility that same year by writing a play of feminist sentiment called *Priscilla Runs Away* which had a triumphant first night and a long run at the Haymarket Theatre. He knew from his own limited experience of the theatre, and vicariously through Arnold's more numerous ventures in that medium, that this was a remarkable achievement, and he couldn't help admiring the Countess's consistent ability to tickle the public taste without pandering to it. Elizabeth meanwhile was reading *The New Machiavelli* with unrestrained admiration as it was published in instalments in the *English Review*. '*You must forgive me for bothering you with my extreme joy over your wonderful Machiavelli,*' she wrote in November, when the serialisation came to its end. '*Never did a man understand things as you do—the others are all guess and theorise—you know—& the poetry of it, and the aching, desolating truth—what one longs to read, written by you, is the story of the afterwards—what happened as the dreadful ordinary years passed.*' She concluded by expressing a hope of seeing him again. He wrote a note to thank her for her generous praise of his book, and added a PS that if she happened to be free one day in the coming week he would be glad to give her lunch and take her for a walk on the Heath, since Jane would be away visiting an old friend in Devon and he would be in need of company. She replied by return of post that she would call the following Tuesday unless she heard from him to the contrary, and was as good as her word.

He took her to lunch at an inn in the Village and afterwards, the weather being fair, for a long walk on the Heath. He learned a good deal about her that afternoon, for she spoke with remarkable candour about her life. She had been born in Australia as Mary Beauchamp, the daughter of a prosperous shipping merchant, a first-generation immigrant who brought his family back to England when she was only three. She and her siblings had a good education in England and for a time in Switzerland, but as a young woman her ambitions and expectations had been very conventional, untouched by feminism and focused on making a good marriage. To this end her father took her on a tour of the Continent where they met and were impressed by Count Henning August von Arnim-Schlagenthin, whose maternal grandfather was a nephew of Frederick the Great, and who, having recently lost his wife, was looking for a new one.

'It was a terrible mistake, and all my own fault,' she said, as they stood on Parliament Hill, looking down on the London plain, veiled by coal smoke like a vast fireplace smouldering under a layer of slack. 'Well it was partly Daddy's for not seeing through Henning's aristocratic façade, but I was in a silly panic about being left on the shelf because my sister and my adopted cousin were already married and it seemed a rather glamorous match at the time. To be fair to Henning, he had his doubts and dragged his feet—I actually more or less seduced him so he would have to marry me. We didn't realise that he was practically broke, and I certainly didn't know what was expected of a German *Hausfrau* or the dreariness of her life. Well, you know something about that from *Elizabeth and her German Garden*. But it was actually much worse—Henning made me cut a lot out of the book before he would let me publish it.'

'How did you seduce him—if I may be so bold?' he asked.

'Henning was in England for a while, dithering about whether to marry me, and I let him know I would be staying one weekend at a hotel in Goring-on-Thames with just a nominal chaperone, and he rose to the bait. I lost my virginity to the sound of the river lapping below my window. It was the only romantic element in the experience.'

'But you went ahead and married him.'

'I had to. I suppose I thought the physical side of marriage would be bound to improve—but it didn't. It was a few minutes' pleasure for him and nine months of pregnancy for me. He kept making me pregnant because he desperately wanted a son. I took up residence in Nassenheide— that's the estate in the book—to get some respite from perpetual child-bearing, because he didn't really like the place, and preferred to stay in our Berlin apartment. Then he took a mistress.'

'And you found consolation in your garden.'

'More in writing about it. The garden in the book is mostly fantasy, really—people who read about it were very disappointed when they saw the real thing. I had resigned myself to living without knowing real love, and like many another woman before me, I sought fulfilment in literary creation.'

'But now you are free to find real love,' he said, smiling, and turning upon her the blue-grey eyes whose gaze he had been told was so hypnotic.

She met it with cool composure, and an enigmatic smile. 'Yes, I suppose I am,' she said. 'If I can find the right man.'

He escorted her to the Hampstead Tube station, and held on to her hand for some time when he took it in his to say goodbye. 'We must meet again,' he said.

'I would like to,' she said. 'I'm living with my sister in Haslemere at present, but I'm looking for a flat in London.'

'Haslemere!' he exclaimed. 'There's a farm near there with a guesthouse where I sometimes go to work. I was thinking of going there again.' This thought had in fact occurred a fraction of a second before he uttered it.

'Well, if you do . . . be sure to let me know.'

'I will.' He raised her hand to his lips and kissed it. '*Au revoir*, then.'

'*Au revoir.*' She smiled, and walked away towards the turnstiles, her neat rounded rear swaying under her tailored coat.

The next morning he scribbled a letter to Jane: '*Work and the gravity of life much alleviated yesterday by the sudden eruption of the bright little Countess von Arnim at 1 with a cheerful proposal to lunch with me & go for a walk. She talks very well, she knows The New Machiavelli by heart, & I think she's a nice little friend to have.*' He thought it prudent to add: '*Her conversation is free but her morals are strict (sad experience has taught her that if she so much as thinks of anything she has a baby).*' After he had posted it he reflected that the afterthought had probably not been at all prudent, and that Jane would immediately guess what was in his mind.

They had not been long in residence at 17 Church Row before he realised that its purchase had been a mistake. The house was too small for their purposes, and he found it a noisy, restless environment for work. The servants went up and down on the stairs all day, and if anyone came into the drawing room, he heard them in his study through the folding partition. There were other disadvantages. The garden was a high-walled yard too small for badminton, and nothing that Jane planted there flourished. The proximity of the picturesque old church and churchyard had seemed an enhancement of the property when they bought it, but on weekdays there were frequently funeral carriages, elaborately decked out with the black trappings of mourning, waiting outside their frontage while services and interments took place, casting an air of melancholy over the street. His main complaint, however, was the lack of a quiet, secluded place to work.

He had accordingly taken a small flat in Candover Street, in the nondescript area east of Great Portland Street, with a perfunctory 'kitchenette', as the agent called it, which he rarely used, a tiny bathroom, and a living room just big enough to contain a desk, an easy chair and a divan bed. The bed was officially for him to take a nap when he needed, or sleep in if he missed the last Tube train to Hampstead after an evening engagement, but it also served for dalliance with various ladies who solaced him for the loss of Amber. These were old flames to whom he sent signals of distress, or new acquaintances he picked up at parties or cafes and restaurants frequented by literary and artistic folk, and they slept with him out of sympathy, or for old times' sake, or because they admired his books, or simply in return for a nice lunch. He did not think his treaty with Jane required him to report these casual couplings to her, but she must suspect that his hours at Candover Street were not dedicated exclusively to work, and it disturbed him somewhat that he was not being open with her. In Elizabeth he thought he saw the possibility of a liaison which he would not be embarrassed to own to Jane and she would be happy to accept. He was in little doubt, from their conversation on Hampstead Heath, that Elizabeth herself was looking for a lover, and had fixed her sights on him as a suitable candidate: a mature man whose intellect she admired and whose amorous appetite was legendary, but who would not wish to make her pregnant.

Accordingly he booked himself into the guest suite at Crotchet Farm near Haslemere for two weeks, to work 'without distraction', as he told Jane, on a new novel. It was another story of a man and a woman each struggling to find personal fulfilment against all the obstacles that a hidebound and materialistic society set in their way, but this time they would not find it necessary to commit adultery in the process because they would get married quite early in the narrative, and find redemption eventually within their marriage.

The novel was indeed to be entitled *Marriage,* and it was designed in part to persuade the British reading public that he was not hell-bent on destroying that revered institution, and to dissipate the aura of scandal that had attached itself to his name in recent years. In the first part of the story, already written, the heroine Marjorie married the hero, a scientist called Trafford, for love in preference to more eligible suitors, but she would fail to identify with his disinterested pursuit of knowledge. To keep her happy, and satisfy her conventional desires, he would give up research and make a fortune from the manufacture of synthetic rubber, but would eventually feel his life had become meaningless and resolve to go and live like Thoreau in the wastes of Labrador to save his soul, Marjorie to his surprise insisting on accompanying him. There they would have an adventurous near-death experience from which they would emerge strengthened and reunited in spirit, and return to England to collaborate on some kind of progressive intellectual enterprise. He had no personal knowledge of Labrador but then neither would 99.9 per cent of his readers, and he was confident he could mug up enough from books to convince them.

He combined work on this uplifting story in his mornings with the conduct of an affair with Elizabeth von Arnim in the afternoons. He called on her at her sister's home, which was only a mile or so distant from the farm, he took her out for walks and excursions in the Surrey hills, and as the early winter darkness fell he smuggled her into his bedroom at the farm guesthouse, and demonstrated to her very satisfactorily how much sensual pleasure she had been denied as the spouse of the late Count. 'I never felt such sensations before,' she sighed after a gratifying orgasm. 'And I never realised a man could go on for so long.' She was frank and very amusing about her late husband's deficiencies as a lover. 'He never removed his nightshirt, and he didn't require me to be naked either—he yanked up my nightdress like a shopkeeper raising the shutters on his premises, pushed my legs apart and got down to business immediately.'

'Which didn't last very long.'

'No, but that was rather a relief, because he didn't smell quite right.'

'And do I smell right?'

'You smell delicious,' she said. 'You smell of honey. I'd like to lick you.'

'Please do,' he said. 'Anywhere that takes your fancy.' And she did.

Although they had spoken on Hampstead Heath of her being free to find 'real love' the words were understood by both of them as code for 'good sex', so it was not necessary to pretend to be possessed by romantic passion to justify their enjoyment of each other's bodies, or to make declarations of undying devotion when his fortnight's residence came to an end. They parted cheerfully, agreeing to meet again when the opportunity arose, but without making any specific plans.

In fact there was a considerable hiatus in this promising relationship. Christmas and its festivities intervened, and then in the New Year he took the whole family, including Fräulein Meyer, to Wergen in the Bernese

Oberland for a winter sports holiday. It was the boys' first experience of skiing and they loved it, until, alas, there was an outbreak of influenza in the hotel which laid them all low, and they spent most of their second week in bed, and more weeks at home recuperating. Meanwhile the Countess had returned to Germany to tie up matters concerning her husband's estate. So he got on with *Marriage* in Candover Street, diverted from his labours by occasional female visitors; among them, most unexpectedly, Amber.

It was entirely her initiative. She wrote asking if they could meet privately somewhere, and although he thought she was taking a fearful risk, he could not deny her. The risk to himself was negligible: if he broke the agreement he had signed there was no sanction Blanco White could invoke except the original threat to sue him for libel over *Ann Veronica*, and it was now too late for that. But she would be putting her marriage in jeopardy by seeing him, and he wondered if it was already in trouble. This surmise proved to be quite wrong.

She came to Candover Street looking happy and well, spoke eloquently of the joy she had in the baby Anna Jane, and showed him a photograph of their child at its christening. 'Christening?' he said, raising an eyebrow. 'Yes, I know,' she said somewhat sheepishly, 'but it's only a social ritual really, and Rivers wanted her christened, so I didn't argue.' All her references to Blanco White were positive. 'He's a good father,' she said at one point, 'and a good husband.' 'I'm glad to hear you say so,' he said, 'since I was in a sense the matchmaker.' 'You were right, Master,' she said. 'It was the only solution.' It gave him a thrill to hear the old term of endearment. But why had she come? She said that she was writing a novel—a new one—and wanted to give him the first few chapters to read for his opinion, but even as he agreed he thought this was more of a pretext than an explanation. He decided that it was simply an internal declaration of independence. A year ago Shaw had written a play called *Misalliance,* privately performed because it was far too risqué to get past the Lord Chamberlain, a kind of highbrow farce about sexual goings-on among a group of socially variegated people. The heroine, an outspoken and shameless young woman called Hypatia, was reported by several friends who saw the piece to be based on Amber. He had not seen the play, but he had read it. The glib young hussy Hypatia was a very shallow version of Amber, but she had one line that struck an authentic note: *'I don't want to be good and I don't want to be bad: I just don't want to be bothered about either good or bad: I want to be an active verb.'*

Amber wanted, had always wanted, to be an active verb, not a passive one. The agreement she had entered into, to cut off all communication with him for two years, was an infringement of her liberty, and this private act of defiance was necessary to her self-respect.

He had cooled a bottle of Mosel in advance of her visit to cover any initial awkwardness or embarrassment at their first meeting after so long an interval. It proved unnecessary but it encouraged an easy flow of conversation. They spoke of old times, sometimes with laughter, sometimes with tears on her part. They sat with their arms round each other on the divan bed, and after a while it was more comfortable to lie down. They ended up performing the best active verb of all. 'I didn't mean to do this when I came here, Master,' Amber said afterwards, 'but I'm glad.' 'So am I, Amber,' he said, and kissed her tenderly.

She visited him again a week later, this time with the intention of making love, but also to say it would be for the last time. 'I didn't want you to think I regretted what happened last week,' she said. 'But if we go on, Rivers is bound to find out, and I don't want to hurt him.' He was glad to agree. He discovered that time had healed the wound of their enforced separation. The bitterness he had felt then was a fading memory, as was the passion of their old relationship, and he had no desire to revive either of these disturbing emotions. He was trying to construct a quieter, calmer life.

Not long afterwards Elizabeth von Arnim returned to England and signalled her availability. She had acquired a flat in St James's Court, Westminster, and wrote to say that she looked forward to entertaining him and Jane there, and perhaps meeting himself alone somewhere else. He invited her to Candover Street, and she arrived one afternoon, smartly dressed as always, but wearing a hat with an opaque veil. 'I feel very wicked,' she said, as she removed this piece of apparel, 'like a character in a French novel.' 'Isn't that part of the fun?' he said, removing some other items of her clothing. 'Goodness me!' she said, helping him with the hooks and eyes on her costume. 'How impatient you are!' 'Well, I've missed you,' he said, 'I've been undressing you in my head for weeks.' 'Have you indeed,' she said. 'Tut, tut.' But he could see she was excited by this badinage and soon they were entwined on the bed in vigorous and joyful intercourse.

After they had slept briefly she showered while he made them a pot of tea, and when he came out of the kitchenette with the tray he found her demurely dressed again, every button and hook secured in its proper place. Perhaps she had found a long hair in the bathroom, or spied a hair-clip under the bed, for she said thoughtfully, as she stirred her cup, 'Do you have other women here?' He did not deny it. 'If you and I are to continue as lovers that must cease,' she said. 'Very well,' he said, smiling. 'Let us make a treaty. I will give up other ladies, but you must accept that I will never give up Jane.' 'Of course,' she said. 'I have no wish to come between you and your family. We must take care that she doesn't find out.' 'Oh, Jane won't mind,' he said, and saw that this reply was a surprise, even a slight shock, to her. 'In fact I'm sure she will approve,' he added. 'I see,' she said, though he was not sure she did.

But he was right, of course. Having long accepted that she could not respond to his sexual needs, and that he would find satisfaction elsewhere, Jane preferred that it was with one person rather than several, someone she knew and respected, who could be relied upon to be responsible and discreet. The Countess von Arnim, or 'little E' as he now began to call her, was eminently eligible for this role, all the more because she declared her intention, while keeping her London base, of residing mainly in Switzerland, where he would be able to visit her without any embarrassing publicity. She had made a good deal of money from her play, and from the sale of the Count's properties, to add to the royalties from her books, and she intended to use this small fortune to build herself a chalet on some mountainside in Switzerland, a country which she associated with happy times in her girlhood. He shared her enthusiasm for Switzerland, and also for house-building, and joined enthusiastically in her search for a site in the Jura, hiking by day and staying overnight in mountain chalet-inns. Fräulein Teppi Backe, who had been governess to her children and was now her companion, accompanied them for appearance's sake, though Teppi was well aware that he found his way to E's room most nights. On two occasions they managed to break her bed, and it amused him to observe next morning the dainty, diminutive Countess, who looked as if she weighed about six and a half stone, coolly reporting the collapse of this item of furniture to an incredulous innkeeper in her fluent but formal German. She couldn't find a site that satisfied her exacting criteria in the Jura, so they transferred their search to the Valais area, and there discovered the ideal situation near Randogne-sur-Sierre, in the foothills below the winter sports resort of Montana, said to be the sunniest in the Alps, with a stunning view over the Rhône valley that opened out to include the Pennine Alps, the

Mont Blanc range and the Simplon. An architect was commissioned, and designed to Elizabeth's specifications an enormous building that was more like a chateau than a chalet, with sixteen bedrooms, four bathrooms and seven lavatories. She explained that she intended to entertain her friends there and to make it a holiday place for her children, and for their families in due course. The building work was contracted and completion promised for the autumn of the following year. It was already named by its owner, *Chalet Soleil.*

Meanwhile he and Jane had agreed that they wanted to get out of Hampstead and find a place somewhere in the country not too far from London where they could recreate the kind of life they had enjoyed in Spade House, perhaps on a slightly grander scale. Visiting his friend Ralph Blumenfeld, the editor of the *Daily Express,* who had a house at Great Easton near Dunmow in Essex, he was much taken with the area—pretty, unspoiled farming country only forty miles from London. Most of the property there was owned by Lady Frances Warwick, who occupied the stately mansion Easton Lodge, and having been introduced to him by Blumenfeld, she agreed to let him have the Old Rectory at Little Easton on a short lease. Landowner and tenant were equally delighted with the transaction. Lady Warwick, reputed to have been a mistress of the late King Edward VII when he was Prince of Wales, was an unusual kind of aristocrat, having been converted to socialism after her marriage, and while continuing to live in patrician style herself was patron and hostess to a large circle of progressive writers and politicians, to which he would be a most welcome addition. To him the handsome red-brick Georgian Rectory, though in need of some modernisation and refurbishment, appeared immediately as an ideal dwelling place. Spacious reception rooms opened off a wood-panelled, stone-flagged square hall, from which rose a broad staircase leading to the upper floors and numerous bedrooms. The house looked across its lawns and over cornfields towards the village, and possessed a large barn in which he immediately saw himself organising games and theatricals. And, vitally, this idyllic place had an excellent railway connection to London via Bishop's Stortford, the trains stopping by request at the Easton Estate's private halt only a mile away.

He signed the lease in August 1911, and they used the house initially as a weekend retreat, but he and Jane both liked it so much that the following spring they made the Rectory—renamed 'Easton Glebe' to weaken its ecclesiastical associations—their permanent home, keeping on Church Row temporarily as a London base, but with the intention of selling it and purchasing the Easton house on a long lease. The boys revelled in the wide open spaces that surrounded the house, and their freedom to explore them. A tennis court was laid out on one of the lawns, and the barn was cleaned and furnished for indoor games and theatricals on wet days. On most weekends they had a party of friends to stay who were always enchanted with and envious of the place. He had a spacious study on the ground floor but intended to create also a secluded suite on an upper floor where he could sleep or write at any time of the day or the night as the mood took him. Jane, as resourceful as always, took on the task of executing his plans, and herself set about restoring the neglected gardens to order.

Meanwhile he accompanied little E to Switzerland to observe the progress of the Chalet Soleil, which like every other building under construction in the history of the world was behind schedule, and would not be completed by the autumn, but was promised to be ready by Christmas. They stayed in a neighbouring chalet owned by the singer Jenny Lind, and spent their days hiking through the foothills and pine woods, taking a simple picnic with them in their rucksacks, and making love after their lunch on mattresses of pine needles covered with their clothes. Little E enjoyed sex in the open air as much as himself, and relished the sensation of sun and breeze on her naked skin. They knew where the local peasants were working and there were few tourists about in early summer, so there was little risk of being surprised *in flagrante*. He took trips with her that year to Amsterdam, Paris and Locarno, where they stayed in grand hotels and disported themselves decadently on sprung mattresses and among pillows stuffed with goosedown, but no lovemaking between them pleased him as much as those rustic copulations on the hillsides of the Valais, rendered all the more natural by the circumstance that contraceptive precautions were, she assured him, no longer required. She had reached that stage in a woman's life conveniently early.

In September *Marriage* was published, and was rapturously received, fulfilling to excess his hopes that it would restore him to respectability in the eyes of the great British public. '*A book that thrills with the life, the questioning, of to-day. Whatever the autumn publishing season may produce, it is not likely to bring us anything more vital, more significant, than "Marriage",'* declared the *Daily Chronicle. 'What a brilliant, stimulating, and even exalting book this is . . . The observation, the cleverness, the almost vicious gaiety, the religious curiosity of the book, are wonderful,'* said the *Daily News. 'Alive with flashes of the most perfect insight at every turn . . . It grips the reader from cover to cover,'* enthused the *Sphere.* He had not had such a royal flush of laudatory reviews since *The War of the Worlds.* Even his old journalistic enemies, the scourges of *In the Days of the Comet* and *Ann Veronica,* were charmed, and purred their appreciation: *'Mr Wells has put all his cleverness into this long story of an engagement and marriage between two attractive and, we may add, perfectly moral young people,'* said the *Spectator,* while *T.P.'s Weekly* described it as *'a thrilling and inspiring book—and one that can be placed on a puritan's family bookshelf'.* He laughed disbelievingly as he leafed through the cuttings sent to him by Macmillan with a congratulatory covering note—even the author didn't think the book was *that* good. But the extravagant praise made up for some of the critical injustices of the past, and he was not going to complain about it.

There was only one starkly dissenting review, albeit in a publication of small circulation. A writer called Rebecca West wrote a withering critique of *Marriage* in the *Freewoman,* a lively little magazine less than a year old which aimed to broaden the feminist agenda beyond the single issue of the vote to include sexuality and culture, and even dared to criticise certain aspects of the suffragettes' campaigns. The previously unknown Rebecca West's witty, combative contributions to this journal had already attracted his attention, beginning with a bold attack on Mrs Humphry Ward, who personified the English idea of a 'serious' novelist, partly on the strength of her genealogy (granddaughter of Dr Arnold of Rugby, and niece of Matthew Arnold) but mainly because her novels were about the waning of Christian faith, and had characters who earnestly debated how its theology could be modernised and its morality preserved. *'The idea of Christ is the only inheritance that the rich have not stolen from the poor,'* Rebecca West asserted in 'The Gospel According to Mrs Humphry Ward'. *'It is now a great national interest (not a faith), and as such is treated with respect, and as securely protected from "modernising" as the tragedy of* Hamlet. *And although Mrs Ward has been "turning her trained intellect" (to quote her publisher) on the universe for nigh on sixty years, that has not struck her. She regards the Englishman as going to church with the same watchful eye for possible improvements as when he attends the sanitary committee of the borough council.'* He knew good polemical writing when he saw it, and chuckled appreciatively. Mrs Humphry Ward was used to fending off the arguments of orthodox Christians on the one hand and of militant atheists on the other, but it was easy to imagine her discomfiture at being attacked from this quite unexpected direction and being portrayed as an ideological robber of the poor. He did not however enjoy being at the sharp end of Miss West's scorn himself. Her review began:

> *Mr Wells' mannerisms are more infuriating than ever in* Marriage. *One knows at once that Marjorie is speaking in a crisis of wedded chastity when she says at regular intervals, 'Oh, my dear! . . . Oh, my dear!' or at moments of ecstasy, 'Oh, my dear! Oh, my dear!' For Mr Wells' heroines who are loving under legal difficulties say 'My man!' or 'Master!' Of course he is the old maid among novelists; even the sex-obsession that lay clotted on* Ann Veronica *and* The New Machiavelli *like cold white sauce was merely old maid's mania, the reaction towards the flesh of a mind too long absorbed in airships and colloids.*

Reading this he felt rather as he had imagined Mrs Humphry Ward must have felt, for he was not accustomed to being likened to a celibate spinster. It was a very long review, and a very thorough demolition of his novel. '*His first sin lies in pretending that Marjorie, that fair, fleshy being who at forty would look rather like a cow—and the resemblance would have a spiritual significance—is the normal woman; and the second lies in his remedy: "Suppose the community kept all its women, suppose all property in homes and furnishings and children was vested in them . . . Then every woman would be a princess to the man she loved." The cheek of it! The mind reels at the thought of the community being taxed to allow Marjorie to perpetuate her cow-like kind.*' The real answer, Rebecca West asserted, was to let women earn their own living.

He might have been more annoyed to receive such a dismissive review by a little-known critic in a journal that he regarded as being on the same side as himself if he hadn't had such a unanimously good press for *Marriage* everywhere else. As it was, he could afford to be magnanimous and admit to Jane, who had read the review first, and passed it to him with the advice, 'You'd better take a few deep breaths before you read this, H.G.', that the woman had put her finger on some vulnerable points in his novel, and certainly knew how to write. This Rebecca West seemed to have an interesting mind and a great deal of self-confidence—wouldn't it be amusing to ask her down to Easton Glebe for lunch one day, and see if she had the gumption to walk into the lion's den and defend herself?

'It seems to me that it is you who will have to do the defending,' Jane said drily. 'But invite her if you like.'

Accordingly he wrote to Rebecca West, care of the *Freewoman*, to say that he had read her review with interest and invited her to lunch to discuss further the issues it raised, adding information about the most convenient trains from Liverpool Street, and how to request a stop at the Easton private station. She accepted by return of post for the earliest of the dates he had offered, the 27th of September. She arrived at one o'clock and they talked with hardly a pause until six-thirty, by which time it was too late for her to return to London, so they carried on talking and she stayed the night.

—And that was how it began . . .

—That was how it began.

—Again! Another young virgin, half your age, bright, impressionable, rebellious, eager for experience—just like Amber. You invite her into your life and of course she falls in love with you, the great writer, as you might have known . . .

—I didn't know. I thought from her review that she regarded me as an old fogey.

—But that needled you, didn't it? The 'cold white sauce' and the jeers at your heroine's conversion to the Endowment of Motherhood, rankled and you wanted to teach this impertinent young bitch—

—I didn't know she was young.

—You could guess that a contributor to the *Freewoman* nobody had ever heard of before was young. And you thought to yourself that you would invite her into your elegant country house, sit her down in your study surrounded by all the editions of your books and other insignia of your fame, and turn on her the full power of your personality, that combination of sparkling intelligence and seductive charm that you knew from experience was usually irresistible to women. The fact that she turned out to be extremely attractive herself made it very easy.

—I had no intention of making her fall in love with me, and I resisted her advances for a long time.

—But eventually you succumbed.

—Eventually I fell in love with her myself.

And made her pregnant, and plunged yourself back into all the complications and embarrassments and time-consuming responsibilities you had experienced with Amber.

—Only this time they lasted longer. A lot longer.

—**Would you never learn?**

—Where women were concerned, it would seem not.

2

One of the many intriguing things he discovered about Rebecca West on the first occasion they met was that it was not her real name. She had been born Cicily Fairfield, the youngest of three daughters of a Scottish mother and an Anglo-Irish father who mysteriously disappeared when she was thirteen and was never heard of until he died in poverty five years later. To her great credit Mrs Fairfield, with very limited means at her disposal, ensured that her three girls received an excellent education. Cicily's two older sisters had both gone to university and one was already launched on a promising professional career in medicine, but she herself had opted to train as an actress—a mistake, she declared, because she discovered that she would never excel in that vocation and dropped out before completing the course. It seemed to him, however, that the training had given her the confidence to express her vivacious personality without inhibition. It had certainly not prevented her from reading a great deal, and she seemed to possess, like himself, the precious gift of remembering everything she read. Astonishingly, considering the wide range of literary and intellectual reference she displayed in conversation, she was not yet twenty years of age. She was, he thought, an exceptional young woman.

Given the way they had been treated by Mr Fairfield, it was not surprising that his wife and daughters were sympathetic to feminism, but Rebecca was evidently by far the most radical and committed member of the family in this respect. She told him she had been an active suffragette for a time, parading and demonstrating and getting roughly handled by policemen, and also joined the Young Fabians, after he had parted from the Society. But she had been dissatisfied with the narrow perspectives of both these groups, and found the circle who gathered around the *Freewoman* more sympathetic to her heterodox feminism. This journal was however regarded at home as having a dangerously immoral tendency and Mrs Fairfield actually forbade her to read it, so when she became a contributor she thought it prudent to use a pseudonym, choosing the name of the radical heroine of Ibsen's tragedy *Rosmersholm,* one of the last parts she had played at the Academy of Dramatic Art, and in due course she adopted it as her own name for all purposes.

'I never liked my real name anyway,' she said as she stirred cream and sugar into her second cup of coffee. She had eaten lunch with himself, Jane and Fräulein Meyer, deftly contributing to the conversation over watercress soup and poached salmon, and afterwards he had suggested the two of them should adjourn to his study and have their coffee brought there.

'No, I don't see you as a Cicily,' he said, 'or a Fairfield for that matter.' Rebecca was fairly small in stature, but solidly built, and had a head of rich dark brown hair with eyes to match, set off by very white skin. Her features were full of character, from the broad forehead to the determined chin, and she had a way of keeping her lips just parted while listening to him as if to inhale more deeply the oxygen of ideas. ' "Cicily Fairfield" is a name I might have invented for a blonde, blue-eyed, English rose in a novel,' he said.

'Yes,' she said, smiling, 'it would have done quite well for your Marjorie if she hadn't had red hair. By the way, I want to apologise for the abrasive tone of my review. I read it through again on the train this morning, knowing that I would soon be meeting you, and it suddenly seemed unforgivably rude. I blushed so deeply that I believe the gentleman in the seat opposite thought I must be reading something very improper.'

'Oh, don't worry about that,' he said, waving his hand in a vague gesture of absolution. 'It's stimulating to have one's ideas challenged so forcefully.'

They argued for a while about whether women could ever get the same satisfaction out of work as men. 'It's not that I believe them to be inferior— not at all,' he said. 'But a man can forget everything else to focus on his work, using sex merely for relaxation and refreshment. Whereas for a woman sex is of paramount importance because it's bound up with reproduction. It's a biological imperative: to find a mate and reproduce—she can't get away from it. That's why I believe in the Endowment of Motherhood.'

'You sound like one of Shaw's characters, Mr Wells,' she said.

'Well, Shaw does have some good ideas mixed up with the silly ones,' he said. 'Have you met him?'

'Once—at a Fabian Summer School,' she said. 'He moved among us like a flirtatious Moses.'

'Very good!' he chuckled. 'But look here, you say at the end of your review . . .' He picked up the magazine from his desk and read out a passage which he had marked: '"*Supposing she had to work?*"—Marjorie, that is—"*How long could she stand it? The weaker sort of Marjorie would be sucked down to prostitution and death, the stronger sort of Marjorie would develop qualities of decency and courage and ferocity. It is worth trying.*"' That's a brutal piece of social Darwinism—you condemn half your sisterhood to disgrace and death by throwing them all into the job market and letting the fittest survive. As a man I'd be run out of town if I dared make such a suggestion.'

'It needn't be as brutal as that,' she said. 'If women were allowed to compete in the workplace on equal terms with men, and men did their share of housework and childrearing at home, all the Marjories might be fulfilled.'

He laughed. 'And I thought *I* was a Utopian!' he said. 'But what sort of work do you have your sights set on, yourself? Writing, I presume—but what kind? Criticism? Fiction?'

'All kinds,' she said. 'And some that haven't been discovered yet.' He laughed again. He liked her self-confidence and her ambition.

They discussed modern literature, beginning with Henry James, on whom she had very decided views, adoring some of his works, especially the stories about writers, but condemning others, including the much-admired *Portrait of a Lady,* on the grounds that the heroine's motive for marrying the odious Gilbert Osmond—that he would make better use of her fortune than she could—was totally unconvincing. 'You'd think it would cross her mind from time to time that he would be a very cold fish in bed,' she said, 'but she never seems to think of him as a lover at all. She has no desire for him—how could a woman marry without desire?'

'Many do, I'm afraid,' he said. 'My own first wife, for one.'

'Really?' She looked intensely interested, and hopeful of further revelations. He inwardly cautioned himself against making intimate confidences to someone he had known for only a few hours, a journalist to boot, and quickly steered the conversation back to literature. 'Writing honestly about sexual desire in novels is always difficult. I'm not very good at it myself, I admit, but then English novelists never have been, not since Fielding. After him prudery and hypocrisy got a grip on our society. You have to go to the French for the truthful depiction of sex in fiction.'

'Have you read D.H. Lawrence?' she said.

'I've read his things in the *English Review*. In fact I was one of the first people in London to hear about him. I was dining with Ford Madox Hueffer at the Pall Mall restaurant, along with Chesterton and Belloc, and Fordie said to us he had just received some poems by someone called D.H. Lawrence which in his opinion were the work of a genius. I remember turning round to the neighbouring tables, full of writers as usual, and shouting out, "Hooray, Fordie's discovered another literary genius! Called D.H. Lawrence!" We had all had a fair amount to drink by then.'

'Well, I think he *is* a genius,' Rebecca said, unimpressed, or at least undistracted, by this burst of name-dropping. 'His new novel *The Trespasser* has some extraordinary rhapsodic passages about lovemaking.'

'Ah, you're ahead of me there. I haven't read it,' he said, wondering how much she knew about lovemaking from personal experience. Very little, he suspected, living at home with her mother and sisters—the unembarrassed familiarity with which she spoke of such matters would be largely derived from her reading.

He was surprised when Jane appeared at the door of his study to ask if they would like some tea. 'Is it teatime already, dear? Could we have it in here?' he asked. 'Yes, of course,' she said. 'But don't forget that Miss West has a train to catch.' 'No, I won't—but anyway, if she misses it she can stay the night. You don't have any engagements in London that would rule that out, do you?' he said, turning to Rebecca, and she smiled and shook her head. 'But I couldn't possibly impose on you,' she said unconvincingly.

Tea came with cakes and muffins, and they discussed the faults of the Fabian and the failure of the Liberal Party to exploit its landslide victory of 1906 to achieve social justice, and the arms race with Germany. She asked him if he thought war was likely, and he said not in the near future, but unless the Great Powers saw sense and made some progress towards world government he predicted that there would be a major war in twenty or thirty years' time. There was a danger that the arms race would itself provoke war by creating a climate of belligerence, stirred up by the press, and the British government was handling the whole business with characteristic folly. He was well primed on this topic, having just put together three articles written earlier in the year for the *Daily Mail* to make a pamphlet called *War and Common Sense* which was to be published soon. He expounded his theory that admirals and generals always fought the latest war with the methods of the last until forced by failure to revise their tactics and weaponry.

'The next war will eventually be won by submarines and aircraft, and we should be spending money on developing them, rather than wasting resources on building dreadnoughts whose only function is to blow German battleships out of the water, or be blown out of it themselves. And instead of conscripting a huge army on the same scale as Germany's, as some people urge, we should form small elite bodies of scientifically trained officers and men armed with the latest weapons.'

'But all this talk of war and weapons horrifies me,' she said. 'As if war is inevitable and the only question is how to kill as many of the enemy as you can without getting killed yourself.'

'Well of course that must be the aim of all warfare,' he said. 'I've invented a game with toy soldiers for my two boys based on exactly that principle. If the leaders of the Great Powers would play like us with toy soldiers, instead of real ones, the world would be a much safer place.'

'There's not much hope of that,' she said with a smile.

'No. And science is developing at such a pace that the possibilities of its application to weaponry are frightening. Suppose we manage to tap the energy that's contained within the nucleus of an atom? There are radioactive elements, like radium and uranium, which produce an enormous amount of energy as they decay, but at an infinitesimal rate, over millions of years. If we could find a way of accelerating that process we would release an extraordinary amount of energy from a single atom. It could be used for peaceful purposes, and transform the world—much more thoroughly than steam and electricity have done. Or it could be used to make atomic bombs.'

'Atomic bombs?' she repeated wonderingly. 'What would they be like?'

'Small bombs that could be tossed out of the cockpit of an aeroplane and devastate a whole city. That's why I believe in the necessity of world government. But I'm afraid that only the catastrophe of a global war will make humanity see that obvious truth.'

At which point Jane appeared again at the study door to say that she presumed Miss West would be staying the night, and would she like to be shown to a bedroom?

Their talk—mainly his talk—continued over dinner, and on the train to London the next morning. Since he had business in town they travelled together and he insisted on paying the difference between her third-class fare and his first-class one. By the end of the journey they were on 'Rebecca' and 'H.G.' terms. She shook his hand at Liverpool Street station and thanked him with obvious sincerity for inviting her to Easton and for the most intellectually stimulating conversations she had ever had in her life.

'So you've made another conquest, H.G.,' Jane observed next day, when he repeated Rebecca's parting words.

'Well, I think I convinced her that there's more to me than she had seen before,' he said. 'More than she saw in *Marriage* anyway.'

In fact it appeared that as a result of their meeting she saw more in *Marriage* itself, for a few weeks later she sent him the proof of another review of the novel she had written for a magazine called *Everyman,* which was shorter but considerably more complimentary than the first one. He wrote to thank her for it, and mentioned lightly that the gratification it gave him had been punctured by a letter about the novel from Henry James, quoting a few characteristic lines for her amusement: *'I have read you, as I always read you, as I read no one else, with a complete abdication of all those "principles of criticism", canons of form, preconceptions of felicity, references to the idea of method or the sacred laws of composition, which I roam, which I totter, through the pages of others attended in some degree by the fond yet feeble theory of, but which I shake off, as I advance under your spell, with the most cynical inconsistency.'* The letter continued for another page or two, repeating in long tortuous sentences the message that Henry James was able to read him only by suspending all his critical faculties. He kissed the rod again in his reply, and thanked James for mingling *'so much heartening kindliness with the wisest, most penetrating and guiding of criticism and reproof. I am, like so many poor ladies, destined to be worse before I am better; the next book is "scandalously" bad in form, mixed pickles, and I know it. Thereafter I will seek earnestly to make my pen lead a decent life, pull myself together, and think of Form.'*

This 'next book', on which he was currently engaged, was called *The Passionate Friends,* and bore a family resemblance to its immediate predecessors. He knew James would hate it, if only because it was in the *'accurst autobiographic form'*, a long confessional letter written by the hero to his son for posthumous consumption. Stephen Stratton was another of his somewhat priggish heroes trying to reconcile his idealism with his sexuality in a world which made such a compromise difficult or impossible. But was it the world, or an inherent flaw in human nature—jealousy, in both the personal life and collective, political life? '*This is the reality of laws and government; this is the reality of customs and institutions: a convention between jealousies,*' Stephen wrote. '*The deepest question before humanity is just how far this jealous greed may be subdued to a more generous passion.*' And that was really the theme of the book. There was some adultery in the plot, but he hoped not to alienate the readers he had won over with *Marriage*. The heroine, Lady Mary, unable to satisfy Stephen's desire without destroying his career by a scandalous divorce from her vindictive husband, was going to commit suicide in the end to relieve the hero of an intolerable choice. Though Henry James's novels often ended with a gesture of renunciation by the hero or heroine, he did not expect him to approve so melodramatic a conclusion, and he was quite sure that Rebecca West wouldn't. But—*tant pis*. He had to write what he had to write, to get it out of his system, and on to the next book. Work, a continuous stream of writing, with occasional breaks for recreation in the form of sex or games, was essential to him if he was not to be overcome by nihilistic despair. As his latest spokesman, Stratton, put it: '*I go valiantly for the most part, I believe, but despair is always near to me, as near as a shark may be near a sleeper in a ship . . . a sense of life as of an abysmal flood, full of cruelty, densely futile, blackly aimless.*' Only continuous exercise of mind and body could keep that black flood at bay, which was why he always had one book on the stocks and another at the design stage.

He was already brooding on the idea he had mentioned to Rebecca West, of a global war fought with atomic bombs, as the basis for a 'scientific romance'. It would have a prologue describing the development of human civilisation in terms of the increasingly rapid discovery of new forms of energy—fire, wind, steam, electricity, and finally atomic power, which at first would transform human life and then threaten to destroy it with atomic weapons. A war would break out in 1958, England, France and Russia against Germany and the Austro-Hungarian Empire. America would be drawn in. Aerial bombing would devastate capital cities, and breach the dykes of the Netherlands, drowning the impotent land armies. Then a truce would be called and a world government emerge. The story might all be told retrospectively in the form of an autobiographical book written in, say, 1970, by a man who had lived through these events.

Miss West wrote promptly to say how much she had relished the quotation from Henry James's letter. '*I laughed aloud at the long postponement of that final "of", which tricks you into thinking he has lost control of his syntax—but of course he never would,*' she said, and he had to re-read James's letter to remind himself what she was referring to, upon which he too laughed aloud. She also invited him to take tea with herself, her mother and sisters, at their house in Hampstead Garden Suburb, as a small return for his hospitality. To refuse seemed churlish, so he went, and enjoyed himself. Mrs Fairfield and her two elder daughters, Lettie and Winnie, were intelligent, cultured women, but in awe of his fame, and astonished that young Cicily (as they still called her, though the secret of her nom de plume was now known to them) had attracted his favourable attention. *'Thank you so much for coming,'* she wrote afterwards, *'Mama and my sisters thought you were brilliant and charming—which you were—and I have gone up enormously in their estimation for having lured you to our humble abode. That you have taken an interest in me has made them believe that I might have it in me to succeed as a writer—and enormously strengthened my own self-belief.'*

Early in the New Year she wrote again, a long letter in which she said that for the past three months she had been unable to forget her visit to Easton and his generosity in talking to her for so many hours. All subsequent conversations with other people had seemed flat and banal, and ever since that day she had been feeding mentally off the ideas and allusions he had thrown off with such casual brilliance. She couldn't bear the thought that this experience might never be repeated, and she was writing shamelessly to ask him if they might meet again, just to talk as they had at Easton, before he forgot all about her. She felt she was on the threshold of a great adventure, a literary career, but she needed guidance and encouragement, and she had no doubt at all that he could give these things.

He skimmed through this letter quickly, then re-read it more slowly. He was well aware, and had known before Jane put it into words, that he had made a conquest of this young woman at Easton. He had seduced her there intellectually, and it would be the easiest thing in the world to do so physically—perhaps that was what she was inviting between the lines of her letter. There was no doubt that she was desirable, with the precious, fragile bloom of youth on her striking looks, and the promise of a passionate nature discernible in the depths of her dark brown eyes. At another time he would have been tempted to take advantage of the opportunity, but he had just achieved a kind of stability in this aspect of his life which he didn't want to disturb. He had a mistress of his own age, sophisticated, discreet, independent, who was approved by his wife, and had obliged him to forswear other women. He did not wish to upset that concord. On the other hand he couldn't bring himself to rebuff the young girl's appeal to his generosity with a flat refusal, and he would be really sorry never to see her again. If he was very careful, and defined his relationship to her strictly as that of a mentor, no harm need be done, and it would be interesting to watch her develop as a writer. He wrote back, *'You're a very compelling person. I suppose I shall have to do what you ask me to do. Anyhow I mean to help you all I can in your great adventure,'* and invited her to tea at Church Row when he was next in London.

—**Fool! Did you seriously imagine you could have private conversations with this girl without emotional consequences? You must have seemed like God's gift to her: literary mentor, father figure and lover all in one.**

—The conversations were to be about books, ideas . . .

—**But it was by a bookcase that you first kissed her, wasn't it? The first time she came to Church Row.**

—I was showing her some of my books about socialism which hadn't been moved yet down to Easton, the ones I read as a young man, Marx and Engels, William Morris and Henry George. I reached up to take down George's *Progress and Poverty,* which was a kind of bible to me in those days, and turned to find her standing very close, and not looking at the books but at me, into my eyes, with a look of such melting adoration that . . .

—**You kissed her.**

—It was impossible not to.

—**And she said, 'I love you.'**

—And I said, 'You're very sweet, my dear, but you mustn't say that. I'm a married man, and twice your age.'

—**But it didn't make any difference. She regarded the kiss as a token of love.**

—Yes, as she told me in several subsequent letters.

—**And you answered those letters.**

—I did at first.

—**You encouraged her?**

—No.

—**But you didn't *dis*courage her.**

—I didn't want to hurt her. I tried to be sympathetic in a fatherly sort of way. I said that I thought she was a very special person, but I couldn't reciprocate her love because of other commitments.

—Didn't you say that you found her willingness to love you was 'a beautiful and courageous thing'?

—I may have said something like that.

—Wasn't that encouraging her?

—I didn't mean it to. Anyway, I stopped replying to her letters.

—Only because Jane told you to.

He handed Jane the letters one day and said with affected casualness, 'What shall I do about this young woman? She's becoming a bit of a nuisance.'

Jane read through the letters. He watched her covertly without being able to tell from her expression what she was thinking. When she handed back the letters, she said, 'How many times did you kiss her?'

'Just the once,' he said. 'She has absurdly exaggerated its significance.'

'I should be very wary of her if I were you, H.G. A girl who calls herself Rebecca West might do anything.'

'What d'you mean?'

'Have you ever seen *Rosmersholm*?' she asked.

'No.'

'Neither have I, but I've read it—just the other day, actually. Ibsen's Rebecca West is a very devious character.'

'I thought she was the heroine.'

'Well she is in a way, but a very flawed one. It's revealed in the course of the play that she wormed her way into Rosmer's house by befriending his barren wife, and then drove the poor woman to suicide by pretending that Rosmer had made her pregnant, so she could have him to herself, and when this comes out they both commit suicide at the end by jumping into the millrace, just as the wife did.'

'Good Lord!' he exclaimed, genuinely astonished.

'It's an odd kind of girl who would rename herself "Rebecca West", wouldn't you say?'

'Well, it wasn't a carefully thought out decision,' he said. 'She chose it on the spur of the moment, to conceal from her mother that she was writing for the *Freewoman*.'

'Even so . . . I would cut the connection with her if I were you. Don't answer any more letters. Go away. You're going to Switzerland soon anyway, aren't you?'

'Yes.'

'That's very convenient,' Jane said. 'Elizabeth will look after you, H.G.'

Chalet Soleil had not been completed, as promised, for Christmas, but it was ready for occupation in the spring. It rose from a steep hillside, three storeys high, vast, many-windowed and balconied under its pitched roof, with a small satellite building beside it called the Little Chalet, which was Elizabeth's workplace and had inscribed over its door the words: 'I HATE THE COMMON HERD AND KEEP THEM OUT.' She was not shy of playing the aristocratic lady, or of covering her buildings with assertive sentiments. Over the porch of the main house was written 'ON THE HEIGHTS LOVE LIVES WITH JOY MAGNIFICENT AND GAY', and above the front door 'ONLY HAPPINESS HERE'—which, so early in its occupation, seemed a little hubristic. The interior of the house smelled pleasantly of the wood of which it was constructed, like a huge cigar box, and was comfortably furnished and equipped for the entertainment of guests. His own bedroom was next door to little E's, and had a special feature which she gleefully demonstrated by suddenly jumping out of a cupboard at him when he was unpacking his valise. She had ordered a secret sliding door to be constructed between the two rooms, mounted on silent castors and concealed behind two cupboards, so that she could visit him at night without any risk of being observed by other occupants of the house.

'Was this done especially for me?' he asked, when he had recovered from the surprise.

'Of course,' she said. 'I don't have any other lovers. I trust you don't either, G.' In response to his familiar name for her, or in retaliation for it, she had taken to calling him ironically 'Great Man', now contracted to 'G'.

'Well, there is a young woman pursuing me in London at the moment,' he said lightly, and told her about Rebecca West.

Elizabeth saw the *Freewoman* occasionally, and the name was familiar to her. 'A clever writer, but there's something rather wild and irresponsible about her articles,' she said with a slight frown. 'I should keep well clear of her.'

'That's what Jane says.' The frown did not disappear. He had noticed before that little E never liked to be reminded of Jane's existence, even though their relationship enjoyed her tolerance. A tiny seed of doubt was

319

germinating in his consciousness that Elizabeth had not been wholly sincere when she said that she had no wish to oust Jane from her place in his life, but for the time being he suppressed it.

The novelty of waiting for Elizabeth to come through the secret door at night was erotically exciting at first, but it imposed on him a more passive role than he was used to. The door could be opened only from her side, and if she chose not to come through it after he had been lying expectantly awake for some time he was left feeling slightly snubbed, and not a little irritated. It was a quite different matter from his old practice, when they were sleeping in the same building, of slipping out into the corridor at night and trying the handle of her room. Whether the door yielded or not on those occasions he was the one taking the initiative, whereas little E's sliding door seemed designed to give her control over their lovemaking. He did not complain, however, and when they went for one of their hikes in the foothills he would sometimes reassert his prerogative as lover by initiating intercourse al fresco. On one occasion this indirectly involved Rebecca West.

Rebecca was now writing regularly for a socialist weekly called the *Clarion* and in an issue that caught up with him in Switzerland he had read a forceful article by her entitled 'The Sex War: Disjointed Thoughts on Men'. *'We have asked men for votes, they have given us advice,'* it began. *'At present they are also giving us abuse. I am tired of this running comment on the warlike conduct of my sex, delivered with such insolent assurance and such self-satisfaction. So I am going to do it too.'* The main targets of her eloquent scorn were journalists and politicians and other public figures who had recently denounced suffragette militancy in fatuous and intolerant terms, but she broadened out her polemic to attack the male sex at large, with effective use of a kind of refrain that punctuated her article in an ascending scale of contempt: *'Men are poor stuff . . . Men are very poor stuff . . . Oh, men are miserably poor stuff.'* He had little doubt that through this article she was discharging the anger she felt towards him for his silence, but being well out of her reach he was able to appreciate her polemical wit.

> *Oh, men are very poor stuff indeed. And I begin to doubt whether they are ever reasonably efficient in the sphere in which they have specialised. They do not claim to be good. Collectively they do not claim to be beautiful, though private enterprise in this direction is brisk. But they certainly claim to be clever. And looking round at that confusion of undertakings which we call the City one*

begins to doubt. One doubts it still more if one ponders on the law,
which men have had to themselves since the beginning. It is prepos-
terously expensive. One could have four operations for appendicitis
as cheaply as one can get rid of one adulterous husband . . .

When he read this out admiringly to Elizabeth she was unsmiling and unimpressed. She regarded herself as a feminist, but of a more subtle and ingratiating kind than Rebecca West. 'Her sentiments may be feminist,' she said, 'but that kind of exaggerated satire will just reinforce male prejudice against women. It's the journalistic equivalent of the vandalism committed by Mrs Pankhurst's suffragettes.'

He couldn't help feeling that there was some jealousy behind her response, and this became obvious the next day when they went for a long walk in the foothills, taking with them a picnic as usual, and a two-day-old copy of the London *Times*, which was delivered to the Chalet Soleil just as they set out. On a grassy knoll with a fine view of the summit of Mont Blanc they had their picnic lunch and afterwards divided the newspaper between them, describing interesting items to each other. It so happened that his portion contained a letter from Mrs Humphry Ward denouncing the moral tone of the younger generation, and citing the articles of Rebecca West in evidence. He read it out, snorting with derision. 'This is obviously long-meditated revenge for "The Gospel According to Mrs Humphry Ward" in the *Freewoman*,' he said. 'Did you read that, E?' 'I can't remember,' she said. 'Oh you couldn't forget it—it was absolutely brilliant,' he said. 'It was the first thing of hers that impressed me.' 'Really? And what was the second thing,' Elizabeth said: 'her face or her figure?' And before long they were engaged in a silly squabble, he accusing her of unfounded jealousy which she was allowing to distort her critical judgment, and she accusing him of lavishing far more praise on the slight productions of a glib young novice than he had ever accorded her own substantial body of work. 'This is absurd, E,' he said, after several sarcastic exchanges of fire. 'Let us drop the subject.' 'You raised it, so I will allow you the privilege,' she said, and resumed reading the financial pages of the *Times* with an air of intense concentration. He did not relish passing the rest of the afternoon in sulky silence, so after a few minutes had passed, he said: 'Let's make love, E.'

'Certainly not,' she said, without looking up.

'It's the only way to forget this silly quarrel,' he said, and with sudden inspiration continued: 'We'll strip off and make love on the newspaper, all over Mrs Humphry Ward's letter about Rebecca West, and then we'll burn it, and our negative feelings will go up in smoke and disappear into the crystal air of these mountains.'

She looked up at him and burst out laughing. 'You're such a rogue, G! Such an artful rogue. It is impossible to be cross with you for long.'

'You're game, then?'

'Of course I'm game.'

So they stood up and faced each other as they shed their garments one by one until they stood naked under the eye of heaven, and he spread the *Times* on the turf with the Correspondence page uppermost and they lay down and made love with Elizabeth's bottom carefully positioned on Mrs Humphry Ward's letter. Afterwards he set fire to the creased and smudged paper with a match, and squatting side by side on their haunches, like a pair of savages, they watched it flare at the edges, and then blacken and disintegrate and blow away in the breeze in glowing fragments, leaving just a little grey ash on the grass.

'There goes our anger,' he said, and kissed her. They returned home to the Chalet Soleil in excellent spirits.

Rebecca's anger was not so easily dealt with. When he returned to England he found a series of letters from her urgently requesting a meeting. He invited her to tea at the new flat he had just leased in St James's Court, Westminster, as a London base in place of Hampstead—at Elizabeth's suggestion, since she had a flat in the same block and it would be, as she said, 'convenient'. The flat smelled of fresh paint, and had not yet acquired a comfortable lived-in look. It was short of furniture, the windows lacked curtains, and the floors were bare of rugs and carpets. He had hoped the inhospitable ambience would inhibit Rebecca from any untoward display of emotion, but she seemed to take little notice of her surroundings. Her dark eyes were fixed on him as she followed him about the flat from drawing room to kitchen and back to the drawing room again (there were no servants in place so he had to make the tea himself), and he glimpsed in their depths a turmoil of emotions—longing, frustration, anger, despair—as he tried to keep the conversation on light or neutral topics. He asked her what she had been doing while he had been away and she said she had been to Spain with her mother. Where? To Valladolid, Madrid and Seville. And had that been enjoyable? No it had not, she had been suicidally depressed most of the time. He pretended not to have heard her, so she repeated the information in a different form: only the fact that she was travelling with her mother had prevented her from taking her own life. And why would she do a silly thing like that? he asked. 'Because you rejected me,' she said. 'You made me love you, and then you dropped me, as a child drops a toy in which he has lost interest. I don't understand you. Why did you kiss me if you didn't want to be my lover?'

He sighed, and shook his head, and made the speech he had prepared.

'My dear Rebecca, you are very young. And being young—and passionate, and beautiful, and dimly aware when you look at yourself in the mirror of the pleasure your body might give and receive in the embrace of another body—you naturally want to experience that pleasure. But it's not necessary to have a great love affair to do that—the great love affair can wait, and I certainly cannot give it to you. What you really want is some decent fun with a nice young man who is at the same stage of exploration and experimentation as yourself, or perhaps a little ahead of you, and who is responsible about birth control. You have been indoctrinated to think that without the emotions of a grand romance sex is an ugly thing. It's not at all ugly—it is beautiful, and one day—' But at that point in his homily the congregation stood up, gathered her belongings, and walked out of the flat without a word.

Soon afterwards she wrote him a long and extraordinary letter. It began:

Dear H.G.,

During the next few days I shall either put a bullet through my head or commit something more shattering to myself than death. At any rate I shall be quite a different person. I refuse to be cheated out of my deathbed scene. I don't understand why you wanted me three months ago and don't want me now. I wish I knew why that were so. It's something I can't understand, something I despise. And the worst of it is that if I despise you I rage because you stand between me and peace.

And it ended:

You once found my willingness to love you a beautiful and courageous thing. I still think it was. Your spinsterishness makes you feel that a woman desperately and hopelessly in love with a man is

323

an indecent spectacle and a reversal of the natural order of things.
But you should have been too fine to feel like that.
I would give my whole life to feel your arms round me again.
I wish you had loved me. I wish you liked me.

Yours, Rebecca

There was a postscript:

Don't leave me utterly alone. If I live write to me now and then.
You like me enough for that. At least I pretend to myself you do.

He read this letter with alarm at first, then with anger, and finally with
relief. It was sheer emotional blackmail. If the stupid girl were really to kill
herself, leaving a compromising letter, it would destroy him: reputation, marriage, career, the liaison with little E, all smashed irretrievably, as she well
knew. But the final lines, and above all the postscript, gave away the hollow-
ness of her histrionic rhetoric. The melodramatic *'If I live'*—a phrase one of
Ibsen's heroines might have flung across the stage—followed by a bathetic
plea for more letters. This girl was not going to kill herself, she was just trying
to frighten him into making love to her, and she would not succeed. He wrote
a curt reply to her letter: *'How can I be your friend to this accompaniment? I
don't see that I can be of any use or help to you at all. You have my entire
sympathy—but until we can meet on a reasonable basis—goodbye.'*

He slightly softened the harshness of this dismissal by adding a postscript to say that he would look out for her articles in magazines; and he
fully expected to hear from her again, a humble, grovelling letter apologising for the hysteria of her previous missive and promising to behave more
sensibly in future if he could bear to see her again, or at least write. But no
such letter came. In July he read some things of hers in the *New Free-*
woman, a successor to the *Freewoman* under the same editorship but with
a more literary bias, which impressed him deeply. The first was an article
about a singer called Nana she had heard in a cafe in Seville, whose sensu-
ous voice and voluptuous figure had held the audience in a sympathetic
trance and given Rebecca a kind of mystical insight:

I remembered how I once saw the sun beating on the great grey
marbled loins and furrowed back of a grey Clydesdale and watched

the backward thrust of its thigh twitch with power. I was then too
interpenetrated with interests of the soul and the intellect to under-
stand the message of that happy carcass: if my earliest childhood had
realised that the mere framework of life is so imperishable and deli-
cious that with all else lost it is worth living for, I had forgotten it.
Now Nana's dazzling body declared it lucidly: 'Here am I, nothing
but flesh and blood. When your toys of the mind and the spirit are
all broken, come back to my refreshing flesh and blood.'

This was remarkable writing for a twenty-year-old girl, even if it was
obviously influenced by D.H. Lawrence, and it showed that Rebecca had
not been so self-obsessed on her trip to Spain as to fail to profit from the
experience. Another essay called 'Trees of Gold' was equally good. He
could not resist sending her a note of congratulation, while making clear
that he had not changed his mind since their last meeting. *'You are writing
gorgeously again. Please resume being friends. You've had time to see just how
entirely impossible it is for you to get that pure deep draught of excitement and
complete living out of me and how amiable and self-denying it has been of me
not to let you waste your flare-up—one only burns well once—on my cinders.
Nana was tremendous.'* She did not reply immediately, and then it was a
very short message on a postcard, thanking him for his encouraging comments and saying that she was now literary editor of the *New Freewoman*,
and exceedingly busy. In the meantime he had read another striking piece
by her in the magazine, a short story called 'At Valladolid', in which a
young woman on holiday in Spain sought the help of a grumpy doctor to
treat an infected bullet wound, sustained in England when she tried to kill
herself after being spurned by a lover. He recognised himself in this latter
figure with discomfort, but also admiration for the precision with which he
was judged: *'Though my lover had left my body chaste he seduced my soul: he
mingled himself with me till he was more myself than I am and then left me.'*

Over the same period that she was writing these literary pieces for the
New Freewoman she was writing quite different but equally brilliant articles
on current affairs for the *Clarion*, sparkling with mischievous wit and revealing increasing disillusionment with the militant suffragette movement—
not on account of its confrontational tactics, but because its intolerant
sexual politics were a mirror image of masculine prejudice. She even dared
to ridicule a pamphlet by Mrs Pankhurst's daughter Christabel that solemnly warned against 'The Dangers of Marriage'. This turn in her thought

delighted him because it accorded very much with his own views, as he told her in a letter congratulating her on this and other pieces in the same journal. Rebecca had hit her stride as a writer, and there was an excitement in following her rapid development almost week by week, preening himself on having recognised her potential in her very earliest work. On the other hand he was slightly piqued by her brief and restrained replies to his enthusiastic letters. He kept expecting she would ask to meet him again, but she didn't, and he felt that he couldn't propose it himself without sending misleading signals (and, to be honest, losing face).

The continual tension of frustrated expectations and conflicting impulses made him irritable and discontented. Supervision of urgent repairs and improvements at Easton Glebe was preoccupying Jane, making her a less attentive spouse than usual, and when he turned to Elizabeth to be comforted and spoiled he was disappointed. She had become increasingly critical of him of late, as if taking possession of 'Chateau Soleil' (as he sometimes ironically referred to it) had inflated her aristocratic pretensions, which after all amounted to nothing more than a fancy name acquired by marriage, and she was forever correcting his pronunciation or table manners and making little jokes about his humble social origins. Once at a London dinner party to which they were both invited, when he was describing a recent visit to Up Park (or Uppark, as it was known now, though he preferred the old spelling and pronunciation), which revived his early memories of the place, she enquired, 'Did you go in by the front door or through the servants' entrance?' and an embarrassed silence fell on the company. 'I was just curious to know,' she said with a shrug, when he reproached her later. She also began to refer to Jane by slightly mocking nicknames, such as 'Wifey' and 'the Keeper of the Scrolls' (a reference to her typing his manuscripts), and to mimic Jane's characteristic phrases and mannerisms. When he protested about this one day in her flat in St James's Court it led to a blazing row in which she as good as said she thought he should divorce Jane and marry herself if their relationship was to have a future. He walked out in disgust, and discovered the next day that she had decamped to the Chalet Soleil. He dispatched a letter into the dust of her departure, apologising for losing his temper, and begging her not to destroy the very rewarding and civilised relationship they had enjoyed for the past two years. *'My wife has every virtue, every charm, only she's as dead as a herring. You're the eyes of the whole universe to me,'* he wrote, laying it on thick, but her reply was long in coming and cool in tone. When he proposed visiting her soon, she suggested a date in November, several weeks away.

Early in October Rebecca West reviewed *The Passionate Friends* in the *New Freewoman*. Spotting the item in the journal's list of contents, he felt a jolt of intense curiosity mixed with apprehension, and turned to it immediately. It was a long article that paired his novel, somewhat demeaningly, with the latest offering by the popular but worthless Hall Caine. He noted with satisfaction Rebecca's comprehensive disparagement of *The Woman Thou Gavest Me* but skimmed through these pages, eager to discover what she had to say about himself. Would she have seized the opportunity to take revenge for his resistance to her appeals for love, by writing a review even more damaging than her first one of *Marriage*? Or would she try to melt his heart with a panegyric? In fact she had done neither. It was a judicious, well-written review which found things to praise generously in the early part of the novel (*'The first chapter, with its brooding over a dear wilful child in gusts of naughtiness and sickness, is among the very greatest representations of childhood'*) but found fault with much of the rest: *'The skin of one's brain is dappled with goose-flesh at the irritating surface of the style . . . Stratton marries a phantom doormat called Rachel who lives, to Mr Wells' eternal shame in one sentence: "It sounds impudent, I know, for a girl to say so, but we've many interests in common."'* What most intrigued him, however, were Rebecca's comments on the sexual and moral dilemma of the protagonists. If, as this pair seemed to assume, she wrote, men require for some great thing they have to do the inspiration of an achieved passion, this places an intolerable burden of responsibility on women. *'Surely the only way to medicine the ravages of this fever of life is to treat sex lightly, to recognise that in this as in philosophy the one is not more excellent than the many, to think no more hardly of two lovers who part soon than we do of spring for leaving the earth at the coming of June.'* This was very much his own hedonistic attitude to sex, which he had always tried to practise with occasional lapses into jealous possessiveness, but never dared to articulate openly in his fiction. He was delighted to find Rebecca sharing it, and surprised too: he had assumed from her passionate declarations of love that she would not be satisfied with anything but total commitment by himself. Evidently that was not true. Was she, he wondered, sending him a message through this review that she was quite willing to figure in his life as a *passade*?

. . .

Not long afterwards he met Rebecca by chance one afternoon in Piccadilly. He was coming out of Hatchard's as she was coming out of the Royal Academy and they saw each other at the same moment, as if some telepathic force had directed and focused their mutual gaze across the road, the cabs and vans and omnibuses passing between them like flickering shapes in the foreground of a cinematograph film. She stood still and waited as he weaved his way recklessly through the traffic to her side. 'Rebecca!' he said, grasping her hand and holding it. 'You look wonderful.' And she did— radiant, vital, beautiful. He had forgotten how lovely she was. 'I've missed you. Why have you been avoiding me?'

'I haven't been,' she said. 'If you wanted to see me why didn't you ask?'

'Well, I've been very busy . . . but never mind. Let me give you tea somewhere—Fortnum's—we've lots to talk about. Your review of *The Passionate Friends* was most interesting.'

'You weren't offended by it?'

'Well, some comments stung, I admit, but I'm used to that by now. And you said some nice things. But look, will you have tea with me?'

'I'd love to,' she said, smiling.

He took her arm and steered her across the road and into Fortnum and Mason's, where they had a sumptuous tea of crab and cucumber sandwiches, toasted teacakes with damson jam, and cream pastries, of which she partook with eager, healthy appetite. She told him about her work on the *New Freewoman,* writing and commissioning book reviews, and he told her about *The World Set Free,* his novel-in-progress about global war fought with atomic bombs. 'Actually, you know, it was through talking to you about the arms race, that day you came to Easton, that I got the idea for this novel,' he said, altering the actual sequence of events, and saw that she was flattered. 'It's one of several reasons why I'm very glad I thought of inviting you.'

'Harold Rubinstein prophesied that you would,' she said, biting into a cream puff.

'Who is Harold Rubinstein?' he asked, disconcerted by this information.

'He's a solicitor, a Young Fabian and a male feminist—he comes to the Freewoman Circle meetings.'

'A friend of yours, obviously.'

'Yes, we met at the Fabian Summer School. He takes me to concerts occasionally when I can find the time.'

'And when did he prophesy that I would invite you to Easton Glebe?'

'When he read my review of *Marriage*. He said you wouldn't be able to resist the urge to meet me and put me in my place.'

'Did he indeed?' he said. He felt a familiar wave of unpleasant emotion pass through him like a spasm of nausea. It was jealousy: a sudden intuition that, if he should decide after all to respond to Rebecca's desire, this uncannily percipient young man would turn out to be a rival, playing the same devious, disapproving role as Clifford Sharp and Rivers Blanco White in previous affairs. If? There was no longer any 'if'. The instant, visceral effect of this insight was a determination to cut out Mr Rubinstein by possessing Rebecca while he had the opportunity. He turned the conversation to her review of *The Passionate Friends*. 'I was very interested in what you had to say about the necessity of treating sex lightly. It's something I've always believed—not always practised, I admit.'

Rebecca grimaced. 'I got into terrible trouble at home on account of that,' she said. 'Mama was very shocked. And Lettie said I was talking nonsense about something I knew nothing about.'

'It's not nonsense at all, but if you're to extend your knowledge in that area, you will have to leave home.'

'I long to. But I simply can't afford it,' she said.

The waitress came up with the bill, and when he had dealt with that he said, 'My new flat is properly finished and furnished now. Would you like to see it?' As she hesitated, he added: 'I'm alone there at present.'

'I'd love to,' she said, and her eyes told him she knew exactly what he meant.

And so the affair began. On that first occasion Rebecca was ardent but submissive: she was overjoyed simply to have his arms round her, glad to know that he found her desirable, willing to do anything he wanted, not taking the initiative herself, following his movements like someone learning the steps of a new dance. But she learned quickly, and the intensity of her desire was thrilling. One day early in their affair when she came to St James's Court there was a servant in the flat—a woman Jane had recently hired to clean and cook when either or both of them were in residence. He received Rebecca in the drawing room and apologised for the woman's presence. 'I didn't know she was coming,' he said, 'I thought it was her half-day off. But come here and let me kiss you.' They sat down together on the sofa and began to kiss and fondle each other, getting more and more excited. Soon he had her blouse undone and his lips on an exposed breast, while his hand was under her skirt and between her thighs. Rebecca began to moan and heave her pelvis against the pressure of his forefinger. 'Take me, have me!' she whimpered. 'You mean now? Here?' 'Yes, yes!' It was impossible to carry her off to his bedroom, where he kept a supply of French letters, without the risk of encountering the servant, but he was too aroused to want to stop, as much by Rebecca's shameless urgency as his own desire, so he hastily unbuttoned and did as she asked. He considered himself a skilled exponent of coitus interruptus, but on this occasion, sprawled on top of Rebecca, with one foot on the floor, he slipped on a rug and the sudden change of position caused him to ejaculate before he could withdraw. 'I'm sorry,' he said afterwards, but she seemed to think he was apologising for the indecorum of their situation rather than the risk of pregnancy. 'It was my fault for leading you on,' she said. 'Imagine if the woman had come in while we were . . .' She giggled. 'I should be ashamed of myself, but I'm not.' He kissed her and suggested she would probably like to visit the bath-room. 'You'll find a bidet in there,' he said. 'I should make very thorough use of it.' She caught his meaning and looked suddenly serious. 'Oh. Yes, I will. Thank you.' But she came back smiling from the bathroom, evidently placing great confidence in the efficacy of a douche, and he did not worry her with his own misgivings. After that he was scrupulous about using a sheath whenever they made love, until in due course she acquired one of the new female devices.

After two years of playful, sometimes decadent sex with little E, who made him demonstrate his whole repertoire of postures, but never wholly abandoned herself, the fierce passion Rebecca brought to the act of love was transporting, reminding him of the ecstasy he had enjoyed with Amber, and yet with a distinctly different quality. Amber he always thought of as an athlete of sex, a kind of Atalanta, clean-limbed, agile, pagan, whereas there was something feral about Rebecca when she was stripped and hun-gry for love. Her body was less classically beautiful than Amber's, but it was sensual, with a full bust, small waist, broad hips and a generously curved bottom. She had a luxuriant bush of pubic hair. 'I was ashamed of it when it first grew,' she said. 'I thought it looked like an animal's fur.' 'That's what's so nice about it,' he said. 'There's something animal about you that is very exciting. Something feline, a kind of contained energy that might show itself at any moment, like the leap of a panther in the jungle. I shall call you "Panther." ' 'And what shall I call you?' 'Call me "Jaguar". We will be two big cats, mating in the jungle.' This childish fantasy pleased them both, and became an essential element of their relationship.

He confessed to Jane that he was seeing Rebecca and discovered that, as usual, she had already guessed something of the kind was going on. 'Elizabeth won't stand it, if she finds out,' she said.

'You don't think so?' he said.

'You know she won't. Are you going to tell her when you go to Randogne?' His visit to the Chalet Soleil was now imminent.

'I don't know,' he said. 'I'll see.'

He went to Switzerland in a state of indecision. He didn't really want to break with Elizabeth if he could avoid it. Irritating as she had become of late, with her patronising little digs at Jane and himself, she was an ideal mistress: an interesting, intelligent companion, and a lover whose attitude to sex as a source of pleasure rather than an expression of deep emotional commitment was one he in principle approved. That she was well-off, and well-connected, and owned a fine house in his favourite part of Europe where he could stay for extended periods for both work and recreation, were also considerable assets which he would be sorry to sacrifice. On the other hand he was enraptured with young Rebecca: he had never met any woman who combined such exciting sensuality with the intelligence, eloquence and wit she possessed, both in speech and in writing. Elizabeth was an amusing conversationalist and a skilful writer, but within modest limits. She was basically an entertainer, skating elegantly on the surface of life, never plumbing the dark depths, never really challenging or disturbing her readers. Rebecca was only at the beginning of her career, but he was sure she would turn out to be the more considerable writer in the long run, and it would be rewarding to observe and guide her development. Must he choose between these two relationships? Or could he somehow contrive to enjoy both? Should he tell little E about Rebecca when he got to Randogne, and risk an irreversible break-up, or devote himself to smoothing over the bad feeling with which they had last parted, and continue to maintain the liaison with Rebecca in secrecy for as long as she was interested herself?

Because he hadn't made up his mind what to do before he arrived at the

Chalet Soleil he succeeded in doing nothing satisfactorily. Elizabeth greeted him graciously but with something less than joy. He sensed she was expecting a humble apology for his behaviour when they were last together, but he felt he had already done that by letter, and that she had not reciprocated with any admission of being at fault herself. The first days passed quite agreeably in their accustomed way, both of them working in the mornings, he in the main house and she in the Little Chalet, then going for walks in the afternoon, followed by dinner and light reading in the evening with perhaps a little music from the piano, which Elizabeth played extremely well. But she did not come through the secret door between their rooms at night. He felt they were both performing parts, outwardly genial but inwardly watchful, circling each other mentally like wrestlers preparing to grapple but never actually doing so. He asked her what she was working on and she said, 'a novel about adultery'. 'The best sport in the world!' he said, meaning to refer to their own civilised and light-hearted indulgence in it, but her answering smile was slightly forced, and he wondered whether she harboured suspicions that he had been unfaithful to her. She asked him if Rebecca West was still 'pestering' him, and he replied accurately but misleadingly that she was not. But when she made some slighting remarks about Rebecca's contributions to the *New Freewoman*, he said that in his opinion, and that of several others, Fordie Hueffer and Violet for instance, she was the most brilliant young journalist in London. 'Really?' she said in a tone of bored scepticism, but she eyed him as if trying to assess the hidden significance of his words.

He had brought the proofs of *The World Set Free* to work on and one evening read some of it to her, but she didn't care for it. 'Why do you smash the world up like that?' she asked. 'To stop humanity from smashing it up in earnest,' he said. 'But there's a kind of joy in destruction in your descriptions,' she said, 'like a naughty boy kicking over somebody else's sandcastle, that they've spent hours building. How could you bring yourself to bomb Paris, beautiful Paris, to smithereens, even in imagination? After all, these bombs don't actually exist, so nobody could really do it.' 'They will exist one day,' he said. 'So you say,' she jeered. Again she did not come to his room that night—or the next. He sensed that she was waiting for him to beg her to do so, but he was not going to crawl to her. Why should he? It was a kind of silent duel between them—who was going to crack first? Who was going to provoke a confrontation and take responsibility for what followed?

In the end it was himself. After the sixth night spent lying fruitlessly awake in the dark, straining to hear the faint sound of the secret door being slid open, he had had enough, and told Elizabeth, when they stepped out on to the terrace after breakfast, that he would be leaving in the afternoon, two days earlier than planned. They were looking down the valley, which was covered at the bottom by a layer of early morning mist like cotton wool. 'Why?' she said, without taking her eyes off the view. 'I don't see that there's any point in my staying any longer,' he said. 'Are you saying it's all over between us?' she said. 'Every night since I arrived I have lain awake, waiting for you to come to my room,' he said, 'and you didn't come. I take that to be a kind of statement.' 'I suppose it is,' she said. 'It's because I'm common, isn't it?' he said. 'No, it's not,' she said, turning to face him. 'You *are* a little common in some ways, G, indeed it's common just to say *"It's because I'm common, isn't it?"* But you're also a genius, and one can forgive a genius for many imperfections. There's someone else, though, isn't there?' 'Suppose for the sake of argument there were,' he said. 'Why should that affect a relationship that has suited both of us very well for the last two years?' 'I know there is someone else,' she said. 'I feel it. I don't like it. I won't have it.' 'Very well,' he said. 'I'll go and pack my bags.'

The Chalet Soleil was reached from Randogne by a little mountain railway that terminated a mile below the house. As he walked down the steep path that led to the station, preceded by a servant with a handcart containing his luggage, he felt sure that Elizabeth was watching him from a window, or the terrace, but he did not look back. The further he left the chalet behind him, the more his spirits rose, and they continued to rise as he travelled across Europe towards London, where Rebecca awaited him. If, as it had turned out, he could not have both women, he had no doubt that he had made the right choice between them. Little E had nothing new to give him. Rebecca was youth, life, and infinite potential.

As soon as he got back to Easton Glebe he told Jane what had happened: Elizabeth was history, Rebecca was the future. 'As you wish, H.G.,' she said, with a sigh. 'But I don't want to meet Rebecca again, and I certainly don't want her staying here.' He agreed without demur to these conditions, and thought he understood the feelings from which they arose. Jane wouldn't be able to relate to Rebecca as she had to Elizabeth, a woman of her own age, or to Amber, a girl she had known from adolescence, who had been almost a surrogate daughter to her. Rebecca—not only young, but assertive and ambitious—would be more of a challenge, even a threat to Jane, if allowed into the ambit of their domestic and social life.

So he had to pursue his affair with Rebecca in a separate zone, and it remained clandestine. He did not meet her in St James's Court any more—there was always the risk of the housekeeper noticing and gossiping, not to mention the embarrassing possibility of running into Elizabeth going in or out of the building when he had Rebecca on his arm. Rebecca had now moved out of her family home into a bed-sitting room in Maida Vale, but he could not visit her there with propriety. For a while they met regularly at the house of a married friend of Rebecca's, Carrie Townshend, and he would take her off afterwards for a few hours to rooms he rented in War-wick Street, Pimlico, whose owner, Mrs Strange, was sympathetic to lovers. There they could act out their Panther–Jaguar fantasy without restraint. She would crouch on the bed, naked, like a panther couchant, with her head up, following him with her eyes as he, naked too, prowled round the room, emitting low-pitched growls, and then he would suddenly pounce, and locked together they would roll about on the bed, or on the floor, lick-ing, biting and digging their claws into each other before he mated with her and they came to a noisy climax. Then she would purr in his arms until they both fell into a delicious sleep. He had never known such liberating sex, sex which acknowledged the animal nature of lust but turned it into a kind of erotic theatre. It provided a private language for their frequent ex-change of love letters. *'There is NO Panfer but Panfer, and she is the Prophet of the most High Jaguar which is bliss and perfect being,'* he wrote to her, and drew a picshua at the end of the two of them as big cats. He wrote of want-ing to nuzzle her *'dear fur'* and of coming up to Town for *'a snatch at your ears and a whisk of your tail'*. But he also wrote more seriously, *'I've been home two hours and twice I've turned round to say something to you—and you weren't there. My dear Panther it's like the feeling of suddenly missing a limb.'* This was no *passade*: to his wonderment he was genuinely, helplessly in love—and for the first time in his life with a woman who if not yet his intellectual equal, might very well turn out to be. She did not flatter him or defer to him or abase herself before his genius, but challenged him and stimulated him by her shrewd insights into his work and that of others. And she could be very funny. She had been taken up lately by Fordie and Violet Hueffer, who were living together as man and wife in spite of ru-mours that he was not legally divorced, and Rebecca's description of being kissed by Fordie, 'like being the toast under a poached egg', had kept him chuckling intermittently for a whole day. When a group of people were discussing Cecil Chesterton's dirty-looking complexion and someone said it was natural, because she had seen him bathing in the sea at Le Touquet and he came out looking just the same as when he went in, Rebecca instantly asked, 'But did you look at the Channel?'

The honeymoon phase of their affair came to an end early in January of 1914, when Rebecca told him she was probably pregnant. They met by previous arrangement at Mrs Strange's house, and as soon as he saw her face he knew what she was going to say. Her period was long overdue, and she was experiencing some morning sickness. 'What shall I do?' she said, weeping. 'You mean, what shall *we* do,' he said, and she smiled gratefully through her tears. 'The first thing,' he said, 'is to arrange for you to see a doctor and confirm it. But we should assume that you are pregnant, and I think I know how it happened.' He reminded her of the occasion in the flat at St James's Court when they had made love on the sofa in his drawing room. 'It was my fault,' he said. 'No, it was mine for urging you on,' she said. 'Well, let's not argue about that,' he said. 'What shall I do?' she said again. 'What you must do is have the baby,' he said. 'You're not thinking of anything else, I hope?' She shook her head, but without conviction. 'Is there any other way?' she said. 'I've scarcely begun my career, and now it's all ruined.' 'Nonsense,' he said briskly. 'And no, there isn't any other way. Abortion is dangerous and a criminal offence. Don't think of it. I'll arrange a comfortable confinement for you in some quiet country place where I can visit, and you can get on with your writing until your time is due. Then you'll have the baby and we will find some worthy couple to adopt it, and you'll be free to resume your independent life again, with me as your lover. What do you say to that?' 'I say you're a wonderful Jaguar,' she said smiling and blinking away her tears. 'But what will Jane say?' 'Jane will take it in her stride,' he said. 'It won't be the first time, I'm afraid.'

In fact Jane came very near to losing her temper with him on this occasion. 'For God's sake, H.G.!' she exclaimed when he broke the news. 'Not again!'

'It was unintentional, of course,' he said. 'My fault—I must take responsibility, and I do. You needn't bother yourself about it. I will make all the arrangements.'

'Well, you've had plenty of experience,' Jane said tartly. 'Don't expect me to buy the layette this time.'

He was surprised how blithe he felt about the situation. But perhaps, he admitted to himself, he wasn't sorry to have bound Rebecca to himself all the more securely by this accident, and he set about making arrangements for her confinement with careful deliberation. It was true, as Jane said, that he had his experience with Amber to draw on, but there was a big difference: in that case they had hoisted the flag of Free Love above the cottage in which she awaited the birth of her child, and paid the price for defying conventional morality. The resulting uproar had put him under intolerable strain, and nearly destroyed his career as a public man, but gradually the episode had faded from the collective memory, and he was now respected and—in most circles—accepted again. He did not want to jeopardise that recovery by another scandal of the same kind. He therefore looked for a location safely remote from London and its gossipmongers, and, after doing a considerable amount of research, settled on the Welsh coastal resort of Llandudno. He invented a fictitious identity for himself as 'Mr West', and obtained details of houses and rooms to let there from local estate agents. At that point, however, he was obliged to leave the matter temporarily in Rebecca's hands, while he made a three-week trip to St Petersburg with Maurice Baring that had been arranged before he learned she was pregnant.

He had known Baring for some years and liked him, in spite of their very different backgrounds and beliefs: he was the son of a banker-made-baronet famous for risky financial speculation, and a Roman Catholic convert. He had been educated at Eton and Cambridge, which he left without a degree, but it must have been out of boredom with the curriculum rather than academic failure, for he possessed high intelligence and an enviable gift for languages which had led to a distinguished and adventurous life as a diplomat and foreign correspondent. He had covered the Russo-Japanese War for the *Daily Telegraph*, staying on in Russia as their correspondent, and had written an excellent book on Russian literature. From Baring he learned that all his own books had been translated in Russia and published in a collected edition in 1909, and were widely read—something he had been unaware of, and which pleased him even though he derived no royalties from the sales. He had expressed an interest in visiting the country one day, and Baring had promised to arrange it, recommending that he go in midwinter in order better to understand the Russian character. 'The climate is utterly different from ours,' Baring said, 'much more extreme. So are the people.'

He certainly found St Petersburg—a hugely enlarged Venice locked in frozen waterways and covered in dirty snow—less like England than anywhere he had visited before, the impenetrability of the language and the strangeness of the Cyrillic alphabet reinforcing its dream-like improbability. *'St Petersburg is more like Rebecca than any capital I have seen,'* he wrote to her soon after their arrival, *'alive and dark and untidy (but trying to be better) and mysteriously beautiful.'* He knew only one person there—Maxim Gorky, whom he had met in New York in 1906, when their respective tours of the country coincided. They found then that they had much in common and got on very well together, though needing an interpreter to converse. As well as both being storytellers from humble backgrounds and with socialist sympathies, they shared a vulnerability to censorious moralists. Shortly after Gorky arrived in New York to an enthusiastic welcome, it was discovered that the gracious lady who accompanied him, Madame Maria Andrevieva, was not his legal wife, and a storm of public outrage was whipped up in the press. The bewildered couple were ejected from their hotel and refused admission by others, and were in danger of being incarcerated on Ellis Island to await deportation, lest they should infect the New World with their depravity, when they were rescued by a rich and enlightened American who took them into his house and entertained them privately for several months. 'The best months of my life,' Gorky recalled with a hearty laugh, when they were reunited in St Petersburg. 'I never got so much written in the time.' Baring interpreted on this and many other occasions when he met writers, journalists, politicians and liberal aristocrats, and without him he would have been lost.

He found the volatile political atmosphere of St Petersburg exciting, and sensed that although Russia was deeply backward by Western European standards there was a readiness for radical change among the intelligentsia which made the Fabians and trade union-backed Labour politicians at home look timid in comparison. Progressive political opinions were not however incompatible with hedonism in St Petersburg. His evenings were crowded with invitations to parties where wine and vodka flowed freely, and suppers in restaurants where the provision of *cabinets particuliers* was more blatant than in London or even Paris. The glittering high-ceilinged dining room of the Hotel Metropole, humming with laughter, chatter, and the music of a gypsy orchestra, had a balcony that ran round all four sides with doors and little curtained windows behind which customers entertained, and were entertained by, ladies wearing flamboyant gowns and a great deal of paint and jewellery.

At another time he might have been tempted to take advantage of this convenient arrangement, but he was determined to be faithful to Rebecca. He wrote to her regularly, combining assurances of his love and longing with practical instructions on what to say to Llandudno landladies. *'You are Mrs West. I am Mr West. Write and arrange that you are to stay at Llandudno until your baby is born. Mr West is in the cinematograph business, and he has to write things. He wants a quiet room to write in and he has to have a separate bedroom. (Though he proposes to spend much time in your delicious bed.) Make this clear and get everything comfortably arranged. That house has to be our home. We have to settle down and work there and love there and live there, and you have to see that it is all right. You have got to take care of me and have me fed and peaceful and comfortable. You are going to be my wife—'* He suspended the rapid movement of his fountain pen across the hotel notepaper, realising that this last was a rash thing to say, but he couldn't cross it out without revealing his second thoughts, and he hadn't time to rewrite the letter—Baring was waiting below in the lobby to take him to have dinner with Vladimir Nabokov, a distinguished criminologist who was apparently an admirer and had a fourteen-year-old son devoted to his scientific romances. He let the word 'wife' stand, but continued in a vein so rhapsodic and hyperbolical that Rebecca couldn't possibly take it literally: *'We will have great mysteries in each other's arms, we shall walk together and eat together and talk together. You are the woman and you are to be both the maker and ruler in all this life. Panther, I love you as I have never loved anyone. I love you like a first love. I give myself to you. I am glad beyond any gladness that we are to have a child. I kiss your feet, I kiss your shoulders, and the soft side of your body. I want to come into the home you are to make for me. I shall hurry home for it. Get it ready.'*

They were reunited in mid-February and spent two days and nights in Mrs Strange's house in Pimlico. When their sexual starvation had been allayed by several bouts of torrid jungly intercourse, they turned their attention to practicalities. Rebecca had not corresponded with Llandudno in his absence, having discovered that the railway connections with Easton were appalling and it would have taken him all day to make the journey. It seemed that his choice of that location had been based on a ludicrous misreading of the timetables in Bradshaw, and instead he now proposed Hunstanton on the north Norfolk coast: equally remote from London, but relatively easy to reach from Easton via Bishop's Stortford. They must go there to look for a suitable dwelling as soon as possible, he declared—but by separate trains, in case they were observed together. Rebecca laughed, thinking he was joking, and when she realised that he wasn't said, 'Aren't you taking discretion to extremes?' 'It's for Jane's sake,' he lied. 'It will save her a great deal of embarrassment if our secret is kept.' 'I had to tell Mother, of course,' she said, 'and Lettie and Winnie.' 'And how did they take it?' 'Badly,' she said. 'Mother feels you betrayed her trust, seducing me after being a guest in her home.' 'But *you* invited me to tea,' he said, 'and *you* seduced *me*—well, pursued me anyway.' 'Quite so. I told her that. It didn't make any difference. Lettie thinks I've been a fool, and that you took advantage of me. I don't think you will be invited to tea again—not until we are married.' 'Hmm, that may be some while off,' he said. 'I shouldn't raise their hopes prematurely.' 'But you said in your letter—' she began. 'I know I did, Panther,' he said quickly. 'But I meant that we would be married *spiritually*. My marriage with Jane is not a real marriage, it's a convenient companionship. We haven't been lovers for years. You are my mate—soulmate and bedmate. One day—when my boys are older—we may go through the tedious legal formalities to satisfy your mother and sisters, but that won't change the nature of our relationship.' He tried to convey the idea he had of the future: two marriages, two homes, one official and sexless, the other secret and passionate. 'Do you mean we should keep the child, and bring it up ourselves?' she said. 'If you wish. It's entirely up to you,' he said magnanimously. 'No, I don't wish,' she said. 'I want to be free to write.' 'Absolutely,' he said. 'But won't I feel sad when it comes to giving him—or her—to somebody else?' 'We'll find a model couple who will let us visit him—I'm sure it's going to be a boy—whenever we like,' he said, 'and take him on treats and holidays whenever we want to. He'll call us Uncle and Auntie.' 'Uncle Jaguar and Auntie Panther!' she said, laughing, delighted with the scenario he had summoned up.

They travelled separately to Hunstanton, met by arrangement in the station buffet, and found furnished rooms to let in a house which was suitable if not seductive. 'Brig-y-don' on Victoria Avenue was a raw red-brick terraced house with bow windows that jutted out into a patch of front garden, and from the first floor gave a view of the Wash and a sideways glimpse of the North Sea, looking cold and grey at this time of year. A summer resort for people in search of a quiet holiday with bracing air, Hunstanton was as still as a tomb in February. Rebecca looked glum at the prospect of spending the next six months there, but he did his best to cheer her up. 'You will get a lot of writing done,' he said, 'and I will spend as much time as I can with you.' He kept his word, visiting her every week for at least two days, often more, and while he was away he stoked the fire of her passion by amorous anticipations of their next meeting: *I shall lay my paw upon you this Wednesday night & snuff under your chin and bite your breast & lick your flank & proceed to other familiarities. I shall roll you over & do what I like with you. I shall make you pant & bite back. Then I shall give you a shake to quiet you & go to sleep all over you & if I snore, I snore. Your Lord. The Jaguar.'* Rebecca sometimes reproached him for writing these naughtily explicit letters, asking him to imagine the consequences if their landlady Mrs Crown should come across one, but he knew that she found them arousing. Their sexual life remained as exciting as ever, and as her belly swelled it became more comfortable as well as conducive to their private fantasy to come to climax in the natural position of feline copulation, Rebecca crouched under him as he covered her from behind, with her head buried in a pillow to muffle her yowls lest they reach the ears of Mrs Crown downstairs. For her benefit and that of the neighbours they acted out the revised story he had prepared of a busy journalist visiting his pretty young wife whom he had brought to this healthy spot from smoky London for her confinement. They took sedate walks arm in arm on the broad beach when the tide was out, or along the grassy cliffs when it was in, filling their lungs with deep breaths of the famous air, and smiling politely at passers-by.

The two clouds that cast a shadow over his spirits that spring concerned his professional life. *The World Set Free* was published and poorly received by the reviewers. The premise of atomic energy and atomic bombs was considered too preposterous to obtain even a willing suspension of disbelief, the message was one they had heard from him too many times before, and his attempt to enliven the narrative at the end by having a wicked German emperor try to sabotage the creation of a world government was deemed more appropriate to a boys' weekly magazine than an adult novel, and likely to inflame the already dangerously overheated popular prejudice against Germany. This reception was a blow to his self-esteem, exacerbated by imagining the smug satisfaction Elizabeth would take from it. But shortly afterwards he received a more wounding blow—more like a stab in the back—from, of all people, Henry James.

James had responded six months previously to *The Passionate Friends* as its author knew he would, professing exaggerated admiration for the ambition of the enterprise but finding much fault with the execution, and he had replied as he always did, admitting his faults in the Master's own hyperbolical manner: '*It is when you write to me out of your secure and masterly finish, out of your golden globe of leisurely (yet not slow) and infinitely easy accomplishment that the sense of my unworthiness and rawness is most vivid. Then indeed I want to embrace your feet and bedew your knees with tears—of quite unfruitful penitence.*' Perhaps he had overdone the imitation of James's epistolary style on that occasion and the older man had noticed, or perhaps it was the Magdalen image that gave his game away and caused offence. But tweaking an old friend's pomposity in private correspondence was one thing—attacking a colleague in the *Times Literary Supplement* quite another. In a long two-part article published in that journal at the end of March and the beginning of April, James surveyed 'The Younger Generation' of British novelists, meaning those younger than James; he and Arnold Bennett, both now in their mid-forties, figured prominently and came in for severe reprimand. They were held up as the most successful of contemporary English novelists, but by the same token the worst, because they set the others such a bad example—sacrificing beauty of form, intensity of effect, all the qualities which made the novel an art, to '*value by saturation . . . They squeeze out to the utmost the plump and more or less juicy orange of a particular acquainted state and let the affirmation of energy, however directed or undirected, constitute for them the "treatment" of the theme.*' James had a good go at Bennett on this score, and then turned to Wells:

> *The more he knows and knows, or at any rate learns and learns—the more, in other words, he establishes his saturation—the greater is our impression of his holding it good enough for us, such as we are, that he shall but turn out his mind and its contents upon us by any free familiar gesture as from a high window forever open (Mr Wells having as many windows as an agent who has bought up the lot of the most eligible to retail for a great procession).*

341

He flushed as he read this, and read it again several times. It was extremely, deliberately insulting, this image of his mind as a receptacle of miscellaneous rubbish carelessly emptied from on high on to the heads of any persons unfortunate enough to be passing below, with the added insinuation of cynical commercial motives in the acquisition of numerous windows from which to perform the action. He showed it to Jane, who laughed. 'Is he referring to slops being emptied from tenement windows, like they used to do in Scotland, calling out "Gardy loo!"' 'I doubt it,' he said, 'but it's quite offensive enough without that interpretation. I can't think what's got into him.' 'Envy, probably,' she said. 'Nobody could envy me the reviews I've had for *The World Set Free*,' he said. 'Envy of your sales, I mean, your fame,' she said. 'That's why he has it in for you and Arnold. You know he always hankered after a big popular success and never got it.' 'You may be right,' he said. 'But basically we have utterly different ideas of what novels are for. We've both been writing increasingly insincere letters to each other for years, and it's a relief in a way that it's finally over. The gloves are off.' Jane looked at him shrewdly. 'I hope you're not thinking of writing to the *TLS* about it, H.G.,' she said. 'You'll only make yourself look small and hypersensitive.' 'No, I'm not going to write to the *TLS*,' he said. 'Good,' she said. 'Don't let it get under your skin.'

But it *had* got under his skin, and he did intend to write something that would relieve the irritation. He went to his study and took from a locked drawer the manuscript of a book he had been working on intermittently, at long intervals, for nearly a decade, provisionally entitled *Boon*. He had no definite plans to publish it when it was finished, if it were ever finished. It was a difficult book to classify or describe—not that he had tried to describe it to anybody. It was a very private, almost secret work into which he periodically discharged the black bile of his feelings about English literary and intellectual life in the twentieth century: satirical, iconoclastic, fragmentary, digressive, bookish, a bit like Swift's *A Tale of a Tub*, a bit like Sterne's *Tristram Shandy*, comparable to Peacock's conversation novels, explicitly indebted to Mallock's *The New Republic*, but more heterogeneous than any of these precursors. It purported to be the 'Literary Remains' of a writer called George Boon, edited by a fatuous hack called Reginald Bliss. Boon was a respected and well-rewarded author such as H.G. Wells might have become had he stayed in Sandgate and pursued the conventional life of an Edwardian Man of Letters. A chapter which sounded like an opening one but in fact occurred halfway through, began: *'There was once an Author who pursued fame and prosperity in a pleasant villa on the south coast of England. He wrote stories of an acceptable nature and rejoiced in a growing public esteem, carefully offending no one and seeking only to please.'* Boon's unpublished literary remains, however, revealed to his editor's embarrassment a much more subversive and anarchic character, who was in a state of raging inner rebellion against the established literary culture and fantasised various projects to satirise and undermine it.

He began to write a new chapter for this book, entitled 'Of Art, of Literature, of Mr Henry James', in which *'Boon sat on the wall of his vegetable garden and discoursed upon James'*, describing the Jamesian aesthetic of fiction in a fashion that became increasingly prejudicial as it went on:

> *He demands homogeneity . . . Why should a book have that? For a picture it's reasonable because you have to see it all at once. But there is no need to see a book all at once . . . He talks of selection . . . In practice James's selection becomes just omission and nothing more. For example, he omits opinions. In all his novels you will find no people with defined political opinions, no people with religious opinions, none with clear partisanships or with lusts and whims . . . There are no poor people dominated by the imperatives of Saturday night and Monday morning . . . Having first made sure that he has scarcely anything to express, he then sets to work to express it . . . He brings up every device of language to state and define. Bare verbs he rarely tolerates. He splits his infinitives and fills them up with adverbial stuffing. He presses the passing colloquialism into his service. His vast paragraphs sweat and struggle. And all for tales of nothingness . . . It is leviathan retrieving pebbles. It is a magnificent but painful hippopotamus resolved at any cost, even at the cost of its dignity, upon picking up a pea which has got into a corner of its den. Most things, it insists, are beyond it, but it can, at any rate, modestly, and with an artistic singleness of mind, pick up that pea.*

Boon was for him a kind of castor oil of the spirit: reading this chapter through the next morning he found he had been purged of his anger and resentment. He spent another enjoyable day in which Boon sketched out a Jamesian novel called 'The Spoils of Miss Blandish', with a plot that didn't begin for 150 pages and concerned the hero's search for the perfect butler.

It was so funny that he longed to see it in print. Perhaps one day he would finish *Boon* after all.

There was a level paddock at Easton Glebe which he had ordered to be mown and marked out as a hockey pitch, and provided with proper netted goals, on which weekend guests were required to play mixed hockey as a condition of their entertainment. Hockey sticks for both right-handed and left-handed persons, padded shin-guards, and a large box of white cricket and tennis shoes of all sizes, were provided. The ball used was a hard leather cricket ball. Grown men—not just London aesthetes, but Members of Parliament, seasoned journalists, and even sportsmen who fancied themselves with a rod or a gun, were apt to pale at the sight of that ball, imagining what damage it might inflict on their persons when propelled by a reckless and undisciplined player, but they were made to feel that they could not excuse themselves with honour. Ladies were given more latitude, but as most of them had played the game at school they were generally more willing to participate. Allowance was made for age. The younger and more vigorous players were forwards, and did most of the running; the more mature played in defence, and the elderly were given extra protective garments and put in goal. He felt obliged to set an example himself, however, and always played forward, while also lending a hand in defence, and refereeing the game at the same time (since he was the only one who knew the rules peculiar to Easton hockey).

'You're going to injure yourself one of these days,' Jane warned him, after a particularly vigorous game, and on the very next occasion, early in June, he did, straining the ligaments in his left knee. The doctor strapped it up, prescribed bed-rest for one week and forbade travel for an indefinite period. This had several inconveniences. It prevented him from improving his skills in driving the motor car of which he had recently taken delivery, a four-seater Willys-Overland with white-walled tyres, which he had christened 'Gladys', and whose gear-change mechanism he had just begun to get the hang of. It also prevented him from visiting Rebecca, which understandably drew some complaint from her, but there was nothing he could do about it except write fervent daily letters, reflecting ruefully that by the time they were reunited she might be too near the term of her pregnancy to find making love comfortable or safe. To keep her now very visible condition secret, Rebecca was pretending to her London friends that she was ill, unable to visit or be visited, and consequently she was lonely. Fortunately her sister Lettie agreed to keep her company while his knee was mending, and the enforced hiatus in their meetings had its advantages in that it enabled him to get on with his main work in progress, another 'prig' novel called *The Research Magnificent*, whose heroine, Amanda Morris, had developed a close resemblance to Rebecca West (she called the hero 'Leopard' and he called her 'Cheetah'). His convalescence passed pleasantly enough, the weekdays devoted to quiet sedentary work, and weekends spent relaxing in the company of visitors who were all the more convivial when they discovered they would not have to play hockey. The weather was exceptionally fine.

Then on the 28th of June the Austrian Archduke Ferdinand and his wife Sophie were assassinated by Serbian terrorists at Sarajevo, and a shudder of apprehension went through the entire continent of Europe. The remainder of the summer was dominated by talk of war. Would there be one, or wouldn't there? And how far would it spread? On the face of it the issue was just a territorial dispute in the Balkans between the Austro-Hungarian Empire and Serbia, but potentially it involved the other great European powers, Germany, Russia, France and Great Britain, who were tied to each other by various treaties and alliances which might drag them into the conflict. Rebecca, after reading a newspaper article which argued that this outcome was inevitable, sent him an anxious letter, but he reassured her: there would be no war. The world was mad, but not that mad. And he genuinely believed this. Although for the past decade he had been predicting a major war, indeed a global war, if mankind did not find a rational way of ordering its affairs and settling its disputes, he had prophesied only to warn, to have his predictions falsified by appropriate action, and he always post-dated the fictional conflagration by a number of decades. That the political leaders of the Great Powers would allow it to happen now, in the summer of 1914, seemed unthinkable, preposterous; and the fact that it was a particularly glorious summer made the threat seem all the more unreal. Day after day the sun rose into a clear blue sky and shone until evening on the ripening wheat of the Essex fields, on the green, well-watered lawns and shrubberies of Easton Glebe, on the damask-covered tea table and the striped deckchairs under the shade of the great cedar. It was idyllic. How could such peace be shattered?

The news however was increasingly grave, and a particular circumstance of the Wells household brought its implications home to them more sharply than to most English families. The previous summer he had decided that his sons needed a new tutor, a male one, more rigorous and highly qualified than Miss Meyer, admirably as she had served them. He had accordingly parted with her on amicable and generous terms and appointed in her place a young German, Herr Karl Bütow, a Pomeranian student of philology working towards his doctorate, to introduce Gip and Frank to Latin and Greek and to establish a more systematic curriculum in other subjects. He was a pleasant young man, kind, courteous, methodical, who did not always understand English humour and English manners, but adjusted uncomplainingly to the peculiarities and whims of the Easton household. He was charmed to discover that the boys had a brown squirrel which they had tamed and trained, called Fritz, and adopted it as his own pet, allowing it to sleep in his room. Karl Bülow was the very best type of German, and having him in the family made the prospect of war more horrible and at the same time more improbable. It was his own conviction that the ordinary people of Germany, people like Karl, did not want war, and that they were being hustled towards it by a combination of Prussian imperialism and the greed of the German armaments industry—'Kaiser and Krupp', in a nutshell—who were trying to get their way by bullying and threatening. Surely, he would say, when the subject came up, as it did every day, surely if their bluff were called, and the Kaiser declared war, the decent German majority would simply refuse to fight? Karl Bütow shook his head in melancholy dissent. 'There is a mood for war in my country,' he said. 'I have felt it. And even those who disagree will not dissent. We are an obedient people.' Like all young Germans he had done his military service, and was liable to be called up in the event of war.

For a few weeks nothing really alarming developed on the Continent, and the English newspapers were more preoccupied with the possibility of civil war in Great Britain, because the Protestants of Ulster, led by Sir Edward Carson, threatened to resist the Irish Home Rule bill by force if it were passed by Parliament. For a while Ireland dominated the headlines and relegated the Balkans to second place. But then on the 23rd of July came the news of Austria-Hungary's peremptory ultimatum to Serbia. 'This is very bad,' said Karl. 'Russia will mobilise in support of Serbia, Germany will mobilise in support of Austria. I will be called up. It is really very annoying. It will seriously delay the completion of my thesis.' He made enquiries and a few days later received an official letter requiring him to return immediately to Germany to report for military service. The whole family and some of the servants went to the station to see him off, and there were tears on several cheeks as the train drew away and Karl leaned out of the window to sadly wave goodbye.

'Well, if there is a war, it won't last long,' he said to Jane, as the train disappeared out of sight in its own smoke and steam. 'Germany will be taking on Russia, France and us, all at once. They can't possibly win. We'll see Karl back at Easton next year.' He spoke more confidently than he felt, for it was well known that the German armies were formidably well armed and trained.

'I hope you're right, H.G.,' Jane said, 'but I feel afraid.'

Many others were afraid. There were reports of people stockpiling food and of a run on the banks as clients tried to convert their banknotes and deposits into gold sovereigns. Rebecca was alarmed and wired him to ask for his advice, addressing the telegram to 'Mr West' in her perturbation. He wrote back *'Keep your gold and cash for your tradespeople until they are reconciled to notes and pay Mrs Crown in notes.'* He jocularly forbade her to go off as a war correspondent, citing imaginary headlines—*'The First War Correspondent With Child. Impression of a Battlefield by a New Comer'*—and concluded encouragingly: *'Prepare your Citizen for the Age of Peace.'*

But this optimistic exhortation was rapidly undermined by events. On Thursday 29th July, Austria-Hungary rejected Serbia's reply to the ultimatum and declared war. On Friday 30th, Russia mobilised in response. On Saturday 31st Germany gave an ultimatum to Russia demanding cessation of military activities. France reaffirmed its support of Russia. Germany shook its fist at France. Great Britain sought assurances from both France and Germany that in the event of hostilities Belgian neutrality would be respected. It was common knowledge that this was the only route by which Germany could make an effective attack on France, and Britain was bound by treaty to defend Belgian sovereignty. France of course agreed; Germany did not respond. On Saturday, the first day of August, France and Germany both mobilised their armies and Germany declared war on Russia. Suddenly Armageddon was at hand.

And yet it was still hard to believe, especially at Easton. August 3rd was Bank Holiday Monday, the day of the annual Easton Lodge Fête, when Lady Warwick opened her grounds to the local populace. There was always a funfair with steam-driven carousels and coconut shies, stalls offering gaudy prizes for feats of strength or skill with hammers, airguns and darts, and refreshment tents offering tea and cakes and lemonade. Lady Warwick's gardens could be inspected for a modest entry fee, the proceeds going to local charities. The Shaws were staying at Easton Glebe for the weekend, and some friends in the neighbourhood, including Ralph Blumenfeld and his son John, joined them that day, which was as fine as its predecessors. After lunch they strolled the mile to the fairground, the ladies tilting parasols against the hot sun, the men in linen jackets and straw boaters (all except Shaw, who sweated conscientiously in his usual Jaeger suit), hearing as they approached the strains of the steam organ, and discussing the war that now seemed inevitable. The crowds in the fairground however appeared surprisingly untroubled by the news, perhaps because they didn't realise its gravity, or possibly because they had decided there was nothing they could do about it, so they might as well make merry while they could. The air rang with laughter, cheers, whoops, and the foot-tapping cadences of the steam organ. He and Shaw went on arguing.

Shaw had come to Easton directly from the Fabian Summer School where the orthodox line was still faith in disarmament, to be magically forced upon governments by co-ordinated General Strikes. 'Sidney Webb refuses to believe that there is going to be a European war, on the grounds that it would be "too insane",' Shaw reported. 'Well, so it is, but it's going to happen. We might have seen it coming if we hadn't been blackmailed to distraction by Carson and his gang.'

'You don't deny, I hope, that we are honour bound to get involved if Germany invades Belgium?' he demanded.

'We haven't always been so scrupulous about national honour if expediency dictated otherwise,' Shaw said. 'The treaty in question was signed eighty years ago in an entirely different Europe, and there was no need for us to bind ourselves to defend Belgium in all circumstances. We were foolishly lured into the diplomatic game of treaties and guarantees and ultimatums that makes politicians feel so important.'

He took Shaw's point, but his sardonic detachment seemed irresponsible. 'Never mind that now!' he cried. 'If the Germans invade Belgium, they will invade us too. We must prepare to resist them. We must get out our shotguns and man the hedges and ditches. If Germany wins this war, it will be the end of civilisation as we know it.'

'It may come to that whoever wins,' Shaw said dourly.

While Shaw's attitude seemed to be 'a plague on all their houses', he himself felt more and more possessed by a violent and very personal anti-German feeling. By provoking this war of uncontrollable scope and scale,

Germany mocked his utopian hopes for mankind. He felt swelling within him a new conviction and a new sense of mission: German militarism had to be confronted and defeated at all costs.

The Shaws left the next day. After he had seen them off at the station he went to the post office and learned the latest news: Germany had declared war on France and, ignoring British warnings, demanded passage for its armies through Belgium. It was now inevitable that Britain would be drawn into the conflict. Rebecca sent a frantic wire saying she was ill, and feared for the unborn child. 'I must go and see her,' he said to Jane, who agreed at once. His knee was now mended, but he didn't feel equal to a long and unfamiliar journey by car to Hunstanton, so he drove the relatively short distance to Bishop's Stortford and left Gladys there, proceeding by train to his destination.

He found Rebecca in bed and in considerable distress, suffering abdominal pains. The doctor had been to see her and feared 'complications', as he cabled to Jane the next morning. She replied: 'I AM FULL OF MISERY AT YOUR TELEGRAM STOP IT ISN'T REBECCA HERSELF WHO IS IN DANGER IS IT STOP I TRY TO THINK THE MESSAGE MIGHT MEAN THE CHILD NOT HER STOP THIS IS HORRIBLE STOP GIVE HER MY DEAR LOVE IF YOU CAN STOP'. Sitting at her bedside he read out this message to Rebecca, who was inclined to regard Jane as a vindictively jealous wife and make occasional remarks to that effect. 'You see?' he said, 'Jane doesn't hate you. She sends you her love.' 'But she says I might die. I think she unconsciously wants me to die,' said Rebecca ungratefully. This telegram seemed to have the effect of making her determined to live, however, and when the doctor called again to examine her he took a more sanguine view of her symptoms and attributed them to indigestion. He also brought the news that Germany had invaded Belgium. Lettie, who had been summoned by Rebecca, arrived from London that afternoon confirming that Asquith had announced that Great Britain was at war with Germany.

'I must get home,' he said to Rebecca.

'Don't go,' she pleaded. 'I feel the baby may come at any moment.'

'It's not due yet.'

'I know, but . . . it could be early. Why must you go?'

'I have to write something about this war, for the *Daily Chronicle*,' he said. He had a lucrative agreement with this paper to write on topical issues any time he felt inclined. 'I can't fight, but I can write, and I can only do that at home. I will leave you in Lettie's safe hands.' And against her protest he caught the last train from Hunstanton to Bishop's Stortford.

It was dark by the time he alighted from the train, and he was grateful for the moonlight supplementing the weak beams of Gladys's headlamps as he made his way back through the country lanes to Easton Glebe. Once he narrowly escaped ending up in a ditch as a fox running across the road made him swerve. He felt euphoric rather than nervous, however, and this unaccustomed night drive took on an epic quality in his imagination, as if he were the commander of an armoured car pursuing some urgent secret mission on the eve of battle. The die was cast. It was war—and he knew how it should be presented to the British people, and how to turn the apparent negation of all his hopes for mankind into a positive crusade.

It was past midnight by the time he rolled up outside the front door of Easton Glebe. Jane heard the throb of his engine and the crunch of his tyres on the gravel, and came downstairs in her dressing gown to let him in. She took him to the kitchen and gave him cocoa and a ham sandwich as they talked. 'Poor dear, you must be exhausted,' she said as he finished the sandwich and drained his mug. 'Come to bed. Sleep in my room tonight. I want to be cuddled.'

'No, I'm sorry, Jane. I must work.'

'Work?' she protested. 'For heaven's sake, H.G.! What work can you possibly have to do tonight?'

'An article for the *Chronicle*,' he said.

They parted with a kiss on the landing, and he went to his own bedroom with its alcove equipped for writing at night: a desk with a green shaded lamp, a spirit stove for boiling a kettle to make tea, a barrel of biscuits, and a bottle of whisky for a nightcap when he was finished. He took off his clothes and put on the comfortable sleeping-suit, rather like an overgrown baby's garment, which he preferred to a dressing gown for these late-night writing sessions. He sat down at the desk, took a clean foolscap block from a drawer, and filled his fountain pen with blue-black ink.

He had already rehearsed the argument in his head on his journey from Hunstanton, and it did not take him very long to write it out. The awesome scale of the war which had suddenly engulfed Europe, and was bound to spread eventually to America in the west and as far as Japan in the east, was a measure of the prize which victory would bring: a permanent worldwide peace. For that reason it was a war which had to be won:

> *There can be no diplomatic settlement that will leave German Imperialism free to explain its failure to its people and start new preparations. We have to go on until we are absolutely done for, or until the Germans as a people know they are beaten, and are convinced they have had enough of war.*
>
> *We are fighting Germany. But we are fighting without any hatred of the German people. We do not intend to destroy either their freedom or their unity. But we have to destroy an evil system of government and the mental and material corruption that has got hold of the German imagination and taken possession of German life. We have to smash the Prussian Imperialism as thoroughly as Germany in 1871 smashed the rotten Imperialism of Napoleon III. And also we have to learn from the failure of that victory to avoid a vindictive triumph.*
>
> *This is already the vastest war in history. It is a war not of nations but of mankind. It is a war to exorcise a world-madness and end an age.*

When he had finished the article, he poured himself two fingers of whisky and sipped it as he read through the draft, making occasional emendations. Then he wrote at the top of the first page in capital letters, '*THE WAR THAT WILL END WAR*', turned out the lamp on the desk, felt his way to the bed, crawled under the covers, and fell into a deep sleep.

He was woken at eight o'clock by a servant with a telegram: 'BABY BOY BORN FIVE MINUTES PAST MIDNIGHT THIS MORNING STOP MOTHER AND CHILD BOTH WELL STOP LETTIE'.

'Is there a reply, sir?' said the housemaid. 'The boy is waiting.'

What he wanted to say could not be passed under the inquisitive eyes of the Easton post office. 'No reply—but here's a sovereign for the boy.'

'A sovereign, sir?' The girl looked shocked, as well she might—it was more than a week's wages for her.

'I mean, a shilling,' he said, smiling and shaking his head, and gave it to her. Later he wrote a letter to Rebecca:

I am radiant this morning. With difficulty I refrain from giving people large tips. I am so delighted that I have a manchild in the world—of yours. I will get the world tidy for him . . . I keep thinking of your dear, dear grave beloved face on your pillow and you and it. I do most tremendous love you, Panther.

Jaguar

—'The War That Will End War . . .' That didn't enhance your reputation as a prophet.

—Oh, don't rub it in. I've lost count of the number of times I've been asked to eat those words. I didn't mean it as a simple prediction—but as an aim. I said in that very first article that we might go under. I just wanted to emphasise what was at stake, why it was worth fighting the war to the death. And I said we must avoid a vindictive triumph if we won—good counsel which was ignored in the event, with disastrous consequences.

—But you ruled out a negotiated peace. *'There can be no negotiated settlement.'* That attitude, which was widely shared, led to a four-year war of attrition, mostly fought over the same narrow strip of territory, and the loss of millions of lives.

—Nobody foresaw it would last so long. And that was mainly the fault of the military establishment, their total lack of imagination about tactics and weaponry. They could think of nothing except an artillery bombardment which was supposed to disable the enemy trenches, but more often than not failed to do so, followed by an infantry charge across no man's land into a hail of machine-gun fire. I invented tanks—I mean the idea of them—in 1903, in a short story called 'The Land Ironclads', but nobody thought of making them until halfway through the war, and they weren't really effective until it was nearly over.

—But your journalism at the beginning of the war brought you into alliance with every dyed-in-the-wool patriot and jingoist in the country. Didn't that worry you?

—Not for some time. You know what it was like in England in the early months—a kind of hysteria gripped the country. The shock of finding ourselves at war was converted into a Crusade mentality. Bishops identified the

Allied cause with Christianity. Men mobbed the recruiting offices to join up. Boys and middle-aged men falsified their ages to get into the army.

—And the Germans were demonised with stories, mostly faked, of atrocities committed in Belgium. Vesta Tilley sang *'We don't want to lose you but we think you ought to go'* at recruiting rallies, and children handed out white feathers to the men who didn't immediately volunteer.

—I never approved of the white feather business. My *Daily Chronicle* articles rode on a tide of popular feeling in which there was a lot of meretricious rubbish mixed up with idealism.

—It wasn't just those articles, though, was it? There were letters to the papers. One to the *Times,* for instance, calling for the civilian population to be armed to resist a German invasion. *'Many men, and not a few women, will turn out to shoot Germans. And if the raiders are so badly advised as to try terror-striking reprisals on the Belgian pattern, we irregulars will, of course, massacre every German straggler we can put a gun to.'*

—I can't defend that. It wasn't really a practical suggestion, and the authorities just laughed at it. But I thought we should demonstrate to the world that the entire nation was committed to resisting German militarism. Very early in the war Charlie Masterman summoned a whole lot of writers to a meeting in Whitehall to ask what we could do to boost morale in the country. We were an oddly assorted bunch, but very distinguished— Robert Bridges, Henry Newbolt, Granville Barker, Barrie, Conan Doyle, Chesterton, Gilbert Murray, John Masefield, Arnold of course, and me, and lots of others I can't remember, some of them liberal, some conservative—and there was no way we would all agree on anything, so I suggested we should each act individually. As I did. In retrospect, some things I wrote in the heat of the moment were ill-judged.

—They lost you some friends: Violet Paget, for instance. She wrote about you, *'he enlisted at once for the Fleet Street front and bid us unsheath the Sword of Peace for the final extermination of Militarism.'*

—She never forgave me for supporting the war. Neither did the Bloomsbury group, but that didn't bother me. I never had much time for them, or they for me.

—And Shaw?

—Ours was always a very combative friendship, punctuated with periods of outright hostility, of which that was certainly one. I attacked him for his *Common Sense about the War* pamphlet in November 1914, and similar stuff. He advised the soldiers on both sides to shoot their officers and go home. Of course that wasn't common sense at all, it was a rhetorical flourish, which enraged public opinion. But basically he was right. The war was futile, and should have been stopped before it became unstoppable. It took me some time to see that. Some time and hundreds of thousands of casualties.

—But you didn't become a pacifist.

—No, but neither did Shaw, for that matter. His real point of view was hard to pin down, as usual. He liked to goad people into re-examining their assumptions, but all he usually succeeded in doing was to annoy the hell out of them. Some of the writers who were at that meeting convened by Masterman wanted him tarred and feathered.

—On the whole, established senior writers didn't come out of the war very well, did they? From the safety of their studies they filled the newspaper columns with patriotic poems and anti-German rants and confident predictions of the course of the war which were invariably wrong. The heroes were the young poets who fought and died, and the conscientious objectors who were vilified and sometimes locked up for their principles.

—I wouldn't disagree with that. It was a queer war—unimaginable horror on the Western Front, and life going on much as normal at home, only a few hundred miles away. Of course there were shortages and so on, and later on a few air raids, but for much of the time, if you didn't read the newspapers and you didn't have a close relative involved, you could forget that there was a war on at all—in fact one *tried* to forget it, otherwise it was too depressing. We went on having weekend parties at Easton all through the war, with hockey and tennis and badminton, and charades and dancing to the pianola in the barn.

—You were fortunate in being, at forty-eight, too old to be expected to fight, and with sons much too young to be called up.

—I was aware of that, aware I was an object of envy, and almost resentment, to friends with husbands or sons at the Front—especially if they were among the casualties. Poor old Pember Reeves, for instance, was completely broken up when his son was killed, and never replied to my letter of condolence. I couldn't blame him. Of course I was affected by the deaths of young men I knew—especially the brilliant young men I'd met at Cambridge, Rupert Brooke, for instance, and Ben Keeling. But as the war got worse and worse I felt my personal immunity undermined my authority to speak about it. I was less and less comfortable as a propagandist, but frustrated in my efforts to find a more useful role. There were frustrations in my private life too . . .

The elation, almost euphoria, he had felt on the first day of the war was produced by the convergence of Rebecca's safe delivery of their child and his vision of a mission for himself in the great historic conflict ahead. But just as the war became bogged down in a costly and indecisive struggle with no happy resolution in sight, so, to compare little things with great, did his relationship with Rebecca. Looking back later, he realised that the seed of all its problems was letting Rebecca keep the baby, but how could he have denied her? When he arrived at Brig-y-don to see his child for the first time she was suckling him, looking down with a fond smile as he lay cradled in her arms, with mouth clamped to her nipple and nose squashed against her generous breast. She looked up briefly to say, 'Hallo, Jaguar,' and returned her gaze to the child. 'What a beautiful sight,' he said, stooping to kiss her forehead. 'Madonna and child.' 'I love him,' she said. 'I want to keep him. I couldn't bear to give him to somebody else.' 'Then you must keep him, Panther,' he said. 'Thank you, Jaguar!' she said, with a radiant smile, and raised her face to be kissed again, this time on the lips.

Later he tentatively restated the case for adoption: bringing up the child would be a time-consuming responsibility, interfering with the literary career she had planned for herself, and making it more difficult to keep their relationship discreetly hidden. But she shook her head vehemently in denial of these obvious truths. One couldn't be writing all the time, and anyway he could afford to provide her with servants, couldn't he? And as to the risk of public disapproval, she didn't care. All she knew was that the baby was her child and she wanted to bring him up. 'All right, then,' he said. 'What shall we call him?'

They agreed to call him Anthony Panther West. Rebecca chose the name 'Anthony' mainly because it had no associations with her family or his. 'Panther' was his own suggestion, a defiant reference to the love which had produced the child. The clerk at the Register Office of Births, startled by the second forename, looked up with his pen poised in the air and asked him to spell it out before inscribing it, with obvious disapproval, on the certificate.

Lettie, who had hitherto shown no sign of forgiving him for seducing her young sister, seemed at last to warm towards him to some extent and thanked him for agreeing to support Rebecca in her desire to keep the child. 'I don't say it's a sensible thing for her to do,' Lettie said, 'but it's generous of you.' 'Well, I'm a rich man,' he said. 'I can afford to give her that.' Mrs Townshend, who arrived on the scene a few days later, approved his decision. *'It was delightful to see R.W. with her boy,'* she wrote. *'It would be a thousand pities to separate them. Suckling is a wonderful calmant. A lover at discreet intervals isn't enough for her: she needs a baby and a home as well. Even as a writer she'll do better work if she has them. I don't know how you're going to manage it.'*

The first task, obviously, was to find a more suitable home than Brig-y-don for mother and child. He accordingly asked Mrs Townshend to look for somewhere at a convenient distance from Easton, and she soon found a substantial detached house called 'Quinbourne' outside the village of Braughing in Hertfordshire, only a dozen miles from Easton Glebe. There he settled Rebecca in September, with a full complement of servants— housekeeper, nursemaid, housemaid and cook—and for a while she was happy. She was infatuated with her baby, pleased to be mistress of her own household for the first time, and even began to do a little journalistic work. But then, as autumn gave way to winter, the disadvantages of her situation made themselves felt. Quinbourne, formerly a farmhouse, was isolated, at the end of a muddy track some distance from the village, and although he was able to run over in Gladys to see Rebecca at frequent intervals, for most of the time her servants were the only people with whom she was in regular contact. The Irish midwife who had delivered Anthony, and stayed on as his nurse, was a treasure, but not intellectually stimulating company. The other women, having guessed that Anthony was his child, and discovered his real identity, began to intimate their disapproval in a multitude of sly hints that she dared not challenge. This petty harassment turned ugly when the house-keeper was caught by Rebecca attempting to pilfer money, and retaliated with blackmail, threatening to tell Jane of the existence of his mistress. The threat was simply dealt with by telling her that Jane already knew, and the woman was dismissed, but she persisted in spreading scandal in the neigh-bourhood. Then one day the cook burst into the dining room and began to make mad, obscene allegations against the nurse and housemaid. It trans-pired that the poor woman had just heard she had lost the third of three brothers killed in Flanders, and had tried to drown her grief in brandy. She deserved only pity and sympathy, but it was an upsetting incident, which further increased Rebecca's dissatisfaction with her situation.

'It's like being marooned on the dark side of the moon here,' she said, developing this analogy from some astronomical remark of his own. 'This house is a satellite of Easton Glebe. Anthony and I revolve round your other life, but we can never share it, and we must remain invisible to your family and friends.' Her sense that he enjoyed another life only a few miles away, full of interesting visitors and amusing entertainment from which she was excluded, was a constant source of niggling discontent, and it was no use for him to say that at present Easton Glebe was made unbearably noisy and inconvenient by the extensive building work that was in progress, and that Jane complained that he was neglecting *her* by spending too much time in Braughing. Rebecca responded by alluding to his 'promise' to marry her one day, and hinted that the sooner he divorced Jane for that purpose, the better. This suggestion he firmly squashed, but he agreed that the current set-up was unsatisfactory, and that she ought to move to London where she would be able to see her friends easily and take a more active part in literary life. The spring of 1915 was devoted to pursuing this plan, and by midsummer she and Anthony were settled in a villa called 'Alderton' in Hatch End, on the northern outskirts of London, with Wilma Meikle, a friend from suffragette days, as housekeeper and companion, and the usual complement of servants. He felt it was still necessary for their benefit, and that of the neighbours, to invent a cover story for this new ménage. Rebecca was 'Miss West', bringing up her orphaned nephew, and he was a family friend overseeing their welfare who occasionally visited and stayed the night in the guest room. This pretence, he strongly suspected, fooled nobody, but respectability was precariously maintained.

There were times when he felt that instead of having a wife and a mistress he had two wives, two households to maintain, two sets of domestic obligations, and not enough sex. When he stayed overnight at Alderton, he had to go through a pantomime of retiring to the guest room, creeping along the landing to Rebecca's room later; and once arrived there he had to be careful about the amount of noise they made. Only in occasional short stays at a hotel on Monkey Island in the Thames, snatched while Wilma looked after Anthony, could they really let themselves go in bed. If Rebecca was happier now, he himself was not.

The war, which he had confidently predicted in one of his newspaper articles would be over in 1915, was going badly, with no end in sight on the Western Front, and the Dardanelles campaign designed by Churchill to end the deadlock was already an obvious failure. He had made a start on a new novel about a prosperous middle-aged author called Mr Britling who had believed the war would never happen, but when it did break out identified enthusiastically with the Allied cause. Britling was to become gradually disillusioned as the sterile destructiveness of the conflict became evident, most agonisingly in the death of his own son on the Western Front, but would grope his way out of despair to some kind of positive resolution. Of what kind, he hadn't yet any idea, being still at the pre-war stage of the story. Mr Britling had *'a naturally irritable mind, which gave him point and passion . . . He loved to write and talk. He talked about everything, he had ideas about everything . . .'* He was a transparently autobiographical figure, even down to his erratic driving and enthusiasm for an idiosyncratic form of hockey, except that he had been married twice and had a grown-up son, Hugh, by the first deceased wife, as well as two young ones by the second one, Edith, with whom his relationship closely resembled that between the Wellses. *'They were profoundly incompatible . . . For several unhappy years she thwarted him and disappointed him, while he filled her with dumb inexplicable distresses . . . Only very slowly did they realise the truth of their relationship and admit to themselves that the fine bud of love between them had failed to flower, and only after long years were they able to delimit boundaries where they had imagined union, and to become—allies . . . If there was no love and delight between them there was a real habitual affection and much mutual help.'* Vainly seeking a woman with whom he could have a totally fulfilling relationship, Britling had been serially and sometimes scandalously unfaithful to Edith, and currently had a mistress who lived in a house within easy motoring distance of his home. She, however, was based not on Rebecca but on little E—*'Mrs Harrowdean, the brightest and cleverest of widows'*—who had seemed just what he needed when she first came into his life, but had proved tiresomely critical and demanding recently, and he was looking for a way to terminate the relationship with a minimum of stress. Britling lived in a place in Essex called Matching's Easy, occupying a dower house which was a faithful replica of Easton Glebe. He employed a German tutor for his younger sons called Herr Heinrich, and a secretary called Teddy, married to a local girl called Letty, who had a sister called Cissie. The novel was a kaleidoscope containing many recognisable fragments of his life, shaken up with some invented ones to make a new pattern. He wasn't at all confident about how it would turn out, but Rebecca was encouraging when he showed her the first few chapters.

.   .   .

Rebecca herself was preparing to write a short book of literary criticism for a series called 'Writers of the Day'. The general editor, who admired her book reviews, had invited her to contribute to the series on a subject of her own choice, and she proposed Henry James—to his displeased surprise, since Rebecca was well aware of how James's treatment of his own work in the *TLS* had offended him. He knew that her admiration for James was far from uncritical, but nevertheless there seemed to him a kind of disloyalty in the dedication she brought to the project, reading and re-reading James's immense *oeuvre* with an assiduity quite disproportionate to the scale of the commission. In this slightly piqued mood he took *Boon* out of its drawer and read its anti-Jamesian polemic as a kind of salve, with such enjoyment that he went on with the book, finding it a welcome distraction from writing and thinking about the war, and brought it to a conclusion, or at least an end, since it remained a collection of disconnected episodes and discourses. He didn't show it to Rebecca—he didn't show it to anybody except Jane, who typed it for him, and Fisher Unwin, who agreed to publish it. He told himself that he didn't want to disturb Rebecca's concentration on her work in progress by his irreverent treatment of her subject, and that the book would have more impact generally if it arrived unheralded and unexpected, but the real reason for not trying it out on other readers, as he usually did with new books, was an intuition that they might advise him not to publish it, a possibility he did not wish to contemplate. When he received the first finished copies in mid-June, and read the title page, he felt a surge of wicked glee.

Boon, The Mind of the Race, The Wild Asses
of the Devil, **and** *The Last Trump.*
Being a First Selection from the Literary Remains
of George Boon. Appropriate to the Times.
Prepared for Publication by **REGINALD BLISS,** *author of*
'The Cousins of Charlotte Brontë',
'A Child's History of the Crystal Palace', 'Firelight Rambles',
'Edible Fungi', 'Whales in Captivity' and other works.
With an Ambiguous Introduction by H.G. Wells.

Much to the annoyance of Fisher Unwin, who claimed it would adversely affect sales, he had insisted that his name should appear only as the writer of the introduction, and that 'Reginald Bliss' must be on the spine of the book. He did not intend that this would deceive anybody as to its authorship: it was a way of indicating that *Boon* was not to be considered on a par with his other literary works, but as a carnivalesque diversion. He turned to a page at random and found Henry James expressing reservations about a proposed conference on 'The Mind of the Race':

> *'Owing it as we do,' he said, 'very, very largely to our friend Gosse, to that peculiar, that honest but restless and, as it were, at times almost malignantly ambitious organizing energy of our friend, I cannot altogether—altogether, even if in any case I should have taken so extreme, so devastatingly isolating a step as, to put it violently, stand out; yet I must confess to a considerable anxiety, a kind of distress, an apprehension, the terror, so to speak, of the kerbstone, at all this stream of intellectual trafficking, of going to and fro in a superb and towering manner enough no doubt, but still essentially going to and fro rather than in any completed senses of the word getting there, that does so largely constitute the aggregations and activities we are invited to traverse.'*

He chortled, and read on, unable to stop from sheer pride and joy in the accuracy of his parody until he reached the end of the chapter. Then he scribbled a note, 'Dear HJ, I hope you will get some entertainment out of this *jeu d'esprit*, H.G.', slipped it into the book, and put the latter in an envelope addressed to 'Mr Henry James, c/o the Reform Club', where he dropped it off the following day. He was aware that Henry James had vacated Lamb House for the duration of the war, and was living in London.

There was a longer interval than he expected before James acknowledged the book, during which he felt some qualms of uneasiness about whether the old man's sense of humour was sufficiently robust to enjoy a joke at his own expense. When, a week into July, a letter eventually arrived addressed in the slanting hand he recognised as James's, he took the envelope (gauging with his forefinger and thumb that it contained several pages) into his study, shut the door and sat down at his desk to read the contents in an uncomfortable state of suspense. The customary form of address— *'My Dear Wells'* was reassuring, as was the calmly courteous tone of the opening lines, explaining a delay in his receiving the book. *'I have just been reading, to acknowledge it intelligently, a considerable number of its pages—*

though not all; for to be perfectly frank, I have been in that respect beaten for the first time by a book of yours: I haven't found the current of it draw me on and on this time—as unfailingly and irresistibly before (which I have repeatedly let you know.)' There was a note of reproach in that parenthesis which gradually became more and more explicit as the letter continued. *'I shall try again—I hate to lose any scrap of you that may make for light or pleasure; and meanwhile I have more or less mastered your appreciation of H.J., which I have found very curious and interesting, after a fashion—though it has naturally not filled me with a fond elation. It is difficult of course for a writer to put himself fully in the place of another writer who finds him extraordinarily futile and void, and who is moved to publish that to the world –'*

He had to put the letter down at that point, and take a turn about his study. No, the old man had not seen the joke, he had not been entertained or amused, he had been mortally offended. He returned reluctantly to the letter: *'and I think the case isn't easier when he happens to have enjoyed the other writer enormously, from far back; because there has then grown up the habit of taking some common meeting-ground between them for granted, and the falling away of this is like the collapse of a bridge which made communication possible.'* There was a nobility as well as pathos about that simile that was humbling, and smote him with remorse. Not that he would withdraw any of his criticisms of James's work in *Boon*—satire was satire, parody was parody, and he had only slightly overstated the reservations that even devoted readers of James had to admit to. But he regretted the hurt to James's feelings and the threatened termination of their friendship. He hastened through the rest of the letter, in which James defended his right to follow the promptings of his own muse however different they might be from his own, eager to draft a reply that would be apologetic and conciliatory without being a hypocritical surrender.

'There is of course a real and very fundamental difference in our innate and developed attitudes towards life and literature,' he wrote. *'To you literature like painting is an end, to me literature like architecture is a means, it has a use. Your view was, I felt, altogether too dominant in the world of criticism, and I assailed it in tones of harsh antagonism. And writing that stuff about you was the first escape I had from the obsession of this war. Boon is just a wastebasket . . . But since it was printed I have regretted a hundred times that I did not express our profound and incurable difference and contrast with a better grace.'* A hundred times was something of an exaggeration, but he signed off sincerely as, *'believe me, my dear James, your very keenly appreciative*

reader, your warm if rebellious and resentful admirer, and for countless causes yours most gratefully and affectionately, H.G. Wells.'

But James was not to be mollified. He sent back a typed letter (with *'dictated'* in square brackets at the top) which began, *'I am bound to tell you that I don't think your letter makes out any sort of case for the bad manners of Boon,'* and continued in the same vein. *'Your comparison of the book to a waste-basket strikes me as the reverse of felicitous, for what one throws into that receptacle is exactly what one doesn't commit to publicity.'* It was notable how much more lucid and direct James's epistolary style had become under the provocation of what he held to be an assault on his most deeply held principles. The letter concluded declaratively: *'It is art that makes life, makes interest, makes importance, for our consideration and application of these things, and I know of no substitute whatever for the force and beauty of its process. If I were Boon I should say that any pretence of such a substitute is helpless and hopeless humbug; but I wouldn't be Boon for the world, and am only yours faithfully, Henry James.'*

He wrote another letter about the possible meanings of 'art' in this context, intended to raise the correspondence above the merely personal, but received no reply. In October he heard that James was in poor health and in December that he had had a stroke. He sent a message of sympathy which was curtly acknowledged by his secretary, Miss Bosanquet. He never heard from James again, nor met him, until his death at the end of February 1916 put an end to any possibility of reconciliation. James had not forgiven him.

   —Hardly surprising, was it? Your caricature of James's fiction was incredibly cruel. *'It is like a church lit but without a congregation to distract you, with every light and line focused on the high altar. And on the altar, very reverently placed, intensely there, is a dead kitten, an egg-shell, a bit of string.'* And then the hippo picking up a pea . . .
   —Well, his comments on me in that *TLS* article were equally offensive. He seemed to forget that he insulted me first.
   —But that was just a paragraph. You went on at him for pages.
   —He went on for much more than a paragraph.
   —But it was mostly fair comment.
   —So was *my* stuff fair comment. It was just expressed in a lively satirical way. And after all I dished out the same treatment to practically every well-

known contemporary writer that you could think of in that book. I even satirised myself in the character of Hallery, who gives a lecture on the Mind of the Race so earnestly boring that the audience walks out.

—**The fact remains that Henry James was the prime target—or that's how it must have seemed to him, and how it would look to any objective reader. Nobody else mentioned in the book has anything like the same amount of space devoted to him.**

—I suppose I got carried away by the fun of the exercise. I persuaded myself that he would enjoy it as a kind of backhanded compliment to his importance and his literary status. After all, he enjoyed Max Beerbohm's parody of him in *A Christmas Garland*—'The Mote in the Middle Distance'.

—**But that was so tender towards the original it was more like an *hommage*. Your parodies were brutal in comparison. It was a mean thing to do to an older writer, much less successful than you in terms of sales and celebrity, and in failing health—**

—James was always complaining about his health as long as I'd known him. When I heard in December that he'd had a stroke, I sent a message of sympathy. When Gosse organised a petition to give him the OM I signed it gladly, and when he got it in the New Year's honours list, practically on his deathbed, I sent him a telegram of congratulation. No response. Two months later I heard he had died. I was sorry we had quarrelled, but it was bound to happen. We were two utterly different writers, with utterly different aims, and had conspired to conceal our differences for too long. The incompatibility of our ideas about the novel was bound to lead to a confrontation sooner or later. It could have been managed more tactfully on my part, as I admitted at the time to him. God knows I was punished for my bad manners.

Boon was a failure. The literary world, or large sections of it, treated him as a pariah, and even his friends were embarrassed by the book. In due course Rebecca suffered too, for when her study of James came out the following year Percy Lubbock and the rest of the Jamesian coterie made sure it was ignored by the *TLS*. It was a miracle of stylish concision and discriminating appreciation, but not a panegyric, and her association with himself was sufficiently well known to damn it in their eyes. The unlucky timing of their respective books had ensured a generally negative reception for both.

In the very month that *Boon* was published Henry James had applied for British citizenship to demonstrate his identification with the Allied cause in the war and, having been largely neglected by the reading public for years, he suddenly became a national treasure who should be treated with uncritical respect, a sentiment his demise powerfully reinforced. It was not a good moment to criticise Henry James.

James's death was announced when he was working on the conclusion to *Mr Britling Sees It Through*. It was a book in which he had invested a great deal of time and effort, and it exemplified exactly that instrumental view of the function of the novel with which he challenged the Jamesian, aesthetic view. His novel aimed to be useful, it had a purpose, which roughly speaking was to wring some kind of positive lesson from the war, but without avoiding or underplaying the horror and the pain. He put Mr Britling through a sequence of attitudes to the war which was very like his own: belated recognition that it was really going to happen, energetic commitment to achieving victory, and then increasing disillusionment, not only with the Allied conduct of the war, but with the patriotic justification of it. Britling came to see the corrupting power of hatred generated by the conflict, and to deplore the demonisation of Germans and Germany which held them wholly responsible for the carnage. The creative freedom of fiction, however, allowed the novelist to put his surrogate under much more pressure than he had ever suffered himself, and thus vicariously earn the right to preach at the end of the book a kind of lay sermon, of daring presumption.

Mr Britling's son Hugh, following the example of Britling's secretary, Teddy, volunteered for military service as soon as he was able, and sent home vivid accounts of the fighting on the Western Front. (There were already plenty of printed sources to draw on for this part of the book.) Then Hugh was killed. The sequence in which Britling received the news and then went out into the dark garden, where *'suddenly the boy was all about him, playing, climbing the cedars, twisting miraculously about the lawn on a bicycle, discoursing gravely upon his future, lying on the grass . . .'* was an imaginative effort to project himself into a situation that was being enacted in real life in hundreds of homes throughout the country every day, and he felt he had done it justice. Mr Britling's recovery from despair was more of a challenge. He presented it in two stages. Teddy was also reported killed, and Britling had to comfort his distraught widow, Letty, who was filled with nihilistic rage against Germans and God. *'The world is cruel,'* she says.

'It is just cruel. As for God—either there is no God or he is an idiot. He is an idiot who pulls off the wings of flies . . . How can you believe in God after Hugh? A God who kills my Teddy and your Hugh—and millions.' Britling says he does believe—but not in the God of the theologians. 'They have silly absolute ideas—that he is all powerful. But the common sense of men knows better . . . After all, the real God of the Christians is Christ, not God Almighty; a poor mocked and wounded God nailed on a cross of matter . . . Some day he will triumph . . . But it is not fair to say he causes all things now. God is not absolute; God is finite . . . A finite God who struggles in his great and comprehensive way as we struggle in our weak and silly way.—Why! if I thought there was an omnipotent God who looked down on battles and deaths and all the waste and horror of this war—able to prevent these things—I would spit in his empty face. God is within Nature and Necessity. Necessity is the uttermost thing, but God is the innermost thing.' 'I never thought of him like that,' says Letty. 'Nor did I,' says Britling, 'But I do now.' And Britling spoke here for his creator. He had surprised himself with a vein of mystical eloquence he hadn't known he possessed, opened up by putting his characters in a situation of almost unbearable distress.

Letty's story was given a happy ending by the unexpected return of Teddy, wounded but alive, but the hero of the book could not be relieved of his grief so easily. Mr Britling's recovery from the trauma of his son's death began when he heard that his former German tutor, Herr Heinrich, had also died, in a Russian prisoner of war camp, and he decided to send to Heinrich's parents the violin their son left behind in the haste of his departure, with a note of explanation that quickly grew into a long letter in which he relieved his own feelings by sharing them. 'If you think that these two boys have both perished, not in some noble common cause but one against the other in a struggle of dynasties and boundaries and trade routes and tyrannous ascendancies, then it seems to me that you must feel as I feel that this war is the most tragic and dreadful thing that has ever happened to mankind.' There were many drafts, begun and abandoned, as Britling worked through the night and into the next dawn on his text, struggling to be honest and to avoid false feeling and false rhetoric—what he referred to disparagingly as his 'tinpot style'. As the letter grew longer and longer it became less like a personal letter and more like a prophetic public utterance. 'Never had it been so plain to Mr Britling that he was a weak, silly, ill-informed and hasty-minded writer, and never had he felt so invincible a conviction that the Spirit of God was in him, and that it fell to him to take some part in the establishment *of a new order of living upon the earth.'* His last paragraph began: '*Let us set ourselves with all our minds and hearts to the perfecting and working out of the methods of democracy and the ending of the kings and emperors and priestcrafts and the bands of adventurers, the traders and owners and forestallers who have betrayed mankind into this morass of hate and blood—in which our sons are lost—in which we flounder still . . .'* But, he reflected, '*How feeble was this squeak of exhortation!'* and left it unfinished. He thought of sending the violin back to Heinrich's parents without a covering letter, but: '*"No. I must write to them plainly. About God as I have found him. As he has found me."'* The book ended with the exhausted Mr Britling standing at the window of his study as the sun rose. '*Wave after wave of warmth and light came sweeping before the sunrise across the world of Matching's Easy. It was as if there was nothing but morning and sunrise in the world. From away toward the church came the sound of some early worker whetting a scythe.'* The image of the scythe pleased him with its ambiguous mixture of associations: the Grim Reaper, swords into ploughshares, the cycle of the seasons promising the renewal of life after death.

When he decided to call his novel *Mr Britling Sees It Through* he believed that by the time it was published the war would be over, or nearly over; but in July, while it was going through the press, the battle of the Somme began, and was still continuing as the book was published in September. When the battle could be said to have finished, which wasn't until November, a million men had died or been wounded on both sides, and nothing had been gained to bring the war nearer to a conclusion. He was apprehensive that in this context his title would seem inappropriately optimistic and adversely affect the novel's reception, which was a matter of serious concern because his financial position was not healthy. His remark to Letty, at the very beginning of the war, '*I'm a rich man*', seemed hubristic in retrospect. All the expenses he had incurred in the last couple of years— the extension and renovation of Easton Glebe, the lavish entertaining there, the maintenance of Rebecca's household, the rental of his London flat, the purchase of Gladys, and the school fees for his boys, now boarding at Oundle—these things, and many others, had drained his savings alarmingly, and he reckoned that he had only £5,000 left in his bank accounts. *The Research Magnificent*, published in 1915, had not done particularly well; unsurprisingly, for it was essentially a reprise of all the other prig novels with more exotic locations. Only his prolific journalism had kept him solvent, and he badly needed a best-seller.

To his immense relief and gratification *Mr Britling* turned out to be just that. It caught perfectly the public mood as the news from the Western Front got worse and worse—it reflected and articulated people's grief for wasted young lives, their anger at the incompetence of their political and military leaders, their struggle to reconcile the monstrous evil of the war with the ideals of duty, patriotism and religious faith which had been instilled in them from childhood. It received rapturous reviews, was praised by many of his old adversaries—even Mrs Humphry Ward—and made the subject of sympathetic sermons in churches. It brought him a huge postbag from appreciative readers, especially from those whose husbands or sons had been killed in the war, many of whom sent their condolences on the assumption that he had lost a grown-up son himself, so vividly had he described Mr Britling's bereavement. The book went into thirteen impressions before Christmas, and had earned him £20,000 in royalties in America by the same date. His financial worries were over, at least for some considerable time.

—So one might say you profited from the catastrophe of the Somme— from the whole bloody war, in fact.

—Well you could say that Homer profited from the Trojan War. It's a paradox of all writing that deals with tragedy: writers take negative experience and turn it into something positive. If it comes off we get praised, and paid for it too. That doesn't mean that *Mr Britling* put me on the same footing as a war profiteer.

—But did you really believe that religious stuff at the end? Or was it an artful device to ingratiate yourself with the British public?

—I believed it while I was writing the book—it wouldn't have worked otherwise. You can't fake something like that. Writing *Mr Britling* was a kind of religious experience for me—what William James describes as 'conversion' in *Varieties of Religious Experience*. When Britling convicts himself of being a 'weak, silly, ill-informed and hasty-minded writer', it's my *mea culpa* as well as his. I was ashamed of some of the bombastic, swaggering stuff I wrote about the war in the early stages, and I wanted to confess. And as I wrote the scene in which Britling tries to comfort Letty I found all this religious language welling up—from my childhood, I suppose, from my mother's piety, which I'd reacted against in youth, but now it seemed the right kind of language. I began to see a way to articulate my secular utopianism in the language of Christianity and make it perhaps more accessible to the mass of people. In *God the Invisible King*, published a year later, I developed Britling's ideas discursively in my own voice.

—**A lot of your freethinking friends thought you'd lost your senses in that book.**

—It went down a treat with the public, though. I remember sending Rebecca a kind of Psalm.

> *Theological books are selling*
> *Selling like Hot Cakes,*
> *And the Breasts of my Mother Land*
> *Are tight with the Milk of the Word.*
> *As for me I lunch with Liberal Churchmen*
> *I dine with Bishops*
> *Lambeth Palace is my Washpot.*

—**It *was* a cynical exercise then?**

—Not at all. I repudiated my conversion later, but at the time I was quite sincere. I could see the funny side of my sudden popularity as a radical Christian theologian, but I was sincere. And whatever you say, *Mr Britling Sees It Through* was a good novel. Britling lives.

—**The last good one you wrote, in fact. The last one anybody would want to read twice.**

—You're probably right.

—**But you went on to write another twenty-two of them. All dead as doornails now. Fodder for the penny tray outside the second-hand bookshop.**

—Yes. But I didn't know that then.

In September 1916 he had several reasons to feel pleased with himself: *Boon* was forgotten; *Mr Britling* was a hit; Winston Churchill wrote to congratulate him on *'the success with which your land battleship idea has been put into practice'* (the British Mark 1 tanks had actually a very limited success in the battle of the Somme, but he appreciated the acknowledgement to his Land Ironclads); and on the 21st of the month he reached the age of fifty in good health. Even his sexual life had improved. In August he had finally voiced his dissatisfaction with the libidinal opportunities of Alderton in a letter to

Rebecca: *'I wish we could fix up some sort of life that would detach us lovers a little more from the nursery. I want to make love to you and be with you as a lover day and night and to have all that more of a lark and companionship than it is . . . You see in the nature of things we haven't much more than ten or twelve years more of love and nakedness and all those dear things. It's a pity to so arrange life that we get nothing better than snatched moments of the night together and evenings with those two appalling bores Wilma and GooGoo.'* (GooGoo being Anthony's name for his nurse.) He asked her to think up some scheme to offload Anthony on to her sisters so that they could get away together, even go abroad. She didn't manage this, but she did agree with his proposal to rent a studio in Chelsea as a love nest. *'Prepare for thorough lickings in the London studio,'* he wrote lasciviously by return. The Chelsea studio fell through, but he found rooms on Claverton Street in his old haunt, Pimlico, which served them for some time as a rather seedy place of assignation. Secrecy and privacy enhanced their lovemaking, but the underlying tensions in their relationship were unresolved.

In the spring of 1917 Rebecca moved with Anthony to Leigh-on-Sea on the Essex coast in order to escape the threat of Zeppelin raids on London. The house was charming but the location badly chosen as it proved to be on the favoured route of the new German twin-engined Gotha bombers, whose airmen used the Thames to navigate their way to London, and sometimes dropped their bombs on estuary towns like Leigh, mistaking them for the outskirts of the capital. *'It is so unpleasing to sit down at dinner with a Gotha trying to nest on the roof and a noise filling the sky as though the Trinity were unskilfully moving a piano,'* Rebecca wrote to a mutual friend, but the insouciant tone was entirely faked, as he discovered when he was staying with her during such a raid. At the sound of bombs exploding in the distance she snatched Anthony from his cot and hid with him under the dining-room table, moaning 'Oh God! Oh God!' as the throb of the planes' engines grew louder, and crying out, 'We're going to die! I don't want to die!' as they passed overhead. He felt some fear himself, but his own way of dealing with it was deliberately to step out on to the balcony and scan the skies, simulating calm, and Rebecca's undignified hysterics upset him.

After his return home he sent her a long letter of complaint about her behaviour which broadened out into a speculation about their innate incompatibility. *'These trivialities seem to have released my mind to look at a whole group of facts that I have refused to look at before. I thought, "Do I love this woman at all?" I thought, "I've made up a story about her and it isn't the* *true one."' What was the true one? What were the facts? That he had an essentially positive outlook, whereas she seemed to attract and embrace negative experience, for example her continuing intimacy with her sisters and mother, who hated him, and the entourage of dreary women servants and companions with which she surrounded herself and discouraged intimacy. *'All the past four years which might have been a love-adventure in our memories, your peculiar genius has made into an utterly disagreeable story— which has become the basis for an utter hopelessness about anything to come. It is your nature to darken your world and blacken every memory. So long as I love you you will darken mine.'* He wrote and dispatched this letter more from a need to relieve his feelings and in the hope of making her more amenable to his desires than with the design of ending their relationship, and he was somewhat shaken when she fired back a fierce response, claiming that she hadn't loved him for the past year, and that she was perfectly capable of supporting herself and Anthony if only he would make an adequate financial settlement on her and stop upsetting her with his unreasonable demands. He replied temperately, *'If I'm not going to be your lover I'm going to be your loving brother. We have told each other some rather astonishing truths. Now let us keep all the appearances going for a time, a little time anyhow, before we change anything.'* By the end of the month the quarrel was over and a truce sealed on the bed in Claverton Street, setting a pattern for the years that followed.

Meanwhile on the bigger battlefield, there was no prospect of a truce, as the armies slogged at each other like weary, bloodied pugilists whose trainers refused to throw in the towel. But it was obvious to him, once America came into the war on the Allied side in 1917, that Germany was doomed, however long it might take, and a year later he had what looked like an opportunity to play a useful part in the final act of the conflict. Lloyd George, who was now Prime Minister in place of the discredited Asquith, had brought two press lords into government—Rothermere as Minister for Air, Beaverbrook as Minister of Information—and Beaverbrook appointed another press lord, Northcliffe, as his Director of Enemy Propaganda. Newspaper men had a better appreciation of his value than politicians and civil servants, and when Northcliffe invited him to join the team at Crewe House as chairman of a newly formed Policy Committee for Propaganda in Enemy Countries, he accepted eagerly. He believed it was vitally important to prepare the German people to accept defeat, by making clear that the Allies would not be vindictive in victory and that the end of the war would be an opportunity to achieve permanent peace for the whole world. He had lately become involved in committees promoting the idea, first floated by Leonard Woolf and others back in 1915, of a League of Nations, which would supervise the post-war peace treaty and guarantee international security on a permanent basis. He planned to use his chairmanship of the Propaganda Committee to ensure that these positive messages were incorporated in the leaflets created at Crewe House and distributed by various means to the soldiers and civilians of the Central Powers. Before long he sent a forceful memorandum from his committee to the Foreign Office, putting forward the arguments for a constructive peace settlement, including a plausible draft constitution for a League of Nations, and received a patronising lecture from the head of political intelligence in response. The Crewe House team nevertheless persisted in promoting the League of Nations idea in their publications, and it received lukewarm endorsement from the government. It was of course essential that British public opinion should be educated in the same direction, but this was not within his committee's scope. Northcliffe and his fellow press lords did nothing, however, to assist the process in their own newspapers: vitriolic anti-German reporting and editorialising continued unabated in the popular press, especially Northcliffe's *Daily Mail* and London *Evening News*. When he wrote to Northcliffe, pointing out the inconsistency, the latter flatly refused to do anything about it, and replied curtly: *'I entirely agree with the policy adopted by my newspapers, which I do not propose to discuss with anyone.'* He realised belatedly that the propaganda produced at Crewe House promising a constructive and generous peace settlement was cynically designed for German consumption only, and that the government was intent on punishing Germany as well as defeating it. He felt exploited and betrayed, and resigned his chairmanship only a few months after taking it on.

Victory came at last, in November, and was made the occasion for an orgy of celebration, when a week of National Mourning for the dead would have been more appropriate, or at least some kind of sober examination of the national conscience. But no, we were going to hang the Kaiser and make the Germans pay. The country was to be made a land fit for heroes—those that were lucky enough to have survived—and God save the King, who rode in a carriage with the Queen through streets crowded with cheering flag-waving patriots to St Paul's Cathedral to give thanks to the Deity for having demonstrated, eventually, that He was an Englishman. That day, he and Jane happened to leave their London flat to return to Easton Glebe. The crowds blocked the progress of their cab and forced them to get out and lug their bags to Liverpool Street station, and he thought to himself, looking at the happy complacency on every face thronging the pavements, 'This is the real people. This seething multitude of vague, kindly, uncritical brains is the stuff that dear old Marx counted on to exercise the dictatorship of the proletariat,' and gave a loud laugh that made Jane, struggling with a valise and hatbox, turn her head and stare quizzically at him.

These disillusioning episodes had, however, positive consequences. His experience on committees concerned with the League of Nations project had convinced him that even their well-educated and well-intentioned members, including himself, were lamentably ill informed about the history of any other nation than their own, while the British people at large knew almost nothing. It was obvious that there was no hope of getting an idea like the League to 'take' unless this ignorance was remedied, and he conceived the idea of an 'Outline of World History' which would attempt to tell the story of all mankind up to the present day within the compass of a single book. By the end of 1918 he had lined up a number of prestigious experts like Gilbert Murray and Ernest Barker to act as advisers and check his drafts for error, and Jane and others helped him with the research, but essentially he intended to write the whole thing himself. He did not of course aim to discover new facts—the facts he needed were already available in encyclopaedias and other works of reference—but to bring them all together in a way that nobody had thought of doing before. As he said in an article in the magazine of the League of Nations Union:

> No one has ever attempted to teach our children the history of man as Man, with all his early struggles and triumphs, his specialization in tribes and nations, his conquests of Nature, his creations of Art, his building up of Science . . . An enormous amount of work has to be done if we are to teach the peoples of the world what is the truth, viz., that they are all engaged in a common work, that they have sprung from common origins, and all are contributing some special service to the general end.

Originally he had conceived it as a book for older children, but as the idea developed it assumed an adult readership too. It was an enormous undertaking which occupied him for two years of 'fanatical toil', as he described it to Arnold Bennett, and ran to three-quarters of a million words, mostly his own. But the effort was fully justified in the outcome. The part-publication of *The Outline of History* sold extremely well, and in its longer book form sold more than two million copies over the next few years in Britain and America, and in numerous translations. His financial worries were now removed for the foreseeable future. He really was a rich man.

—You were also a famous man. Probably, as a result of the *Outline*, the most famous writer in the world in the early twenties. Surely Orwell was wrong in saying you ceased to influence young people after 1920?

—I was famous for some time after that, in the sense that the man in the street almost everywhere knew my name. My newspaper articles were syndicated all over the world, and my books continued to circulate in cheap editions and influence and educate people, including young people. But I was no longer someone whose latest work you had to read if you wanted to keep up with fashionable ideas and trends, and this became more and more obvious as time went on. At the beginning of the 1930s I published two enormous compilations, *The Science of Life* and *The Work, Wealth and Happiness of Mankind*, to form a trilogy with *The Outline of History* summarising modern knowledge about mankind—historical, biological, and sociological—but they weren't so successful. Later I tried to interest publishers in the idea of an encyclopaedia which would include *all* knowledge, but there were too many difficulties about copyright. My idea was that it should be free. I imagined an international Encyclopaedia Organisation that would store and continuously update every item of verifiable human knowledge on microfilm and make it universally accessible—a world wide web of information. I wrote a book about it called *World Brain,* but it didn't catch on. There was a journalist once who called me 'the man who invented tomorrow', but people weren't interested in my tomorrow any more. I was a child of the Enlightenment, a modern Encyclopaedist, an heir of Diderot, but the horrors of the Great War had undermined faith in Reason. Intellectuals looked for salvation to fascism, or Soviet style communism, or Christianity, Roman Catholic or Anglo-Catholic, to all of which I was opposed. Between the wars I was increasingly a lone voice, crying in the wilderness, as a thinker.

—And as a novelist?

374

—As a novelist I was old hat. Avant-garde experimental writers made the running in the twenties—James Joyce and D.H. Lawrence and Virginia Woolf. It was all stream of consciousness, symbolism, myth, not much story and not many ideas, not what I called ideas. Even Dorothy Richardson started to impress people with her interminable epic of navel-gazing, *Pointed Roofs*. It was Henry James's theory of the novel taken even further, fiction aspiring to the condition of lyric poetry. And the new writers liked to define themselves in opposition to old fogeys like Arnold Bennett and me. That essay of Virginia Woolf's on 'Modern Fiction', for instance, accused us of being 'materialists'—'*the sooner English fiction turns its back upon them . . . the better for its soul,*' she said. Lawrence famously attacked Galsworthy, who was often grouped with us, and he put his boot into *The World of William Clissold*, my most ambitious novel of the twenties, in *The Calendar of Modern Letters*. He said the book was all 'chewed-up newspaper and chewed-up scientific reports, like a mouse's nest'.

—**And eventually Rebecca had a go at you. She mocked your love scenes**—'*the passages where his prose suddenly loses its firmness and begins to shake like blancmange*'. **She called you 'the Uncles'—you and Bennett and Galsworthy and Shaw.** '*All our youth they hung about the houses of our minds like Uncles . . .*'

—That was in 1926. We had split up by then. Calling me 'Uncle' was a coded way of saying that it was final.

He lost count of the number of times they were on the point of splitting up, only to pull back from the brink and give the relationship another chance. One of the most serious crises of this kind followed from his visit to Russia in the autumn of 1920.

He had taken a keen interest in the March and October Revolutions of 1917, and wrote to his old friend Maxim Gorky in March of the following year to applaud the new Bolshevik government's peace treaty with the Central Powers, '*showing the world the way out of the slaughterhouse*'. Gorky for his part was a huge admirer of *Mr Britling*—'*It is beyond doubt the best, boldest, most just and humane book written in Europe during this accursed war!*' he wrote, and arranged to have it translated and published in Russia, where it was apparently received with acclaim. So important did he believe Russia would prove to be in the politics of the post-war period that he persuaded Sanderson, Oundle's progressive headmaster, to arrange for Gip and a few other interested boys to be taught Russian: the first time, apparently, that the language was taught in any English school. By 1920 it seemed to him that Gip would benefit by a visit to Russia, and he was also intensely curious to see for himself what life was like under the Revolution. A man called Kamenev at the Russian trade delegation in London had already contacted him to suggest an official visit. Beaverbrook was eager for him to write about it for the *Express,* which would more than cover his expenses, and he might get a book out of the trip as well. He accordingly wired Gorky to say that he was 'coming to have a look at Russia' with his son and, as he had hoped, Gorky generously offered to accommodate them at his home in St Petersburg. This proved to be a large apartment-cum-editorial-office of many rooms, where a shifting population of shabbily dressed poets, novelists, intellectuals and female assistants nested. It was a much more authentic and less closely supervised vantage point from which to assess the state of the country than the large hotel that was normally provided for foreign visitors.

Gorky was a person of high standing in Bolshevik Russia. His internationally acclaimed stories and plays about the plight of the lower strata of society under the Czars, and his record of personal suffering in those days, had made him the literary figurehead of the Revolution, and he used his position, to the detriment of his own creative work, to help and protect writers and artists of all kinds. In spite of poor health—he had only one lung as a result of a failed attempt to commit suicide in youth—he worked long hours editing, publishing and organising, finding work and shelter for many who would otherwise have perished in the chaotic conditions of life in post-revolutionary Russia. One of Gorky's assistants was a young woman who lived in the apartment on Kronversky Prospekt, called Moura Budberg.

He met her, unforgettably, on the day of his arrival. She came into Gorky's untidy office, every surface of which was heaped with books and papers, bringing some proofs from the printer. She was tall, with dark eyes and black wavy hair. That she was wearing a British military waterproof over a shabby black dress only enhanced her striking looks, and made her seem like a female personification of the Revolution—Hope defying Privation. 'This is Moura,' Gorky said to him. 'Moura—H.G. Wells.' Gorky added something in Russian to the young woman, who replied in the same language, and then shook his hand. 'We have met before,' she said, to his astonishment. 'Really?' he said. 'Yes, when you were in Russia in 1914, with Maurice Baring.' Her spoken English was strongly accented, but fluent and confident. 'Well, I'm embarrassed to say I don't remember,' he said, staring and trying to recall having seen her face before, 'but I met a great many people on that trip.' She smiled. 'It is not surprising. I was wearing a long silk gown at the time, and a great deal of jewellery. It was a big party at the home of my father, Ignaty Zakrevsky, but I was introduced to you as Marie von Benckendorf. My husband, Count Ivan Benckendorf, was a diplomat. We were in Petersburg on leave from the Berlin Embassy.' 'That does seem to trigger a faint memory,' he said, for politeness' sake, though the names meant nothing to him.

Gorky observed this exchange smiling genially but uncomprehendingly under his heavy broom-like moustache. He said something in Russian.

'Gorky says I am to be your official interpreter and guide for the duration of your visit,' Moura said.

'I'm delighted,' he replied. 'Thank you very much.'

'It will be a pleasure,' she said.

For a day or two he had long conversations with Gorky, made rather tedious by the necessity of interpretation, and also, to be honest, by their content, for Gorky was anxious to give his visitor a positive view of the Bolshevik state and to excuse in advance the imperfections which he might encounter, so their meetings consisted of homilies from his host rather than interactive dialogue. It was a relief to get out of the apartment and form his own impressions with Moura as guide, sometimes with Gip, but more often on his own because some young people in Gorky's entourage took his son under their wing, which was better for the improvement of his Russian. She escorted him to the House of Science and the House of Literature and Art, to the Mariinsky theatre and the Nevsky Prospekt, for walks along the embankment of the Neva, to St Isaac's Cathedral, which was being converted into a Museum of Atheism, and to the sadly neglected Summer Garden, where the leaves were already falling on the overgrown footpaths. Without her company he would have become depressed and homesick.

Petrograd, as it was now called, was a war-worn shadow of the St Petersburg he remembered from 1914. There were practically no shops open, because there was nothing available to buy or sell except tea, cigarettes and matches—and, rather poignantly, cut flowers. The streets had a blank shuttered look like an eternal Sabbath in a provincial English town. Food was rationed by the government, but what was available barely kept the population above the level of starvation. The whole economic system of manufacture, credit and trade had ceased and it was impossible to replace any commonplace utensil or commodity. New clothes were unobtainable: even Gorky owned only one suit, which he wore all the time. The roads were pitted with deep cavities like shell holes, the drains had collapsed and the wooden pavements on many streets had been torn up for firewood. The tramcars were free but grossly overcrowded, and there were numerous accidents to passengers who clung to the outside and fell off, probably weakened by hunger. The people on the streets looked grim, perhaps at the approach of winter, perhaps from malnutrition, but more likely it was their apprehension that the country was in a state of ruin from which it was difficult to see how it could ever recover. When he said as much to Moura, she looked cast down. 'Is that what you are going to tell the British people when you get home?' she asked.

Unlike the Bolshevik officials he met, Moura was not a fervent propagandist for the Revolution, and in fact seldom made political comments of any kind, but he was aware that if he made a very unfavourable report on the country when he got home, as Bertrand Russell had recently done, much to the displeasure of his hosts, she might incur some blame. 'What I will tell the British people is this,' he said. 'Firstly, the ruin I see all around me here is not, as they have been told by most of their politicians and newspapers, the fault of the Bolshevik government—it was caused by the total collapse of the rotten capitalist-imperialist Czarist regime under the impact of war. And secondly, I will tell them that the Bolshevik government has so far prevented the country from falling into absolute anarchy, and is the only possible government for Russia for the foreseeable future.' Moura gave a nod of approval, and seemed satisfied.

He had spoken sincerely, but he did not unsettle her by pointing out that the Bolsheviks were severely handicapped in the monumental task of reconstruction by their doctrinal allegiance to Marx and Marxism. The Revolution that Marx had predicted should have begun in the industrialised countries of Western Europe, where there was an educated urban working class of the appropriate critical mass; instead it had actually happened first in Russia, whose population consisted mostly of an agrarian, superstitiously religious peasantry, neither able nor willing to exercise the dictatorship of the proletariat. Uneasily aware of this anomaly, and of their isolated and vulnerable position on the political map of Europe, the Bolshevik leaders he met invariably asked him when the revolution was going to begin in Britain, and were disbelieving or despondent when he assured them that there wasn't the slightest prospect of it happening.

Early in his visit Moura escorted him to a session of the Petrograd Soviet, which he had been invited to address. 'Will you be translating my speech?' he asked her the day before. 'No, there is an official interpreter,' she said. 'How can I be sure that my words will be translated accurately?' he said, remembering Bertrand Russell had complained that his speech to the same assembly was altered in translation to appear much more flattering about the state of Russia, and reported thus in the newspapers. 'The best thing you can do is write your speech and I will translate it and give it to the interpreter to read out,' she said, which she did, rather to the latter's consternation. She was implicitly colluding with him to prevent any manipulation of his words, an action which required considerable courage given her situation, and the episode had the effect of reinforcing his growing attraction to her. In the course of their perambulations he learned something of her history, which was both sad and dramatic. Her husband was dead—murdered, she said, on their estate in Estonia after the Revolution by some peasant with a grudge—and her wedding ring had been sold for food long ago, with all her other jewellery. Her aristocratic family had lost all their wealth and property, and were dead, dispersed, or like herself had thrown in their lot with the Revolution to survive. He gathered that she had two children who were being looked after in Estonia, and whom she longed to see again, but it was impossible for her to leave Russia and an attempt to do so had led to her being jailed for a time, after which she had been in considerable jeopardy until taken under Gorky's wing.

He made a short trip to Moscow with Gip, primarily to meet Lenin, who asked the usual question about the imminence of a revolution in Britain, but was too shrewd and sophisticated to show any surprise or disappointment at his answer. Lenin spoke excellent English and was altogether much more relaxed and less doctrinaire in conversation than he had expected from the pamphlets and speeches issued under his name. Nevertheless the interview was unsatisfactory. There was no meeting of minds: Lenin wanted to talk only about the electrification of the Soviet Union, his grandiose plan to modernise the vast territory of Soviet Russia by throwing a web of cables and pylons across it, a project ludicrously beyond the country's industrial capacity for the foreseeable future, and was uninterested in his own belief in global collectivism and a massive programme of education that would move mankind forward on its evolutionary path towards that goal.

He was glad to go back to Petrograd for a few days before his planned return to England—to Petrograd and more particularly to Moura, whose company he had missed acutely. Her enigmatic smile, her dark lustrous eyes above the high Slavic cheekbones, and the soft curves of her body where the thin black dress clung to it, stirred in him a desire which he felt intuitively she reciprocated. The idea of parting from this bewitching woman without having made love to her, and in all probability never seeing her again, tormented him. What had so far restrained him from making the attempt was the thought that she might be Gorky's mistress, but he had detected no sign of it in their behaviour when they were together, and Gorky's common-law wife, the actress Maria Fyodorevna Andréeva, whose presence had caused all the trouble in America, was serenely in charge of the apartment in Petrograd. He decided that his scruple was unfounded and unnecessary.

On the last evening of his stay some bottles of wine and vodka were mustered to accompany a farewell feast consisting of five tins of sardines and three jars of stuffed peppers, obtained through some shady connection of Gorky's. Afterwards, in the relaxed mood engendered by the food and drink, when Gorky and 'Andereyevna' had retired and Gip had gone to bed in the room they shared, he began to flirt discreetly with Moura on a sofa in a corner of the large living room, and then, encouraged by her response, less discreetly. The circumstances were propitious: the electricity supply had been shut down—a frequent occurrence in Petrograd—and the room was romantically lit by candles and firelight. The others still up were getting drunk on vodka, sitting in a circle round the fire, chatting and occasionally singing in Russian. 'Do you sleep with Maxim, Moura?' he asked. She opened her eyes wide and laughed. 'Of course not, Aigee,' she murmured. 'He sleeps with Andereyevna, and I sleep on the ottoman in Molecule's room.' Molecule was the nickname of a young medical student whom Gorky had taken under his wing. 'But Molecule is not here tonight,' he pointed out. 'No, She has gone to her friend Tatlin, the artist,' Moura said. 'So you will be able to sleep in a proper bed tonight,' he said. 'Yes,' she said. 'And you will be alone.' 'Yes,' she said. She looked into his eyes and smiled. They understood each other.

Some hours later, when he was fairly sure everyone in the apartment, including Gip in the bed beside his, was asleep, he left his room and felt his way barefoot through the dark corridors to Moura's. He had a story ready if he should be intercepted, that he had lost his way looking for the WC, but even so his heart beat fast, for he would hardly be believed, and the consequences would be deeply embarrassing. The risk he was taking, however, enhanced the ecstasy with which it was rewarded when he reached the safety of Moura's room. She had the softest skin he had ever encountered. She murmured incomprehensible but exciting Russian words and phrases as she reached her climax and he released the pent seed of three weeks' abstinence into a sheath he had prudently brought with him from England.

He did not feel guilty about being unfaithful to Rebecca. In his mind and in his memory, as he travelled back to England, that act of love in Moura's dark bedroom (he had not seen more than dimly what she was like, naked) in the heart of dark, ruined Petrograd, did not belong to the familiar world of ordinary adultery, of hotel bedrooms and *cabinets particuliers* with pink lampshades and plush upholstery, but to a realm that was exotic, adventurous, almost imaginary, where the constraints of domestic ties and loyalties were suspended. It was perhaps for this reason that when he saw Rebecca shortly after his return, at the flat in Queen's Gate, Kensington to which she had moved after the war, and gave her an account of his trip, he rashly did not conceal or minimise the part Moura had played as his interpreter and guide, but on the contrary described her talents with such enthusiasm, and showed such knowledge of her remarkable life, that Rebecca's suspicions were aroused, and she suddenly said: 'Did you sleep with her?' Some foolish impulse of honesty made him answer, 'Yes.' As he saw her face go white, and then red, with shock and anger, he said, 'Just once,' and added foolishly, 'On my last night.'

There followed floods of tears and a tremendous row, which ended with her declaring that she intended to take a handsome young lover herself at the first opportunity. 'And I won't have any difficulty finding one.' 'Don't say that, Panther,' he said. 'I couldn't bear it.' 'Why shouldn't I? It's tit for tat.' 'It's much worse for a man,' he said. 'Ha!' she cried, addressing the ceiling. 'Is this the great critic of the double standard speaking?' And then, looking at him with fierce hatred, 'Why don't you go home to your frigid wife, and tell *her* all about Moura. *She* won't mind.' Rebecca retreated to her bedroom, locking its door and leaving him to let himself out of the flat.

He went home and immediately wrote a letter, begging her not to carry out her threat: '*I love you and want to keep you anyhow, but I know that in spite of myself I shan't be able to endure your unfaithfulness. I am horribly afraid now of losing you. It will be a disaster for both of us. It will cut the heart out of my life. I don't think it will leave much in yours.'* When she didn't immediately respond he sent more letters, decorated with drawings of heartbroken Jaguars gazing mournfully at the turned backs of unforgiving Panthers. *'I am almost unendurably lonely and miserable,'* he wrote. *'I've done no end of work and good work. The Outline of History is going to change History. It doesn't matter a damn so far as my wretchedness is concerned. Righteous self applause is not happiness. Russia excited me and kept me going. Now I'm down. I'm alone. I'm tired. I want a breast and a kind body. I want love. I want love that I can touch and feel. And I don't deserve love. I've nagged at and bullied you. I've not kept faith. You are probably the only person who can really give me love and make me love back. I don't believe I'll find you next April. If I don't find you then I hope I'll find Death.'* This last sentiment was overstated, but he was due to make an extended lecture tour in America in the New Year and Rebecca was about to visit a friend on Capri, so he was frantic to be reconciled before their long separation commenced. Rebecca eventually surrendered to his epistolary siege, and peace was made between them, sealed in the usual way.

Rebecca went off to Capri in November, leaving Anthony in the care of a boarding school, but he became ill himself and had to cancel his American tour. Then Rebecca's friend on Capri also fell ill, and Rebecca was obliged to stay on, for weeks that extended into months, to look after her—or so she claimed in her letter. The worm of jealousy had entered their relationship with her threat to retaliate for his infidelity, and he wondered whether the young novelist Compton Mackenzie, who was living on Capri and whom she mentioned as having been kind to her, was part of the island's attraction. He therefore proposed to join her in Italy at the end of January, which would be good for his health, and they could both get on with their writing under the mild winter sun. They met in Amalfi and occupied adjoining rooms at the Hotel Cappucini, 'Miss West' posing as his secretary and companion; and all was well until a retired English major among the guests recognised him and made an unpleasant scene in his cups one evening, complaining of 'adulterous couples' polluting the moral tone of the establishment. Another English acquaintance turned up at the hotel not long afterwards, and soon every guest in the place was aware of their identities. The sense of being the object of their prurient curiosity made him irritable and prone to make scenes himself, as Rebecca bitterly complained. 'Even when people are nice to us, you snub them and make me feel awful,' she said after he had behaved badly to a harmless brother and sister from Croydon who accompanied them on an excursion to Paestum. They left Amalfi after a month and moved on to Rome and Florence, still bickering between bouts of lovemaking, and making critical remarks when, as was their custom, they showed their work-in-progress to each other.

Rebecca had had a deserved success in 1918 with her first novel *The Return of the Soldier*, a short, exquisitely written tale of a soldier who lost his memory as a result of a battle wound and recovered the happiness of his first love in consequence, only to forfeit it when, through the intervention of his embittered wife, he recovered his memory and was sent back to the Front to a probable death. It was a timely book which was highly praised and sold well, but Rebecca was struggling with her second novel, a dark, complex work called *The Judge*, while he himself was writing a riskily confessional novel called *The Secret Places of the Heart*. The hero, Sir Richmond Hardy, a world expert on fuel, was having a nervous breakdown due to overwork and the frustration of his efforts to establish international control of the earth's resources of oil and coal, and sought help from a psychiatrist, who agreed to conduct the therapy while accompanying him on a motor tour of the West Country of England. Hardy's sexual history was not unlike his own, a mixture of casual promiscuity and an unsatisfied longing for the perfect mate, and he currently had a mistress called Martin Leeds who annoyingly fell just short of this ideal. In the course of the motor tour Hardy met and fell in love with an enchanting young American woman and had many profound conversations with her about the meaning of life and his mission to save the world by the sensible management of fuel. In the last part of the novel they would be tempted to have an affair but abstain for the highest motives, and Hardy would die shortly afterwards leaving Martin to make a very late appearance in the book, regretting that she hadn't fully appreciated his merits when he was alive.

There was an autobiographical source for the American girl: Margaret Sanger, the controversial leader of the birth control movement in America. He had signed a petition long ago protesting against her persecution under American law for distributing information about contraception, corresponded with her subsequently, and finally met her in the summer of 1920 when she was visiting England. He found her extremely attractive, and sensed that he could easily have initiated an affair with her, but constraints of time and circumstance as well as conscience prevented him from acting on the intuition. Rebecca had not met Margaret Sanger, but had corresponded with her at his suggestion to obtain advice on the latest methods of female contraception, and was aware of his admiration for the American woman. He knew that Rebecca would read this personal history into the parts of the novel he showed her, and hoped that she would infer, and give him credit for, a wholly chaste friendship with Margaret. She did not however appreciate her own part in the story, which was mostly off-stage. She declared that 'Martin Leeds' was the most improbable name for a female character in the history of fiction, and tactlessly laughed aloud while reading chapters into which he could not recall putting any jokes. He retaliated by criticising the structure of *The Judge*, which started with a fine dramatic situation—a judge picks up a prostitute whose husband he sentenced to death ten years earlier and the woman plans to murder him in revenge—and then worked further and further backwards into the past. 'The writing is all very fine, Panther— lots of vivid local colour—but you are keeping us waiting impatiently to rejoin the opening scene, to discover what happens next. What does happen?' 'I haven't made up my mind yet,' Rebecca said sulkily. 'That's why you keep going backwards,' he said.

After they returned to England, conscious that he had not been the easiest of travelling companions he wrote a letter thanking her for 'two and half months of almost unbroken happiness', to which she replied tartly that she wished he had expressed this gratitude at the time, since it had not been evident from his behaviour.

—There was a pattern here, wasn't there? You were always trying to persuade her to extricate herself from domestic and family ties, to go away with you on your own, but whenever she actually managed it you behaved deplorably. The same thing happened a year later—only you were even worse. You went to America to report on the Washington Peace Conference, had a fling with Margaret Sanger, went about the country being lionised, and sailed back to meet Rebecca in Gibraltar for a holiday in Spain. But you made the holiday sheer hell for her. As soon as you transferred to the *Maria Cristina* in Algeciras, you started throwing your weight about, to her acute embarrassment.

—I wasn't well. I was exhausted from all the travelling, and I had a sore throat.

—You ordered the manager of the hotel to phone the Admiral of the

Fleet at Gibraltar Harbour for a naval doctor to attend to it. 'Just tell him it's H.G. Wells who is ill,' you said. 'He'll send someone immediately.'

—That was a little presumptuous, I admit. But the retired English doctor they dug out from the foothills behind Algeciras was a hopeless quack—he could only prescribe a gargle for my sore throat.

—Perhaps a gargle was all that was required. When you moved on to Seville you treated Rebecca so rudely in public that the English chaplain there took her aside and offered to wire her parents to come and fetch her. In Granada you walked out halfway through a party with dancers and poets given in your honour by Manuel de Falla. When you got to Paris on the way home you refused to take Rebecca with you to visit Anatole France because, you said, she was not good-looking enough.

—So she claimed. I may have said she didn't look smart enough. We'd just arrived in Paris—her clothes were creased and her hair needed doing.

—That was still insulting.

—She could be just as personal. She said I was getting a paunch.

—And so you were! You can't deny you behaved abominably on that trip.

—I was in a strange state in those years. I was having a kind of extended nervous breakdown, like Sir Richmond Hardy. I was outwardly successful— 'the most famous writer in the world'—but inwardly dissatisfied. The praise I got was not the kind I wanted or from the people I wanted to get it from. It made me arrogant and irritable—I was aware of that, but I couldn't control myself at times.

—Why on earth did Rebecca put up with you? Again and again you had tremendous rows, again and again she would say she'd had enough, and again and again you would wheedle your way back into her favour and her bed.

—I wasn't always as difficult as that time in Spain, and even then we had happy interludes, days when we got on very well together and enjoyed ourselves. We were both exceptional people and we knew it. We were interested in the same things, we stimulated each other intellectually and creatively as well as erotically—it seemed destiny that we should be lovers. But yes, in retrospect it was surprising how long we stayed together, because we were temperamentally incompatible. Rebecca's sensibility was essentially tragic. Jane was right—it wasn't accidental that she took her assumed name from Ibsen. All her life she liked to act out the part of the tragic heroine, with tears, hysterics, melodramatic gestures . . . I hated her when she was like that. My temperament is essentially comic—I want life to be enjoyable, I like festive occasions and happy endings, I like sex and games, and when things go seriously wrong in my life—I don't mean things like a sore throat, but a real disaster—I try not to let it show to other people.

—So why did the relationship last as long as it did?

—Basically because Rebecca went on hoping that I would divorce Jane and marry her. That's why she would put up with my moods, and make up after our quarrels. And it wasn't a one-way process. More than once I wrote her a letter saying I thought we should probably part for the sake of both our sanities, but she never wrote back saying unequivocally, 'Yes, I agree, let's do it.'

—Perhaps that was because those letters of yours were never unequivocal. They were full of fond nostalgic memories of your happy times together, and admissions of your sins against her, and expressions of your undying admiration for her. They were more like love letters than end-of-the-affair letters. No wonder she hesitated, when you proposed separation, to take you up on it.

—She hesitated because she still hoped to marry me. She didn't really believe that I would never divorce Jane. To my mind, we had a potentially perfect relationship when it started: Jane to look after my creature comforts and organise my professional life and be the perfect hostess for the entertaining that we both enjoyed; Rebecca to be my lover, fellow artist and soulmate. But she wasn't satisfied with that role alone—she wanted both, and Anthony gave her a kind of right to both, she thought. He was the incarnation of her claim on me, and he was a constant bone of contention between us even after we split up: arguments about how much I should contribute to his education, whether I could adopt him, and—when she blocked that—what access I could have to him. I'm afraid he had a pretty difficult childhood, Anthony. When he was very young he thought his mother was his aunt and I was his uncle, and then Rebecca told him she was his mother but he should still go on calling her 'Auntie', and then years later she told him his uncle was really his father.

—It sounds like a Freudian nightmare. You and Rebecca could hardly have done more to make him neurotic in later life if you had tried.

—I admit some responsibility for his later fecklessness. But he rarely reproached me. He always idolised me and blamed his mother for his upbringing, which was unfair on her, and embittered her towards me for a long time. It was all a mess and a muddle, that triangular relationship, an

386

unholy family. It would have been better for Anthony if he had been adopted by a nice couple of caring responsible parents as I had intended, or if Rebecca and I had parted much sooner.

And the parting itself was never a clean, decisive break. It was impossible to put one's finger on a particular letter or remember a particular conversation of which one could say, 'That was it. That was the irrevocable statement of intent to separate.' Not even the Hedwig Verena Gatternigg affair had that effect.

This youngish Austrian woman—she was in her early thirties, and married to an officer on a Danube patrol boat in the shrunken post-war Austrian navy—came to London in the autumn of 1922 with an introduction from her mother, whom he knew slightly, and called at the flat in Whitehall Court which was his London base at that time, to propose translating one or more of his books into German. On that occasion Jane was with him and they gave tea to Frau Gatternigg. She was pretty, with long-lashed brown eyes under a lustrous head of hair, and an elegant figure—but also a withered hand which gave her a certain pathos and made him sympathetic to her request. Her spoken English was excellent. As she was interested in education, he suggested she might translate *The Great Schoolmaster,* a book he was writing about Sanderson of Oundle, who had died suddenly and dramatically of a heart attack earlier that year while giving a public lecture at which he himself was presiding. He gave her a carbon copy of the chapters that Jane had already typed out, and she returned a few days later to ask some questions about the text. On the next occasion she called (this time without an appointment) Jane had returned to Easton, and Hedwig Verena made it very clear that she wanted more than German translation rights from him. 'I want you,' she said, showing she had read *Ann Veronica* attentively.

It was not in his nature to reject a frank advance from a woman, face to face. The propositions which he received occasionally by post from strangers were a different matter, and these days he seldom followed them up; only recently he had declined one from a writer called Odette Keun, whose book *Sous Lénine, My Adventures in Bolshevik Russia,* he had reviewed favourably when it was translated from the French and published in England. She had thanked him effusively for the review, and declared herself a devoted admirer of his work, who had dedicated an earlier book to him without his knowledge; she was at a loose end with nothing to live for, and asked him to come to Paris and give her two or three days to make him happy. Intriguing as the offer was, prudence counselled against accepting it for several reasons. He replied that he already had a lover to whom he could not be unfaithful, and she accepted this virtuous excuse with resignation. Frau Gatternigg, appealing to him in person, was a different proposition, and he thought that if he rejected her overture she would be bound to attribute it to revulsion from her withered limb and be deeply hurt, so he responded gallantly. In fact when she was naked in his bedroom he found her deformity invested her with a novel and slightly perverse fascination which made him particularly vigorous. She for her part was passionate and effusively grateful, and if he had never seen her again he would have had only agreeable memories of the occasion and almost counted it as a good deed.

Unfortunately she began to pester him with love letters and urgent requests to meet him again, some of which he weakly indulged, and once she tricked him into an assignation by telling him she was staying near Easton with a married couple who were great admirers of his work and would be thrilled to meet him. When he responded to this bait by driving over to the house, Hedwig Verena opened the front door, dressed in a filmy tea gown and little else, and led him immediately upstairs to a bedroom, explaining that her married friends were away and had left her to look after the house. He felt increasingly uneasy about continuing the affair, if one could call it that, but unable to bring it discreetly to an end, until to his relief she finally went back to Austria.

He was unpleasantly surprised to receive a telephone call from her on an exceedingly hot day in June of the following year, when he was on his own at Whitehall Court. 'I'm back, H.G.,' she said. 'When can I see you?' 'You can't, Hedwig,' he said. 'I'm sorry, but I'm much too busy, and will be for the foreseeable future.' Undeterred she came to the flat soon afterwards, pretended to the maid who answered the doorbell that she had an appointment, and was shown into his study. When she tried to embrace him he backed off and held up his hand. 'No, Hedwig.' 'But I love you!' she exclaimed. 'I'm sorry,' he said, ' I do not love you. I never loved you, and I never said I loved you. We had an enjoyable *passade* last year, but that was all it was.' Upon which she sat down, uninvited, and said sulkily, 'You are very cruel, H.G. You are very cold. It is because of Rebecca West, is it not?' 'What do you know of Rebecca West?' he said angrily. 'What everybody in London knows, that you are her lover,' she said, smiling maliciously. It seemed to him that her withered hand now gave her a sinister, witch-like appearance. She added: 'Perhaps I will tell her that you were *my* lover last year.' 'Are you trying to blackmail me?' he said, standing over her threateningly, now really angry. 'No, no, of course I would not, I am joking you,' she said, making a rare idiomatic error. 'But I would love to meet her and talk to her about books and ideas. Perhaps I could interview her. Give me a letter of introduction to her, and I promise not to mention that we had what you call a *passade*.'

In the end it seemed the only way to get rid of her, so he scribbled a brief note of introduction to Rebecca and sent Hedwig round to Queen's Gate, instructing the housemaid not to admit her if she returned. He learned later that Rebecca received the visitor with much puzzlement, and that her maid was so concerned by the latter's appearance and manner that she went out into the street to check that a constable was on point duty at the corner in case he should be needed. Hedwig chattered away in a bizarre fashion, praising Rebecca's work extravagantly, inviting her to borrow her flat in Vienna, describing in detail an unhappy affair she had had with an English diplomat there, and gesturing so wildly that she sent a sewing-box flying to the floor and broke it. But she kept her promise not to reveal her intimacy with himself, and Rebecca, after suffering a fervent embrace, eventually managed to ease her out of the flat.

That evening he was in his dressing room, changing for a dinner with Lord Montagu, the Secretary of State for India, and wondering how he would bear a starched shirt and dinner jacket for a whole evening in the stifling temperature, when he heard the sounds of someone being admitted to his study. It was Hedwig. Unfortunately the maid had gone off duty without passing on his instruction to her substitute, and Hedwig had talked her way into the flat. When he entered the study she was standing in the centre of the room facing the door, wearing a waterproof raincoat, and he just had time to reflect that this was a strange garment for such a hot day before she threw it open to reveal that she was naked except for stockings, a suspender belt and high-heeled shoes. 'You must love me!' she cried, 'or I will kill myself. I have poison. I have a razor.' He instantly grasped the urgency of getting not only help but also witnesses to the madness of her behaviour. He went to the door and called down the passageway to the maid to summon the hall-porter of the building, but when he turned round Hedwig had already thrown off the waterproof and slashed her wrists and armpits with a cut-throat razor.

Fortunately she had not severed an artery, but she was bleeding profusely when he took the razor from her, propped her up in an armchair and covered her with the waterproof, having checked that there was no vial of poison in its pockets. 'Let me die, let me die,' she declaimed, and as others arrived, 'I love him, I love him.' The hall-porter, an ex-army sergeant-major, proved to be a model of calm efficiency in summoning the police and the ambulance service, and Hedwig was whisked off to the Westminster Infirmary, from which he received in due course a telephone message that she was not in danger. This was an immense relief: if she had succeeded in committing suicide he would have been finished. There would have been an inquest and a public scandal that would have made the Amber Reeves affair look petty in comparison. Even so he was well aware that the press could make something very damaging out of the incident if they wished, and his solicitor Hayes, whom he contacted by telephone, agreed. 'We must try and persuade your friends in the Newspaper Owners' Association to suppress the story as far as possible,' he said. 'But I'm afraid there's bound to be something in the papers tomorrow.'

And indeed there was. The police and the ambulance men had seemed sympathetic and discreet, but a reporter on the *Star,* a popular evening paper, got wind of the story the next morning, perhaps from the hospital, and having ascertained from Hedwig Verena's landlady that she had visited Rebecca West earlier, went round to Queen's Gate with a photographer in tow and asked her for a comment and a photo of herself with Anthony. She shut the door on them and phoned him in a panic asking him what had happened. When he explained she said, 'Oh my God! What shall I say to them?' 'Nothing—send them round to me,' he told her, knowing they would not be satisfied until they got something to print, and gave a short dignified statement when they arrived. 'It is true that a young woman entered my flat uninvited and threatened to commit suicide, and actually attempted to do so while I was seeking assistance. Fortunately she did not succeed, and she is being treated in hospital for minor injuries. I do not wish the matter to be talked about, and I do not intend to add to the snowball of rumour.'

He telephoned Rebecca and arranged to meet her in Kensington Gardens that afternoon to discuss the situation. She was not as angry with him for sending Frau Gatternigg to her as he had feared—but then she had no idea of his previous relationship with the woman; as far as she knew, Hedwig's invasion of his flat and demented behaviour was totally unexpected.

'I'm sorry you've been dragged into it, Panther,' he said. 'There will be a report of some kind in the *Star* this evening. Hayes says the best thing we can do is to dine out conspicuously and go on to a theatre, behaving as if nothing serious has happened and we are not in the least disturbed.' They carried off this performance—rather well, he thought—at the Ivy that evening, and later at Wyndham's Theatre, knowing that the Late Evening edition of the *Star* was on the streets outside, with a long and fairly accurate account of the incident under the headline, '*WOMAN ATTEMPTS SUICIDE IN FLAT OF H.G. WELLS*'. It mentioned that this person had '*visited the home of a well-known woman novelist in Kensington and acted in a strange manner*' on the same day.

A few other papers repeated the story the following morning, but with no more details, and mercifully there were no journalistic sequels. He blessed his good relations with Beaverbrook and Rothermere, both of whom promised to help when he appealed to them, and instructed their editors that 'H.G. Wells is not news for the next two weeks.' Hedwig, having been advised that she would be liable to prosecution for attempted suicide, returned to Austria as soon as she was able. Before the end of Beaverbrook's and Rothmere's helpful embargoes, the story was, in journalistic terms, dead.

—**You were very lucky.**

—I was. Mind you, Hedwig had no real intention of committing suicide. She'd had some practice in cutting herself without doing serious damage. I discovered later that she'd used the same trick before, in Austria, when she was spurned by some lover.

—**Your account of that episode in the Postscript to the Autobiography is very misleading as regards Rebecca's part in it. You say there that you discovered, when you met her in Kensington Gardens, that Hedwig '*in the rôle of a literary admirer and possible interviewer, had visited Rebecca the previous day—I suppose with the idea of staging a triangular situation*', as if you yourself had nothing to do with it.**

—I didn't feel it was relevant.

—**It was very relevant! Rebecca's involvement was what made the story potentially so sensational. It wasn't just a matter of a famous writer and a deranged fan—as you say, it became a triangle: the famous writer, his mistress and a jealous rival of the mistress. And it was all your fault.**

—Yes, quite true.

—Why on earth did you send the woman round to Queen's Gate? Anything might have happened. She might have attacked Rebecca.

—I honestly don't know. I was desperate to get rid of her, and it was fearfully hot that day in London—ninety-two degrees. I sometimes think the heat made me almost as deranged as Hedwig. Of course, I didn't yet know how dangerous she was, but it was certainly an irrational thing to do, sending her to Rebecca. When I came to write up the whole episode I really couldn't explain it, so I left it out.

—In other words, you were too embarrassed to admit your folly even in these allegedly candid confessions?

—I suppose so, yes.

—She told people later that it was the Hedwig episode which finally convinced her that you were completely selfish and didn't really love her, and that she would have to break with you.

—Not true, actually—or only half true. I was selfish, but I did love her. And anyway, she didn't break with me immediately.

—No, she went for a cure to Marienbad with a friend, and you followed her there and made a nuisance of yourself as usual.

—I did. The rope that held us together was fraying, but it wasn't quite severed. After that we had a short holiday in Swanage with Anthony, for the boy's sake, and were quite happy together for a few days, until she raised once again the question of my divorcing Jane and I refused, so we went back to bickering about the terms of my support for her. She wanted me to settle £3,000 a year on her. I gave her a large lump sum instead and said I would look after Anthony's school fees. She was thinking of making a life for herself and Anthony in America, where she had good contacts in journalism, and went off for a long lecture tour there in the autumn of '23 to assess the opportunities. She stayed until the following spring and decided in the end that she didn't want to emigrate, but it was clear from the sparseness and the tone of her letters that when she came back to England, she wasn't coming back to me. And yet . . .

—And yet?

—It wasn't easy for either of us to write *Finis* under our story. The world was full of men she couldn't talk to as she talked to me, and of women I had only a brief and simple use for. I went to Lisbon where the Galsworthys were wintering and paired up with a very pleasant red-haired young widow who was as much in need of consolation as myself, but it was only a *passade*.

Rebecca, I gathered later, had experiences of a similar kind in America, all of them ephemeral and some alarming and upsetting. When we returned to London in the spring we were both very much aware of each other's presence, and occasionally we met—once by chance in the theatre, and a couple of times by arrangement—and actually made love again, but it was different, we couldn't revive the old Panther–Jaguar intimacy, we had hurt each other too much. In September Rebecca went off to Austria with Anthony and some friends, and I decided I would make a journey round the world, a project I had often planned and never followed through, but first I had to go to Geneva to address the League of Nations Assembly.

—**Where Odette Keun turned up.**

—She'd heard somehow that Rebecca and I had parted and she'd read in a newspaper that I was going to be in Geneva, so she hastened there from Grasse where she was living at the time, and called me up and invited me to meet her at her hotel that evening.

—**And instructed the reception desk to send you up to her room, where she had turned out all the lights and was waiting for you behind the door, doused in jasmine perfume and wearing only a negligee, and led you like a blind man straight to the bed.**

—It was clever of her, because her face was not conventionally pretty, as I discovered next morning: she had a prominent nose and a rather long chin. But she had a supple, slender body and she was like a monkey on heat as a lover. She'd been converted to Catholicism as a young girl and spent three years in a Belgian convent preparing to become a nun before she was dismissed for allegedly tempting a priest to kiss her, after which she made up for lost time by acquiring sexual experience from some fairly louche characters in Marseilles and Paris. I discovered that she wasn't French, but the daughter of a Dutch father and an Italian mother, brought up in Constantinople. She was a fizzing cocktail of mixed genes and cultures, but intelligent and articulate and she had read nearly every book I had written.

—**So when she said she adored you and wanted to devote her whole life to serving you on any terms you prescribed, you succumbed, and went to Provence with her after your speech to the League of Nations, and rented a *mas* called Lou Bastidon in the hills outside Grasse, looking down over orchards and olive groves towards the Mediterranean, and you liked the situation and the climate so much that for the next nine years you divided your time between France and England, most of them in a** *mas* you had built to your own design called Lou Pidou, which had a plaque over the fireplace, *'Two lovers built this house.'*

—Odette's idea, which I indulged, but we had such fierce and frequent rows that I kept calling in the stonemason to remove it, and then requesting him to put it back again when we were reconciled, until he got fed up and refused to do it any more. But I really don't want to talk about Odette.

—Why not?

—Of all the women I've known well—and known in the biblical sense—she's the only one whom I remember without any affection at all. With amusement at times, at the outrageousness of her behaviour, and bitterness often, but not affection. There were other women I parted from unhappily, but who subsequently became friends again—Isabel, Rebecca, and little E, for instance; even Hedwig, who recovered from her madness and sent me a nice letter of apology. I met her years later with her husband and advised her about getting a novel published. But Odette nearly drove me mad with her moods and her jealousies and her demented behaviour, which became worse and worse as time went on. I made a treaty with her at the beginning of our relationship, that she would be my companion in France but not invade my life in England, and was free to do what she liked while I was away from her. To make her independent I gave her a regular income, and the usufruct of Lou Pidou. For a few years she kept to the agreement, and wrote obsequious letters to Jane assuring her that she was looking after my health and general welfare. Jane was quite happy with the arrangement, since it meant she could go off to Switzerland for her holidays while I was in the south of France, winter sports and mountain walks now being too strenuous for me, and she considered Odette much less of a threat to her own status than Rebecca had been. She even gave us a nice picture by Nevinson for Lou Pidou. But after Jane died, in '27, Odette became discontented. She wanted to be openly recognised as my companion, in England as well as France.

—She probably hoped you would marry her.

—And perhaps I would have done—God help me—if she'd played her cards right and been sweet and tender to me in my grief, but she couldn't control her egotism, her competitiveness, and her temper. She badgered me and teased me, she showed off to my friends when we entertained them at Lou Pidou, and delighted in shocking them by using four-letter words which she falsely claimed I had taught her, and by making embarrassing allusions to our sexual habits. She complained that I spent too much time away from her and that she was lonely in Grasse, so I acquired a flat for her in Paris, where I could visit her more easily for short periods. Still she wasn't satisfied, and broke the terms of the treaty by following me to England. I threatened to leave her, but she didn't believe that I would sacrifice Lou Pidou, and persisted. In the end I did give up Lou Pidou—with great regret, for I loved the place—because I couldn't stand the relationship any longer. It was as if the monkey had climbed on to my back, and was digging her claws into me all the time. I had to be free of her. But still she tormented me—she settled in London and spread malicious gossip about me, and about Moura, who I had linked up with again. She went to Amber Reeves's house one day and proposed that, as two women who had been wronged by me, they should go round to my flat and shoot me in revenge: she actually had a small revolver, which Amber relieved her of and handed in to Hampstead police station later, pretending she had found it on the Heath. Odette published a book called *I Discover the English* in which she said Englishmen were unimaginative lovers who made the sexual act as boring as cold suet pudding, knowing that readers privy to our relationship would take the remark as a reflection on me, and she threatened to sell my erotic letters to her, a piece of blackmail I defied her to carry out, for I was not ashamed of them and they would have demonstrated conclusively that our sexual antics, so far from being like cold suet pudding, would have made Etruscan vase-painters blush.

—**And she wrote a review of** *Experiment in Autobiography,* **called 'H.G. Wells—the Player', published in three parts in** *Time and Tide.*

—Yes.

—**Which you allude to dismissively as 'very silly articles' in the Postscript, though they weren't silly at all.**

—They certainly didn't constitute a review in the normal sense of the word. They were eight thousand words of character assassination, an act of spiteful revenge—and not just Odette's. The Literary Editor of *Time and Tide* then was Theodora Bosanquet.

—**The devoted secretary who typed Henry James's last pained letter to you.**

—Exactly. She'd been waiting for nearly twenty years to punish me for *Boon,* and now she saw her chance—hiring my discarded mistress to review her ex-lover's book. It was a disgraceful abuse of editorial power. Rebecca was appalled when she read it and wrote me a sympathetic letter. She was on the journal's board of directors, but it was too late for her to do anything about it.

—You must admit the piece scored some palpable hits. Shall we have a look at it again?

—I'd rather not.

—Then I will. She begins by paying tribute to the influence of your early work. *'It is quite impossible that anyone outside those generations which he was freeing should understand the wildness of the glory and happiness of our relief. I remember when I read, as an adolescent, that noble work* First Things and Last Things, *I sobbed with the ecstasy, the almost intolerable sense of organic liberation that it brought.'* She anticipated what Orwell said about you: *'It would be no more than justice to give his name to the twenty-five years between the 'nineties and the War. For it was he who largely wove their intellectual texture.'* But she has an interesting theory about what motivated you. She describes you as a genius who in early life was trapped in an environment that was impoverished in every sense—materially, spiritually, culturally and sexually—and that when you managed to break out of it, you were for ever afterwards trying to take revenge on the world that had nearly condemned you to obscurity and an early death. *'His motivation was first and foremost the revolt of a powerful and outraged ego.'*

—Ha! She had a nerve to talk of outraged egos!

—*'He had suffered in his mind and his body—I have heard him say many times with an undiminished indignation, that if he had been properly nourished in his childhood he would have been in his prime several inches taller.'*

—And so I would have been.

—*'His perpetually vibrating physical and sexual vanity, always clamouring for satisfaction, is also the result of a body humiliated in young manhood.'*

—Rubbish!

—You don't admit that there was something compulsive about your womanising—as if you had to seize every opportunity to prove your virility?

—I just happen to enjoy sex, and if I found a woman with the same appetite I had fun with her. I never forced a woman in my life, and I've had long-lasting friendships with women who turned me down.

—But a contradiction runs through your thinking about sex. Sometimes you say it should be regarded as just fun, a healthy form of recreation, like golf; at other times, with a beloved partner, it's the most sublime physical, emotional and spiritual experience attainable, a portal to the Lover-Shadow.

—True. I oscillated between those two attitudes to sex without ever reconciling them—but that's the human being for you. We're a bundle of incompatible parts, and we make up stories about ourselves to disguise the fact. The mental unity of the individual is a fiction. There is simply, in the human machine, a multitude of loosely linked behaviour systems which take control of the body and participate in a common delusion of being one single self. I explained all this in a doctoral thesis 'On the Quality of Illusion in the Continuity of the Individual Life in the Higher Metazoa, with Particular Reference to the Species *Homo Sapiens*'—successfully submitted to the University of London in 1943.

—The examiners could hardly fail you, given your age and distinction, but they were obviously somewhat baffled by the argument.

—Well, perhaps its time has not yet come.

—Isn't there some truth in Odette's theory that your career was shaped by a desire to bring down the social system which nearly stifled your potential?

—I wanted to save future generations from being stifled.

—But she says you were always essentially a 'player', not a leader, someone more interested in winning than constructing, and constantly moving on from one game to another, and *'What he did not make, in any country, was a school, a following, a consolidated nucleus of disciples— without which there is no perpetuation of any idea . . . He was a paradox; personally, an anarchist, incapable of inner discipline, or submission or respect to a system of team-work, who tried to press a world order upon others.'*

—Have you done?

—Not quite. Listen to her last paragraph. *'As he stands now, near to the finish of the contest, he sees the trend of happenings leading away from his own lines; men who are the foes of his thought have become the rulers of nations and have beaten his Utopia. He can no longer shape minds or inflame devotions. This was not inevitable. He had the brain, he had the vision, he had the ability. But that thing which makes the common man endure for an end; which makes the nobler man die for an end; that thing which is integrity of doctrine and selflessness of idealism; that ultimate genuineness which in the last analysis alone makes for permanent force and influence in life—in no form and no measure has he ever had it at all. It was only a game. He was only a player.'* No doubt that judgment was motivated by personal spite and resentment. But aren't you haunted by the fear that Odette may have been right?

—No. I never had disciples because I never wanted them. They turn liberation into tyranny. Jesus was fine until he got disciples. I may have failed to change the world, but I did infinitely less harm than those rulers of nations who, according to her, writing in 1934, had succeeded—by their 'integrity of doctrine and selflessness of idealism'. Who did she mean? Hitler and Mussolini? Stalin? The rulers of Japan? Look at what they have done to the world between them. And don't bother me any more.

PART FIVE

n the spring of 1945, the façade of Hanover Terrace looks much as it did a year before—if anything, even shabbier and in more urgent need of repair. Most of the windows are still boarded up, for V1s and V2s continue to fall on London throughout March, the last spasm of German defiance as the Allied armies advance inexorably from east and west. There is no longer any suspense about how the war in Europe will end—only about when, and whether the Russians or the British and Americans will get to Berlin first, and whether Hitler will be captured alive. People study the maps on the front pages of their newspapers, shaded and cross-hatched in black and white, with broad curved arrows showing the movements of the various armies, all pointing towards the same target, every day a little closer, and keep their ears cocked to the nearest radio for the latest bulletins. There is a strange mixture of weariness and tension in the air, like a deeply drawn-in breath waiting for release. It would be premature to express joy or triumph at the news of each new advance, each new tally of German prisoners taken, while V-weapons still fall at random on London, and loved ones serving in the forces in Europe and the Far East are still in jeopardy.

H.G. certainly manifests no such emotions as he scans the daily newspaper and, fatigued, lets it drop to the floor. The prospect of final victory does not excite him. The news seems more like tidings of defeat to him— the defeat of his own utopian dreams for humanity's future. The photographs of the bombed German cities, Dresden especially, showing block after block of skeletal buildings, mere façades like stage sets, their roofs and interiors all burned away, appal him, and the fact that he prophesied such devastation in his fiction is no consolation. Thirty or forty years ago, in novels like *The War of the Worlds*, *The War in the Air* and *The World Set*

Free, he described the mass destruction of great cities, the crowds of panicked refugees choking the roads, the collapse of civil order and the descent into barbarism, which is the spectacle Europe presents today. In many respects his imagination leapfrogged the First World War in those novels, and made them more prophetic of the Second. He always struck a note of hope at the end of those books, that a benign new world would arise from the ashes, but he has no such optimism now. As he has written in *Mind at the End of its Tether,* at present with his publishers, '*the limit to the orderly secular development of life had seemed to be a definitely fixed one, so that it was possible to sketch out the pattern of things to come. But that limit was reached and passed into a hitherto incredible chaos. The more he scrutinized the realities around us, the more difficult it became to sketch out any Pattern of Things To Come.*'

Of course it is good that the Allies are going to win the war—in a narrowly personal sense because both his name and Rebecca's were known to be on a list of 2,000-odd people who would have been immediately arrested by the Gestapo had Germany successfully invaded England in 1940, but also for more universal ethical reasons. When the first pictures of the liberated concentration camp at Belsen are released in mid-April, and the full horror of Nazi ideology is revealed, not in skeletal buildings but in skeletal human beings, some barely alive, staring gauntly into the camera, others dead and heaped in piles like refuse, and as more details emerge about the extermination camps in Poland discovered by the advancing Russians, their gas chambers, incinerators and ash heaps, the justice of the war is irrefutably confirmed. Nevertheless the fact that it happened at all, that it was necessary only twenty years after the First World War, was a defeat for civilisation, and one he takes personally, since he spent so much time in the intervening years working for peace. It seemed symbolic that in September 1939 German tanks rolled into Poland and Stukas dive-bombed Warsaw just as he was preparing to address the PEN Congress in Stockholm on 'The Honour and Dignity of the Human Mind', obliging him to cancel his speech and, like the rest of the delegates, scuttle home to a precarious safety. Now the Human Mind is at the end of its tether, or at least his own is.

As Hitler's genocidal persecution of the Jews becomes more and more the central fact of Nazi iniquity in public consciousness, he is uncomfortably aware that certain aspects of his own treatment of Jews in his fiction and non-fictional writings have given offence to Jewish readers in the past and are likely to be held against him more widely in the future, especially some passages in a book called *The Anatomy of Frustration* published in 1936, where, while condemning the Nazi persecution of the Jews in the strongest terms, he asserted that *'this must not bar Gentile writers from the frankest and most searching criticism of the many narrowing and reactionary elements still disagreeably present in the Jewish tradition'*, invited Jews to consider whether the long history of their persecution did not show that these elements were inherently provocative, and suggested that the ideology of National Socialism *'is inverted Judaism, which has retained the form of the Old Testament and turned it inside out'*. That these and similar opinions were attributed to a fictitious persona called William Burroughs Steele, whose unfinished encyclopaedic masterpiece he himself was supposedly summarising, would not provide him with an alibi.

A couple of years ago he had initiated a correspondence with Chaim Weizmann, the leader of the Zionist movement, but also a first-class chemist for whose scientific work he had great respect, in which he apologised for having *'through my own ready irritability and tactlessness, aroused the resentment of Jews who are essentially at one with me in their desire for a sane equalitarian world order. For centuries the Jewish community, whatever its Old Testament tradition, has been the least aggressive of all nationally conscious communities. <u>Mea Culpa</u>.'* He invited Weizmann to publish the correspondence, but as far as he knows the hint was not taken. And even if it were to be published he does not suppose it will excuse him in the eyes of posterity. If you write as much as he has written in his lifetime, and as hastily, you are bound to make some mistakes of judgment at times. It took him a long time, for instance, to recognise how completely Stalin's police state had betrayed the ideals of the Russian Revolution. But at least he was never taken in by Mussolini and Hitler, as many British pundits and politicians were.

The war finally comes to an end with Hitler's suicide on April 30th and Germany's unconditional surrender on May 7th. May 8th is declared Victory in Europe Day, and celebrations throughout the land are described on the BBC's Home Service as they happen. There are crowds around Nelson's Column in Trafalgar Square and in the Mall in front of Buckingham Palace, where the King and Queen come out on to the central balcony with their two daughters, accompanied by Winston Churchill, to wave and receive the cheers of their subjects. There are local street parties for children, and parades of the Home Guard and Boy Scouts and ARP wardens on village greens. As night falls bonfires illuminate the bomb sites and lights blaze from the uncurtained windows of houses. A month later there is an Allied Victory Parade down Whitehall, columns of soldiers, sailors and airmen and women auxiliaries from all over the Commonwealth saluting and saluted by the King with the Queen standing beside him. The mood of these celebrations is less hysterical than those he remembers from November 1918, partly because the war against Japan is not over yet, but there is always something morally repugnant about them. 'Those who win wars are the dead and the wounded,' he says to his night nurse, who witnessed the parade in Whitehall and enthuses about it when she comes on duty. 'The dead can't parade and the wounded usually don't wish to or cannot.' 'Well, there's some truth in that, sir,' the woman says, but she looks as if she feels snubbed.

The more others rejoice, the more misanthropic he becomes. He writes to Bertrand Russell in late May, *'This vast return to chaos which is called the peace, the infinite meanness of great masses of my fellow creatures, the wickedness of organized religion, give me a longing for a sleep that will have no awakening.'* There is an echo in this last phrase of some lines written by the wife of Thomas Huxley for his tombstone, which he found in his mother's workbox after her death, written out on a piece of cheap notepaper in her slanting hand.

> *And if there be no meeting past the grave,*
> *If all is darkness, silence, yet 'tis rest;*
> *Be not afraid ye waiting hearts that weep,*
> *For God still giveth his beloved sleep*
> *And if an endless sleep He wills, so best.*

It had surprised and rather pleased him to discover that his pious mother had towards the end of her life apparently entertained doubts about personal immortality without being unduly disturbed by them, and he wanted to have the lines inscribed on her tombstone too, but the vicar vetoed the proposal. They have been in his head lately because he looked them up to quote in an article for the *Cornhill*, an ironic self-portrait entitled 'All's Well That Ends Well: A Complete Exposé of this Notorious Literary Humbug', written in the persona of a highly prejudiced biographer called Wilfred B. Betterave. *'Such is the squalor of this man's circumstances and character,'* Betterave wrote, '*I had little reason for supposing, now that he had lived down so much, that he would consent to see it all dragged into the light of day. I put it to him as gently as possible. To which he responded: "Why!—you were made for the job. Let yourself rip. You have* carte blanche. *See that the mud flies, my boy. You will have quite a market for it and some of it will stick. Some of it ought to stick. I'm not all that proud of it myself."* '

Early in July a general election is held, ending years of coalition government and restoring party politics. There is a widespread desire for change in post-war Britain which makes Labour supporters hopeful, but also a general presumption that Churchill's success as a victorious wartime Prime Minister will ensure a Conservative victory. His own sympathies for the Labour Party have ebbed and flowed erratically over the years. When he was in the Fabian he changed his mind more than once about whether the Society should throw in its lot with union-dominated Labour, finally deciding against the idea, but in the 1920s he stood twice as a Labour candidate for the University of London seat, coming bottom of the poll on both occasions. Subsequently he left the Party to promote his own 'Open Conspiracy', a political movement which never had more than one member, namely himself, and never existed outside the covers of his books. The modern Labour Party is very much a Fabian creation—most of its leading lights and potential ministers have been active members, and the fact that Lord Beveridge, whose 1942 report on reform of the social services is the blueprint for Labour's policy, was the young civil servant who helped Beatrice and Sidney Webb to compose their *Minority Report on the Poor Law* twenty-five years ago, illustrates the genealogy very clearly. To vote Labour in the forthcoming election would be to concede that the Fabians were right all along about how to achieve the aims of socialism, and he was wrong—but who else can he vote for? Not the old Liberal Party, which is a spent force. 'I think I will vote Communist,' he says one day to a startled Gip and Marjorie. 'But you detest the Communist Party, H.G.,' Gip says. 'The Roman Catholic Church is my *bête noire* and the Communist Party my *bête rouge*,' says Marjorie, with an air of quoting somebody. 'Who said that?' he asks. 'You did, in *'42 to '44*,' she says, referring to a book of his occasional wartime writings which she typed. 'Well, I don't like the Party as such, but there are some decent people in it. Find out for me who the Communist candidate is in this constituency,' he says. But there is no Communist candidate in the Marylebone constituency and he is obliged to support the Labour candidate, which turns out to be not such a bitter pill to swallow after all because she is Elizabeth Jacobs, the granddaughter of an old friend, the short-story writer W.W. Jacobs who died a couple of years ago, and she is well to the left of the Labour Party spectrum. Marjorie drives him to the polling station but he is too weak to walk inside, so the Returning Officer brings his ballot paper out to the car and a box for him to put it in. 'Is this allowed?' he asks, only half joking. 'Probably not, Mr Wells,' says the Returning Officer, 'but I'm prepared to bend the rules for you.'

The next day it is clear that, to general astonishment, Labour has won a landslide victory and Clement Attlee is Prime Minister instead of Winston Churchill. For the first time Great Britain has a government with a proper mandate to create a socialist state, unlike Ramsay MacDonald's two hamstrung and compromised minority governments in the 1920s. It has a far-reaching programme which includes the nationalisation of key industries, redistributive taxation, free education up to university level, a national health service, allowances to families for each child payable to the mother, and state pensions for all. It is a prospect that would have excited him forty years ago, when he was advocating just such policies, but now he cannot rouse in himself any expectant enthusiasm. It is not that he questions the values these policies are based on—clearly they promise a fairer society in the future; it is that he no longer believes in the future—that is to say, a continuing reality which will provide a firm foundation for progress. Reality as empirically perceived and understood by ordinary rational people now seems to him as insubstantial as the images reflected on the wall of Plato's cave—or, to use a more contemporary analogy, as the flickering shapes and shadows of the cinema screen, an analogy he has used in *Mind at the End of its Tether*.

> *The question 'Is this all?' has troubled countless unsatisfied minds throughout the ages, and, at the end of our tether, as it seems, here it is, still baffling but persistent. To such discomfited minds the world of our everyday reality is no more than a more or less entertaining or distressful story thrown upon a cinema screen. The story holds together; it moves them greatly and yet they feel it is faked. The vast majority of the beholders accept all the conventions of the story, are completely part of the story, and live and suffer and rejoice and die in it and with it. But the sceptical mind says stoutly,*

'This is delusion' . . . *Hitherto, recurrence has seemed a primary law of life. Night has followed day and day night. But in this strange new phase of existence into which our universe is passing, it becomes evident that events no longer recur. They go on and on to an impenetrable mystery, into a voiceless limitless darkness, against which this obstinate urgency of our dissatisfied minds may struggle, but will struggle only until it is altogether overcome.*

On August 6th there occurs an event which seems a further confirmation of this bleak vision: the American air force drops an atomic bomb on the city of Hiroshima. Tens of thousands of people are killed instantly, and several square miles of buildings levelled to the ground, by a single bomb dropped from a single plane flying at high altitude. A passage from his novel *War in the Air* comes to mind, the description of the destruction of New York by the German airship fleet, *'one of the most cold-blooded slaughters in the world's history, in which men who were neither excited nor, except for the remotest chance, in any danger, poured death and destruction upon homes and crowds below'.* Those German airships were of course using conventional bombs; it was in a later novel, *The World Set Free*, that he anticipated the discovery of nuclear fission leading to the development of atomic bombs, and imagined their awesome destructive power, which would finally abolish the already much violated distinction between combatants and civilians in wartime.

He had written those books to warn of the inevitable consequences of applying advances in science and technology to weaponry unless and until war was abolished by the establishment of a world government. A few weeks earlier another event had taken place which seemed a promising step in that direction: the signing of the founding Charter of the United Nations organisation by fifty member countries. It was a cause for which he had worked all his life, and he had personally played a leading part in drafting the Sankey Declaration of Human Rights which was incorporated into the Charter. But he had no faith that the United Nations would in the long run prove any more effective than the League of Nations. The procedural rules of the Security Council required unanimity from the five permanent members, the so-called Great Powers, which meant that any one of them could veto a proposal they deemed damaging to their interests, and there were signs that the Great Powers were already falling out over the political settlement of the post-war world, Soviet Russia in disagreement with Britain, the USA and France. The falling-out could easily lead to yet another war, with a deadly new weapon available to the combatants.

But the immediate effect of the atom bombs dropped on Hiroshima and, three days later, on Nagasaki, was to bring the Second World War to a swift conclusion. Only a few voices were raised in the Houses of Parliament and the press questioning the ethics of such massive and indiscriminate destruction of human life. The general reaction of the Allied nations was joy and relief, and it is one he understands and to a large extent shares. It was well known that the imperialistic, militarist autocracy that ruled Japan under its allegedly divine Emperor was determined to resist an Allied invasion of its mainland to the bitter end, no matter what the cost in human life, a resolution it had already demonstrated in the ferocious battle of Okinawa, sending hundreds of young men to their deaths in kamikaze attacks on the Allied fleet. It was grimly amusing to reflect that he had prefigured these fanatically brave pilots in his description of Japanese fighter aircraft in *The War in the Air*, flying machines which had flexible curved wings like butterflies, and fuselages that their pilots straddled like horsemen, charging the giant airships with rifles in one hand and drawn two-edged swords in the other. Thousands, perhaps tens of thousands, of Allied servicemen, mostly American, would have been killed in an invasion of Japan before it was conquered. Who could blame the USA for saving those lives by a show of force which even the stubborn Japanese leaders would recognise as irresistible? Who could blame the Allied servicemen, and their families and friends at home, for suppressing any qualms about the mass liquidation of Japanese civilians in their relief at having the shadow of death lifted from themselves?

He has a personal interest in the end of the war against Japan, because Eric Davis, the husband of his and Amber's daughter, Anna Jane, is one of its casualties, to an extent as yet undetermined. Eric managed to escape from Singapore, where he was running a radio station, just before the British garrison surrendered in February 1942, and led a group of his staff on a perilous escape to Java, where they continued to broadcast until the Japanese occupied that country too, and then he disappeared without trace. Anna Jane carried on working in India, where she has a government job, in a state of horrible uncertainty about his fate, and he feels all the more sympathy for her because he seriously misjudged Eric Davis on first acquaintance. Back in 1930, when she was a student at the LSE, and announced her intention of sharing her life with Eric, he tried to dissuade her from doing so in a long and—in retrospect—rather pompous letter. Though she had known for some time that he was her father, and seemed comfortable with the idea, this was the first occasion on which he explicitly invoked his paternity to give authority to his advice. Anna Jane however was her mother's daughter—determined, fearless, independent-minded—and rejected it, politely but firmly. Eric subsequently vindicated her choice by having a useful career, and by demonstrating impressive courage and resourcefulness in wartime, not only in the aftermath of the Singapore debacle, but before that by his conduct on the liner *Benares* when it was sunk in the Atlantic in 1940 by a German U-boat with great loss of life, including eighty children being evacuated to Canada. He shepherded passengers into the lifeboats, several times refusing a place for himself, and survived by clinging to a raft through a long dark night. It was a story that made him more conscious than ever that he and his sons, mainly through the chance of birth-dates which excused them from military service, had never been tested by such dangers in either of the two world wars they had lived through. In correspondence with Anna Jane he encouraged her to hope that Eric was a prisoner of war, but as the years passed with no news, this seemed less and less likely. Anna Jane says in her recent letters that she is resigned to his being lost, but it would be surprising if she does not privately dream of some happy ending like the return of Teddy in *Mr Britling Sees It Through*. Perhaps at last there will now be some reliable information about what happened to Eric that will, one way or another, bring her peace.

As an ordinary human being, then, identifying with the feelings of those who still believe in the reality and continuity of events, he cannot sincerely condemn the dropping of the atom bomb. But to the scientific philosopher the invention of the bomb itself—the release of such awesome energy by breaking into what had once been regarded as the smallest irreducible unit of matter—evokes only dread, and the mushroom cloud over Hiroshima is an ominous apocalyptic sign, not just of the end of the world but of the universe.

> *Our universe is the utmost compass of our minds. It is a closed system that returns into itself. It is a closed space-time continuum which ends with the same urge to exist with which it began, now that the unknown power that evoked it has at last turned against it. 'Power' the writer has written, because it is difficult to express*

this unknowable that has, so to speak, set its face against us. But we cannot deny this menace of the darkness. 'Power' is unsatisfactory. We need to express something entirely outside our 'universe' . . . But if we fall back on the structure of Greek tragic drama and think of life as the Protagonist . . . we get something to meet our need. 'The Antagonist', then, in that qualified sense, is the term the present writer will employ to express the unknown implacable which has endured life for so long by our reckoning and has now turned against it so implacably to wipe it out.

Gip, who is proofreading *Mind at the End of its Tether* with increasing dismay, sitting in Marjorie's little office in Hanover Terrace, reads this passage aloud to her. 'What's got into H.G.? This is pseudo-mystical drivel, like some kind of cosmic Manichaeism,' he says. 'What's manic . . . thingummy?' she asks. 'I wish I could stop the publication of this book,' he says, ignoring her question. 'It will only damage H.G.'s reputation. It's a repudiation of everything he has worked for all his life.' 'You can't stop it,' she says. 'It's how he feels. It's what he believes now, whether you like it or not.' 'But he's a sick man,' says Gip. 'He knows he's dying—it's no wonder he's depressed. Remember Karenin in *The World Set Free*?' 'I can't say I do,' says Marjorie.

Gip's own memory of the scene in question is somewhat vague, so he goes to H.G.'s study, the author himself being in bed and probably asleep, finds a copy of *The World Set Free*, locates the relevant pages, and when he has read them, takes the book back to enlighten Marjorie.

'After the world is devastated by atomic warfare, the nations see sense and make peace. A world government is established, and a splendid new civilisation begins to emerge from the ruins of the old.'

'That sounds familiar,' says Marjorie, but Gip ignores this faintly subversive comment and continues his summary.

'One of the most inspiring leaders of the new order is a Russian intellectual called Marcus Karenin, a key member of the World Education Committee. He's a congenital cripple with an extraordinary mind. Towards the end of the story he is very ill, in a sanatorium in the Himalayas, where he is due to have an operation which may or may not prolong his life, and various characters make a pilgrimage to hear his words of wisdom while they can. He tells his secretary Gardener that he hopes to die under the surgeon's knife. This is what he says: *'I hope he kills me, Gardener . . . The*

410

thing I am most afraid of is that last rag of life. I may just go on—a scarred selvage of suffering stuff. And then—all the things I have hidden and kept down or discounted or set right afterwards will get the better of me. I shall be peevish. I may lose my grip on my own egotism. It's never been a very firm grip . . . I do not see why life should be judged by its last trailing thread of vitality . . . Remember that, Gardener, if presently my heart fails me and I despair, and if I go through a little phase of pain and ingratitude and dark forgetfulness before the end . . . Don't believe what I may say at the last . . . If the fabric is good the selvage doesn't matter.'

Gip looks up from the page. 'You see, Marjorie?' he says triumphantly. 'It's as if H.G. foresaw his own final illness, and left us a warning: *"Don't believe what I may say at the last."* This cry of despair –' Gip slaps his hand down on the galleys of *Mind at the End of its Tether* '– is not the true voice of H.G. Wells.'

Anthony has a different theory about H.G.'s gloom. He sees his father less frequently these days, because he no longer lives in Mr Mumford's on the other side of the wall at the end of the garden, but with Kitty and the children, having been reconciled with her some months ago, and he has been very busy in the Far East department of the World Service as the war against Japan reached its climax. But he still calls at Hanover Terrace occasionally, chats with his father and exchanges views with Gip and Marjorie, if they happen to be there at the same time, about H.G.'s state of mind and body. When Gip shows him the manuscript of *Mind at the End of its Tether,* and repeats the argument he put to Marjorie, that its extreme pessimism and renunciation of H.G.'s progressive humanist principles are effects of his physical debility and should therefore be ignored, citing the words of Karenin in support, Anthony shakes his head.

'No,' he says. 'I've only skimmed through the book, of course, but I'd say that it expresses a very real, very personal despair.'

'About what?' says Marjorie.

'About the way his reputation has declined, and his audience has dwindled.'

'Oh, come!' Gip protests.

'Did you read 'The Betterave Papers' in the July *Cornhill*?' Anthony asks.

'Yes, of course,' says Gip. 'But that's entirely ironic. Betterave is a caricature of H.G.'s enemies, a bigoted reactionary who appropriates and exaggerates every insult and slur my father suffered in his lifetime, and so makes them look ridiculous. Irony is saying the opposite of what you mean.'

'It can also be a way of saying something you *do* mean, indirectly. There are criticisms of his own books in that piece towards the end, which are too accurate to be interpreted as irony. On *William Clissold*, for instance . . . Is there a copy of the *Cornhill* here?'

There are several of the author's complimentary copies in the office, and Marjorie hands one to Anthony.

'Listen to this,' he says, turning to the end of the article: ' "The World of William Clissold *is a vast three-decker, issued in three successive volumes of rigmarole, which broke down the endurance of readers and booksellers alike."* You can't call that irony—it's absolutely true. And so is the rest of the passage. *"It marks the collapse of an inflated reputation. After that Mr Wells might write what he liked and do his utmost. It was no longer the thing to read him. Reviewers might praise him and a dwindling band of dupes might get his books. They vanished from the shop windows and from the tables of cultured people . . ."* And then he lists a number of his later books, with their awful off-putting titles, like *The Autocracy of Mr. Parham*, and *The Bulpington of Blup*. And he goes on: *"People whom once he had duped would perhaps mention him as a figure of some significance in English literature, but the established reply of the people who no longer read him and had nothing to say about him was simply the grimace of those who scent decay. 'Oh, Wells!' they would say, and leave it at that. So that Wells decays alive and will be buried a man already forgotten."* That's not Betterave speaking, that's H.G.'

'It's not all like that,' says Gip.

'No, it's not,' says Anthony. 'There's some good knockabout fun earlier that you can call ironic. But it's the ending that leaves the deepest impression.'

'Well, he won't be buried—or cremated—as a forgotten man,' says Gip.

'No, of course not. There will be obituaries, tributes. And some of his books will endure: *The Time Machine, The Island of Dr Moreau, The War of the Worlds, Mr Polly,* maybe *Tono-Bungay* . . . but they're all early ones. *Mr Polly,* is, I suspect, the last of his novels that has never been out of print since it was first published, and that was 1910—correct me if I'm wrong.'

'You're probably right,' says Gip. 'But I think you're reading too much into "The Betterave Papers". It's just a squib. *Mind at the End of its Tether* is a much more worrying work to me, because its pessimism is so extreme.'

'But H.G.'s best work *was* essentially pessimistic,' says Anthony. 'It was inspired by ideas like entropy, the randomness of evolution, the innate folly and vanity of mankind, the possible ways in which the world could end, or human civilisation be wiped out. His true vocation was to work that vein of inspiration, producing novels that would last, that would become classics. But he got distracted by his involvement in politics, his sense of vocation changed, he started to believe in Progress, and he began to write books which expounded various ways of achieving it. He claimed he wasn't interested in creating enduring works of art in fiction, but in responding to pressing social and political concerns, like a journalist. He quarrelled with Henry James about that, and picked over the bones of their disagreement years later in the *Experiment in Autobiography*. He was unrepentant then. But lately—as *Mind at the End of its Tether* shows—he's lost faith in Progress, or in the perfectibility of man, which comes to the same thing. For nearly half a century he campaigned for World Government on the assumption that the only people capable of achieving and running it would axiomatically be enlightened, selfless, reasonable. But recent history has demonstrated that they are much more likely to be ruthless tyrants or, worse still, enlightened, selfless, reasonable people who *turn into* ruthless tyrants.'

'Tyrants can be defeated,' Gip objects. 'We have defeated Hitler.'

'Yes, but at what a cost . . .' Anthony says. 'I think it all became too much for H.G. in the end, the evidence of the power of evil in the world, mocking his belief in Progress. It wouldn't be surprising if he felt he had wasted his energies and gifts as a writer propagandising for a lost cause. If he had listened more carefully to Henry James, he might not be so depressed about the reception of his work today.'

'Isn't Henry James just as out of fashion today as H.G.?' Marjorie says.

'Perhaps he is,' Anthony says. 'But he still has his devotees among the literati, and according to my mother American universities teach him as a great writer.'

Gip gives a snort of derision. 'The world would be just the same if Henry James had never written a word. You can't say that about H.G.'

'How *is* Rebecca?' Marjorie asks Anthony, thinking it is time for a change of subject.

'Very busy,' says Anthony. 'She's doing a lot of work for the *New Yorker* these days. The editor really loves her stuff.'

'That's nice,' Marjorie says.

'Yes, I wish she could pull a few strings for me in that quarter,' says Anthony wistfully. 'The *New Yorker* pays extremely well.'

In September Rebecca publishes a report on the trial of the traitor William Joyce, 'Lord Haw-Haw', in the *New Yorker,* and sends a copy of the magazine to him when it comes out. *'I had to file it the day after the trial ended,'* she says in her covering letter. *'Harold Ross told me, "I know of only five or six writers in the world who could have written such a thorough and journalistically competent story in such a short time, and of no other who could have equalled it in literary excellence."'* Her pride in this accolade from the notoriously demanding editor is justified by the article. She conveys the character and appearance of each of the major players in the drama vividly but economically—for a drama is what a treason trial at the Old Bailey necessarily is—and achieves some degree of empathy with them all, even the central figure, the man who taunted British listeners throughout the war with his propaganda broadcasts from Berlin. Many people—though not himself—found something horribly addictive about those broadcasts, which was usually attributed to Joyce's strange nasal drawl and unpleasant wit. He was like a pantomime villain, a man they loved to hate. So far from frightening the British public with his gloating celebration of Nazi victories early in the war, he strengthened their determination to resist; but there was a temptation to gloat in turn now that he stood in the dock, which Rebecca deftly avoided in her article. She brought out the strange twists and paradoxes of his early life and upbringing and showed how they made him first a fascist and then a traitor. She picked her way ably through the complex legal argument which dominated this first trial, as to whether the child of Irish parents born in the USA could be deemed a traitor to the United Kingdom. The judge ruled that he could, but Joyce was granted leave to appeal, which is where her article ends. Writing to congratulate her he says that he enjoyed reading it, but would enjoy seeing her even more. She replies apologetically that she is too busy at present, keeping track of the appeal, and preparing to report on another treason trial for the *New Yorker.* *'Ross cabled me "We want whatever you want to write on the Amery trial",'* she declares exultantly. Clearly, she is enjoying a surge of success and confidence as a writer, and he is glad for her.

. . .

Rebecca is too busy to visit him, but fortunately Moura is not. She moved back to London at the end of the war, into a new flat in Kensington, and calls in frequently to sit by his bedside or—if he is up—joins him in the small sitting room or the sun lounge, relieving his boredom and Marjorie of some secretarial duties. When it is necessary to write to correspondents in French or Russian she can take his dictation down in the appropriate foreign language. She gives him news of her children, Paul and Tania, and Tania's family, and commiserates with him over the sad news about Anna Jane's husband, Eric, now known to have died when a ship on which he was escaping from Java in 1942 was sunk. She entertains him with anecdotes about the people she knows and meets at parties and receptions in London and invites to her flat for sherry, for she has an amazingly wide and promiscuous circle of acquaintance that includes Russian exiles, British government officials, foreign diplomats, writers, artists, actors and film-makers. She brings articles she has clipped out of newspapers and magazines which she thinks will interest him and reads them aloud. Sometimes they just sit in contented silence for minutes at a time, like an old married couple for whom sex is a memory and only companionship remains—which indeed is exactly their case, except that they have never been married. They do not talk about the past very much, for there are too many minefields in that territory: buried crises and quarrels and infidelities and unsolved mysteries which it would be foolish to dig up now. But when she has left him, after squeezing his hand and stooping to kiss him goodbye, his mind often goes back in time to recall various moments in their shared experience.

For twenty-five years Moura has been woven into the fabric of his life, at first a bright thread that appeared and vanished again for long intervals, but later as a more and more prominent motif. They corresponded only occasionally after that memorable night in Gorky's apartment in Petrograd, during the years when he was involved with Rebecca and Odette, and Moura was secretary and companion to Gorky in Sorrento, where he had gone to live for his health with Lenin's and later Stalin's permission. They did not meet again until 1929. In the spring of that year he went to Berlin to deliver a lecture on 'The Common Sense of World Peace' at the Reichstag (an inauspicious venue in retrospect), unaware that she was eking out a living there as the literary agent of Gorky, who had been persuaded by Stalin to return to Russia the year before. At his hotel he found a note from her saying she would be at his lecture. He could not spot her in the audience as he spoke, but she was waiting for him at the back of the hall afterwards, tall, beautiful, and alluring as ever in spite of her shabby, well-worn clothes. 'Aigee,' she said, smiling, as he came up to her with his arms held wide to embrace her, and her pronunciation of his name acted on him like an aphrodisiac injected straight into a vein. For the next two days, until he had to return to Lou Pidou and Odette, they were lovers again.

At that time, eighteen months after Jane's death, he was in an unsettled emotional state. Odette was eager to occupy the vacant space in his life, but he was growing increasingly tired of her whims and tantrums. She had become a kind of nagging wife without the rights of a wife; but instead of doing the sensible thing, which would have been to drop Odette and take up with Moura now he had found her again, he carried on for some years a covert, quasi-adulterous affair with her, conducted through assignations in various Continental venues. In retrospect he couldn't really explain his behaviour to himself, except that he foresaw the difficulty of cutting loose from Odette without losing Lou Pidou, but when eventually he made that sacrifice in 1933 it seemed absurdly obvious to him that Moura was the love of his life and the woman with whom he wanted to spend the remainder of it, and he courted her accordingly. Moura was perfectly happy to be his acknowledged mistress, but insisted on retaining her independence. She refused to live with him, and she was always moving about, going off on foreign trips of her own. He did not suspect her of being unfaithful, for she was not promiscuous. She told him once that she had slept with only five men besides himself: a man called Engelhardt she claimed to have married and divorced before she married Benckendorf but who he suspected had been a lover, her husbands Benckendorf and Budberg, Bruce Lockhart, and an Italian in Sorrento, whom she did not identify. All of them she said were either dead or no longer in a relationship with her, and he believed her— until he caught her out deceiving him about a visit she made to Moscow in 1934.

He had arranged to go there himself in July of that year to interview Stalin, having recently interviewed Roosevelt in America for the same journalistic project. It had occurred to him that it would be interesting, in view of the economic Depression now affecting the whole world, to question the leaders of the two great countries, one capitalist, one communist, to ascertain whether these ideologies could learn lessons from each other, and his name was still influential enough to secure the prompt agreement of both parties. Remembering how useful Moura had been to him as interpreter and guide in Petrograd in 1920, he wanted her to accompany him to Moscow, but to his annoyance she refused, saying that she feared she would be arrested if she returned to Russia and then, when he offered to obtain the necessary clearance, insisting that she had to go to Estonia to see her children, who were still living there in the care of their faithful Irish governess, Micky. Typically, she gave no reason other than that she simply *had to*—and set off a week or so before his own departure. It was agreed however that he would join her on his way back to spend some time at her country house, and he was sufficiently mollified to see her off to Tallinn from Croydon airport. Moura promised to write to him in Moscow.

Instead of Moura he took Gip with him on the trip and was grateful for his company, but his son's Russian was limited, and he felt helplessly dependent on a guide and an interpreter whom he did not trust, aware that he was being manipulated by Intourist for propaganda purposes but unable to do anything about it. The interview with Stalin was just as frustrating as the one he had had with Lenin years before, the Soviet leader showing no interest whatsoever in any kind of rapprochement with liberal capitalist democracy. Afterwards he drafted a more flattering journalistic account of Stalin and Stalin's Russia than he really felt, unwilling to give encouragement to right-wing British pundits. In fact he was depressed by the uniformity of opinion he encountered everywhere. Even Gorky spouted the Party line relentlessly when he visited him in his spacious dacha in the country outside Moscow—conformity being the price of his privileges, no doubt. They had a sterile argument about free speech, which Gorky claimed was a luxury that Russia could not yet afford. In the course of the evening he happened to mention to his interpreter Umansky that he was stopping in Estonia on his way home to stay with his friend Baroness Budberg, and Umansky said, 'Oh, she was staying here just a week ago.'

He was speechless with surprise and shock for some moments. 'But that's impossible,' he said at last. 'I received a letter from her sent from Estonia last week.' The Intourist man Andreychin said something in Russian to Umansky, who looked disconcerted and said, 'Perhaps I was mistaken', stonewalling all further enquiries on the subject. At dinner, from which Umansky absented himself, he said to Gorky through Andreychin, 'I miss our previous interpreter, Gorky,' and his host, taken by surprise, said, 'Who do you mean?' 'Moura.' There was a hurried exchange in Russian between Gorky and Andreychin, at the conclusion of which the latter said: 'Gorky says she was here three times in the last year.' Further enquiry revealed that the first occasion was at Christmas when she had allegedly been with her family in Estonia—'I *always* spend Christmas in Estonia,' she had declared—and the second when he was in America to interview Roosevelt. The third was the previous week. 'Gorky says you should not mention these visits in Estonia or England as it might cause her some embarrassment,' Andreychin told him. 'Obviously,' he said, though the implication most obvious to himself at that moment was that Moura had deceived him.

There had always been rumours that Moura was Gorky's mistress, and he realised now that Gorky must be the anonymous Italian lover on the select list of men to whom she had given herself. He would not have minded this concealment if the relationship was finished, as she had claimed was true of all those she mentioned. But clearly it was not finished. What other reason could she have for returning so frequently to Russia to see Gorky? Well, there was another possible reason, Gip pointed out, when they discussed the matter privately: she could hardly have crossed the watchfully guarded frontiers of Russia so frequently without the co-operation of the authorities. Wasn't it possible that she was a Soviet agent, passing information about leaders of opinion in Western Europe, including himself, to Soviet intelligence? It was a plausible theory, but he was reluctant to accept it. If it was true, he told Gip, then she had only used her 'information' as an inducement to obtain a visa, and as far as he himself was concerned the NKVD were welcome to it. But Gorky had quite enough influence of his own to facilitate her entry into the country.

Gip had to return to England shortly afterwards and for the rest of his stay in Moscow he was in a torment of jealousy, weeping and raging alone in his hotel room, unable to sleep, plotting all kinds of punishment and revenge. He actually drew up a codicil cutting Moura out of his will, which he got witnessed at the British Embassy, and changed his itinerary so that he could return directly to England to pursue other sanctions against her. But in the end he couldn't wait to confront her, changed his travel arrangements again, and sent her a postcard giving her the time of his arrival in Tallinn, mentioning that he had heard an absurd rumour that she had been in Moscow lately, so that she would have an uncomfortable inkling of what was in store for her.

Of course it also gave her time to compose herself and prepare an excuse, but he was surprised all the same by how serene she seemed when she met him at Tallinn airport and kissed him affectionately. In the taxi to the city he said, 'That was a funny story of your being in Moscow.' 'Yes—where did you hear it?' 'I can't remember—it was just something I overheard.' 'I can't imagine where it came from . . .' And so they fenced for a while until he said, 'Moura, you are a liar and a cheat. Why did you do this to me?' She had a story ready, of course. 'The trip was arranged suddenly after I got to Estonia,' she said, 'that's why I didn't tell you about it.' 'Why then did you arrange to have a letter posted to me in Moscow from Estonia in which you said nothing about it?' Moura was imperturbable. 'Let us have lunch in Tallinn and I will explain.' He couldn't help laughing at her. 'You remind me of the wife in the *Illustration Française,* discovered *in flagrante* with a young guardsman, who is putting on his trousers in the background, saying to her husband, "Just give me time and I can explain everything."' Moura smiled good-humouredly and said, 'I know a very nice restaurant with a lovely garden.'

They were seated in the shade of an awning like a great sail and served an excellent lunch of grilled crayfish, accompanied by a deliciously crisp white wine. Relaxed and refreshed by these agreeable circumstances they began to chat amicably as if nothing had happened, until he perceived the danger and called the meeting to order. 'And now, Moura, for your explanation.'

She said that the opportunity to go to Moscow had arisen suddenly and unexpectedly. Gorky had obtained permission from the Russian Foreign Office, and she longed to see the country again after her long exile, but she hadn't told him about it or arranged to meet him in Moscow because if they had been seen together suspicions might have been aroused.

'What did you think of the country after—how many years away?'

'Ten years. I was disappointed, to be honest.'

'Moura,' he said. 'Why do you keep on lying? You have been to Russia three times this past twelvemonth.'

'No,' she said. 'Who told you that?'

'Gorky,' he said, and described the occasion. 'No,' she said, shaking her head. 'There must have been some mistake by the interpreter.' Her effrontery was remarkable and compelled a certain admiration. 'Anyway,' she said, 'why are you so upset, Aigee? You don't suppose Gorky and I are lovers, do you?'

'Of course I do!'

'Pooh! Gorky has been impotent for years,' she said. 'Everybody knows that.'

'Well I don't,' he said, taken somewhat by surprise. 'But why should I believe you, when you lie to me about your three trips to Russia this year?'

'That is a mistake by the interpreter,' she repeated.

'Moura, if you can prove it to me beyond dispute—by getting Gorky to write me a letter, for instance—I will believe you. Or get Andreychin on the telephone so we can both speak to him. You can phone him this evening.'

'Very well,' she said calmly.

But predictably, no proof was ever forthcoming. There was difficulty making a telephone connection that evening, the letter from Gorky never materialised, and after a while he became bored and somewhat embarrassed by his inquisitorial role. It was impossible to resist the lure of Moura's bed in the warm summer nights of Estonia, and when they returned to England they slipped back into their old relationship. It was never quite the same for him: an element of doubt and distrust always tainted it, and for a time he was deeply depressed by the experience, which had shaken his own faith in himself—not just the discovery that he could be so blind in the most intimate relationship with another human being, but also the violence of his reaction to the disillusionment. For only the second time in his life he was seriously tempted by the idea of suicide, a mood he was able to throw off only by writing *Experiment in Autobiography,* in which he attempted to make an honest analysis of his life and character.

He was never quite sure whether Moura had told him the truth about her relationship with Gorky and her trips to Russia in 1934, but gradually he became reconciled to not knowing whether she was telling him the truth about anything. She regarded reality as something that could be patted and prodded and twisted like a child's modelling clay to produce all kinds of interesting and attractive shapes according to the needs of the moment, and if you challenged the accuracy of her representations she would just smile and fall silent or change the subject. The embarrassment of the untruth thus exposed somehow became yours and not hers. It was, he suspected, a peculiarly Russian trait. She was a free spirit who would never be netted and tamed, and his long effort to make her commit herself explicitly and irrevocably by marrying him was always doomed. There was an almost ritual demonstration of this in 1935, when he said to her one day, 'Let us at least get engaged, Moura. Let's invite our nicest friends to a big lunch and announce our engagement', and to his surprise and delight she agreed. Accordingly a private room at Quo Vadis in Soho was booked, and their friends invited to an Engagement Party, but just before the guests sat down she said to him, 'Of course, Aigee, I am not serious about this.' 'Not serious?' he said, aghast. 'No I will make a speech telling everybody that it was a joke, an excuse for a nice party.' And so she did, and he had to smile and pretend that he had been complicit in the joke all along to avoid a public humiliation. He never did discover whether this had been her intention all along, or whether she had decided to cancel their engagement as she walked into the restaurant.

After that he abandoned all hopes of matrimony, and settled for the loose association which was the only one she would accept: she was his companion and lover, but would not cohabit with him and remained free to come and go as she pleased. She was, he was fairly sure, faithful to him, and if he was unfaithful to her, as happened occasionally, and she found him out, she teased him rather than reproached him for it. The main thing is that, in her own inscrutable way, she loves him, and the fact that she continues to visit him in his impotent dotage and be kind to him is probably as much as he deserves from any woman, if not more. He is grateful to her for it.

Mind at the End of its Tether is finally published in November and passed over in silence by most of the press. A few short notices regret that Mr Wells seems to have given up hope for civilisation, the human race, and the universe itself, and one says that these incoherent ramblings by a once distinguished thinker will embarrass his admirers and encourage his detractors. Gip had warned him that this would be the tenor of the book's reception, trying to persuade him not to publish it, so he is neither surprised nor disappointed. As usual, the publication of a book acts as a kind of purge or evacuation of the intuitions, anxieties and obsessions which motivated its composition, and he is no longer oppressed by the cosmic despair expressed in *Mind*. Not that he feels any more hopeful for the future of the human race, but it doesn't bother him so much. He has delivered his opinion—let the human race make of it what it will. He has nothing more to say.

He can still however be coaxed into collaborating with others to intervene in matters of public interest. In that same month the trial begins of Nazi war criminals at Nuremberg: Goering, Hess, Ribbentrop and the rest of the villainous gang. Some fastidious legal brains have questioned the legitimacy of this unprecedented tribunal, but the crimes in question are also unprecedented and there is an irresistible will throughout the victorious nations to punish them. It is essentially Nazism that is on trial. 'The *wrongs we seek to condemn and punish have been so calculated, so malignant and so devastating that civilisation cannot tolerate their being ignored,'* the chief American prosecutor declares on the opening day, all the evidence being taken from '*books and records which the defendants kept with their Teutonic passion for thoroughness'.* The trial proceeds into the New Year at a snail's pace, hampered by the involvement of four different legal teams from the four Allied countries. In February there are rumours that the Russians are trying to suppress certain documents that concern German–Russian relations going back to the 1920s and '30s. A petition is organised by a group of prominent persons in Britain and America that includes Professor Joad of the BBC's *Brains Trust* and the novelist Arthur Koestler, asking the Nuremberg Tribunal '*to make public all documents proving or disproving the alleged campaign between the NAZI party, Trotsky and other old Bolsheviks convicted in the Moscow trials',* and he is invited to add his signature. He is glad to do so, because the suppression of free speech, and the manifestly rigged show trials of alleged traitors, has always been his most serious objection to the Soviet regime under Stalin.

His opinion was reinforced by reading *Animal Farm,* George Orwell's clever satire on the Russian Revolution and its subsequent history, which his own publisher in recent years, the enterprising Frederic Warburg, brought out in August 1945 after T.S. Eliot had rejected it for Faber. According to Warburg, after a slowish start the book's sales increased steadily in the following months as more and more East European states were taken over by Soviet-controlled communist regimes, including Poland, the very country whose independence Britain had entered the war to defend, and the benevolent Uncle Joe of Allied propaganda began to assume a sinister aspect. *Animal Farm* is now a best-seller, which serves Eliot right. If one of his critics was to triumph over the other, this is the way round he would have chosen.

Moura enjoyed *Animal Farm* when he lent her his copy, but to his surprise she is displeased when he shows her the petition to the Nuremberg Tribunal which he has signed. 'You should not concern yourself with such matters, Aigee,' she says. 'You know nothing about them. And anyway what have these documents to do with what the Nazis did in the war? It is all old history—why rake it up now?' She is unusually grumpy for the remainder of her visit, and leaves earlier than usual. When he mentions this uncharacteristic behaviour to Anthony, who drops in to Hanover Terrace later that day, he gives a knowing smile and says, 'Moura is probably worried that her name might turn up in those documents.'

'Why should it?'

'She was probably spying for the Russians on the Germans in those days. Or for the Germans on the Russians.'

'You shouldn't say such things, even as a joke,' he says.

'I'm not joking, H.G.,' Anthony says. 'And I'm not the only one who thinks Moura is a spy.'

'Is, or was?'

'Both. Do you mean to say you never suspected it?'

He does not answer the question. There was of course the episode in Moscow in 1934, and Gip's interpretation of it.

'I don't mean she's a spy in the classic sense,' Anthony goes on, 'stealing the blueprints of secret weapons and that sort of thing. More likely she just keeps her eyes and ears open on the cocktail party circuit and at those little soirées of hers, and passes information that might be useful to the Russian Secret Service.'

'If this is so well known that even you know about it, why hasn't she been arrested?'

'Perhaps she was, and MI5 turned her.'

'Turned her?'

'Maybe she's a double agent.'

He stares at Anthony, but his son does not blink, or break into a grin that would declare, '*Only teasing.*' 'Bah!' he exclaims at last. 'I refuse to believe it. It's all nonsense.'

'Well, have it your own way, H.G.,' says Anthony. 'I didn't mean to upset you. I assumed you always knew much more than I did. And you know I like Moura awfully. I have a tremendous respect for her.'

'Moura's family was destroyed by the Revolution. She never believed wholeheartedly in communism, even if she had to pretend to while she lived in Russia, and she got out as soon as she safely could. Why would she become a Soviet spy?'

Anthony shrugged. 'Who knows? She was in deep trouble in 1918, wasn't she—over the Lockhart plot? Maybe that gave the NKVD some kind of hold over her.'

'They weren't called the NKVD in those days,' he says pedantically. 'They were called the Cheka.'

After Anthony has left he stays in his armchair, tugging the rug more closely round his legs, staring into the dully smouldering fire—a few knobs of coal covered with dusty slack—and brooding on this conversation. The more he ponders the more horribly plausible becomes the scenario that Anthony has suggested. Moura was certainly compromised when her lover Lockhart was arrested in 1918 for alleged involvement in a plot which narrowly failed to assassinate Lenin. Lockhart, a British agent sent to Moscow as a diplomat with instructions to encourage the Bolsheviks to re-enter the war, claimed in his memoirs that he had nothing to do with the assassination attempt, and he was eventually sent back to England in exchange for a Russian spy. Moura was arrested with him and imprisoned for a short time. She was lucky to be released—people were shot out of hand for far less in Russia in those days. But perhaps she wasn't lucky—perhaps she had agreed to work for the Cheka as the price of her freedom. It would explain the otherwise surprising fact—which he had taken at the time as a stroke of luck—of her appointment as his interpreter and guide in Petersburg in 1920. She could have been instructed to befriend the influential British visitor and report to the Kremlin on his activities and attitudes. Did she pretend they had met before, in 1914, in order to win his trust? Could it be that she even made love to him to secure it? The thought pierces his heart like a dagger. He cannot bear it. He will not believe it—why would she give herself to him with such a calculating motive when there was no reason to think they would ever meet again? But some collaboration with the Soviet Secret Service would explain not only her three visits to Russia in 1934, but possibly other journeys she had undertaken alone over the years. Was this the real reason why she had always refused to marry him or live with him—so that she remained free to travel back and forth between Russia and England without his knowledge? He had discovered, or thought he had discovered, that she was deceiving him with Gorky in 1934, but now he stares appalled, trembling, dizzy, into the vertiginous abyss of a different, deeper deception beneath it: the possibility that their long love affair had been from the start directed and determined by the expediencies of her personal survival. In a way it is a possibility that he had always been aware of subconsciously, but denied or suppressed, refusing to put all the available clues together because he would rather be a jealous lover than a political dupe.

'Goodness, what's the matter, H.G.?'

Marjorie is in the room and is stooping over him with a look of great concern.

'Why are you crying?' she says. She takes the silk handkerchief he wears in his breast pocket and gives it to him to wipe his eyes.

'Nothing, nothing,' he mutters. 'I'm tired. I want to go to bed.'

He wakes suddenly in the middle of the night and is instantly reminded of his conversation with Anthony and the new narrative of Moura's life it prompted. He goes over it again and again, adjusting and emending it, revising and expanding it, in the light of newly remembered facts. If it is true, then she has made a complete fool of him. He has to know if it is true. The next time Moura visits him he will confront her once more and demand to know the real truth. He rings for the night nurse and asks for a sleeping draught, knowing that he will not get back to sleep otherwise.

He wakes again when the nurse draws the curtains of his bedroom to let in the grey light of a damp March morning. She helps him put on his slippers and dressing gown and steers him across the room and into the bathroom to pee and put in his false teeth. Then he gets back into bed and she places his breakfast tray with tea and toast and a boiled egg across his knees, and puts a folded copy of the *Times* on the chair beside his bed. As he slowly consumes the food, his thoughts travel in the same groove as during the night, but with a different, more forgiving tone. After all, how else could Moura have survived all the dangers and crises she had encountered in her lifetime except by compromise and deception? But if he were to confront Moura with this new narrative of her life and she admitted it was true, it would be the end of their relationship. Does he really want that? No, he does not. He values her companionship, he looks forward to her visits, they are among the few things that make his tedious existence tolerable, as his life seems to stretch on and on against all reason and expectation. It is apparently his fate to die very very slowly, to sink inch by inch towards oblivion, in a succession of days and nights that are all the same except for the sparks of interest and the warmth of human contact that visitors bring to him, Moura above all. He does not want to lose her. He will swallow his pride, he will sacrifice the satisfaction of knowing the truth—what good after all would it do him now? He will accept living on, and dying, in a state of uncertainty.

To his surprise, for he did not expect to see her again so soon, Moura returns later that morning, bringing with her a bunch of early daffodils that light up the room like a torch. He is in bed when she breezes into the room, for he seldom rises before the afternoon. 'Hallo, Aigee! You were not expecting me, I know, but I was in a cross mood yesterday, and left sooner than usual so I have come to make up for it. Here are some nice signs that spring is on the way.' She stoops to kiss him on the cheek.

'Thank you, Moura, that is very sweet of you,' he says, and watches her, bulky under her shapeless shift dress, but still graceful as she moves about the room, finds a vase, fills it from the bathroom, and begins to arrange the flowers.

'How are you today, Aigee?'

'Much as usual,' he says. And then to his horror, he hears himself saying without any premeditation, 'Are you a spy, Moura?' The suppressed desire to know the truth seized his vocal organs and made them utter the question he had decided not to ask.

Moura does not reply at once. She continues to arrange the daffodils and is silent for so long that he thinks perhaps she did not hear the question, or that he only imagined that he had asked it. But then she speaks.

'Aigee . . . That is a silly question. Shall I tell you why? Because if you ask that question of someone and she is not a spy she will say "No". But if she *is* a spy she will also say "No". So there is no point in asking that question.'

'No, of course not,' he says. 'Forget I ever asked it.'

'I have forgotten it already,' she says, with a smile, and removes the newspaper from the chair next to his bed to sit down beside him. 'Would you like me to read you something from the *Times*?'

'Yes, please,' he says. 'Read me the obituaries.'

On August 6th, Rebecca West returns to England from Nuremberg, where she has been observing the trial of the Nazi war criminals to write an article for the *New Yorker*. She is flying from Berlin to Croydon in a British civil aircraft. A newspaper briefly scanned in the Berlin departure lounge reminded her that this day is the first anniversary of the dropping of the atom bomb on Hiroshima, but she does not think of that as she gazes out of the plane's window at the Kent coastline sliding slowly past under the Dakota's wing. She is thinking about a very unexpected and very passionate love affair she has had during the past fortnight. Was it only two weeks ago that she flew in the opposite direction in a Royal Air Force plane with a group of journalists on the same assignment as herself? It seems impossible that so much intense experience could have been compressed into so short a span of time.

Not that the trial itself had much intensity. It has been going on for nine months and is not expected to reach a conclusion until several more have elapsed. With so many defendants and four teams of prosecutors, each with its own legal tradition and code of practice, and given the tribunal's anxiety to be scrupulously fair to the defendants (apart from the Russians, who regard the whole event as a show trial with a foregone conclusion) its progress has been painfully slow. Somewhere in the daily tedium of the proceedings the catalogue of evil that was being investigated had ceased to have emotional impact. Those who had attended from the beginning were clearly suffering from atrocity-fatigue, and simply longing for it to be over—all except the defendants, in whose interest it was to spin out the trial for as long as possible, since most of them were likely to be hanged at the end of it. In a curious way, the defendants were controlling the trial, and punishing the prosecutors with boredom. The courtroom was a citadel of boredom. Not of course for herself, to whom it was all new and fascinating, but it would need all her literary skill, when she came to write her article, to compensate for the lack of drama.

Outside the court, there was a quite different atmosphere. The lawyers, the servicemen, the journalists, the officials and civilian secretaries, relieved their boredom in the most obvious way, in sexual love—especially the Americans, who were the dominant presence in the Allied community, numerically and economically. There was hardly a man among them who wasn't separated from a wife or sweetheart thousands of miles away, who wasn't spiritually sick from a surfeit of war and exile, and who didn't seek comfort and release in the arms of any available woman. As soon as she arrived she could almost sniff the heady scent of erotic arousal in the air, and before long she was overcome by it herself.

Francis Biddle was one of the chief American prosecutors. He was a virile sixty, lean, handsome in spite of a balding pate, intelligent and cultured, full of energy and wit. She had known him and his wife Katherine in Washington and Philadelphia between the wars, and liked him immensely—his wife less so. Katherine had joined him in Nuremberg for a while, but had returned to the States to look after their children, as he told her almost as soon as they met. It was her first working day. 'Rebecca!' he cried, spotting her in the crowd outside the court building, and came across to kiss her on the cheek. 'It's wonderful to see you. You're as beautiful as ever.' 'No, I'm not, I'm a frump,' she said, quite sincerely. He laughed. 'We can fix that.'

And he did. He got her a precious card admitting her to the PX, a passable imitation of an American department store which had miraculously materialised in bomb-damaged Nuremberg, complete with soda fountain, where she could get her hair done and buy nylon stockings and lingerie and other clothes that were unobtainable in England even if you had the coupons. Coiffed and manicured and dressed in a New Look summer frock she could almost believe his insistence that she was a woman who had 'let herself go' in the drab environment of austerity England and was now restored to her ripe beauty. He rescued her from the crowded dormitory-style accommodation where she had been billeted with other women journalists, and brought her to the Villa Conradi, an impressive Italianate residence in its own park where he and the other senior American lawyers lived comfortably, and led her to a spacious, high-ceilinged bedroom, with a highly erotic painting of Venus and Mars facing the bed that was a pictorial declaration of his hopes and intentions. He soon confessed that he hadn't met her by accident on her first day—he had seen her name on a list and looked forward eagerly to their reunion. He had followed her life at a distance through her books, especially *Black Lamb and Grey Falcon*—which he claimed he and Katherine loved so much they would read it aloud to each other—in the hope that one day they would meet again. 'I always had a yen for you, Rebecca, but I never had the chance to act on it, until now,' he said, the second time he kissed her, this time mouth to mouth. When she raised the subject of his wife he waved her scruples away. 'Katherine is a good buddy and a great mother, but that's all there is to our marriage these days. She never liked sex much anyway. Wouldn't do it for eighteen months after our second was born.'

She had had no lover for a considerably longer period, and had resigned herself to celibacy for the remainder of her life, but the opportunity of one last lovely fling with so charming and attractive a man was too tempting to refuse. So she abandoned herself to it, and gloried in it, and gave thanks to the goddess beneath whose image she enjoyed it, night after night. But now it was all over. 'Or is it?' she wonders, looking down at the green and brown quilt of English fields, and the ribbons of winding road with little toy cars crawling along them. When they parted that morning, Francis urged her to come back to Nuremberg for the verdicts, which would probably be some time in the fall, and promised to write in the meantime, maybe even make a quick trip to England himself. The idea of going back to Nuremberg for the verdicts makes good journalistic sense, and she is confident that Ross would commission a second article. Perhaps after all, she thinks, as the captain instructs the passengers to fasten their seatbelts, and the plane tilts downward to begin its descent, perhaps this relationship need not be just a brief flare of passion, but has some way to go yet. It has certainly given her a new lease of life. Henry will be waiting at the airport to meet her. Will he detect in her face the lineaments of gratified desire?

She has a pleasant surprise at Croydon: not only Henry, but Anthony and Kitty and her two grandchildren are also there to greet her. It is good to see them all happily together after the upsets of the recent past. Caroline holds a hand-made placard, 'Welcome Home Granny'—in imitation, no doubt, of many such signs she has seen decorating the homes of returning servicemen. If only they knew what Granny had been up to in Germany! Everybody comments on how well she looks. 'It's all the wonderful food I've had,' she says. 'There's no rationing for the Yanks in Nuremberg.' Henry stares at her with a puzzled frown for a moment, and then says, 'You've got a new hairdo, Rac.'

'Yes, do you like it?'

'Very nice.' He kisses her on the cheek. 'Have you had an interesting time?'

'Very interesting.'

'Good, you must tell me all about it.'

She tells him about the trial as he drives them home, and mentions that she met an old friend from before the war, Francis Biddle, one of the chief American prosecutors.

'Well that was nice for you.'

'Yes, very nice,' she says. She is back in England. Nice-land. Henry-land.

Soon after she gets back to Ibstone House she rings up Marjorie to enquire about H.G.'s health. 'There's no change really,' Marjorie says. 'He gets out of bed and comes downstairs for a few hours, but most of the time he keeps to his bedroom. I think he's getting weaker by infinitesimal degrees, but it's hard to tell. He said one day, "I'm waiting on the banks of the Styx for that bloody ferryman to come. I wish he'd hurry up."' 'Oh dear, how sad,' Rebecca says. 'I'll try to come and see him. I took some photos of the courtroom in session at Nuremberg he might be interested to see.' 'He would like that,' Marjorie says. 'Perhaps the week after next,' Rebecca says. 'I must write this article for the *New Yorker* while it's all still fresh in my mind.'

For the next six days she works hard at her article. She describes Francis's manner, seated on the high bench at the top of the courtroom, '*like a highly intelligent swan, occasionally flexing down to commune with smaller waterfowl*', and smiles to herself imagining him reading that. He sends her an erotic love letter, and she replies archly reproving him. He writes again, asking her to let him have a letter that he can show to Katherine—he has mentioned her a lot in his letters home and he is afraid Katherine is getting suspicious. She feels a little chill as she reads this and does not reply.

On the seventh day after her return from Germany she wakes feeling unaccountably anxious and apprehensive, and sits at her desk all morning without being able to produce anything worth printing. The waste-paper basket fills with screwed-up balls of discarded foolscap. In the afternoon she asks Henry to drive her to the head of a valley three miles away so that she can walk home downhill. It is a fine day, warm but not too hot for comfort, with small fluffy white clouds moving slowly like grazing sheep in a clear blue sky. Her mood of the morning begins to lift. Perhaps it was provoked by Francis's rather demeaning request for a letter to show Katherine. It had lowered him in her esteem, and reminded her uncomfortably of the triangular relationship between herself, H.G. and Jane in years past. What slaves we are to our genitals, she thinks, what quantities of time and energy and spirit we waste on contriving their conjunction with another's, and then on concealing it. I should break with Francis now, but I am too weak, and so the affair will drag on for a while until he decides not to jeopardise his marriage any further. And so it goes on between men and women, always has and always will.

As she approaches the house, Henry comes out to meet her with a grave expression on his face. 'Marjorie phoned,' he tells her. 'H.G. died this afternoon.'

'Oh my God,' Rebecca says. 'I must have had a premonition this morning.'

Marjorie gives a very detailed account of H.G.'s death when Rebecca phones her that evening. 'It was quite sudden and unexpected. He'd kept to his bedroom for the last week or so, but he sat up at his table for meals, and read the papers and did the *Times* crossword as quickly as usual. The day nurse was off for two hours this morning, so I popped in and out to see him several times, and he seemed just as he had been for ages. Perhaps a bit more tired—and more gentle. He could be very irritable at times. But when I did some little thing for him he said, "Thank you, Mrs Wells", and smiled at me. Nurse came back on duty, and I went home at lunchtime feeling quite happy about him. Then at four o'clock nurse phoned me to say he was dead . . .' There is a pause while Marjorie evidently stifles some tears. 'Sorry,' she says, and continues. 'Apparently he rang for her and sat on the edge of the bed and asked her to help him take off his pyjama jacket, as if he was going to get dressed. But then he put it on again and got back into bed. He said to her, "Go away, I'm all right," and lay down and closed his eyes. Ten minutes later she looked in, and he was dead.'

'He died alone, then,' says Rebecca.

'That was what he would have wanted,' says Marjorie. 'He always hated being ill, being pitied. He just slipped away when no one was looking. His expression was quite peaceful.'

'Yes, I'm sure you're right,' says Rebecca. 'I'm glad for his sake the end was peaceful and painless.'

Nevertheless, she thinks, as she replaces the telephone in its cradle, there is a poignant absence of poetry in H.G.'s passing. That the writer who imagined so many violent and sudden deaths in his stories, deaths of individuals and massacres of crowds, the destruction of armies and fleets, the inundation of whole populations, and the death of the planet itself, should leave this life in so quiet and banal a way seems somehow anticlimactic. But perhaps not inappropriate. His life was like that of a meteor, or rather a comet—he explained the difference to her once, and she can hear his voice now, the voice of a born teacher. 'They're both astral bodies that invade the solar system from time to time, lumps of rock and ice from God knows where in interstellar space. But meteors burn up when they hit the earth's atmosphere and leave a white trail in the night sky we call a shooting star, or they're larger lumps of rock that sometimes impact on the earth—meteorites. Comets enter our planetary system on eccentric orbits of their own. They consist mostly of ice and dust which vaporise as they pass near the sun and create a sparkling tail which can be millions of miles long and visible from earth with the naked eye, until they disappear, for hundreds, sometimes thousands of years, before they reappear.' That seems to Rebecca a good analogy for H.G.'s career, and as a writer she depends upon metaphor and simile to give things meaning and definition.

H.G. was like a comet. He appeared suddenly out of obscurity at the end of the nineteenth century and blazed in the literary firmament for decades, evoking astonishment and awe and alarm, like the comet of *In the Days of the Comet* which threatened to destroy the earth, but in fact transformed it by the beneficial effect of its gaseous tail. H.G. also aspired to leave a transformed world behind him, and even if he didn't succeed (who could?) he had a liberating and enlightening effect on a great many people. As time went on his imagination and intellect dwindled in brightness, gradually people ceased to look up and stare in wonder, and now he has passed out of sight. But there are eccentric orbits in literary history. Perhaps one day he will glow in the firmament once again.

ACKNOWLEDGEMENTS

My primary sources for this novel were numerous works of fiction and non-fiction by H.G. Wells referred to in the text itself, most importantly his *Experiment in Autobiography* (2 vols, 1934) and the 'Postscript' to it, about his sexual life, which he wrote for publication after he and the women mentioned in it were dead, and which was published in 1984 under the title *H.G. Wells in Love,* edited by his son G.P. Wells; also *The Correspondence of H.G. Wells,* edited by David C. Smith (4 vols, 1998), the letters collected in *Henry James & H.G. Wells: A Record of their Friendship, their Debate on the Art of Fiction and their Quarrel,* ed. Leon Edel and Gordon N. Ray (1958), and in *Arnold Bennett & H.G. Wells: A Record of a Personal and a Literary Friendship*, edited by Harris Wilson (1960), and letters not included in these collections which are quoted in some of the biographies of Wells and others listed below.

Among biographies of H.G. Wells I found *The Time Traveller: The Life of H.G. Wells* (1973; revised 1987) by Norman and Jeanne MacKenzie, and *H.G. Wells: Aspects of a Life* (1984) by Anthony West, especially useful, supplemented by other books including: Michael Coren, *The Invisible Man: The Life and Liberties of H.G. Wells* (1993); Lovat Dickson, *H.G. Wells: His Turbulent Life and Times* (1969); *H.G. Wells: Interviews and Recollections,* edited by J.R. Hammond (1980); Andrea Lynn, *Shadow Lovers: The Last Affairs of H.G. Wells* (2001); Gordon N. Ray, *H.G. Wells and Rebecca West* (1974); David Smith, *H.G. Wells: Desperately Mortal* (1986); Antonina Vallentin, *H.G. Wells: Prophet of Our Day* (1950); Frank Wells, *H.G. Wells: A Pictorial Biography* (1977); and Geoffrey West, *H.G. Wells: A Sketch for a Portrait* (1930). The most recent biography, *H.G. Wells: Another Kind of Life* (2010) by Michael Sherborne, was published as I was finishing *A Man of Parts,* but not too late for me to take advantage of his meticulous scholarship; it contains many facts unobtainable from previous biographies, and enabled me to make numerous corrections and additions of detail to my novel. Among reference guides to Wells's life and work I am indebted to John Hammond's *An H.G. Wells Companion* (1979) and *An H.G. Wells Chronology* (1999), and Geoffrey H. Wells's *The Works of H.G. Wells 1887–1925* (1926). Critical studies of H.G. Wells from which I profited include: Bernard Bergonzi, *The Early H.G. Wells* (1961); John Batchelor, *H.G. Wells*; Peter Kemp, *H.G. Wells and the Culminating Ape* (1982); and *H.G. Wells: the Critical Heritage*, edited by Patrick Parrinder.

Biographies of, and autobiographies and collections of letters by, people who knew Wells with varying degrees of intimacy, were valuable sources of information. They include: Tania Alexander, *A Little of All These* (1987); Enid Bagnold, *The Autobiography of Enid Bagnold* (1969); Barbara Belford, *Violet: The Story of the Irrepressible Violet Hunt and her Circle* (1990); Nina Berberova, *Moura: The Dangerous Life of the Baroness Budberg*, translated by Marian Schwartz and Richard D. Sylvester (2005); Julia Briggs, *A Woman of Passion: The life of E. Nesbit* (1987); Bernard Crick, *George Orwell: A Life* (1980); Margaret Drabble, *Arnold Bennett* (1974); Gloria G. Fromm, *Dorothy Richardson: A biography* (1977) and (ed.) *Windows on Modernism: Selected Letters of Dorothy Richardson* (1995); Ruth Fry, *Maud and Amber: A New Zealand Mother and Daughter and the Women's Cause 1865 to 1981* (1992); Victoria Glendinning, *Rebecca West: A Life* (1987); J.R. Hammond, *H.G. Wells and Rebecca West* (1991); Michael Holroyd, *Bernard Shaw* (3 vols, 1988–91); R.H. Bruce Lockhart, *Memoirs of a Secret Agent* (1932); Lucy Masterman, *C.F.G. Masterman* (1939); M.M. Meyer, *H.G. Wells and his Family* (1956); Doris Langley Moore, *E. Nesbit* (revised edn. 1967); Berta Ruck, *A Storyteller Tells the Truth* (1935); Carl Rollyson, *Rebecca West: A Saga of the Century* (1995); John Rosenberg, *Dorothy Richardson: The Genius they Forgot* (1973); Bonnie Kime Scott (ed.), *Selected Letters of Rebecca West (2000)*; Keith Sinclair, *William Pember Reeves: New Zealand Fabian* (1965); Karen Usborne, *'Elizabeth': the Author of* Elizabeth and Her German Garden (1986); *The Diary of Beatrice Webb*, Vol. 3, 1905–1924 (1984), edited by Norman and Jeanne MacKenzie. Several novels in Dorothy Richardson's autobiographical novel-sequence, *Pilgrimage*, notably *The Tunnel* (1919), *Revolving Lights* (1923) and *Dawn's Left Hand* (1931), portray H.G. Wells in the character of 'Hypo Wilson' with what he admitted was, at least in the first of these books, 'astonishing accuracy', and provide insights into the nature of her relationship with him and Jane. *Agent Moura:*

My Secret Agent Auntie—Baroness Moura Budberg, a documentary film made for the BBC in 2008 by her great-great-nephew, Dimitri Collingridge, and available on DVD, was of great interest to me.

Other books and articles I read or consulted in connection with this project include: Ruth Brandon, *The New Women and the Old Men: Love, Sex, and the Woman Question* (1990); John Carey, *The Intellectuals and the Masses* (1993); Margaret Drabble, 'Introduction' to *Ann Veronica* by H.G. Wells (Penguin Classics edn, 2005), and 'A Room of her Own' (on Amber Reeves), *Guardian* (2 April 2005); Samuel Hynes, *The Edwardian Turn of Mind* (1968); Edward R. Pease, *The History of the Fabian Society* (1916); W. Boyd Rayward, 'H.G. Wells's Idea of a World Brain: a Critical Re-Assessment', *Journal of the American Society for Information Science* 50 (15 May 1999); Katie Roiphe, *Uncommon Arrangements: Seven Portraits of Married Life in London Literary Circles* (2007); Miranda Seymour, *A Ring of Conspirators: Henry James and his Literary Circle 1895–1915* (1988); and Philip Waller, *Writers, Readers, & Reputations: Literary Life in Britain 1870–1918* (2006).

I am very grateful to A.P. Watt, acting on behalf of the estate of H.G. Wells, for permission to quote extensively from the works and letters of H.G. Wells, and from letters of his wife Amy Catherine Wells; to the Society of Authors acting on behalf of the Bernard Shaw Estate for permission to quote from his letters to H.G. Wells; and to Dr Dusa McDuff for permission to quote extracts from three letters of Amber Reeves. Extracts from articles in *The Young Rebecca* (© Rebecca West, 1982) and from a personal letter of Rebecca West (© Rebecca West, 1974) are reproduced by permission of Peters, Fraser and Dunlop (www.pfd.co.uk) on behalf of the Estate of Rebecca West.

Quotations from letters are very useful in a novel of this kind because, as well as revealing the personality and motivation of the characters, they provide evidence to the reader of the factual authenticity of the narrative. There were a few occasions however when I felt obliged to compose fictional letters or fragments of them, either because the originals were unobtainable, or because it seemed the most plausible means for information to be passed from one person to another. All have some basis in the biographical source material; none is attributed to H.G. Wells. They are as follows: Rosamund Bland to H.G., telling him that her mother has found a compromising letter from him (p. 182); Sydney Olivier to Wells, warning of Hubert Bland's accusations of libertinism against him (p. 183); Dorothy Richardson to Wells, informing him of her miscarriage (p. 199); Edith Bland to Jane Wells, attacking her for condoning H.G.'s womanising (p. 205); Maud Reeves to the Wellses, asking if Amber can stay with them in the Easter vacation of 1908 (p. 221); Rebecca West to H.G., following his visit to her family home (p. 316) and her response to his report of Henry James's comments on *Marriage* (pp. 315–16).

I am grateful to the staff of several libraries whose resources assisted my research: the London Library, the University of Birmingham Library (including its Special Collections department), the Folkestone Library, the Birmingham Reference Library, The British Library (including its Sound Archive where I was able to listen to a BBC radio interview with Amber Reeves recorded in 1970), and the Women's Library of London Metropolitan University. Paul Burns, the owner of H.G. Wells's former home, Spade House, Sandgate, now a residential Care Home for the elderly, kindly suspended his normal rules and allowed me to view and photograph the exterior of the house and its gardens. Andrea Lynn and Michael Sherborne gave me invaluable help in tracing copyright holders of quoted material. I am very grateful to those who read this book at various stages of its composition and commented helpfully on it: Bernard Bergonzi, Maurice Couturier, Jonny Geller, John Hick, Geoff Mulligan, Claire Tomalin, Paul Slovak, Tom Rosenthal, Mike Shaw, and, as always, my wife Mary.

D.L.
October, 2010

Contents

4 Chapter 1: The President

12 *Do you want to run for president?*

14 Chapter 2: Washington, D.C.

22 *Let's explore the White House!*

24 Chapter 3: A Hard Job

32 *The US Congress*

34 Chapter 4: Exciting Times

42 *Would you like to be the president of the United States?*

43 The President's Quiz

44 Glossary

46 Guide for Parents

48 Index

Words in **bold** appear in the glossary.

Chapter 1
The President

The president of the United States of America is the leader of the country. Being the president is a very important job.

The Presidential Seal is the official symbol of the president of the United States. It shows an American bald eagle and 50 stars for the 50 states.

Barack Obama
44th president of the United States, 2009–2017

Every four years, **citizens** of the United States **vote** to choose their president. Americans must be at least 18 years old to vote. They vote for the person who they think will do the best job.

These are some past presidents.

George Washington
1st president, 1789–1797

Abraham Lincoln
16th president, 1861–1865

Franklin D. Roosevelt
32nd president, 1933–1945

John F. Kennedy
35th president, 1961–1963

George H.W. Bush
41st president, 1989–1993

If you want to become president, first you need to **campaign**. This means asking people to vote for you in the **election**.

You need to tell people what
you would do for the country
if you were president.

Bill Clinton campaigns
in 1996.

The person who wins the election becomes president of the United States.

Abraham Lincoln takes the oath of office in 1861. The oath of office is the promise made by every new president to do what is best for the United States.

The new president must
promise to do what is best
for the country.

Do you want to run for president?

You need to have lived in the United States for at least 14 years.

You must have been
born a citizen of
the United States.

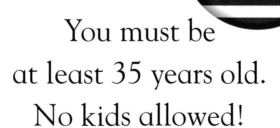

You must be
at least 35 years old.
No kids allowed!

Chapter 2
Washington, D.C.

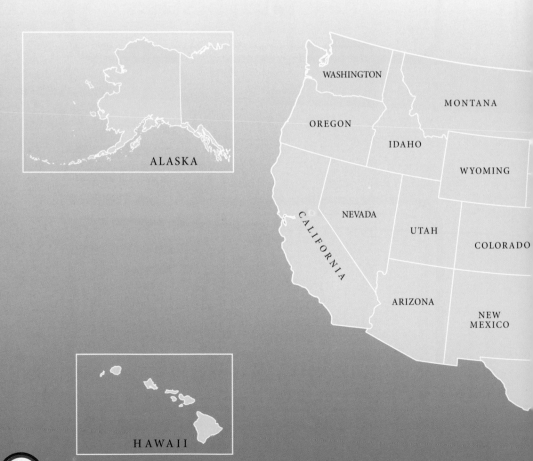

The president lives in Washington, D.C. It is the capital city of the United States of America.

This map shows the United States of America. The capital city, Washington, D.C., is marked with a star.

The United States **government** is located in Washington, D.C. The city was named after the first president of the United States, George Washington.

The Washington Monument was built in honor of George Washington.

There are many **monuments** that honor past presidents in Washington, D.C.

This statue of Abraham Lincoln is part of the Lincoln Memorial.

The president's home is the White House. It has been home to every American president—except one!

George Washington didn't live in the White House. It was still being built when he was president!

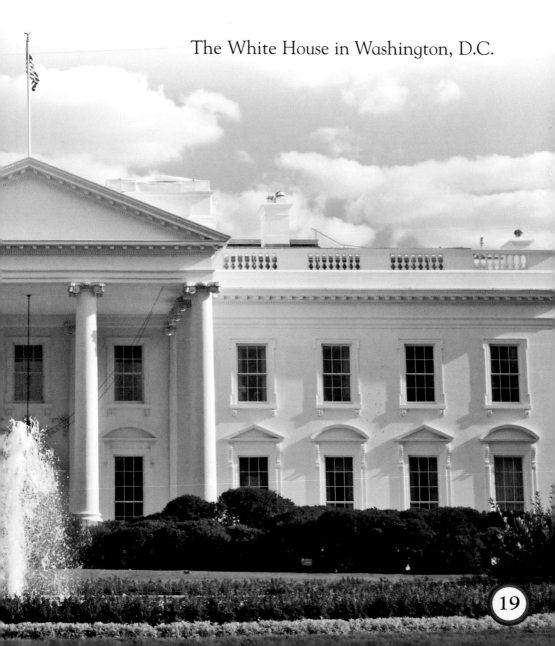

The White House in Washington, D.C.

The president's family lives
in the White House, too. The
White House has 132 rooms,
so there's plenty of space to
live, work, and play.

John F. Kennedy watches his children, Caroline
and John, play in the White House in 1962.

Barack and Michelle Obama pose with their daughters, Malia and Sasha, and their dogs, Sunny and Bo, outside the White House in 2015.

Let's explore the White House!

The president's main office is the Oval Office.

The president meets official staff in the
Cabinet Room.

Bedrooms for the president's family and guests
are upstairs.

Chapter 3
A Hard Job

Ronald Reagan at work in 1982

A good president tries to do what is right for the American people. The president has to make some tough decisions.

Air Force One—the
president's airplane

The president often travels on
Air Force One to meet leaders
of other countries. They try to
find ways for our world to live
in peace.

Barack Obama with British Prime Minister
David Cameron in London, England, in 2016

The president is in charge of the American **armed forces**.

The armed forces keep Americans safe.

George H. W. Bush with US soldiers in Saudi Arabia in 1990

The president works with Congress to decide on the **laws** for the country. Congress is made up of people elected from the 50 states.

IN GOD WE TRUST

Jimmy Carter speaks to Congress in 1978.

31

The US Congress

- Congress is made up of the Senate and the House of Representatives.

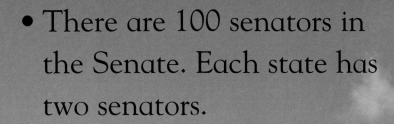

- There are 100 senators in the Senate. Each state has two senators.

- There are 435 representatives in the House of Representatives. States with a lot of people have more representatives than states with fewer people.

The Capitol building in Washington, D.C., is where Congress meets.

Chapter 4
Exciting Times

Being president is hard work, but it is exciting, too! There are lots of fun **traditions**.

Franklin D. Roosevelt throws a baseball at an All-Star Game in 1937.

Barack Obama throws the first pitch at the 2009 Major League Baseball All-Star Game.

The president hosts fun events
at the White House, such as
the Fourth of July barbecue.

The president also gives awards, such as the Medal of Freedom, to people who do great things.

Barack Obama hosts a Fourth of July barbecue at the White House in 2013.

The president meets many people and listens to what they think the country needs. The president also gives lots of speeches. Imagine the whole country listening to what you have to say!

George W. Bush speaks to people in New Hampshire in 2004.

The president works
for the American people.
They count on the president
to do what is right for the
country. It is an important job!

Barack Obama meets children on
Earth Day in 2015.

Would you like to be the president of the United States?

What would you do for the country?

The President's Quiz

1. How often do Americans vote to choose their president?

2. What is the capital city of the United States?

3. What is the president's house called?

4. What is the president's main office called?

5. Who does the president work with to decide on the laws for the country?

Answers on page 45.

Glossary

armed forces
the military organization that
protects the country

campaign
when a person who is running in
an election asks for votes

citizens
people who are legally part of a country

election
when people vote for who they want
to be in charge

government
group of people who run a city, state,
or country by making decisions
for its people

laws

rules of a country or state that people live by

monuments

statues or buildings that honor someone or something

traditions

events that have been celebrated in the same way for many years

vote

to choose a person you think should win an election

Answers to The President's Quiz:

1. Every four years **2.** Washington, D.C.
3. The White House **4.** The Oval Office
5. Congress

Guide for Parents

This book is part of an exciting four-level reading series for children, developing the habit of reading widely for both pleasure and information. These chapter books have a compelling main narrative to suit your child's reading ability. Each book is designed to develop your child's reading skills, fluency, grammar awareness, and comprehension in order to build confidence and engagement when reading.

Ready for a *Level 2* book

YOUR CHILD SHOULD

- be familiar with using beginning letter sounds and context clues to figure out unfamiliar words.
- be aware of the need for a slight pause at commas and a longer one at periods.
- alter his/her expression for questions and exclamations.

A VALUABLE AND SHARED READING EXPERIENCE

For many children, reading requires much effort, but adult participation can make this both fun and easier. So here are a few tips on how to use this book with your child.

TIP 1 **Check out the contents together before your child begins:**
- read the text about the book on the back cover.
- flip through the book and stop to chat about the contents page together to heighten your child's interest and expectation.
- make use of unfamiliar or difficult words on the page in a brief discussion.
- chat about the nonfiction reading features used in the book, such as headings, captions, lists, or charts.

TIP 2 Support your child as he/she reads the story pages:

• give the book to your child to read and turn the pages.

• where necessary, encourage your child to break a word into syllables, sound out each one, and then flow the syllables together. Ask him/her to reread the sentence to check the meaning.

• when there's a question mark or an exclamation mark, encourage your child to vary his/her voice as he/she reads the sentence. Demonstrate how to do this if it is helpful.

TIP 3 Chat at the end of each page:

• ask questions about the text and the meaning of the words used. These help to develop comprehension skills and awareness of the language used.

A FEW ADDITIONAL TIPS

• Always encourage your child to try reading difficult words by himself/herself. Praise any self-corrections, for example, "I like the way you sounded out that word and then changed the way you said it, to make sense."

• Try to read together every day. Reading little and often is best. These books are divided into manageable chapters for one reading session. However, after 10 minutes, only keep going if your child wants to read on.

• Read other books of different types to your child just for enjoyment and information.

Series consultant, **Dr. Linda Gambrell**, Distinguished Professor of Education at Clemson University, has served as President of the National Reading Conference, the College Reading Association, and the International Reading Association.

Index

Air Force One 26–27

armed forces 28–29

baseball 34–35

Bush, George H. W. 7, 29

Bush, George W. 39

Cabinet Room 23

campaign 8–9

capital city 15

Capitol building 32–33

Carter, Jimmy 31

citizens 6, 13

Clinton, Bill 9

Congress 30–33

election 8, 10

government 16

House of Representatives 32–33

Kennedy, John F. 7, 20

laws 30

Lincoln Memorial 17

Lincoln, Abraham 7, 10, 17

map of the United States 14–15

Medal of Freedom 37

oath of office 10

Obama, Barack 5, 21, 27, 35, 37, 41

Oval Office 22

Presidential Seal 4

Reagan, Ronald 24

representatives 33

Roosevelt, Franklin D. 7, 34

Senate 32–33

senators 33

speech 38

states 4, 30, 33

vote 6, 8

Washington Monument 16

Washington, D.C. 14–17, 19, 33

Washington, George 6, 16, 19

White House 18–23, 36–37